PREY

Marko Delacroix #1

Alaska Angelini

PREY
Marko Delacroix #1
Alaska Angelini
Copyright © 2014 by Alaska Angelini

ISBN: 9781530507450

All Rights Reserved

Prologue

From the depths of the underground he came, a monster moving amongst the shadows. Stalking every living thing like the predator he was. The dark suit and fedora couldn't hide what anyone who got within a ten-foot radius would feel. And he could have had them. Could have torn them to pieces with his razor sharp fangs. He wanted to. But they wouldn't be his meal tonight.

I would.

Even lying in bed, the covers pulled up to my neck, I saw him getting closer. Shared his vision. His thoughts. He was coming for me. I could feel it in my bones and not just because his arrival was my greatest fear. My blood was literally calling him. Every beat of my heart was like the sweet bells of my church, luring in the faithful servants of the Lord. Luring in him. I was Marko Delacroix's salvation. His continuation amongst the living dead. But I wouldn't be for much longer. Tonight, I would die. He'd kill me. And then I'd be replaced.

How did I know? Because with every leisurely step closer, he projected more images into my mind. Of my last breaths. Of my legs and arms intertwined with his as my pulse weakened. Slowed. Stopped. He wanted me afraid, just as much as he wanted to soothe those fears and seduce me when he got inside my home. Oh God, and seduce he would. My body burned for him as much as I was terrified of the creature who fed from me. He was nothing short of the devil in my mind. A man whose looks and touch could bring the highest pleasure. But one that would ultimately be my demise.

One might wonder why I didn't run or hide if I knew the end was near. It was simple. I couldn't. Not only because he could track me down, which I found out the hard way, but because it was physically impossible to go far. I was helpless to flee. With the insertion of his fangs weeks ago, came something more lethal than any poison to shock my system or make me crave him. It was what happened to my brain. I could think. I could carry on with my routine. Yet, when it came to defying him, my mind wouldn't allow me to. I was powerless. Under his control.

Prey.

Chapter 1
Marko

Like a merry-go-round, our game went around and around. Predator—prey. Vampire...human. I walked the streets, a fiend for their blood. The beat of their hearts, a soft melody for the killer that lurked within. Laughter drifted by as couples and groups stepped out of the surrounding nightclubs and restaurants. It was an aphrodisiac to the overwhelming temptation streaming through. The scent of their skin blanketed the area, mingling with aromas of food I no longer remembered the taste of. But for some reason, tonight, I didn't care about what I lacked from my past. Each person stood out. Distinct. Different. The saxophone playing on the corner lifted my spirits even higher and for the first time in months, I could feel a smile pulling at the corner of my lips.

I pushed my hands deeper into my pockets and continued my stroll amongst all the party-goers. Most were young—college age. Not necessarily my cup of tea, but I'd put off feeding for weeks. I was looking for a change from my routine. Something new. Something...exciting. Boredom for a vampire wasn't a good thing. For me, everyone I saw was a meal. If I wasn't a Master and part of *le Cercle*, I'd be half-tempted to walk through one of those door and paint the room red. As it was, we had enough trouble without me adding to it. A vampire attack wouldn't fare well mere days before our big announcement. Our acceptance back in to society. It was already in the works. The details were unimportant as I spotted a petite blonde staggering from the exit of an Irish Pub.

My pace stayed slow and I stopped, scanning the crowds. Even though she was an easy target, I didn't want her. My taste didn't run for the weak or inebriated.

So, why was I here, amongst all these drunks?

Seconds went by while I spun around in a circle, taking in the busy street. I found my focus stopping back on the girl. A low groan poured through my throat and I knew.

I was in full-blown massacre mode. It was the reason for the happiness and had I not known better, the results would have played out differently. I was almost past the point of being able to control myself and I couldn't keep doing this. It wasn't that I felt bad for taking what I needed, I was just losing interest. The lack of excitement was driving me under. Making me delay what had to be done.

Anger had my eyes narrowing and my steps were fast as I made my way to the blonde who'd somehow stumbled around the corner. I could use any excuse I wanted, but I didn't bother. She'd take the edge off. I needed that. Then, the real hunting could begin.

I broke around the brick, inspecting the dim road. Sporadic groups headed toward the clubs resting on the main street, but I paid them no attention as I swept the drunk girl into my arms. I never broke my stride, moving more toward the darkness. A delayed gasp had me looking down. For the briefest moment, she struggled against me, but when her blue eyes rose, she stopped. The pull was automatic. Her tightened features loosened as she stayed trapped in my gaze. The will to keep her there was second nature and so much easier due to her intoxication.

"You looked like you needed help." My French accent pushed through thickly as I felt my fangs began to lower. The scent of liquor poured off her in waves and it was almost enough to cause me to drop her and keep walking. Wine, I could do. Cheap whiskey was my biggest turn off.

The girl licked her lips, nodding. "Yes," she said, breathlessly. "I need…help."

My attention came up and I took one last look around. "Good, because I'm going to fix everything for you right now." The seductive drawl was gone, placed with an annoyance over what I was about to taste. There was nothing appealing in the least about what I was about to do. The flavor of her blood would be tainted. Bitter. Yet, here I was, spinning the defenseless blonde toward the dark alleyway between the buildings that faced the next block. At my broken connection, she began to move.

"Wait," she said, shifting. "What are you—?"

I didn't give her time to continue. My hand locked over her mouth and I slammed her into the wall with enough force to leave her dazed. The palm of my other hand settled over the low-cut dress and I let her racing pulse fill me. My fangs shot down and I dove forward, embedding them in the junction of her neck. A small cry vibrated my insides and I soaked it in while her blood rushed out over my tongue in a gush of warmth. The taste was almost enough to make me break away, but the need couldn't be denied. I forced myself to suck, half sighing in relief, half hating that I'd resorted to this particular person. Flashes of who she was tried to force through, but I brought up my wall, ignoring what I didn't care to see.

"Mmph." Muffled words and sobs were followed by thrashing, but I continued, ignoring her fight to survive. Sympathy or regret didn't exist here. Only death.

Heat traveled down my throat, coating my stomach. I fought the urge to gag, the lesson automatic. Tighter my hand clasped over her thin lips and I dug my fangs in even deeper. There was no gentleness in what I was doing. Only impatience as I felt myself become somewhat sated at her slowing heart. *Thump. Thump.* I became one with the beat. Enjoying what I was hearing, despite how unsatisfied I was. Nothing existed in the moment I was a part of. No members. No trouble amongst our underground city. This was all I knew. All I wanted to know.
Thump………Thump.

I broke away, letting her fall to the ground as I sucked in air. It only intensified the sourness and I growled at the sorrow I felt at having to stop. Happiness these days could only be found in those precious seconds of feeling as if I were doing something right. Something I was meant to. When all you've ever known is hell, it doesn't take much to entice you to join. But I wasn't merely a follower floating through this nightmare. Someday, I'd rule it. It was only a matter of time.

The crunch beneath my fingertips vibrated through me as I broke her neck, fulfilling the inevitable. Nothing existed but the emptiness that consumed me. I needed more. To have someone new. Someone…clean. My arm came up and I wiped the blood from my lips and chin. No more delaying my feedings. I didn't like to settle in whom I chose. I shouldn't have to.

The fedora sat angled on my head and I fixed it, waltzing back onto the dimly lit road. My eyes were already scanning for the person who would wash the taste out of my mouth. Younger vampires didn't mind cheap blood. I, on the other hand, knew the difference. Centuries had shown me the way. That, and a lot more.

I pulled out a pack of cigarettes, lighting one as I headed further from the downtown area. My walk was leisurely. The cool night breeze swept away the earlier anger and I relaxed. Homes crowded along the intersecting road and I turned left, keeping my head low as I tuned into my surroundings. Dogs barked in the distance, but faded the further down I got. They knew a threat when they felt one and it bypassed the need to bark. They'd be hiding. Cowering at my presence. They were smart, unlike all the possible victims I passed. Most humans lacked a sense of real danger.

Bells chimed in the distance, mingling with the scattering leaves that blew from the trees. It stole my attention and I glanced up at the tower of the cathedral. As I broke onto the next block, I pulled the collar of the trench higher on my neck. Just the view of the church left an uneasiness creeping over my skin. Regardless, I tuned it out, more interested in the commotion on the grounds.

People were emerging from the opened double doors, joining the group already standing out front. The menu wasn't selective. Some were old. Others young. They were all dressed nicely, but not appearing as if they'd just left service. The humming of a few told me they'd just been to choir practice. I'd come across this group before, but only once when most of them were already driving away. I always took this route. It led back to the tunnel I preferred to use to go back home.

An older man laughed, reaching for another gentleman's shoulder. It grabbed the attention of a younger girl who joined them. My head was shaking no before my brain could even consider them as my prey.

"Surely, we can ask," one of the men said. "Let's go find Father Moretti."

They girl followed as they headed up the steps, but my stare stopped on the woman coming down. Dark hair swayed around a pair of slim shoulders, covered by a red, long-sleeved blouse. Her pale skin stood out in contrast, even in the darkness. Immediately, I knew I wanted her. There was no explanation other than my captivation, and I clutched to it, not breaking my gaze. She smiled, reaching out and hugging an older redheaded woman. I saw nothing but the way her long locks kept blowing, twisting and twirling around her. It was so long, surely down to her waist. I could see it haloed behind her on the sheets as I loomed above, ready to take her as my own. The images had me licking my lips, still entranced with every move her body made.

"I will," she assured the woman. "You take care." Even as she spoke, she was stepping more toward the end of the grounds. She reached up, waving, and I felt my adrenaline begin to surge.

I stayed on the other side of the street instead of heading closer, not braving the holy ground she still stood on. Wind whipped harder and the scent of her skin with the smallest trace of her essence had my eyes widening. With all the people there, I knew it was hers. *Floral.* Lavender, maybe, with a hint of jasmine. A trace of…strawberries. Ones she'd probably eaten earlier, before she walked through those doors. And cleanliness. Her blood was so fucking pure of most of the contaminants humans usually held; the craving was undeniable.

My fangs pushed into my bottom lip and I kept my distance, waiting until we came upon more homes before I jogged to her side of the street. A gust sent a stronger fragrance to overtake me and my eyes closed at the monster I felt unleash. Had I thought I'd been temporarily sated by the blonde I'd had not fifteen minutes before? It didn't feel that way. My feet were moving faster. Gaining ground. I saw nothing but the tease of her neck as we hurried along in tandem. Her face was of little consequence in that moment. All I knew was the blood that kept calling me. Sound barely filtered through my bloodlust. It was her soft voice that shredded through my resolve. My steps faltered, slowing, as I realized she'd paused to answer her phone.

"Hunter, I'm so excited to hear from you. I was just at choir practice. I even talked to your uncle for a little while before I left. He misses you so much." Her pause and laugh had me cocking my head to the side. Something about it was appealing. Beautiful, even, if something as unimportant as a laugh could be described as such.

"You're...home?" Her tone dropped in surprise. "Like, at your moms, or...?" She leaned to the side to look past a truck parked further out of a driveway. Her hand dropped immediately. One second, the woman was at a standstill, the next, she was sprinting faster than I could have imagined her capable of. My toes pushed into the cement, ready to chase after her, when I caught myself. The last thing I wanted to do was bring attention to myself. Especially since she was on the phone. Luckily, she didn't run far. Just four houses up. A man was already waiting on the front steps, a large, dark green bag at his feet.

"Tessa!"

A squeal came from the woman as he jumped down to meet her. I instantly hated him. The explanation didn't matter. He was holding my meal and that was enough. And that hair. Fuck if he wasn't clutching it as his arms locked around her.

Tessa. My fists clenched and I narrowed my eyes even more.

"You were supposed to let me know when you were coming so I could go with your family to the airport. God, I missed you." She hugged on tighter as he spun her around in a circle.

"I wouldn't let them spoil it for you. I wanted it to be a surprise. Tell me you haven't changed your mind about wanting a roommate." He let her down, nodding to his bag by the door. As he went back to give her his attention, his stare came up to mine. And held.

"Of course I still want you to stay. I already have your room set up." Her smile was still in place as she turned to see what he was staring at. My steps were slow as I neared the sidewalk that put me in front of her home. Green eyes met mine and her full lips separated. In what...? Interest? Fear? I knew they could feel the uncomfortable aura I threw off. Especially with the mindset I was in.

Her instincts had her hand coming to the arm of the man she called Hunter, but she didn't turn from me. Instead, her mouth closed and her eyebrows drew in the smallest amount. I didn't wait to see what other expressions she'd have. I kept my speed the same, tipping my hat to them as I walked past.

"Let's go inside," he breathed out.

Footsteps told me she was obeying, but at this point, I didn't care. Only one thing reigned supreme in my mind. *They weren't staying in the same room.* And I had every intention of making sure she made it in there. The smile returned and I let it fill my face completely as my mind raced. I always did like a challenge, and I needed one. First, I'd have to figure out a way for her to invite me in Maybe not tonight, but soon. After that, she'd be *mine*.

Chapter 2
Tessa

Butterflies fluttered around my stomach while I led Hunter into his room. They'd been there since I left the church. The weird prickling sensation eased a little and I turned and gestured to the full size bed resting in the far corner. "It's not much, but I think it'll do for now. You can decorate however you'd like now that you're here."

The thud from the bag dropping to the floor made me jump, but I didn't understand why. My smile was in place, but I felt off—skittish.

"It's perfect. You outdid yourself." He walked to the dresser, picking up a picture of us that was sitting on top. It was of senior year, right before he left for the Army. He looked so much younger then, and definitely lankier. The large arms and wide chest he had now had me shifting on my feet. Although we'd kept in contact over the phone and through letters, it was hard to imagine he was the same Hunter I'd known so long ago—my best friend since childhood. Even the pictures over the years didn't do justice to the man standing before me now.

He laughed, setting the picture frame back down. "The good ol' times. Look what I have." His hand reached to his back pocket and he brought out his wallet, pulling a photograph free. I gasped and stepped forward, taking it from him.

"Your senior prom. I can't believe you've kept this in your wallet," I laughed, shaking my head. "I look horrible. My hair is just…ridiculously big."

"Your hair? Look at me. Could I have been a bigger dork?"

Harder the laughter came, until we were both collapsing to the bed. Hunter moved on his side, propping his head up while he held the weight with his fist. His flexed bicep had my eyebrow raising as I met his blue eyes.

"I never saw you like that, and I can tell you now, you're definitely not a dork. Every girl in Austin is going to be banging down our door. I'm going to have to keep a pair of earmuffs in the bedroom just so I don't get woken up by all the knocking."

Hunter rolled his eyes. "Oh, please. You're just trying to butter me up because you know I brought you presents."

My smile dropped. "You didn't." I was already flying up and diving toward his bag. A large arm wrapped around my waist, pulling me back to the bed. I laughed, feeling like we'd moved right back into being kids, not a thirty year old man and a twenty-eight year old woman. It all came in a rush of giggles while he tickled me. Weight settled on the top of my chest and Hunter's serious expression had me blinking past the changing atmosphere. It only lasted for a few seconds, but our stares were locked and it was almost impossible for me to look away. The butterflies exploded back within while he eased up, looking at the window. I didn't miss the way he pulled at the shirt around his neck.

"I'll just get them." The smile was back and he didn't take his eyes off me as he made it back to his bag and started digging through.

Slowly, I pushed to sit. The previous excitement was gone, leaving me with a mix of uncertainty. Hunter and I had been here before. Shortly before he decided to go into the Army. It was the whole reason I thought he was running away. Taking my virginity hadn't gone as we both thought it would. For months, we had avoided each other. It wasn't until he wrote me after boot camp that we started talking again We'd both agreed we hadn't made a mistake. There was no one else we would have picked to be our firsts, but had it come naturally and not been forced on both of our parts from peer pressure, maybe it would have ended in something other than tears and distance.

"There's quite a bit, so you'll have to bear with me." Four packages were pulled out and placed next to me. One of the wrapping papers looked old and worn. It was even torn in a spot at the corner. The next three had two corners that were the same. I smiled as he sat down beside me, causing the bed to shift. "Here," he said, picking up one with red and green older style Christmas paper. "Open this one first. I got it three years after I left."

My mouth parted. "That long ago? Why didn't you ever send it? Or any of these?"

His lips pulled back into a smile and his head dropped while he shrugged. "Maybe it was my way of making sure I made it back to give them to you myself. I'm not even sure that makes sense."

Reaching out for his hand, I brought it to my lips, forcing the tears that clouded my eyes not to spill over. Hunter had seen so much fighting during his time of service. I couldn't even imagine all that he'd witnessed or been forced to do, but I knew whatever it was had changed him over the course of time. I'd felt it. Picked up on the troubles he held within while reading his letters.

"You've been so brave. What you've done for this country—what you've all done—hasn't gone without appreciation. Thank you." My lips pressed into his knuckles and he looked up, turning my hand to place his own against mine. Our grips tightened and he let go, nodding at the package.

"Open it."

All I could do was grin as I reached down and pulled at the tape that secured it. A small black box had my pulse jumping and I shot my gaze up, only to see his attention on the box. I swallowed hard, popping the top. A heart hung on a silver chain. What I saw wasn't cheap. My hand rose to my mouth and I couldn't stop myself from bringing it down and sliding my fingertips over the diamonds surrounding the pendant.

"It's beautiful. Hunter…I can't believe you'd buy me something like this."

"What can I say, I saw it and it reminded me of you."

I pulled the necklace free and unclasped it. "Will you put it on me?" My voice almost gave out at the explosion of my pulse. I swallowed hard, not sure what had caused it. Sure, I was surprised by the gift, but I couldn't help but feel like it was triggered by something more. Something…threatening.

"You bet." He stood, coming over and taking the ends. As I held my hair up, I shivered at his breath brushing against the back of my neck. It clashed with an odd prickling against my skin and I tried not to shift uncomfortably. My reactions had to be just nerves. It was Hunter who was with me. There was no reason to fear anything or feel uncertain.

The width of his chest was eye level and I closed my lids at the smell of his cologne, trying to calm myself and focus on him. Was this really the boy I'd grown up with? Although the familiarity was there, our closeness felt off. Sure, I was attracted to him, but it didn't feel right. Didn't feel…real. I loved Hunter. He was my best friend, but could we ever be more? The unexplainable fear left me unsure.

"There." He stood and my hand came to my chest, feeling the weight that settled against it from the heart. The next box was placed before me and I nervously pulled at the paper. Seeing the keychain of New York, I glanced up at him.

"You remembered," I said, lowly.

Fingers rubbed over his short hair and he laughed. "You always wanted to go there. You can't imagine how guilty I felt going without you."

"I'm glad you got to see it. Maybe someday I'll get to go."

Blue eyes rose to mine and he gave a sharp nod. "You will. I'll take you. It'll be fun. And, you'll sing."

A burst a laughter came from me at that.

"I'm serious," he went on. "If I'm going to take you, you'll stand up at one of those lounges and you'll sing for me. And not one of those choir songs I used to get to listen to. You'll sing my favorite and blow all those New Yorkers away."

Heat rushed to my cheeks and I reached out, pushing against his shoulder playfully. "You flatter me, but I'll tell you what. If we ever do go to New York, I'll sing you one song. One," I emphasized.

His eyes searched mine and I looked away at the uneasiness. I couldn't stop the tingling in my stomach. My skin was practically vibrating at the intensity. The need to flee left me confused. I glanced toward the window before facing him.

"I'm holding you to that." Hunter rotated his shoulders and rubbed against the back of his neck, reaching out with his other hand to give me the next gift. As I opened it, I couldn't stop the nervousness from stealing some of my enthusiasm. I loved each one and the more time that went by, the antsier I became. And I didn't appear to be the only one. As I unwrapped the teddy bear, he stood up to pace. It didn't take me long to follow.

"Thank you so much. I love them." My arms lifted and I pushed away the need to stop myself. Instead, I let him embrace me. Long arms pulled me in close, wrapping around me. Fingers buried in my hair while his other palm came to settle on the small of my back. I felt so small, yet safe, in those seconds. The moment he broke away, the tingling came back. Heaviness pulled at my stomach and I licked my lips, reaching over and collecting all the gifts.

"I'll just put these away. Would you like some coffee?" My smile lit up. "Actually, I know the perfect thing."

I raced in my room, setting the bear on my bed and the rest on my dresser. Mid-step to leave, I paused, turning to try to look outside. Adrenaline spiked and fear exploded, causing me to shake. I forced my feet forward until I was able to pull back the curtain. My reflection stared back at me and I cupped the glass, looking out. My fenced in backyard was empty from what I could see. My head shook and I turned around, nearly screaming as I faced Hunter.

"You hear something out there?" He moved in around me, glancing out.

"No, I just thought I'd check things out. That's what you get for moving in with me. I spook over everything. You should know that. I have weapons hidden all over this house."

He laughed, wrapping his arm around my shoulders and leading me back to the living area. "You can stop worrying now. I'll protect you."

Something in his words comforted me and I let myself try to relax as I headed over and pulled open the fridge. The cake sat at the bottom, still in the Tupperware I'd placed it in. It would never make it to the fancy tray I bought. If I knew Hunter, the cake wouldn't last past tonight.

"German chocolate?" His eyes were big and he was already walking forward.

"Your favorite, just like my mother used to make."

A moan came from his mouth and the cake was suddenly gone from my grasp. "Oh my God, you have no idea how many times I've dreamed about eating this. Seriously," he said, looking over from the small round table at the side of my kitchen. "When I was overseas, I'd wake up smelling chocolate. It was the oddest thing."

I reached over, bringing out two forks and joining him. The utensil was pulled from my hand and he didn't even wait for me to get a plate. I laughed, digging my fork in for a bite, too.

The mouthful brought out another moan and he closed his eyes, chewing slowly.

"Good?"

His finger rose silently, telling me to hold on. I took a bite, waiting.

"Heaven. And you're an angel for making this for me."

"I don't know about that. I just know you."

Hunter's head tilted as he glanced over. "You do know me. And I, you." Silence grew between us and I tightened my grip on the fork as Hunter looked as though he wanted to say something, but was holding back. I wasn't sure why that scared me.

Knocking had both of us looking toward the door.

"Are you expecting someone?" He stood and so did I.

"No." I took a step when his hand settled over my shoulder.

"I'll get it."

I felt myself following behind him, even though my legs almost felt like they were sinking through quicksand. Everything within told me to run. To hide. But another part of me kept going. Hunter looked out of the peephole only to pull back and pause. The hesitation sent my heart racing even more than it already was.

"Who is it?"

My whisper was drowned out by my pulse and I could feel my whole body inexplicably shaking. And those butterflies…they were back. I could even see Hunter trembling slightly as he reached for the knob. He turned to me, his brow creasing. "No one's there. At least…not anymore."

Chapter 3
Marko

Pitch black surrounded me as my eyes snapped open. Just like the tides were pulled by the moon, I felt the gravity of its presence, bringing me out of deep sleep. The covers flew back at my throw and I jumped from bed. Light flooded the room from my silent order and I stalked to the closet where I kept my clothes, grabbing the first suit I came in contact with.

Even in my dreams, I saw her. That smile, that intriguing look in her eyes as she stared at the stranger who'd suddenly became part of her life. *Hunter.* The interaction I saw between them in my mind had me snarling. From what I'd witnessed while looking through the windows, they'd known each other for quite a while. Prom. How old was a person when they went to one of those?

My head shook, suddenly not caring. Those gifts. They didn't come from just a friend. And I saw the way he looked at her. The man was gone. In love. The realization left me moving faster.

Was he with her now? The curiosity between them had been a plaguing thought. Last night, I'd been unable to leave. It wasn't surprising for our kind, but I thought I had better control over myself. One street over and I came doubling back, running as fast as I could like a gone man myself. To be denied something when I wanted it didn't happen. It never took me more than a few minutes to connive my way into a woman's home or bed. I couldn't stand that I hadn't had the opportunity yet. If I had, I'd have been allowed inside. Tessa would have sated me. And oh what a night that would have been. I could have drank her within an ounce of her life, leaving her flirting with the edge of death. Temptation to give her my own blood to bring her back so I could do it all over again teased me. Perhaps I would. Then I'd feed from her every night until I lost interest.

I slid my shoes on, walked into the bathroom, and wet my face. As I combed my hair back, I blindly went through the motions, still seeing no one but her. Those lips. Her big green eyes. That fucking hair. How would she look, moaning and crying under me? It had been a while since I'd been with a woman. But I could see myself fucking her. Hurting her as I did so.

A silent laugh shook my chest and I spun, leaving my quarters. The moment I broke from the tunnel that made up the hallway, I was faced with long tables and a shorter one at the end. Vampires fed while their blood slaves rested at their feet. It wasn't tradition to drink from them in public. That would only be in private, and another way to put the slaves in their place. They weren't worthy enough to display such a sacred act in front of the members. It just wasn't done unless you were one of the leaders.

Three from *le Cercle* still sat at the shorter table. They glanced up at me, pausing from their feeding of a woman, sprawled out nude before them. Blood stained the bottom of their pale faces and I nodded in acknowledgment as I continued. The markets and stores were open, but only a few of the slaves were actually shopping. It was still early, but life had already began in our world. How I had forgotten the ways so quickly? Months of not caring left me sleeping as much as I could, and now, here I was, eager to break into the world we spent the majority of our time trying to avoid. Not anymore. Soon, we'd all be one.

"Where do you think you're going?" The words were spoken slowly. I turned, spying Marie Bardot...my biggest enemy, if I were to have one. Her beauty was undeniable, her mask of innocence being the death of many men. My acceptance into *le Cercle* wasn't taken lightly. Especially since she believed my place should have gone to her. For all intents and purposes, if one was counting years, perhaps. But my power outweighed hers and for her only having forty years on me, it wasn't surprising. We all came into our strengths at our own time. Although I suspected she'd reached hers long ago.

"I do believe I'm going out for a bite to eat. Do you have a problem with that?"

She shrugged, swaying her hips as she walked closer. There was nothing seductive about the look she displayed—fangs elongated and she fixed me with a stare that held every ounce of contempt she harbored. "Maybe. More whores? I have to say, it's becoming to you. Puts you right in your place."

My fingers locked around her throat and I smiled threateningly, moving in close. "If you don't keep those lips closed, I might just bite them off. Watch yourself."

I let her drop to the ground, ignoring the four men who were suddenly at my side. They would have killed for her, or at least tried. And they wouldn't have known any different. Their Mistress was their life. She owned them and they depended on her blood. Not only for their increased life span, but because they were bonded males. Three drinks from her and they were stuck for life. She'd be able to read their thoughts, speak to them internally, and command them to do her will. Unless she killed them, which happened a lot with Marie. All she had to do was whisper the word *death* and they'd drop on command. It was a system I was happy not to be a part of. One I tried to avoid at any cost. Yet...hadn't I just teased the idea of giving Tessa my blood? One exchange would let me track her. Provide me glimpses into her thoughts. Not very clearly, but enough to give me some clue as to what she was thinking.

I turned, ignoring the hiss behind me as I headed for the tunnel that would lead out. Usually I would have taken the stairs and gone through Kline's home, but Tessa was closer to the south exit and I was growing impatient to get to her. It only made me wish to give her the first exchange even more. It would be so much easier than guessing whether she was home.

My footsteps pounded into the cement flooring of the tunnel and the moment the fork appeared, I turned left, breaking into a dead sprint. I didn't stop until moonlight shone through the grate above. I climbed the ladder, pushing up the metal and stepping through. The street further ahead was relatively silent and I scanned the darkness, putting the cover back down. Light was nonexistent here for a reason and our inside men made sure it stayed that way.

Houses sat off in the distance and I walked toward them. Whistling filled the air and it took a moment to realize it was coming from me. Content...finally. A warmth rested within. I couldn't remember the last time I was so excited about prey.

Finally, a game I could get back into. It was easy if you had a target you were interested in.

Will I have her tonight? The plaguing question repeated continuously.

A van went by and I watched the houses illuminate in front of me. A car was parked in my prey's driveway and the whistling stopped as I noticed its headlights were still on. Was she leaving? Damn, the lack of control I had. It caused me to grind my teeth together.

I came to a stop, stepping closer to the trunk of an oak tree resting next to the sidewalk. A bang had me turning to the side so I could listen. Although I was houses away, I could have been right next to them for how good my senses were.

"I shouldn't be gone long. An hour or two tops." Hunter's voice had my lip peeling back in aggravation.

"Take your time. You haven't seen Devon in a while. I'll be here."

"You sure you don't want to go? I bet he'd love to see you."

She made a sound of disbelief. "I don't think so. I have a lot of things to do anyway."

"Okay…well, I'll be back. Lock that door," he said, stepping into view.

A laugh I knew all too well echoed out. "I always do. You both be safe. See you later." Hunter got in the passenger side and the door to the car sounded, followed by the house's door. I waited while the sedan drove off in the opposite direction before I stepped out and continued forward. Had I thought my night would be good? It was only just beginning. Now…*that invitation.*

I licked my lips, feeling my fangs retract. Music met me as I headed up the sidewalk. I kept my steps light to take it in. The piano was slow and haunting. Every stroke of the keys drew me closer and I found myself trapped in the tune. Just when I thought I couldn't like it anymore, a voice broke in, rooting my feet to the top step. The lyrics were of love. Of loss. My hand grabbed the rail, suddenly noticing it wasn't a tape or recording I was listening to, but Tessa. I blinked past the spell quickly wrapping around me. My hand rose and still, I couldn't make myself ruin something so beautiful.

Dishes clinked in the background and although she wasn't singing loudly, the power she held was a force all of its own. Hadn't Hunter mentioned something about having her sing for him? Ah. New York.

My fist connected with the wooden barrier at the thought and I breathed through the sudden anger of them having anything to do with each other. The following raps were slower. Lighter. Composure settled over me and a smile pulled at the corner of my mouth as the curtain pulled back, only to swing as she let it go.

"Yes?"

The door remained shut and I cursed in French under my breath. "I'm sorry, I'm in a bit of trouble. You wouldn't happen to have a phone I could borrow, do you?"

Shuffling had my eyes flickering.

"I saw you last night."

My smile returned. "Yes, I just moved in down the street. I'm afraid my power is out and I don't have any candles or a phone to call for help."

The door cracked and green eyes studied me suspiciously. "Your power?" She opened it even more, glancing around the surrounding houses.

"Everyone's seems to be working okay."

I shrugged, turning to look behind me. "I'm not sure why mine is acting up. You see, I just moved to this country and I'm afraid I'm not really sure who to contact concerning certain things. I'm sort of…lost."

When I faced her, she was finally looking toward me. My excuse was shit, but I got what I wanted—her attention. I locked stares with her and watched her shoulders soften almost instantly.

"Would you mind inviting me in? I could really use your help."

"Invite you in?" Her words were slightly slurred, drawn out while she stayed trapped in my gaze.

My cock hardened and I stepped in closer. "Yes. I'd really like to come in. If you approve, of course."

Tessa blinked heavily, shaking her head. My lips separated in surprise. I felt floored. Not many women could break through my powers. I didn't like that she could. It made me feel weak. Something I knew I wasn't.

"You said you needed candles, right? Hold on." She threw me a smile, shutting the door in my face. More shock registered and my jaw tightened as anger surfaced. Seconds later, she reopened the door, holding two small candles and a phone in her palm. "There you go."

"Bathroom?" I took what she held, waiting. If she denied me this, I was in trouble. I couldn't keep coming over every night with a fucking excuse.

Tessa glanced behind her, toward the right, and turned back to me. "I don't know."

I turned up the charm, trying to drown out any warning she may have felt. "It won't take long. I promise."

"I don't usually let strangers in my home."

I cleared my throat, trying to get her to look back in my eyes, but she resisted. "Oh, but mon chaton, I'm no stranger. We met last night. Besides, I have a feeling we'll be seeing a lot of each other. You have nothing to fear from me."

Dark hair fell over her shoulder and I could see her nervousness. "You promise to make it quick?"

"Absolutely," I reassured.

"Okay. Come in." The smile she gave was so forced, it made mine grow as I looked down at the threshold and stepped through. There was no going back now. I'd forever have access into her home, no matter whether she wanted it or not. My instincts flared and a voice within taunted me to attack. To pin her down and fuck her right there on the floor while I sucked the very life from her body. Something unknown had me following the direction of her finger.

"Down that hallway. First door on the right."

"Thank you."

Light flooded the room as I flipped the switch and enclosed myself inside. The blue and white flowered shower curtain wasn't what I had expected. I pulled it back, peeking inside. A bottle of shampoo rested on the edge and I picked it up, opening the cap to inhale the scent. The smell I associated with her rushed back. My fangs immediately came out and I bit at my bottom lip, ready to tear out of there to get to her. Instead, I placed the bottle back, walked over, and flushed the toilet.

As I washed my hands, I stared at my reflection. Dark hair was windblown and I raised my hand, fixing the piece that escaped and hung over my forehead. My brown eyes darkened for the smallest moment, only to go back to normal. I turned off the water, leaving me in silence except for the piano piece that still played in the background. My eyes closed and I could so easily hear her pacing. I took a few seconds, not caring about time or whether Hunter would come back. Tessa's scent surrounded me and I tuned into the fast beats pulsing in her chest. With the piano, I could have listened forever. At the small sound of anxiety she made, my lids lifted and I walked out. Whether it was relief or fear I was faced with, I wasn't sure.

"Good, you're done." Her feet shifted and she glanced toward the candles and phone on the coffee table. I studied the blue couch positioned by the wall next to it. It was old, but in fairly good shape. As I looked around even more, I noticed she seemed to like the color blue. Artwork hung on the walls…shades of the color in swirls with random lines shooting through them. My interest piqued even more as small wooden figures became visible on the shelf at the far corner. They weren't beautiful. More…rugged and old. Who was this woman to collect such odd things? I couldn't believe I even wanted to know. She was a human, nothing more.

"You sing?"

Tessa's lips parted and a blush came to her cheeks. Innocent. Sweet. *Blood.* I stepped closer and she immediately took a step back. Wariness had her hand coming to her chest and I knew she was feeling me at my worst. I wanted her so fucking badly, I couldn't control myself. I didn't want to. I was tired of the questions and interest in what I knew was nothing but a fucking meal.

"I…" She took another step back. No, this wasn't going to end well for her. Not like I teased when I refrained from attacking her to begin with.

Her mouth opened again, as if she were going to stay something. My head shook slowly and I tilted my face, forcing her to look back into my eyes while I closed the distance between us. Her body language said it all. *I had her.*

"So beautiful," I whispered, trailing the backs of my fingers down her cheek toward her lips. "Would you like to show me your room, Tessa? I think I'd like to see it."

"My room?" The repetition was common. I knew her mind was trying to process an answer, but she'd have nothing register except what I commanded.

Tessa took a step to the side of me, and another. I grabbed her hand, making sure not to break our connection. Slowly, I walked with her down the hall, all the while basking in the way she stared into my depths. Here, I could make her do anything I wanted. The possibilities were endless.

The doorknob connected with my palm and I twisted, pushing it open. The light was on and I left it alone, not wanting to miss a thing. The moment we stepped through, her scent surrounded me. It was the strongest I'd ever experienced from a human. Her domain was like a treat all on its own and I suddenly didn't ever want to leave. To smell that year after year would have been the closest to heaven I would ever get.

My legs connected with the bed and I sat down on the edge, pulling the back of her thighs so she could stand between mine. "Tonight, I'm going to make you fall in love with me, mon chaton. Then, in a few weeks, when you feel you can't live your life without me, I'm going to kill you."

I pulled against her hand, making her lower the top part of her body until she was at my height. "Now, kiss me." My hand cupped her cheek and I drew her closer, brushing my lips against hers. To wait for her was pure torture. As my tongue slid over her lips, I quickly learned the true meaning. A moan left me and I crushed into her hard, unable to wait a second longer. I never broke our stare as I sucked against her tongue. My fingers buried in her long hair and I deepened our kiss, feeling myself get lost in her flavor. I could have gone a million years without food and never been hungrier than I was in this moment.

"God, you taste so good. I can't wait to taste you everywhere." I reached down, sliding my hand under her shirt. Smoothness, so hot it stung my cool skin, met my fingertips and I closed my eyes, savoring her heat. So easily, I could imagine my cock buried within her. She'd burn me everywhere and I was looking forward to it.

Whack!

The hit across my cheek left me in a surprise stupor, triggering the rage I kept bottled inside. It was enough to break the spell she'd put me under. And how was that even possible? She should have been under my control. Not the other way around.

Movement showed her lunging to the top side of her mattress and I grabbed her body, spinning it to slam on the bed. I dove forward, feeling pain burst into my shoulder. I looked down at the small kitchen knife she'd stabbed me with. Pink lips separated and I groaned as I lifted, pulling the blade out and dropping it to the floor.

"Big mistake, mon chaton. *Big.*" My knees pushed her legs apart and my fangs came down. I didn't wait. Couldn't.

Chapter 4
Tessa

Had I ever known pain? I wasn't so sure as something sharp pierced my neck and what resembled fire began to seep its way into my body. My mouth opened to scream, but nothing would come except the thrashing while I fought to find air. A deep sound sent vibrations down every inch of my limbs and the stranger on top of me hooked his arm behind my knee, pulling my leg up as he moved against my most private area. Sensations shot throughout me and the pleasure mixed with the pain, leaving me fighting to decipher what I was feeling.

How did I make it stop? How did I get free?

Sucking was combined with a caress of his tongue and he arched me even more, pushing us deeper into the bed. I heard myself moan before I could process that I had. My arms shot out to the sides of me and my back bowed off the mattress until all my weight felt to be on my head. As he stole my blood to become one with his own, I didn't have to question what was happening. Information began to filter through, leaving me crying out in agonizing noises at what I knew was feeding from me. It didn't seem real. Or possible.

A gasp filled the room and he nuzzled into my neck, rubbing his face back and forth against me. The small sob that escaped had the creature's head lifting. Blood was smeared across his chin and cheek. Only then did tears began to flow.

"I'm not done," he said, lowly. "Not even close. But it doesn't have to be like this. It can be good…for now."

He licked his lips and glanced down at where I'd stabbed him. My hands curled into fists while I tried to stop the tears. At the fangs coming into view, my strangled denial filled the room. Anxiety had me frozen. I battled, trying to push him off or attempting to attack him again. Would he kill me? Words came rushing through and I recalled him saying he was going to—in a few weeks.

My hands shot up against his chest just as he sliced his bottom lip with his sharp fang. Blood dripped onto my chest while I fought to squirm from under his large body.

"Once I give this gift to you, you're going to want me all the time. More so than what you would have felt from the bite alone. It'll be better for both of us."

I shook my head frantically.

"You don't have a choice," he growled. "Bend to me. Enjoy what I want to give you."

Fingers sunk into my hair at the crown of my head while he cut his lip even more. His other hand latched to my face, holding me completely still. The steady stream that started flowing over my neck left me fighting with everything I had, but the force was immoveable. I opened my mouth to scream just as his lips massaged into mine. Blood washed over my tongue, leaving behind a metallic taste that made me ill. My teeth slammed shut, barely missing his lip, but still, he held. Pain pushed into my cheek and I tried with every ounce of strength not to cry out like I wanted. It didn't work. I choked at the amount and texture that caught in the back of my throat.

"Swallow," he snapped, clamping his hand over my mouth. My head turned to the side and I could feel the warmth flow down my throat. Like an electrical current, something almost alive rushed through my insides, jolting me with every zap.

"Oh....yes. Already I can feel you," he whispered. "And soon, you're going to know nothing but me. You're going to love me, Tessa."

My head was finally able to move and I turned it to the side, trying my best to throw up. It didn't work as whatever was happening sent my body into spasms. Sensitivity heightened to almost painful portions and I felt my eyes widening as a bloodcurdling scream left my mouth. If it was from the fear or an involuntary action, I didn't know. Suddenly, I was starting not to care.

Heat formed in the pit of my belly, growing and expanding outward with every breath I took. My gaze turned to the vampire hovering above as deep pants left me. He was attractive. More so now than I remembered before. I faded deeper into a blissful state, caught up in his full lips, now healed. Adoration had me taking in every expression he made. The sexy smile. The way he stared at me like I was the only woman he'd ever wanted.

His hand came down and his fingertips turned my face. I couldn't stop myself from moving into his touch. A lick over where he'd bitten had me moaning and my hand blindly reached for him. How was this okay? His breaths brushed against my skin and I felt my eyes roll at the ecstasy of something so small. This was wrong…yet, my body, and now my mind, started to believe it was right.

"Yes," he said, grabbing my wrist and pulling me to sit up. "Touch me, mon chaton. Let me feel your hands on me."

Need surged as the fear disappeared. Had he just been looking at me fascinated? I felt in awe of the power beating against my insides. Impatiently, he shrugged off his jacket and I reached for the buttons on his shirt. With each one giving beneath my fingers, he watched me even harder. I kept eye contact, unable to break away. Not because it was like before, but because I couldn't dare turn from him. I let the last button slide free and rose to my knees, pushing back the bloody torn material until his chest became exposed. My fingers immediately traced over where I had stabbed him. Nothing. He didn't bear a single mark. Thoughts wouldn't come, only actions as I slid my palm up to cup his neck.

Somewhere deep within, something off began to push through, but I continued, leaning forward. Our lips met and I felt his arm come around my waist, bringing me in closer. The need that consumed me had never been this strong before with a human.

As if he picked up on my thoughts, he smiled. "It's my blood in you. Our connection is unbreakable now. Even after I leave, you'll yearn for me."

The words were of little importance when all I wanted to do was feel. Tingling began to take over the outside of my body and I ran my fingers up, burying them in the length of his hair. I could feel myself growing so wet. I craved touch. Wanted nothing more than to have him explore every inch of my body.

As if he'd read my mind again, he pulled at the hem of my shirt, easing it up until he joined me on his knees and pulled it off. White material blurred in my peripheral vision as he threw it to the floor and I felt a fog move in. I tried to blink it away as I stared up at the man who towered over me. He tightened in my hair, tugging it back as he bent down to kiss my exposed neck. I couldn't stop myself from reaching for his shoulders to pull him in even more as he paused over my pulse point.

"Oh God," I moaned. "Please." I longed for his bite. Knew nothing but what it could bring.

The grip tightened even more in my hair. "I want to drink every drop of your blood, Tessa. To have you nearly lifeless in my arms." He groaned, slamming me to the bed and meeting my mouth with a brutality I couldn't have cared less about. I could taste blood. The flavor was suddenly so different from before and it didn't matter if it was mine or his.

My nails raked along his back, the desperation within me heightening to proportions so extreme, I begged for something I didn't even know. I liked this. Even wondered why he hadn't found me sooner.

The hardness of his erection pushed in between my legs and I cried out, tearing at his back with a force I almost couldn't believe.

"I'm going to make your death the sweetest of them all. God, I see it. I wish I could show you." Dark hair fell forward as his head lifted. A battle seemed to play across his features and he gave a hard jerk, as if to make whatever he was thinking disappear.

"I need…" My hips arched and my head turned back and forth.

"Your body wants my bite, but all you're getting right now is my cock."

With a pull, the button on my jeans popped free and my zipper broke. I felt my hand fly up unexpectedly. Tightly, I grasped his wrist, holding it with all the strength I possessed. The vampire stopped, his eyes narrowing as he looked at me.

"Impossible." The one word sent my eyelids fluttering. He let go, covering me with his weight. "Stop thinking. Kiss me. Let me taste you."

A warning echoed through and I didn't understand it. I hesitantly lifted my head, meeting his lips. At the taste of his tongue, I momentarily forgot everything. I could feel my pants being pulled down and off. And then…his. He began to position above me while I took in both of us wearing our undergarments. Regardless of the fact that I wanted him, uneasiness surfaced once again. My shoulders shifted and my eyebrows drew in, confused. The man above paused.

"What the fuck?" French broke through and somehow, I knew what he'd meant without ever learning the language. "Mon chaton, look at me." Pressure latched onto my chin, pulling up so I had to face him. Pain registered at the force and I glared at the unexpected feeling. What had happened? I'd been so blissful. So…

"That hurt," I ground out.

"God dammit." More French. As I began to sit, he dove forward, locking his hand around my throat. "Perhaps the fight would be better than seduction. Thing is, Tessa," he said, hissing my name, "if I take you that way, I'll rip out your throat before the real fun can even begin. Do you want that? Do you want to die tonight?"

Did I want to die?

"Who are you?" The question was out before I even knew I'd thought it. It was enough to have his shoulders drawing in. Fingers wove through his hair and he pushed from the bed, grabbing his clothes. There was anger, but something else.

"I don't want to kill you yet. If I have to fight you, I will. Obviously, you're not going to comply. Your subconscious wouldn't have broken through if that were the case."

"I don't want to die," I mumbled.

"Too bad."

I ignored him, feeling a little security now that he was backing off. "You didn't tell me your name."

He glanced up as he slid his leg in his pants. "You really want to know my name? I don't see why. You'll be dead in a few weeks anyway. Hell, I don't even know why I'm explaining anything to you." His head shook in annoyance as he worked his fingers on the clasp, adjusting the waistline at his slim hips. "Marko. Marko Delacroix. And you're Tessalyn Antoinette Kennedy. Twenty-eight years of age. Soon to be twenty-nine. If you live that long.

"You were raised in this city and never have plans of leaving. Although, you do wish to explore New York someday. But not as a singer," he said, rolling his eyes.

"Your best friend is Hunter Anthony Moretti. You've known him since you were seven. You teased the idea of marrying him someday until you lost your virginity to him at the tender age of sixteen, and your desire suddenly wavered. You graduated top of your class. Were offered a free ride to the University of Texas, yet you work as a receptionist at a car dealership. You don't speak with your parents anymore, not that you really did growing up. You find they're too in love with each other to share it with their only daughter, so you pushed them away long ago, never caring to try to strengthen it yourself. But you've always preferred to be alone so it never really bothered you. Am I getting this right?"

Tears burned my eyes at the ugly way he spoke of my life. Whatever had been wrong with me before sobered with his words and I was thankful for it. I hesitantly climbed off the bed, trying to push my own anger away. I wasn't so naïve to know if I attacked him, it would be the death of me.

"My blood told you that?"

I slid on my shirt as he reached for his. The tears were threatening more by the minute while what was happening—what had almost happened—started to sink in.

"No. I watched your life play out. It's deep in your eyes. The details did get filled in from your blood though, even though I already knew the majority of it."

My lips separated and I lowered my head. This vampire, Marko….this killer, knew every detail of my life. Had seen it. Twisting in my stomach had me feeling sick. The thought of his blood in me had me spinning to race to the restroom. I gagged as an arm looped around my waist, holding me while I started to fight against him.

"You're just in shock. It'll pass. And when it does, it'll be of little consequence. You'll want nothing more than to taste me, just like I already want to taste you." I thrashed again, unable to help it. "I'll be back tomorrow night." His hand came around, grasping my throat. "You will be more compliant then. You will wait for me at the door and you will let me in, or you won't like the consequences that come with me forcing my way inside."

Fear engulfed me and the trembling came back in full force. "Please don't come back. Please. I'll pretend none of this ever happened. I won't say a word." My voice cracked as the tears finally broke free and streamed down my cheeks. A laugh filled the room and I was tossed to the ground, as if I were nothing.

"I'll be back. And don't think about running. You won't make it far." He grabbed his jacket, sliding it on as he surged from my door, slamming it behind him. Sobs wracked my body so hard, I fell forward, resting my forehead on hands that seemed to try to claw their way into the carpeted flooring. For minutes, I felt myself fall apart. I was confused, scared. Fear had sunk its claws just as deep as Marko's fangs and I had no idea what I was supposed to do now.

Chapter 5
Hunter

"Tessa?"

I looked down at the knob, confused as I pushed the door closed. Hadn't I told her to lock it? I knew I had. I turned the dead bolt, shaking my head. *Women.* Didn't last night teach her anything? A stranger could show up at any time. With the phantom knocker, I would have thought she'd have taken the scare a little more seriously. One time would have been odd. Three times, throughout the span of a few hours...it wasn't natural. Hell, had she not convinced me that kids had done this before, I probably wouldn't have left to begin with. A bad feeling was in the pit of my stomach and I couldn't shake the weird sensation. Even under heavy fire overseas, I never once felt the fear I did last night. It rocked me and I didn't like it. I wasn't one to get spooked easily, but anyone that hid themselves from the view of others wasn't right in my book.

"Tessa?"

The house was dead quiet, causing me to walk faster. I pushed open the bathroom door, moving my head back as a wave of steam rolled out. She'd just gotten out of the shower. And a damn hot one at that. My shirt was suddenly too tight against my neck and I pulled at it as teasing images of her body underneath mine played out. Damn. How many times had I fantasized about making up for our first time? Too many. And it wasn't just correcting my mistake that made me want her again. I loved her. Always had.

My arm rose to knock when I paused at the sniffling. *Was she crying?* I moved in closer, tilting my head to give myself a better angle to hear. The sob had my hand rapping against the wooden divider that separated us.

"Tessa? Can I come in?"

"One minute." Shuffling was followed by another sniff. My lips tightened with uncertainty and I knocked again.

"Tessa, are you okay?" I grabbed the knob and paused, debating whether I should risk getting her even more upset.

I drew my hand back just as it swung open. Her dark hair was wet, hanging down in loose curls that stopped just above her waist. She hugged the white, thick robe she wore tightly to her body as she moved back. It was a silent admittance into her room and I stepped inside, feeling my heart break at the anguish that pulled her features in. She was on the verge of completely breaking in front of me and I had no idea what had caused it or how to help.

"What happened?" My voice was quiet, almost too afraid to increase in volume for fear of pushing her too far.

Tessa's foot rose, as if she were going to step forward, only to drop. Her fists clenched, but reached toward me. I didn't need her asking for me to know what she wanted. My arms lifted and she rushed into them, throwing herself into me with enough force to almost push me back. Sobs shook her body violently and I held tightly, trying to swallow past the tightness in my throat.

"God, Tessa," I breathed out. "Jesus." My knees felt weak, yet rage rushed through me. I couldn't stop myself from scanning her bedroom for some sort of explanation. Her bed was stripped completely and I felt myself stiffen, trying to imagine what would cause her to be suffering as she was.

Fingers dug into my back while she tried to move into me closer.

"Tessa, you have to talk to me. Tell me what's wrong. What happened?"

The crying got harder and I pulled at her arms, trying to unwrap her from me. It hurt worse than seeing her break down, but if I didn't find out soon, I'd snap. Someone had obviously hurt her in some way, whether it was physically or mentally, and I wanted to know who.

"Please," she begged, pulling against me even firmer.

"No. Look at me," I said, angling her face up. "I'm here now. You're okay. Just talk to me. Tell me what happened. I won't let anyone hurt you, if that's what you're afraid of."

When she continued reaching out to hold me, I swept her in my arms, bringing her toward the bed. Screams had her thrashing in my arms and I nearly dropped her at the violent outburst. Dots of blood soaked into the mattress had my arms nearly giving out. The yelling disappeared, drowned out from my pulse as I let go of her legs and reached forward, pressing my fingers into the half-dollar sized amount. Crimson stained my fingertip and bile pushed at my throat as I realized how fresh it was. God, if I hadn't left…If I…

"Hunter, we have to leave. Hunter." The sobs came back and I looked down into her red-rimmed eyes, numb from the fury within.

"Where are you hurt?" My hand came out to tear at the robe but I closed my fist just as I connected. I didn't want to imagine my biggest fear. It was wrong that I prayed she'd been merely injured over my assumption.

"We have to go," she said, dragging it out.

"Who?" I exploded.

Tessa's mouth opened and a rush of air came out, but nothing in the form of a word. Her eyes darted back and forth and the panic resurfaced. "Ah…." Again, she seemed to struggle with her words.

"Speak. What happened? Did someone…rape you?"

Just the words left me in a place I couldn't ever remember being. My hands gripped her shoulders and I groaned at the frustration I felt. Why wasn't she saying anything helpful? "Tessa," I said, shaking her. "Talk to me God dammit."

"I…can't," she whispered. "Hunter…I can't." The crying was stopping as something altogether baffling began to happen to her state of mind. Whispering left her mouth and it almost appeared as if she were talking to herself. A crazed laugh came through and she shook her head, shrugging out of my grip as the sobs quickly replaced it.

I reached for my phone, knowing I needed to call the police. She needed an ambulance. Doctors. "You're in shock. I'm going to get you help. Maybe one of the cops can get you to tell them what happened."

Her head shook and she used the sleeve of the robe to wipe her nose. "No one can," she managed. "It's an amazing trick, really. It makes perfect sense why they're such a mystery."

"They?"

Tessa went to speak, only to close her eyes. "Forget it."

"No I want to know. Who hurt you? If you were raped, we need to get you help." My voice had softened and I noticed her mouth had twisted.

"No one raped me, Hunter."

My head shook and I pointed to the mattress. "Something obviously happened. If you weren't raped, then you have to be hurt. Are you dressed under the robe? I want to see."

White came to her knuckles as she grabbed at the collar of the cotton, holding it together tightly. "I'm not hurt. The blood doesn't belong to me." Even though I got the impression she was lying, I continued.

"You hurt someone?" The rush of words had her shaking her head. "Fuck, you're being so difficult. Why can't you tell me? You were begging that we needed to leave when I arrived and now you want to pretend nothing happened. You were a damn train wreck not even a minute ago."

Tears overflowed and I threw my hands up, stepping back. My teeth clenched and I forced myself to keep going. "Tell me this. If you won't reveal this person—"

"Can't," she burst out as a sob broke through.

"Okay." I lowered my head, breathing deeply through the irritation. "If you *can't* reveal this person, is it because you're afraid they will hurt you again?"

Silence.

"Tessa, are you afraid they'll come back?"

Silence.

Dark hair spun as she went to the closet and threw the doors open. She reached on her tiptoes and pulled out new sheets, laying them on the dresser as she swept through the door and into the restroom. A wet washcloth was in her hand and she leaned over the mattress, beginning to scrub out the stains.

"Go ahead and go to bed, Hunter. I'm getting tired and I'll be doing the same here shortly. Let's just forget this ever happened."

"Forget?" Shock filled my tone and I took a step back. "You were always so strong. I've never known anyone to back you into a corner this way. And you have *me*. Do you think I can't protect you from this person?"

Tessa's eyes rose to mine and her face grew pale. "No, Hunter. Even you can't protect me. Goodnight."

A response. A reaction. Nothing would come as I stared at her in utter astonishment. The surprise didn't last long. I surged forward, pulling her from the bed and carrying her to my room. The robe flew up past her knees as I tossed her on my mattress.

"I can't protect you? You don't think so? I reached under my pillow, pulling out one of my guns. It was habit. Something I'd picked up years ago. It made me feel safe after what I'd been through and seen.

I placed it on the dresser, opening the top drawer and pulling out another. The heavy thud was replaced with another from the second drawer. And then the third. By the time I made it to my closet, I didn't have to move a thing. A rifle case rested against the bottom wall, courtesy of my mother earlier that day, and case after case of handguns sat along the top.

"Tell me again that I can't protect you. Say it, Tessa! I've killed plenty of times before. I'd do it again in a heartbeat if it meant stopping someone from harming you. That shouldn't even be a question in your mind." I sat on the edge of the bed, reaching out to touch her face. "You *have* to know that."

As her eyes searched mine, I watched her shut herself off.

"How can you kill something that can't be…" she trialed off.

"That can't be what? Killed?"

Her eyes snapped up, but she stayed quiet.

"If that's the case, then let me think." As crazy as it sounded, I didn't dismiss the possible answer. I knew Tessa. She'd been terror-stricken and was still in shock. Whatever she couldn't speak of affected her more than she could even show. I took a deep breath and stretched out on the bed, pulling her down beside me so I could hold her in my arms. "Everything can die. It's all about finding the right way to make it happen. Give me time. If there's something that can be done, no one will try harder to find the solution than me."

Chapter 6
Marko

To say I was addicted to the taste of her wasn't enough. I was consumed by her sweetness. Crazy to the point of madness, just to her moans. It was one thing to tempt the killer in me, quite another to become the obsession of my monster.

Even as I paced the grate outside the tunnel entrance, I knew it was pointless. I felt trapped in between where I needed to go and where the vampire in me wished to be. Hunter was home. I could feel it in my blood that now resided inside of Tessa. From distraught to somewhat peaceful, she clung to him for stability. The desired effects I'd wanted to get out of the exchange didn't happen. My meal didn't bend to me and although I'd heard of it happening before, I never in my wildest dreams would have imagined it happening to me. And from her, of all people. It pissed me off. Made the challenge even greater. To kill her wasn't enough. There was nothing satisfying in that. I wanted her to love me before I drained her. To...

A frustrated sound had me kicking at the dirt. Women fell in love with me all the time. Maybe I clung to that part of humanity the most. The beast within was the one who twisted the sweet act into something that fit who I'd now become. I'd never once felt bad for the murders I'd committed and I wasn't about to start now. So, what was I still doing here, pacing around a clearing just outside of the homes that surrounded me? Why did I leave to begin with?

I slowed as pieces began to fit into the puzzle of my mind. For so long, I'd done things my way. Apparently, with the boredom, it wasn't working anymore. If I tried to be genuine, to show emotion and act as though I truly cared for her, perhaps I could get her to ease to the influence of the bond for it to really snap into effect. Wouldn't it be the ultimate victory? My head shook while I battled with how stupid that sounded. No. It would be pathetic. I didn't act out anything for anyone. Especially not a human.

Time passed and I pushed from the curb I'd been sitting on. There was a calmness within. It told me Tessa was probably deep in sleep and I couldn't stand it. To know I was out here obsessing over her and she was oblivious to it enraged me. I felt myself walking back toward her house before I processed doing so. To question whether I lost my mind was pointless. My actions proved I had.

Lights flickered on as I passed a house and my eyes narrowed. If I kept up this weird stalkerish behavior, someone was bound to call the cops on me. The last thing I needed was to worry about human laws. Especially so close to the big news.

The room I knew to be Hunter's was illuminated from the inside and I could feel myself being pulled in that direction. The blinds were closed and my jaw tightened in aggravation. I kept walking, making my way to the front door. I adjusted the tie to the new suit I wore and cursed myself for the millionth time for not staying in my room. My hand rose to knock and I almost rolled my eyes as the door swung open. Staring down the barrel of a gun wasn't amongst my favorite things, but I wasn't afraid.

"It's nice to meet you, too, Hunter. Is Tessa home?"

Blue eyes glared at me as he pulled the hammer on the back. "It's almost one in the morning. She's sleeping. What is your business with her? And why at this hour?"

I put my hands in my pockets, raising my eyebrow. "It's one in the morning and I'm here to see Tessa. Our business is our own. If you don't mind, I'll just wake her up myself."

The barrel pushed closer to my face. "I don't think so. She's not feeling well. Besides, I've seen you before. Last night. You were walking by."

"No," I said, shaking my head. "I was making sure she made it home safely from choir practice. When she saw you, I decided to let you two have your moment and I left. Now, I'm here to see her again and you're going to move out of the way and let me do that."

Confusion and uncertainty pulled at his expression. I knew he was questioning whether I spoke the truth.

Footsteps sounded in the distance and my smile appeared. Her pulse became mine, racing in my chest as she got closer. I closed my eyes, willing it to slow. To calm. I knew it would have the same effect on hers.

"If you don't mind," I said, nudging my head to the side. "Tessa would like to see me now. Wouldn't you, mon chaton?" My voice was just loud enough for her to hear. The footsteps continued and Hunter turned, giving me a view of her in a long white nightgown. Her dark hair was in a mass of frizzy, soft curls around her. Her skin looked radiant in the light and I knew it was because of my blood. A weird tingling erupted in my stomach and I pushed my way past Hunter, no longer noticing he was there. Tessa licking her lips brought me closer. Fear was present, but something else. Something I couldn't quite figure out, nor cared to. All I wanted was to be back on top of her. Back tasting her mouth as I breathed in her scent.

"I've come to apologize for my behavior earlier. I'm sorry. I should have never reacted the way I did. I'm ready to make it up to you. I owe you that much." My hand outstretched and I knew I wasn't quite making sense to her, but I didn't mean to. What I spoke of was for Hunter's benefit. I wanted him hurt. To be…jealous of something that didn't truly exist between Tessa and me.

A hand gripped my arm and I felt the strength behind the pull trying to turn me around. It failed. My head cocked to the side and I slowly stepped to face him. "Yes, Hunter?"

Whatever he was going to say didn't come. More confusion pulled at his features and he lowered the gun. "I don't think I got your name."

"Marko Delacroix," Tessa said, lowly. "It's okay, Hunter. We'll just go talk in my room."

"Who is this guy?" he asked, stepping in closer to her. "You never mentioned him. Is he your—"

"Boyfriend?" I cut in. "Why, yes, I am. I have to admit, I'm a little upset she hadn't mentioned that part already."

As my eyes connected with hers, she lowered them instantly. I could see the uncertainty emerge within her. Felt it as she tried to decide the best route to take.

"I didn't find the right time. I…" Her eyes squinted and she shook her head. "Marko, can we talk in my room?"

"I'd love to." My attention went to Hunter long enough to throw him a smile. The upset expression only had mine growing. "It was a pleasure meeting you," I said, turning my back and heading down the hallway. At the smell of Tessa's room, my cock hardened in anticipation. I continued in and shut the door, locking it. Tears were already pooling in her eyes.

And here I was, facing my biggest challenge concerning prey. A deep breath left me and I lowered to my knees, looking up at her. "Come here. Stand before me."

"Why did you have to do that?" she rushed out quietly. "Why come back? I begged you."

"Come," I said, more forcefully.

In slow steps, she made her way closer. I couldn't stop from clenching my jaw and jerking her the rest of the way. My face instantly buried in her stomach and I breathed in deeply, letting myself disappear as our heartbeats became one. The act was something I still couldn't wrap my mind around. It was almost like I'd created something. A new life *within* someone. I loved it. Basked in the new sensation as it took me over.

The pressure of Tessa's hand settled on my head and although the hesitation was there, I felt her need to comfort me. The human span of emotion was baffling. I'd been a human once, but from what I remembered of my past, no one ever helped me out. There was no act of kindness given to me by anyone else. Yet, I'd repeatedly made it clear that I meant to kill her and here she was, stroking my hair. Perhaps I didn't need to try to force the bond that would never be. Could she already be feeling what I wanted her to? Not love yet, but something bordering it.

Footsteps pulled me from the moment and I tried to ignore Hunter in the distance.

"You're lonely."

My head snapped up and my lips peeled back in distaste. "I beg your pardon?"

"You're...back. That tells me you have nothing or anyone else to go to. You're like a lost a puppy, albeit a rabid one. But I think you're in need of company. Of attention."

"That's the most ridiculous thing I've ever heard. I should kill you right now for comparing me to..." I pushed to my feet, crossing my arms over my chest.

"A rabid dog? You have to admit, you sort of resemble one with the whole bite thing."

I scowled. With every step I took forward, she took one back. "Maybe you're right, since the only reason I'm here is to finish my meal."

Her eyes dropped and the fear came back. My pulse thumped and I closed my lids, taking a deep breath and focusing on bringing it back down.

"Will you kill me tonight?"

"Probably."

Annoyance quickly took over the *creation, the one heartbeat* I'd been so proud of. I pushed my palm into my chest. "Fine. No, I won't kill you yet. Tonight, I just want you."

Tessa glanced at the bed. "You can't have me that way. I'd prefer you just killed me, if that's the case."

Anger was quickly taking over the nice behavior I'd been forcing myself to show. "You have no say. You will give yourself to me and you'll damn well enjoy it."

"Will I?"

My eyes tore from the wetness surrounding the light stain on the mattress and I lunged forward, yanking her into my body. "You looked to be enjoying it just fine before."

"That was from your blood. Not you."

Our eyes held and I wasn't sure whether it was her fear or my anger causing me to shake at our racing pulse. "Perhaps I should get you to drink it again."

Even as I spoke the words, they sounded unsure. Weak. I didn't want to have to exchange again and definitely not this soon. At the rate I was going, I was going to be in over my head before the sun set tomorrow.

"If I give myself to you, will you leave me alone? Let me live?"

My head shook and my subconscious answered before I could. "Death *will* find you. There may be an illumination, but there's no light at the end of the tunnel...not for you, mon chaton. Not for anyone."

Tessa's lashes lowered as she seemed to go into her thoughts. I let go as her head bowed. Our disconnection had her turning and walking to the dresser. As her eyes came up and she looked at me through the reflection, I felt rooted. Green kept me trapped as her hands messed with something on the top. And like that, she dipped her head, and I blinked past the confusion. I knew she had no special powers. It was our blood. It was bringing us closer. Even so soon.

Pale skin became exposed as she began unbuttoning the top of her nightgown, but I barely noticed as she turned to face me. The thickness of her lips thinned into a smile and it seemed genuine. It made no sense.

"Well?"

My gaze traveled down past her neck, to the cleavage of her breasts, stopping at the rosary. I swallowed hard, looking back up to her face. I waited for the urge to distance myself and met her smile when it didn't come.

"I think you may have beautiful breasts, but I can't see them." Her expression melted and she reached for the material, hugging it closely as I came to stand before her. I pushed past her hands, grabbing the necklace and twisting the beads around her neck tightly. "Now, I do believe I'll partake in what you were so enthusiastically offering. First, a word of advice," I said, lowering to whisper in her ear, "never use anything holy against a vampire. You're only going to piss it off. As you can see...it doesn't work." With my jerk, I broke not only the rosary, but the damn heart chain she had fastened around her neck. I tossed them to the ground, crushing my lips into hers.

"I hate you," she whispered, breaking away. "Someday, I'm going to kill you."

I laughed, leaning back and cupping her cheeks. "That makes both of us. But in the meantime, we fall in love."

"I could *never* love you."

The phrase had all amusement leaving and it was partly because I believed her.

My fingers slid into her hair and I gripped, holding her gaze to mine. I felt the minute she slipped under my control. "You will love me and you're going to make an effort right now." I loosened the hold, but kept my hands in place. "Now, stop talking and kiss me with every ounce of passion you possess."

Knocking didn't have me turning away. My hands followed her face forward and I met Tessa's lips with all the false eagerness I could feel coming from her. Weight from her arms wrapping around my neck couldn't have been more perfect. If it were only real...I wasn't sure why I wanted it so much, but the need was powerful and it taunted me.

"Tessa?" Jiggling sounds erupted in the background, but I ignored it, pulling her in closer with the palm I slid to her lower back. The taste of her almost had me closing my eyes. I fought the urge, moaning as her tongue massaged against mine.

"Tessa, open the door or I'm breaking it down."

I groaned, pulling back. "Tell him you're fine."

Suddenly, I didn't want to stop. I'd had every intention of letting him see us kissing, but my lust for her outweighed my greed. My cock ached to be inside of her. The real her.

"I'm fine, Hunter." The monotone voice seemed to work and it almost gave the impression that she'd been annoyed. Heavy footsteps pounded down the hall and I pulled her mouth back to mine, stealing one more kiss before I turned away. Tessa blinked a few times and I caught her fist as it flew in my direction. "Stop doing that."

"Kiss me for real then. Like you want to."

Again, seriousness took over her features. It was the same expression as before, when I couldn't comprehend what she was thinking.

"What if I said, in some small way, I do want to kiss you?"

A heavy thud in my chest had my hand lifting. Was that from her or me? "What's stopping you?"

Disbelief had her growing angry. "You've got to be kidding me. You come in, force your blood on me, bite me," she ground out, "and you expect me to want you? You have no manners. You're rude, cocky, and an arrogant asshole. Not to mention, all you seem to be focused on is *killing* me. I'm supposed to just jump right in bed with you and fall in love?" Sarcasm was thickly laced in her words. "I don't know what sort of women you've been with, but that kind of charm doesn't work on me."

The verbal knockdown to the proverbial pedestal I felt I stood on left my arms crossing. "How would you expect me to act if I were trying to get you to fall in love with me?"

Shock turned to irritation. "You'd have to give me space, for one. And be caring and sweet. Neither character trait is one I believe you possess. And, you wouldn't want me dead."

"How can you say I'm not caring or sweet? I gave you part of me. I've *never* done that with another human before. Or anyone, in general! Apparently, I care."

Tessa glared. "About yourself. God, are you delusional or just out of touch with reality?"

"Apparently delusional because I'm putting up with *you*. No one has ever talked to me this way. I can't believe I haven't killed you yet."

A drawn out groan came from her lips and she walked over, grabbing the fitted sheet from her dresser. As I watched her put it on, I tried to understand what she wanted. It was everything I wasn't, yet I was sitting here contemplating trying to act it out. This wasn't me. Since I'd been tempted by her scent, nothing had been me. It didn't make sense.

"I'm staying the night." I kicked off my shoes, making her stop. "I'll sleep in your bed, but I won't touch you."

"Yeah, right. I wish you'd just leave. If it weren't for Hunter…" she trailed off, looking over at me. "You touch me and I'll scream."

"And you'll both die. You're safe for tonight, Tessa, but not for long."

Chapter 7
Tessa

Three days and I almost convinced myself I'd made the entire thing up. If it weren't for Hunter's constant questioning about Marko, maybe I could have forgotten about the vampire completely. But I doubted that. He turned my world upside down, yet made me question who he truly was. A part of me felt as though I couldn't fault his behavior. After all, if he were as bad as he made himself out to be, or as bad as I had made him out to be, wouldn't I be dead instead of at work? Wouldn't he have bitten me again that night, instead of actually letting me sleep? *Good?* No. I knew I shouldn't let myself even think that. Sympathy could be a killer and I'd surely be the victim if I held onto those thoughts.

Marko Delacroix was not to be trusted. He wasn't a pet I could tame and love. There was a monster under his curious exterior and no amount of training him to be civil was going to change that. The root of his behavior spoke for itself. Even though I hadn't seen him, it didn't mean he wasn't there. I still got the tingly sensation once the sun went down and I couldn't deny that I felt him watching. My skin crawled. Fear left me shaking while my heart raced. Yet…what kept me alive, beating so heavily in my chest, called out for him in sadness. How?

The phone ringing had me reaching for the receiver. I cleared my burning throat for what felt like the million time. I couldn't think of anything but him and it was driving me crazy.

"Hampton Auto Sales. This is Tessa, how may I direct your call?"

The greeting came out, even as I tried to figure out what it was that was so intriguing about this vampire.

"Hello, I came across an ad you posted about a used…"

Nothing existed after that. I didn't care. I was already reaching for the button. "Please hold while I pass you over to sales." For the first time, I didn't wait for them to say thank you. My internal ear vibrated and I wedged my finger in the center to give a quick push. "Sales, line one." I put the receiver down, wondering why I'd come in at all. I didn't feel good and I couldn't concentrate for more than a few seconds at a time. It was as if I were on auto-pilot and my mind was wrapped around the predicament I was in.

"Hey, Tessa."

My eyes rose to Jared, one of the salesmen, as his arms settled over the counter I sat behind.

"Hey," I said, trying to smile. "Going good today?"

"Eh, maybe. I have a couple coming in at one to look at the daily special. I think I pretty much have it in the bag." He leaned more forward while he glanced toward the small group of other salesmen bullshitting by the door, waiting for more customers to show up.

"Listen, Tom, Will, and I are heading to Joe's Cavern for lunch. You want to come?"

Realizing I had no idea what time it was, I immediately looked at the clock. "Actually, I can't. I have errands to run today."

It was a lie, and the first one I could remember telling concerning something so small. Guilt ate at me while I gave him a sad look. "Maybe tomorrow. I'm not feeling so well anyway."

"Hope it's not that flu that's going around," he said, already leaning back.

"I sure hope not." I cleared my throat again, rubbing my hand along the length of it. The phone ringing had him grinning and throwing me a wave as he started walking back toward the group. "Hampton Auto Sales. This is Tessa, how may I direct your call?"

Silence.

My eyes shot from the buttons I'd been staring at to the white wall before me. The company posters didn't register. Didn't even exist. I tried to catch my breath as a weird fuzziness wrapped around my brain.

"Hello?"

"I need you to come to me."

The receiver almost fell from my hand and sweat began to coat my palms. "I…"

"Will come to me," he growled. "This is not a request, mon chaton. I need your blood. You *will* come."

No, repeated in my head, but somewhere deep down, I knew I couldn't deny him. Not only because a small part of me got sickly aroused at the thought, but because my brain was denying me the right to choose.

"I don't want to," I whispered.

There was a moment of hesitation before he let out a deep breath. "I can't wait any longer. You got your time these last few days. Now it's your turn to give me mine."

If I'd been afraid before, it didn't compare to the realization that I'd be in his territory. I liked familiarity. The safe haven of my own home. I was a person of habit. I still drove the same car my parents got me in high school. Still lived in the first home I'd managed to get by myself. Shit, I was still working the same job. I didn't like new.

"Can you wait until tonight so you can come to me?"

Somewhat of a groan came through and his throat sounded raspy and deep as he answered. "No. It has to be now. I'm going to give you an address. Write it down."

My hand was shaking so badly, I nearly dropped the pen I'd picked up. "Okay." Weak. God, I suddenly felt so much sicker. I didn't want to do this. More sweat drenched my body and I could feel my cheeks burning.

"Fifty-two thirty-four West Oak Drive. You'll knock on the door and tell them Kline sent you. You'll say that every time I want you to come to me. Then, you will ask to see me. My first name only, Tessa. You have to say it exactly like that or else you will be killed. Now, repeat what you'll say so I can hear."

Deep breaths left me while I felt myself stand in panic. "Kline sent me." I swallowed past the sudden scorching in my throat. "I'm here to see Marko."

"Just like that. Now, hurry up, I'm hungry."

The line went dead, but I couldn't hang it up. I stood frozen, afraid as I dreaded what was to come. Why couldn't I tell him no? Why did I completely lock up any time I tried to mention him or expose what he was? I was a prisoner inside my own body and I didn't like it.

"Jeez, you okay, Tessa?"

Trembling had me battling to get the phone on the hook while I stared at Carlos, the finance manager.

"No, I have to go home. I think I'm getting the flu."

"Oh, damn. You look really pale. Do you need someone to drive you home?"

I shook my head. "No, I don't live far."

"Alright, then. Be careful. I'll let Abby know to get the phones."

My purse was already in my hands and I nodded, pulling the post-it note with the address and name free. "Thank you. Hopefully I'll feel well enough to come in tomorrow."

If I wasn't dead. I couldn't think of that now. I broke around the counter, fumbling for my keys as I spouted a few goodbyes to the guys standing by the door. The moment I got in my car, I looked down at the address. West Oak. I had no idea where that was. Austin was big. Hell, it could be anywhere.

I pulled out my phone, mapping the address, all the while trying to stop the constant shaking. Marko's location was a good fifteen minutes away. Where I lived and worked close to downtown, he was more toward the outskirts. I frowned as I tried to memorize the turn offs. It wasn't too complicated and didn't look to be too far off of the freeway.

The car's engine came to life at the turn of my hand and nausea swept through while I made my way out of the parking lot. Music filled the interior lightly and I reached forward, turning it off, not able to stand the smallest interruption. The traffic stayed at a steady pace and with every mile I got closer, the worse I felt.

Fever seemed to settle over me and I seriously wondered whether I really was starting to catch this flu Jared had mentioned. Or…was it Marko? Shit.

My hand shot to my mouth and I tried to stop from being sick. The wave came out of nowhere and I tried my best to keep my focus on merging to the exit. Swallowing, I managed to keep it at bay, but I knew if I didn't stop soon, I'd be in trouble.

"Please, please." The word mumbled from my mouth as more saliva had me in tears. I hated being sick and it couldn't have come at a worse time.

I turned, making sure I was clear as I pushed the car faster toward the intersection. The light was green and I turned left, going under the overpass. West Oak was the third street down and terror mix with dread as I scanned the addresses on the expensive bricked-in mailboxes resting in the front. As luck would have it, the two-story mansion was the third one down and I pulled in, watching as a black iron gate rolled back at my arrival.

Faster, my heart pulsed while I came to a stop in front of the large French doors. My hands were trembling so badly by the time I grabbed my purse that I fought to get the strap to sit on my shoulder.

Would this place be the death of me? Was this why he wanted me to come? He could hide the evidence here. I might never make it back out of those elaborately carved doors.

The closer I got, the more detail came into view. I forced myself to remember the words I needed to say while my feet became heavier. Warnings to run screamed in my brain and I silenced a sob at what I was doing. Having no choice was the worst feeling in the world and it crippled me internally.

My hand rose, knocking three times in quick succession. I stepped back, glancing behind me. I wanted to flee so badly. Why couldn't I?

A creak had me jumping and spinning forward. An older man in a uniformed suit stood, staring at me blankly. More nausea came and I licked my lips, searching for what I was supposed to say. "Kline sent…me. I'm here to see Marko." The words stuttered out and I reached over, holding onto my purse like a life vest.

"Come in." The door opened wider and walking past the threshold was like walking into a brick wall. A sound escaped my lips as the man's hand grasped the underside of my arm, gently leading me forward.

"The first time is always the hardest," he said quietly. "Marko will be in his room." He led me into a large kitchen and opened a stainless steel metal door. The thickness as he pulled back had my eyes widening. *Holy shit.* What was he hiding down there? Or…who?

I stared into pitch black, shaking my head. "Where will he be?"

The man's eyes lowered. "Feel for him. You'll find your way."

Feel? For what? All I was experiencing was the dreaded flu. I kept quiet as I stepped down to the first step. A rail rested to the side and I held onto it as I walked down three more. Air brushed my hair forward and I nearly screamed as the door secured loudly behind me. Darkness was all I suddenly knew and I flickered my gaze around, seeing nothing. Anxiety had me wanting to lower so I could curl into myself. I didn't want to continue. Something was down there. Something *very* bad. But I couldn't leave. My feet wouldn't allow me to. Even now, they continued at a slow pace, betraying what my instincts kept trying to warn me about.

Light appeared the further down I went and sounds began to make their way to me. Talking. Shuffling of some kind.

My hand pushed to my stomach as the need to heave began again. I paused, inhaling deeply, trying anything to make it pass. The stench of mold mixed with the smell of cooking meat and it didn't help. Confused, I stepped down even more. The stairs had seemed to go multiple levels and my weak legs were feeling every one of them.

The bottom of the steps were lit up and I placed my foot down onto them, ducking my head to see through the opening. My lips separated and I gasped, moving down even more, not believing my eyes.

A mass of people scurried in and out of doors, some with bags in their hands, others holding what looked to be fast food. Amazed, I eased past the entrance, too shocked to take in much else. It was baffling. A fucking underground city. And I was almost positive I was looking at humans. Some were in suits and some were average, everyday people. Women laughed, talking with one another as if they'd known each other forever. Shit….maybe they did.

My head shook and I walked in deeper, stopping as I spotted large tables a good distance away. They sat empty, but there was energy around a smaller one at the end that I didn't like. It scared me, just as much as the dark tunnels that broke off in all directions.

One man between two of the shops pushed from the wall and I saw his lip pull back threateningly as I weaved through. It was enough to startle me in a place that almost appeared so normal. I walked faster, trying not to be too obvious as my pulse raced and my body vibrated in warning. I knew with my reaction, he had to be a vampire.

Feel for him.

God dammit. I felt lost, scared, and sick. Nothing else.

I glanced behind, watching shadows play off the creature's face as he leaned further down. The black hood he wore concealed everything but his features and even those were hard to distinguish. The large open area wasn't lit very well. The shops held most of the brightness, but not as much an aboveground home would. Outside of the businesses, one could easily find areas to hide.

A dark tunnel stood ahead and I wanted to double back to where all the humans were. It had to be safer there. Why were my feet refusing to let me? Again, I stared back, noticing his lip curling higher. The man was gaining on me. If I went any faster, I'd be running. Should I run?

I didn't think. I pushed from the balls of my feet and raced for the tunnel ahead. My flats slapped against the cement and I held in the scream that wanted to come at the man breaking into a quick run. The speed was so fast, it was shocking. He'd catch me and I knew what he was capable of.

Light disappeared as I broke through the tunnel entrance. I had no idea where I was going. But, I didn't have to. One minute, I was running, and the next, a door opened and an arm shot out, wrapping around my waist. Air exploded from my lungs at the impact and I was dropped to the ground roughly. My body locked up at the speed he displayed as he reached back in and slammed the vampire down right next to me. There was no gentleness in his actions. Crunching from the vampire's skull connecting with the floor left me scooting back. Blood sprayed out as Marko's fingernails extended out, shredding the monster's neck.

"She is not to be touched. Ever," he roared. "You be sure to spread the word to all of your little friends. If any of you so much as think about coming near her, I'll kill you myself." The vampire was thrown from the door, bouncing off the far wall. I crawled back even more as Marko slammed the barrier closed behind him. My head shook continually as I took in the new side to the man who now stood before me. Fangs, I knew he had those. Razor sharp nails, inhuman speed...*power*?

"Stand up, mon chaton. Come to me."

My head kept shaking, even though I somehow managed to get to my feet. Dark circles rested under Marko's eyes and there was a tinge of paleness to his full lips. His bare chest heaved, the lean muscles tightening as he glared in my direction.

"Your blood has made me sick. Look at me. I'm a God damn mess." The words were spat and I couldn't help the joy, yet offense, I got out of his statement. I moved more toward the door, only to stop at what lay outside. Was the injured vampire still there? Was he even hurt anymore?

"If I'm making you sick, why do you want more? You should let me go."

In four large strides, Marko made it to me, jerking my arm, causing the contents of my purse to scatter across his floor. I didn't even have time to scream as he tossed me on the large bed.

"I'm sick because I've put off taking more from you. Do you know what that's done? I should have never of given you my blood. Had I known this was what would happen, I would have avoided it at all costs. I'm *not* weak."

The heel of my shoes pushed into the firmness underneath me while I made it to the large wooden headboard. "You're not weak." I managed.

"Oh, but, mon chaton, right now, I am. I haven't slept in days. You blood will not allow me to. Each drop taunts me to take more. I crave nothing but your taste on my tongue. And you're going to give it to me."

"No." My throat closed, not allowing me to say any more. Vibrations from his agitation and anger left me looking for an escape even though I knew there wasn't a way out. Not from what had to be done.

Marko's legs hit the edge of the mattress and his eyes cut right into my very soul.

"I'm going to sit on the bed and you're going to straddle me. And you're not going to move. If you do, I *will* kill you and that time isn't here yet."

I gripped the pillow melded against my hips. His knee came down and he crawled forward. I couldn't stop myself from watching his shoulders flex with each lift of his hand. My foot pushed in more and I moved my head back as his face came in, pausing before he rubbed his nose along my neck.

A deep groan sounded and his palms wrapped along my waist, spinning me to fit on his lap as he settled against the headboard. Pressure pushed to the middle of my back while he drew me in.

"I don't want this," I whispered through the fear. I knew the pain would be excruciating and with how bad he looked, accompanied with his warning, there was a chance he wouldn't stop drinking until I was dead.

"Shh." My hair was brushed back while he adjusted my neck. "You may not want it now, but you're about to be begging me for more. The first time was the worst. Your body rebelled against the unknown. Now, it longs for nothing more than my bite. You can deny it all you want, but you know I speak the truth. My blood calls you back to me, as yours does with me. We'll never be the same, even if I did let you go. The only way to stop the connection is through death. Yours…or mine."

My eyes closed and I lowered my chin to rest on the top his shoulder. Coolness swept down the side of my throat and I couldn't remember feeling the marked difference in his temperature before. He'd always felt cooler, but never this much.

"I'm sick because of what you're feeling, aren't I?"

"Yes, and had we been bonded, I would have never gotten so bad. You would have known when I needed you. I could have told you without having to speak a word."

My eyes opened, but I didn't see the headboard before me. "Bonded?"

"Three times ingesting my blood. It's something you're never going to have to worry about. Now, relax and embrace what I'm about to do. The acceptance will help."

I slammed my fist against his chest, but didn't move. "I don't want to accept. I want to go home."

Pain exploded at my hair being pulled and I felt my back connect to the mattress. The force knocked the air from me and still, he pushed into my chest until I was sure my bones would crack. Air refused to come while he made sounds full of pain. My hands continued to beat against him as my own agony took over. The humming of his voice eased as he lifted and pinned my wrists with one of his hands.

"Your aggression is only going to make it worse, but I'm afraid it's too late."

The burning in my throat was undeniable and I knew it was his pain. My face turned to the side just as the bite caused my legs to kick out. Stinging brought tears falling free and his thighs pushed mine further apart while he ground his hard cock into me. The pleasure that exploded within sent my hands flying up against his hold. Surprisingly, he let go. Even more shocking was when I moved my hands to his back. For the first time since I'd met him, the fear dissipated completely. My hips arched and I felt myself move against him, suddenly needing more.

Vibrations from his moans intensified the passion that swept through me. I wrapped my arms around his neck, lacing my fingers in his hair, drawing him in deeper. Tugging against the button of my slacks pulled me from the bliss, but I didn't dwell on it or fight as I let him work them free. My hips even lifted to help him move them down. Marko broke away, meeting my eyes. What lurked deep within the depths pulled at me, but it had nothing to do with the trance I knew he could have put me in. There was something else. Something more that I couldn't even begin to grasp.

"Marko?"

"No." His head shook, cutting me off from saying…I wasn't even sure. My slacks were removed and my arms lifted as he took off my blouse. What we shared in that moment was only one thing. Need. And I was just beginning to feel the effects of it. Would it grow? Have me sick and obsessing over him all the time? The questions were there, but didn't last as he leaned in and unclasped my bra while pushing me back to lie down.

Warmth was back in his touch and I trembled for an entirely different reason. Lips pressed into my chest and I gripped his satin comforter while he made a path toward my breast. At the prick of his fang over the fleshy area, I gasped, moaning at the lust that built.

"Feels good, doesn't it, mon chaton? I know it does. I feel your pleasure."

A smile pulled at the corner of his mouth and he licked the bead of blood that began to surface. It was so wrong, yet so right. What I saw should have turned me off, but I wanted more. Wanted him to pierce every inch of my body if it meant I'd feel the desire that existed now.

"We shouldn't…" I slammed my mouth shut, not wanting to hear the denials anymore. Whether we should or not, I wasn't going to fret on it. Contact was something I hadn't had in years. I missed it. Even more so in the moment. And hadn't I fantasized about something like this happening? God, I had such dark, twisted thoughts and they were nonstop. Especially now that Marko had come into my life.

Suction pulled my nipple into his mouth and I cried out, arching. Fuck, if I were going to die at some point, maybe going this way wouldn't be so bad. My mind slowed as the thought rolled back through. How many other women had thought the same thing?

Marko picked up the change in my mood and I saw his eyes narrow. He was back on me before I could process movement.

"Don't you dare pull back now. I know you want this. I'm going to *make* you want it."

Fangs embedded back in my neck and I clawed at his shoulders, feeling him move to the side. It appeared as if my raking downward left him uncomfortable or he could at least feel it. He had said he was weaker...I didn't care. Let him hurt. Like before, ecstasy ruled over everything. Thickness from the poison that rested within him increased into my system and the swirl of his tongue left me rocking against him even more. For what felt like forever, he drank. When he broke away, he reached up to the wounds and ran his finger over them. In slow movements, he drew across my chest, a grin appearing as he did so. At the last line, he sucked the remaining crimson away.

"That's better now, isn't it, mon chaton?"

All I could do was nod. I knew nothing but wanting his hand to lower so we could continue. When he did so, I couldn't reach for him fast enough. He stayed propped on one side while he kissed me and undid his pants. The pressure of his fingers rubbed over my panties, teasing my opening. I made a sound into his mouth, gripping his shoulder tighter. How many years had it been since someone had touched me there? The answer didn't come. Couldn't, as he slid my panties to the side and rubbed along my slit.

"You're so wet and hot." He brought his digit to his mouth, closing his eyes. The loss of contact wasn't missed for long as he worked his pants from his legs. His hand returned and I dug my nails in again as he slid one inside of me. "And...tight. Fuck." French poured from his mouth as the thrusts became deeper. He rocked in their motion, building me even higher before he slid in another.

"You want me?" Both of his fingers that had been inside of me pushed into his mouth and he sucked on them again before separating my thighs wide and moving down.

"Yes." The answer was obvious. I was gone. Completely oblivious to anything but what I was experiencing.

Kisses along my stomach moved to my thighs and I cried out from the pain as his fangs sunk into the sensitive skin. The draw of his sucking felt odd in that location and the top part of my body shifted, but the pleasure was just the same, if not more.

Desperate for something I couldn't even begin to process, I pulled at the material of my panties resting at my hip. Relief took over as he reached over and jerked them free. The burn from the friction sent heat where the lining had rubbed and torn. White cotton was thrown to the side and he inhaled while he broke the seal of his lips. I watched his tongue lick over the wound, closing it. I knew from the first night that it wouldn't take long for the bruising and punctures to disappear completely.

"Open wide for me, mon chaton." He was already moving closer to my pussy and although my hesitation was obvious, I obeyed. Only once had I let someone taste me there and the boyfriend I held for two months hadn't impressed me. But at the first trace of Marko's tongue up my inner folds, I knew this was different. Maybe because I wanted it. Wanted…him.

My head lifted higher and I rose to my elbows, watching as he sucked me into his mouth. I bit my lip and started rocking my hips as he teased and moved down, outlining my entrance. The width of his tongue flattened and he used his thumbs to spread me, licking his way to my clit. Flicks over the sensitive bud tightened my stomach even more and I fell back to the bed as my need increased. Over and over, he teased me, until I was gasping to catch my breath through the orgasm that beckoned.

"You're going to come now." His thumb took over for his tongue, rubbing over my clit. I moved to meet his finger as it glided back into my channel. The thrust surged deep and I plunged down with each increase of motion. Dark hair fell over my face and I didn't care to push it out of the way. The orgasm was right there and I didn't have to search it out as spasms shook my body.

"Marko." My hands reached out for him as I moaned and screamed through each jerk. He moved in almost immediately after I finished, not denying me the closeness I needed from the best pleasure I'd ever experienced. My deep breaths were cut off by him easing his weight down and kissing me. The passion he displayed…the need he put into meeting and teasing my tongue left me even more lost to him. My heart swelled in that moment, beating furiously in my chest as pressure pushed against my pussy. I felt myself stretch and I gasped at his size. I was wet, but it wasn't enough. He withdrew, inching in even slower. Stinging caused me to jerk and I couldn't stop the whimper.

French came out through his tightened jaw. A string of curse words were met with him cupping the side of my face. "I don't want you to hurt right now."

Tenderness left me even more in awe. I couldn't stop staring into the depths of his eyes. Was he being sincere? Playing his game to make me feel this way? "Don't stop," I whispered.

Lips met mine and I held onto him tightly, matching his desire. I felt myself get even wetter and my push down evoked a moan from Marko. Inch by inch, he took his time. His hips moved so erotically and with each withdrawal, the urge became more intense. I rotated mine, crying out as he broke through uncharted territory and buried himself in me completely.

"Oh…God," he said, drawing the words out and pushing back in just as deep. My teeth bit into his shoulder and I sucked against his skin, wanting to taste him like he did me. The internal craving was undeniable. I wanted all of him and if I didn't have his blood, my brain couldn't process what would happen. I *had* to taste him, no matter what I had to do to make it possible.

My teeth sank in hard and the action had Marko's fingers fisting through my hair, holding me in place. I pushed harder, until I was biting with everything I had. Aching registered in my teeth and gums, but I couldn't stop. The tiniest jerk to the side had a tinge of warmth flowing through my mouth and even though my mind eased, my eyes widened. But not from the fear of what was happening. Power slammed into me just as hard as he began to. For the life of me, I didn't let go or stop sucking as another orgasm built.

Adrenaline kicked in while I tried controlling the euphoria that began blanketing me. I wanted to enjoy this, but something larger was beginning to mess with my mind. The top half of my body twisted uncontrollably and I barely noticed as spasms had me screaming through their strength. The room swayed and I was able to turn back to Marko even though I felt as though I were falling. If the pleasure wouldn't have been so good, I would have been terrified. Instead, my emotions weren't my own. The blood that was working its way through me ruled. Tessa was disappearing and I held onto that as Marko's cock swelled. More French surrounded me and I knew they were sweet words of love. Ones…he wasn't positive he meant. I was as sure of that as I was mysteriously understanding his language.

Black dotted my vision, making pieces disappear. I gasped as his voice grew louder in my head and began to blur together. It all mixed around, distorted, only to go back to normal. The room began to fade and I sunk my nails in one last time to try to hold on. For the life of me, I knew I wasn't going to be able to.

Chapter 8
Marko

We were one. *Thump-thump. Thump-thump.*

My lids opened and I lifted from nuzzling Tessa's neck, a smile coming to my face. I knew I'd have her, but it was how much she wanted the sex that left me happy. Maybe I hadn't expected so much passion. From the glimpses of her past, she hadn't enjoyed fucking very much. Hell, she'd only been with two people and the first was just once. The second...well, he didn't last long in or out of the bedroom.

I pushed up completely, taking in the dark hair covering her face. The word MINE was written across her chest in blood. The claim made my smile grow bigger. Tessa still laid there, breathing heavily. She had to have been exhausted with as much blood as I drained from her. Hell, I'd needed it. Taking Boyd out for trying to attack her left me lightheaded. I couldn't ever remember being so weak. And it showed. Not only in my appearance, but in everything I did. Even talking had become a chore.

Tightness pulled at my back and I paused midway in removing the long curls covering her face to look over my shoulder. Damn, she'd gotten me good. My eyes narrowed only to flare open at the bite mark on my shoulder. The memory of me pulling her in slammed into me like a freight train. I fingered the bloody indents, watching the dark substance slide over my finger at the swipe.

My head spun back to face her and I swept her hair back, immediately turning her face to look at me. Dark pupils were dilated, nearly taking up the entire green area. My head shook with what I already knew.

"Hey." I tapped against her cheek and her lips separated. The deep breaths went from her nose to her mouth as she gasped. My brain reeled as I tried to figure out if this was common with a second exchange. "Tessa." I tapped harder and she blinked. A small strangled sound, almost like a whisper, sent a small dose of panic rushing through me. I wanted her dead, but not like this. Maybe not even for another few weeks. Shit!

I reached down, picking up my pants and sliding them on. I didn't think as I grabbed one of my shirts and pulled it over her head. Her body wasn't necessarily limp, but it wasn't reacting either.

"Tessa. God dammit. Tessa," I growled louder.

"You…" Again, she blinked. Calmness over her potential death faded, replaced by the anger again. Two fucking blood exchanges. I didn't want this. The obsession I felt for her went past the point of controllable. I hadn't lied to her about not sleeping. I couldn't knowing she was there with Hunter. And it wasn't just him. It could have been any man and I would have felt as strongly. I stalked her house until the last minutes before sunrise. Nothing mattered but her and I hated it. Who was this person that had taken me over? I didn't know him. Didn't want to! She was ruining me. She was…winning. But what was I supposed to do? Kill her to stop the process? Bond her and make her my concubine? I nearly laughed. That sure as hell wasn't happening. Blood slave? Eh. Keep her here so I could at least sleep? That was tempting.

"You…" Tessa took a deep breath and tried to sit, but fell back to the mattress. My arm latched onto her bicep, pulling her up. Her cheeks flushed even as her skin glowed vibrantly. "You're…staying away from me…after this," she said, slurring. "And you're not keeping me…here. God, I have the worst headache."

"Wait." I slapped her hand away before it reached her head, forcing her to look at me. "You were reading my mind?"

I knew she had. There'd been no reason for me to close myself off before. Now, I'd have to remember to. There were too many secrets she couldn't know.

You're staying away from me after this. The words came barreling back. "You are not one to tell me what to do. Whatever I decide will be done and that's the end of it."

I barely caught her fist as it flew toward my face. The power was amazing. I noticed she was bouncing back. And fast.

"Stay the fuck away…from me." Motionless, she stared, and I couldn't ignore the tears pooling in her eyes. They tugged at my heart and I could have cursed the new sensations brought on by our growing bond. I'd hurt her feelings from my cruelty. Could read her thoughts as she internally broke down, regretting what we'd just shared. Regretting opening herself to me.

"I told you that you were going to fall in love with me, mon chaton. The process has started. There's no stopping it. *Especially* now."

"Wrong," she said in French, pulling at her hand. "I've walked away from people I held more love for than the speck of emotion I feel for you. That was real love. You poisoning your way into my heart will not make it flourish. More like wilt until it feels nothing but death and hate. Congratulations," she spat, "you're getting part of your wish."

I let go of her, not believing what I was hearing. She'd slipped into my language. Spoke it as if she'd been born and raised in my country. And I knew she didn't even realize it.

I pushed from the bed, not able to stop staring at her.

"By the way," she continued, climbing off the other side and grabbing her slacks, "the bite was better than *you* were. So much better. Maybe we should just stick to that from now on."

The lies I so clearly registered had me flying over the mattress to tower above her. "If that's the case, maybe I should fuck you again. It might possibly change your mind. Or maybe I'll give you to the vampire who followed you back here for his gang to work over. I bet they'll do a better job fucking you."

My hands locked into her hair on both sides of her head as I lowered to eye level and projected visions into her mind of some of their work. The multiple bite marks and tears into flesh made some of the women unidentifiable. That was of course after a few of them raped their victims. Not Boyd, but the others.

Tessa's hands flew up, slamming into my forearms as she cried out. "I want to go home," she said, trembling violently. "I want to leave."

Even pissed, my obsessive side refused the idea. But it had to be done. I had to figure out a way to deal with her absence better than the last time. I had to break away and hunt, whether I wanted anyone else's blood or not.

I let go of her and stepped back. "You know your way out. Go."

Tessa's lips separated and she looked down toward the door. I felt her fear as if it were my own, and I didn't like it. The emotion left a sour taste in my mouth and I swallowed, trying to wash it away.

"Go," I urged. "No one is stopping you. *Yet.*"

Tessa jerked off my shirt, changing it for her own. Even as she did, I felt my body stir. Fuck, I wanted her again. And more powerfully than before. As she came around to my side, her steps were slow. I watched her pick up the contents of her purse and toss them inside. Even with my blood, she was still sore from how hard I'd fucked her. My mouth tightened at the softening in my chest and I leaned down, picking up her wallet and handing it to her. She wouldn't meet my eyes and I nearly made her. If it weren't for the pain she felt—I felt—I would have. It was all too real. Too new.

I threw up my wall, closing off that side of the exchange as much as I could. The dull emotions were a mild annoyance, but still effective. Dammit. Feeling wasn't something I wanted. *This* wasn't what I wanted.

Knocking had us both looking over. I tuned into the presence, immediately standing. Tessa joined me, throwing me a confused look as she did so.

"Who's Marie?"

My eyes shot to her and I groaned at not guarding my thoughts—again. The feelings I could easily remember to block, the thoughts were going to take some practice. "The devil," I mumbled under my breath. "Stay here and don't move."

I grabbed the shirt Tessa threw on the floor and slid it over my head. The fragrance that engulfed me hit hard. I paused, taking in my prey's scent. God, she smelled so good. If it weren't for who was at the door, I would gladly end this little charade between Tessa and I and take her again. As for Marie, I knew she wasn't going anywhere until I addressed her, which I was dreading. Tessa made me feel weaker, softer, than the vampire who was meant to be heartless. I couldn't stand that Marie might pick that up.

My hand pulled at the knob and I opened the door enough for Marie to see me. Red stained her lips and the long black sleeves of her dress hung loosely as she crossed her arms over her chest.

"Yes?" I brought up my eyebrow in annoyance.

Up and down, her head moved, trying to peer around me. I kept my place, not allowing her access.

"What is it, Marie?"

The curiosity wavered as her smile stretched wide and she met my eyes. "I heard you had company. I wanted to meet her. Or him. I'm not judgmental. I like both, too."

My low growl had her eyebrow raising.

"*Oh.* Someone's a little territorial. You've shared with me before."

"Have I? Well, that was longer than I care to remember back to. I don't share my meals anymore."

Marie leaned in toward my chest, inhaling deeply. When she pulled back, she was licking her lips. "Meal…or more? I think I smell her in you. And she's absolutely…delicious."

"You don't worry about that," I cut in. "She's *mine*. Back off."

I slammed the door, taking in Tessa's nervous expression. She went to walk around me, but I subconsciously stepped in her way. The narrowing of her eyes were mirrored by my own as I followed her more right.

"Move, Marko."

Still, she spoke in French, and it turned me on even more. When was the last time I'd actually been able to carry a conversation in my native language? Fuck, it had been so long ago. I switched over, too, studying her face as I began to talk.

"Where will you go? Home? Will you shower and try to erase what just happened?"

A hardness took over and there was that dull pain again.

"I never want to remember this. Ever."

My eyes closed and I wasn't sure if the ache was from me or her. No one had ever had the power to hurt me with words. "You don't mean that. I felt how much you enjoyed yourself."

"For the millionth time, it wasn't you I enjoyed, it was your poison. Now, if you'll excuse me, I think I'll go take that shower."

My feet stayed fixed to the floor, cemented in place at her hate. Racing thuds were shaking my chest and I knew the beat wasn't my own. The loud bang of the door followed her out of my room and I fought not to rush after her and drag her back in by that fucking beautiful hair of hers. Power surged as I tapped into myself, testing the new form of our bond. I knew I could send her images. I'd heard stories before. But I wanted more. My eyes closed and I explored my mind, trying to push into hers. To see what she saw. Darkness surrounded me and…nothing. I closed my fists, trying harder. Her pulse escalated and I waited for her thoughts to start. Random words skidded through and frustration led me walking to the door.

"So stupid. I can't believe I allowed that to happen. Years of celibacy down the drain for another asshole. I'm never going to learn. To make things worse, this one's the biggest of them all! What the hell was I thinking?" She paused and my head lowered. *"I wasn't. That's the problem. His bite drugs me. Makes it impossible for me to think rationally. No more!"* she yelled. *"Marko Delacroix is history. Kill me? I'd like to see him try."*

My eyebrow rose and I tried not to laugh. Tessa had no idea. Or maybe she did. I could so easily race back out there and snap her neck and there was nothing she could do about it. Her life was in my hands. I had the power to decide her fate. Maybe I'd show her exactly how lucky she really was. Then I'd end her life.

"Wait." Silence. *"Who is that? Are they coming my way? Oh, God, they are. Shit!"*

My head lifted as I waited.

"What a darling little thing you are." It was a woman's voice.

"Smells good, right?" Another woman.

"Like Marko."

The voice had me squinting with my eyes closed, trying to decipher who it was.

Tessa's thoughts came back through. *"If I tell them to go away, how pissed are they going to be? They're vampires. Do they want to kill me, too?"*

"I'm sorry, I'm late. I have to go." Tessa sounded winded.

"Surely you have a little time. Beatrice, lean in closer and tell me what you think. Is that two exchanges?

My eyes flew open and the door hit the wall at my jerk. My feet wouldn't move fast enough as I pounded down the hall and broke into the main room. People were out in droves, walking amongst the stores. I felt for Tessa, spotting her as two of the members of *le Cercle* led her toward the table.

"Tessa." My voice was deep, controlling, as I approached, grabbed her arm, and pulled her toward me. The fear of me was in her eyes, but she didn't stop from slamming her elbow into my side.

"Don't you even start. I'm going home." She turned back to the members. "It was so very nice to meet you both. I hope you have a wonderful day." With that, she turned and walked at a fast pace toward the stairs.

Beatrice shook her head. "Your blood is strong within her. Should we be expecting her at your feet soon?" Valencia's stare was hard and Beatrice's wasn't any different as they waited. My gaze fixed on Tessa just as her feet disappeared into the darkness. If I said yes, there was no going back on my word. There hadn't been a slave amongst members for as long as I could remember. Most had concubines who sat at their designated table, but a slave…they were so beneath us.

"Hesitation. You haven't decided."

My jaw clenched and I jerked my gaze back to them. "No, I know what I want. She'll be dead before the month is out."

Chapter 9
Hunter

My hand clenched around my gun as my eyes stayed glued to the television. Surely there was panic in the streets. This couldn't be true. How? But I knew it was. The announcement was on every station. And from the President, no less.

This has been a big year of a change. Of growth. We've come so far in both understanding and adversity. What we thought was unacceptable fifty years ago has shown in these days that we can do anything. Be anyone. I know the uncertainty is there. It was for me at first, too, but I ask that you try to be understanding. Everything will go on as normal. The term vampire may sound scary, but these people are already here. They work at our hospitals. They teach at our colleges. Night classes, of course," he said, laughing. *"But, in all fairness, I ask that you refrain from judgment or panic. We're an accepting generation. Keep that in mind.*

I hit the power button, shaking my head. I'd seen the same clip at least half a dozen times. Still, it was hard to believe.

"We're an accepting generation." The sarcasm was thick in my tone. "Ridiculous. Accepting, my ass." I reached forward, grabbing my beer. The door opening had me pushing to my feet.

"Tessa. You're home early. Did they let you go because of the news?"

Her eyebrows drew in, confused. "What news?" Her purse fell to the counter and she was already heading for the hallway. I stood, following.

"The vampires, of course! Tell me you haven't heard about it?"

Her feet stopped, but she didn't turn around. "Vampires?"

"Yeah, they exist. Our President wants us to be accepting and allow them into society. Can you believe that shit? Fucking *vampires*." I took a drink, laughing and shaking my head at the same time. "Are they insane? I think our government has lost their fucking minds. Vampires. As in fanged individuals. And they want us to just go about our day as if nothing is the matter." I couldn't stop saying it. The shock and fear was present and my laugh following was doing a good job trying to hide it.

"I knew," she whispered. "I…" Tessa turned around, a pained look on her face. "I knew."

My smile faded and I tried to process her words. "You…knew? You know a vamp…" Flashes of the blood on her mattress sent my eyes going wide. "Your boyfriend?" I spat. "Marko? Marko's a vampire?" Of course he was. It explained the weird feelings. The blood. The way he looked at her like she was a fucking steak.

Deep breaths left me as I stepped closer. "You begged me to leave. You begged me and I didn't help you…and he came. You insinuated killing something that couldn't die. Jesus fucking Christ, Tessa! Why didn't you tell me? He's not your boyfriend at all!"

Tears clouded her eyes, but didn't fall. "I was physically incapable of telling you, Hunter. As in, the words wouldn't leave my mouth no matter how hard I tried.

Even now, I can barely talk about it. I feel a lock in my jaw. A lack of air in my lungs. You have no idea how hard this is for me!"

In all the years I had known Tessa, in all the fights we'd had, never once had she raised her voice so loud or forcefully at me. I put my gun at the small of my back, pulling her in close. "I'm sorry I didn't help you. I didn't know."

"It's fine. It doesn't matter anymore anyway."

"Why is that?"

Silence left her parted lips and she shut her mouth, letting her forehead drop to my chest. "I'm in trouble, Hunter. Let's just leave it at that."

My frame stiffened and I brought her head up with my finger. "Trouble, how? With vampires...or Marko?"

A sorrowful expression crossed her face and I hated how she couldn't just say it. "The first?"

Her head shook.

"Then Marko. What is trouble? Like, he won't leave you alone? Or, he wants to still hurt you?"

"Let's just forget about it. I've had a long day. I'm going to take a shower before I start packing."

My hand pushed into her back, not letting her leave yet. "Pack? God, you are in trouble. You're trying to run from him. You..." I thought back to that night. She'd been so deathly terrified and in shock. Then, he'd come back and spent the night. I had stayed up and watched him leave before sunrise. It made me sick. Made my hate for him so much more. But the threat was there and it went beyond what I thought at the time. He was more than a jealous boyfriend. He was...

"You think he's going to try to kill you."

Again, she pulled back. "I have to pack."

She didn't have to say any more for me to know what I spoke was the truth. A jerk had Tessa pausing and she reached forward to unhook the material of the blouse that got caught on my belt buckle. I glanced down, unable to miss what was so clearly on and between her breasts.

"What the hell is that?"

Harder, she pulled, tearing the shirt as she spun for her room.

"No way," I said, following. "You're going to show me."

The door hit my palm as she tried to shut it and I didn't wait. I was tired of being the nice guy. It was getting me nowhere with her. A damn vampire had more pull over the woman I loved than I did.

"Show me, Tessa, or I'll look for myself."

Dark hair spun as she turned to face me. The anger she displayed was like I'd never seen. From fear to fury, this vampire brought out the worst in her.

"You want to see?" she yelled. "Fine. It's not like I haven't had to do something I didn't want to already today." Her hands tore at her shirt and she tossed it to the floor, surging forward. "You see that? Do you see what he's done to me!"

MINE.

My stomach dropped and I tried to breathe through the combination of emotions. "Is that your blood or his?"

She walked over, pulling open her drawer. "It's mine," she said, quieting. "It doesn't matter. I'm finished talking about it. I have to leave before the sun sets. If I don't, he'll be back. Not like this is going to work anyway. He'll find me."

"And I'll kill him. So help me, Tessa, this man…*this thing* better not come near you again. *Ever.* He's so dead." My hand came to mouth as I fought the urge not to slam my fist into something. Vampires, real. And one was already trying to stake its claim. No wonder Tessa had been so withdrawn from me. Hell, I couldn't have a five minute conversation without her shoulders caving in and me losing her to her thoughts. And it was him she was thinking about. That made it even worse.

"I'll start packing while you take a shower. I want that off you. Just tell me where we're going."

Tessa's anger was gone completely as she came back to face me. "Distance isn't going to matter. I don't know why I'm even flirting with the idea. He *will* find me, Hunter."

"How do you know?" My head shook and she licked her lips as her eyes looked upward, full of tears.

"Because he's telling me he will, right this very moment. He hears me. Hears us. He says if I go, I'm in big trouble."

The world could have dropped from under my feet and I wouldn't have been any more surprised than I felt. Telepathy? God, if he could read her thoughts, he'd know our next move. Our location for sure. Unless…

"Go get in the shower."

I didn't say anything as the tears spilled over and she obeyed. The moment I heard the door shut, I threw her closet open. A suitcase sat at the bottom and I pulled it out, throwing it open and tossing handfuls of clothes from her intimate drawers, along with shirts and jeans from her closet. When I couldn't fit anymore, I zipped it up and rushed it outside to her car. My eyes scanned the surroundings, even though I knew he wouldn't be coming yet. The sun was out. We were safe during the day.

I bounded up the stairs and went into my room. My green bag was still where I left it on the floor. Clothes I hadn't put away yet were resting inside. There wasn't much, but apparel was of little importance. What I needed was room for my guns. If what I knew of the myth was accurate, the best I'd do was slow the fucker down. But if it wasn't that way, maybe I stood a chance.

Four cases fit easily in my bag and I scanned the stuff my mom had brought over. My head shook. It wasn't good. I'd have to get online and search out what people knew of killing vampires. There was the old, wooden stake through the heart, but did that even work? I supposed it wouldn't hurt to try. But where the fuck was I going to get stakes? Make them?

I picked up the bag and jogged it out to the car. The shower was already off and I knew it wouldn't be long before we had to leave. But where? Shit, I had no idea. If it meant keeping Tessa safe, I'd scour every inch of this world to find places to keep her hidden. I may not have had a lot of money in the bank, but I had enough to keep us under the radar for a while. But then what? I didn't have a job. Not yet. Only interviews set up starting as early as next week. That was here, though. And I couldn't leave to work if it meant stripping her of her protection.

My feet pushed into the soft earth as I made my way to the back and threw my bag in.

Plans could come later. Right now, I had to focus on her. Besides, what was I running from? If he was going to come for her, why prolong the outcome? I'd kill him and then she could go back to her normal life. Back to hanging out and laughing with me. We could pick up where we left off so long ago. Then, I'd show her how things could be different. She might like to try. I knew I wanted to see whether our chemistry was still there. I thought I'd felt it the first night. Before…

The door slammed shut at my push. *Before* that bastard attacked her and marked his territory across her fucking chest. God, I could still see that word. *Mine.* Fuck him. Tessa was my first everything. If she belonged to anyone, it was me.

I rushed through the front door and rounded the hallway just as she was walking into her room. She was already dressed, like I knew she would be. Since I'd been here, she rarely came out of the restroom not wearing either her clothes or a robe.

The situation couldn't have turned out any more perfect. I stopped in my room, grabbing one of my ties from my interview suits and headed back to her room. She was staring at her opened closet that was a mess. Hangers dangled from others. Some were scattered on the floor. I didn't wait. I slid the tie over her eyes, pulling the back of her head to my chest.

"You're coming with me. Don't you dare take this off until I tell you. If you can't see, neither can he."

"But…" Tessa didn't fight as I stepped back, knotting the tie. "Hunter, I think he can feel me. He knows things. You don't understand."

"Let him look. If he's that good, I'll kill him. It works out either way."

Chapter 10
Tessa

To truly love a monster made me question whether Marko was the evil one at all. Maybe it was me. Maybe my yearning for something forbidden had finally caught up with the present, and all those dark fantasies I tried to keep buried were finally materializing around me. I wasn't good. Not deep down. Regardless of my life in the church, I was a beacon of endless dark, fucked up fantasies. The thing was, Marko had to have seen it from the beginning. He didn't speak the truth out loud, but it didn't mean he hadn't been aware. I couldn't stop the images I saw in my head of the two of us. Of me coming all over his cock repeatedly while he painted my body with blood. It was sick. Wrong. Yet, here I was, blindly staring toward the window, daydreaming of what I knew shouldn't be. And he was seeing it all. His moans broke through my lustful fog, making my cheeks heat in mortification. I couldn't believe I was doing it once again. That I was doing it at all. Never before had I thought about bloodplay, but it fit in with the twisted thoughts I had around sex and power. With him, it was just so right. Natural, even. And I couldn't stand it.

Why? Why was this happening? I didn't want to feel for this monster. So, why was I inviting death in at every opportunity? To him, I was teasing him with what he ultimately wanted and for some reason, I had no control over it. Maybe I wasn't thinking it at all. Maybe he was somehow making it happen. Perhaps it was his projection.

Fuck, I didn't know. Control over my mind was gone. I was doomed. Doomed to die in his arms as he sent me over the brink of pleasure. He'd make me beg for death just as much as I'd be begging for him to end this torture. He was the devil. He had to be.

My head turned away from the open blinds as I silently prayed to make it all stop. If God heard me, he wasn't helping. For some reason, it didn't surprise me. Not with my lack of faith. For so long, I'd tried to understand, but I just couldn't ever convince myself to believe. Nothing made sense. Especially now.

Hunter was sitting on the bed next to mine, messing with his guns. I tried to ignore how they made my anxiety worse. I'd never trusted them. Too many times, I'd heard of one accidently going off and killing someone. Despite my fears, I couldn't deny their presence did make me feel a little more at ease. Bullets might not kill Marko, but maybe it would give us enough time to escape.

Hunter glanced over, his brow creasing as he stared at me. Whatever was on his mind was consuming him. He kept silent a lot and constantly messed with his weapons. I wasn't sure where his head was at and I was almost afraid to know. Whatever he'd been through in his time of service had left its mark. I could see that now, I just wasn't sure how deep his scars ran. Was this situation with me making him worse? It had me questioning whether I should look for a reason to break our ties together. I didn't want Hunter suffering because of me. And he surely would if he got in the way with Marko.

"I still think we should have left after the first night."

The statement came out of nowhere and he turned back to his guns. I instantly frowned as I recalled fighting against him as he tried to get me to head back to the car.

"I told you, it's pointless. We're away from the city. That's what counts. Besides…I don't want to go further. I just want…" He knew what I wanted. I wanted to go home. I hated being out of my element, regardless of what that meant. But I'd stay here because it was my only way to protect myself. At least, until Marko came to get me. If he was even going to. Since I'd left, he refused to speak. It didn't mean he was giving up. He wouldn't. The blood told me that.

"Tessa, when was the last time you went out and did anything? Lived? Seen another state or went to an amusement park? The beach isn't but a few hours. Have you gone in the last decade?"

My head lowered and even though anger surfaced, I pushed it away. "It's hard for me to do anything. I don't know why. I guess I've let my life slip away in routine."

"Come with me," he urged. "Let's just…go. We may be on the run, but what an adventure we'd have. I'd show you things. It would be only me and you. We used to be so close. Think about it. Me. You. Together. Just—"

"Trying to outrun a vampire who could easily track me in a day," I said, interrupting. "It won't work. I can feel him, Hunter. He knows where I am. It's only a matter of time before he loses patience and when he does, my life—and probably yours—is in his hands."

"Bullshit," he exploded. "I refuse to believe he's that powerful. God, I almost wish he'd fucking come so I could put an end to him once and for all. The hate I have for that motherfucker has no bounds. I want to kill him, Tessa. I want to…" he trailed off, angrily turning back to his guns.

This new side of Hunter had my eyes moving to stare at the bed in surprise. I'd never seen him so enraged. The red of his face, the crazy look of his eyes…it scared me.

The sound of the clip slamming into the gun made me jump and I glanced over as he picked up the next weapon. I licked my lips, unsure of what I should do. Should I say something to ease the tension I felt surrounding us? I knew it would have been for the best, but the words wouldn't come.

"There has to be more people who are in the same predicament. I'm going to find them, Tessa. And then we're going to team up and we'll kill them all." His mouth opened, only to shut. The wary expression he threw had me knowing where his thoughts were. Hunter didn't trust me. Whether it was because Marko could read my thoughts or because I was connected to him now, I wasn't sure. Probably both.

"I would try to kill Marko if it came to it," I whispered. "I don't want to die."

A sympathetic look crossed his face and Hunter stood, coming to sit on the side of my bed. His hand reached out, grabbing mine.

"You didn't ask for this to happen. God, Tessa, I shouldn't have left you alone. This is my fault. If I had stayed—"

"No," I rushed in, shaking my head.

"It is," he continued. "I won't let him kill you. I can't." Tears came to his eyes and he lowered his face. "If you die, I'd be responsible. It'll be like I was the one who…God," he growled. Seconds went by while he stayed lost in his thoughts. "No. Marko will be the one who ends up dead. I can't lose you," he said quietly, looking back up. "I *refuse* to lose you. Whether that be to death or him, it doesn't matter. He may have your mind, but he won't have you."

My hand reached forward to cup his cheek and he immediately moved in to rest his forehead against mine.

"Hunter?" I closed my eyes, searching for the words. Was I supposed to ask if he meant as friends in general, or that he didn't want to lose me because he felt there'd be something more between us? The timing felt so awkward. Almost as much so as being close to him did. My mind was screaming for me to put distance between us, but for the life of me, I couldn't help but think that was Marko's blood talking. Not me.

"You're so tense against me. Stop worrying so much," he said, pulling back to look in my face. "You always worry. For once, put some faith in me. Let me take care of you. Let me be the one who worries."

If only it were that easy.

"For once, believe I'm capable of taking care of myself. I've never needed you to save me, Hunter. Not even when Jimmy Thompson pushed me down at the park when I was nine."

"But I did, didn't I?" he said, smiling. "I gave him quite the black eye, if I remember correctly. And then there was Steven Bishop in high school who you dated for all of four days. I beat the snot out of the asshole, too."

My eyes rolled and I laughed. "I slapped him first, if I recall. You didn't even know what was happening when you flew across the cafeteria."

"Didn't have to," he said, picking up a strand of my hair and twisting it around his finger. His stare rose as he continued to play with it. "You were crying and that was all I needed to see. No one hurts you and gets away with it, Tessa. No one. Not even an undead bastard like Marko. Mark my words, I *will* kill him."

As I stared into his eyes, I believed him. And I couldn't stop the aching in my chest at the thought. The conflicting craziness only left me angry. If I didn't die, I might just end up in a mental institution. My brain felt like it'd been tossed in a blender, right along with that damn beating thing in my chest that ached for its supplier.

Marko was nothing more than a dealer, serving me false emotions with ecstasy-doused injections. Poison to my heart. Addiction for my soul. And I was eating it up with all the desperation of a junkie.

My hands drew back and I clasped them in my lap as I let Hunter's words really sink in. I couldn't deny the panic that skidded through me at the mere thought of him killing Marko. How could I want to defend someone who wanted me dead? What a trick these killers had up their sleeves. And as evil as it was, I longed to join them. Somewhere deep down, I was beginning not only to have the need for Marko…but for *them*. For a life below the surface. The clear revelation had me pushing to the far side of the bed and standing. I glanced at Hunter's confused stare and tried to give him a reassuring smile. God, who the fuck was I becoming? I wanted Marko dead…but I wanted him to love me, too.

"Can you hear him right now or something?" Hunter stood as I began pacing

"No. He hasn't talked to me since we left. I'm just stretching my legs real quick."

The answer seemed to calm him and I kept my head down as I forced myself to stop and crawl back in bed. If he thought there was something wrong with me, he'd feel the need to be more on guard. Saliva filled my mouth and I swallowed past the increasing sensation. I could feel myself getting hungry, but not for food. *Marko.* I'd felt drawn to him before, but not like this. Never like this. And he was taking other people. It was a betrayal of the worst kind, considering the ties we held, yet it was also relief.

Chapter 11
Marko

Words were powerful things. Some could evoke the most sincere form of love while others could start the deadliest wars. What Hunter spoke was neither. His threats were equivalent to a pesky bug buzzing in my ear. Sure, they made me furious, but that's not what made me decide to kill him. It was taking Tessa away from me that had been the last straw.

Murder wasn't something I did often. At least, not outside of feeding. But there were times like this one that rubbed me the wrong way. Now, I was going to have to break my streak of days of distancing myself to go get her and bring her back. But, to where? Here? Her home? Fuck, I didn't know.

I sighed, pulling the redhead's face more to the side. The screams were muffled under my palm, but I didn't pay attention as I listened to Tessa and Hunter talk.

"Tessa, you need to try to eat. You haven't eaten all day."

"I'm not hungry." She yawned, moving her thoughts internally. *I feel like I have enough of his blood in me to last at least a week without eating, Hunter. I feel stronger after I taste Marko. The need for food doesn't exist. Only....him.* She sighed out loud. *God, I hate him. Love him...*

My eyebrows drew together and I glanced down at the pale neck before me. Why did I care that she was falling for me? I shouldn't have. All the women loved me after my bite. *Although, they never hated me.* But they'd never had my blood. I couldn't let myself get caught up in this. It was my own fault and now I had to pretend that what we shared wasn't real.

I projected the scene around me into Tessa's thoughts, hearing her catch her breath at what she saw. I didn't contemplate right or wrong, or pay attention to the sickening of my stomach. My fangs elongated and I dove down, biting and drawing against the woman's vein hard. Sweetness with just the smallest amount of tart had my claws coming out and I let the tips push into the woman's cheek, breaking the skin. A strangled cry came from Tessa and I eased my hands from the woman's lips, letting the cries of agony shine through. *"Please. Oh...God! Please. I don't want to die!"* I wanted Tessa to see what was coming. Wanted her to experience just a small taste of what I'd put her through when the time came.

Sobs grew heavier and fists were weakening as they slammed into my arms. I looked at the cement before me, not seeing it. I never saw anything in these moments. Where I usually closed myself off to feel my prey, I instead went back to Tessa. She was crying hysterically and I could hear Hunter buzzing around, calling out to her. But she didn't speak. Didn't think past the shock. I knew she was waiting to see what I was going to show her next. And I would. Fucking Tessa. She pissed me off to no end. Playing the willing captive as Hunter led her nearly twenty miles away. The distance caused me to bite down harder. God, I was going to make that bastard pay.

Beating weakened against my lips and I blinked, only just realizing the girl was almost unconscious in my arms. My claws ripped down past her jawline, making her body jolt. I could hear my thoughts turn to full-fledged yelling at my anger. *Humans aren't fucking concubine material. They're not. They're nothing! Only food.*

Whether the woman fainted or passed out was beyond me and I didn't care. I took one last draw and waited. One set of beats. Two. I let Tessa feel the last seconds of her life and oddly, in the moment, me and mon chaton almost felt like one again. My eyes closed as I fought the guilt over what I was doing. Over what I'd done. It was Tessa's guilt for me. Not mine. I didn't regret anything.

I licked over the wounds, willing them to disappear, and let her dead body drop to the ground. I cut off my thoughts, bringing my wall so fucking far up, Tessa would never get past it. One of the collectors quickly ran over and grabbed the redhead, pulling her by the legs and disappearing back into the dark tunnel. I hadn't had my meals brought to me in years, but knowing Tessa wasn't home had me not caring. I wasn't up for hunting tonight. I didn't even have to feed, but if it diluted her even more from my system, I'd do it. Even though it fucking killed me.

My strides were fast as I entered the heart of our underground city. The members of *le Cercle* glanced over to me from the small separate table meant just for us. I knew they felt my rage. It had to have been following my presence like a fucking black, deathly fog. My stare connected with Julius, the leader, and raspy words forced their way into my mind.

Sit. We feed. And then we plan.

I stayed perfectly composed as I continued to the stairs. *I've already fed. Inform me of when we meet. I need out.*

No. I said you sit and feed again.

The anger intensified and I rounded back, slamming my shoulder into a young vampire, sending him falling backward. Slaves and vampires of all status parted in my path and I zeroed in on the members who watched. They didn't change expressions or appear fazed by the wrath I so clearly wanted to cause. But they wouldn't. They were smart, keeping their thoughts so enclosed within, no one but maybe Julius would ever hear them.

I pulled out the chair at the end, taking my seat. All nine members were present and seated accordingly, waiting for me—the tenth.

Julius rested in a wing-backed, red, velvet chair at the head of the table. Next to him, on both sides, were Bufar and Anastasia, next to them and working down, Natalia and Valencia, Beatrice and Demetrius, John and Zachariah…and at the very end, facing Julius…me, the newest member of *le Cercle*.

"Feed." Julius may have been referring to everyone, but his eyes stayed on me. Just like they were meant to. It was the reason the newest member always sat his opposite. My every move was to be watched and it left my skin crawling.

I looked down at the two women who lay nude on the table, the soles of their feet connecting as their heads rested in front at me and Julius. We all had our feeding locations. Mine being the best. A reward for making in into the elite group. It would last until one of us got killed or were replaced. Then we'd move up one spot until only the last was left with new members. The cycle would be never ending, just like it had been for thousands of years.

My hand buried in the brunette's long hair and I tried with everything I had not to imagine Tessa. I failed.

Visions exploded before my eyes and I was suddenly in the hotel room where she and Hunter were staying. I was there…yet, I wasn't. Everything was in black and white, like an old photograph. Tessa sobbed heavily, her arms tightly around Hunter's neck while he cradled and rocked her. His stare stayed transfixed straight ahead. It said he was ready to kill me for what I was doing to her. And suddenly, I knew his mere threats weren't going to be enough to sate the rage he harbored inside. He was really going to try to kill me, just like I had every intention of killing him.

The black and white room warped, twisting and morphing before leaving me off-balanced in the blur of commotion. A street appeared and I was standing in the middle, somewhere downtown, while chaos and fighting produced blood splatter at every angle. Puddles formed as skin was shredded. *Vampires versus humans.* And it was real. I could feel it deep within my bones and it sent off a slow, deep panic. This was bound to happen at some point, but I could feel the shift and it wasn't in our favor.

Movement showed through the thick cluster of people. It was a man. He was tall and wore a black hoodie. His face was painted evilly, like someone long dead. The rotting flesh appeared as black painted holes and he had lines over and below his lips. The demented skeleton snarled with the predatory moves he made. Dark circles under his eyes made the shadows play around his face even more and all I could do was stare, warily. The threat was buried deep within his eyes as he stalked toward me. No amount of face paint could disguise the depraved person who came to meet me head on. *Hunter.* He wasn't the person he was now. The gone man in love was now replaced with a gone man set for death or revenge. Whatever came first. From the expression he was giving me, he wasn't planning on the death part.

Colors swirled around me again and I felt like my insides were dropped hard from some faraway place. The jolt left me feeling a second of hollowness within. It jarred me to the core, leaving me empty for the first time in my life. Sweat poured from my skin as I inhaled deeply and shot to my feet. Heads spun my way, but only one knew what I saw or what happened. He knew, because he was responsible for it. Only he'd have that sort of power.

I swallowed hard, still trying to catch my breath, even though I didn't necessarily have to breathe. My feet stumbled back and I pushed my damp hair from my face. I couldn't stay here. Not right now.

I have to go. The mantra repeated, but I meant it for only one—the man whose pale blue eyes still held mine. Seconds went by before his hand gestured a dismissal. I turned, rushing for the stairs. I wasn't sure where I was going or what I was even doing. All I knew was I had to get out.

Whispering hummed around me as I headed past the shops. They knew something was wrong. That I was Julius's focus at the moment. I couldn't stand it. I'd done so well to stay out of the attention of the gossiping droves of our population. Now, I'd be the fucking focal point. And it wouldn't even be good gossip. *Tessa.* This was her fault.

My feet pounded up the stairs, taking three at a time. The moment my hand connected with the door, it slammed open at my force. I didn't say a word as I broke through the front door and scaled the large, iron gate. The need to run sent me taking off at a speed I hadn't had to use in as long as I could remember. Where I was going, I didn't have a clue, but my feet seemed to know which direction to take me in. I ran, and ran, letting my mind return to the one person who might have ruined everything. Fuck, she'd ruined *me*. Even now, I could feel myself aching for her smell. I felt homesick for a place I barely even knew. Her. Why was this happening?

"Marko?"

I slowed, feeling my heart race. I hadn't been reading her thoughts, only thinking of her, and now she was calling out to me. My legs slowed and I breathed in deeply, looking down the road at her house. Homesick…God, was I really here? I hadn't planned it, yet I knew where I was going to.

"Tessa," I answered…waiting.

"I was just seeing if you were still there."

The lights were already out on most of the houses, and I frowned as I bounded up her front steps. My eyes closed and I grabbed the knob, willing it to unlock. The door swung open at my push and I shut it behind me. Even inches inside, I could smell her. A calmness slid over me and I headed for her room.

"I'm here." God, I was here. And she wasn't. *"You're in so much trouble. You know that, right?"*

Silence, even in her mind.

A deep exhale left me as I lowered to her bed. Out of all the places to go to, I'd come here. Damn, I needed help. Advice, but from who? I had no friends. No one I could trust. Even in the vampire world, everyone looked out for themselves. No one cared about the problems of other's. They had their own, and if you showed weakness, they'd set out to destroy you even faster. I'd lived the life for so long, it was all I knew.

"Marko?"

"Yes, Tessa?"

The softness was in my words. I was mentally exhausted after that vision. I wanted to kill her almost as much as I teased the idea of loving her. Love, such a ridiculous word. But here, sitting on her bed, trying not to think about what I'd seen and how I wanted to keep her, I could almost make myself believe I'd been somehow swept away by the foolish emotion. If I weren't a realist and knew I'd just turned into an obsessive stalker fixated on good blood, I'd do something stupid like bring her home with me to stay.

"Why show me that girl? Do you think I don't know what I face?"

"Being reminded isn't a bad thing."

"It was wrong and you know it."

I kept silent, trying to find the words to deny it. *"It wasn't wrong at all. It was reality. I felt how upset you were and it didn't bother me in the least, mon chaton. Sure, you feared for the girl, but let's get down to the ugly truth. Even if I was your Master and you were my blood slave, that doesn't mean I'd solely feed from you. Even if you had me, you'd never truly have me. Besides, I don't want you that way. You'd be much better suited for a night to remember than anything long-term."*

"I hate you."

A smile came to my face. *"So you've said a hundred times in the last few days. You've also said you loved me almost as many."*

"That wasn't me you were hearing, Marko, it was yourself. Your blood. The real me doesn't love you at all. How does it feel to know that the one thing you want the most is nothing but a big, fat lie?"

My eyes narrowed and the hurt had me lashing out. Maybe I did know it was all fake, but hearing it, facing it…knowing what I felt was true and hers wasn't… *"If there's nothing for me to work for any longer, perhaps I should just kill you now."*

"So you've threatened since I've met you. Anyway, I'm done arguing with you. Why don't you tell me what made you choose me?"

The top half of my body fell back onto the mattress and I stared up at the dark ceiling. Even though I was beyond pissed at her smart ass mouth, I could still see her hair flying back from the wind…her exposed neck. My need for her suddenly became something more. Something far past the point of being obsessive. *"Your smell. Lavender with a hint of jasmine. And I used to like strawberries. You ate some before you left for the church. The combination caught my attention."* My hands shook and I clenched them through my impatience.

"Oh, you're right. I think I did have some." She paused. *"Marko, there's something I need to get out."*

"What?"

"I don't think you're entirely bad."

"No? You sure about that?"

"Yeah, I think so. You're cruel and an asshole at times, but I'm starting to see something else. Well, not see, but feel. You want me. I know you do. I'm not so sure it's the blood making me pick it up either." She broke off and I could tell she was choosing her words carefully. *"But, I'm confused about everything. I don't know because even as I think it, all I can see is you and that's not helping me figure out these feelings. Your face…well, we both know how insanely attractive you are. And the accent. That's really hot. And I guess you have this dangerous, sexy air about you that would have not only me, but all the girls swooning."* She paused and I realized my lips were pulled back on the side. *"The smile. I can see it on your face so clearly. That's what gets me the most, I think. It's like…although I know you're a killer, there's this side of you. I feel like…if I could tap into it, I could change you into such a good man. The one I've always dreamed of. In reality, that's the downfall. That's what I think maybe gets us all. We want to save the bad boy. And even as I sit here and my brain tells me you can't be redeemed, my heart aches to become the one you truly need. The one to make you better."*

My smile melted and I knew the aching within my chest was a combination of both of us. It was so crippling that my hand rose to push against it. Was this how it was to be human? I'd all but forgotten. Never really wanted to remember the pain, but here it was. The vampire said I needed to put an end to it. The real Marko, the one who once existed, clung to the sensation.

"You can't save me, mon chaton. It's impossible. You will die at my hands. And I know it won't make things better, but you're the first one who's made me contemplate my timeframe. I…" What the fuck was I doing? I couldn't be telling her this stuff. I shouldn't have even been saying or thinking it. God dammit. What was I doing?

"A small part of you truly doesn't want me dead," she whispered. *"You want to keep me. You worry about your status. About what everyone will think if you take a human concubine. Is that like a wife?"*

Tightening took over my jaw and I sat up, feeling adrenaline kick in. The realization put into words nearly made me sick. To hear the truth of it so loud and clear…I felt exposed. I felt…weak within my race—again. Vampires took human slaves, but never a human concubine. It was forbidden. Unheard of, even. It was like a human marrying their pet. It just didn't happen. *"I can't stand that you read my thoughts so easily."*

"You can read mine."

"That's different. You're the prey."

"In your eyes, yes. I see that now. I feel what you do. But I'm a person, Marko. A living, breathing person with feelings and wants. You've seen my life. You've told me about it. I know when you viewed the years I've lived you didn't feel much, but those were my memories you saw. Through each one, I experienced either happiness, heartache, or sadness. And it makes up every ounce of the person I am today." She paused and I strained to hear the next part of her confession. *"That person has you contemplating more time. Does that mean nothing to you?"*

My head lowered and I leaned forward, burying my fingers in my hair. *"It's the exchange of blood, Tessa. Nothing more. It's not real."*

"Are you one hundred percent sure of that?"

"It doesn't matter," I said, getting angrier. *"It's done. You die. That's not going to change."*

So be it. You leave me no choice. It had been a private thought. Not part of the conversation. My brow furrowed and I gripped to my hair tighter.

"What's your next move? More days at the hotel you're staying at?"

A sarcastic laugh came through. *"I knew you knew."* Silence. *"No. I'm going to join the church. You can't get me there. I'll be safe. I'll live."*

My head shot up and I felt my eyes widen. *"You can't join the church. You don't even believe in God. Funny since you've made your whole life revolve around Him."*

"You know, Marko, I never understood religion, but I'm really beginning to believe it wasn't as farfetched as I'd imagined. I mean, look you at. You exist. Why couldn't God?"

The anger intensified. If she was speaking the truth, she'd be right. I *would* lose her. The mere thought that she'd be gone and not even dead, and at her choice, sent my vampire into a frenzy. I'd never lost when it came to my prey. Never been bested at my own game. Especially with a woman who'd taken in my blood twice. This obsession would never end. It would literally drive me crazy, just like it was doing now. Dead or bonded. There was no in between.

"You come home. Stay here. I'll leave you alone."

"You lie."

My fist slammed into the top of her dresser, sending it to cave in the middle. The large hole was nothing compared to what I could do if I really wanted to unleash the fury I held inside.

"You'll never make it to that church, Tessa. I'll kill everyone around you. It's home or I unleash a hell storm you could have never thought possible. And

before you think you'll do it in the day when I can't get to you, think of all those humans you spotted living below. There's thousands more who don't. You are not safe anywhere you go. Not even behind holy walls. Picture your loved ones. Think of Hunter. I had every intention of killing him. If you come home, you have my word he lives. And not the word of the vampire. I give you my word as Marko Laron Delacroix, son of Laron Marko Delacroix, Hunter will not die at my hand. Not because of this."

Her fear was back. I could feel the tingling in my chest. The trembling of my hands. She believed me and suddenly, I believed myself. I could still have her brought to me if she tried to hide in a church. Tessa was mine.

"What of me?"

My eyes rose to the mirror, taking in my reflection. *"We continue. You still have weeks. That doesn't mean you live. That just means you can rest assured that you have time."*

"Hunter won't let me go" The thought had me narrowing my eyes. *"Hunter isn't your keeper, Tessa. I am. You'll come home. He'll either follow or he won't. Regardless, you'll be here."*

"I don't think so. That gives you access to me at all times."

"I have access to you now! You think being twenty miles away makes a difference? I've been telling you to come home, but I think you neglect to see who you're truly dealing with. Perhaps I'll show you." My eyes closed and I searched out our connection—the one I could tap into when I needed to be fed. She wasn't technically bonded to me, but she held enough blood that I knew she'd feel my call, even the smallest amount, if I forced it out. Normal vampires wouldn't have the capability, but I wasn't normal. I was a Master Vampire and part of *le Cercle*. That alone spoke of my status and power.

Heat began forming in the pit of my stomach and I concentrated harder, letting the burn grow within until it scorched my insides. A small sound echoed in my ears, but I didn't stop. I'd call her to me right now if it was the last thing I did. Fuck tomorrow. Fuck being separated. She was inside and connected to me like no one had ever been and my greed ruled. Not sanity or morality. If I wanted to twist her body and mind into a million pieces before I suffocated her with my obsessive ways, so fucking be it. Let me go crazy before I ended this sweet torture.

"No, please," she begged. *"I don't want to go. Marko, please don't do this."*

My eyes opened and I cut them up to look back into the mirror. A smiled pulled at my mouth as I stared at myself. *"Better not wake Hunter on your way out. I'll be waiting."*

Chapter 12
Tessa

Contacting Marko had been the biggest mistake of my life. For some reason, I thought I could pull out more of the good I kept glimpsing. Make him understand why he couldn't continue down this path. I felt his confusion concerning me and I'd tried to play on it. Now, it was backfiring in my face. Hunter was going to be so pissed off when he woke up and I was gone.

I cut off the ignition and looked toward my house. Marko was in there waiting for me. He might as well have been standing next to me for the amount energy I felt. I hated being this connected to him, yet I couldn't deny the tinge of excitement of seeing him again. I'd left days ago, ready to never see him again, and now look at me. I was panting like a bitch in heat. My body was the enemy. It knew who it belonged to. And if Marko decided to bite me, he'd have my mind. He'd have all of me.

The squeaking of my car door broke though the silence and I didn't bother shutting it quietly. Marko knew I was here. His excitement matched my own, but for a completely different reason. To him, he'd won by getting me here. The trick he'd done had been nothing but a new way for him to play with me. Now he'd probably do it all the damn time. And I'd come running like the mindless twit I was. Our world was doomed. We'd all be slaves if the vampires had their way. They'd rule and we'd never stand a chance.

I threw open the front door, letting it close loudly behind me. Marko leaned against the edge of the hallway wall, a smug smile on his face that I didn't like at all. It stirred my anger to no end. I didn't think as I reared back and threw my keys at him. Had I contemplated, I didn't doubt my hand would have frozen up, just like my mouth did when I tried talking about certain things.

He deflected the metal easily and it made me angrier.

"Are you happy?" I exploded. "Is this what you wanted?"

Up and down, his eyes traveled over my body. *Lust.* But I doubted it was all sexual. It was my blood and the smell of my skin that he craved. It was the pull. The feeling we were caught up in.

"Come here."

My head shook as I glared. And just like that, I was going.

"I hate you. God, I do."

"I could change that," he whispered.

Not again, what are you doing! His thoughts came rushing through and I smiled at his slip. He looked confused, only to turn angry.

"You're just as trapped as I am," I said, shaking my head. "I have to obey when I don't want to and you're starting to *feel* what you don't want. Are you afraid, Marko?"

"I don't know what you're talking about. I fear nothing."

Against my better judgment, I stepped closer. "Afraid of falling in love with me? Your plan is backfiring and I'm not so sure either of us are going to come out of this with the results we want."

"Wrong. I don't lose."

"You just did," I said, lowly. "You could have beat your biggest fear had you let me go. You could have continued on with your life and nothing would have changed. But this," I said, gesturing between us, "isn't going to work for you or me. Either I die, or we bond. Neither of us wants either one."

Marko hands were around my neck before I could even process him moving. "You know nothing," he growled, squeezing tighter. "Maybe I'll just kill you now and be done with this once and for all."

Air refused to come as tears burned my eyes. My nails clawed into his wrists and I thrashed against his hold, trying my best to break it before I became too weak. With the force he held, it wouldn't be long.

"God, your heart calls to me. Such a beautiful melody it sings when you're so close to death. Will it sound just as sweet when the rhythm stops?"

Pressure built in my face and a gurgling sound came from my mouth. My legs were getting so heavy. My ankle twisted to the side as numbness started to sink in. Still, I clawed against him, even though my fingers almost refused to obey.

"Please," I begged in my head. *"Don't do this."*

"I'm sorry, mon chaton." Something flickered behind his eyes and he eased his grip, allowing me the smallest amount of air as he drew my face closer with his hands and pressed his lips against mine. "God, I really am."

A silent sob left me and I closed my eyes, trying to face my death while he still allowed me enough oxygen to stay conscious. As I went over my life and mindlessly fought, it only made me cry harder. Nothing. I'd accomplished nothing worth anyone remembering. Hunter would be heartbroken, but other than him and my parents, no one was going to miss me. The closest I'd ever gotten to being in love was to the man who wanted me dead. And that didn't even count. It wasn't real love. Like Marko had said, it was an illusion.

"Part of it is real," Marko said, interrupting my thoughts. My eyes opened, but it had been almost impossible. I was so tired.

None of it's real. I don't love you and I'm sure not going to die thinking I do.

His hands loosened even more and air rushed in, burning my throat. What looked to be sadness filled his face, but I wasn't sure with the anger that kept coming back.

"You do love me. At least a small amount."

"No," I forced out through the rawness.

"Yes," he said, tightening his hands. "I'm not feeling this for nothing. You love me."

I closed my eyes, clearing my thoughts. I would not give him the satisfaction of killing me for the reasons he held to.

"Tessa." He shook me hard, choking me even more. The urge to gag was automatic and my knees gave out. Spots appeared, even in the darkness. Panic set in, but I fought to surrender to his will.

I hit the ground hard as he let go. My limbs were tingly and numb and coughing wracked my chest. Loud popping had my eyes subconsciously flying open. Blood webbed out, soaking through Marko's white button up shirt. Somehow,

I managed to turn my head. Hunter was standing at the door, a gun held out in front of him and he was gaping. Marko stepped over me slowly.

"I told Tessa I wouldn't kill you today. You are so fucking lucky."

More popping had Marko jerking the smallest amount. I pushed against the floor, trying my hardest to get to my feet. Bullets fell at Marko's feet within seconds and his ability to heal was faster than before. Whether it was because he'd been expecting the shots Hunter fired at him, I wasn't sure.

"Impossible," Hunter breathed out, moving to the side. More rounds were fired until he was pulling against an empty clip.

"You can't kill me," Marko said, reaching out and snatching him by the throat with only one of his hands. Hunter was lifted off the ground while he held the vampire's wrist. Red filled his face as he kicked against the vampire's thigh and thrashed.

"I could put you through the brick exterior of this home right now if I wanted to. Maybe I'll just settle for the floor. A broken back isn't death, right?" A smile came to his face and I forced a scream that had him pausing.

"Don't. Just name it." I stumbled, falling, but managing to make it to his feet. Hesitantly, I reached forward, wrapping my hands around his thigh and placing my forehead against it. It took every ounce of energy I possessed, but I could feel myself getting slowly stronger. "Anything. Just don't hurt him." The plea was almost silent, but I knew he heard it.

Hunter went flying across the room, landing hard and sliding through the small dining room area. Marko had me around the waist, carrying me through the front door immediately as I watched Hunter try to stand.

"Tessa, don't!"

Darkness cloaked around us as my house faded in the distance. I knew we were going at a fast pace, but it all blurred together while I watched Hunter race outside. We were right there, just past the lawn, but he acted as though he never saw us. Maybe he didn't. Maybe he had pretended not to. It wasn't like there was anything he could do anyway.

I swallowed constantly as we continued, disappearing from my street and coming to a grate resting on the side of the road. Marko reached down, removing it. He never let go as he turned and climbed down the ladder. As he replaced the grate, we were face to face. I shouldn't have been able to see in pitch black, but I could, which told me it was due to Marko's blood.

"Don't look at me like that. He shot me and all he got was tossed around. He's lucky I didn't crush his windpipe."

Bars pressed into my back, but I barely felt them as we kept each other's stare. My mouth opened to speak, but I knew it would hurt too badly. Instead, I used my thoughts.

Thank you for not hurting him worse. But you can't believe that's the only reason I'm upset. God, look what you did to me. You just fucking..." My body shook as fear left me wanting to get far away from him. *"Why are you bringing me here?"*

Marko took a deep breath and leaned his forehead against mine, trapping me between him and the bar behind my head.

"I shouldn't. I...fuck, how did things go so wrong? Do you see what you're doing to me? The deep growl left me shaking even worse.

"Let go of me and walk away," I managed, lowly. "You're the one doing this. Not me. Let. Me. Go." The last was silent.

A battle played on his face as his eyes darted between mine. "I...*can't.*" Pain laced his words and I saw through the mask he relied on. His nature. He truly couldn't help himself when it came to staying away. Emotions I knew weren't mine pushed through and I could feel his dilemma as if it were my own. Everything he was, everything he used to be that he could barely remember. He knew nothing but the vampire that stood before me now. And he was trapped by a hunger so intense, my human mind couldn't even begin to grasp the vastness. If I died, this would end for him. He'd have no more obsession. No more arising problems in his community. He'd be free. *And lonely.* An emotion he couldn't really remember feeling. Even though he craved to kill me more than anything, he wanted to keep me, too. Even if it was until whatever we shared ended.

The wave of information dissipated as fast as it came and I knew he'd made it happen. He wanted me to understand. To somehow...help him? Desperation was all he had left and I didn't have an answer that made any rational sense. If we continued to have any sort of contact, he *would* kill me. He wouldn't be able to take the effects of his condition indefinitely. He'd snap like he'd just done and I'd be history. Unless...

No. My head shook. *I'd rather die than be bonded to him.*

A growl had his hand going back to my throat, but he didn't squeeze. "I can still read your mind. Your refusal is starting to make me want it even more. What's a bonded human if I can get rid of this...insanity? I could still kill you. All I'd have to do is whisper one word into your ear and you'd drop upon hearing it."

"Where's the fun in that? You like to play with your food, Marko. We both know that."

He stepped down from the ladder, pulling me into him. "I do. I especially like to play with you."

The hand that was still on my arm moved over to the swell of my breast and I turned away, not making it far before he spun me into the wall.

"Maybe bonded won't be so bad. It's not like I have to make you my concubine. You could live your life, I'd live mine. I'd just take you when I want."

My hands pushed against his pecs. *"But I don't want you."*

"Lie," he whispered, pushing his knee between mine. "You want me in all ways. I can smell your arousal, mon chaton. Even as hurt as you are, you want me so bad, you can't stand it."

"I can't stand you," I forced out. *"Do you think I like being choked, threatened, and stalked? I want to live my life without that sort of risk. I want to get married and have children. I want a husband who loves me passionately and not just because I'm lunch."*

His face buried in my neck as if what I said had nothing to do with him. Lips trailed up my throat, kissing over the soreness his fingers had brutally caused. From rough to gentle, he flipped his switch quicker than I could adjust to.

"That's not in your future, Tessa. You might as well put that out of your head now." He pulled back, staying close as he dipped forward, rubbing his rough cheek against my face. "Even if I did let you go, bonded, do you really think I'd allow another man in your home or your bed? The obsession may fade, but you still belong to me. If you live, you'll always be mine. I won't share. Not for anyone."

My hands flew out angrily and tears burned my eyes. Even if I did make it out alive, he'd always be there. I'd never be rid of him unless I figured out a way to kill him first.

"Such dangerous thoughts you cradle with so much love in your mind. You'd rejoice in my death, but not for long. You're tied to me now, Tessa. *If* you survived my demise, you'd never be happy. You'd likely go insane. Our blood is one now. Dependent on each other until the tie ends. Face it, mon chaton. Your happily-ever-after isn't so happy after all."

My dreams, my hopes for the future, it all came crashing down around me as I looked into his eyes. I felt numbness sink in, all the while, heartache. It couldn't be this way. I refused to let it be so. "Kill me," I said, struggling against him. "Kill me right now. I will not live a life that revolves around you. I choose my death for *me*. Not you."

An angry hiss blew against the side of my face and stinging rushed to the surface of my scalp at him jerking my hair. I cried out, preparing for the worst. Sirens registered in the far background just as his fangs buried in my neck. My body spasmed and then melted into him. The reaction was automatic. At the thickness that entered, I moaned through the instant ecstasy. It had his arms wrapping around my waist and drawing me against him.

Each bite was better than the last and I let out soft sounds as he tugged at my vein with his soft suckling. Where I expected a hard, rough last few minutes, it was beginning as anything but.

Lower, his hand moved. Sharp fingernails registered over the small of my back and I reached for his shoulders, holding tight as I waited for him to shred my skin like I saw him do to the other woman. Where fear should have registered, it didn't. I knew it was because of the poison he was pumping into me. His blood within had me giving myself over freely, for whatever that may have been. Here, I was his. And I liked that.

My shirt eased up while my heart raced in anticipation. Tingling prickled every inch of me as he ran the pointy tips up my side, adding pressure in the smallest amount. The swirl of his tongue brought my breasts pushing into his chest, urging him on. The nails retracted and his fingers squeezed into my back.

"You love being mine. Let me hear you say it."

Hardness pushed against my pussy and I move my hips, wishing he'd end it now, before we were too far gone. I couldn't stop the impatience that had me pulling on him. It was a bad sign, even if I couldn't hold onto that feeling.

"Say it, mon chaton." The words were spoken more forcefully in my mind. A moan followed and I could feel him tugging at the lining of my pants until he had them off. Within seconds, he ripped my panties free. If he'd heard my thoughts on wanting to die now, he ignored them.

"Yes, I love being yours." And like that, the words came whispering out without my permission. Even as I said it, I was pushing on my toes to try to get him inside of me faster.

Marko broke from my neck, breathing heavily. His mouth crushed into mine while he pushed me deeper into the wall. I drank him in…drank *me* in, as I felt his cock spring free against my lower stomach. A distinctive taste coated my tongue and I turned to the side, breaking our connection, only to come back and meet his stare head on. Who knew death could taste so sweet?

We held each other while he lifted me and rubbed the head of his cock against my wet opening. The thickness over my clit caused me to jump at the sensitivity but left behind a need that overpowered the one only moments before.

"Give yourself to me," I begged. "Just…" frustration seemed to cloud the passion and I wasn't sure where it had come from. What was I pleading for? His cock? His heart? The smallest amount of humanity hidden within his darkness? Escape?

Marko inched his way into my pussy, turning his face into the other side of my neck. I held to him, letting myself enjoy the way he stretched me to fit around him. My hips arched even more and I felt him surge forward. A loud groan vibrated my neck and he reached around with his other hand, smearing the trail of blood from the open wound left behind. The warmth stretched down toward my breasts and he went back, collecting more on his fingers. My lips separated as he pushed the pad of his index finger over my bottom one. He thrust his cock hard, moving his finger to my top lip. All my fantasies came rushing back. My tongue hesitantly darted to the edge, collecting the smartest amount of my blood. Marko's breath hitched and his mouth dove forward so he could kiss me again.

"You drive me crazy, Tessa. If you only knew what I was really thinking… I see you. The real you. The Tessa no one else knows, who you try never to think about. The one you've denied this whole time. I want to bring her out. To explore every dark fantasy she's ever had."

The rocking of his hips increased as passion exploded between us. Tighter, I held him, suddenly not wanting to ever let go. Acceptance of my secrets, something I never thought I'd have. Every element of who Marko was took over my brain, numbing and drowning out the world. His breaths were mine. The sensations shooting from his cock to his sac, all the way to the base of his spine…they twisted my core making my orgasm flood to the surface. Even my own blood was something I felt I had to taste. It made no sense and yet, I understood him better than I understood myself.

Dark love. It was growing. Getting overwhelmingly stronger with every increased slam of his cock.

"Tessa," Marko moaned, drawing more mindless patterns over my skin with my blood. His finger stayed close to my pulse, never moving far for long.

"It's almost time," he continued. "I can feel the call. It's…so strong." The last came out through clenched teeth and I searched for fear. It had to be there somewhere amongst the release that so desperately wanted to come. Why wasn't it? Why was I even wondering? I should just close my eyes and enjoy dying this way.

As the smallest amount of control I held dropped, I felt my lids obey. Bliss was all I felt as I tuned into the tingling and heat increasing by the second. Marko pushed deep, grinding his pelvis into the top of my slit. I sucked in air, ready to scream when he viciously bit down into my neck. My whole body locked up despite the spasms trying to force their way through. Tears poured from my eyes while I willed oxygen to come. Seconds went by before I was gasping through the burning of my throat. My nails were tearing into Marko's neck, but he didn't stop. Didn't even seemed fazed as he bit down harder.

A strangled cry escaped and small dots of lights broke through the darkness. All my mind could process what that this was it. The love I'd experienced not moments before registered and a sob somehow managed to echo out around us. I felt cheated. Heartbroken that it hadn't been real. And that I was going to die right now, never getting to feel real love for him. Why did I want to save him, even as he was killing me? *It was obvious.* Because we—humans—were blind to the true evil surrounding us. We were the light. Where we gave and loved...others, like Marco, thrived in the darkness of taking. They'd possibly come to rule this planet and when they did, they'd only then realize it would never be sustained. It was only a matter of time before they killed all their prey and then themselves. They were doomed and so were we.

"Mmm-mmm" Sounds of denial came from his mouth as he fucked me harder, nearly crushing my hip as he gripped through the furious thrusts.

The dots were fading along with the room and I blinked heavily through the blank void taking over. My fight was gone and I was ready to go. Nothing existed past the mix of melancholy. It was bittersweet and unbearable all at once. I was a part of so many different levels and I let each one of them be my focus instead of the monster who fed from me. Our ties were ending as my heart slowed. I couldn't even feel the beats anymore. God, I loved him. Did he know? Could he feel how I ached for what he was doing?

Tears trickled down my face and I felt it all end in a long, drawn out fade of sensitivity. Weight became non-existent and my heart shattered as I realized I was going. His arms were disappearing and so was I. And there was nothing I could do about it.

Chapter 13
Hunter

All I could do was pace as I watched the cops stare at me skeptically. It made no sense. Without her here to verify she'd been kidnapped, they couldn't do anything. What the fuck was that supposed to mean?

"She's been kidnapped by a fucking vampire. Kidnapped, as in gone. How is she supposed to verify that?"

They didn't break their gazes as they continued to look at me like I was crazy.

"Vampire!" I yelled. "Look at the bullets on the floor. They're flat and covered in his blood. Look at my God damn neck where he choked me! He took her and he's going to kill her and there's nothing you can do?"

"Sir, you need to calm down. We can take a report, but as of now, there's no evidence that there is indeed a missing person."

"Because she's missing," I exploded. "What the fuck is wrong with you?"

"You have a good night, sir."

My mouth dropped to the floor as I watched them leave through the door. For minutes, I'd argued my case and apparently, blood and bruises weren't enough reason to search someone out. It infuriated me. Left me pacing even more as I clenched my fists, over and over.

The sound of the car driving off was a bigger blow. It made the anger worse and I didn't even begin to know where to search for Tessa. How did he do it? Take the bullets at such a close range without even blinking? Fuck, I don't think they even penetrated past his skin. It scared the shit out of me. How did they die? They had to fucking die. Nothing was immortal. Nothing, but God.

My feet carried me to the room and I pulled back the drawer, grabbing my rosary. Tessa and I had matching ones, a gift from my uncle, who was a priest. She'd been so excited when she'd noticed ours matched. The thought only led me back into the living room faster. I collapsed onto the sofa, lowering my head and rubbing my fingers over the beads as I began to pray. God, she had to be safe. Her neck had been so red and bruised already. And her eyes…

The busted blood vessels had frozen my trigger finger for a split second when she'd looked up at me. I'd never imagined I'd see Tessa so physically hurt and helpless. As she'd driven away, I couldn't believe she'd left to begin with. What in the hell had she been thinking coming back here? She knew he wanted to hurt her and she'd walked right into it.

My eyes squeezed shut tighter as I tried to stop the racing of my mind and focus. I could only get the beginning of the prayer out before I drifted back into random questions. I didn't understand it. Couldn't begin to grasp how this was happening. Nothing was making sense anymore. How had we, the government, allowed this to happen? It was like everyone was brainwashed.

The door slammed open and I jumped to my feet. Marko came to an abrupt stop, appearing disoriented. Blood was smeared across both of their faces and Tessa lay, looking lifeless in his arms. Her pants were on, but missing the button on the top. Her shirt was torn and…blood. So much blood covered the top half of her body.

The beads fell from my hands and the fear that engulfed me wasn't from the vampire, but the way she looked. The bite on her neck was more than puncture wounds from fangs. Every indent of his teeth was shredded into her skin. Bruising was so thick around her entire throat, only small blotches of pink skin were visible.

"Jesus," I breathed out, wiping away the tears already pouring free. My soul was mourning. Broken at seeing the woman I loved lying there almost lifeless. "Give her to me." I reached forward and he bared his fangs, letting out a deep threatening sound.

"Get. Back."

The warning physically slammed into my insides, almost bringing me to my knees. The shock was enough to make me fall the entire way. Not only was he powerful on the outside, but the inside as well. There were so many things that encompassed his kind.

"Please. Just let me have her. I think she may still be breathing. Let me help her."

"She's alive, barely."

My cry of frustration filled the living area and Marko stepped even closer to the door. I could tell he wasn't right. His deep breaths, the way he kept his fingers on her neck, only to lift and begin to kneel as if he wanted to put her down. He was torn on what to do and I had to try to convince him to let her go.

"Listen to me," I said, quietly. "You're here. You came back and she's not dead. Just put her down and leave. I'll take good care of her. I promise."

"I don't want you to take care of her," he exploded.

My hands shot up as I clenched my teeth. "Someone has to. She's hurt. Let me get her help."

Marko's eyes closed and he brought her head up to lean against his. French poured from his mouth while he began to rock back and forth. There was such anguish in his tone that it only made me angrier. My steps closer brought his eyes snapping open and they held a warning that caused me to pause.

"Take her to holy ground and keep her there for as long as you can. I'll be back and next time, there will be no stopping me."

Fuck holy ground, I had to get her to a hospital. I'd worry about a church after she was well enough to leave. Then, I'd take her. First, I had to get to her.

"Let me have her." I stepped even closer, holding my arms out toward him. Cautiously, he made his way to me and I watched his fingers tighten on her as I got within distance. I swallowed hard, lunging forward and pulling against her arm. He held onto her for another split second before letting go. Tessa's weight came crashing into me and I lowered her to the ground, checking her pulse first. She didn't move. Barely looked like she was getting any air.

"Wait!" Marko lowered, shoving his hand into my chest hard enough to make me fall back. His eyes came up to me as he lifted her head and ran his tongue over the large wounds of her neck. Within seconds, I watched as it began to disappear.

No wonder…

Deep breaths left me while I stared in shock. Even the bruising in the general vicinity was beginning to disappear.

"She needs time, but she'll live. Her heart already beats stronger. If she didn't have so much of my blood in her, she'd be dead right now. Get her to holy ground and fast. *Not* the hospital. Holy ground."

Marko stood, spinning for the door.

"Your blood? What exactly does that mean?"

He opened the barrier, looking back over his shoulder toward me. "It means, she belongs to *me*." The deepness of his tone had goose bumps rising on my skin, but it didn't stop me from shaking my head.

"Tessa was mine before you ever came along. You can't take that away."

His lip peeled back while he narrowed his eyes. "I already have."

****

"Tessa?" My hand held onto her tighter as I looked up into the candlelit room my uncle had set us up in. Deep breaths and groans came from her mouth. I could tell she was dreaming, but she had yet to wake up. "Tessa, honey."

Her lips separated, free from the blood that had been smeared around them when we'd left her house. The moment I had her in bed, I'd made sure that I cleaned all of the dark substance from her body. It made me sick to imagine what she must have gone through. How terrified she must have been before and after I'd shown up. God, they'd just…disappeared when they flew out the door. I searched everywhere around the grounds and they were gone. How did he do it?

"Marko?" The nearly silent plea grated my ears. Surely she hadn't meant that the way it sounded. She should be screaming his name in terror, not looking for his assistance.

"Tessa."

My uncle's presence moved in from behind the chair I was sitting in and I glanced back, frowning at him.

"You're positive it was a vampire?"

My head nodded and I looked back toward her. "I saw his fangs. The bite was horrible before he made it disappear. I can't believe this is happening."

Silence met me and I didn't turn back to see if he was still there. He seemed to come and go, hovering just far enough away where I felt I had my space. My world was falling down around me and nothing was processing right.

A painful sound was accompanied by her features drawing in tight. My hand settled on her chest, trying to calm her. I could hear what sounded like yelling in the background, but I ignored it as I focused on her.

"Tessa, honey, it's okay. You're safe now."

"No." Her head shook back and forth and I could tell she was coming to. "Shh."

Uneven breaths left her while she became more active in her movements. "Marko?"

"No," I said, firmly. "He's gone. He can't hurt you anymore. Tessa, open your eyes."

She kicked her legs, forcing herself to her side. The gagging had my eyes widening and she breathed in shakily while she thrashed even more violently. The scream that left her made the hair on my arms standing on end.

"Get me out of here!" The scratchy plea had Marko's words coming back to me. She'd taken his blood. If he couldn't be on holy ground, apparently she couldn't either. But why didn't he know that? Had he wanted her to die this way? In so much pain? "Hunter!"

I scooped Tessa in my arms, grabbing the sheet and throwing it over her as I sped past my uncle and bounded down the steps that took me to the first floor. She was beginning to claw at her face and chest. I tried pinning her arms between us while my shoulder dove into the large wooden, swinging doors that put us through the entrance.

"Please," she sobbed.

Her voice was about gone by the time she finished. The cool night air hit us and I didn't stop running until I made it to the sidewalk. My feet stopped abruptly at Marko's stalking figure. His eyes practically glowed in the dimness and a deep sound that I knew was hostile was coming from him.

"Leave." I receded to the edge of the lawn, battling on what I should do. I could avoid him easily, but that would possibly kill Tessa.

"I said leave!"

His stare stayed on her, the menacing sounds dying as her body calmed. She was unconscious again and it only worried me more. Apparently, the only reason she'd been awake to begin with was from the pain she had been feeling.

"Marko," I said, louder, trying to break his fixation on her.

"I can't leave her. It won't *let* me leave her," he said, more insistently. "Fucking…Christ. Her pain is mine. Her…" Words were broken as his hand came to his mouth. "She's already dead. I should have just killed her when I had the chance."

Had Tessa not been in my arms, I would have gone at him with everything I had. He deserved to die, but I wanted his death to be slow. Drawn out and torturous. "You come near her again, I *will* kill you. There has to be a way and you can bet I will find out what it is before the night is over. You're going to be the one to die and I'm going to be the one who does it."

Marko's eyes rose to mine and he glowered as he came closer. "Someday, you may try, you may even think you stand a chance, but I assure you, you will *not* win."

I studied his stature. The way the top half of his body was leaned more toward me. There was such confidence in his tone that I almost believed him. But he didn't know me or what I was capable of. And it was only a matter of time before he found out.

Chapter 14
Marko

Bells rang out loudly, filling the street with the sweet sound of the hour. The night was almost over and the sun would soon rise, driving me back to my underground prison. Once a home I'd enjoyed, now…my eyes lifted from Tessa to the bell tower. Now I found myself wanting something more. Something I shouldn't want.

I let the images of her singing in the choir project in front of me. She'd been happy to use her voice for something people enjoyed. It was the only place she'd allow anyone to hear her without fear of criticism. It kept her coming back. That, her love of Hunter's uncle, and the aggravation of not understanding religion. She'd tried so hard to make sense of it, but the questions kept coming. The doubt. She'd been raised attending this very church and loved it. Now, she'd never be able to walk through those doors again. I'd hoped with her disbelief that it would allow her entrance, but I was wrong.

At the first ounce of pain her mind registered, I was pulled from the tunnel I held myself up in. My feet moved on their own accord and I let them as I tuned into her discomfort. The more she experienced, the clearer it became. There was nothing she could do about what she was feeling. She wasn't conscious. Her mind wasn't processing words…it left me in a panic. I felt the burn. It encompassed my insides like liquid fire traveling from limb to limb. That shouldn't have happened. I could live through her death, but apparently not painlessly, if anything holy was involved.

The run to the church was a blur as my main focus became saving her and myself. I didn't think I'd die, but my blood had been boiling within us both and that wasn't a good sign. And then, my yells had started. They poured from me, laced with panic. I'd almost risked going to her. Had been right there and would have, had mon chaton not woken up and pleaded through her pain.

"Marko, you have to leave."

He was right, I did. Not because he said so, but because it was getting too close to the sunrise and I didn't want to risk getting caught in the first rays. It wouldn't kill me, but it could weaken me if I stayed in it too long.

I lowered my gaze back to Tessa's limp body. Her heartbeat was steady, even, but not nearly as strong as it usually was. Everything within me pleaded to take her back with me and it had nothing to do with killing her. I'd already been there tonight and repeating the experience surprisingly didn't appeal at the moment. Not that I hadn't been to heaven while listening to her flirt with death. It had been the happiest moment of my life….for all of ten seconds. Knowing I'd never get to taste her again, or even see her again, sent my heart plummeting to my toes. I'd stopped and held her, begging for forgiveness for who I was. But it didn't matter. I'd be back to try again. I knew that just as much as I knew I'd do whatever it took to make it happen. Even risking holy ground if it stood between me and her.

My foot stepped forward and I caught the priest standing on the stairs. Muscles contracted in my throat and I swallowed past the sensation.

"I want to tell her goodbye."

Hunter's head went back at the snort. "I think you've already done that tonight. You're not getting close to her again."

My jaw tightened as I stared at the distance separating us. I didn't feel comfortable getting any closer, yet I felt myself take two more steps. "I gave her back to you. All I want to do is tell her goodbye. You have my word that I won't be back for a while."

"No."

My eyes rose to his and I used my pull to have him come to me. Stupid human. I'd given him a damn chance.

Although I spoke French to Tessa, I kept my eyes locked to Hunter's.

"Mon chaton, I have to leave you for a while. I'm afraid when you hear from me again it won't be good. I'll want to kill you again. And I may just succeed. Do what you have to do to protect yourself." My head lowered, breaking eye contact and I kissed her forehead. I knew I still had a few seconds before the daze wore off on Hunter.

"I'm afraid you may have won the love part of our game. I think mine for you may far exceed yours for me."

Maybe it was just the blood talking, but I did feel as though I loved her. If the obsession had driven me to it or somehow manipulated my way of thinking, I wasn't sure, but I didn't care. I was a torn man—half killer, half lost soul. Humanity was apparently within me somewhere, but it wouldn't win any more than she or any other human would against our kind. And maybe Tessa was right. Maybe it would be the end of us all.

Hunter stepped back, shock on his face as he stared at me. I frowned, turning and walking back toward her house. I'd have to pass it to get to the entrance of the tunnels.

"Marko?"

The call had my head spinning and my heart racing. The whites of Tessa's eyes were still red in places from the blood vessels that had burst when I choked her. They hadn't healed yet and the sight made my stomach twist sickeningly. Fuck, I'd destroyed her. What the hell was I that I could do something so hurtful to someone that obviously meant a great deal to me?

"You're wrong," she said in French.

I took a step back, my head shaking. I didn't want to hear her say she loved me. Not after what I'd done. She should hate me. Fear me. I knew she was incapable. That we both were trapped in the whirlwind of the bond trying to force itself on us.

"Prepare yourself for my return. You're going to need to."

I turned, pushing my legs to run as fast they could. If I heard another word, another declaration of her fake love, I'd slice my wrist open and force my blood into her mouth whether she wanted it or not. Which, I knew in my heart, she didn't.

That was suddenly becoming the biggest burden I harbored.

The grate bent at my grip and I pulled it free, forcing myself inside. As I put it back in place and jumped down, I came face to face with Julius. He didn't say a word. He didn't have to. I was in deep shit and I knew it. I'd attacked a woman and manipulated two cops to try to cover my ass, but that was beside the point. We were at a critical point in our coming out and instead of playing it safe, I, a member of *le*

Cercle, would be once again in the mouths of my community. Word traveled fast and I knew it wouldn't take long to make the rounds. We had slaves who worked in the police force. Surely, they'd heard the report of a vampire being involved in crime.

"Come."

The one word had me nodding. Darkness closed in around us as we headed through the tunnels and he didn't stop until we broke to the right and then right again, taking us even further away from the heart of the underground city. Doors appeared and we headed to the one at the back. It was his. I could feel his energy pouring from the walls as if his mere presence left the powerful impression that would forever exist.

Light filtered from the room as he pushed the door open. I walked inside, not sure what to expect. Would he kill me? He easily could. It would solve all his problems…and mine. Somehow, the thought wasn't altogether unpleasant. At this point, I was willing to take any relief I could get.

His eyes scanned the holes in my shirt, but he already knew what happened. Had probably seen it in his mind the moment our stares had connected at the entrance.

"You wanted to see me?" His question left my lips separating. Of course he'd know. It wasn't even important I tell him. My intentions, my thoughts, my plans were his to sort through at any given moment.

"Yes. I need to be on lockdown for a while. I…" I cleared my throat, still tasting Tessa. The craving hit hard, already returning even though I'd just gotten more than enough of her blood. "I'm not well."

He nodded. "So I see." A large desk sat in the far corner and he pulled out the chair, sitting down. "You face quite the decision ahead of you. Do you really think being restrained is going to stop the inevitable?"

"No."

"Then why spare her any more time?"

The aching was back in my chest, taking me over. Wrong and right collided, combining into one until I didn't know the difference between them. Why was it such a complicated decision?

"Something is wrong with me." The words sounded foreign as I faced my leader. Weakness wasn't permitted and I knew I was risking my chair by even speaking the words. Would he throw me out? Make me an outcast to all of those who lived in our world?

Julius held out a pack of cigarettes and I walked forward, grabbing one. As I lit it, I inhaled deeply. He put the pack back down and continued to stare. He wasn't smoking, but he must have known I needed one.

"Your troubles will pass. But only when you do something about your problem. Until then, you will suffer, and I will not help you."

I gave a quick nod, facing the fact that Tessa would only have the time I was physically able to give her. Then…she'd die. It's what she had wanted when faced with the choice tonight. And I'd taken it into consideration. Given her what she wanted, despite what I truly did. She didn't want this life and I wasn't going to force it on her, no matter how much I now wanted to keep her. It wasn't guaranteed that I'd even still feel the same way for her when the bond went through. The attraction might disappear completely on my part and she'd be stuck loving a man who felt nothing. She didn't deserve that. She didn't deserve death either.

"Thank you for your time." I bowed, turning and heading to the door.

"Marko." I stopped and turned to face him.

Light eyes narrowed as he stared at me. What he saw, I was afraid to know.

"You should be aware that there's a stir at The Craze. Boyd and his punk friends have started inviting humans to join in their festivities. So far, it remains under control, but you know Boyd. He's too newly turned to control his urges, as I believe you got to witness the day Tessalyn Antoinette came to see you. He has to be watched and I want you to be the one to start doing that. We have quite a long time before we begin the next phase of our plan. I want as little instances as possible before that happens."

As if I didn't have enough to worry about. Couldn't he see I couldn't even control myself?

"It'll be done. I'll start first thing tomorrow."

"See that you do."

I shut the door behind me, taking one last drag of my cigarette before dropping it to the ground and grinding it with my shoe. If I was meant to watch Boyd, at least I'd have a distraction from Tessa and maybe that would buy her a little time.

Whatever her plan was, I sure hoped it was good. Maybe if she put up some form of fight, it would help ease the guilt. Unless, of course, she figured out how to kill a vampire. Or Hunter did. Then I was in more trouble than I'd bargained for.

Chapter 15
Tessa

Five days and I was still alive. I hadn't heard from Marko since he'd left and I wasn't sure whether I would again. He didn't try to communicate with me, nor I with him. From how close to death I had been, you couldn't tell it by looking at me now. The evidence was as gone as my heart. Gone, for him. *Love.* He'd warned me and I thought he'd been full of shit, but the longing was proof that I was beyond help. How did I let this happen? I knew it was because of his blood, but why couldn't I have been stronger? My anger had no bounds, except for the emotions that pulled me back to him. I was lost.

My arms held the pillow tighter as I stared toward the light shining through my window. Hunter sat at the small desk he'd pulled in from his room and now he barely left my side, day or night. All he did was research and chat with other vampire-haters who held a group. Most had never even seen a vampire. Hunter's dilemma, *or mine*, made him popular extremely quickly. Why anyone believed him was beyond me. He could have been lying for all they knew, but they held firm in their interest and excitement on what he'd do to get rid of the vampire population around the area. I had a feeling they were already discussing a *save the world* campaign. It left me in a weird place. Although I knew vampires weren't good, I saw their world. They had a way of life that left me interested to discover. Not all of them could be bad. They had people to feed off of. If they stuck with that, couldn't they keep their way of life under control? They'd stayed secret this long.

"Hey, Tessa, listen to this." Hunter spun in the chair and it took everything I had to sit up and face him. I had no will to do anything. It had been taken when Marko walked away from me. I hated that. Hated that during the heat of some induced passion, I'd taken his blood for the second time. Had I not, I wasn't so sure this would be happening. I hated even more that he'd given it to me to begin with, but…I pushed away the thoughts as Hunter began talking.

"I just got a message from a guy I was stationed with back in two-thousand-five. He's stationed at Fort Hood now. That's roughly an hour away. He's come face-to-face with a vampire. Said he and a few of the guys there have been looking into ways to kill them. They have a few ideas." He smiled. "I knew reaching out to my old friends was bound to pay off. I got this. It's already beginning."

A shiver raced down my spine and Hunter frowned.

"You okay? You haven't really said much lately."

"I'm fine."

I turned, already ready to lie back down when he kept talking. "Tessa, I know I've been around Marko, but I have to make sure. How do you know you're in the presence of a vampire?"

"How do you know you're in the presence of a vampire?" I repeated the question, feeling the all too familiar terror creep in. The one I had felt while underground in the midst of them all. The redhead girl came to my mind, too, and I let the two of our experiences combine as I tried to make my answer as clear as I could. My palms began to sweat and I clasped my hands together. "The fear emits a sensation like a tuning fork. It goes right from your chest, down to your stomach, leaving your pulse exploding. Once you feel the hum throughout every inch of your body, intense tingling takes over like electrical currents zapping your whole internal system. You shake uncontrollably and sound dissipates until all you can hear is the racing of your heart. When you think you can't bear another minute, you're left without a choice. They only show themselves the moment you let your guard down. And when they do, they bring a level of fear you never even thought could exist. That's where they want you. That's where you're at when you die."

Hunter's eyebrows drew together and I looked down, remembering I'd been almost dead not long ago and that wasn't necessarily how I felt. Then again, regular people wouldn't be under the passion I had been in. They wouldn't hold the vampire's blood that masked the true terror.

I eased back, turning toward the window again. *Vampires.* For once, since I'd met Marko, I wished I could forget. I knew regardless of anyone mentioning them or not, the knowledge would always be there. The constant reminder only hurt worse at the thought. Especially since there was nothing I wanted more than to be amongst them.

"Tessa, I'm going to start making dinner. You're going to try to eat tonight, right? I'm starting to get worried."

"I'll eat," I said, quietly. Anything to make him go. I just wanted to be alone and go over what had happened. I had yet to be able to process anything. The tears were there, so ready to spill that I was going to drown if I didn't release them soon. I'd never been a person to wallow in emotions, but this was different. The blood was finding ways to constantly refresh the pain until I wanted to scream through the torment it was putting me through. Marko didn't even have to be here for him to find a way to make me suffer.

The door stayed open and Hunter's footsteps led him further away. I heard myself sigh as the first tear rolled free. I didn't sob or make a sound. I held in everything I could, minus the streams starting to run steadily over my face. Why did this have to be so hard?

Banging from the kitchen had me wiping my hand across my face. I knew Hunter wasn't coming, but I couldn't help myself from wanting to hide my feelings. Even as I made the tears disappear, new ones replaced them. Minutes went by while episodes of heavy, silent wracking of my chest were replaced with moments of strength. They went back and forth until I somehow managed to get control. I pushed myself to sit and watched as the sun lowered even further in the sky, until it eventually faded.

Marko would be getting up soon. Or was he already awake? I hadn't once gotten the urge that he needed to feed. Not even the smallest tickling in my throat. That obviously meant he'd been taking care of that with other prey. They'd be dead now, put out of the misery I was forced to endure. It made me angry and I pushed myself from the bed, walking to the restroom to wash my face. As I stared at my reflection, I shook my head, hating what I saw. So weak. So…pathetically weak. I frowned, catching my thoughts. I sounded like Marko…I could feel the coldness within. His blood. It was changing me in more ways than one.

"Tessa, dinner's ready."

Hunter's voice was right outside of the restroom. I took a deep breath and threw open the door. The smell of chicken didn't appeal in the least, but he'd worked hard to make it so I'd force it down. Food was the last thing I needed. The urge to eat wasn't there anymore. My mind revolved around one thing and I couldn't understand it. If I was human, why did I crave blood? Was it from the changes within me from Marko's blood dominating, or the internal call that I needed to finalize the bond?

It had to be the latter. The pull was killing me. It only made sense.

"Looks good," I said, making myself smile. It was enough to tug at my lips and Hunter returned my expression with an even bigger one. I felt myself soften. He really was a great guy. And he'd done so much for me since Marko left me bloodied and broken—a whisper from death.

I picked up the fork and knife, cutting into the chicken. Flashes had my hands freezing. It was of a woman. One I felt I knew, but I'd never met before. What looked like an antique portrait of her face staring at me repeated, over and over, until I wasn't afraid of seeing her anymore. I was left more curious as to why it was happening.

"You okay?" He paused in chewing and I nodded, taking a bite. As my gaze rose, I caught Hunter staring. I paused mid-bite.

"I never asked you how things were going. You mentioned having a job interview in a few days. Tuesday, I believe."

His mouth tightened the smallest amount. "I'm not going. It's too soon."

"Too soon?" My head shook. "It'll be daytime. I'll be fine."

"Like you were that night when you left?"

My head lowered. "I had no choice. Even if you had been awake, I would have left. You don't understand."

"Explain it then. I feel lost, Tessa. I'm trying to give you time, or at least, hoping you'll open up to me, but you're so closed off."

I took another bite, chewing slowly. The moment I swallowed, I looked back up. "He has the ability to call me. I have no choice but to go. My body obeys whether my mind wants to or not. We share things. Thoughts, if we choose to. He can talk to me and I to him. But we haven't since…" I trailed off, stabbing my fork through another slice.

"Holy shit." He took a deep breath. "I can't believe you were actually able to tell me all of that."

I paused, cutting my gaze up to his. "Me too, now that you mention it."

"Must be because everything is going public."

"Must be," I repeated.

Knocking had Hunter pushing from the table. He pulled a gun from the back of his waistline and I felt my heart explode.

"Just a precaution," he said, quietly. "It won't kill them, but it makes me feel better."

I nodded, turning in my chair as he started for the door, only to stop. My skin tingled and fear slammed into me just like I'd described to him. I rose, reaching for his arm.

"Don't answer it," I said, breathlessly. "You can't…"

Hunter's hand was shaking as he reached behind my neck and pulled me forward, kissing my forehead. "It'll be okay. Just stay here."

Slowly, he headed for the door and I could see how physically hard it was for him. He pulled back the curtain, glancing out. When he turned to me, I could see the confusion on his face.

"It's a woman. She's surrounded by men."

"A woman?" I swallowed hard, heading for the window. I peered out, nearly gasping at the face. It had been the one I saw flashes of. My hand reached for the door handle and Hunter grabbed my bicep.

"Maybe we shouldn't answer."

I knew he was probably right, but I couldn't stop the curiosity of why I'd seen her. Did it have to do with Marko?

More knocking had me shrugging. "It's okay. I think I might know her." It was a lie, but not entirely. Hunter let go and I unlocked the dead bolt, easing the door open a few inches. "Can I help you?"

A big smile came to her face and I took in the black floor-length dress she wore. It hugged to her curves, displaying cleavage that was half hidden by her long, dark hair. She was beautiful. More so than what I'd seen of her in my mind. Her red lips surrounded perfectly white teeth. Ones that didn't appear to have fangs, but I knew they'd come when blood was her desire. Marko's were the same way.

"You must be the Tessa I keep hearing so much about. My name is Marie." She leaned in, inhaling deeply, right at chest level. I leaned back, a little surprised. "Oh yes, I smell Marko in you. You favor him, more so than your own scent. You've exchanged twice. I'm impressed. He's finally coming around."

"I'm sorry, what can I help you with?" I didn't want Hunter hearing this.

"Right," she said, glancing toward my best friend. "I'd hoped to prepare you for my arrival. It worked. You're calm and I'm glad."

All I could do was nod. It was also something I didn't want Hunter to pry into.

"Well, the way I see it is you're one of us now and we're all very close in the community. At least, we try to be. I'm a part of a little get-together and I wanted to invite you." She paused, her lips separating. "I'm sorry, I feel so rude, please excuse me, it's been awhile since we've met new company. I forget my manners. Please, let me introduce you to my men." She turned to the side, starting from her left and working right. "This is Kevin, Stephen, Denton, and Jose." They nodded and gave me a smile. I knew they weren't vampires immediately. Each of them held a glow, regardless that they were all a different ethnicity. It was a lot like the one I had. Their all-black clothing only intensified it and as I studied each one, I realized just how big they were.

My eyes glanced back at Hunter as he stared at the woman cautiously.

"Are they your bodyguards?" I asked, still confused.

A giggle came from her lips. "In a way. They're bonded to me. We all share a very close connection."

"Oh. Wow." My mouth parted in shock and I looked back up, seeing them differently. Four men. I couldn't even begin to understand how that worked. Especially if passion was involved. I hadn't thought a vampire could bond with more than one person at a time. Apparently, I didn't know much of anything concerning them.

Visions flashed of all four of them together. One fucking her pussy and another in her ass, while she sucked one's cock deep in her mouth. The one I knew to be Jose was getting his cock sucked by the one buried in her back entrance. My cheeks burned as I blinked hard and jerked my head back, looking down at her.

"You can thank me for that later. So, what do you say? Do you want to come to my get-together? I think it would be great fun and I really would love to get to know you better. It won't be like that," she whispered, "just as friends."

Hunter's hand gripped the back of my shirt, but I paid it no attention. "I'm sorry, I can't. Marko and I…" I searched for the words, not even beginning to know where to start. "We're not—"

"He tried to fucking kill her," Hunter exploded. "Almost did. And now you're here. I don't think so."

A sad look came over her face as she kept her stare on me. I was cautious to fully meet her eyes. I knew the power they held. I could feel it.

"It happens sometimes. But only when two people who match up perfectly are meant to be," she rushed in. "It's very rare, but it does happen. You have to understand what he's going through. It has to be excruciating for him."

"For him?" Hunter said, sarcastically. "Maybe you missed the part where Tessa almost died."

Hunter had me shifting uncomfortably. His anger was so thick, I could almost feel it. Combined with the power of the vampire before me, I was a Goddamn ball of nerves.

Marie glanced up to Hunter, but she kept quiet as she looked back at me. "I'm sorry, may I come in? New shoes, and it was a far walk," she said, displaying one of the black stilettos.

"Can't do it," Hunter said from behind me. "It's against house rules. No inviting vampires into your home. Then you can come and go as you please, even if we don't want you to."

"Really?" I said, turning around.

"Yeah," he said, quietly.

No wonder Marko was so intent on me inviting him in. And to think I could have prevented this.

"I'm sorry," I said, shaking my head. "Surely you understand."

Her bottom lips came out almost as if she were pouting. "I understand. You haven't had a very good experience with our kind. I assure you though, Marko is the exception. And he really can't help it. The fact that he even stopped shows how much he truly does love you. If he didn't, you'd be dead."

My heart dropped even as my chest crushed around it. I felt Hunter's hand grip to my shirt tighter.

"Listen," she said, softly. "I'd love for you to come to this party. And you don't have to worry about Marko, he's not even in our part of the city right now. Our leader has him babysitting some newbies so they won't get into trouble. He'll be gone the entire night." She leaned in closer. "The pain will ease being with your kind. I know you must ache for him. I can't even imagine what you're going through."

I stepped back more into Hunter's hand. I did fucking hurt and I wanted it to stop. Besides, I wanted to go back. The pull was pleading for me to. Even if it did terrify me to be close to so many people who could kill me, the temptation was irresistible. I belonged. Nothing had been truer.

"What sort of party is it again?"

"Tessa," Hunter exclaimed. "You can't be serious about possibly going?"

I glanced back, frowning. He didn't understand. Even I didn't get why I was asking.

Marie's face lit up. "It's Crystal's birthday. We're having a girls-only night together. I can't wait for you to meet her. We've been best friends for…well, ever. I think you'd really like her. There are so many people I want to introduce you to."

I smiled and tried to ignore that it was genuine. "It sounds fun, but I don't know. I'm not sure I can."

Marie pressed her lips together and leaned in a little closer. "I promise you have nothing to worry about. Marko may be powerful, but you'll have me and all my friends protecting you. Even he can't compete with that. Besides, think about yourself. We both know you need this. I can physically feel what you're holding in. I don't know how you're managing."

Fuck, I didn't either.

"Trust me," she continued, "everything will be okay. Come to your new home, even if it is only for the night. Let Marko's blood get what it needs. Comfort in the right atmosphere. A feeding of sorts. And your aching will ease some. At least temporarily."

"It will?"

"Tessa," Hunter snapped, pulling back at the material, "you can't go with her. Have you lost your mind?"

Marie's eyebrows rose in what looked to be disbelief. As if she was surprised I'd allow him to talk to me that way. She turned her head to look down to the side and I felt my shirt tugged back again. I spun on Hunter, suddenly not able to deal with his grabbing on me or telling me what to do. "I don't feel threatened. I think this will be okay. You heard her. Marko's not even there."

"What if it's not okay? What then, Tessa? She's a vampire. Are you ready to trust them all because of what she says? Maybe you're her next meal. Did you think of that? Just because she's female doesn't mean she won't eat you alive."

I rolled my eyes. "Hunter, she has four men to feed from, why would she want me? It's ridiculous. I've been there. I've seen their city. It's just like here. The only difference is their diet. Sure, there are drawbacks obviously, but they can't all be bad based off one person. That's like saying everyone on earth is like the serial killers held behind bars. We both know that's not how we all are. Besides, you heard her. Marko can't help it. I believe that. I've heard his thoughts. Felt what he has. It's beyond his control. Please just stop worrying, I'll be protected."

"My men will watch out for her, I promise," Marie said from behind me. "You have nothing to fret over. We'll have her home before sunrise."

Hunter shook his head at me. "This is a bad idea, Tessa. I can feel it."

He was right to worry and I knew it, regardless of what I tried to force myself to believe. I'd been raised to have faith. Although I hadn't found it in what I wanted, a piece of me clung to what instinct tried to convince me of. "I feel like it's not a bad idea, Hunter. I need this. Here," I said, placing my hand on my chest, "I *have* to go."

His eyes shut and he took a few steps back. "I really wish you wouldn't."

I turned back to Marie. "What do I wear? I really don't have anything…" again, I looked at her dress, "like…that."

"Don't even worry about it. I have plenty of things for you to choose from. We'll have you fixed up in no time. Why don't you go slide some shoes on. We'll head out."

I nodded, closing the door. Hunter had his arms crossed over his chest, glaring. "Don't do it, Tessa. Please. I'm begging you. Stay. *For* me."

My eyes closed and I lowered my head. "I wish you could feel what I do. My mind needs to go. It's like, I can't not go."

"Is he calling you again?"

Immediately, my head shook. "No, this is me. I just feel like it's something I have to do. Please understand. I'm…fucking dying inside." Even as I said it, more tears surfaced.

"If you go, you might be dying for real. You're going to get yourself killed and there's nothing I can do about it. Nothing but force you to stay whether you like it or not."

I cocked my head to the side as anger sent one of the tears spilling over. I quickly wiped it away. "This is my decision. I understand you're afraid, but I'm telling you, you have nothing to worry about. I *will* be home before sunrise."

"And if you're not?"

I sighed, not even wanting to think about the possibility. "Then I am so sorry and stupid for not listening. But I'm going, Hunter. I have to. I really do."

An aggravated sound left his mouth and he walked into his room, slamming the door. My flats were still by the far wall and I slid them on, looking down at the large denim button up blouse and black tights I wore. I looked a mess, but I didn't have the strength to change. I'd have to use every ounce I did have once I got to the underground city and I was hoping just being there would reenergize me. The sluggishness was taking its toll.

"Perfect." Marie beamed as I stepped out and shut the door behind me. I hugged my arms to my chest as we walked our way down the street.

"I'm so excited you're going. We're going to have so much fun. I just know it. But most importantly, you're going to feel better."

I tried to pretend to be happy, but now that I was out of my home, nervousness was kicking in. I could feel her energy so much stronger without my walls blocking the extent of it. It had to be the rule Hunter had spoken of. There was obviously something up with it. A protection precaution of some kind.

"How many people are going to be at this party?"

We got to the end of the road and turned. It wasn't long before I was faced with the same grate Marko had taken. My pulse exploded and I didn't want to go down there. I couldn't face the spot where I'd almost died. Yet, I had to. I couldn't go on with the way I had been, so empty and exhausted. Something had to change and I had to face my demons.

"I have no idea how many people she invited. She said it was a girl's get-together. Knowing Crystal, there might be quite a few."

One of the men took off the grate and I was lifted before I could say anything. My eyes shot to Marie's nervously.

"It's okay, Tessa. This is normal. My men and I will take good care of you. Trust me."

Chapter 16
Marko

Lights strobed through the large, underground two-level club, illuminating the foggy effects. Pink and blue colors shot around the room as the seductive tune echoed against the cement walls. Each beat of the heavy bass slammed into me as my eyes stayed focused on Boyd and his group of vampires. Humans mingled in the mix, stirring an aroma thick of lust. Here, they wouldn't feel fear, when they should.

The club was a playground for fucking. It was all passion and feeding. They loved the danger, the unknown, as their bodies swayed and rubbed against the hard muscle and curves of the strangers they were so easily accepting. In the eyes of the earlier generations, we were gods. A prize to be won. And they didn't hesitate to make their interest known if they had one.

My hands gripped into the railing of the balcony from the second story, watching the edge of Boyd's mouth pull back as he flirted with a blonde college-aged human girl. He'd done exceptionally well when it came to not attacking them. Why he'd gone after Tessa was still a mystery. Maybe he'd gone too long without feeding when she appeared. After all, she would have been the only one not bonded in our city. It was an open invitation. But here, these humans didn't carry any vampire blood within them, and he was so composed. Relaxed, even.

I brought my glass to my lips, drinking down the expensive liquor. The taste was bland, despite the punch it had. It wasn't what I wanted.

Laughing from a rather large group had my gaze drifting over and I took in the mix of vampire and humans, not having a desire for any of them. I'd fed twice today, just like I did every day to try to curb the cravings for Tessa. It was working to an extent, but I still couldn't stop the obsession that left me desperate to go to her. Awake, asleep, she was all I saw. All I dreamed of tasting.

My heart jumped and my eyes flickered and narrowed for the briefest moment. I swallowed, placing the glass down. I couldn't stop my fingertips from reaching up and pressing against my chest. That hadn't been *my* pulse skipping.

I pushed it away, refusing to pry into Tessa's thoughts or emotions. It was the hardest thing of all. I knew it would take the smallest switch and her mind would open for me, but I couldn't do it. If I did, it would all be over with. The obsession would grow and I'd leave here with only three things on my mind—to taste her, to fuck her, to kill her.

As my heart took turns going up and down in rhythm, I held to the rail like a fucking anchor. Where was her sadness? It had grown on me even though I hated it. But, now…she was different. Sweat was starting to drench my shirt and my throat began to burn at the need to taste her. I grabbed the drink, throwing it back and slamming the glass down. The music began to play a new song and dark lyrics were an aphrodisiac to the fantasies playing in my head. Her fantasies. Blood. I'd cover every inch of her body in crimson and take my time licking it off. Fuck, I wanted to. *She* wanted me to.

The door flew open and another large group poured in. Long, red hair waved out around a pair of bare shoulders and Crystal had me groaning in irritation. Her men and a large number of women surrounded her. Spying Marie left me even more agitated. My heart thumped in a steady, hard cadence and I shifted uncomfortably. A loud laugh shook Marie's chest as Crystal said something in her ear. Marie turned in a complete circle, only then viewing who she'd apparently been looking for. Maybe I didn't have to see. Maybe I already knew. Lavender and jasmine took me over without even getting the smallest trace. I felt the rail on the top of the balcony bend in my grasp.

Dark hair swayed as Tessa was pulled forward. My lips parted as I moaned through her appearance. Black shadowy make-up decorated her eyes and her lips were the exact color of blood. She looked so different and yet…like my darkest dream come true.

Her black dress only went down to mid-thigh and clung to her breasts and hips, accentuating her small waist. The vast amount of cleavage had my fangs elongating. My eyes ate her alive as a smile came to her face. Marie was whispering something and the vampire's fingertips slid along the side of Tessa's throat while she pulled her in even closer. I watched the smile on Tessa's face fade into uncertainty. What the hell was that conniving bitch telling her? I wanted to know. Instinct told me to listen, but the price that would come with doing so wasn't something I could risk.

My mind cleared and I snapped my eyes to Boyd. He was staring at Tessa just as intently as I had been. He pushed from the chair, entranced. I got ready, just in case. But he didn't run to her. His steps were determined, but slow. I couldn't stand it. The predator in me flared, ready to claw him up until nothing was left just for having his eyes on what was mine.

Marie held Tessa's hand as she brought her to a table full of gifts. I knew there'd be a party tonight, but in no way had I ever thought the events would begin like this. What in the hell was going on? I almost didn't need to ask. Marie had gone to her. I knew the woman better than most. She thrived at being in the middle of anything she deemed exciting. My stir in the community must have fit the bill. And she was smart enough to know my prey was at the root of it.

I pulled back on my hands and threw my legs over the side of the balcony, landing on the story below. Boyd was getting too close and I had no control as I began to zero in on him. He seemed to catch himself and stop, but his feet were already on the go again. He pushed past two human women, halting ten feet from the table.

"Marie." His voice called out and she turned, her smile fading as she spotted him. Protectively, her arm came out to Tessa, pulling her into her side. I tilted my head in surprise. There was a sense of possession in her stance that I didn't like. And it was real, not just for show. It was as if she were claiming Tessa for her own.

"What?" The one word had a warning laced within and Boyd shifted as he took a step closer, only to retreat. I could feel Tessa's fear. Knew she was trembling at the young vampire's insistence. She'd feel his need for her, if that were the case.

"May I come closer?" His eyes went to Tessa, only to return to Marie. The brunette vampire turned toward my prey, her eyes searching Tessa's face. Slowly, she reached up, cupping her cheeks. So tender….so wanting, herself.

I pushed a couple who had gotten too much in my space away from me. My fangs were still out. Still ready to tear anyone apart if they so much as made the wrong move.

"I can see his intentions. Boyd wants to apologize for attempting to attack you that first day you came here. Are you okay with that?"

Even through the music, I could hear Marie's soft voice.

"But…you told me Marko was watching over Boyd. You said I wouldn't have to see him."

Marie's thumb caressed over her cheek bone. "I didn't know he was watching over him *here*. Sweetie, don't even give him any mind. My men nor I will let anyone hurt you. You trust me, right?"

I nearly laughed at that. Like they could stop me if I wanted mon chaton. The declaration challenged me. Made me almost want to prove Marie wrong.

Tessa only glanced up into her eyes for the briefest moment before she nodded.

"Good." She turned to Boyd. "You may come." Marie broke away and Boyd eagerly walked forward. His breaths were light. His intentions…not quite clear. Was he genuinely sorry? He knew he was on my bad side, but did he care? He was a vampire. I knew he'd only look out for himself. I would have if I were him.

"I do want to apologize." Boyd stepped closer and I circled to the side, placing myself next to a crowd, but leaving myself just enough distance to move in fast if I needed to. "My actions were…deplorable. I'm not usually like that. It had been a rough few days and I…" his head shook. "I'm truly sorry I scared you like that."

Tessa nodded a little fast. "I believe you. The cravings must be hard for you."

Relief flooded his face and he smiled, moving closer. "You have no idea."

Marie grinned as she leaned against the table and I moved a little further back, staying out of view. It didn't stop the bitch from seeing me. Marie's smile fell until all that was left was the side of her mouth, edging into an evil grin. My head shook in disgust as I went back to Tessa and Boyd. I knew Marie was up to no good, hoping she'd see a blood bath on my part. She wanted me to fall. She wanted my chair. If Tessa's life was what took it, she'd sacrifice my prey in a heartbeat. *Or would she?* I couldn't ignore the protectiveness I'd seen before she noticed me. Maybe she was just as confused as I was?

Lights flickered over the dark waves down mon chaton's back and I tried to break the lust that had my eyes traveling to her hips and ass. Fuck, I could bend her over and drive my cock right where it needed to be. Right where it was meant to be.

"Do you dance?"

Boyd's question had my claws extending the smallest amount.

"Oh, no," she laughed. "I can't. I'm horrible at—"

"You *have* to dance," Marie cut in. "Not now, but at some point tonight. This is a party," she laughed. "You can always dance with me if you feel uncomfortable with anyone else." She glanced to Tessa's neck and I saw her lust as clear as day. What was Marie planning? Was it just to destroy me in the eyes of our community or was there something more going on that I couldn't quite comprehend?

"Maybe later," Tessa said, shyly.

"We have all night. No rush."

Boyd shrugged. "And I'm always down to dance, too. Just nod or call out to me if you decide."

"Thank you." Tessa's hands locked in front of her, clasping tightly as he walked away. The uncomfortable sensations prickled my skin and all I wanted to do was sweep her in my arms and take her back to my room. The underground club wasn't far from there. Two tunnels, our main door…and we'd be isolated. Alone.

A new song started and a large part of the party group cheered, pulling at each other as they made their way to the dance floor. They were all high on something or another. Mostly speed, *X*, or some other substance ingested through their slaves. Once it was in the blood, it was a quick fix for the vampires. A taste of the forbidden for someone not worried about overdose. Not that the effects would last long or even be that strong.

Tessa glanced around, taking in the bar area. Marie stepped in closer, coming up from behind. What she whispered, I wasn't sure. It sent Marie's hand up and one of her men came forward. The order was made and he walked to the bar, waiting as one of the four bartenders listened.

"You're going to love this drink," Marie said, wrapping her arms around Tessa from behind. "They call it The Shaker. It's the closest to what you need. It's going to make all that pain just…disappear." Marie's lids closed and she moved in closer to Tessa's neck, inhaling deeply. Heat balled in the center of my stomach as my eyes narrowed. I didn't wait. I projected my warning along the vampire's skin with just enough brutality to let her know I was serious. Marie's eyes snapped open as she jumped at the shock. Her other three men pushed to her side, having felt what their Mistress did. Her head moving back and forth stopped them from coming toward me.

Tessa shrugged out of the hold, turning and grinning. "Maybe just one drink. Then I should really be going. I feel bad for leaving Hunter alone."

"Hunter is doing fine. He's a big boy." Marie glanced down, only to look back up, questioningly. "I have to ask. Hunter's a very attractive man. Have the two of you ever considered…you know."

Tessa's lips pursed and I could tell she didn't want to talk about it. "We're best friends. That's where it ends."

"But aren't you at least a little tempted? I mean, a woman has needs."

"My needs don't revolve around Hunter that way."

A slow nod was all Marie gave while her eyes scanned over her men. "Do any of mine attract you? I don't mind sharing."

Rage exploded within and I held to Julius' order for stability. God, I'd kill Marie if she tried to push Tessa on one of her slaves. There wouldn't be enough people able to get me off all of them if the time came.

"I don't think…" The words were rushed out when Marie's finger settled over Tessa's lips.

"You don't understand our ways. I see that now. I apologize if that came out crass. You see, we're all very open sexually. I think you'll soon find that out. Nudity is not something we gape at or feel uncomfortable around. Sex is just passion. Here, we embrace it. Live it to the fullest." Her shoulder came in closer to her face as she gave a half shrug. "I have four men, what does that tell you?"

Even in the dim atmosphere, I could see Tessa blush.

"Sweetie, you're one of us now. You can be or do whatever it is you want. No one will stop you or judge your actions. *Embrace* your new life. You have vampire blood within you. We're like sisters now."

It was the stupidest thing I'd ever heard, but it made sense to Tessa. I could feel it. She suddenly wanted this. Wanted this…life. Fuck, what had my blood done to her? It was warping her thoughts. Had changed who she was. There was no going back. This *was* the new Tessa. In truth, she was part of our community now. Could be for good, if I accepted her as mine. Even if it was just as my blood slave and not my concubine.

Tessa's head shook as she started to say something, only to stop when she reached for the glass handed to her.

"I'm sorry, Marie. Nothing against your men. They're all very attractive, I just don't think I can."

"No worries. Drink. When the pain fades, we'll have this conversation again."

Tessa was already sipping from the straw and I watched as the red liquid rose to her lips. The slow, deep sucking didn't go unnoticed by my cock. God, how it looked like blood. *It could be my blood if I wanted.*

My eyes closed as I tried to erase it from my mind. I had to stop watching. If I didn't, I was going to do something I regretted and I couldn't ruin her life that way.

Boyd was back in his group. Back to talking to the human females who were turning into nothing but groupies for our kind. Although he appeared to listen, he only had eyes for my Tessa. And not even in a threatening way. More curiosity. Maybe he was wondering the same thing I was. What was it about her that called to our dark desires? Was it her beauty? She wasn't overly beautiful, but attractive, none the less. Was it her blood? Her scent?

A sigh escaped me. I knew it was, but what was so gripping about it? She was pure human. There was nothing else within her that lurked in the shadows. It just had a distinct attraction that appealed to us. There was no other way to explain it. She just smelled good. Like a juicy steak to a starving man. And we were all starving for her. Especially me.

"What's in this? It's really good."

I didn't even have to be next to them to hear her voice. I was so in tune with my prey, everything she felt, every sound she made. We were one.

"A little of this, a little of that. Good, right?"

Tessa laughed, a lightness pushing through the heaviness we'd both experienced the last few days. It helped me relax and I leaned against the far wall, taking turns looking between her and Boyd, who were now at opposite ends.

"I like it. Kind of fruity with a slight twinge of…" Her head shook. "I can't put my finger on it.

"Blood?" Marie's voice had my spine stiffening and me and Tessa both suddenly feeling sick. "Kidding," she said, laughing. "Although, I bet you really could go for some right now. I know I could."

"Why is that?" Even as Tessa asked, I watched her lick her lips. The bond was getting to her, too, And badly.

Marie's shoulders swayed to the music and she glanced toward the dance floor before turning back to Tessa. "It'll always be a craving of yours now. You've tasted power. Marko's blood has corrupted your own and it wants to take over. The withdrawals for more will always be there, but what you have going for you is us. We're your support system. Human, vamp, it won't matter who you consume. If you don't want to be bonded, your best bet is human, but ties to close friends are good, too. The world is at your fingertips, all you have to do is choose and enjoy the ride."

Seriousness came over Tessa's features, but Marie didn't let her dwell on it. "Drink up. Soon, we dance."

Tessa's eyes scanned the area constantly. I noticed the more she sipped on the straw, the more she began to rock and sway with the songs. What the hell was in that drink? She didn't consume alcohol often. I'd seen it in her memories. But she seemed to get a little too relaxed, a little too fast. Was I overreacting?

I headed to the bar, watching as the vampire behind the counter looked up at me nervously. Guilt? It wasn't that. It was my presence. He'd know my status just from the vibrations I threw off.

"Do you put blood in The Shaker?"

His lips parted and he quickly shook his head. "No. We're not allowed to do that. Not since humans come here now, anyway. Just liquor and juice."

I nodded, staring back to Tessa. "You know Marie. You made those drinks for Denton, correct?" My finger pointed and he looked in the direction of Tessa.

"Yes…sir."

"And you're telling me it was just juice and alcohol you placed in those glasses?"

His hands shot up. "I swear it. Nothing else."

"Thanks." I headed back to the middle of the room, watching each sway of Tessa's body. Her hair rocked back and forth to the side, teasing over the exposed cleavage of her breasts. Her lids were heavier, giving her a dreamy appearance while she stared at the dance floor. No way was she feeling that good on three-quarters of a glass. Did humans have that low of a tolerance? I hated not knowing, and I wouldn't unless I got closer. If I did…there'd be no going back. My skin itched to have a taste. To feel her pulse against my fangs.

Marie took Tessa's empty glass and grabbed her hand, laughing and pulling her to the dance floor. There was no hesitation on my prey's part. Her happiness radiated from her like a net, entrancing and trapping me completely. I could feel the lust thicken within. It caressed my skin with need. Left me breathless as I moved in closer. Fuck, I'd never seen her like this. So carefree. So…full of life. Even in her memories, she'd never been without some form of burden. Even if it was her own anxieties, which she had a lot of. Now, she suddenly didn't.

Marie came to a stop in the middle of the dance floor, pulling Tessa in close. The sway of her body had Tessa's moving in tune almost automatically. I stepped quickly to the side as I tried to get a better view. Fingers pushed Tessa's hair back as Marie kept her focus on my prey's face. Her eyes…she wanted so badly to trap

Tessa within her stare. My prey was smarter than that. It made me feel happy. Safer, for her being here.

Words came from Marie's mouth that I didn't catch it. I'd been so fixated on the sway of Tessa's body that I barely noticed her lips had moved from my peripheral vision.

A laugh poured from Tessa's mouth and she spun around, giving Marie her back as the vampire pulled her in close. I saw the change sweep through Marie's expression and rumbling vibrated my chest as warnings exploded out from my body. The fight to give in was there, written all over her fixated eyes, but I didn't trust her not to succumb to the temptation. She would at some point if she kept torturing herself this way.

Tessa's arms shot up as a new song came on. One she appeared to know. Her hair swung out as she turned back to face Marie. The vampire genuinely laughed at my prey's excitement and I felt the threat lessen. It was a back and forth battle for us all, apparently. Me, Boyd, Marie…and I was in the middle. The cause of it all.

My heart was racing and I tried to calm myself. Having Tessa so exposed in this atmosphere left me wanting to protect her more than kill her. The realization was like a weight lifting. As long as I stayed far enough away from her, she was okay.

More songs came and went, and hours past as I watched. Content as I could be while continuously scanning the crowded two-level room. The night was ending without incident and I was glad for it.

The third glass was taken from Tessa's hand from Kevin. He and the other men were close by Marie's side, which put them close to Tessa. But I didn't feel a need to worry about them. It was Boyd who was also on the dance floor with one of the blondes that kept my attention. The constant swallow was a sign I knew too well. It was getting time for him to feed, and with him being new, the urges came a lot sooner than mine. He'd be edgy. Not in control of what he needed.

I took in Tessa on one side and Boyd on the other. I wondered if I could get to him without my prey spotting me. If I waited much longer, it might put me too close.

A group of four had taken residence next to me and I walked around them, moving along the length of the elevated floor to the end. Boyd didn't know I was monitoring him, but he soon would.

Five males in his clique stayed close and I tapped one's shoulder, signaling to Boyd. His arm instantly drew back from my touch, as if he feared it. And he should.

"B," he yelled.

Agitated eyes snapped over and I knew the aggression was because it had broken his attention from what he wanted.

Mine.

"What?"

The gesture the friend made had Boyd's gaze flashing over. With only a few inches of elevation from the floor, my eyes were level with his. Had I been on the dance floor, I would have towered over him.

"Fuck," he groaned, weaving through the people in between us. He came to the edge, shaking his head. "I wasn't going to hurt her, I promise."

"No, you weren't. I wouldn't have let you." I grabbed his arm, pulling him down from the group. "Time to feed. Pick someone and head to the back. If you don't, you can take one of the suppliers. I'm not having a scene break out because you're too preoccupied on what belongs to me to take care of yourself."

His arm yanked against my grip. "What are you, my keeper?"

I laughed at his attitude. It was his vampire pushing through. The one who longed for the fight. For the kill.

"Ass in the back and feed or you're out of here and I put you in lockdown."

There was a slight hiss from the threat, but he spun around, heading in front of the dance floor to make his way to the feeding rooms nestled in the back.

"Boyd!" Tessa's hands shot up, waving him over. I felt my stomach drop through the floor at the panic that surged. His face spun and the tightening of his fists told me he wanted to run. To go at her with everything he had. My feet began to move, but not nearly as fast as I wanted them to. He took one step. Two.

My hand latched onto his throat, holding tight as I spotted his fangs. I didn't get a chance to look back to see if Tessa was staring at me. His palms wrapped around my wrists and I rushed us to the back, throwing him into the first room we came to.

"Feed," I ordered. "Or so help me, you won't see tomorrow."

A woman was sitting on a small bed in the corner, her knees to her chest. Just like the ones we fed from on the table for meals, she was a supplier. A slave to our entire vampire community. She gave freely, lusting from our bite, not caring what happened before, during, or after we were finished. This would be how the humans would all turn out in the end. Our slaves.

The woman stood and Boyd's glare went from me to her. I slammed the door leaving him there, only to become faced with another glare. One that stopped me dead in my tracks. She didn't say a word. Maybe she didn't have to. I felt her anger and fear. Her heartbreak concerning our situation.

"Did you come here to die, Tessa? You couldn't have just waited for me to come to you first."

My body was already hovering over hers. When I'd taken the steps that separated us, I wasn't sure. Her scent called to me. Left me in a fade as I reached for her waist, pulling her against me. Shaking vibrated my fingers and hummed through me. Her pulse was racing, drowning out the bass that bounced from the walls. For seconds, she just stared. The longing in her eyes begged me to put an end to it all. She didn't want to feel this anymore than I did.

"Tessa, you naughty girl." Marie stepped up from behind her and I had to tear my eyes up to face the bitch whose fault this was. "Come, sweetie, I'm getting bored. Let's head out."

Tightly, my fingers increased in pressure and I nearly moaned as Tessa's head lowered against my chest. It was submission in the purest form. She waited for my direction and it fucking killed me. My fingers broke free and I reached for her face, digging my fingertips into her cheeks as I held on.

"I *forbid* you to come back here. Now go, mon chaton, while you still can."

I let go, sweeping past them like my life depended on it. In a way, it did. But it was hers I was more worried about. And I knew she didn't have long. I was losing the fight, and Marie was all too aware.

Chapter 17
Tessa

Tears built in my eyes as I watched Marko stalk away. What was I doing? Did I want to die? Fuck this bond that was hell bent on destroying me. There was nothing worse than having no control. I couldn't stand it. I couldn't even remember the walk from the dance floor to Marko. I was just suddenly…there. Looking up at him like some sappy, suicidal idiot. God, I wanted to escape. To run so far away and never come back. Well, the rational side of me anyway, which wasn't really making an appearance at the moment. Everything was a blur. Even the walls as I held to Marie and stumbled through the tunnel.

"I hate him," I said, for what I knew to be at least the third time. "I really do."

"We all do, sweetie." She laughed. "Trust me."

"I do trust you," I said, glancing up. "And I probably shouldn't."

Marie's smile disappeared the smallest amount. "You're smarter than you look, but I don't plan on hurting you. At least, not at the moment."

I felt my eyebrows draw in and a burst of giggles left her.

"Joking. Jeez, lighten up. You're too serious. Besides, if I wanted to hurt you, I've had plenty of opportunity. We both know that. I meant what I said. You're supposed to be here and I want us to be friends."

Both sides of my mouth pulled back into a grin. "I want that, too."

"Good. Then we both have nothing to worry about."

Light broke through as we came into the heart of the city and my feet slowed at the sound of music. My eyes scanned the room, spotting the group immediately. They held the oddest array of instruments. One was playing an accordion, another, what looked to be an old washboard, and there was a banjo player and a violinist. Together, they were brilliant. Beyond amazing. So much so that I picked up my pace and broke away from Marie, heading toward the far cement wall where they stood.

"I know this song," I said, moving closer.

"They sing it all time. Let's go lie down in bed. We'll talk."

"No, wait."

I barely heard Marie call me as I approached. The tune I knew, but never had I heard it played this way. It was different. Sad and upbeat at the same time.

A vampire with a big beard looked up at me and I gave him a big smile as he continued with the lyrics. I could feel Marie come to a stop behind me, but I didn't care. For the first time in my life, I wanted to sing. And I was far from a place of worship. It didn't matter. Maybe it was because I was shitfaced drunk. I'd probably regret it in the morning, but what if I didn't have the morning? I could easily die at any time and I wanted to sing.

"When was the last time you lived?"

Hunter's words pushed through and when the man broke off and pointed to me, I didn't hesitate to join in with him. Surprise shot to his face and I didn't even get embarrassed. My hands clapped and I laughed as I felt their spirit lift. The music that had been beautiful before, took on a whole new life. The volume increased, as did their beat, picking up tempo as they smiled and stomped their feet to the rhythm.

I let my voice ring out. Loud. Uncaring. *Free*. God, I felt so fucking free. It was the place. It was my new blood. Regardless of what happened with Marko, I was home, and I knew it.

Clapping and laughter behind me had me spinning toward Marie as I continued to sway and dance with the other men. Shock. Yes, she sure had it on her face. But surprise, too. I knew I sang well. I wouldn't deny that. But something about how uplifted everyone was suddenly, how the environment wasn't so dark, just left me invigorated. This place wasn't so bad. It just needed to be lit up on the inside. It didn't have to be dreary and about death. It didn't. They drank blood. So what. I'd done it and still wanted more, but there was at least a little good here. I was witnessing it firsthand. And no one was trying to rip out my throat or attack me. We were just a group of people having a fun time.

The song began to end and I laughed, kissing the lead singer's cheek as I stepped back. My small wave had them all returning the gesture and I wrapped my arm around Marie as she waited for me to take my place at her side. Which, at the moment, felt perfectly normal.

"You are amazing. I didn't know you could sing. And so well," she gushed.

I shrugged and laughed, suddenly feeling the embarrassment start to sink in, but didn't dwell on it.

"Thanks. I sing…" I trailed off, sadness taking over at the realization. "I used to sing for the choir. I guess I can't anymore."

"Church choir?" Marie's head shook, panicked. "Don't go there, Tessa. Don't ever go back there."

My shoulders sagged as we headed toward the same hall Marko's room was in. I didn't even hesitate in my steps as we continued in the darkness. One of the men pushed open the door right past Marko's and I could have rolled my eyes at the irony. As we headed inside, my feet finally dug in and I came to a stop.

"Marie…" My eyes shot to her. "You're the devil."

"I beg your pardon," she said, offended.

I lifted my hand. "I'm sorry. That didn't come out like I meant. You came to Marko's door while I was in there. He thought your name and when I asked who Marie was, he said the devil. It was you."

She let out a loud laugh and kicked off her shoes. "Indeed. Talk travels fast here. Besides, I heard you moaning as I walked by. I knew he'd been fucking someone good, so I thought I'd mess with him. I do that a lot. It's fun."

"To mess with Marko?"

"Well, yes, of course. He's so uptight. It's fun to pick at him every now and again. We get bored down here. It adds excitement. Especially since I know he doesn't like me. It makes it that much more fun."

I stepped out of the shoes and hugged my arms over my chest. Now that we weren't dancing, I was cold. It was always cooler down here. Especially now.

"Ah, take that off and come get under the covers. You're shaking."

Marie let her dress drop to the floor and I paused.

"Oh, come on," she said, walking over to the bed nude. "I'm not going to bite you. Or touch you, if that's what you're worried about. Marko would try to kill me and I'm not looking to fight tonight. I just want to talk and the best way to do that is comfortably. So…take off that dress and come lay down with me."

"But." I looked at the men, unsure. Noticing that they only had eyes for Marie, even though I felt uncomfortable as hell, I pulled the zipper free. The dress dropped to the floor and I rushed to the bed, diving under the covers she held up.

"Braver than I thought, too," she said, smiling. "I didn't think you'd do it. You take orders well. You'd be a good slave."

My head drew back and I shook it. "Not really. Obviously." My hand gestured to the door and Marie rolled her eyes.

"That has nothing to do with you whatsoever. Marko is…how do I say this without pissing myself off? Guess there's really not a way," she sighed. "Marko is the epitome of a leader. Someday, he will be. Probably not for another couple of hundred years, but mark my words, he'll go far. He has the power. He has the focus. And he knows it."

"Leader?" My eyes lowered to the bed. "No wonder he doesn't want a human concubine."

"Concubine?" Marie burst out. "He put you in the role of his concubine? Or thought it?"

My head shook, not wanting to tell her too much. Especially if I was wrong. "No. Not really. He's just thought about it a few times. About how humans weren't concubine material. They were food."

"He was angry, though?"

Marie's face was focused, serious, as she stared at me.

"Well, yeah. Very angry. He's always angry concerning me."

She sat up, letting the blanket fall to her waist, exposing her breasts. "He loves you. Like…*really* loves you."

I nearly laughed, but hadn't I thought the same thing? Even called him on it? I knew he battled with feelings for me, but it was an illusion. Marko may have let me live up to this point, but he was still choosing to kill me over keeping me. That alone spoke for itself.

"I don't want to talk about him anymore. He's going to try to murder me anyway." I yawned, snuggling into the pillow. "Let's talk about something else."

Marie turned from me and glanced over at her men who were in the process of removing their clothes. Denton looked up and I could tell she favored the dark skinned man over the others. He nodded and my eyes widened as I realized they'd been communicating, just like me and Marko.

"I'm going to give you a gift, my new friend. I think I'd like to keep you around for quite some time. What you choose to do with it is up to you."

"A gift?"

"Yes." Denton walked up, holding a small silver dagger. There was nothing fancy about, but I knew what I was looking at wasn't cheap. There was history behind the weapon that I wasn't sure I was comfortable with. I could feel my heart pick up speed at her taking it and holding it out to me.

"Keep it close to your side. Cherish it. It's a beautiful protector. And a blessing never hurt anything. Maybe keep that in mind, but not too close, if you know what I mean."

My lips separated as I let the heavy metal slide over my fingers. "You want me to—"

Marie's finger pushed against my lips. "Shh. We don't speak words out loud here. The walls can sometimes have ears. Look into my eyes and let me erase this conversation. You won't even remember having it. You'll just know what you'll need to do."

Aching settled back in my chest, but my true self somehow pushed through. For the first time, I connected with the depths of who Marie was, and then…nothing.

Chapter 18
Hunter

Tessa held my stare, neither of us ready to give way to the other. Our arms crossed over our chests and I adjusted mine, raising my eyebrow as she mirrored my actions. If I wasn't so pissed, I might have laughed at our ridiculous confrontation, but I was. Downright livid, and she knew it the moment she staggered through the door.

The anger hadn't come right away. Not even close. First came lust at the revealing, little black dress. Then came shock that it was actually her I was looking at. That's when the anger broke through.

"Well," I said, widening my eyes. "You going to explain?"

The sun lit up the house brightly. Lit up, because I'd opened every fucking curtain and blind just to see the moment she came walking down the Goddamn street. *I'll have her back before the sun rises*, my ass!

"I fell asleep at Marie's. Truthfully, I'd have come home a lot sooner had I not drank so much. So, please, Hunter, not right now. My head hurts and I feel like I'm going to throw up."

"You drank?" The surprise was deep in my words. Of course she drank. She wasn't dressed like she'd spent the last few hours at a church convention. "I thought this was a girl's get-together. A birthday party or something."

Tessa's eyes closed for the briefest moment. "It was. But at a club."

"A club," I repeated, having flashbacks of myself at clubs. I hadn't been in years, but I did go through a period where I liked to go out and have fun. I'd just grown out of it.

"Yes, a club. It's not a big deal. I won't be going back."

"Oh." I stood a little straighter, feeling relief begin to take over. "Well, that's good. Did you see Marko?" The words came rushing out and I wanted to kick myself. The question had been driving me insane all night. I hadn't even been to sleep yet and I was exhausted and cranky from lack of caffeine. "Of course you didn't," I said, under my breath. "You wouldn't be here right now if you did."

Tessa's head lowered and she hugged her chest tighter. The cleavage drew me in, but I tried like hell to ignore the way my body reacted to hers. Now wasn't the time.

"Actually, I did. I spoke with him."

"What?" I leaned down to be able to see her face, but Tessa lifted, looking at me.

"I was stupid. I saw him and I barely remember even chasing after him. I don't know what I was thinking. Well, I wasn't, I was drunk. He's the one who forbade me to go back."

My mouth opened, only to shut. Then it opened again. "He could have killed you! Tessa, oh my God, what in the hell is the matter with you? Do you want to die, is that it? Do you have some sort of death wish that I'm not aware of? What…" My hands stood, hovering in the air, looking just as lost as I felt. It didn't make sense why she'd be so stupid. Didn't having her throat nearly ripped out count for anything?

Tessa kicked off the stilettos she wore and dropped a few inches in height. "You don't understand, Hunter. To be there...I felt..." Her head went back down. "I feel like I belonged. Like it's the first time in my life I actually fit in somewhere."

I rubbed against my short hair, trying to understand. "It has to be him. He has to be using some sort of power or magic to lure you there."

"No, he's not," she said, angrily. "He doesn't want anything to do with me. I do believe it might be his blood in me, though. It's made me part of their world. I think I'm meant to be there." She glanced up, frowning. "I didn't even want to come home, Hunter." My silence had her taking a few steps toward the room. "I'm going to take a shower and climb into bed. I just want to lie down."

This couldn't be what things were coming to. I was losing my best friend to not only Marko, but...to them. Would she leave the world above for the one below? Alienate all humans until they turned her into a monster, too? Misery never held such a crippling sensation than when it was paired with betrayal. I hated him for choosing her. For not only turning Tessa away from me, but from everyone.

I didn't serve my country for twelve years to come home and have my dreams destroyed by a blood sucking monster. Marko Delacroix would pay. They all would.

"Tessa, wait." I pushed into her room, making her jump as she tried to cover herself. The black, lace, sexy panties were see-through and went down in a *V*, displaying the firmness of her stomach and accentuating the curve of her hips. The strapless bra pushed her generous breasts together and I mourned for something I would never know. Tessa had been so young when we'd lost our virginity to each other. There wasn't much to appreciate then, but now...fuck, I'd worship her body like it was the most prized possession in this world. And in mine, it was.

"Hunter." Her eyebrows lifted while she waited for me to leave. My head shook and I surged forward, jerking her into my body and pressing my lips against hers. I held, waiting. As my hand slid in her hair, I felt her pull back. Our eyes searched each other's and I knew. It sliced like a blade right through my heart. *Tessa wasn't mine anymore.* She'd never be again. It wasn't like I could remove Marko's blood from her body. She'd never be the old Tessa again. Never love me like I loved her.

My hand dropped from the dark waves and I pressed my lips together, still feeling the tingling from the kiss she never returned.

"I'm moving out. I won't witness your self-destruction. You're going to die and I will never be able to help you when you won't even help yourself."

Bile burned the back of my throat. I didn't want to move out. Couldn't imagine leaving her defenseless to die at the fangs of that vampire.

"I think it would be best," she whispered.

Even as she said it, I couldn't believe what I was hearing. My statement had been meant to gauge her reaction on where she stood, and it was all too clear. My Tessa was already gone. She had died the day I'd left her to visit a friend. The night Marko somehow conned his way inside of her home. Tessa was dead.

A fog clouded my mind and I turned, slowly walking from her room. The constant heaviness in my chest drifted to my stomach and entered each of my limbs. This was my fault. I'd felt the evil in him that night he'd been following her. Somehow, I knew, yet still, I had left.

Thoughts blurred while I pushed my door open and looked around the space she'd made up just for me. I could still see her that first night, laughing and so excited at my arrival. I'd stood a chance then. She was still my Tessa in those moments.

Grief had tears burning my eyes. I reached for the dark green bag I'd come with, so full of hope for my future. Didn't I fucking deserve it for what I'd been through? What I fucking had to do and what I saw? I pulled the top open, tossing it on the bed, now drowning in my sorrow. The bathroom door shut and I listened to the shower turn on as I pulled my clothes from the drawers.

The sound of faint singing had my head bowing and the tears dropping to the floor. What happened to New York? To my dreams of taking Tessa to the smoky room of a lounge and listening to the singers, knowing they couldn't hold a candle to the woman who'd be at my side. I wanted to see her stand on the stage. To blow everyone away with her beautiful voice. We could have had such an amazing time. Fuck, an amazing life. I wanted to show her so much. All I wanted was for us to happy. God dammit!

Those vampires were going to pay. Every single one of them. I'd figure out a way to end their lives if it was the last thing I ever did. Their blood was going to puddle in the streets. I'd soak the city of Austin in my enemies by the time I was finished. There wouldn't be a vampire alive who didn't know who I was. They'd fear me…because they'd be next.

Chapter 19
Tessa

Singing had always been my escape. My make-everything-disappear-and-leave-me-in-this-moment-forever route. Dismissing Hunter so coldly had broken my heart. God, I loved him. And that was the true kind. It was pure, focused solely on my feelings for everything that made him the person he was. Knowing he was leaving so devastated killed me. All I wanted to do was rush out, apologize, and beg him to stay. Regardless of what he believed or thought, I was terrified of what was happening to me. That night Marko had almost killed me had been the scariest moment of my life. I felt torn on what I needed to do and what I felt I should. I was so scared to face this alone. Hunter had always been there for me when I needed it the most, but I couldn't allow that anymore. The underground called to me as if it were my home. The one I'd always longed for but could never find. I'd always struggled with finding my place in the world. To feel like you never fit in was the worst. But there, even afraid amongst the people surrounding me, the calling was all too clear. To keep Hunter as I was battling the realization was wrong.

And then there was Marko. I longed for him. Loved him. And didn't. Beneath it all, my mind still held onto what and who he truly was. I'd never be able to forget or forgive his actions, but I couldn't necessarily blame him either, seeing as it was in his nature. Nothing was right. Not the facts. Not the emotions. And definitely not my behavior.

A sob left me and I put my hand over my mouth, letting myself sink to the floor of the shower. My mind was literally going to drive me crazy. Everything congealed into the biggest mindfuck I could think of. What the hell was I going to do? Marie wanted me to come back to her place tonight for more stories. She used Marko as my crutch and I let her. To learn more about him was something I felt I needed to do. But the other half of me wondered why I was even going to bother. He'd kill me. I could feel it in my soul. I wouldn't be here much longer. So what was I doing wanting to go back to the underground? I should be spending time with Hunter and my family. Except, my family was overseas right now and Hunter was exactly where I needed if I wanted him to survive. He'd fight for me for all the wrong reasons and I couldn't allow that. I knew he wanted a future for the two of us, but I couldn't give it to him. My heart wasn't my own anymore. Besides, he would be safer away from me. I didn't want him to die, too, and he would if he stayed under my roof. Marko might have said he wouldn't kill him before, but that didn't apply anymore. Hunter was fair game and I couldn't be responsible knowing I'd been the death of my best friend.

Another sob left me as I let the water pour down over my back. Minutes went by, then what felt like hours. The water was like ice and I numbly reached over, turning it off. Still, I sat, shaking from the cold. To say I felt alone was an understatement. I *was* alone now. So what did I do?

I stood, pulling back the curtain and grabbing a towel. The moment I opened the door, I knew Hunter was gone. An eerie silence rested throughout the house and as I peeked through his open door, all the drawers were still open and empty. My heart instantly broke. I wiped away the new tears and forced myself to face this by myself. It was for the best, I'd never needed anyone. I shouldn't start now. Hunter would be safe. That was the most important thing.

Thoughts began to invade as I headed to my room. My bed stood ahead of me and I pulled back the covers, not even bothering to get dressed. I climbed in, removing the towel and snuggling in as I stared toward the still open curtains. It didn't take long for heaviness to pull my eyes closed. Marko was already waiting for me, but not like I had dreamed. His fangs extended and he smiled evilly as he began to circle around. A groan came from my mouth as I tossed and turned, trying to make him go away so I could fall asleep.

"Tessa."

I jumped at his voice and wondered if I had somehow slipped into real sleep and dreamed it.

"Yes?" I refused to say his name in case I had been mistaken. The last thing I wanted was for him to think I was reaching out to him. Especially after our run in at the club.

Silence. My fist slammed into the pillow and I turned to my stomach.

"I think I'm going to be coming for you soon."

I stiffened, only to hold my pillow tighter. Tears threatened but I held them off. I would not shed a tear over this. For Hunter, I would, but not for Marko.

"I know."

"That's it? You know?"

My eyes rolled, erasing any sadness and quickly turning it to annoyance. *"What do you expect me to say? Oh no, please don't kill me. Is that it? You want me to beg for my life? Sorry, Marko, you're not getting that from me."*

More silence. Minutes went by while I stared at the remaining leaves swaying on the nearly bare tree in my yard.

"Marko, I need to ask you a favor."

"What?"

One of the leaves fell from the branch and I watched it float through the air. I almost felt like I was falling, too. Maybe I was in more ways than one. *"I need you to give me more time. I want to start spending time in your city."*

"Have you lost your mind? You can't just come down here to hang out. That's not the way it works, Tessa. You'll be killed faster than you can imagine."

I had lost my mind, and it was his fault, but I knew he was right. It would only take an instance like with Boyd for my life to end before Marko got his chance to do it himself.

"I belong there. Even Marie says that's where I should be. I'm only happy when I'm underground. Give this to me before you try to take my life. If I get killed, just think how much easier it'll be for you. You can go on without a care in the world."

A low sound came through as I waited.

"It would be far from easy for me, mon chaton. I'd destroy anyone who wanted to hurt you. If they killed you, there'd be nothing of them left by the time I finished. Your death will come from no one but me."

"Will you give me time?"

"It means that much to you? Darkness in some underground city full of monsters?"

"More than you know."

He let out a deep breath. *"How long?"*

My eyes closed. Was he letting me decide the day I got to die?

"Yes. I am. Or, at least, I'll try. There's no guarantees. After last night, you're lucky I didn't take you while you slept in Marie's bed. I thought about it, and she wouldn't have been able to stop me. Not her, or her men. You play a very dangerous game coming so close to your killer. But you're a masochist. It makes sense."

"Excuse me?" I sat up, staring blindly ahead.

"You like pain, mon chaton, and the sad thing is, I'm the perfect person to give it to you. But we'll never know that life. Now, give me the day you wish to die."

I paused, not even wanting to think about his words. Dark fantasies didn't appeal when facing death. *"Wednesday sounds like a good day to try to kill you."*

A laugh echoed around me. *"I'll see what I can do about giving you your chance."*

"Marko?"

"Yes, Tessa?"

Loneliness was invading and I didn't want to let him go. Here, he couldn't hurt me.

"Do you think your kind will ever be able to come to peace with us?

"No. It's impossible. You can't be on good terms with food."

"But, you're wrong. So many vampires have blood slaves. They don't kill them. Why can't each vampire be designated a donor so the world's population will be safe? It might work. Sure, there will be a few who break the rules, but what if something like that could be set up?"

He paused. *"We already have that for those who choose not to hunt prey. But you miss the point. It's not who we are. We have to hunt, Tessa. It's part of who we are."*

"Who you were. If your leader made it mandatory—"

"There would be war between us vampires. I, for one, won't stand for it," he snapped. *"We're already caged underground. To take the little freedom we have, it can't be that way. We're killers. It's what we are."*

The anger had me becoming quiet. There was no use arguing about something he was so passionate about. He'd refuse to listen to my side and I wasn't going to waste my energy trying to convince him that peace would be better for everyone involved.

"Will you be here tonight?" The deepness in his voice told me he wanted me to be. He wanted me, period.

"Marie wants me to stay at her place again."

A curse came through in French. *"She using you, mon chaton. You know this, though, don't you."*

It wasn't a question. We both knew I did. *"I like her."*

"You want to change her. Make her like you so you can see that we're not all bad. I'm telling you, we're not good. You can't save us."

"You're probably right. That doesn't mean I can't have hope. I happen to think there's a reason other than your blood as to why I'm being pulled to the underground. I'm curious to see what it is. If it's nothing and I die before anything really comes out of it, at least I'll be in a place where I belong."

"You really feel that way?"

"Well, yeah. I'm excited about going back. Nervous, but excited."

A few seconds went by before Marko cleared his throat. The burn had my heart sinking. "You need to feed."

"Yes. It'll be twice today. And I'll still have to feed while you're here. It'll help. At least, I'm hoping."

Hoping…I wasn't. And how messed up was that? I wanted his fangs back in my neck. I wanted him to feed from me and only me. I was his and he didn't even want me that way. Not without the price being my life.

"Stop it," he hissed. "You say Wednesday, I say right now if you keep up those thoughts. You don't feel like I want you, but we both know that's the biggest lie there is. It's how much I want you that is our problem."

"Marko, if we hadn't done the exchanges and you didn't want to kill me, do you think you'd still want me?"

He sighed. "I don't know. Probably not."

His answer could have been him ripping my heart out of my chest for the hurt it caused. The shock came in pulses of agony that left it hard to breathe. I hated this bond that kept trying to bring us together. What I hated more was the real me who still lurked around, not strong enough to overpower his hold.

"Tessa—"

"Don't," I said, interrupting. "Get out of my head now and leave me alone until you're ready to kill me. But just so you know, I'm not going down easily. It may be hard to defend myself, but I will not be an easy victim. You tell me to be prepared, I say to you, pray, Marko Delacroix. Your days may be numbered yet."

"I hope you fight, mon chaton. And I do pray you feel justified in trying your hardest when you take your last breaths."

I threw the covers back, going to my closet. Nudity didn't matter. If someone saw me, fuck it. I had to get out of here. I needed to live. I needed to start planning.

Chapter 20
Marko

I sat at our table in the heart of the city, listening to the musicians off in the distance sing their tunes. Some were fast paced, some riddled with portents of the end being near. There was so much passion in their lyrics. Why I'd never paid attention before was beyond me.

People bustled around, doing their daily shopping. Some for fresh veggies in the market, brought down from above. Others glanced around the racks of clothes and shoes. While slaves sipped their gourmet coffee at the round tables inside, my eyes narrowed, wondering what it was like to be them. It would have never crossed my mind before, but I couldn't help wondering how they went through their day to day. Tessa…she was making me contemplate all sort of things and I wasn't sure what to think about it.

Laughter from an older woman and a younger man had my attention going to them. I knew they were owned by two different vampires, yet they could have been best friends from the looks of it. There was happiness here where I'd somehow convinced myself only darkness existed.

Movement coming up from behind would have normally left me on edge. From the scent, I knew it was Marie. I kept my back to her as she stopped at my side. Distaste flashed over her features and she unwantedly kneeled. She wouldn't have been able to speak to me as I sat at this table otherwise. Whatever she wanted had to have been important if she felt the need to lower for me.

"What is it?"

Dark waves fell over her shoulders while she shifted. "Your girl."

I figured as much, but I had no idea what she was referring to. "My prey. Go on."

Marie looked up, meeting my eyes. "I thought of killing her last night. Would have, if…"

My fists clenched as I glared down at her.

"I like her," she continued. "Sure, sexually, but I mean as more. Like…as you would a friend. Like humans feel between each other. She makes me laugh. No one does that. Not like she does." Marie took a deep breath, shaking her head. "Did you know she sang with the vermin?" Her head gestured behind her to the band that was playing. "I don't think they've bathed in months, but as we were walking up, she looked at them like they were a treasure. She got so excited and began singing with them at the top of her lungs. I was floored at first, I'll admit. And not just because the human can sing, but because of her behavior. I was sure the drinks had made her lose it. But she had so much…spirit. I'd never seen anything like it. Her happiness made me happy. Like…before this life."

I blinked, repeatedly, not believing what I was hearing. Tessa sang? "Show me." I extended my hand and Marie clutched it tightly. Images exploded before me and so clearly I could see Marie trying to steady a very upset, but numbly composed Tessa. The music was nothing but a nuisance in the background and I knew it was because it was from Marie's point of view.

Tessa's feet slowed as they approached and she disconnected herself from me, or Marie, as it was. Loud lyrics were being projected through the upbeat, yet sad tune.

"I know this song," Tessa said, moving in closer.

"They sing it all time. Let's go lie down in bed. We'll talk." I felt the lust in me. The need to touch Tessa and sink my fangs into her neck as my hand explored her body.

"No, wait," Tessa mumbled.

The men glanced up to mon chaton, one smiling as his head moved with the beat. Quickly, hers moved in rhythm and she began clapping her hands. The nod of his head had her voice picking up on the next round of the lyrics. Disbelief hit me hard, right along with awe.

As Marie stood there listening, watching, Tessa's hair began to sway. The tempo picked up and one of the men became enthusiastic as he played the accordion he held in his hands. She immediately began to dance with him while they sang. The power of her voice left me breathless as its beautiful tone wrapped around my heart, squeezing tight. The other member's excitement shone through their music and they were all starting to sing together.

I watched in my own amazement, suddenly realizing that even though I'd seen every aspect of Tessa life, I didn't know her at all. Had never seen her let go and become so carefree. And there'd been times she'd been drunk before. But she'd always stayed reserved. Always uncomfortable. Even in her own skin. Here, she was alive. *Thriving.*

My hand pulled back, unable to watch any more. Marie shifted, a slight sheen appearing on her forehead. Her strength didn't compare to mine. It had taken a lot out of her to show me up to that point.

"Julius saw her," she whispered. "He came out and watched."

I couldn't stop my eyes from widening through the doom I felt. Julius wouldn't stand for her causing a stir, and from the people I could feel coming from the tunnels behind Marie's presence, I knew it had done that.

The band pulled me from the moment and I looked over toward them, seeing them entirely differently. The blank stares as they played appeared in contrast to the show I'd just witnessed. Where their clothing was in tatters and dirty, I barely even noticed when Tessa had joined them and unlocked their passion.

"She's coming back tonight, or so she said this morning before she left."

"She is," I confirmed. "Someone," I stressed, "convinced her that this is where she belongs."

Marie twisted her lips. "Well, she does. Although, I had ulterior motives at that point." A shift had Marie edging closer to me. "Let me try to erase your marks. I'll give her my own. She can become my slave."

I was leaning forward in my chair before I could help myself. "Give her your blood to try to erase mine? You know very well mixing vampire blood could kill her. Especially since yours is weaker."

"What could it hurt? You have no intention of bringing her in and I can't keep having her here when you're just going to end up killing her anyway. Let me try."

My hand gripped around her throat, squeezing as the threat warped in my chest. "No. You will not take her death away from me. If you give her your blood, she *will* die. If you go against me and try, your death will be next. By me."

Marie jerked from my grasp, pushing to her feet. Dark material from her full-length dress flared as she spun and stalked toward our tunnel. I could feel her anger. She wanted my prey as her own. For friendship and more, I didn't doubt, but I couldn't allow it. If Tessa did live through the exchange, her staying here as someone else's slave would drive me crazy. I wouldn't be able to have her. She'd be in love with Marie and no one else would matter. It would be worse than killing her.

I sighed, turning to look back at the band. Their songs had awakened something in mon chaton. She rarely sung in front of people, but here, she had. And it hadn't been shyly done. Her voice had carried down these tunnels like an amphitheater. And I'd missed it. Damn Boyd. At least I didn't have to worry about him for a while. He'd been banned from the club for the next few days due to his actions and now I could get a break. But what was I supposed to do when Tessa explored our city? Hide away in my room? Perhaps. And she'd be right next door. Fuck. She wouldn't make it to Wednesday. I knew this like I knew the sunlight was beating down on her skin even as I contemplated my actions. The slight warming had me closing my eyes, basking in something I would never feel again. To do so through her was such a comforting feeling.

"The boy begins."

My eyes opened at Julius' voice and I turned my chair back toward the table to face him as he took his seat.

"Hunter?" I asked, confused. He wasn't a boy, but a man. In Julius' eyes, I could see where he'd think so.

"Yes. I dreamed of him. Saw…"

Julius' long, dark hair rested over his shoulders as he leaned back, lacing his fingers before him. "She's rejected him. He feels she's lost to us already. He begins."

My eyes lowered as his disapproval shot through me. I knew he wasn't happy with the situation that I had caused.

"Hunter doesn't stand a chance. He's a human." Even as I said it, the flash of our meeting on the street broke through. I didn't like it. Couldn't stand that it had even gotten that far. The enemies had been winning. If they did win…"I'll take care of him before this gets out of control."

"Be sure that you do." He reached for an empty glass, sliding his hand over the top. Wine rose throughout and he rotated the dark liquid in a circle, staring into its depths. "She will kill you," he said, glancing back up at me. My stomach dropped and I shook my head, not believing.

"Impossible." My voice sounded distant as I tried to process the thought of dying. Especially at Tessa's hand. She loved me. How could she kill me?

"I assure you it's not. You *will* die, Marko."

Julius' prophesies were always told in riddles, but I had a feeling this time, he was speaking the truth. It left me unnerved. I'd gone so long thinking I was invincible. To know that I wasn't, and that I'd be killed by a human woman who I happened to have feelings for, left me in a daze of confusion.

"You underestimate her because of the love you've created within her heart. Her love will be the death of you, and it brings more problems than you can imagine. You should have never given her your blood. But it's done and you won't live past tomorrow night. The rest, we all wait out."

"Tomorrow night? So soon?" I shook my head. How was she going to do it? There weren't that many ways, but apparently she was going to figure something out. I couldn't let that happen. "No, I'll kill her first. Tonight. Then it'll all go away."

Those light colored eyes rose to mine and he slowly shook his head. "It will not. The events are already set into motion. And you will not harm her. I forbid it. You gave her your word and you will keep it. Besides," he said, turning toward the band that stayed leaning against the cement walls, playing their somber tunes, "tonight will be...quite interesting to see. I happen to look forward to it."

I knew better than to ask why. My fingers gripped the chair as I stood. "Thank you," I said, bowing. "If you'll excuse me. I have some things to take care of."

"Yes. You do." His hand flicked out toward me and I turned, heading toward my room. My heart raced frantically, my throat burned, and I never wanted to kill Tessa more than I did now. The vampire within wanted to take out the threat before the threat could take out me. But I'd been told no. It didn't sit well. What if she tried to kill me tonight and I'd just die tomorrow? Dammit, I didn't like this. Especially since my feelings for her kept pushing back through.

"Fuck," I growled, slamming my door open.

One look at my bed and I slowed. I could still feel her underneath me. Still taste her blood on my tongue, as if it was the only one meant to be there. This room had never been the same. Tessa had claimed the space, just like she was about to claim my life. I was as good as dead, and according to Julius, tomorrow night it would be for real.

Chapter 21
Tessa

Life. It had taken me twenty-eight years to truly begin to live it. The city had always been beautiful to me with the slight hills and active community, but I'd never been a part of it. I still wasn't. But it didn't mean I couldn't begin to enjoy myself. If Austin was known for anything, it was for music, the eclectic people, and the food.

Today, I'd immersed myself in all three. The cool air had invigorated me and taken me to the park to enjoy viewing the pet owners play fetch, to walk down the river, to watch a band play live outside a café. And it had led me to the place I was sitting in now. Tattoos had always been something I wanted to get, but never had the strength to do. So many times growing up, I'd heard my father always stressing about how the body is a temple. God wouldn't want you to graffiti the church so why would he want you to do the same to your body? It had been nonstop and the main reason why I never gave it thought. Here, now, I was done putting off what I wanted. Fear wasn't going to rule me anymore. Or religion. I couldn't see God casting me to hell for putting ink into my body. There were worse sins than that. Like holding vampire blood and liking it. I was doomed already.

Buzzing faded in and out and I gripped to the paper, staring at the French words as I waited for the tattoo artist to call me back. My pulse thumped steadily in my chest from fear of the unknown. Would it hurt badly? Well, yeah, that was a stupid question. But I knew it would hurt me more than most and I didn't care. The location was key.

I read the paper for what had to be the hundredth time. The words were spelled right. Everything, including the size, was okay. The man had already drawn the words up for me. It was all but done. And there was no chickening out.

"Tessa, why don't you come on back?"

My eyes rose to the big, bald man who had tattoos from his neck down to his fingertips. I couldn't see what his clothes concealed, but I was guaranteeing they ran down his legs, too. And I liked it. Liked this man with the big beard. Bruce.

I stood, following him past some cubicle style rooms. A girl was getting her bellybutton pierced and I felt my lips separate in surprise as I hurried by. How bad would that hurt? Should I get mine done, too? My head shook as if my mind had already decided. Maybe if I lived.

We passed a room where a man was getting his back tattooed and I watched the artist wipe away the black ink with a paper towel as he lowered and began to tattoo him even more. Bruce turned left and walked to a desk-style table in the back of the room. My eyes went to the chair and I gripped the paper even tighter.

"Why don't you come stand over here? Show me exactly where you want it and I'll place the design on and see if we have it in the right location."

"Alright."

I swallowed hard as I came to stand before a wall-length mirror. My hand pulled my long hair to the side and shakily, my finger rose to point to my neck, just below my pulse-point. "Here," I breathed out.

"You got it." A smile came to his face and he rubbed some stuff on my skin as he got the design in place. When he stepped back, I looked at the letters on my neck. I nearly gasped as my imagination brought them to life as the real thing.

"Perfect," I said, returning his smile.

"Great, why don't you climb up and I'll get things ready."

The black leather chair was cool as my shirt rose and it met my heated skin. "Bruce?" I looked at him while he messed with the packaged needles. His head turned and he glanced back.

"Yes, Tessa?"

I couldn't stop my eyes from going to his arms. "How long would it take if I wanted to get my forearm done? From wrist to elbow, all the way around?"

"Depends," he said, fixing the tattoo gun. "What are thinking of getting?"

"It's hard to describe. I want good versus evil. Angels and…demons. But with music and roses mixed within."

"Sounds interesting." He sat down on a chair, spinning toward me. The sound of the gun had me looking over at it cautiously. "If you want, I can draw something up for you. It'll take a few days, and maybe even a few tries, but I like the concept."

I didn't have a few days. Not if I died.

"I might have to leave for a while. How about you keep my idea in mind and when I get back, I'll let you know. Then we can make it happen."

He rolled the chair he sat in closer. "Sounds good to me. Now, do me a favor and lean your head more toward me. Just try to relax."

I nodded, turning in toward his chest. The rock band that was on the front of his shirt became my focus and I clenched my fists tight as the buzzing got close to my ear. *Marko.* My eyes flew open wide as I realized he'd feel what I did. The thought only began to register as the needles connected with my skin. My whole body jolted from the pain, but I kept still as the needles branded me. My mind opened and I tried to hold in the smile as my heart began to explode in rhythm. It wasn't all from me. Curiosity left my mind completely focused on the connection Marko and I shared.

"Tessa?" Panic and anger. The mix had my eyes narrowing as my hands gripped tighter to the armrests of the chair. *"Answer me, mon chaton. What in the hell is going on?"* More buzzing filled my ear and even through the pain, I could feel myself relax. It reminded me a little of Marko's bite. The initial sting. It was heaven.

"Tessa!"

Fear overpowered his tone now. Interesting. But probably because he thought I was getting hurt and he was upset it wasn't being done by him. The need to shake my head at my fucked up situation almost came. Instead, I breathed through the new surge of pain.

"Almost halfway," he said, wiping over the letters.

Bruce's voice had Marko's growing quiet, but not for long.

"I know you can hear me, God dammit. So help me, if you don't answer me…"

A smile surfaced and I bit my lip as the burn grew. A growl came from Marko and I could hear noises in the background, which rarely happened. Usually it was just his words. But…crashing. He was going crazy. Good. He deserved it for what he continued to do to me.

"Do to you? Mon chaton, speak. I'm only catching words here and there." He paused. *"You have two minutes to tell me what's going on or I'll send someone to get you. And I will. They'll drag you back here by that long hair of yours and I will…"*

"Kill me?"

"Not tonight."

His words threw me off. I expected an angry response. There was no anger anymore. Just…uncertainty?

"What is that sound? What's happening? You're in pain. Why?"

I stayed quiet, a frown sliding into place.

"Do you need help?"

"No. I'm perfectly fine." I laughed out loud, not able to process the ridiculousness of his question. My killer wanting to turn into my knight and shining armor. In what world did that happen?

"Laughing, now that's something I've rarely come across," Bruce said, quietly, above me. "Crying. Yelping. Now those I've heard, but laughing is new."

"Sorry, I was thinking about something."

"Well, I'm glad it was keeping you distracted. We're all done. Why don't you take a look."

The sound of wheels rolled across the floor, and I sat up, standing and walking back to the mirror. I tried to close off my thoughts as much as I could.

"Oh, it's beautiful. Thank you." I refused to read the words, too afraid he might hear. Marko would only get to see it in person and he wouldn't know about it a moment before. Somehow, I didn't doubt he was going to hate it and that made me even happier. This was for me. Not him.

"Good, here, let me put this on real quick. You'll need to be sure to do the same thing, and often."

Bruce rubbed some Vaseline over my neck and taped on a small piece of clear plastic wrap to cover it. As I followed him to the front and paid, I thrived from the soreness. Loved it even. The feeling followed me all the way through downtown, until I was walking past my church. The choir members were all inside. Their cars filled the parking lot on the side and I longed to go in there with them. The hum of their powerful voices brought tears to my eyes and even across the street from the church, I could hear one of my favorite songs pouring through the propped open front doors. Aching in my heart nearly brought me to my knees. I'd never know what it would be like to sing in there again. Never know the life I'd held for so long. It was gone now. Just like this level of the world would be, whether I lived or died. I wouldn't be here much longer. I knew that in the depths of my soul. This place wasn't for me.

I jogged across the street, slowing as Father Moretti exited onto the steps.

"Tessa, wait."

My head lowered and I kept walking until I reached the sidewalk. He was already jogging my way and I didn't want to talk to him. Yet, I felt like I needed to. Something deep within pulled at my mind and I tried to figure it out as I pulled my hair to the front to cover my neck. I couldn't stop the guilt that ate at me. For so long, I'd tried to be such a good person. That was gone now.

"Father." My voice was low and I couldn't ignore the sadness it held.

"Hunter was just here asking if I'd heard from you. How are you?"

"I'm okay."

His eyes glanced down toward my neck and I hugged my chest tighter, hoping my hair would cover it. My mouth opened and I wasn't sure what I was going to say. The feeling of déjà vu had me blinking past the confusion. "Since I can't go inside, will you meet out here with me tomorrow? I need …" I had no idea what I needed, but still, I spoke, as if it had been programmed for me to say. "I need some guidance. I've missed being here and…" Like time stopped, my hands were heavy as I reached into my purse, pulling out the dagger that rested inside. I wasn't sure where it'd come from, but I knew it was important. So…important.

Marko.

I cut off my thoughts as best as I could, trying to disguise the panic that burst through me. This was it. This was what I was supposed to do. "Maybe if we can talk like this it will help me. I really wish I could now, but I have some errands I have to take care of. I wish you lots of blessings." My hand trembled as I held out the dagger toward him. "Lots and lots of *blessings*."

Father Moretti took the dagger, looking down at it. His mouth opened, only to close as his stare connected with mine. I fought so hard to hold in the tears, but they escaped at the realization of what I was doing. The real Tessa knew this needed to be done, but the part that loved Marko mourned for what had to take place. "Can you meet me again tomorrow? Say…four?"

"Four. I'll be here." He held up the dagger, nodding his head. "I accept your blessings and I'll offer some of my own."

Chapter 22
Marko

What the hell was Tessa up to? It was driving me crazy. God dammit, my neck was still hurting. The dull ache had me constantly rubbing my hand over the sensitive area. And I knew she was okay. Not being tortured or fed from by another vampire like I feared at the very beginning. It would have hurt her badly had she been forcefully attacked…*like I'd done with her the first time.*

I cut off my thoughts. I would not feel bad for taking her as I did. It hurt her, but she liked it now. And I hadn't done it forcefully since. Not like that. She should feel lucky. Had anyone other than me fed from her, she'd probably already be dead. At least I was giving her time. Something I'd have taken back if I would have known my life depended on it. God, what the fuck was I going to do? I wasn't ready to die. I was meant to take Julius' position someday. I couldn't do that as a pile of fucking dust.

My feet pounded against the concrete as I paced the length of my room. I had to come up with a plan. And I didn't have one. There were only two options and I knew which way I was leaning toward. *Death.* Tessa had to die. If I bonded her to me, it would ruin everything. Not just for her, but for me. How could I focus on myself if I had to look out for someone else? I didn't want the companionship or responsibility. Not really. But this fucking bond was trying to force itself on me. What a mistake. I should have never given her my blood. Lesson learned. After I killed her, I'd never do it again. Not to a single person.

Once again, I rubbed over my neck. Damn woman. Typical of her breed to find ways to hurt me without actually physically doing so. Maybe it was her way of getting back at me before I ended her life. Well, if this was it, she was in trouble because it wouldn't keep her alive. Of course, it was affecting me from coming up with a plan so maybe that was her intention all along. To distract me.

My eyes shot to my door, blindly taking it in as my thoughts broke through.

If I was meant to die tomorrow and I couldn't kill her tonight, that didn't mean I couldn't find a way to end her life after sunrise. She was coming back tonight to explore our city. I'd tempt her to stay with me. I'd seduce her and come morning, I'd feed…and end it.

Twisting in my stomach seemed to pull some invisible thread on my heart. Mourning. Fuck no. I would not grieve for mon chaton. I shouldn't feel this sorrow. She wasn't even dead yet.

An aggravated sound tore from my mouth as I headed for the door. Knocking had me coming to a stop before I could even get there. I tuned into the surroundings, cursing at Marie's presence. Couldn't the woman leave me at peace? Jesus. What was wrong with her?

I took the few steps, opening the door. Marie's eyes were still slightly swollen from sleep and her hair was a mess around her. The black silk nightgown she wore left her bare feet exposed and I noticed she tapped her foot.

"What?" My agitation was thick and it had her lip pulling back in anger.

"I want to speak to you about Tessa again."

"There's nothing to talk about. She'll be dead soon and it'll be like she never existed." *Lie,* my mind whispered. Nothing would be the same if Tessa was gone. I would grieve her death just as I was already doing. It very well might fucking kill me. Mentally, I knew I was so much more attached to her than I wanted to face. Maybe it was the bond and the effects would end the moment she died, but I wasn't betting on it. God, I loved her. I fucking did. The realization was enough to leave my knees weak and me gripping the door for some form of strength.

At the silent stare Marie continued to give, I opened the barrier and she immediately swept past me. As I shut the door, I noticed her nails were slightly elongated. It went to show just how off her mental stability was. Marie was upset, and not just a little.

"I ask that you reconsider your plans for Tessa." Her eyes cut over, but went back to staring at the floor. "I ask…I ask…" Again, she came to look at me. "I had a dream."

It wasn't a secret that Marie had visions like Julius. It was what almost had her taking my position, despite that I was stronger. Hers weren't as accurate as Julius', but pretty damn close. It was enough to have me stepping closer.

"What did you dream?"

Marie sniffled, wiping her eyes before the tears could escape. "War comes."

My head shook. "We've known that now for hundreds of years."

"Soon," she emphasized. "Like…really soon. I don't know exactly when, but I know Tessa is alive when it happens. God, she looks so different. If you could see her…what the fuck happens?"

I couldn't stop my eyes from widening. "So, she lives? Does she kill me?" Dammit, I couldn't breathe. Julius was right. I was going to die.

Marie glared. "Would I be asking you to rethink your plans for her if you were dead?"

"Wait." I moved in closer. "You mean, we're both alive?"

"Marko! Pay attention. That's not even relevant. You love her, yes?"

I opened my mouth, only to close it. "No. It's the bond. It's not real."

"Good. Then give her to me," Marie sobbed. "If you kill her, or keep her, we're doomed. We may be doomed anyway."

"What are you talking about?"

There's a monster who wants her. A human. I can't see his face. Just the one he paints on." She shuddered. "If you make her your slave or concubine, he will take her. And he will kill her. She will die, Marko, right in front of you. And it will destroy you. Then, we will all die."

Marie brought her hand out toward me. "Watch it. See it. You have to see!" Hysterics were setting in and I couldn't stop the uneasiness at witnessing her so upset.

"I don't want to see."

"Marko. *Please.* You have to watch it."

My head shook slowly and I stepped further away from her. "You have to stop worrying. She will not live past tomorrow. Tessa will die and there will be no war."

"She will *not* die, Marko. You may, though. Your future is not for certain in my dream. Tessa's is, but not yours. That could have been me taking your place. Or Julius. Anyone watching Tessa get killed, for all I know. Just because I assumed it was you means that you taking that position is not certain. You know that and so do I."

"So, if it could have been you, why should I give my permission to allow you to take her as your slave? Then that means it'll happen for sure."

A hiss came from her mouth and she let out a small scream. "I don't know! They never make sense. All I know is that man is going to kill Tessa and we're going to lose. I don't want either to happen."

"They're not going to, God dammit. Hunter won't kill Tessa because I'm going to kill both of them myself. Now, leave my room and get yourself ready. We feed soon."

Marie took a few steps and stopped. "Tessa could very well kill you. Just so you know, my money is on her."

"Then you're going to lose. I don't have plans on going anywhere. Better remember that."

Marie's lip pulled back in anger. "Neither does she. Brace yourself, Marko. Our girl has more strength than you know, and quite the trick up her sleeve. I bet you won't even see it coming."

My door slammed behind Marie and I walked to the bed, collapsing on the edge of it. I leaned forward, burying my fingers in my hair. Damn women. Why were the two who held the most presence in my life determined to kill me?

I tuned into Tessa, despite knowing I shouldn't. I'd done so well with beginning to ignore her that now I was starting to think it had been a mistake. She could have been plotting my murder this entire time and I would have missed it.

"Red or black? Hmm..." She paused, leaving a moment of silence. "Black. Marko would like the red too much."

My eyes rolled as I fell back to the bed. Maybe Marie was right. Sure, Tessa loved me in the way of the bond, but if it were more, she'd have chosen the red so she could please me. Why couldn't she love me that much? I probably would have done it for her if I knew she liked something…which is why I'd probably be the one who died. Fuck. She won. I did love her more than she loved me.

"No." I stood, closing off her thoughts again. It was stupid to even have done it to begin with. Once I fed, I'd stay in my room. Julius would have his wish and I'd let Tessa live. We'd make love, we'd cuddle, make love again…and then, when the sun rose, I'd do it. I'd kill her.

Chapter 23
Tessa

Darkness settled around me as I gripped the flashlight tighter. Light broke through at my push of the button and I could feel my skin crawling as I forced myself through the tunnel Marko and Marie had brought me to before. Coming alone was the scariest thing I'd ever done. Scarier than going through the large house Marko had ordered me to...was it only weeks ago?

My deep breaths surrounded me and I jumped as I saw a rat scatter past my foot. A scream almost broke past my lips but I held it in, making myself go faster. Sounds echoed from far away and I let the realization that it was the band I'd come across with Marie to help ease my fears. I was meant to be here. Marie had said so herself. Fear wouldn't keep me away. Even now, shaking, I still felt the relief of getting closer.

Illumination shone in the distance and I turned off my flashlight, trembling as the darkness swallowed me whole. Small sounds had me looking over my shoulder, regardless of whether I couldn't see anything.

The lyrics grew louder and I felt myself humming to the tune. I didn't know it, but their style had a way of sucking me in. Noises grew, telling me that life in the city was well underway. The sound of voices only grew with every inch I got closer. I stopped, easing the flashlight to rest just on the edge where the light shone through. I'd grab it before I left. Just the small act helped fuel my positivity over the situation. I could do this.

As I broke past the walls of the tunnel, my feet came to an abrupt stop and my whole body froze. The tables that sat within the large space were full of vampires feeding. I immediately spotted Marko at the smaller one and his head turned toward me, along with everyone else's. Silence left me unable to run or move forward. With so many vampires focused on me, my whole body shuddered. What would they do? Was this the end for me? God, what had I been thinking? It had never dawned on me they had a schedule. And here I was, interrupting it.

As the faces stared, one man rose from the end of the shorter table. Marko's head snapped over to him and I saw the worry reflect on his face. Long, black hair rested over his lean shoulders and he looked dressed from another time. Power pushed against my skin and my eyes immediately lowered as he walked over to me. The closer he got, the more my knees gave out. He wasn't within ten feet before I dropped, hanging my head at his arrival. I couldn't breathe. Couldn't think as I kneeled and waited for the worst.

"You are not uninvited. Stand."

I glanced up, somehow managing to get to my feet. As his hand came out, I eased mine forward, hesitating before sliding my fingers along his pale palm. He paused, pulling my hair to the side to look at my neck, now free of the wrapping. A smile pulled at the corner of his mouth, and it didn't look very nice. He let go, adjusting the dark strands back into place.

"You want to be here, yes?"

Only then did I let my stare connect a little longer with his. "Yes."

"Come. You will kneel by me while we feed. Then, you are free to roam as you wish. You will be aware that you are responsible for yourself here. Expect no one to help you. You chose this. No one else."

I swallowed hard, nodding. "Thank you."

His face stayed devoid of emotion. "Do not thank me. You may soon regret coming here. After tonight, you may never want to come back."

Whispering increased and I glanced around the large room as the vampire led me to stand next to the chair he had risen from. I immediately fixed my red sundress so I could kneel, noticing many others in the same position. Was this how the blood slaves behaved as they waited for their bonded to finish?

Marko shifted in the chair and my eyes took in his feet from underneath the table. He didn't speak to me in my mind and I took that as I sign not to speak to him, either. Music began to play again and I listened to it while I stared at the floor. Had I lived a life here, would this have been how it would have turned out? Marko sitting in his chair and me kneeling? Life going on as everyone took their place at meal time? Or, if I didn't belong to Marko, but stayed here on my own, what then?"

"You'd be on top of this table," the man said, from beside me.

It took a few seconds to realize he was talking to me. My head lifted and I blushed as it became clear he'd read my thoughts. I'd seen the nude women on the table, even though I'd tried to avoid it. But…

I lowered my head back down. So that was the price of staying here without a vampire to take responsibility for me. I'd become a slave to all if I chose that route. Not that I'd live, but if Marko somehow allowed me and I wanted to stay—

"No," he cut in, quietly. "You've exchanged twice. No matter how tempting your smell, your blood will not taste good to others. You're damaged goods for anyone but Marko, Tessalyn Antoinette."

At the sound of my first and middle name, I couldn't stop the slight fear that encompassed me. My mother only said that when I was in trouble, and it wasn't often. And, damaged goods? Another thing I associated with my mom. She'd said that exact thing to me when she discovered the blood on my sheet from my first time—with Hunter. I'd been damaged goods then. I didn't like the thought that I was put back into that place all over again. If I was damaged, it was Marko's fault. He'd done this to me. Forced his blood upon me for no other reason but to evoke passion where it hadn't belonged. Now, I'd die because I wasn't worthy enough in his eyes to become his blood slave. I hated him almost as much as I loved him.

Love…I shouldn't even call it that. What he made me feel wasn't worthy enough to be considered love. It was like he said—an illusion. We didn't know each other enough to love, and what we did know was nothing other than an unstoppable force, hell bent to tie us into a situation we didn't want. Or, him, anyway. I was past the point of being able to decide. I knew the person I was now wanted this life and him. Or more, needed us to be bonded while I stayed here. But I couldn't let it happen. I refused.

A sigh left me and I interlaced my fingers as I continued to stare down. Maybe I'd talk more about it to Marie. Surely, she might have a solution. A sputtering in my mind had me looking back up. Another feeling of déjà vu settled over me. Had I talked to her about it already?

A few vampires rose from the long table and walked away, their slaves following behind. Minutes went by while I let myself stay consumed. It wasn't until dark hair appeared in my peripheral vision that I let my stare rise.

Marie smiled and I returned it, jumping as a hand settled over my shoulder.

"You may go. Remember, you're responsible for yourself." His lids lowered until they were slits as he stared down at me. For the life of me, I couldn't break our connection, but I knew he wasn't pulling me under like Marko had done. I still had control over my mind. Seconds went by before he nodded. "Go."

"Thank you." I stood, trying not to wince as I straightened my legs and fixed my dress. My eyes went to Marko's intent stare and I quickly turned, racing toward Marie. The moment she slid her fingers through mine and led me toward her room, calmness surfaced. Friends weren't something I ever had a lot of, but I felt a kinship with the dark haired female vampire and it had come fast and hard. Something about her put me at ease.

"I wondered if you'd come," she said, looking back as her men moved in behind us. "I'm glad you decided to."

Even though there was something off with her mood, I gripped her fingers tighter. She pushed her door open and the large bed came into view. Immediately, I felt a blush surface. God, had I really slept in between her and her men in that big thing? Heat flushed my cheeks. I had, and it had felt like the most natural thing at the time.

"So, tell me, what do you feel like doing tonight? You name it and I'll make it happen." Her smile was forced as she walked over to her closet, throwing the door open.

"Anything I want?"

My question had her pausing and looking back over her shoulder, suddenly beaming at me.

"There's a mischievous you within that question, Tessa. I like it. What do you have in mind?" The smile faded and her head cocked to the side as she came back to me. "What is that on your neck?"

My hand rose, pushing beneath the denim collar of the jacket I wore over my dress.

"What was that?" she whispered.

I lowered my hand, pulling back my hair and turning my face so she could see.

"Oh…Tessa." Her eyes shot to mine as I let my hair drop. "Does he know?"

"No," I said, quietly. "And I don't want him to yet. Not until—" I cut myself off. "Marie, I need to speak to you about something I did today, but I can't. I mean, it came out of nowhere and…"

"Shh." Her fingers came to my lips. "I already know. You're doing the right thing." While we held each other's stare, I felt her fear concerning the situation. It took me a few seconds to nod past it. Marie let her fingers slide down and she placed a quick kiss across my lips. I couldn't help the weird heaviness that filled me as she spun around and walked back to her closet.

"I don't know what I want to do tonight. Or if I want to dress up. I just feel so—"

"You have to dress up. It'll make it more fun. We'll go back out and you can sing with the vermin. Or, we'll…" Tears filled her eyes as she turned and stepped closer toward me. "I know you're scared and you want to talk about what's going to happen, but we can't. There are things I want to tell you, too, but that isn't allowed." She paused. "I have many gifts. One is seeing the future. And…I had a dream last night."

I blinked past the shock.

"What about? This place? Marko?" I glanced back up. "Me?"

Marie grabbed a fancy red dress, not much different than the color of the one I was already wearing. "All. All and more. Let's not talk about it. My skin grows cold at the thought. Come." She pulled me toward the vanity that rested against her back wall and turned toward her men who were standing guard against the wall next to the door. Their behavior sometimes confused me, but I didn't question it.

"Out," she ordered. The demand was so different than the way she talked to me. There was another side of Marie. Marko had hinted as much, and maybe Marie's intentions weren't all good concerning me, but I couldn't help but like the side of herself she displayed. And maybe she did like me a little. It appeared so.

My blood. The words barreled through and I suddenly knew. That had to be it. Did she want me that way? Julius had said no other vampire would have liked the taste, but maybe it was more the call than the actual feeding. The temptation of the smell. But would she do it just to experience the flavor, or would she do it to kill me, like Marko? My hand came out and I stopped before we got all the way to the vanity's chair.

"Marie, what are you true intentions for me? I know you didn't come to me just for the party. There's something else."

Her lips separated and she looked down at the dress in her hands. "You're right. I wanted to…kill you. To get back at Marko in any way I could."

"Do you still?"

Her eyes lifted and she shook her head. "No. I'd have you for my own slave if it were possible. Marko will not allow me to, so I'll spend all the time I can with you before the end presents itself. For either you or him."

I swallowed hard. "I die on Wednesday. Or, at least, he'll try. I don't have plans on dying anytime soon."

Marie's eyes flickered and they studied mine for a few seconds before her smile returned. "Wednesday…my money's on you. And that's all I'll say. Now, let's get you dressed. We'll talk more later."

I nodded, letting my denim jacket and dress drop to the floor. The atmosphere changed as Marie's eyes traveled over the expanse of my neck, down to my chest. She stepped back, quickly turning to the closet. When she returned, she held matching lingerie. The strapless red silk bra was met with a pair of barely existent panties. With each article of my clothing that fell to the floor, I couldn't stop the shaking. I pulled up the panties, slowing as I reached for the bra she'd sat on the vanity.

"So beautiful," she said, shaking her head. "How I wish I could keep you."

"If he allowed it…how would that be possible?"

To be a slave was something I had to do. I'd never be able to go back to living a human life after I knew of these ways. Of this place. To be Marie's might not be so bad. We were friends, or could be, if we were given more time. And if I didn't have this pull toward Marko, he wouldn't want to kill me. I could live.

Marie's hand pushed back the hair covering one of my breasts and my breath hitched as her fingertips moved down the center of my chest. Where I hadn't expected to feel arousal, I did. My breasts began to feel fuller and I licked my lips, wondering what was going to happen.

"We've talked about this before, although you probably don't remember. You'd have to take my blood, and I yours. My blood would fight against Marko's. His would probably win."

"What does that mean?"

Her touch was making me even foggier in my mind. I bit my lip as she brought her thumb down to tease my hard nipple.

"Holding two vampires' blood doesn't fare well for humans. Unless the vampire who exchanges the second time is stronger, they'll die. If I tried to win your blood and failed, your death would be mine. Marko will not have it."

The roll of her thumb had a moan coming from my mouth. Blindly, I reached for the chair behind me as she stepped in even closer, adding just the smallest increase in pressure to the tight nub she now pinched between her fingers.

"I wish I were stronger. I keep thinking that maybe if I tasted your blood, took Marko inside of me, too, I might be able to defeat his marks on you. God, it's so tempting, Tessa. I'd love to taste you."

Her lips moved toward mine and I jumped as someone pounded against the door. "Marie!" The name was said threateningly and I knew whose voice it was. She pulled back and dropped her hands, sighing. I quickly put on the strapless bra as she made her way to the door. It was swung open wide and although I felt the need to conceal my body, seeing Marko's lips part was enough to have me not moving.

"Yes, Marko?"

He didn't answer her. Didn't move as he stared at me.

In heavy breaths, I tried to prepare myself for what would happen. I knew that look. Knew where it was going to lead. He wasn't quite himself. His vampire was taking him over. I could already see his fangs coming down.

"No—"

Before I could finish, he was through the door and on me.

"You like her touch? You want her as your Master instead of me?" Fingers buried in my hair as he trapped my arms with one of his, wrapping it around my waist. I thrashed, but it didn't stop him from slamming me into the wall to try to get closer. Not once did he break his stare from my eyes as he glared. Through it all, I saw his lust. He wanted me just as much as he fought the need to end my life.

"You will not kill her in my room!" Marie's words had the arm around me loosing and him pulling back just the smallest amount.

"You," he said, spinning us around, "I should kill you right now. You know better."

Marie's head shook. "Don't you preach to me about what I know. You gave her your blood, damn well aware of the purpose. You don't want her. *I do.* Now, let her down and go before I have you thrown out."

"Oh, I'm going, but not without her. I won't have her head filled with things that could very well kill me. And you'd tell her." His head shook. "Not happening, Marie. You want my chair and you'll do anything to get it. I won't die because of your schemes."

My legs kicked against him as I pulled at his hold. "I don't want to go with you, Marko. The man said I could explore the city. I know he's the leader. Do I need to find him and tell him that you're denying me of what he said I could do?"

Anger turned to rage as he looked down. One minute, I was within his grasp, the next, I hit the ground hard.

"Wednesday is no more. You will not make it out of this city alive. I won't let you."

The words induced an anger I couldn't stop myself from feeling. They ate at my sanity. Twisted my psyche until I couldn't even process what I was doing. I was over this. Done with the threats.

"No." I pushed to my feet, my eyes wildly searching the room. A pair of scissors sat on the vanity and I grabbed them, immediately slashing them in his direction. The pressure from his hand catching my wrist was crushing and I screamed as I went wild to get out of his hold. My leg kicked against him and at the swing of my free arm, I felt the blade connect against my forearm, slicing through my skin. A scream forced its way out, but I couldn't focus on the pain. Not when all I knew was ending the man's life before me. Love or hate, it made no difference. Just freedom from his threats.

"Stop it," he growled as I pounded into his chest and neck. The scissors fell free from my grasp as he squeezed tighter and I barely noticed all the blood covering his white button-up shirt from my hits.

Movement from Marie had my gaze flashing over and I could feel myself stop mid-swing. Her eyes were wide and devoid of any color. The black center had completely taken over everything but the white. Fear had my pulse exploding. One second, Marko was holding onto me, the next, he was spinning for Marie's neck as she shot in our direction.

"Get to my room, mon chaton, now!" Marko slammed her to the ground, forcing her over and placing his knee to the middle of her back. Growls came from her mouth and I grabbed my dress, terrified. But I didn't go to his room. Couldn't.

I pulled my sundress over my head and raced through the door. Darkness swallowed me up and I let it as I ran through the tunnel. I couldn't remember ever feeling so afraid. Marie hadn't been herself. Hadn't even looked like I'd seen Marko when he was at his worst. Had he been holding back with me the entire time? I knew he had.

Light met me as I broke into the heart of the city, but I saw nothing as I sprinted past the still occupied tables. Large crashes erupted behind me and fear left me moving at a faster speed than I could imagine. But it wasn't fast enough. Weight crashed into my back and I yelled in pain as I slid against the floor. Stinging flared over my chest at the cement burning my skin, leaving behind a heat so intense that I feared the damage it had caused.

I was rolled over by a vampire with light colored hair, but the room spun so fast. Whoever was on me was pulled off, only for more hands to start clawing at me. Faces appeared all above, crowding me while I kicked and swung. It didn't stop the long nails from lacerating my side as I tried to fight them off. Cement tore into my exposed shoulders, pulling my dress high on my waist as someone grabbed my foot, freeing me, but only for themselves.

My screams echoed around and I twisted, able to make it to my knees before someone else grabbed at my dress. I was ripped up to stand and I sobbed as a loud roar vibrated my skin, leaving it feeling as if it were melting beneath the voice. God, I really was going to die tonight. Just not by who I thought.

Chapter 24
Marko

My growl couldn't be held in as I threw people out of my way to get to where Julius held up Tessa's bloody body. The vampire within wanted her for himself, but the male who harbored such a close bond felt the need to protect what belonged to him. Just like I'd done concerning Marie. Sure, I had wanted Tessa, and had almost lost control, but in feeling Marie's threat as she rushed toward us, there was no comparison. I had to protect mon chaton.

The back of my fist caught one of the snapping vampires in the face and I threw another out of the way, managing to get to the front of the line in a sea of hungry predators. Julius' eyes narrowed as they landed on me and I panted at the sweet aroma of my prey's blood. Her red, torn dress was saturated in the dark substance. Even in my bloodlust, I felt my stomach twist in heartbreak. *I'd done this to her.*

"I want to go home," she said, weakly, trying to break Julius' hold. "Please."

"You won't make it out of here with the amount you're bleeding." He kept his eyes on mine as he lifted her forearm with the deep scissor laceration. A strangled cry left her mouth as he ran his tongue over the deep cut, making her shudder. The warning I shot him couldn't be hidden as my head lowered and my eyes cut up. My breaths became heavier while I focused in on him. I was ready to die if he went further, and I surely would if I attacked like I wanted to.

"I've seen many things in the last few weeks concerning this woman. Before you even met her, Marko. My curiosity is piqued as to why. It intrigues me even more that her blood tells me nothing." His hand tightened roughly on the back of her neck and he lifted her a few inches from the ground, tearing a piece of her dress away that hung loosely at her side. Again, his tongue closed one of the wounds, this time, on her side. I couldn't help the steps I took forward.

"Let me have her." My hands reached forward and Tessa screamed as his grip loosened but caught in her hair, letting her toes barely touch the floor as he held her captive. The black French words on her neck had my eyes going wide and I felt myself gasp as I read them.

Love you to death.

Time stopped as I stayed frozen by the power of her statement. Death on her part or mine? Did it even matter? God, she'd marred her skin to prove a point to me. To express her emotions and view on the two of us. And here she was…

"Julius!" My body shook as power coursed through me. My eyes went from Tessa to my leader. I wasn't sure why this was happening. Why I was defending a human to the one man who I shouldn't have challenged. I should be walking away and letting him have her, whatever that meant. Still, I held my hands outward, taking in the words I'd be forced to see next time I wanted to feed. *Every* time I wanted to feed.

Cries came from Tessa's mouth as she struggled against his hold, clawing at his arms until he gave her a good shake. Slowly, he lowered her to the ground, turning her to face him. Tears streamed down her face and her fear was my own.

"You will attempt to kill Marko Delacroix tomorrow night. You will ~~succeed~~ and he will be no more. When that happens, you will come back and meet with me. After I do what is necessary, you will take his spot at my table."

"What!" He was going to change her? And give her my chair? I surged forward, feeling myself come against an invisible wall.

"Go home, Tessalyn Antoinette. I'll see you tomorrow after sunset."

Tessa took one last look at me. A sob escaped and she held her heart as she walked backward toward the tunnel. Even after all of that, she still didn't seem to want to leave. Her hair flared out as she spun and raced into the darkness. My legs felt like they were going to give out. *Love you to death.* Over and over, the quote repeated in my head. It was the perfect phrase and went both ways. I'd love her to death, too.

Minutes went by while Julius stared at me. What did he see? Her making it home? The future? My death?

A ripple of energy blasted through the room as he let the wall drop and I edged around him, ready to go after Tessa. Her blood still scented the surroundings and I was more torn than ever. If I waited until tomorrow night, I'd be dead for sure. But if I took care of our problem now, or even waited until the day after, perhaps the future would change. It was known to do that.

"You will not be leaving," Julius said, sternly. His hand waved and two of the higher members of *le Cercle* came forward. "Put him in lockdown. He's not to be fed the entire time. I'll release him at sunset tomorrow."

My mouth opened and he stepped forward, pushing his hand against my stomach. "You didn't feed when Tessa was here, either. Good."

I pulled hard at both sets of hands that held me. I knew I could have used my powers, but it was pointless. He wanted me to ravage her. To truly have me tear her apart by the time I got into her home. Yet, he knew I'd lose...maybe part of him hoped I wouldn't? Or maybe he just wanted the challenge to be real. I wasn't sure of his motives. Nothing about his prediction made sense. Tessa couldn't kill me. The odds were against her and if she had some sort of plan, I'd have caught something. Wouldn't I?

Julius bent down, picking up the shredded part of the dress he had thrown down. It was completely soaked in her blood.

"Put this in there with him."

The cloth was grabbed and I shrugged even harder, breaking their hold. "I can walk on my own. I won't fight you."

Nothing. No skepticism, no reaction whatsoever to my words. They kept quiet as I began heading to the far tunnel that led to the cells where the most unstable vampires were kept. I rounded the corner, feeling the members close ~~behind. Tessa's essence~~ taunted me. Made me want to rear around and shred the two vampires behind me to pieces to get back to her. ~~I couldn't. I'd be doing~~ enough damage tomorrow and it wouldn't even truly be my fault. Julius was determined to have me at my worst and for the first time, I feared for mon chaton. Even knowing she was fated to kill me, I suddenly didn't want to hurt her. Not deep down. My instincts wanted me to, but the man who was being brought out little by little ached at the thought.

Bars stood ahead in the distance and I pulled at the collar of my shirt, noticing that not only was the cloth going to trigger me, but I wore her blood. The front of my shirt was completely soaked in it. Fuck, I had to get it off the moment I was in there. I didn't want to do this. I didn't want to be trapped with her blood calling to me. How was she even doing? Julius had closed her deepest wounds and I knew my blood would help her heal faster, but mentally, how was she?

I watched the door open on its own, knowing one of the members behind me had unlocked and opened it with their mind. My legs were heavy as I walked through, spotting a row of small cells leading down into the distance. Thick bars sealed off each space and even with as powerful as I was, I wouldn't be able to escape.

One of the doors opened in the front and I stared at the empty cell. Less than twenty-four hours and I'd be free again. I could do this.

My hands shook as I watched the bloody piece of dress get thrown in. Just the slight breeze of it passing sent my fangs pushing into my lip. I stepped through the threshold and squeezed my eyes shut as it slammed behind me. The ripple that tingled down my back brought out a groan. The invisible shield was in place and it would hold the scent in.

I walked forward, tearing my shirt off and tossing it down to the floor. Red stained my chest and I rubbed my hands over it, feeling my pulse increase as I did so. God dammit, I was fucked. *She* was fucked. I didn't care what Julius or Marie saw, I would not die tomorrow. I knew this like I was certain Tessa would.

Slowly, I headed toward the cement wall, pushing my palms against the cold surface as I let her take me over. I opened myself to mon chaton completely, even though I knew I shouldn't. I had to feel her heartbeat. Her pain.

And it was intense.

The physical aspect was there from her injuries, but it was the mental portion that had me worried. God, she was so fucking scared and close to breaking. Seeing her held before me and the terror on her face, it didn't hold the reaction I would have thought it would. Fuck, I'd stood up to Julius to try to get her back because of it. And her…wearing that fucking dress. The red one she said she wouldn't choose because I'd like it. She was trying so hard to be strong, but she couldn't fight the bond. It was another reason I knew she wouldn't be able to kill me. It would be impossible for her to. She was a sitting duck, just waiting to get devoured by the evil monster inside of me.

"Tessa?"

Her heartbeat increased. But nothing. No thoughts. No words. I focused harder, waiting to see if she'd say something. She didn't.

A few minutes went by and I called to her again. The jump in pulse repeated, but nothing.

I knew the area I was in wasn't blocking what we shared from the tie, but something had to be. Her? Had she somehow discovered a way to keep her thoughts from me? It didn't seem possible. Nothing with her did. Even Julius made it seem odd that he got nothing from her blood. Something about her intrigued him. Enough so that he wanted to replace me at the table. He had to know something about her that I didn't. She was human. I was one hundred percent sure of that. So what was it?

I paced, trying to ignore the dark red cloth from the corner of my eye. I stared ahead and with each turn, found just how hard it was for me to disregard. The sweetness pulled at my core and I heard a sound escape. God, what was I going to do?

After I do what is necessary, you will take his spot at my table. Julius' statement came surging back into my mind and it sent my anger flaring. How could he think turning Tessa would make it acceptable for her to take my spot? That position would go to Marie if I died. Tessa wouldn't even be able to function for the first year after her change. His words didn't make sense, and yet, I knew he had meant what he said. Fuck! I couldn't stand this. Already, I could feel my skin turning hot at the confinement. The trapped sensation left me in a craze and the evil part of me was creeping in. Obsession with my prey was pushing back through worse than ever and I yearned to smother mon chaton in my passion. To wrap every part of who I was around her until she couldn't breathe past the potency of who lurked inside.

"Tessa? I waited and said it again, this time more forcefully. The isolation crept in, even more without her response. Over and over, I called out to her. Each time getting more uncontrolled and frenetic. Not a single thought appeared. Hours went by and I sat in the corner, staring at the bloody material that left me fevered. It taunted me to be held so I could breathe the sweet smell in deeper. Its intoxication of my space would have me gone soon, and there'd be no coming back until the deed was done.

"Tessa!" Desperation left my internal voice cracking. I began to go to her dress, only to stop myself. I had to drown out the smell. Buffer it somehow.

"Oh God, Tessa, please answer me. I...need you." My hands came up to my face, cupping around my nose, trying my damnedest to make the scent fade, even just a little. Minutes went by and nothing worked. I tried not breathing, but I couldn't calm myself enough to focus on stopping what came so naturally.

I pushed from the floor to stand again and slammed my fist in the cement wall as hard as I could. Small pieces flaked away and once I started, I couldn't stop. Chips fell into chunks, but I knew the wall was so thick I could spend years going at it and never break free of the prison that held me. Blood ran from my knuckles and I looked at it in horror as her scent mixed with mine, perfuming around me, so delicious and tempting. My tongue ran over the substance before I could even process what I was doing. The smallest taste sent my nails extending and a hiss exploding from my mouth.

Power surged through me with the likes I'd never felt before and I projected it out in an explosion as I yelled through the overwhelming craving. The ripple against the shield blew back against me, slamming me into the wall. The action only had me lifting and charging right at the bars, over and over. Pain engulfed my shoulder but it didn't stop me from yanking against the thick metal that my hands could barely fit around.

Small sobs broke through and I suddenly realized she'd felt my pain. How long had she been crying? I didn't know.

"Marko?"

The soft tone of her voice left me breathing out raggedly. I fell to my knees, noticing my stomach clutch to my ribs with the deep inhales.

"I'm so sorry, mon chaton. Run and don't ever stop. God...fucking start running."

Fire enflamed my throat and I looked over. Not inches away sat the piece of her dress. I groaned through the torturous spasms that contracted the muscles as I tried to swallow the need away.

"We can't put this off any longer. I'll be waiting."

My head lowered to the floor and the monster in me began to take over completely. I was disappearing as my mind spaced out. Any humanity I held was vanishing to the place it had been before, for hundreds of years. That Marko wouldn't exist come sunset. The Marko I was just before I met her wouldn't either. I'd never been made to go through anything like this and I feared what I'd become once this was over. Something was happening. I was changing. There would be nothing left of Tessa when I got done with her, and I knew if I didn't have her in my life, there was no hope for anyone. Julius would have to keep me here or kill me. No one would be safe. I'd be the monster both vampires and humans feared.

Chapter 25
Tessa

The levels of fear that existed always seemed to amaze me. When I thought I couldn't be any more afraid, something came along and proved to me that the sensation ran to depths our human minds couldn't even begin to process.

As I looked in the mirror, staring into my nearly black eyes, I couldn't stop the chattering of my jaw. My whole body continued to jerk and shake violently and I knew it was because of Marko's state of mind. He wasn't right. Hadn't been now for hours. And it was only getting worse. The fact that I was changing because of how far gone he was terrified me the most. I looked every bit the demon I had no doubt resided inside of his body. And I wasn't even his kind. The blood within in me was enough to change who I was. It knew its true Master and rushed through my veins, calling to the one man I feared, yet loved, more than anyone. Even in my last hours, I couldn't deny what was true. I loved Marko Delacroix and no amount of fear or hate would be able to get rid of that.

"I want you taste you, mon chaton. I want to tear you apart."

My eyes closed. The mantra had been repeating now for hours. Every few minutes, he'd say something along those lines and I'd continue to ignore him, but the threats didn't come without consequence. Nausea left me lightheaded from all the shaking and regardless that the sun was up, safety wasn't present. My throat burned horribly. My vision was only what I could describe as 3D. It left me completely panicked and anxious.

What was I going to do?

I opened my eyes, turning to look at the clock. The smallest detail became apparent in everything my gaze moved across and I knew this was how it must have been for the predatory vampires. The ones who were in the middle of hunting. They wouldn't miss the smallest thing. Not a move, breath...*or their victim's pulse point. I bet it looks beautiful hammering away on the side of their neck.* I ripped myself from my thoughts, staggering backwards. God, had I thought that? The bond. It was making my own cravings for blood come back. It wanted me to take Marko's.

A moan poured through and I knew he'd heard me.

"You want my blood? I want to cover you in yours."

A small sound escaped and I tried to stay focused. My eyes darted to the clock again. Almost four.

Cautiously, I headed into the living room, trying my best to keep my balance with how different everything appeared. My sunglasses rested on the counter and I put them on, grabbing my purse. There was no way I could let Father Moretti see me like this. He'd think me evil. Shit, I *was* evil. I was beyond help, whether I lived or died.

The sweater I wore was big and I hugged it around me, trying to keep warm through the shaking. Especially now, walking out into the cool air, I could feel the trembling getting worse. My jaw was going crazy, but it didn't compare to my vision. I could barely keep my eyes open from the sensitivity to the sun. Tears escaped as I squinted. Cold and blind. Fuck, I didn't like this.

"I'll warm you up. I'll make you burn for me."

Dammit, I was breaking concentration. My brain was beginning to lose focus with my lack of sleep. I hadn't dared get in bed last night for fear Marko would slip in. Now, I was feeling it and badly. I was exhausted from being on guard the whole time.

"Keep talking, mon chaton. Fuck, your voice does it for me. I've missed it so much. I can't wait to hear your screams against my fangs. You're going to scream so loudly."

Back and forth, he went. Good and negative. I couldn't stand it. I forced myself to block him out even more. I felt him fade, but not entirely.

"Mon chaton, don't stop now. Mon chaton! You better say something." A growl began to take over the ending and I ignored him as best as I could as I approached the church. My vision began to warp and I felt my feet slow. No matter how hard I tried, I couldn't get closer to the grounds. It was physically impossible while I was so taken over.

"I'm going to bleed you dry for not answering me! Fuck!"

My eyes scanned the area, not seeing Father Moretti. I knew I was early, but I was hoping he would have been waiting. I wanted to be back within walls. Back in the security of my home.

"Tessa!" The demonic voice didn't even sound like Marko. It sent chills up my spine and made more tears cloud my eyes. They slid free from the burning and I lifted the glasses, trying to wipe away the wetness. A sob was right there, but I held it in. Shit, what had happened after I left? I had been so sure Marko would come for me. Since he hadn't, was it because his leader told him not to? Marko had called him Julius. And the vampire wanted me to come back to take Marko's place. I knew that meant he'd want to change me into one of them, and I didn't want that. Hell, at this point, I didn't ever want to go back underground. Especially after how I'd seen Marie. I had trusted her, even just a little, and at the first scent of my blood, she'd snapped.

The hope I held that vampires could be good if helped the right way seemed pointless. One cut on my arm and the underground city had turned into complete and utter chaos. There was no way vampires and humans coexisting could work.

And hadn't I heard Hunter mention at one point that vampires worked in hospitals and other places at nighttime? How was that possible? It didn't seem real to me. It couldn't have been that way if they were so quick to attack.

"You're so smart. Keep talking. Let me hear your suspicions. Think about anything. Just don't stop."

My head shook as I realized I'd slipped back into letting him in. *"Marko, what's wrong with you?"*

"Oh, God, yes. Talk to me."

"I am, and I asked you a question. What's wrong with you? Answer or I start ignoring you again."

He paused. *"Lockdown with your bloody dress. God, it smells like you're here with me now. Talk to me more."*

The tone of his voice was changing again. Growing unrecognizable. Something told me to stop. That I was going to make it worse. This was nothing more than a tease to the animal that wanted to kill me, but for the life of me, I couldn't refrain from the questions that flooded through.

"Lockdown? Like...in a prison?"

"Sort of."

"How long will you be there?"

He laughed, moaning again. *"Not much longer. Will you sing for me like you did with the vermin? I want to hear you sing before I kill you."*

He saw that? Or did he hear about it? *"Fuck you. I'm finished. I'm sick of listening to your threats."*

Any questions I had vanished with his words. It was pointless to try to carry on a conversation with him with the way he was.

"No. Don't you dare stop talking to me. Tessa. Tessa!" The force of his yell echoed inside my head and I reached up, pushing my palm against my temple as he seemed to go crazy again. Father Moretti pushed through the doors of the church and my hand shot up at him. I reached deep within and tried to close off my thoughts completely. If it was ever important for me to guard myself, now was the time.

"Tessa." He rushed up, wiping the sweat from his brow. There was a tint to his skin, as if he were blushing, but I knew it had nothing to do with that. He had been putting everything he could into blessing my secret weapon and I couldn't have been more thankful. I was going to need every bit of holiness I could get to fight the demon that resided within Marko.

A black box rested in his hand and he slowly brought it out before him. Before he could open his mouth, my hand flew up and I pressed my finger against my lips. "Thank you so much," I whispered. "I..." the urge to throw myself into his arms was there, but the pure aura that radiated out prevented me from it. I held out my purse and he placed the box inside.

"If I'm able, I'll see you soon." For no reason other than my own comfort, I kept my voice low. It didn't stop him from nodding or seeming to somehow understand.

"I'll look out for you," he said, matching my volume. "Come back soon. Tonight, if you're able."

All I could do was nod as I took steps backward. My heart was racing and I could feel the presence of the dagger, even boxed up. I didn't like it. It made me feel even more scared, but for an entirely different reason. I wasn't sure what I feared more, it or the vampire determined to put an end to my existence.

With a quick wave, I spun around and raced toward my house. I felt my wall come down the moment I pushed through my front door. Yelling broke through the mental exhaustion and I locked the dead bolt, heading for my room.

"Love you to death, Tessa. Love you to death. Love ME to death."

My head shook as I placed the purse on my comforter and stared at the box. Marko continued, chanting the words over and over. Letting his voice deepen, only to go back to normal. It seemed to last forever. Until...he stopped. With his eerie silence, I looked up, right to the window. In roughly three hours the sun would set.

Then, he'd come.

Chapter 26
Marko

Blood poured from my arm, the cuts already beginning to heal as I carved in new ones. *Love you to death. Love you to death.*

There wasn't an available space left on my right forearm except closer to my wrist where I'd first begun. The words were fading, allowing me to go back and start all over again. *Love you to death.* God, I did. I loved her so much in the moment that I couldn't think past wanting to show her *just* how much. *To death.* Yes, it was going to be glorious. The best death that could ever be done. I'd make it perfect. Slow.

The small chunk of cement tore into my skin as I began to leisurely slice the *L* at my wrist, engraving what I never wanted to forget.

Blood pooled just above the cut and I felt the warmth run in a river over the side of my arm. With as much as I'd lost so far, I'd be famished come time to feed. I'd take every last drop she had to give, even if it killed me. Oh, but what a sweet death it would be. To have her consume my body as much as my mind, there'd be nothing more heavenly.

The *O* was deep and I moved to the next, so focused on the *V* that I never heard the clothes hit the ground. It was the breeze that brushed against my skin that had me surging to my feet, ready to attack.

"Get dressed. It's almost time."

My eyes stayed narrowed as Julius crossed his arms over his chest. I didn't break his stare as I crouched down and snatched the suit from the ground. I knew my trench and fedora was present, but I was focused on nothing but the threat that stood before me. And leader or not, Julius was my enemy. We were all against each other here.

"It's done. I was right."

I kept silent as I took off the pants I was wearing and exchanged them for the new pair.

"The old Marko is gone. Dead." He smiled. "Reborn into what you need to be. This, right here. *You* increased your growth. Can you feel it? Try to clear your mind and let yourself realize just who you are now."

What he spoke sent my core burning as I tapped into my powers robotically. Adrenaline spiked and I gritted my teeth at the vast sensation of pin pricks. I'd…been here before, long ago, when I'd first come into my powers. It lasted for what felt like forever, but in reality, only the first year. Then rebirths came every few hundred years and I wasn't sure why I hadn't connected the dots before.

"How does it feel to die?"

"I knew she wouldn't kill me." I somehow managed the words past the thickness in my throat.

"Oh, she very well may end your life tonight. That I can't see."

"You said you were going to change her."

He laughed. "She needed confidence. We both know she doesn't stand a chance."

"No, she doesn't."

I shoved my arm in the sleeve and he tilted his head as he watched me. "You do realize that you underestimate her, correct?"

"No." My head lowered as I began buttoning the shirt. I didn't want to talk. I wanted to focus on killing mon chaton in my head. Julius was fucking with my concentration. I knew nothing but her, and him getting in the way, even if it was just in the way of my fantasies, was not only dangerous for him, but for me.

"You do. She's not unprepared, Marko. This, I do know. She plans to kill you and she might just succeed. If she does, and she comes back here without you, I *will* turn her. Her blood may not speak to me, but I know it. I know it like my own."

Even though his words shocked me, I barely registered them as a low rumbled vibrated my chest. "She doesn't want this. Did you not see her fear?"

"I care not for her fear. It will fade. If anyone can stop this friend of hers, this Hunter, it will be her."

I blinked as my mind tried to clear out Tessa, but it was almost impossible. Her name was on repeat, circling and forcing its way through so that nothing else mattered.

"Marie. She dreamed."

Julius' fists clenched and I watched the anger seep into the muscles of his face.

"She didn't tell me this."

I reached for the trench impatiently, not caring. "Probably because she thought you already knew. Hunter will kill Tessa, so says Marie. If mon chaton is your savior, then the battle is lost. We will all die. But I hate to tell you, she won't live past tonight."

"Her first test. I guess we shall see."

The shield rippled, disappearing under the wave of his hand. I didn't wait to jerk my fedora off the ground and take off in a sprint. Nothing mattered but Tessa. And I'd get to her soon. The sun may have still been out, but I'd be waiting at the exit for the light to disappear, and when it did, my prey would finally become everything I wanted, and more.

Music poured through the heart of the city as I ran through. The instruments stopped, their lyrics of the end of the world dying off as I faded into the distance. Maybe everyone knew what was to come. I didn't doubt it after the mess that had happened yesterday. But I couldn't think about that now. Let them know. Let them see what happened when I got my mind set on destroying someone. I'd come back soaked in her blood and there'd be no question whether I was someone to mess with. Death would follow me everywhere I went. And it would begin with her.

Darkness swallowed me up as I hit the tunnel. The pounding of my shoes echoed around me and I broke to the left, already seeing the light up ahead. The silhouette standing just outside of it had me slowing as I approached.

"Marko…you're early. I…" Fear engulfed Marie's face as she tried to look for a way around me.

"You were going to try to save her before I was set free. Is that it? You want her for yourself?" My hand locked around Marie's throat as I slammed her into the cement, baring my fangs at the rage that engulfed me. "I lost my chance to kill her yesterday because of your attack. And you're back, to what? Get to her before I can?!"

Nails dug into my wrist and she squeezed with impressive strength, but not enough. I gripped tighter, rearing back and slamming her even harder into the wall.

"You touch what's mine, you beg me for the person who my blood gives life to, and then you try to steal her from me?"

Sounds came from Marie's throat as she thrashed in my hold.

"If you weren't part of Julius' plan, I'd fucking kill you now. Do you hear me? You'd be lifeless at my feet."

Footsteps pounded in the distance and I knew it was her men coming. The vampire within craved their fight. Needed it more than anything to sate the obsession that was driving me crazy. Had Marie not been here, I might have just risked the damage of the sun to get to Tessa. At least now I had an excuse.

"Don't," she whimpered, trying to break free.

"You will remember this day and what happens when you cross me." I paused, staring into her depths. "You…have crossed me…haven't you?" Something was there, hidden just in the shadows that rested deep within her soul. I couldn't see it, but the presence wasn't entirely concealed. Marie was smart. She knew how to guard things. "What is it, Marie? What would you like to tell me?"

The pull appeared when before, it wouldn't have. I thrived in my new powers, clutching to the connection and diving into her thoughts. Blindly, I lifted my hand to seal off the tunnel from her men as I pushed through, weaving past the beginning moments of her life. I didn't care to see who she was. There was only one person I yearned to know about, and that was Tessa.

Moans poured from her memories, deep and so full of pleasure, my body couldn't help but respond. I knew they were of mon chaton when she'd come to my room. It was the day of the second exchange.

Louder, they became, until I stood outside the door, listening. Waiting. Marie paced, unsure whether to knock and interrupt from her jealousy, or bask in the sounds she only wished she were a part of. Me…she wanted *me*.

I pushed into the fogginess I'd tapped into harder, feeling her change from wanting me, to curiosity over the woman. *Concubine.* The plans she'd thought exploded into my mind. Marie wanted to use me to get stronger. For us to become one so my blood could feed hers. But at the first scent of Tessa, everything changed. It baffled her. *It floored me. Why?*

Her blood may not speak to me, but I know it. I know it like my own. Julius' words broke through and I lost the connection, too in shock to continue. Even as I tried to decipher his words, the new vampire within me kept trying to break through so he could take over. It was hard to concentrate.

Her blood. The call. Tessa may have been human, but so had Julius once upon a time. Or even his creator. Who was to say Tessa didn't come from one of their lines somewhere? He'd called her Tessalyn Antoinette from the beginning. Like, he'd known she was his kin. If she had been anyone else, he wouldn't have cared. But he wanted her tested…

I swallowed hard, feeling myself begin to sweat. I was wrong. I had to be. Even as I thought it, rationality drifted away. My blood cravings intensified and I longed for Tessa. Needed to taste her. To completely consume her.

"How? How did you?" Tears streamed down Marie's face and her hand tried breaking mine free completely. I blinked, barely realizing Marie was still in front of me. There was no thinking involved. My hand pushed into her hair and with a jerk, I snapped her neck, letting her fall to the floor. It wouldn't kill her, but it would take a few minutes for her to come to.

As for her men…I turned, watching them collapse, dead. The lesson would suit her well. She'd mourn their loss and see firsthand what our true way of life was all about. For so long, she'd been the more powerful one over others, pushing them around, taking what she wanted. It was time for her to see the repercussions that would follow from her actions. She fucked over the wrong vampire by trying to get to Tessa first. I was finished with her and anyone else who got in my way. The new me was meant to rule. The right way. No one or nothing would stop me.

"Cross me again and see what happens. Vital to our plan or not, you won't survive what I have planned for you if you think to betray me again. All for a fucking human."

I stood, regretting not prying more into her thoughts when I had the chance. Maybe I'd missed something. Something important. I was in such a rush to get to Tessa, I was moving through everything in a powerful, newborn haze. Murderous hate poured through my veins, feeding me on. Driving me insane. I crouched, glaring up at the grate, watching the sunlight fade as the sun lowered more in the sky. Calm mixed with the need to slaughter, and the trance that settled over me had me rocking on my heels while I waited. *Love you to death. Love you to death.* Yes, I would love her to her death and I'd enjoy every second of it.

My fangs elongated at the intensity of my need and I closed my eyes, feeling for mon chaton. A moan nearly left me as her fear oozed into my body, exciting the new person inside of me. Again, I felt myself dwindle away to become the monster I'd been when Julius came to me in the cells. It was so easy to slip back into that mindset and I knew it would stay like this for some time. With new formed power came bouts of insanity. Tessa was going to find out firsthand just how dangerous that could be. And I wouldn't know what happened until I cleared. If…I even found myself enough to come back.

Chapter 27
Tessa

From the depths of the underground he came, a monster moving amongst the shadows, stalking every living thing like the predator he was. The dark suit or fedora couldn't hide what anyone who got within a ten foot radius would feel. And he could have had them. Could have torn them to pieces with his razor sharp fangs. He wanted to. But they wouldn't be his meal tonight.

I would.

Even lying in bed, the covers pulled up to my neck, I saw him getting closer. Shared his vision. His thoughts. He was coming for me. I could feel it in my bones and not just because his arrival was my greatest fear. My blood was literally calling him. Every beat of my heart was like the sweet bells of a church, luring in the faithful servants of the Lord. Luring in him. I was Marko Delacroix's salvation. His continuation amongst the living dead. But I wouldn't be for much longer. Tonight, I would die. He'd kill me. And then, I'd be replaced.

Or so he thought…

I gripped the blanket tighter, holding on for dear life. I wouldn't die tonight. Julius said I wouldn't. So why was I so afraid? I knew why. Because Marko wasn't himself. He was the epitome of evil and I was his target. I didn't want him to die at my hands, or at all. I knew the man inside, who I'd fallen in love with was somewhere underneath the surface. The one that protected me, even from himself when he could help it. But no matter what I did tonight, he wouldn't be present. In a sense, Julius had been right. Marko was dead. I'd killed him when they locked him away. To think that was what the leader meant only had me shaking worse. I held to the fact that he promised to change me when I returned. That meant I would live, or so I hoped. Little did he know, I wasn't going back. I'd run—now. I'd leave and pray to God every day that they wouldn't find me. Let them think Marko killed me. I didn't care. As long as I didn't have to become part of them.

My eyes closed, trying to feel him. I couldn't anymore. It was like our bond was already broken. If it weren't for the feeling in my heart, I might have just believed that. But I knew the truth. Marko was on his way to me and somehow, he'd managed to turn himself off completely. Would he use the front door? Burst through my window like the evil creature I knew he was at the moment? His state of mind left me absolutely terrified beyond comprehension. My situation had scared me straight and I just hoped it would continue to last long enough to allow me to end his life. It was him or me.

Images began to filter through my mind and I saw my house come into view. A sound left me as I felt under my pillow. My cry increased at the slight sting against my fingertip and I went back to clutching at the blanket, shaking violently.

Flashes of blood splattered over my vision and I nearly screamed at how real it looked. As if the red substance had gotten in my eyes and blurred everything together. I pushed to sit up and flipped on my bedside lamp. My whole body locked up at seeing Marko in my doorway. I'd never heard it open. Never heard a sound except my own racing pulse.

The fedora fell to the ground and he let his trench coat follow. He was so calm...it scared me even more. I kept my hand under the blankets as he began taking off his suit jacket and shirt. The crazed look in his black eyes left me feeling even more nauseas. The fire in my throat was so intense, swallowing was impossible.

"Mon chaton, I'm disappointed. You make this too easy."

The demonic voice was back and I clutched the white nightgown that pooled in my lap. My knees drew up as he neared. I took in the muscles flexing on his bloodstained chest as his movements changed. He was waiting for me to try to run. Prepared in case I had plotted a last minute escape. Maybe that's what he wanted, but I refused to give in to him. I stayed still as his hand connected with the mattress, trying my best to stop the nerves that wracked my body. Like the animal he was, he graceful prowled over me, until his forehead was pushing mine down into my pillow—hard.

"You're so afraid. I can smell your fear. It's so thick and sweet. But it's not enough." His black eyes opened and connected with mine. I refused to hold his stare for long. Couldn't, as my whole body jolted through another wave of terror. The reaction left me angry and my palm shot straight up into to his cheek as I tried to put distance between us. He didn't even budge.

"You will not get from me what you want. Now, get off."

A deep inhale was followed by him ignoring me. He let out a sound, somewhere between a moan and a sigh as he flattened his hand against the side of my face and sucked against my jawline. Slowly, I moved my fingers underneath my pillow while he pulled the covers back to climb underneath.

"Marko?"

There was no response as he continue to suck his way down my skin. Long nails brushed against my outer thigh while he eased the side of my nightgown higher up my hip. Pleasure sparked, but I pushed the fake sensation away.

"Marko."

More of his weight lowered and his hard cock moved along my pussy. The temptation to close my eyes and give in was overwhelming. His fixation influenced my thoughts and I fought the bond as best as I could. I had to find some way to distract him.

"I've thought of nothing but this moment now for hours. Moan for me. Let me hear your voice." The hand on my head slid higher as fingers weaved through my hair. At his other thumb pressing into my lower stomach, I exhaled through the change in emotions.

"I'm going to kill you," I whispered. "You think you're going to win, but you won't."

There was a hesitation as he jerked on my hair, making me face him. An evil smile was on his face and with each shake of his head, he glared even more. "Spread your legs and let me fuck what's mine one last time. I'll love you to death, mon chaton. Just like you want. Love you to death," he repeated, twice more.

My fingers rose a little higher under my pillow and he yanked hard, turning and exposing my neck completely. If he sunk his fangs into me, it was over with. I'd lose my fight. I'd die. He'd kill me and I wouldn't even fight back.

"I will," I whispered. "God, I will. I'll love you to your last breath and then I'll hate you for eternity. Dear Heavenly Father, I ask that you seal this place from all evil. That you—"

Marko's head came up and his hand slammed over my mouth. He looked uneasy and I couldn't stop now. My insides were burning just as the mere words and my throat felt like it was closing, but it was *working*.

That you...ah....

My fingernail brushed against the dagger resting under my pillow as I fought to make more words appear in my mind. It was as if my brain was shutting down, trying to protect Marko. But I couldn't stop now. If I could distract him just a little longer...if I could pierce his heart...I knew this would be over. He'd die. The pain of touching it left my skin on fire. I tried my best to get as close I as could without warning him, but I knew my time had run out.

"Lord Jesus, in your Holy Name, I ask..."

The beast within him flared as he pushed up higher from my chest and his lips peeled back to reveal his fangs. The internal scream at how terrifying he looked broke off my thoughts and my hand shot up to grip the dagger tightly.

Like a blur, I saw him coming down for my throat. I didn't even have time to think as I extended my arm up to meet him in his quick advance. The double sided hilt that overhung the handle pushed back against my hand from the force and a gasp broke through the loud roaring in my ears. I wasn't sure if it was mine or his. My chest exploded in an inferno, burning from the inside as if someone had dropped a torch down my throat and let it settle deep within the center of my being.

Gargling was followed by a groan as Marko lifted off me, staring down at the buried blade. His eyes weren't black anymore. And he was blinking...confused.

"Mon...chaton?"

My heart shattered and I sobbed as he fell to my side. A broken up breath had his hand rising and pulling the hilt. As the blade slid free blood poured from his chest.

"Oh...shit. Ahhh! Fuck." His head lifted, only to fall back and I could barely focus myself. I was going to be sick from the intense burning. It enflamed my soul, leaving a piercing shriek coming from the depths of some faraway place within me.

"Tessa?" A hand pulled against my arm, bringing me closer toward him, but I couldn't bear the smallest touch. The agony was moving, growing, threatening to consume me. "Mon chaton. Oh...please."

We both cried out as he tried to lift me into his arms. Even he didn't have the strength, which told me the damage I'd truly done. We were both going to die, and there was nothing either of us could do about it.

"Two minutes," he breathed out. "If I'm not dead by then, I...won't die."

I gagged as the flames rose higher, incinerating my throat. He may have had two minutes, but not me. I knew my life was disappearing with ever second.

"Uhh, shit. Shit!" His leg jerked as he kicked out. The sway of the mattress had my eyes rolling back. Even my breath leaving me became unbearable. I was melting on the inside. Everything was turning into a pool of blood that was beginning to rise up to coat my tongue.

A hand grabbed my shoulder and Marko managed to pull me up to cradle over his chest. It was enough to have a small amount of crimson running out onto his chest. Speaking was impossible. Moving was nonexistent. I was trapped within the shell that held me. All I wanted was it to be over with. If he was already growing stronger, I hadn't killed him. Only myself.

"You're not going to die," he breathed out, reading my mind. "I won't let you." His arm rose, but fell back on the mattress as he took in two ragged breaths. Another groan left him and I felt my body convulse for the smallest second. I managed to cry out as multiple spasms coursed like electricity, shocking me back to awareness. My arms thrashed and I clawed at my skin, trying to make the burn stop. It was happening. I was getting ready to die and there was nothing I could do about it.

"Keep still, mon chaton, you're only going to make it worse. Let your body heal you."

A scream was my only response as I twisted, rolling off of him and onto my stomach. My knees immediately curled in.

"Jesus." The bed dipped as he cried out, rising to his knees. "I'm proud of you. But you missed my heart. Now, up."

I locked more into myself, not wanting to move. Breathing was almost impossible but I took deep breaths, getting nothing more than enough oxygen to stay conscious. Panic made the gasps faster and I flew to my knees as my survival instincts kicked in. Marko's fingers embedded in my face while he edged in close, holding me still.

"You may hate me when this is said and done, but I don't care. The feelings I have for you now, the *love* to spare your life, may not exist after the bond is complete. You have to know that before I start. Your love may fade, too. But I leave neither of us a choice. Your human life is now over. Tonight, Tessa dies for real. She can never come back here." His eyes were turning black again and I knew he was slipping away. His words weren't his own.

Claws extended and I tried to shake my head. After being attacked in the underground city and seeing everything I had, I didn't want his way of life. Didn't want him. I knew the love I felt wasn't real and if securing the bond would make that become my reality, I didn't want to be trapped in an endless life down in hell with him. I'd rather die. At least there I'd be at peace.

"Too bad," he said, reading my thoughts. "You're *mine*. I won't let you go. From here on out, we're blood bound. Forever tied to one another until I decide otherwise."

He slammed me to my back as crimson poured from his wrist and forearm. I fought the advance with every ounce of power left. My hands shot up while I screamed and tried to push him away. I failed. Marko gripped my face harder, nearly crushing my jaw as he drowned me in his blood. And he didn't stop until my throat started to open back up. Adrenaline was so powerfully racing through my arms and legs, I was fighting harder than I ever had. But my fight stopped with an internal tug that nearly ripped open the center of my chest.

My arms locked up and I felt the pattern of my heartbeat change as his blood flooded my stomach. The pulse slammed once. Then, in a set of three, only to return to a two-count rhythm. I sucked in air as the electrical currents shocked me with a force I hadn't known existed. It left me shooting to my side and screaming as I tried to get in a fetal position. For minutes, I thrashed back and forth, unable to control my limbs. Glimpse of love and hate shadowed Marko's face and I wasn't sure how this was going to end. Would the new, evil him try to kill me the moment I came to? That Marko wouldn't want this. Wouldn't want *me*.

Aching registered over every inch as my movements slowed. Twitching turned to shakes until it finally began to stop. A low hiss turned into a growl, pulling me from the exhaustion.

"Tessa? Tessa, I have to talk to you!" A loud crash had my head turning toward the door, but for the life of me, I couldn't react. My heart ached as I feared for my best friend. Hunter stood there, his eyes flaring from surprise to rage. Panic was present, and I had no doubt it was from what he was witnessing. But there was something else. A new found confidence in the way he held himself. Determination as he took a step closer.

"You're fucking dead," Hunter yelled, staring at Marko.

A twinge in my stomach had me crying out and clutching to my bloody nightgown. Marko pulled me into his arms, holding my head locked in his grasp as he moved in next to my face from behind. I couldn't stop the jolts against him from the pain of the increasing ties. "You kill me and she will die. We're bonded now. That's *forever*. Face it. Tessa belongs to me. You'll never have her now."

"*Watch* me. I'll never let her go. Not to you."

Hunter reached behind his back but the next thing I knew, glass was shattering and gravity was gone. Darkness registered and Marko clutched onto me as he scaled the fence. I knew where we were headed. Lights from the houses blurred by at inhuman speed and I watched my home and Hunter's emerging body fade away as we raced for the safety of the tunnel. My life as a human was over. I was a slave now. Marko Delacroix's slave, and he'd been right on one count. Things weren't the same now that I could feel our connection intensifying. But was it better, or worse?

Lies. Scandal. His past.

Like a tidal wave, his mind subconsciously opened to me, revealing secrets I could have never imagined. And now I was a part of them. I was tied to his deceit. Wrapped up in his lust. And headed for one hell of a war with none other than my best friend, and there was nothing I could do about it. I was bound—blood bound.

To be continued…

Blood Bound

Marko Delacroix #2

Alaska Angelini

Blood Bound
Marko Delacroix #2
Alaska Angelini
Copyright © 2014 by Alaska Angelini

ISBN:

All Rights Reserved

Chapter 1
Tessa

To lose one's self, even temporarily, was the worst thing a person could experience. I'd been there. Suffered, unable to voice my fear or concern over a situation. And where most people would have pulled through and moved on, I couldn't. If ever I was trapped before, now I'd sunken as far as the pits of hell. And quite literally.

The underground city I was being pushed toward laid ahead and I'd never dreaded a return back to a place more than I did now. I could feel the vampires' presence crowding in against my skin, making it tingle in warning as I got closer. But I was helpless to flee. I was blood bound to a Master who had made me his blood slave and there was no turning back. Marko Delacroix owned me and only death would set me free.

"Faster."

His palm pushed into the middle of my back, nearly making me fall. Dread had my feet unresponsive and I moved even slower. To fight against him now was pointless. I wanted to, but I knew better. My body was barely healed as it was. Not minutes ago, I had been on death's doorstep, spitting up blood. Now, his blood was healing me, making me even more loyal to the one person I'd like nothing more than to cut ties with. I may have still had feelings for him, but the emotions were a twinge of what they'd been before. I served him. That's all I knew at the moment. I'd be the keeper of his deepest, darkest secrets. A vessel for his lust. And the supplier of his meals. But I would not love this version of him. I couldn't. I was trapped, lost…out of answers and ideas.

Monsters came in many forms and my new Master was at the top of the food chain. The evil now resting inside of him didn't hold a candle to the Marko I'd met at the beginning. The one who almost killed me, but found it within himself to let me live. This new Marko…he truly did scare me. Black still held the color of the brown eyes I once was in awe to look into, and his face didn't reflect the devilish smile that tried to charm me, regardless that he didn't like to. No, that Marko was dead now. Whatever had happened to him when they locked him away was beyond me. And I was too afraid to ask. Truthfully, I didn't want to know. Julius mentioned turning me into one of them and having me take Marko's place, but that's the last thing I wanted now. I couldn't be evil. Couldn't be one of them. I'd kill myself first.

"I can still hear you," he growled. "Be careful how dark you let those thoughts go. You see slicing your wrist, do you know what I see?"

Fingers weaved into my hair, jerking me back until his face was buried in my neck from behind. "I see blood. I see finishing what we started."

My eyes narrowed even though I couldn't see him. "Are you threatening me? I figured at least that would end now since you finally trapped me into being yours." Even though I knew I pushed him with my words, I couldn't contain the anger.

"You *want* me to end your life. I see it buried deep within your mind, Tessa. I know where your thoughts are going to go before the words even form to leave your mouth. But you will not die so soon. You once said I liked to play with my food. We both know you were right. After we meet with Julius, I think I'll do just that."

Despite the fact that he was holding my hair, I gave a good pull. His words sickened me. This Marko sickened me. "Rape me if you feel so inclined, but I will not submit to you in that way. As my duty, you may have my blood, but I will never again willingly give you my body."

"Do you think I need permission to take what's mine? I'll fuck you right here if I want."

Even as he spoke in that deep tone, my body came to life without my consent. It had me tugging against him harder in an attempt to separate us. "You can barely stand, more or less get your cock up. I feel your pain, or do you forget the bond we now share? Let go and get this over with."

"My cock is going to be filling that smart ass mouth of yours before the night is over. Mark my words, Tessa. You're going to learn very quickly who you serve and what that entails."

"And you forget Julius wanted me to take your spot. Maybe I'll become the stronger one and I'll let you serve me."

I launched forward at his push and slid to my knees. The burn from the cement cut into my skin and I knew he'd broken the surface. It was enough to have a sob escaping, but not from the pain. It was from the anger and unfairness that was my new life. If only Hunter would have gotten to me faster, before the bond, I could have been spared. Hunter could have killed him for good.

A roar sounded behind me before I was picked up and slammed into the side of the tunnel. It came with enough pain to have me whimpering. Although it was pitch black, I could see the outline of Marko's features and the slight illumination from his black eyes.

"Take it back," he said, digging his fingers into my face. "You love me. You do." Hurt flashed across his face and it was nearly enough to stop my heart. This new monster wouldn't have cared…

"Marko?" The tears escaped at me wishing the old him rested somewhere within the demon that had taken over. If only the one I'd grown feelings for would come back, then maybe things wouldn't be so bad. My hand unclasped from one of his wrists and rose to trace over his slightly rough cheek. After a few blinks, his anger returned and he reared back from my caress.

"You're going to pay for that. When I kill Hunter, I'm going to make you watch. I'm going gut him alive right in front of you while you scream for me to stop. And I won't. I might even make you help."

I sobbed angrily, kicking my leg into his thigh. There was no point in arguing. I wanted away. To hurry up and get out of this tunnel and into his room so I could close myself off. Surely, he'd have to talk with Julius. That could buy me some alone time before I had to endure another second of being in his presence.

"So quick to escape your new Master." He moved in closer, inhaling deeply against my neck. At the push of his hard cock against my pussy, I turned, groaning in aggravation, and pleasure. "How I long to taste you. I'm starving for your life. Starving to death," he whispered.

The grip loosened while he let my body sink into his. Again, he ground his cock against me, sparking lust deep within my core, even as his voice changed more to the Marko's I missed. "I know you want my bite. You want that sweet sting and I'm going to give it to you right now. Fuck, you smell so good. You make my mouth water. All I can think about is how much I want you. You fighting me makes me want it even more."

My head shook, trying to move him away from my neck. "I fight because I can't stand this. I do not want you."

"Liar," he moaned. "You do, I can smell your arousal. You want me and I want you, too. Something tells me I love you, but I don't know how I could. Maybe if I got my fill of you, tasted what you're made of, I'll remember."

Thoughts faded as the temptation of his words sunk in. If he did taste me, would the old Marko return? Would this demon vampire be sated and go away? If that didn't work, he could very well kill me from taking too much blood.

"Not here," I managed. "You need to feed, I feel that. But let's go to Julius first."

Vibrations shook my body at his warning. "I say what we do. *Not* you."

I fell to the ground, grunting at the impact. Throbbing flared in my leg and I scrambled to my feet to get further away from him. I didn't want him changing his mind. If I was going to die, it sure as hell wouldn't be in these tunnels. I'd almost been killed here before. It wasn't a memory I wanted to repeat.

Light rested ahead and with each step I took closer, music began to register. Exhausted and sore, I tried to push myself faster. It had been too long since I'd slept. I'd expected Marko to come for me the night I was attacked. The delay until the following night left me restlessly anticipating his return and the lack of sleep was taking its toll.

"Wait." Marko rushed forward, cupping my shoulder and spinning me around to face him. "I'm curious to see something. You go first. I'll be behind you shortly. You are not to look back. You are not to say a single word. Not one. Not to Julius or anyone. He'll be waiting for you. Now, go."

My mouth opened to ask questions, but at his anger, I turned and headed through the entrance of the tunnel. A few steps in and the music slowly died. Heads began to turn in my direction and Julius spun around from a far table to look at me. Fearfully, my hands came up and gripped the bloody, ripped nightgown I wore. It was from Marko's wound and the last blood exchange, but they wouldn't know that. They very likely thought I'd been successful in killing him.

Quickly, Julius began walking to me, such grace and poise in each step. I felt myself stumble, but continued ahead. My eyes searched the surroundings, taking in all the vampires and slaves standing around. Had they been waiting for the result, too? It only made me more curious about what had happened after they attacked me.

"You live."

Although his tone sounded unsurprised, I found my eyes stopping on Marie's sobbing form. She'd been sitting in the chair Julius had been hovering over. Her shoulders sank in and even as she returned my stare, she cried harder.

"Look at me." Julius' anger had me tearing my gaze away and I met his light blue eyes for only a second before I lowered them to stare at the onyx brooch pinned in his cravat. "I said, look at me."

The warning was all too clear, but Marko's words had me locked into his orders. My gaze stayed transfixed ahead and my lips were involuntarily sealed shut.

"I won't ask you again. If I have to force you to obey, you're going to regret it."

My pulse jumped and my mind was empty as I stood there. I knew Marko was making it impossible for me to think. I wasn't sure what he was hoping to get out of this or what he wanted to see, but using me as a pawn didn't make me the least bit happy.

"That's it." Bony fingers wrapped around the back of my neck and he spun us, leading me toward one of the halls in the back. "You don't want to show me what happened, I'll see for myself. Then, you'll be punished as you wait out your fate."

Somehow, a small sound broke free of my lips and I searched for the words to tell him no. Fear shot through me and I tried to fight his grasp, but I couldn't.

"There'll be no need for that."

Marko's deep voice echoed from the walls and his body stalked forward, dried blood moving with the powerful muscles of his bare chest and stomach as he advanced. Julius' grip tightened for only a moment before he let go completely.

"And here I thought you were dead."

"So little faith in the man who will someday be leading us. I told you before, I have no intention of dying, and I won't."

Julius smirked. "Had you been so powerful, you would have killed her, yet the two of you are now bonded. And you expect me to have faith?"

All emotion melted from Marko's face. When his black eyes met mine, I couldn't help but feel my stomach drop. If my new Master hadn't been having second thoughts about keeping me, he sure as hell would now. Weakness wasn't something he liked and Julius had brought me into it.

"You'd have me kill your kin? I thought I was doing you a favor." Marko grabbed my bicep, pulling me to his side. The pressure of his fingers almost brought me to my knees. The statement succeeded and I would have hit the ground had it not been for his tight grip.

"Tessalyn Antoinette is not *my* kin," he said, smiling. "But I do know whose she is."

"Kin?" Marko's memories hadn't told me that. My gaze went between them. Although Julius glanced down to me, Marko stared at our present leader. "I'm kin to someone here?"

The smile grew bigger while he turned his attention back to Marko. "You're kin to one of us, yes. But you don't need to worry about that now. In time, things will reveal themselves. There's no rush. Why don't you two go clean up? The night is still young. Marko, I expect you in the meeting room in an hour."

The grip around my arm tightened and with a nod, Marko turned us and headed toward the tunnel where his room rested. My eyes went back to Marie as she continued sobbing. What was she doing, sitting out here crying? Although I was afraid after the last time we were with each other, my heart ached to go to her. Something was wrong. Something was very badly wrong.

Darkness came within the distance and I looked over my shoulder as Julius made it back to her side. The tunnel entrance cut off my view and I pulled against the grip as we disappeared into the pitch black.

"Marko, wait."

He didn't even react as he threw his door open and pulled me inside. I couldn't stop the scream from exploding from my mouth—Marie's four bonded men, dead on Marko's bed. Their pale, lifeless bodies left me jerking hysterically against the vice that gripped me.

"Oh…God." My mouth opened and a shuddering breath left as I tried to figure out why they'd be here, in Marko's room. And then I knew. The truth left me cold and growing still. Silent sobs wracked my chest and I let my face slowly rise to the creature standing next to me. The hardness behind his stare wavered the smallest amount before it reappeared. Maybe I'd imagined it, or maybe I just wanted to believe he regretted what he'd done. Either way, I'd never wanted to get away from him more than I did in that moment.

"Why?" I sniffled, wiping the tears from my face with my free hand. My heart ached for Marie. What could she have done to deserve having her bonded killed? It didn't make sense. It left my mind reeling with questions I couldn't decipher. "Why would you do that? She loved them. They…adored her. Why would you—" At my voice cracking, I let the anger force its way past my lips. "Why! Answer me. Answer…you…insufferable, disgusting—"

Gravity disappeared as Marko's hand latched around my throat and slammed my body diagonal, across all four of their laps. One minute, I was screaming in horror, the next, stinging locked my arms and legs from his fangs brutally embedding in my neck. I gasped and dug my forearms into his shoulders, trying to break him free.

Hard tugs on my vein left tears flowing down the sides of my face. I hated him. Wanted nothing more than for the bastard to feel how deep my aversion ran while he took my very life from me. My eyes closed while I let my loathing seep from me in waves, praying he felt it down into his evil, black soul. What seemed to last forever went by and my lids blinked weakly. The sucking softened and I felt sicker knowing he wasn't going to finish me off.

"I will hate you until the day I die. And then I will hate you for an eternity after that."

Marko broke from my neck, meeting my gaze. "No. You will love me. It says so right there on your skin."

"That was for the old Marko. I did love him to death. Now, I'm left with you, and I will hate you with every last breath I take."

Whether my words affected him was beyond me. He lifted and I tried not to be sick as I scrambled from the bodies. Bile burned the back of my throat and all I wanted to do was stop this nightmare.

"I want Marie. I want to go to her."

Marko spun on me, his lips peeling back as he took a step forward. "She will not want to see the murderer of her bonded. I may have killed them, but their deaths are yours. *You* did this, Tessa. Had she not tried to make it to you first, her men would still be alive. You killed them through me and she very well knows it.

Chapter 2
Marko

Who was Tessa to make me feel bad for what I'd done? This woman, this…slave, she was nothing to me. A peasant to the Master who towered before her. Her mouth was crass, her manners deplorable. Yet, she stood up to me as if I were beneath her. As if I were the filth caked to the bottom of her dirty feet. It enraged me, made the vampire within beg to end her life, and I would have if not for…something. I knew I'd drank too much of her and I'd had no intention of stopping, yet I did, and I couldn't understand why.

A sob left her lips as her head turned toward the door. There was such yearning, such melancholy pouring from her that it only increased the rage. This ungrateful wench should have been kneeling before me, not begging to go to Marie. *I* was her Master. No one else. I fucking…loved her, even if I didn't understand it. And this was how she behaved? How she treated *me*.

Knocking on my door had her taking a step forward. I didn't have to tune in to know who it was. "Stay and be quiet. It's not who you wish it to be."

The collectors swept in as I swung the barrier open wide. I knew it was them because I'd called the servants, even as I took my slave's blood. To feel her hate…a part of me wanted to somehow erase it from within her, even as I tried to block it out any way I could.

"Take them out and bring new sheets to fix my bed."

Two human men walked forward, moving into action at my orders. They weren't much different than the suppliers who fed our kind. Instead of their blood paying their way, they were muscle, offering their services in exchange for our bite.

A small sound came from Tessa and I noticed she'd moved to lean against the far wall. The haunted look only registered for a moment before I moved my gaze over her body. The full shape of her breasts was the first thing to pull my attention, but I tore my thoughts from imagining what they looked like. Blood, old and new, stained her once white nightgown and I let it sink in. The sight didn't bother me in the least, but how disheveled she'd appear to everyone else did. If she were to be my blood slave, she would reflect me. Her appearance was important. I wasn't just anyone. I'd rule this place someday and she'd damn well represent that behind, and outside, my door. I couldn't stand that the collectors were seeing her this way. Or that anyone had to begin with.

"Come."

My voice had her glare cutting over from the bodies. Her seething didn't ease as she came to me. It was apparent she didn't want to obey, but I was leaving her little choice. I grasped our connection, holding it tight until she followed me into the restroom.

"You will take a shower and clean yourself. I will be back with new clothes. You are not to leave our room."

Our. The realization had my lips separating as something tugged at my brain. Tingling rushed through my stomach and I placed my palm against it, willing it to stop.

It didn't work.

"Marko?"

"Shower."

A small cry left her lips and she clutched her stomach, doubling over. Her large inhale had me gritting my teeth against the twinges that also began to surface within me.

"What's…happening?" Tessa's knees gave out and she fell to them, curling into herself and resting her forehead on the cement. Her yells were followed by her throwing herself to the side as her legs kicked out through the electrical currents within. I felt them zapping me, stabbing throughout as they branched out toward my fingertips and toes. The strength behind the flow was enough to have me baring down on the countertop.

"The bond," I breathed out. "Fuck." I paused as I let the time we'd been together sink in. I hadn't drank when I forced my blood on her. I'd only just done that. So…the completion of the bond would only just now come to pass. No wonder she wasn't in love with me like she should have been. She was somewhat of her true self for now. But not for long.

"I thought we were already—" Her stare shot up to mine. "You just finalized it? Jesus, we weren't bonded before then? You…" Anger and devastation drew in her features as she managed to get to her feet. The swing of her fist was automatic and it caught my bicep as she drew back to swing again. "Why? I don't want this. I hate you! I want to go home!"

My hand easily deflected the next blow, but it was for nothing. Weakness and spasms already had her sinking back down to the ground.

"Just face it, you're mine. What you want is no longer of concern. Your life is to please me now. That's it. You are no one. A slave. *My* slave."

"I could have been a wife. A mother. You stole that from me." She wiped the tears away shakily, coming to her feet. "I will never forget this. Ever."

"Yes, you will," I said, stepping around her and pulling the shower door open as I turned on the water. "A few hours from now, you will know nothing but me and your duty. Besides, from what I can remember, at the rate you were going, you would have been a spinster, if anything. You've never even loved before me."

Tessa shook her head, glaring in my direction. "You are so wrong. Why do you think you want me and Hunter so far apart? He loves me and I've always loved him. As a friend, yes, but I think if we both want to be honest, I loved him quite a bit more. After all, I did invite him to live with me. Do you think that was for nothing? I've often flirted with the idea of trying to have a future with him, but I never got the chance to test out how we were together. You ruined that before it could ever begin."

The revulsion and truth she cast in my direction had me lunging forward and taking ahold of her roughly. "Mention him one more time and see what I do." Tessa nearly fell as I pushed her in the shower. Immediately, guilt swarmed me. I blinked past feeling confused. She was a slave. It shouldn't matter how I treated her, but for the life of me, I couldn't look at her face. I knew she felt what I did. Whatever the sensation had been was already fading as I slammed the bathroom door closed behind me. Two of the bodies were already gone and the collectors were out of sight. I walked to the closet, grabbed a T-shirt, and pulled it on, trying my best not to let her words affect me.

Fucking Hunter. I was going to kill him. The need to see his blood on my hands almost had me racing for my door to take care of it now. If it weren't for the fact that I'd have to leave Tessa alone, I would. Besides, I had other stuff to take care of. She needed clothes and it would take time to make what I imagined her wearing. The apparel would have to suit my status and that meant it would have to be specially made.

Darkness encompassed me as I broke into the hall and kept my focus ahead, dismissing the stares cast in my direction the moment I entered the heart of the city. My eyes scanned the glass windows and I walked past a boutique and salon before I barged through the door of George's. The dress shop and tailor was one I'd been to for more years than I could remember and I knew if anyone could help, it was George.

"Master Delacroix." Joanie hung up the blouse she held and rushed toward the counter. The smell of fear overwhelmed me and I pushed it aside. Although I knew her, I couldn't really remember who she was. It was the same for the vampire I was searching out.

"I need George."

I blinked past the deepness in my voice and rotated my shoulders as my mind became fuzzy. The new powers were obvious and although I could barely recall how I'd gotten to this point, something within told me everything would come back. I was on auto-pilot in a way, still here, still…new.

"Master Delacroix." George's voice had me turning around, watching as he entered the store. I took in his short height and dark skin. He was stylishly dressed in a suit that melded to his lean frame. I dressed similar. It represented status. Elegance.

"George, I need you to put something together for me. An outfit for my slave. She'll require it by the next meal time. I'm also going to need a complete wardrobe for her. Fitting of my standing, of course."

The vampire nodded as he came to kneel before me, bringing his hand to hover over his head. "If you'll just show me what you'd like, I'll start on it right away."

The jolt that went through his body as his fingers settled over my palm brought on a smile. I let the images pour through into his mind's eye hard and clear. My powers were so much more than I could have dreamed and this was only the beginning. I knew that. And soon, everyone would see just how much when we all met up again. I'd no longer be number ten. Where exactly I would advance to was just too exciting for me to think about. This was what I longed for the most. What I had focused on my whole vampire life.

"She's to wear something like this for meals. I want the hooded tops only in silk. One of every color you can produce. Black undergarments. All of them. More like shorts. These are only for meal time. As for the others…" I let my voice trail off, unsure of what I wanted Tessa to wear as every day intimates. Lingerie? Fuck, it did appeal. I let them pour in his mind, just in case. "The wardrobe, I'll leave up to you. Make it the best."

My hand slid free and George groaned as he pushed to his feet. Sweat rested above his brow and I took pride in what I'd caused.

"I'll have Joanie deliver them to you the moment I finish."

"Thank you." I stepped back, spinning around to survey the area. Marie's head was lowered to rest on the table where she resided alone. I refused to dwell on Tessa's words as I headed back to the room. *Insufferable, disgusting…*

Had she felt my internal reaction to her aversion? I didn't think so. If she had, she showed no surprise over the weakness I'd harbored. The pain in my chest had been the main reason I'd snapped and taken her the way I had. I'd wanted to teach her a lesson. Make her hurt the way she'd hurt me. I didn't really know her other than a feeling she gave me, yet it was unfair and irritated me that she had that sort of control. And still, I was weak. Still…she was alive.

My hand slammed into my door and the collectors moved out of my way as they carried the other two bodies over their shoulders. For smaller men, they struggled with Marie's giants. It should have made me think or feel something, but it didn't. I headed back to the restroom. There was only one person on my mind and even being gone the small amount of time I had, she left me racing back to her.

"What are you doing?" The voice was sharp as I entered. Steam rolled along the ceiling and I shut the door, meeting a pair of wide, green eyes as she peeked out of the glass door. Her hand came up to cover her generous breasts and I couldn't stop my body from reacting. Even enraged at her talk of Hunter, I didn't want to push away the lust taking me over. I could feel myself softening the smallest amount and there was nothing I could do about it.

"Ma minette."

Tessa's head reared back, only to start shaking. "You have the wrong person. I'm mon chaton. You know, kitten without the endearment attached to it? Bond or no bond, I'm nothing dear to you so there's no use even pretending."

Anger had my upper lip twitching and I jerked at my belt, freeing the clasp on my pants and letting them slide to the floor. In one hard pull, I freed the leather and took off my shirt. She stiffened as I began stalking in her direction. Her anxiety perfumed around me and my vampire thrived from the mix of her different scents.

"You asked what I was doing. I think it's about time I collect what else you own me for bonding you. I do recall a few kinky memories locked away somewhere in my mind. I believe they came from you. Let's see just how much you truly get off on the darkness you hold within."

The slam of the shower door had me surging forward and pulling it open. Water immediately shot in my face as Tessa held and aimed the shower head right in my direction. A scream left her while she tried to escape my advance.

"You think water is going to stop me? Give me that." I grabbed the handle and pulled it free of her grasp. Water dripped from my hair and face and I fought the urge to throttle her. I very well couldn't take a beaten slave before the members — especially with what she'd be wearing.

Tessa edged to the door, staying close to the wall as she did so. My eyes narrowed and her feet came to a stop. The sway of her breasts left me so hard, I had to force myself to meet her eyes.

"We both know very well that I don't want this."

"You lie. You want me. Come, let me feel. I bet you're getting wet just from the thought."

"From the shower," she rushed out. "Which I'm finished with, by the way, I think I'll just go to bed now."

I stepped closer, inhaling deeply. Immediately, I frowned. She didn't smell right. At least, not what I expected. Something pulled at my memory while I searched for what was missing.

"Lavender with a hint of jasmine...and strawberries," she said, lowly. "That is what you're missing. That's what called you to me." Tears welled in her eyes and I felt her pain. Felt my own. My hand clutched the belt tighter while I waded through what felt like quicksand in my brain. Her words left me soft—again. Left me aching for something I didn't understand.

"Do you not remember anything?"

There was her love for me. It was buried deep down and was so small, I couldn't fathom how we'd even gotten to this stage. Why would I bond a woman who didn't love me? Who loved another man? Surely, I was smarter than that.

"Show me." My arm went out and I pulled her nude body into mine. My hand slowly lifted and I weaved my fingers into her wet hair. So gentle. So...loving. What the fuck was wrong with me? Although I questioned it and knew I should right my wrong, I couldn't as I stared into her depths. Seconds went by and...nothing. My fingers tightened and I squinted as I tried to push into her mind.

"Impossible."

"You can't see?" There was desperation there and already, she was shifting in my embrace.

"You can read my thoughts. Does it look like I can see anything?"

"I'm thinking it. I'm showing you," she said, pleadingly. "You have to see." The last broke off as her thoughts engulfed me. But not the right ones.

He has to see. I don't want this Marko! I could handle the other, but not this one. I don't want him!

I had the belt around her throat before she could continue. Immediately, her hands flew to the leather and she tried pushing her fingers past the hold I continued to tighten.

"You don't want me. I *get* it. But what you neglect to see is the moment I don't want you, you're dead to me. In every sense of the word, *mon chaton.*"

Although fear tinted her gaze, there was so much strength aimed toward me. It was enough to cause my hold to loosen.

"I already asked for death over this. You gave me hell instead. Now, I will be an angel amongst the demons and *I will* rule. Good always prevails. You watch and see."

I couldn't stop the laugh that bellowed out. "To rule, you'd have to be a vampire." I leaned in closer, until our faces were but inches apart. "And I won't release you to Julius. *Ever.* Besides, you will not be who you are right now if you were turned. You'd be one with evil. You'd change completely." I loosened the belt even more and pulled it free. "You'll never win, Tessa. Not over this world and not over yourself. Your life is what I make of it from here on out and if you want to continue breathing, you'll keep in my good graces. Which better start soon. I already tire of you."

She went to open the door when my arm wrapped around her waist and I yanked her back to me. The feel of her hot skin against mine sent my blood racing. She may not have smelled the same, but I still responded to her more than I could comprehend. It didn't make sense. None of it. Yet…I couldn't deny how deeply I was drawn to her.

"You forget what I'm here for. You're not going anywhere yet." I took in the way her hard nipples rose with each deep breath. It left me licking my lips. Fuck, to taste her skin. I wanted to. Every single inch.

"And I said you weren't getting that from me."

My hand slammed over her mouth while I turned her around and pulled her back into me. I couldn't stop my other hand from gripping her stomach, squeezing through my need. Throbbing pulsed through my hard cock and I couldn't stop from grinding it into her lower back. I was dying to fuck her. The desperation hooked into my insides, warping my mind until all I knew was the rebellious slave in front of me.

"If I want you, I take you. That's just how it works. And I do want you, ma minette."

I let my hand drift down to fit over her swollen folds. A small lunge had my arms moving with her failed escape and it only had my hold tightening.

"You like this," I said, lowering next to her ear and removing my hand from her mouth. "You dream of being taken this way. I've seen it."

"You've seen nothing," she said, panicked. "Marko did, not you. If I have to be here, I want him with me instead. Him, *not* you!"

The thrashing increased and I felt her tinge of arousal fade. Along with it…mine. Her reaction left me pissed. He was I and I was he, yet I didn't know him, aside from the few memories I could barely decipher through the fog. The fact that I was even giving any of this thought was just baffling. I wanted her. Therefore, I should just take her. She was a slave. A human. She was nothing important, regardless of what I felt.

"You have until the count of three to become still and accept what I want to have. If you fight me and deny what your body craves, I will discipline you the only way I know how. Take it from me, you don't want that. Or…maybe you do."

"No. I don't want *you*," she sobbed. "This can't be how my life was supposed to turn out. I want to go home. I want…" I knew *who* she wanted and just the reminder—again—left me seeing red. But it didn't last.

Her words became unrecognizable as weight settled into my hold and her head dropped into the spray of the shower. Dark hair was pulled down by the flow of water and I blinked, even more confused on what to do as she became limp and cried. Were humans always this emotional? It left my skin crawling. Repulsion soared at her weakness. Yet…it hurt to see her fall so far from the woman who fought me on the way in here not an hour ago.

Hour.

"Shit," I breathed out, releasing my grip and watching her fall to the shower floor. *Julius.* How could I have forgotten about our meeting? How? I knew how. I'd thought of nothing more than fucking this human since she had taken me over. She was all I knew. All I'd wanted to know. To kill. But I hadn't killed her. I'd bonded to her and I couldn't remember exactly how or why I'd given her my blood. We were just there, and then she was mine. The pain had been a good distraction to the questions and now they were beginning to eat away at me.

My eyes narrowed as she edged to the back wall. Tears still poured down her face and I took in how swollen and red her eyes were. I tuned in and explored our connection, feeling her emotions, her exhaustion. I had done well blocking her out. So well, I almost forgot I could read her if I wanted.

"You haven't slept in a long time."

There was hesitation as her eyebrows drew in. "No," she said, sniffling. "Have you changed your mind? "

My lip pulled back at the relief in her tone. "Only because I have to go to this meeting. But I'll be back and I *will* finish what I started. I'm far from done with you for the night."

"So, I can go?"

The internal pull I held onto dropped, allowing her the right to leave, and she instinctively felt it. The shower door flew open and she grabbed the robe hanging on the outside of the glass. She was out of the restroom before I could tell her that was my damn robe. A snarl left me and I lathered on the soap, cursing myself for the millionth time on how I let this happen. Nothing made sense and I was at the point where I didn't want it to. I wanted this bonding over with. More, I unexplainably yearned for her to accept it. For her to love me.

Chapter 3
Tessa

The slam of the bedroom door had me peeking out from the blankets I'd been curled in. Although sleep beckoned, I couldn't ignore the part of me that screamed to run. I knew it was pointless, but shouldn't I at least try? I couldn't just lie down and give into this life—especially if that meant being continuously raped by Marko. It was bad enough I had to be his supplier, but to give him my body, too? God, I couldn't do that. True, I responded to him, but that was only because of the bond. He wasn't Marko. Not really. I could already feel myself becoming attached to him and I knew it wasn't what I wanted.

My heart raced as I threw back the covers and pushed to sit on the edge of the bed. I tried my best to block the thoughts urging me to stay. Not only because my mind was already starting to have second thoughts, but because I couldn't allow him to hear. The simple fact that Marko hadn't come bursting through the door yet gave me hope. It led me to stand.

What do I do? Where do I go?

I headed over to his closet. It was still nighttime. I could wait for first light, but that only meant I'd have to endure the sexual advances before then. No, I had to leave now. If I stayed, I'd give into him. A part of me wanted to. Wanted to…stay and serve.

T-shirts and jeans hung on one side while suits rested on the other. I grabbed a black shirt and let the robe drop to the ground as I slid it on. It swallowed me, almost going to my knees. My eyes scanned the rest of the apparel and I let out a groan. Didn't he own a pair of sweat or jogging pants? I didn't see anything I could wear.

I rose to my tiptoes, pushing clothes folded on the top shelf around. My fingers connected with a pair of silk pajama pants and I grabbed them, pulling them on. My heart slammed in my chest as I broke for the door. I didn't think. I knew I couldn't go through the heart of the city. It would be too risky and he'd possibly see me leaving. Instead, I turned, running past Marie's door and heading deeper into the darkness. Where it led, I had no idea.

Sounds dissipated and I held my hands out in front of me as I ran as fast as I could without risking injury. My breaths grew louder and deepened until they were all I heard. What felt like forever passed as I kept going further into the darkness. The tunnel rounded and broke off, but I stayed straight. Traffic sounded above and began breaking through the silence. I squinted as a small glow rested ahead. It only caused my adrenaline to soar even more. I felt for Marko's connection, but didn't pick up anything at all. Whether he was coming for me and didn't want me to know, or he'd closed himself off to me altogether, was the biggest question I held.

Fear left me sprinting toward the light and staring up at three glowing dots. I knew it was a manhole, but where would it place me? I felt so disoriented.

A ladder stood ahead and I climbed up, pushing my hand against the heavy metal, groaning as I hooked my arm around the thin bar and pushed with everything

I had. As I managed to slide it over, voices broke through from the distance. It took me a few seconds to gain my bearings from the weight.

Slowly, I peeked my head out, noticing I was in the center of downtown Austin, right on the corner of the street. A couple slowed to stare and I didn't wait for their reaction. I climbed out, not bothering to return the circular metal to fit back on the hole. People watched and I kept my head down as I began to run in the direction of my house. I still had no idea where I was going, but if I could get to my car, I'd have a beginning. That was the most important part.

Laughter poured from one of the clubs I passed and I raced around the crowd waiting to get inside. As I broke around the corner, I slammed into what felt like a brick wall. Air exploded from my lungs and a cry broke from my lips as I began to crumble to the sidewalk.

"Jesus, are—"

My mouth dropped open as my gaze connected with Boyd's. Immediately, his hands tightened on my biceps.

"Tessa…are you okay?" The vampire was already walking around the corner to see if there was anyone behind me. "Who are you running from?"

I jerked at my arms impatiently, unable to break the connection. He held on more secure, pulling me more toward him.

"Let me go, please," I rushed out. "I—"

"You're running from him." A smile came to Boyd's face as he brought us deeper into the shadows of the nearby street.

"Please. I'm begging you."

Something flickered behind his eyes and I wasn't sure what he was thinking. All I knew was this vampire had already tried to kill me once. He'd apologized for it, but that didn't mean I could trust him. Besides, if he was up here, he needed to feed.

"You know I can't let you go if you're running from Marko. He's a member. One of my leaders. I'd get in a lot of trouble if I set you free and he found out."

My head shook a little too quickly. "I'm not running. I was heading back to my house to grab some stuff while he was in a meeting. I wanted to be back before he returned, that's all."

The smile returned as he leaned in, breathing deeply. "You lie. Damn, it smells so sweet."

"I'm not. I…"

He moved in closer, his upturned lips lowering into an expression I wasn't so sure I liked. "Then I'll accompany you back to your place while you get what you need. Afterward, I'll take you back underground."

Fear engulfed me, causing me to tremble. Thoughts went a million miles a minute and all I could do was nod. "Okay. I'd like that." *Lie*. But if I could at least get inside my home, I could shut him out. He couldn't walk past my door if I didn't invite him in. But how did I get rid of him after that? How did I make it to my car without him stopping me?

Fingers laced with mine and I looked down, only to peer back up at him uneasily.

"As a precaution. Appearances are everything, you know."

"Appearances?"

He let me lead as we headed toward my street. "You know, if people think things are okay between us, they won't give us a second thought. Out here, I have a pretty alarming aura. It draws attention. I'm hoping to drown it out a little, being out here with you."

"Oh." Did it really matter how anyone viewed us? I couldn't quite understand it as he rubbed his finger up mine. All I knew was it left me even more edgy. As we turned and headed toward the church, I licked my lips, letting my mind race. Would Father Moretti be watching? Would Hunter be inside? Hunter could help me escape. Hunter…

No. I quickly cut off my thoughts. If I dragged my best friend back into this, he'd die this time for sure. I would not be responsible for that. I couldn't. I…loved him. Sure, as a friend, but breaking things off and having him move out, all the while trying to protect me, stirred something I'd pushed away a long time ago. I missed him and I couldn't stop the weird tugging in my chest when I thought about the longing I felt to have him back. He represented life. Something I didn't have anymore.

We stayed on the opposite side of the sidewalk as we walked past the entrance. The whole cathedral was lit up brightly and Boyd shuddered next to me. I glanced up at him as he rubbed the back of his neck. The moment we got past the grounds, I pulled at his hand and we jogged across the road. Two houses hadn't gone by before my feet dug into the cement. Two silhouettes were walking through the darkness, right toward us. My heart exploded in rhythm and I felt my breathing hitch. My head shook back and forth and I knew before the taller one even stepped into the light.

"No," I groaned.

But it was too late.

Illumination from the street lamp lit up Marko's enraged face and I took a step back at him baring his fangs, angrily. Julius was standing next to him and they both looked downright pissed.

"I was just helping her retrieve some of her clothes." Boyd jerked his fingers free and I heard him swallow hard as he stepped away.

"I'm sure that's all you were going to do," Julius said, walking forward. "As for Tessalyn." His light blue eyes pierced mine and it was enough to almost bring me to my knees. I looked down, noticing the light from the street lamp flicker above. Our shadows blinked repeatedly, until….darkness. The light went out, leaving the night to swallow us up whole. Even the power inside the houses were off. Eeriness settled, almost appearing to push into my skin like a living thing. Dogs were suddenly silent. No one came from their doors to see about the outage. It was like time stopped. Like…life wasn't existent past the people who stood before me.

"If you run away again without the intention of coming back, the consequences you will face will fail in comparison to anything Marko will put you through." Still, he came closer. "You are on very thin ice with me, human. You're lucky I don't kill you right now. Instead, I'll show you what happens when you betray your kind."

Long, thin fingers reached toward my face and no matter how much I tried, I couldn't move away. They pushed against my temples and images exploded in my mind. I could see my mother and father. They were laughing, leaving what looked to be some cozy little restaurant in what I assumed was Italy, the last place I knew them to be. A neon light stood above the entrance of the door they exited and within a few steps, I saw a man step from the shadows at the end of the building. The pale skin and black eyes told me immediately what he was. Neither my mother nor father's steps faltered. They were too busy communicating over what looked to be an enjoyable conversation.

Subconsciously, my hand reached out and my lips separated in a silent warning. They had to run. To look up! I knew why the vampire was there. He was going to hurt them. Kill them.

"Mom. Dad!"

Their pace never changed and my fingers closed into a fist as I screamed louder. They were so close. So oblivious to the evil before them.

"Shall I have him end their lives?"

The scene disappeared as I gasped for air. Aching took over my lungs and I wasn't sure how long I'd been holding my breath.

"No. Please." Tears rolled down my face and felt myself fall to my knees. Defeat left me weaker than ever. "I'll go back. I won't run away again. Just…please, don't hurt them."

"Let's hope for their sake you're telling the truth. Next time, I will make you watch as I have them killed." One minute, Julius was there, the next…gone. My eyes searched the surroundings wildly and I squinted as the overhead light flickered back on. Boyd was gone, too. Marko was the only one before me and I was terrified at what I saw. His black eyes narrowed as he came forward, pulling me to my feet by my hair. A scream wanted to come, but I held in sound the best I could as he transferred his grip to my arm, leading me back to the entrance of the underground city.

Silence settled around us and as we passed my house. The living room light was on. Everything within me wanted to break away and rush for my door. Was Hunter still there? Had he accidently left it on after he went looking for me? Stinging burned my eyes and grief over my previous life consumed me. It broke my heart with every step that took me further away from my yard. I didn't fight Marko as he nudged me toward the opened entrance to the grate, or even when he led me back to his room. The moment his bedroom door shut, the cold that seeped into my skin was enough warning that a storm was about to hit. I tried not to shiver at the frigid temperature, but failed.

"You…*embarrassed* me. You…*humiliated* me!" he roared. "I leave you alone for the briefest amount of time and what do you do? What do I *hear*? Julius, asking me if I was aware my slave was a traitor. *My* slave! Me, the future leader."

Marko pushed me roughly toward his bed as he glared. Fear had me continuing on, but not easily. I didn't want to get on there. Didn't want to be anywhere near it or him while he was this angry.

"You are going to learn to behave tonight or else I'll beat you every night until you do."

As he went to the restroom, I pulled back the covers, jumping underneath despite not wanting to. I didn't like what he'd said and to pretend I wasn't scared was absurd. I was terrified beyond belief. I didn't want to get beaten. Not the way he'd made it sound.

Marko emerged with the belt and I slid closer into the middle, trying to get away from him. He dove forward, ripping me off the bed and pushing me to lean over the side before I could barely process what was happening. The first crack of the leather against my ass had me jumping and screaming against the fire lighting a path across me. Even with the pajama bottoms on, I'd felt its force. But it didn't buffer for the second. Marko yanked the material to my ankles and reared the belt back again. And again. I cried out, clutching to the comforter as he connected for the fourth time.

"You will get this every night until you learn to behave. I will not be embarrassed and I will not be disobeyed. Answer if you understand."

Whack!

"Yes," I sobbed, jumping again at the contact. "I understand." Fingers traced over the tender skin and even though it hurt, I couldn't deny that it also stirred some twisted sort of arousal deep within. With him touching me now, it only ignited it even more.

"Please." I shifted under his touch, well aware I wasn't wearing any panties. I didn't want him to discover what he was evoking even now as he grew closer to my pussy. Shame had the tears rolling free, but I made sure to hide the fact by holding in the sob that wanted to escape.

"No. You're going to feel and be quiet while you do so."

I buried my face deeply into the blanket, trying to disappear from the moment. How could I like this? How, after everything he'd done to me, did I want him to continue? I knew why. I was still praying the nicer Marko was somewhere deep within. The longer he was away, the more I feared what was to come. And still, even as I mourned for the life I had before Marko, my resolve against the entire situation was fading. I thought when he bit me the effects had been immediate. Now, I knew that wasn't the case.

Chapter 4
Marko

Heat warmed my skin and I suppressed the moan at what was before me. Spanking Tessa with the belt may have been to punish her, but I couldn't deny how much I enjoyed it. Seeing her pussy glisten from the wetness of what I'd done was only making it harder for me to stay angry.

Why the fuck had I tuned her out? If I had just dealt with what I was trying to escape, I would have known. I could have stopped her before Julius had to inform me of Tessa's betrayal in front of all the members. They laughed. They…thought it a hilarious that I couldn't even control a mere slave…and here I wanted to rule a city. Jesus, I could truly beat her for all the rage I felt in that moment. But here, now, I was finding it hard to keep that mindset when I was faced with something I'd yearned for from the moment I saw her in her bedroom. I wanted her. I wanted her so fucking much, I couldn't think about anything else.

"Please…don't." A sniffle followed the weak words and her emotions became mine. She didn't want me to stop. Well, she wanted *me* to, yet she didn't. She wanted the old me back and felt if we continued, he'd show himself. God, how wrong she was. Didn't she know he didn't exist anymore? Wouldn't, probably ever again.

"Spread your legs. Let me see what I've acquired by making you mine."

Her head shook even as she obeyed. I knew it was in part because of the order. She had to do it, whether she wanted to or not, but at this point, deep down, she was beginning to want to.

My hands lowered and I used the pads of my thumbs to rub over and spread her swollen folds. She was so hot and wet. So unbelievably soaked. I gritted my teeth to stop from rushing. I wanted to taste her, wanted to fuck her so fast and hard to punish her even more. Yet…I forced myself to go slow. To explore her pussy and take my time.

"You want me. Admit it right now. If you lie, I'll know, and I'll spank you again."

Her hesitation had my hand coming down over the welts and bruising already marring her skin.

"Ahh…I." Her hips arched and I spread her folds wider, moving my thumbs down past her opening, toward her clit. The small circles of pressure I added just outside of the sensitive bud made her pleasure quickly become my own. The more I evoked, the more I continued with my actions.

"Answer."

"I'm…not sure."

"Wrong." I spanked her again. "Tell me you're going to behave. That you're going to be an obedient slave and give me what I want."

Tessa's head lifted. She'd pushed the lust away to think over my question and I didn't like it.

"I don't know."

I dove forward, placing my palm against the side of her face so her head was back down and immobile. "You don't know whether you're going to behave and obey?"

Whack! Whack!

Her hips jerked underneath my hovering frame and she let out a sob, even as her head applied pressure against my hand.

"I don't want you to keep touching me. I've changed my mind."

"Your mind now belongs to me. And I say you're going to lie here and let me play with my pussy. Mine, Tessa. All mine. Even *that* doesn't belong to you anymore."

Whack!

My palm connected again and I moved to stand, forcing her legs wide to give me a better view. A groan poured through her mind and French filled my head as she turned her face more to where she could see me.

"Someday, I hope our roles are reversed. You will feel what it is to be powerless to me. No matter what it is concerning, your pleas of mercy will go unheard. I'm going to make you suffer and I'm going to enjoy every minute of it."

A small laugh left my lips while I circled her entrance. I knew she was referencing Julius' statement on her taking my place, but that was over now. She was a slave and always would be. *My* slave. "If it's like this right here, I do believe I might enjoy it. Just as you are."

"Asshole."

"Yes, I am that. Now, be quiet and let me revel in this."

Her face turned away and I felt the tension throughout her ease. The more I touched her pussy, the more she gave in. She did want this, regardless of her threats or words. I felt it. Knew where she was inside of her mind.

"What happened to the meeting? Don't you have to go back?"

The distraction had my palm slapping down on the other side of her ass and her words dying off with a small cry.

"Meetings don't take long. I know what I need to. We're expecting guests soon. *Le Circle* from further north. Dallas, to be exact. And you're going to be on your best behavior. That is, if I even let you out of our room."

I slid two of my fingers into her channel, feeling the wet warmth encircle me as I buried the length inside of her. Tessa rocked, stiffening when she seemed to catch herself. My eyes closed, soaking in how hot and tight she was. Although I knew I'd fucked her before, I couldn't really remember it. Blurry flashes were all I could make out and I felt the beast in me come alive at wanting to experience the real thing.

"Don't let me out. I don't want to meet them."

My teeth grinded while my lids lifted. I reached up, pulling her hair back and slamming my fingers into her hard as I began to thrust. "Do you not learn? I said to be quiet. Besides, the decision is mine. You should be proud to have me as your Master. Do you know who I am? Who I'm going to be?"

Tessa moaned as I increased the speed. Her pleasure was building by the second and she was fighting as best as she could. *"Of course I don't know, not that I think you really know who you are either."*

I snapped at her internal thoughts. "That's it."

I slipped free and ripped at my clothes, removing them. I was done with her attitude. Everything she said or thought pissed me off. All I wanted to do was enjoy her body and she had a way of making me continually question myself. I didn't like it.

"Remember what I said about that mouth? You're about to find out first-hand when to keep it closed."

I threw my pants across the room and lunged, grasping her arm as she tried to escape off the other side of the bed. The fear in her eyes only drove me on. I tuned in, reading her clearer than I ever had. Fighting me was her way of justifying what she knew she was giving into. *This version of me. This life.* But it didn't matter either way. Her thoughts poked at something within and I couldn't stand her screwing with my head. It was foggy enough—thoughts, actions. Since I'd taken her, I was having to focus twice as hard. It was just making the effects worse.

"Open." I pushed her down on all fours before my kneeling frame and locked my thumb and index finger on both sides of her face where her jaw hinged. She let out a sound as I forced her mouth open.

"Fight to breathe, if you must, but no more words will make it free. This, I assure you. If you fight, bite, nip, I'll make those spankings feel incomparable to what I do next. Now, gagging," a smile pulled at my mouth, "feel free to do as much of that as you'd like."

The hand I had on her face lowered and I grabbed my cock, tracing the tip around her now willfully separated lips. Her eyes stayed on mine and I saw the rebellious side of her shine through, but I also saw something more. Something I knew she harbored. She was a slave through and through. Human or not, she'd obey, and she'd do it because it was what she needed. And Marko…yes, she still longed to see him break through. She watched. Waited. And I knew she'd be disappointed.

"Wider."

The growled command sent her glaring even harder, but she did it.

I slid the head in and almost all of my tension eased as her tongue glided against the underside of my cock. The heat had my fingers tightening and I moaned as she added the slightest amount of suction. The intensity behind our connection left me breathless and I blocked out how my heart seemed to stop for the smallest moment. The vampire in me surged to the front and I jerked her head back even more as I pushed to the back of her throat. Her hands shot to my thighs and her nails dug in as I began to thrust, barely letting her catch her breath while I fucked her mouth.

Tears escaped and ran down the far sides of her cheeks as she fought the gagging. I couldn't stop myself from reaching forward and collecting the new tear so I could taste it. A large inhale filled the room as I pulled out to the edge of her lips, only to go even further.

"Ma minette, I do have to say, this may not be so bad. Silent. Obedient. Gagging on my cock." I bit my lip, slapping against her wet cheek as I kept my length buried in her throat. "Keep this up and I may let you live after all."

The hurt flashing in her eyes slit my heart clean open and I couldn't stand it. I knew she wanted her precious, sweet Marko, but I was here to show her that he wasn't coming back—ever.

"Fuck you."

My stare widened for the briefest moment and I tightened my jaw as I pulled her up and slammed her on her stomach.

"Couldn't resist the rebuke, could you? You want it, you got it."

"No!" Tessa thrashed wildly and I hated that when she lost her arousal, so did I.

She managed to somehow roll to her back and I wrestled to grasp her hands as she slammed them into my shoulders and chest.

"Promise me love, deliver me *death!* Do it. Say the word that kills me. Release me as your slave and stop the torment for us both. You don't want this, don't want me, and we both know it. Besides…I don't want you."

I froze on top of her, unable to stop the odd tightening in my stomach at her request. My lips separated and I searched my mind to end everything now. To put me out of the misery I felt I'd been through for longer than I could grasp. Slaves were easily obtainable. Why should I keep this one? Even as I thought it, the question was clear to me.

Wider, my mouth opened, and I shut it, swallowing hard. The smile that appeared on her lips had me even more confused.

"I knew it. You can't do it, can you?"

I tightened my hands on her wrists, cutting my stare down threateningly. "What I *can* do is make your life a living hell. You might want to take a minute to think about that."

Soft lips pressed into mine, so gentle, barely brushing against the surface. When she broke the kiss and stared up at me, I couldn't think to speak—couldn't react as my heart beat wildly in my chest.

"My Marko is still in there. I love you," she whispered. "A part of me really does."

Hungrily, my mouth found hers. Regardless of whether I felt she meant the declaration entirely, I couldn't think past it. Didn't want to face that she was once again lying, or choosing another side of me over who was actually before her now. I didn't care. She said she loved me. Had anyone ever told me that before? Did it matter? It was her, and somehow, that meant everything.

I rotated my hips, lifting just enough to ease the tip of my cock into her channel. The tightness had my lips breaking from hers so I could suck in air while I inched inside.

"Mon chaton, fuck, you feel so good."

"Marko." Tessa moaned deep in her throat, pulling her hands against my grasp. The moment I let go, they came to my back, the nails burying in as she urged me in further. And I gave it to her. I couldn't stop the silent request. My mind was getting fuzzy again and nothing mattered but her. What happened to making her pay? To teaching her a lesson?

"Look at me," she whispered, cupping my cheek. As my eyes searched hers, I pushed deeper, dying to get back and kiss her. She exhaled at whatever she saw and I felt my brows draw in as I slowed.

"Why are you sighing?"

Fingers traveled from my cheek to trace across my lips. "I feel you so strongly right now. Like the way things were before you changed. I feel your love.

And I feel mine returning so much so, nothing is beginning to matter but you. I should be scared that I'm vanishing. Terrified, even, but I feel no fear. Just my need of you." Tears welled in her eyes, but didn't spill over as she held my stare. "Please don't hurt me anymore. You've won. You have me. Now love me, too, with everything you have."

The room spun and I fought to get control over my pulse. It was going crazy in my chest and nothing I tried could stop the fireworks going off inside of me. My teeth nipped at the side of her hand as I searched for a response. The taste of her skin had my fangs lowering the smallest amount. Thought disappeared completely as she moved to run the pad of her finger over the sharp tip. The vampire within me reared to the front as she pushed up. Her essence exploded, sending sweetness coating my mouth. Slowly, she traced her blood over my lips, pulling my head down and licking it off. Light took over my vision, accompanied with flashes of the two of us that I couldn't quite make out. I blinked through the colors, slamming harder into her as she moaned.

"This is why I fell in love with you," I breathed against her lips. "This is the real you I'm meeting. I think I understand now."

Tessa blinked and her lips separated. At the surprise she wore, I felt myself slow, but I couldn't stop. "This isn't the real me, Marko. This is just your version of me. And you've never told me you love me. Not like…that."

All I could do was stare into her green depths. I couldn't very well tell her now. I didn't know her. The emotion was there, but I couldn't say the words. I didn't feel like it was my place.

My hand settled over her mouth and I rested my forehead against hers, closing my eyes as I tried to forget everything we just shared. My thrusts stayed steady and I tuned into what she was feeling as I built her back up. Flashes of the outside of her house projected before me from nowhere and I could see myself stalking back and forth in the backyard, staring at her window. Seeing her move through her routine. The obsession accompanying the vision was automatic and it engulfed me, effecting my movements, making it better for her.

Closer, I got to the glass, watching as she messed with something on the dresser. Even with the barrier between us, I could smell what I longed for. *Her.* Lavender and jasmine. Her blood…

My eyes flew open, disrupting the memory, and I growled as I rolled, pulling her on top of me. But I didn't let her lift up. My arms wouldn't let go as I held her to my chest and pushed into her pussy faster.

"Oh, God…Marko?" The rise in her tone brought me back to reality and I could feel her channel clenching around my cock. I didn't think. Couldn't, at the internal frenzy leaving me a mess.

My hand squeezed into her thigh while the other grabbed onto her bicep. I didn't wait to lift Tessa to sit on my face. I had to taste her. Taste every drop of what I'd done.

I sucked against her clit, quickly moving to thrust my tongue into her entrance. Although my hands gripped her hips, I didn't have to tell her to move against me. Tessa leaned forward, holding onto the headboard while she rotated. The screams were immediate. My claws came out as the first wave of her orgasm hit and I felt my eyes go wide.

I remembered this. Her flavor. *Her.* It was more than memories. It was so real, snapping my vampire into possessive mode.

A small cry followed the spasms as they ran their course and still, my tongue searched for more of what made her, her. Crimson raced down toward my face. I blinked past the shock that I'd broken the skin on her legs. My claws were still out—still ready for more.

Tessa tried to lift and I shook my head slowly, meeting her stare. I was gone, unable to break free from what I knew was mine. Even her blood didn't appeal as much as her cum in the moment and there was nothing that would stop me from having more.

"Your…eyes. Marko?" Her voice was deeper, huskier, as she watched me. The impatience was laced throughout, but I hardly noticed.

To answer would have taken me away from what I was doing. It was as if I were locked in place—there, but not—as I sucked against the top of her slit. I had to get her ready to come again. I had to...love her. Show her…

Chapter 5
Tessa

Brown, not black. Although I shouldn't have given in to either one, the small amount of love for the real Marko had gotten me to this point. Faith in finding *him* had me obeying when I wanted nothing less. Well, I'd wanted it, knowing it was wrong, but I couldn't help but think that my actions would trigger some sort of response. And it had. Not much, but something about what we were doing was working. I could feel my true Master lurking somewhere deep within and I wanted him back. If I had to be bonded to this vampire and stuck in this life, it had to be the original one I served.

Heat reignited in my core as his tongue swirled around my clit, never staying long from my entrance. I gripped the headboard tighter, moving just the slightest amount with the pleasure he was building all over again.

The stinging in my thighs was down to a dull throb, but I didn't care. It had been what triggered my orgasm to begin with, and in truth, I liked it more than I was ready to admit to myself.

"Tell me something," I breathed out. "Say anything."

Still, he remained quiet as he continued. I knew it was my Marko, but something was off. Desperation began to filter though as I tried to figure out how to keep him here.

"Please," I begged quietly. "Say something."

"Quiet." The vibrations of his order had my lids closing all the way and a sigh of frustration broke free. If I rebelled, I knew the new Marko would come back and I wasn't ready for that. Obey…yes, I had to.

I opened my eyes, connecting back with his as I let what he was doing come to the forefront. No more thinking. The best thing I could do was live in the moment. Take what I could from the real him. It was the only way I'd get even the smallest amount of peace in this existence.

"I love you," I whispered again.

The first time had been to gauge his reaction, to see if I could bring him back, and it had worked. Although my statement was genuine to a degree, I couldn't help but use it to try to pull him back to me. That had been the main thing he'd wanted to begin with—for me to love him. Now, here I was, telling him to his face and he was responding. I had to continue to say what I thought he believed.

"Do you love me?" I asked, moving against him faster as he circled around my clit. Tighter, I held the headboard as I waited.

Nothing. Just the brown eyes proving who he was.

"I know you love me. And someday, you'll tell me and we can be happy, like we were supposed to be."

He blinked rapidly and I bit my lip as heat built in my core. A moan poured from my mouth and I leaned more forward.

"It'll be just me and you, forever, like I know you wanted. You love me. Let me hear you say it." The last died off in a plea and there was no mistaking the way my voice cracked. I may have started this with other intentions, but the newly bonded slave secretly wanted to hear his admission. Something was happening to me, no matter how much I kept trying to push it away. Ever since Marko had bitten me, I slowly felt something different stirring deep within my mind. I was falling for him all over again, but this time, there'd be no going back. The small part of me that loved him had my mind not only facing the fact, but it was ready to grow and lock me into the realization. I'd be there forever. A lost slave in love with her Master, regardless of who she was before, or who she secretly wanted to be. What if I didn't have a voice when this was finished? Or a fight when I truly didn't want something? Would I know the difference, or would I be too much of a zombie?

Tear burned my eyes. I wanted the old Marko back before it happened, if that was the case. At least there was a chance that he'd treat me somewhat humane. At least he'd show me some sort of love. This new one wouldn't. He'd degrade me. Abuse me. He'd—

One minute, I was holding on, the next, I was on my back and Marko was inches from my face, baring his fangs.

"He'd what? What else were you going to say?" Black eyes flickered with anger and I felt my lips separate in fear from the aura he threw off. It left me shaking. I was faced with my biggest nightmare and I wasn't sure what to do.

"He'd…never be able to love me. Could you?"

His furrowed brow eased and slowly disappeared. I sucked in air as he thrust his cock back into me.

"You're a slave. Masters don't love slaves the way you speak of. We feed from them and fuck them. That's all you're good for, *mon chaton*."

Looking into the face of the man I was beginning to love, when it wasn't him behind the exterior, killed me. My body responded to his, but my mind didn't. At least…so far. Soon, I wasn't sure whether I'd have a conscious at all.

"Accept your place," he said, lowering to bury in my neck. "You're no one to me and never will be."

My shoulders jerked underneath him, but he slammed into me even harder. Lips kissed against my neck and I braced for what I knew was coming. Where he was brutal in his words and actions, the bite was gentle. I barely felt his fangs puncture my skin. Ecstasy triggered my orgasm and my channel clenched around his cock as my screams were pleasure filled. I couldn't stand it, even as I ate up the bliss with everything I had. But so did he. I felt his moans against me and basked in knowing that even with his hateful words, he couldn't deny how he softened when it came to my blood.

The thrusts slowed until I felt his cock swell inside of me. Intentionally, sadistically, I raked my nails down his back as hard as I could. The trigger was automatic. Warmth shooting into me had a moan escaping my lips no matter how hard I'd tried to hold it in. The last thing I wanted him to know was that I liked what we'd experienced, and now he'd think just that.

"Off," I snapped, already wiggling to disconnect us.

Weight shifted and I used my hands to force him over the rest of the way. Marko rolled to his back, laughing loudly as he pulled his pillow in behind his head.

"Never again," I said, sliding off the side of the bed. I headed for the restroom and surprisingly, he let me go. The door slammed behind me and I cursed the fact that there wasn't a lock. Not that it would have kept him out anyway. God, what was I doing? I'd found out what I wanted. My Marko was still there, but how was I going to get him back without resorting to fucking and falling in love with the other him? I just didn't know.

I turned the shower on, mindlessly losing myself in my thoughts as I cleaned up and tried to wash away any remnants of what was left behind. By the time I opened the door, Marko's light snores filled the room. The temptation to slam it again and wake him up pushed to the front, but I was over fighting. Maybe I'd wake up in the morning and the old Marko would return. Then, we could figure out what we were going to do about this war with Hunter.

My stomach turned and I walked over, grabbing my pillow. I'd seen an extra set of blankets at the top of his closet when I'd been looking for clothes. I took them down and got dressed, placing them on the floor. There was no way I was sleeping in the same bed with him.

As I pulled up the blanket, I let Hunter consume me. Not the part that longed for him. I couldn't go there; it would hurt way too much. My curiosity of an *us* was fading by the minute and I was losing all interest for anything that wasn't my Master. It killed me, but there was nothing I could do. What I focused on was what I saw of the upcoming war in Marko's memories. Hunter's appearance scared me. The dark clothing, the face paint. How had he gotten so bad? Did I have to ask? Was it just from not being able to help me, or was something else going to happen to destroy the loving, selfless man I'd known?

He'd been ready to die or kill in his state of mind. And from Marko's impression during the vision, Hunter might very well kill us all. Us…because I was one of them now. If my Master died, I very well would, too. I knew this. Not only from stabbing Marko and being so close to death, but because I could feel it. My life really was in Marko's hands and his survival meant my own. Suddenly, I didn't want to die. I meant what I'd said while he was fucking me. If the old Marko returned, I wanted to continue on and see what happened between us. I knew there could be love if we truly gave it a shot. Well, if *he* ever did. *Love.* Yes…the emotion was strengthening within me and I was starting to drown in it. Every second that went by made it grow. The bond had me and I was its prisoner. For life.

****

Knocking had me groaning as I turned and pulled the covers over my head. Shuffling sounded and I tried to push it away as I fought to get back to the dream of Marko I'd been having. He'd been telling me something, but even now, I couldn't remember. It was frustrating and I tried to block out the voices humming in the distance.

Darkness began to pull me back under and the weightlessness of unconsciousness beckoned. The nudge against my leg had my eyes flying back open and my body jolting from the surprising fear.

"What do you think you're doing sleeping down here? Get in bed."

I pulled the covers down to see my Master holding some sort of outfit against his side. My head shook and I brought the covers back up.

"That wasn't a request, ma minette. Ass in the bed."

A frustrated sound left me as I pushed to my feet and collapsed to the far side he'd left unoccupied. I didn't want to be in the bed with him, but his order was clear and the slave in me obeyed.

"Take off the clothes. You will not sleep wearing any. That is also an order, in case you missed that."

I didn't bother opening my eyes as I stripped off his big T-shirt.

"Do slaves usually sleep with their Masters?"

"This one does." The bed shifted and my body slid the distance that separated us as he climbed in and pulled me into his side, curling around me. The need to fight wasn't there. Sleep was already coming back, regardless of the closet light he'd left on, and something about the closeness made me feel protected when I should have feared it the most.

"Your dreams invade me. I can't sleep but off and on. I find it fascinating what runs through your mind when you're so deep under."

My eyes opened, but their weight left me fighting to stay awake. "What was I dreaming? Me and Marko…" I forced myself to glance back, "we were talking. What about?"

He laughed and I immediately frowned.

"You have such high hopes for a future between us. You do realize, with my status, I will have to take a concubine and probably find little use of you after that, right?"

My pulse spiked through the pain filling my heart. *Humans aren't concubine material.* How many times had I heard him think that?

"Will you release me then?"

"By death?" He snuggled in closer and all I could do was blink past the question. "I will not kill you, ma minette. I like having you to come back to. Besides, concubines are far from love matches. We'll feed from each other's power. That's it. It's a marriage of convenience, more than anything."

My mouth opened, only to shut.

"You want to know if we'll have sex. I'm sure we will. And maybe I'll even like her. Possibly fall in love. It's been known to happen at times."

"Can a bond be undone?"

Marko got quiet behind me. "I will not release you, Tessa. *Ever.*"

"But, can it be undone? I know Marie spoke of one being taken over before a bond was set into place, but ours is done. Can it still be erased?"

His arm settled between my breasts while he gripped my shoulder. "It can, but the vampire would have to be stronger than me. There's not very many of those, and let's face it, the chances of one strolling through and picking you out of everyone else is slim to none. They'll feel my attachment to you. Their request would be enough to kill over."

"But…if I found someone and they wanted me, would you let me go?"

I tried to turn to face him, but his grip tightened. I almost couldn't believe how compliant he was being to begin with. I hadn't expected that. Rage, yes. Punishment, possibly.

"No. You stay with me. Until death."

I wanted to fight, wanted to go at him with everything I had, but I didn't. The slave in me felt quite the opposite. She wanted to turn and thank him for not wanting to be separated. Fuck, had I fallen so far in only a few short hours of sleep? At his behavior, maybe we both had.

Chapter 6
Marko

I was weak. Even after all the hours of healing, I could still feel where the dagger had caused damage. The pressure around where the wound had been left a hollow feeling. Left me pissed, even more than I already was. And there was really no reason other than the change going on within me, but it was enough to have me snapping at Tessa for the second time in the last ten minutes.

"Hair out. I want it to show."

The silk hood that covered her head fell back at her push and she glared at my reflection as we stood in front of the mirror together. She hadn't spoken to me once since we woke up in each other's arms. I'd liked it, until I realized just how much.

"Here," I said, spinning her to face me. "It's not that hard to listen, yet you make everything impossible." I pulled her long hair from the back to the front, allowing it to cascade down her chest. A long curl fell over the member's brooch in the middle and I fixed it, feeling a smile pull at the corner of my lips. "There. Perfect."

I lifted my eyes, taking in the green silk before staring into her green depths. Her eyes were a darker color than what she was wearing, but it made them glow. She was beautiful, even more so than I could remember. I swallowed hard and she leaned forward, kissing me before she spun and padded out of the bathroom, barefoot.

I took in her ass, barely hidden from the black shorts. They'd turned more into panties, thanks to George, but I didn't care. I couldn't wait to show her off.

"Ma minette."

Tessa turned, silently looking at me as I tugged at the collar of my button-up shirt and came forward. "Best behavior. Obey every single thing I say. It doesn't matter what it is. Understood?"

"Of course, Master."

Distaste pulled at my lips, but she was right. I was her Master and addressing me as Marko couldn't happen in public anymore. How she knew that was beyond me.

"Follow behind and close. You will hold your head high even as you keep it down. You are of more worth than you know and you will act like it. You've probably seen that you're the only slave who will be at our table." I messed with her hair, keeping my attention off her face. "The concubines sit the closest at the table next to ours, but they don't join in our seating. When we get to our table, you sit only after I do. Unless I tell you otherwise. You are not to look around, especially toward them. It is an insult because even though you have status over the commoners, you will never hold their rank. Do not mess with your hands or fidget in any way. I need your obedience. We have a far ways to go, you and I, and if you want us to both find some form of peace in this arrangement, you'll be the epitome of elegance, grace, and…" I trailed off, meeting her eyes. I wasn't sure why I was rambling or where the nervousness was coming from. It wasn't her. She was as calm as could be. Something was off within me and I wasn't sure what it was. I wasn't acting at all like myself, but I knew it wasn't the old Marko either. "You know what I speak of. You know how important this is. You can feel it here," I said, resting my hand over the member brooch.

"I will make you proud," she said quietly. "*And when you get a concubine of your own, you will release me. Others will see I'm a good fit.*"

Once again, her thought threw me. How in the hell had she accepted this life so soon?

My jaw tightened and I stopped myself from throwing her over the bed and lighting into her ass. No matter what she thought, I'd never give her up. I couldn't even grasp why she'd think I'd even want to. But I couldn't worry about that now. I had enough on my mind. Like appearances. My chair would lift tonight and I'd move up in seating. How far, was what concerned me the most. Just how powerful was I becoming compared to the rest?

"Let's go," I ground out.

I adjusted my jacket and opened the door, waltzing through. I tuned into ma minette's presence and slowed my pace until I felt her right behind me. The large tables were already occupied and I caught Marie's stare for the briefest moment before I focused in on Julius and two other higher ranking members already standing in their places. Standing, because we wouldn't sit until I was seated, according to Julius' decision.

"*Stay behind me while we wait.*"

Tessa remained quiet while we came to stand behind the tenth chair. Julius' eyes found mine and I noticed his were slightly narrowed as he took me in. Fear or anxiety was no more. I wouldn't let my nerves get the best of me. I was meant for this part. To thrive in power. Nothing and no one would get in my way and I'd continue to prove that as I made my way to the top.

Three members exited the far tunnel in the back, where the strongest of the Masters were held. I'd be moving there now. I could feel it as I took in their uneasiness. The vampire within flared, causing my power to surge throughout my stomach and chest. To tap into what I held would have been heaven, but I wasn't there yet. Wouldn't be until Julius felt for himself. Which he had every intention of doing shortly.

Valencia and Beatrice took their positions, as did Demetrius. John and Zachariah followed shortly behind. Their heads stayed down as they took their positions.

"We all know Marko has been reborn. His powers grow and there's to be a change in seating. First." He held out his hand. I removed my jacket and walked forward, forcing my energy back on Tessa so she'd know not to leave my chair. As I took off the cufflink and rolled up my sleeve, I held my head high. Julius' nails extended and I stopped, lifting my arm.

The cut was deep and fast. I remained transfixed to his stare as his lips connected with my skin. The slight widening of his eyes was followed by his head tilting the smallest amount.

"Interesting." He licked over the wound, sealing it shut. I stepped back, fixing my cufflink back into place. "Take Demetrius' place for now. Your power comes in faster than I expected. You'll change again in the next few days. We'll monitor you at each meal time."

I held in the smile. Number seven, and I wasn't done. Not even close, I could feel it.

The shift in seating was followed by Tessa coming to stand behind me once again. Julius took his chair first and the rest of us followed. Ma minette was all grace as she lowered to kneel at the side of my chair. Two nude suppliers were already sprawled out on the table, the soles of their feet touching. And suddenly, my mind sputtered. Thigh. My feeding position had gone from neck to thigh.

I lifted my gaze to the blonde resting on the table before me. Her body was curvy, her face, attractive…yet, I couldn't imagine feeding from her. And especially her inner thigh.

Fuck. At the jump of my pulse, I pushed the thought away. I'd *have* to feed from her. I was not weak for my slave, and no one at this table would think I was. Not for a second.

The gesture was given by our leader to begin feeding, but he didn't move. He waited, watching…me. I knew I had all rights to feed from Tessa here, but I couldn't if I wanted to stay in control and show them I was meant to rule.

My hand settled on the woman's ankle and her thighs spread wider. She already knew the routine. Beatrice moved in, already taking her position, as did everyone else—everyone but Julius and me.

"Marko, send me your slave."

I stopped my slow advance and turned to our leader. Possessiveness flared, causing me to tense. Tessa didn't move, but I could feel her anxiety. We both knew what Julius' intentions were and although I could deny him, I wouldn't.

"Go." My voice was stern as she glanced up and met me with fearful eyes. She didn't want to go to him. Didn't want to leave my side. And fuck if I wanted her to. She was *my* slave. *"Go, ma minette. Now."*

Tessa stood, keeping her head down as she walked to Julius. I could feel the eyes of the community on her while she made her way to his chair. There wasn't a moment of hesitation on Julius' part as he wrapped his arm around her waist and pulled her into his lap. Her hood fell back and the glance into his face was enough. My mind fizzled out and I lost our connection as he kept her eye contact. Words poured from his mouth, but I couldn't hear them. No one would have been able to. He had her in his own protective bubble and he could do whatever he wanted to her. No one would have been able to stop it—especially not me.

Sickening churned in my stomach as his lips drew even closer to her. My nails extended while I breathed through the rage pushing its way through. Feeding became nonexistent. I couldn't do anything but watch every move he made toward my slave.

Slowly, he brushed the hair from her neck and traced his fingers over her throat. Her lids drew down lower and burning filled my throat as I watched Julius move in and sink his fangs into the one spot only mine should ever breach.

Tessa's body jolted and then melted into his chest as he cradled her close. I could see his eyes flickering through different emotions. The fascination he had with my slave's blood was something I didn't like. Something…I feared. What were his reasons? What was he trying to see or discover?

A small cry came from the supplier and it pulled me from the murderous frenzy taking me over. My grip disconnected from her ankle—she was lucky I hadn't crushed the bone. To sit still was taking everything I had. My minette was gone from me completely in the moment and I couldn't stop the mourning tugging at my heart. How, in one day, did I go from not liking her, to feeling my old self's emotions of love? It wasn't full blown yet, but I knew if I kept Tessa with me for a long enough period, she'd win this new version over, just as she did the last. She was mine, no matter the mindset, and no matter how much I wanted to push her away. I wasn't sure it would work in the end. I wasn't even sure I wanted to keep her at a distance, even though I knew I should.

Minutes stretched out and even though Julius finished, he still kept the two of them isolated as he continued to speak with her. His eyes came to me at random moments, but barely. Whatever they were conversing about, it was in-depth enough to steal his attention.

I leaned back in the chair, crossing my arms over my chest. I didn't miss Beatrice's raised eyebrow. She was surprised by my lack of feeding, but I didn't care what she thought at the moment. I only had hunger for one and now I'd miss feeding from her too because of Julius. He'd taken enough blood from her that I'd have to wait a few hours before I could take more.

"Are you going to let the Black Prince feed from your slave, too?"

A warning came from my throat as I scowled at Beatrice. "Sayer will not touch my slave. He is not my leader."

"We'll see when the time comes." The vampire's attention stayed on me, but I went back to Julius as he sat Tessa up higher on his lap. Her lids were still heavy and I could tell she was barely able to stay upright. My teeth slammed shut at how much he'd taken from her. She still wasn't all the way healed from our incident and I'd bled her out enough last night. Now this? She'd be out of commission for at least two days. Unless…my cock hardened instantly.

I shifted in my chair, noticing vampires were already leaving the area. While I waited for Julius to finish, I forced myself to focus on the pairs, taking in every little gesture they made regarding their slaves. A frown came to my face and I could see their longing. They didn't like not feeding or being close to what was theirs any more than I did. Why had I not noticed this before?

Tessa's voice broke through in agreement to something and my head jerked around. She stood with Julius' help and her face lowered as she tried to walk. I pushed from the chair, catching her as she started to fall after only a few steps. Her weight wasn't even felt as I glared toward my leader. The smile on his face was enough to stir the evil within me and I tore my gaze from his before I got out of hand.

"Let's get you to bed." Without concern as to what the community would think, I swept her into my arms and walked at a fast pace toward my room. The moment my door shut, she sobbed, burying her face in my chest.

"I'm sorry. I tried to walk."

Confusion had my eyebrows drawing in as I lowered her to the comforter. "Shh. It's not your fault." I removed my jacket, pulling the buttons of my shirt free in my haste to take it off. My heart was racing and I swallowed hard as I let my nail lengthen. When our eyes met, my pulse spiked harder than I could ever remember. The cut on my forearm felt like nothing due to my impatience. "Drink."

One word, and she didn't hesitate to grab hold of me. Her head lifted and my eyes rolled back as her lips settled over the wound and suction pulled against me. *Thump-thump. Thump-thump. One. We were one.*

The thought stirred something, but I was so lost in the moment, I didn't care to tap into it. Our moans were followed by her tightening her fingers. I could feel her strength already starting to return. My eyes opened and I was in no hurry to stop her from continuing. There was something about her taking my blood that just did it for me. Maybe because she was a human and there was something forbidden and taboo in that aspect. Regardless, I let her continue until she broke away, gasping.

"Thank you," she breathed out. "That's much better."

"I didn't do it for you. I did it for *me*. I need to feed later, too, you know."

My eyes blinked, and even as I spoke to her harshly, I knew it wasn't me speaking the words. Pain washed over her face and I felt myself push from the bed, walking away. Silence settled between us and I headed to the closet in a daze, taking off the suit and exchanging for a pair of pajama bottoms and a T-shirt. I wasn't in the mood to do anything but lay in bed and stare at my slave. Maybe hold her while I contemplated what I'd do concerning Hunter. Just the name had my fangs coming down and me fading out even more. Deep within, I knew I needed to get rid of him fast, before he did something stupid. Something like in Marie's vision. Keeping Tessa safe was my last thought before the darkness in me once again took over. I was gone.

Chapter 7
Hunter

Underground city. Tessa had mentioned it and I knew one existed, but the question was…where? Just underneath? If I went outside and opened a manhole, would I find it? I didn't think it was so easy, and even if it were, what did I do once I was there? I may have been gung-ho about killing vampires, but I wasn't stupid enough to think I could take on a city of those monsters by myself. I'd need help. I'd need…

Shavings of wood fell to the floor as I finished off another stake and placed it in the Tupperware of holy water. On Tessa's table, to be exact. Leaving was impossible. I couldn't very well just disappear and carry on if there was a chance she'd come back. Marko could get to me if he wanted, but I didn't see him returning. He'd think me long gone, if he even cared. He had her now. He had the woman I loved, so why would he return?

Aching filled my chest as I thought over the hell that filled the last few days. Was Tessa dead now? I couldn't believe that. He said they were bonded. Did that mean she'd live past this? And what if I did kill him? Was he telling the truth when he said if he died, she would, too? It was a sickening thought. The last thing I wanted was to kill the woman I loved. It was the opposite of what I was trying to accomplish. My heart beat for only her and I was willing to do anything I could to get her back.

I pushed from the chair, pacing the length of the kitchen and small dining room area. There were too many questions and each one brought me further into the darkness I tried every day to escape. Reconnecting with old friends was great, but I'd held on to one dream. One that was now in the gutter thanks to that blood-sucking bastard. I had to get Tessa back. Had to make him disappear so she and I could move on with our lives. Hopefully, in the direction I wanted, but if not, as long as she was free from him, that would work, too. I just wanted her happy by her own free will, and until she was separated from Marko, she'd never have that.

Duty. I'd always felt a sense of it toward her. Time hadn't changed that, and wouldn't. I'd grown up believing the two of us would be together someday. Even when I enlisted in the military and we weren't talking, the thought never wavered. My distance was meant to help her heal and get past the shock of us losing our virginity to each other the way we had. God, I'd been so fucking stupid back then. So…impatient. I'd hurt her, and if she knew how deeply I regretted that, maybe she would have…fuck, maybe nothing. But she'd never know if I didn't figure out a way to find and get her back.

My phone sat on the table next to the stakes I wasn't even sure would work. It brought my attention back to the dagger my uncle had blessed. With the blood on the mattress, I wasn't sure if it came from an injury or him forcing more down her throat. I didn't see anything wrong with him physically, but then again, I didn't doubt he'd already healed. What had happened before I'd gotten there? It left me even more anxious.

I snatched my cell and pressed Tom's number. My plea for Tessa was running through the church like wildfire. If someone ran into her, they were supposed to call me. If I couldn't be reached, they were to call Tom. Although my phone hadn't rung, I couldn't resist seeing whether he'd heard anything.

"Hunter, how are you?"

My head shook at the greeting, even though my tone didn't reflect my sour mood. "I'm doing great. Any news?"

"Nope. Not a word. Nothing on your end?"

"No." I paced, walking to the front window and pulling back the blind to glance out. "Sorry to bother you, I just thought I'd check real quick."

What sounded like a door shut in the background. I stepped back, impatiently heading back to the kitchen.

"No problem. Feel free to call at any time. But if I hear something, I'll let you know right away."

"Thanks. I'll let you go. You take care."

"You, too."

A sigh left my mouth and I pushed the button, ending the call. Aching filled my chest. It hurt not hearing any news. Was she okay? Was she trying to escape or find someone to help her? Was she dead?

Again, my eyes went to the dagger. Dried blood covered the blade, but that could have been from anything. Marko could have used it to cut himself to force-feed Tessa for all I knew.

Slowly, I reached forward, picking it up.

She'd brought it to my uncle with every intention to end the vampire's life. That told me she didn't want what she'd been kidnapped into. So what the fuck was I doing here? What was I waiting on?

My stare drifted down to the black gear I wore. Maybe I knew this was what was going to happen even before I had gotten dressed. Duty. Love. There was no avoiding it. No putting it off.

I tucked the dagger in my belt and grabbed a gun, placing it in my holster and shoving another at the small of my back. The large knife fastened at my side could possibly do damage too, I just had to remember the most important part—no eye contact. After the church incident with Marko, I knew how easy it was to lose in their game. Marko could have killed me then, when he hypnotized me, but he didn't. I was lucky. But I'd be even luckier the next time we met. This time, he wouldn't come out unscathed.

A slight shake of adrenaline left my hands fumbling as I checked my flashlight. Nothing scared me, but going against the undead sure as hell did. Anyone would be stupid to think this mission wasn't suicide. They were too strong—mentally and physically. No wonder they had us under their thumbs. If we didn't stand together and do something about them, it wouldn't be long before we were all turned into Tessa. *Food.*

I walked out the front door, closing it behind me. The sun wasn't far from setting and my heart raced even faster. I should have done this earlier, or prolong it until tomorrow morning, but I couldn't. My feet were already walking in the direction I'd seen Tessa and Marko head toward too many times to count. If only

I'd seen where they were going. They never made it past Tessa's yard before they disappeared into thin air.

I kept a fast pace as I headed down the sidewalk. Only half a block went by before I had the option to turn left or right. A field stood ahead and the slight hill was devoid of any trees or shelters. Just tall grass.

I spun in a circle and licked my lips. Dammit, I had no idea what I was doing. A drain rested along the curb and I bent down to look inside. I sure as hell wouldn't fit though that. For some reason, I crossed the street, collapsing on the curb bordering the field. Did they turn left or right? Both just led to more residential streets. Surely he didn't stay in a house around here?

Mindlessly, I shook my head and stopped as something had me turning to look off to the side. A grate sat a few feet back. The bent bars had me slowly coming to my feet. There was blood smeared on the edge and I…knew. My breath caught and I hesitated for only a moment before I reached forward and yanked it free. The sun was getting lower and I scanned the area, not seeing anyone in the distance. Did I do this? Go below ground where lord only knew how many vampires were waiting to make me their meal?

Tessa. God, I had to. She was down there and she needed my help, whether she thought so or not. I knew she had ties to Marko, but I couldn't ignore her own internal need to kill him. He was evil. They all were and they needed to be stopped.

The ladder leading down drew me forward and I cautiously lowered, placing the grate sideways over the top. For the life of me, I couldn't shut myself in with them. It wouldn't be for long. Just enough time for me to explore and see if I ran across anything. My gut told me I would. To not listen to it could be the death of me. My instincts had saved my life more than once and tonight, I'd rely solely on what they told me to do.

Pitch black rested ahead and I pulled out my flashlight, already feeling sweat surfacing on my skin. The beam revealed a cement tunnel a good ten feet tall. I stayed in the middle as I moved forward as quietly as I could. Elevation appeared in spots and I could tell from the last small rise that it was dropping. I was headed deeper into the earth. Entrances opened up to the side of me and I shined the light, seeing it led further back to more locations, but I kept straight.

Minutes went by and the tunnel ended, only to break off. Left or right? Darkness was prevalent in both directions and I wasn't sure whether I should go any further. If I got lost in here, it would take me forever to find my way out. *If* I found an opening at all. I might die from a vampire attack before then.

A sigh left my lips and I pulled at the collar of the long-sleeve black shirt. Something sounded in the distance and my hand went for my gun, changing at the last minute to grab the handle of the dagger. A rat ran across the light and I shook my head.

"Fucking shit."

My fingers fumbled with the compartments in my belt and I opened a pocket, pulling out a small piece of chalk. Not once had I thought I'd need to use it, but now I was glad I'd taken my friend's advice so long ago and kept it with me. He'd used it plenty of times in the mountains of Afghanistan and it had worked.

Trembling had taken over my hands and I crouched, drawing a line at the bottom of the angled paths. As I stood and replaced the chalk, I looked both ways again. More sounds tapped in the distance and I turned left, heading in the direction. If someone was there, I'd face them head on before I let anyone sneak in behind my back.

With each step, my pulse increased, and I couldn't ignore how my body positively hummed down here. Tuning fork. Yes, Tessa had nailed the description when she'd explained it to me. There was something down here; I could feel it down into my very bones.

A curve rounded me more to the right and I clicked the flashlight off as voices in the far distance forced my feet to stop. It didn't seem to be coming toward me, just more…staying stationary. Quietly, I inched forward to hear more of what they were talking about.

"You wish. You lucked out, dumbass. Taking Master Delacroix's slave to her home so you could feed from her. You're an idiot, Boyd."

Laughter from multiple males brought me closer. *Delacroix*…Marko. They had to be talking about Tessa. Had she tried to come home and I missed my opportunity to try to save her? My gut clenched.

"Shut the fuck up. She said he was in a meeting. The last thing I expected was for him and Julius to show up."

"And he knew," someone piped in. "You know, Julius saw your intentions. I'm surprised he allowed you to run off like you did. You'd surely be dead meat or in lockdown if Master Delacroix had his way. He's already watching you like a hawk."

A growl sounded and I kept my hand on the dagger as they continued.

"I can't fucking help myself when I'm around her. Her blood. God dammit. It just…drives me insane. Even with her bond, I still feel compelled to taste her. It's like heroin to me. I just…Jesus, why don't any of you feel it?"

A moment went by before someone new spoke up. "I do, I'm just not an idiot like you. I hear she has kin within the community."

"She's not a vampire, stupid ass." *Boyd?* Had that been his name. It was definitely his voice responding.

"She doesn't have to be one of us. Vampires were human, once upon a time. Sometimes, the lines cross, become one—the *purest* line. Did it escape your notice we have visitors coming? One of them may very well have one of those lines."

"The Black Prince," Boyd said, lowly. "It has to be. Fucking Christ. With someone that powerful, it would make perfect sense why we're all attracted to her. She'd hold power, even as a human, yet she'd have no idea. God, can you imagine if she were turned. She'd be—"

"Unstoppable," someone said, cutting in.

A few sounds of agreement echoed and I brought my fist to my mouth. My Tessa coming from a line of vampires? No way. That couldn't be true. If they made her one of them…

Nausea had me closing my eyes.

"Master Delacroix won't turn her," someone said, breaking the silence. "Do you see how he protects her? His bond runs deep. He'd lose her if that were the case and he won't do it. I'm telling you. He's like…obsessed. He scares the shit out of me. If I were you, Boyd, I'd stay as far away from her as you can. It's not worth it, man. If you so much as place a fang in her…he'd rip the motherfucker clean out of your mouth. You'd be lucky to have a jaw left—period—by the time he got done with you."

"I'm not afraid of him. My powers are increasing by the day. You watch, in another half century or so, I'll be a member, and when I am, I'll move up like him. I'll be more powerful, too."

"Moron," someone said, lowly. "You're powerful, yes, but nowhere near member-worthy, and you probably never will be. It takes special blood. The right mix to grant a vampire that much power. You're a mutt. You come from a peddling vagabond. You're not nobility like he was, Boyd. Face it. They're all royalty and we're the peasants just trying to survive. We serve them. End of story."

"Fuck you. It doesn't matter who he was before he was turned. He just lucked out in that department. You'll see, I'll be a member someday, and when I am, I'll remember this conversation."

Feet began to shuffle and I eased back, still crouched.

"Time to feed. They're already seating and I'm not being late this time. Our leader has eyes over all of us and I'm not pissing him off."

"Ooh, do you think Julius will feed from Master Delacroix's slave again? Did you see Marko? I thought he was going to attack Julius."

The voices grew quieter as they moved farther away. I longed to hear more, but knew I shouldn't risk it.

"What I'm more interested in is to see if Julius offers his slave to the Black Prince. Now, that will be interesting."

I stopped my slow steps, realizing they were going too fast for me to keep up. Black Prince, slaves, Masters…my mind was having one hell of a time trying to wrap itself around all the terms. What I hated the most was having Tessa involved in any of it. I had to get out of here and come up with a real plan. I knew where they were now. I'd come back and next time, I'd be better prepared. Preferably with back up. It was time I reached out to my friends. If we could pick off a few at a time, we'd make progress. It was a start, and I was more than happy to finally begin.

Chapter 8
Tessa

Whack!

Blood filled my mouth as my vision blurred to the side. The black velvet settee wavered before me and I knew one more hit would do me in. The whole left side of my face throbbed and my eye was swelling shut.

"Did you not think I wouldn't know? That the news wouldn't get back to me?" The deep voice had me turning from the antique furniture to face a man with olive skin and black hair. His clothes were dated. Historic. Edwardian period, but I wasn't sure. French filled my ears as he continued and I knew he was my father, but I held no love for him. The hate festering inside left my blood boiling to degrees I'd never experienced before.

"You will go back to Pierre-Louis' home and you will ask for his daughter's hand. You will not ruin her reputation. My reputation!"

I stood straighter as I wiped the blood from my mouth. Fear was non-existent, only rebellion.

"I will not. She came to me. It was she who threw herself into my arms when I told her no."

Whack!

An explosion of lights registered and my knees hit the floor hard. A groan came from my mouth as I pushed back to stand. The moment my shaky legs managed my weight, I was hit again. My arm took the impact of my weight as I ended up back on the floor. I clenched my teeth against the soreness of past beatings—ones I somehow knew hadn't happened that long ago.

"I don't care who did what. You were spotted together by their staff. The damage you've already caused by not asking is done. You will go back and you will offer a proposal of marriage or you can leave my home and never return. Your choice."

My mother's soft cries had me looking toward the doorway. She stood there, wringing her hands in her long, silk gown as her lips quivered. I knew she wanted to speak out. I also knew she wouldn't.

I forced myself to my feet and swayed as I brought my attention back to my father. He was ready, waiting for me to give him a reason to hit me again. And what wanted to leave my lips would surely do just that. But I stood taller for my mother and accepted what I knew I didn't want. "I bid you a goodnight. I'll head to Chateau de Petit now."

"As you should," he bit out. "Now, get out of my sight and don't return until you make amends and fix this."

A nod was the only reply I could give as I turned and headed for the door. The moment I left my father's study, I let the anger fill me.

"Get my horse ready," I snapped to Francois, the butler, and continued up the grand stairway to my room. The reflection staring back at me was one I didn't recognize, but had seen before. Swelling was prevalent around my eye and bruising

was already setting in. And my father wanted me to appear before them this way?
God, I fucking hated him. They'd know. Everyone knew.

I poured water into the basin, washing the blood smeared across my chin.
The need to run, to say to hell with being the Duke was right there. Duc de
Delacroix. I didn't want it. Didn't want this life—especially with that conniving
bitch, Adelais, as my Duchess.

A sharp pain had me wincing as I patted my face dry. The ride was another
few hours. I'd be lucky to make it by sunset. Dammit, I didn't want to go back.

Knocking had me heading for my door. Where I expected my mother, I was
surprised to see my father standing before me instead. Apparently, he wasn't done.

I took a step back, watching the colors fade out as he rushed forward with
the intent to hurt me even more.

Just as the man I knew to be Marko's father got to me, my body jolted
awake in a mass of deep inhales. Sweat drenched the sheet wrapped around me,
trapping my arms from being able to move. From…defending myself. I cried out,
thrashing, as a hand clutched my shoulder.

"What do you think you're doing?" The roar of Marko's voice had my head
snapping in his direction and I could see his own fear. He was soaked in sweat, too,
and there was a paleness to his already fair skin. Tears blinded me as I ached for
what he'd been through. But I knew it hadn't just been a simple beating he'd gotten
from his father. Something told me things had gotten worse. So much worse. And I
wasn't sure it had been in his father's favor.

"I'm sorry. I didn't mean to. I…" Scratchiness had taken over my words and
the sobs filling me left them almost unrecognizable. I felt as if I'd betrayed my
Master. As if I'd somehow spied on his most secret moments. It left me torn to
reach out to try to comfort him or hide from the wrath I was sure to come.

Marko's hand reached for his chest as his eyes searched the room. I knew he
was deep in thought. He didn't remember that moment. Somehow, I knew that. At
least, he hadn't since he'd been reborn. But I'd brought it back, and the anger
starting to mask his face made me wish I hadn't.

"He deserved to die. I'd kill him again. I should have killed them all."

The covers flew back as he strode across the room, nude. The slam of the
bathroom door left me jumping at the impact. If I could have fled, I would have, but
I knew it was pointless. I was going to have to face his rage when he returned and it
was something I didn't want to have to do. Even bonded, even…obedient, the
longing to go home was still nestled deep within me. It was always fluttering
around, but never within reach for me to grasp.

The shower sounded and I eased from the bed, rushing to the closet to dress.
Only a few outfits had come in so far and I was left grabbing the first one I could
get my hands on. A deep wine colored, long-sleeved dress that was tight at the top,
baring my shoulders, but flowed loosely around my legs. It was too formal in my
opinion, but everything that rested on hangers was. By the time I got it on and fixed
my hair using the vanity the suppliers had delivered, the shower ended. I kneeled at
the foot of the bed, patiently waiting to brush my teeth. I didn't have to wait long.
The door swung back open and Marko's feet came to stand before me.

"Such a good little slave. You may go now. Then, you'll face me."

I knew he'd been reading my mind, probably had been the whole time he had been gone. It drove me to my feet, rushing into the restroom. Even as I prolonged the confrontation, I knew it wasn't worth it. When I headed back into the bedroom, Marko was already dressed and sitting on the edge of the bed, placing on a cufflink. His dark eyes rose to mine, but didn't appear as black as they usually did. It made me feel braver as I went into position before him.

"Your dreams may end up getting you into trouble, ma minette. Whether you know this or not, what you did was intentional in your mind. You subconsciously sought out my past and found a piece of it. I suggest you not do it again. I'm aware you saw things when I placed the final bond on you that night in your room. I saw them, too, even if I don't remember the details of them yet. But we will never speak of what we saw. *Ever.* Do you understand?"

Flashes of the massive, gruesome killings during his newborn years assaulted me, as did the plans Julius had discussed with the members on what was to come. So many things filtered though and I tried to block them out as I nodded my head. Marko held secrets, ones that went against our leader, and we couldn't risk them becoming exposed. "Yes, Master. But..." The assertion came and I couldn't deny I was dying to learn more. I was quickly realizing that although I'd seen visions of his past, I hadn't seen everything. Not even close. And I wanted to know who he was.

"You're in awe of my status." Marko turned away from me, grabbing his suit jacket and sliding it on. "It was not everything it was cracked to be, Tessa. It was a curse."

"Which one is worse, the one of your past or the one you're living now?"

Black eyes snapped over to me. I couldn't help but lower my head at his anger.

"I'm sorry, Master. That was out of line." Cautiously, my head lifted. "How long were you Duke before...?" The question was one of many bombarding me all at once. Did he marry the girl who'd thrown herself at him? What happened after he killed his father?

"Ma minette, enough. I said we weren't talking about it. Besides," his head shook, "the details are not all there and I don't want them to be. Forget my past. I have."

A frown came to my face and I folded my hands in my lap, staring down. Had the woman been beautiful? Surely, he would have married her. Even if his father had been killed by him, Marko still would have had to go about his duties. And if he did marry her, did they have kids? What kind of father would he have been? Surely, better than his own.

"In the corner!"

My bicep was grasped and I was ripped up. Fire flared over my ass at the spanking and Marko pushed me into the corner, adding pressure to my shoulder to make me kneel. His offence at my thoughts left my head spinning.

"Until you learn to listen, you'll stay. Now, stop thinking about me and worry about yourself. You're on the verge of being in a lot of trouble if you continue."

"They're just questions. Ones I have a right to know."

My head was pushed harder into the corner as he crouched behind me, moving in next to my ear, "You *have* no rights, slave. The sooner you get that through your thick skull, the better. Silence, manners, obedience, your blood, and your body. Those are what I want from you. Nothing more. Not your love, not your compassion, and most of all, not your pity or concern."

"I don't pity you," I said quietly. "I just care for you. There's a big difference. My questions are nothing more than a way I wish to grow closer to you. But you're right, I shouldn't bother. After all, I'm no one. Not your concubine, that's for sure. I doubt you'd treat her this way."

A growl sounded behind me and I gritted my teeth as I waited for the punishment I feared would come. I didn't have to wait long. Marko grabbed my hair, turning me to face him. Lips crushed into mine harshly and I cried out at the cut sending blood to wash over my tongue.

"Maybe you won't have to wait long to find out."

My breath caught and I jerked from his hold, turning back toward the corner. Anger had tears burning my eyes and I could feel myself shaking from how badly his declaration affected me. *I bet my next Master will treat me better than you. In fact, I know he will.*

"Wench!" Marko gave my head another push as he stood. Cement connected with my forehead and I made a frustrated sound as I slammed the side of my fist into the wall. But I didn't move, didn't stand and face him like I wanted to. Even as I felt the harsh feelings toward him diminish, my own declaration sounded in my head. Someday, I'd make him pay. Someday, our positions would be reversed.

Chapter 9
Marko

Another Master better than me? Tessa had no idea how good she had it. And bringing my future concubine into it? Any other Master would have beat her for the word even leaving her mouth. *Better* than me…? I wanted to laugh. The stubborn woman just didn't get it. Hell, she probably never would and I'd be forced to listen to this forever. No. It would get worse when I did find a partner. Dammit. I wasn't looking forward to that either.

"Wench…no…more like witch! You probably trapped me into this bonding. Put some sort of spell on me and I just can't remember you doing it."

"How *dare* you!"

Tessa spun around to face me and I lurched forward. The action had her quickly turning back around and sinking to her knees to face the corner, but I didn't stop my advance. I lowered, returning to the side of her face, trying to ignore the way her new soap left me softening. *Her.* Yes, I'd finally gotten to have her the way I wanted and every small whiff of her essence had me going crazy to have her again.

"You get up one more time and I get the belt."

Frustration emanated from Tessa in a thick aura of pressure and I knew from the vibes she threw off she was past the point of being merely angry. Ma minette was downright fuming and for some reason, it made me happy. I didn't understand it any more than I understood her or the bond we shared.

"I hate how much I love you."

I smiled, nuzzling behind her ear. "No, you love how much you hate me. You love this right here, whether you want to admit it or not."

"Wrong," she snapped. "If you only gave me the chance, I'd show you what real love was. This," she said, facing me, "this is not the best conditions to make me love you. A slave I can be. Kneeling before you would give me pride, but the verbal and physical abuse will not get you my entire heart. Don't you want me to love you? I thought…" her head rested against the cement wall as she stared at it in a daze. "Marko wanted me to love him. Maybe it was my definition I clung to and he saw something entirely different. I don't know."

"He *is* me, ma minette. Stop talking about me as if we are two different people. And I've already told you what I want. Love is not something I need from you."

"Lie," she whispered, facing the wall. "That's the only thing you wanted from me. That, and my blood. You have my blood at your disposal. My love, you will never truly have. Not like this."

I slid my hand over her bare shoulder, trying to ignore the way her words messed with my head. As my body moved in and molded behind hers, Tessa stiffened, but didn't try to stop me from getting closer.

"But you do love me. And I'm going to show you just how much." I eased us to stand, still staying behind her with my arms over her shoulders. I let her watch as I placed a cut between my thumb and index finger. "You're going to drink and you're going to have so much love for me, you're not going to know what to do with it. Artificial, real, it makes no difference. Love is love and I have yours."

Tessa dipped down to slip under my arms but I had her slammed down on the mattress before she could escape. Even as I forced her jaw open and thrust my wound to bleed into her mouth, my mind exploded with only one question. *What the fuck was I doing?* I didn't know. This wasn't me. It couldn't be.

"It's not real," she mumbled against my hand as I applied pressure to keep it in place. The words were muffled, but I heard her thoughts loud and clear. I knew the truth and I couldn't stand it. Her love wasn't mine. Not the real version. Hunter had more than I did. The truth was written in her eyes when she came down from the drugging of my blood. I saw it so clearly. Could feel it in my own thoughts. It was driving me crazy. Blood. I'd have to keep her under. Have to make her love me all the time. Or, at least, until she fell in love with *me*. That was bound to happen...wasn't it?

"Drink!" I cut the top edge of my hand more, trying to ignore how the truth was getting to me. *Hunter.* I had to wipe out not only him, but the hold he had on her subconscious. And her heart.

Lips settled over my skin, but there was no satisfaction in what I felt. The hard look staring back wasn't fooled by what I was doing. Neither were my true feelings, however deeply buried they were.

Adrenaline began making my heart pound faster and I pulled my hand back, a smile tugging at my lips. "There. Now, go take your place back in the corner and don't move until I tell you to. You'll do the time for your smart mouth and when I let you up again, you'll be better. Won't you." It wasn't a question. Tessa blinked and her breath came out in a slow, deep rush.

"Yes, Master."

I stood, watching her make her way back to her spot. Conflict had my mouth twisting, but I pushed it away as I sat on the edge of the bed. Memories of her dream broke through and no matter how hard I tried to bury them back down, the blood covering my fists as I pounded them into my father's face wouldn't disappear.

"See," I gritted out, swinging continually. "I'll make a great Duke. The most powerful one to ever rule. I'll eliminate all problems. I'll make them disappear. I'll make you disappear! No one will stand in my way of getting what I want anymore—especially you."

A grunt came from my father's mouth as his hands tried to fend me off, but there was no stopping the events taking place. I was gone. So far gone, I could barely grasp the amount of fury I held.

So many emotions filled me at once. I pushed from the bed, but I was blind to my surroundings.

"Marko, what have you done?" My mother pressed herself against the wall, skirting deeper inside, but not closer. Terror filled her eyes as she stared at my father's bloody, broken face. I couldn't move, frozen in position on my knees. My eyes lowered as I stared down at my battered hands. The crimson had me shaking my head as I searched for something to say. The boy in me wanted to apologize. To beg for forgiveness. The man who'd been born with his first murder managed to force himself to stand.

"I've done nothing. You haven't seen anything. Retire for the night, mother. I'll see you in the morning. Have your food brought to your room."

Terrified eyes stared between me and my father and she nodded quickly, running out of the door and shutting it softly behind her. As my attention went back to the damage I'd done, I couldn't stop the smile etching in. My time was now and I'd show them all who Marko Loren Delacroix really was. My father's reputation would mean nothing compared to his heir. They'd respect me. They'd fear me if they didn't. A father dead. A son reborn.

Deep breaths pulled me back to the room and I watched as Tessa pressed her hands flat against the walls on each side of her. I walked forward, noticing she shook the closer I got. By the time I lowered directly behind her, the trembling was near violent.

"What's the matter, ma minette? Are you afraid of your Master? What did you get out of seeing that? Have some of your questions been answered?"

Silence lasted for all of a few seconds before her breath shuddered. "I expected some trace of remorse. Some…form of conscience. You liked killing him and I got the impression he wasn't the only person you hurt while you were still alive. Am I right?"

I could tell from her tone that she wanted me to ease her biggest fear, but I couldn't. I didn't really know. "I was never a good man. He made sure of that. Stop trying to romanticize me. You're only going to let yourself down."

"No," she said, shaking her head. "You can't be all bad. I felt your good. I know it's in there somewhere."

My arm wrapped around her waist as I kneeled behind her, molding myself to her small frame. "Keep telling yourself that, Tessa. You can con yourself into loving an evil vampire who you wish was once noble and chivalrous all you want, but we'll both know it's a lie." I moved her hair out of the way, kissing her neck as I went back to holding her. "Whatever you want to believe, love, I don't really care."

Slowly, my tongue traced over the tattoo, letting her flavor soak into me. The consumption of my slave would intoxicate me. It would push away the past and I was okay with that. The present was more important to me anyhow. The old me was dead and I wanted everything attached to him to stay buried. Nothing good came out of those dark years of being Duke. I knew that as much as I knew the hole I'd dug myself into had been the result of my death. I'd made a deal with the devil and, like all contracts, my fate couldn't be voided. My sentence was damn near eternal and I'd accomplish here what I couldn't do there. I'd rule.

"Marko." A moan came from Tessa as I pushed my hand between her legs, rubbing her pussy through her dress. I knew my blood was buffering the way she felt about me and I let it. She loved me again. That's all I cared about. This was where I wanted her. This was where I *needed* her. God, I did. I fucking needed this human to love and accept me.

"Tell me you're mine."

I added more pressure over the top of her slit and nipped at her neck, suddenly remembering Julius had fed from her. The realization began to sink in, even as I continued on. It made me want to stop. To physically fight through the anger of someone else feeding from what was mine.

"I'm yours. You know I'm yours."

"I do and you'll always be. I'll never let you go."

"Please..." Her hand grabbed my bicep and I wasn't sure whether her response was a plea for me to release her or keep her. I didn't let my fear overshadow what I wanted to believe. Tessa loved me. She'd always love me. I'd make sure of it.

Chapter 10
Hunter

Pictures. They were piled to the rim of the box sitting at the top of Tessa's closet. I scattered them out over the surface of her bed, smiling as I looked at our earliest memories of each other, down to the pictures I'd sent her when I was away, serving our country. She kept every one. Had even written the dates of when she received them on either the back or bottom. The little hearts surrounding the dates had me smiling even bigger. Why had she done that? God, I could only wish it was for the reason I prayed for. Had she loved me all along?

A sigh broke from my mouth and I grabbed a picture taken of the two of us not long before things went bad. Love shone through both of our eyes as we stared and smiled at each other. We were sitting on Tessa's parents' porch swing and her mother had snapped the Polaroid. At that point, we had the world before us. A future both of us no doubt had carved into stone. Yet, it hadn't been. I'd cast it deep within the depths of some bottomless pit to likely never be retrieved. Had I not ruined things between us, how would our future have turned out?

I knew. I'd have still joined the military, but I wouldn't have been alone. Tessa would have been mine. I'd have asked her to marry me in a heartbeat and go on the ultimate adventure. We would have been happy. Probably parents now. It could have been great. Picture perfect, just like the memories in her box. Why did fate always hand me the short end of the stick? Hadn't I done enough good to find some sort of happiness? It was the question that plagued me the most. How much good did someone have to do before it was returned to them? I'd fucking put my life on the line for people. Some I didn't even know. And where had that gotten me? Nowhere. I had nothing. My dream was gone, just like she was. And if I'd heard correctly, getting Tessa back would be impossible. It didn't mean I was going to give up, but I wasn't optimistic.

I glanced at my phone, knowing there was still no news. It was pointless for me to call Tom. He'd have dialed me in a heartbeat if someone knew anything concerning her. So, what did I do besides wait? My friends were all working. Until they had the time to come, I was by myself. I'd done all the research I could. Talked to everyone I'd connected with online. I was in a waiting game that made each minute feel like an eternity and that wasn't good for my mind. How many times had I been in the position to wait things out? In the Army, overseas…too many. And most hadn't come with good results.

I yawned, scooping the pictures in a pile. There was only so long one could sit and dream and I'd done my fair share today. It was time to call it a night, even if I knew sleep wouldn't come for quite some time.

As I stood to place the box back on the shelf in the closet, I caught sight of what looked to be a journal. Although my mind said not to even head in that direction, I was already placing down the box and stepping forward. One quick flip through and my heart began to beat wildly. I'd just hit the jackpot into Tessa's most intimate hidden thoughts and I wasn't sure what to do about it.

I headed to the bed and sat down, placing the small butterfly print book in front of me. If I did this, I'd be a dick. It was wrong, but didn't I deserve some glimpse into the woman I'd dreamed of making mine? What if she didn't love me at all? What if…

A long exhale broke through and I picked it up, flipping to the first page.

Dec 5th

Dear Journal, dear me,

You would think years of holding the same job would give me satisfaction, and in a way, it does, but where I am headed? The older I get, the more the question eats away at me. Who am I? I feel so alone. I feel so…empty. Is this my life? What I'm meant to do until my dying days? Growing up, I never would have thought so. I used to have dreams. Now, I live my days in lonely house.

I scrolled through, browsing. Some passages were long. Others short. Spotting my name, I stopped.

Dec 19th

Mr. Peterson came into the dealership again today. He comes in every Thursday, and every Thursday, he asks me out on a date. I wonder what he'd say if, for once, I told him yes? The thought is intriguing, even if going on an actual date with him isn't. I need excitement. I need…something.

Hunter hasn't called in a few weeks. He mentioned something about not being able to for a while. Does he know how scared I am for him? He's different, I see that, but still the same. I guess he's just grown up. It's hard to imagine, even with the pictures he sends. And what pictures those are. I can't help but blush with each one. He sure did grow up. I wonder whether he'll look the same in person? I'm not sure, but I'm dying to find out. Is it wrong for me to still want him? Sometimes I feel as if it is. He's probably moved on. Probably dated plenty of women since he left Austin. Why would he come back? And to me, of all people? To him, what we had was probably nothing more than a silly childhood crush. To me, those years forever changed my life. No one compares to him. Men, they're all charm and no real commitment. Hunter was true. Hunter will make some woman extremely happy someday.

I blinked past the words and reread it again. I wasn't sure what to think, but I decided to read more. I got lost in Tessa's words. In her every day mundane life. Choir practice seemed to be the epitome of her existence and even that wasn't always happy. She questioned herself a lot. Questioned life and religion in general. As I neared the middle, I caught more than just a mention of my name, but what looked to be pages filled with me.

March 9th

I asked Hunter to move in with me today. It was a bold decision, but one I couldn't resist. He gets out in only a few short months and he mentioned returning to Austin. He seems excited about it and my question just came from nowhere. I feel so giddy right now. I'm getting my best friend back!

I knew he wouldn't want to move in with his parents. He didn't sound enthusiastic when he mentioned going back to his childhood home, but he seemed happy when I offered for him to stay here. Had he been? I think so. Maybe it was my excitement pouring through and I missed his lack thereof? Damn, maybe I should have paid more attention. What if he just didn't want to hurt my feelings?

Well, what's done is done. I'm excited and maybe a little greedy to have him back, but I'll take it. I'll take him. Damn, that sounded bold. Although, maybe not far off from the hidden truth? Here I am, laughing out loud. And clapping! I put down my pen to clap! Almost twenty-eight years old and I'm acting like the teenage girl he once knew. I have to admit, it feels good to be happy again. Hunter make me happy. I've missed him so much.

Poor guy. He has no idea the mess he's coming to, being here with me. I'll probably bore him to death. No, I'll cook for him. He'll be glad to be here. He always did like food and I've gotten good at baking.

And...I'm rambling. And blushing. I know I sound absolutely ridiculous. Friends, Tessa. That's the most you'll ever be to him. Even losing your virginity to the guy didn't help him fall for you. Playing the needy wanna-be girlfriend won't either. Stick to friends or you'll run him off again. Friends are good.

My head shot up and I slammed the book closed. She'd lost her virginity to me in an attempt to get me to...commit?

There were no words. No thoughts as I came to the realization of how everything went down. After I'd hurt her, I pulled away. Tried to give her time to get over the shock of what we'd done. I wanted her mind to heal as well as her. And she thought I'd...what? Used her? Didn't want her after that? Fucking shit. And I'd left shortly after. Without so much as trying to push to the bottom of our problem. She loved me. Tessa loved me and I felt it in my heart. The lack of communication had kept us separated for years. If only I would have confessed. If I would have taken leave and rushed back here to tell her I was sorry and I wanted her to come back with me...we'd be together right now. So...what did I do? How did I fix this?

I pushed from the bed and slid my shoes on. It wasn't too late and even though I was tired, I had to find something to occupy my mind—anything that would help me come up with a solution. Marko, he was my biggest issue and I had to figure out a way to kill him. Yes, Marko had to die. Then, Tessa would be mine.

Chapter 11
Tessa

"Kneel."

The deepness of Marko's voice cut right though me as he towered above, glaring. Since Julius kept drinking from me, he refused my blood. Even after continually giving me his own. Days of hunger had turned him into an animal and I wasn't sure what was going on with him internally. It was impossible to know since he'd somehow grown strong enough to block himself off from me. I'd even tried to ask what it was, but he wouldn't talk. Wouldn't even take me when I actually offered past the fear that he may truly hurt me or someone else. Anyone within a five-foot radius was his target and he'd dropped more than one vampire when he'd taken me into George's to get adjustments on the new outfits from my wardrobe. Everyone feared him and after what I'd seen from his past, I knew why.

Sapphire silk haloed around my face and fell more forward as I went to my knees and bowed my head. I was past the point of fighting with him. At least, while he was in this mindset. I was brave, but I wasn't naïve.

"You will stay just as you are while I go feed. Do not move. Do not so much as shift your weight to ease the pain. You will not accompany me at the table tonight. You will stay right here and wait for my return."

My lips separated in disbelief and I scrambled my thoughts for what I could have done to upset him as much as I did. It had to have been me. The change got worse after I took his blood for the third night in a row, after Julius took mine. Maybe he hadn't wanted to give it, or maybe…did I take too much?

"Yes, Master." The response was automatic and I kept my stare fixed, losing myself to my mind. Something I was good at lately. I'd been told to kneel repeatedly over the last few days, but never while he left me alone. Shit, he *never* did leave me alone. Only when I had to go to the restroom, but he was still always here. Always hovering, waiting for my return. And now, he'd be making me stay in the room by myself?

Pacing, not feet away, disrupted my thoughts before I could even really get lost in my safety zone. I blinked, but stayed still.

"Do you remember yet?" he asked, coming to a stop before me.

"Remember?"

"What Julius says to you after he feeds?" Marko kneeled, gripping my face and bringing my head up. "You say you don't remember. Has it come back?"

Nothing had come back from those moments. I had no idea what our leader said or any memory of the feedings. The only thing I recalled was him pulling me into his lap. Then, nothing, until Marko carried me into the room.

"I don't."

"Prove it."

Black eyes stared intently into mine and warmth circled my belly as he grew closer. I tried to blink but couldn't. He was reading my memories, I knew he was, but I could still think—still control everything but my eyes.

"I don't know what he said," I repeated, lowly. "I wouldn't lie to you."

His hand pushed off from my face, nearly knocking me backward as he stood. Anger within me flared, but faded just as fast. I hated how the more time that passed, the more I couldn't control my feelings. The bond was complete and I knew this was as far as it went. I'd die for him. Kill for him. Give myself over freely to the worst monster he was capable of being…I would love him. And love, I did. Each morning I woke up, I was lost to him even more. Regardless of who he was or how he treated me.

"I can't stand that he's tasted you. That he's had his hands on you." Marko stopped just before the door and spun around to face me. My breath hitched and I dropped my gaze.

"Get up. If I go out there without you, it'll just make me look weaker than I already do. If he can feed from you at the table without anyone making a fuss about it, then so can I. You're *my* slave. Fuck all of them. If I want to strip you bare and fuck you right there while we all feed then I will. No one tells me what I can or can't do—especially when they probably want nothing more than to do it themselves. And he probably does. I bet he dreams of having what's mine. I can almost guarantee he wants to claim you as his own. But I won't let him. I won't let anyone have you. If that's the death of the both of us, so be it!"

Marko surged forward, ripping me up to stand and pushing me toward the door. His words scared me. I knew he was unstable due to his lack of feeding, and more than likely paranoid, but I couldn't get over just how much. Dammit, I had to get him to take my blood and fast. Preferably without anyone else getting hurt. He was getting worse, out of control with his suspicions—they were nonstop. Only yesterday, he nearly killed one of the male suppliers for looking at me too long. This had to stop.

The door swung open at his pull and I rushed out, right into Marie. We hit hard and I nearly fell. If it hadn't been for Marko catching me and pulling me back into him, I would have.

"I'm sorry," I said, lowly. "I didn't mean—"

"You don't apologize to her," Marko said, interrupting me and stepping around. "She should be apologizing to *you*. You are above her, slave. Now, let's go."

His annoyed command had tears blinding me as I gave her a sad look and followed. She gave me…nothing. And that hurt even more. Did she blame me for her the death of her men? Hell, I knew she did. I could see it in her cold expression.

The tables were almost entirely full and everyone but Marko was already seated at the members' table. I stopped at the seventh chair while he hung his jacket on the back and made his way to Julius. My head stayed down even though I longed to look back at Marie. How mad would she be if I tried to talk to her? Would she attempt to kill me? A few minutes went by before Julius' voice took me away from my thoughts.

"Impressive. Move to the fourth. I'm afraid we're not finished yet."

Gasps resounded through the large space and I walked around to the other side of the table, making my way to the fourth chair. The moment everyone went to sit, so did I. A hand locked on my bicep as I was halfway down and I paused, letting Marko bring me back up. I didn't connect with his gaze, no matter how much I wanted to.

"Tonight, you're mine." Hands grasped onto my hips and he easily lifted me to straddle his waist as he sat down. My heart exploded in rhythm and only continued to get faster as he reached up and pushed the hood back. Shallow breaths left me while he slid his hand against my neck and pushed the long length of my hair back over my shoulder. French words entered my mind and I soaked in each one like the neglected slave I was.

"Tonight, I have you in all ways, ma minette. Now, lower to my chest and let me taste what I own."

Fingers tightened into the hair at the base of my neck and I couldn't stop the arousal blossoming within me. I gripped the lapels of his jacket, easing against my show of weakness—my love for the one man I shouldn't display any form of affection for in public. My grip was affection. I should have been limp. Giving, to him. But our bond had me wanting more and I couldn't deny it.

The trace of his tongue over my pulse point tickled my skin, igniting a fire in the pit of my belly. I wanted nothing more than to rock my hips against the hardness I could feel under my ass. Slowly, he trailed down, kissing right over my tattoo. The one I got in an effort to save my life. I wanted to give him pause. To leave him shocked long enough for me to stab him, but it hadn't worked out that way.

Love you to death.

With one last show of tenderness, fangs sunk into my neck. I didn't so much as flinch as they reached their desired depth. It was a perfect harmony of predator and prey. He had my life in his hands and he could easily kill me, but I knew he wouldn't. It wasn't necessarily trust. I didn't have that option. It was a sweet, poisonous submission. The bond and his venom had me putting my life against odds I had no control over. It left me an enamored zombie. I wasn't in my right mind, I knew that. Yet…somehow, my brain had convinced me I was okay with the outcome. I had this new love for him. That was enough.

I melted down into Marko's body completely, basking in the pleasure rushing through. But it wasn't like before. It intensified my arousal, but didn't make it unbearable to the point of me going crazy to have him. This one was different than the others. It made me realize that there had to be different bites. It fascinated me, when I should have been worried about it.

Swirls of his tongue had my lids closing and me relaxing even more. Safety cloaked around me and I loved being in the arms of the vampire who held me. The more time I spent out of his room, the more I could see how different he was from everyone else. Marko was definitely leader material. Marie was right on that account. He was meant to rule. But would I still be at his side if the day ever came? Surely not. He'd have a concubine by then, not a slave. A ruler wouldn't resort to such low status. Julius might have fed from me, but he had the right and I wasn't by his side every night. I had no doubt I was just a lesson to Marko. One I didn't quite understand yet.

"You think too much, ma minette. But your thoughts are enlightening. Perhaps you are *a lesson. We all have to learn them in our own way. But I'm not worried about that right now. Think more on how honored you feel by being my slave. I like hearing you say that. You're learning your place.*

Lips broke from my neck and his tongue slid over the wounds, making me shiver with the increasing lust. I blinked, unsure of what to do. I knew I should get down. He was done with me. It would only be right. My foot dropped, but his hand eased against my lower back. It was a clear sign for me not to move. Again, I lowered to his chest, waiting for my next instruction while soaking in the small happiness the action gave me.

"Our guests arrive tomorrow. They will be staying a few days. There's plenty to go over and I expect you all in the meeting room at two. Marko." My body stiffened the smallest amount at Julius' voice calling him out. "Your new room has been set up not far from mine. You'll move in there tonight."

"Of course." The depth was seeping back in my Master's tone, but it was a different kind. One of authority. I knew the move was what he'd been waiting for. Happiness bubbled within and I held in my smile.

A tap to my leg had me standing and Marko immediately followed. "Two." He nodded, grabbing his jacket and spinning toward our hall. I followed, keeping my head down until the darkness overtook us. The moment he shut the bedroom door behind us, I was swept into his arms.

"It's happening. Finally. Do you know how long I've waited for this, ma minette?"

"Four hundred years?" The change in his mood left me unable to do the actual math. It threw me off. I hadn't heard him so enthusiastic since I'd been here and although I was hoping for him to be in a better mood after feeding, I would never have guessed it would be this much.

"I'm not that old. But it sure felt like that long." A laugh poured from his mouth and the mattress shifted under our weight. I took in his smile, losing myself to how attractive he truly was when he wasn't ready to kill me or someone else. It made time slow. Left me just as in awe as his venom did. I could see myself being able to truly love this vampire at his best. If only he could be more like he was now all the time.

"Marko?"

"Yes, Tessa." Lips pressed into mine and I forgot what I wanted to ask as I opened my mouth to him. My stomach growling had his head rearing up. For seconds, he just looked at me.

"You haven't eaten…in days."

"I haven't been hungry. Well, until now I guess."

The torn expression he held was one I carried myself. I didn't want him to stop. Didn't want him to disappear back into the monster he'd exposed me to. I'd gone this long without food, what was a few more hours?

"I guess I forgot as much as you did. We can't let this happen again. You may be strong, but you'll grow internally weak if you deny yourself nourishment. Your body still need nutrients I can't provide."

He lifted and led me to the closet where he grabbed a hanger holding a pair of black slacks and a pearl colored silk blouse. The sleeves had slits along the top and there was a circle cut out of the back. It looked elegant. Almost…

"Fit for royalty," he finished my thoughts. "As well as you are, in a sense. Why don't you get dressed and I'll take you to get something to eat."

"Down here?" I couldn't help but ask as he stared me over.

"No. Tonight we celebrate our advance to the top. We're number four, ma minette. *Four*. And I have a feeling I'll be at least number three before this cycle of my rebirth is over. It'll take a few more months to kick in, but it'll happen at some point. I guess I have you to thank for the speed."

Heat rushed to my cheeks and I took the hangers from his grasp. He opened a drawer and pulled out white lingerie. I blushed even more as I took them too. The moment the restroom door was closed behind me, I couldn't help but let my smile surface. This was the Marko I had been waiting for. My only concern was, how long would he stay around this time?

Chapter 12
Marko

Leading my slave through the heart of the city looking as beautiful as she did gave me such pride, I couldn't even grasp the enormity. I was on top of the world at Julius' news and nothing was going to hold me back from having a good time. Not Dallas' *le Circle's* arrival. Not my plans for Hunter. Not even Julius' odd fixation on Tessa. Tonight was our night and I had every intention of showing her a good time.

Her blood made my heart float even lighter and I held my arm around hers tightly as we took the stairs to Kline's. I wanted so badly to press her against the wall and drink in her taste. To slide my tongue against hers as I shredded the silk that covered her large breasts. The flavor of her skin was the only thing I wished for at the moment and I would have made love to her for hours had her wellbeing not made itself known.

Food. How had I forgotten her needs? She was human. Not a vampire. I had responsibilities now that existed outside of my own. It was important I keep them well in mind if I wanted her at her best. After all, she was every bit as important as myself when it came to moving to the top. I couldn't do it while being miserable, and I surely would be if Tessa wasn't by my side. I needed her presence like I needed her blood to survive. The days and bond had taught me that. Even if I didn't show her how much I realized it.

The door opened at my push and one of Kline's servants was already waiting for our arrival.

"The car is ready for you in the front, Master Delacroix. It'll take you wherever you need to go."

My response wasn't needed and he knew that as he led us to the front door, opening it just in time for us to make it through. A black limousine had Tessa slowing enough to pull against my arm, but she didn't break away as another servant opened the door for us. I let her climb in first and I followed.

"What do you like to eat?" My question tore her wide eyes away from the lit up bar resting off to the side.

"I…ah, healthy? I don't eat much meat."

"Italian?"

A smile came to her face, nearly stilling my pulse. "What about French?" She bit her lip and I didn't miss her hidden meaning. My hand locked on her inner thigh as I pulled her closer.

"You're about to have all the French you can swallow, but for food, you'll eat Italian."

"Yes, Master," she lipped, silently.

"Take us to the best Italian restaurant this city has." I rolled up the divider, giving us privacy. I had Tessa straddling me before she had a chance to move. "And, you," I sucked at her bottom lip, "you're going to eat everything I order and I'm going to taste again."

Her smile had me mirroring the action. The beauty of my slave left me speechless and I couldn't move for several moments as we stared into each other's eyes. Why hadn't I done something like this before? Tried to make her happy instead of robotically compliant and miserable? Ah, the haze. I tried to ignore the constant fuzziness as I leaned forward and drank her in, adding pressure to her lower back to bring her pussy down on me even more. The slacks had me breaking away long enough to look down. The agitation only drove my mouth back into hers harder.

"I want you."

My declaration sent Tessa's nails pressing into my shoulders. The limo made its way to the freeway and our kisses turned more passionate. I couldn't stop myself from unbuttoning her blouse and pulling her breast free from the white silk bra. Her moan was spontaneous as I sucked her nipple into my mouth, biting against the hard tip with just enough force to have her hands sliding more toward my neck.

"Marko, please."

"Please what, ma minette? Please give you my cock? Or please make you come?"

"Both." Her hips rotated and a groan came from my mouth.

"Not yet. There will be plenty of time for that. Now is not it."

One last suck about did me in. I could easily make the limo drive around until we were finished, but I wanted her fed. *I wanted to take care of her.*

I pulled back, swallowing hard. Stopping was torture and these weird needs pushing in were even more so. I fixed the buttons on her blouse and eased her back next to me. I couldn't stop my brow from furrowing at the sudden changes within. I knew the old Marko had made appearances here and there, but this was entirely me. And she wasn't showing any form of rejection.

"You look upset." The quiet tone had me shaking my head and taking her hand to add assurance. God, who was I suddenly? I didn't even know. One minute, I was throwing her around, putting her through pain, and the next, I was passionate and caring. If she wasn't getting whiplash, I sure as hell was.

Buildings rose on both sides of us and I took a deep breath as we pulled into the entrance of what looked like a large hotel. Tessa stiffened beside me and the door opened before I could ask or open my mind to read hers.

"Good evening. Welcome to Buccio's."

I stood, nodding, and turned to help Tessa out. Her eyes darted around nervously, but she took my arm as I led her to the main door.

"What is it?"

Anger laced my tone and I tried to rein it back in. If my slave was upset over something, there was a reason, and I wanted to know what it was.

"My parents. This is their favorite place. They come here a lot."

"Oh." I shrugged it off. "Well, we both know there's nothing to worry about. They're not in the country."

"No, but…" she trailed off as I led her inside. The lobby was somewhat packed and I followed the sign bringing us toward the restaurant. There was no point in going further in our conversation as I stopped at the host.

A petite male smiled and I glanced around before addressing him. "Table for two. The most secluded seating you have." There was a hesitation as he looked over his computer.

"I'm sorry, sir. Did you have a reservation?"

"A what?"

"A reservation, sir. That area is booked for the night. The table was occupied not half an hour ago. I can try to squeeze you in at a different table, but it may be a long wait."

I laughed, drawing his attention. His eyes met with mine and I leaned forward, lowering my voice. "I don't think you understand. I'm a *very* important man and I require that table at its earliest convenience. You will make it happen. Now, put Marko Delacroix in for the next reservation and we'll just take a seat until our table becomes available."

The boy's fingers typed away, even as he stared at me.

"Is it done?"

"Yes, sir. Marko Delacroix, back booth, VIP section."

A big smile came to my face at the VIP. "Perfect. Thank you for that."

My eyes broke contact and I spun Tessa around, leading her to a small loveseat set off to the side. The leather was slightly cool against my hand as I rested it behind ma minette's shoulders. The way she leaned into me, molding her body against mine sent another surge of pride through me. With her hair piled high on her head and the tattoo peeking out at every turn of her face, I couldn't ever remember being so happy.

"Marko, do you think it's a good idea that we're out?"

"What do you mean?"

Tessa rested her head against my chest and I couldn't stop myself from cupping the side of her neck to hold her to me.

"I don't know. It just feels odd being up here."

I laughed, kissing the top of her forehead as she looked up. "Because you know where you belong. You're afraid of this place and that's okay, but you worry for nothing. I assure you, I can take care of us if anything happened." My smile faded. "You do believe I can take care of you, right?"

"Of course," she said, lowly. "It's just—"

"Tessa!"

I felt her stiffen beside me as her head snapped to the side. A woman, not much younger than her came forward, wearing black pants and a red button-up shirt, just like the uniforms of the other waiters and waitresses.

"Shit," Tessa mumbled under her breath. *This is what I was afraid of. Her name is Chloe. Her parents are best friends with mine. They own this restaurant.* She stood and I followed. "Chloe, how are you?" Tessa smiled, hugging her and instantly jerking back. The heat burning into my chest was one I felt from her. I saw a chain on the girl's neck and knew a cross had to have been hidden under the blonde's shirt.

"I'm doing great. How are you? I haven't seen you in choir practice the last couple of weeks. Father Moretti said you were sick. I went by your house to check on you, but Hunter said you weren't home."

Tessa's hands clasped together and her smile wavered only for a moment. "I was pretty sick, but I'm doing better now. Thank you for coming by, I'm sorry I missed you. I…don't live there anymore. Did you say Hunter was still there?"

"Oh…well, yes, last time I heard. But maybe he's moved out? I'm not sure." The blonde's brown eyes darted to me nervously, but she went back to looking at Tessa. "Are you coming back to church soon?"

"I'm afraid not. I live too far away now. I'm going to have to find me a new one, I suppose."

"That's so sad. I'm going to miss you. We all will."

"I know. I'm sorry. Please, let me introduce you to my…boyfriend. Chloe, this is Marko. Marko, Chloe."

I shook her hand, even though she hesitated. I knew being so close to me was making her feel uncomfortable, but she was actually getting it pretty easily. I was in too good of a mood to throw off the vibes I'd surely reflect now that I was even more powerful.

"Pleasure," I said, wrapping my arm back around Tessa. As I looked at our surroundings, they continued to talk. Mostly about Hunter, who I didn't care to hear about. Anything involving him would just piss me off and the night would be ruined. I had a hard enough time controlling my anger to begin with. The evening was going too well to have it fall apart now.

"You should probably get back. I think someone is looking for you," Tessa said, pointing to a couple scanning the room.

"Oh, right. Call me. Maybe we can hang out sometime." Chloe was already walking backward and I could feel ma minette relax more with each step she took.

"Sounds great. Tell your parents I said hello."

Blonde hair spun in the ponytail as the girl nodded and waved, walking quickly back through the tables. The tension in Tessa's body left as she turned back to me. "I'm sorry about the whole boyfriend thing. I wasn't sure what to say."

Boyfriend. Such an odd word. So…juvenile for how far we'd come. "I half expected you to tell her I was your fiancé. Isn't that more appropriate?"

Tessa's eyes went wide and she shook her head. "I'd never say that."

Offence had me cocking my head. "No? Am I not good enough for a human to marry?"

"Of course you are. Just…"

"Not you?"

Tessa pulled her arm free from me, angrily. "I'm not putting a claim on you that I will never have, is what I meant. Besides, boyfriend is more fitting. It's about as serious, status-wise, as we'll ever be."

The temper in me only intensified as I caught her meaning. The hurt that washed through me was hers and I couldn't stand that I was still confused about these feelings. Humans weren't concubine material. To marry a human would just be…wrong. It would be weak. And yet, if I had to choose someone, ma minette wouldn't be so bad.

Who was I kidding? I loved her, though I shouldn't. My heart raced for only her and the vampire within wanted nothing more than to stomp her feelings into the ground and prove to the both of us how wrong this truly was. She was a slave…and here, I was using my status to try to woo her. The truth was, I wanted to use what I could in an attempt to win her over and it was all for nothing. Tessa and I would never be together as man and wife, or Master and concubine. We wouldn't, so what was I doing? I sighed. I was trying to do something only my blood could do. I just wanted it to be real.

"Marko Delacroix."

My fingers wrapped around her bicep as I led her to follow the host. Our booth sat in the very back, secluded from the rest of the room by a wooden wrap-around divider. I let go, letting Tessa scoot in the U-shaped cushion as I entered on the other side. She stopped next to me, lowering her head as she picked up the drink menu.

"Your waiter will be with you shortly." The boy walked off and I rested my forearms on top, trying to gain my bearings. My vampire didn't want to be pushed out of the way, only causing the all too familiar rage to fester within as I battled him.

"Marko, do you want to leave?"

Tessa's voice was quiet as she gazed over. I knew she could feel the agitation. It radiated from every pore on my body. I pulled at the tie, reaching down for the menu and scanning over it.

"You will eat."

Voices hummed around me, making my skin crawl and my fangs lowered the smallest amount before I managed to get myself under control. What it was I needed, I wasn't sure. These spouts of uncontrollable anger were something that kept happening and it would go on for a lot longer.

Footsteps approached and I knew the waiter was coming before he even made it around the wall.

"Good evening. My name is Joe. Can I start you off with wine or—"

"Red. Most expensive bottle you have. And there will be no need to come back. We're ready to order now, so get your pen ready." My stare lifted and he fumbled with the pen nervously. "Prime New York Strip, medium. Steamed broccoli and rosemary potatoes as sides. Veal Piccata. Chicken Parmesan. And…" my finger scanned over the menu, "balsamic-glazed salmon," My mouth tightened as I glanced to Tessa. "Scratch that, ma minette is allergic to salmon. Just the others."

"Yes, sir."

The waiter shuffled off and I turned, raising my eyebrow. "Allergic to salmon? Who is allergic to salmon?"

"Me," she said, smiling.

"You do know you probably aren't anymore, though, right?"

"I'm not risking it."

"As you wish. But I bet you'd have really enjoyed it."

Something flashed behind her eyes and I heard what she was thinking before she even said it. *Will you eat?*

"I'll try a little, not that I'll taste it," I answered. "Of course, if we eat off the same plate and take bites at the same time, I'll taste it through you. I have to say," I said, feeling the anger ease a little, "I'm a little excited about that part. It'll be interesting to experience."

"I can't wait to see your expression at the first bite." The dazzle in her eyes brought me to her even more and I felt myself fall back into the enamored mindset I'd been in when we left the underground city. My gaze lowered to her lips and I leaned in, pressing into her gently. The returning footsteps didn't break the concentration I kept on her face.

"You're beautiful when you're happy. I think I'd like to keep you this way."

The confusion was apparent while she looked at me. "Marko, your…eyes. They're brown. How long have you been back? I didn't notice the change."

I blinked, turning from her to her blonde friend, who had suddenly took over the place of our waiter. She smiled, but looked at Tessa a little nervously as she set down the glasses. I took the bottle from her hand, gesturing that it was okay to go.

"I don't know what you mean. I'm the same as I've been since we left."

"I can't believe I didn't notice. Do you think you're back for good?"

There it was again. Annoyance. "I'm the same as I was hours ago. I'm not the Marko you're looking for, ma minette. Let it go. I'm here to stay."

"But…"

She stayed quiet, grabbing the glass of wine I offered and sipping from it. The taste as I mimicked her actions was pure heaven and I leaned back against the chair as she drifted deep into her thoughts. Ones I blocked out intentionally. I didn't want to hear the comparison of myself. Let her worry over it, I wasn't going to bother.

"What do you like to do for fun? Do you have any hobbies? Do you like music?"

The questions weren't what I was expecting. My eyes took in her curious expression and I took another sip of the wine while I thought over what I could remember from my past. "I like music. Mainly classical, but I guess there are some songs I've heard over time that I enjoy. I like to read. I think I used to do that a lot. Well, obviously before you came along."

"Read? What do you like?"

I turned to face more toward her, unable to help but wonder what she was up to. "Why don't you tell me more about you?"

A sarcastic laugh filled the space between us. "You already know everything there is to know about me."

Did I? I supposed I did, subconsciously, but I still wanted to hear it. "Enlighten me."

"Alright. You know I sing. It's my passion. I've always enjoyed it, but I've never had the courage to really do it in public before. I read, also, but I guarantee you it isn't the same genre as you. I sometimes go on baking sprees, even though I barely touch what I make. I'm downright boring," she said, laughing.

"Will you bake for me so I can taste it?" The smile surfacing on my face couldn't be held in. Even knowing what she spoke was the truth, it was different to hear her tell it. It was almost like I was learning about her for the first time.

"If you'd like."

"I think I would very much like to see you do it. Tell me more."

Tessa and I both lifted our glass of wine and the same time, the actions coming so natural. My body just responded to her innermost thoughts automatically. As she began to talk again, I stayed transfixed. I even found myself laughing harder than I could ever remember. As the blonde placed the food on our table, we both grabbed our forks. She never wavered from the flow of our conversation, and I never wanted her to stop.

"So, that was my first and last time to ever try water skiing and I don't regret the decision one bit."

I laughed, bringing the steak to my lips as she did. At the flavor bursting over my tongue, my eyes rolled back and I moaned through the new experience. God, how had I forgotten how amazing this was? It was unbelievably rich and juicy. And so tender. And once again, I had her to thank.

"Good, right?"

I swallowed, pulling her to me and crushing my lips into hers. Food had suddenly become the biggest aphrodisiac ever to exist and I was dying for more. More of it and more of her.

"Again," I said, licking across her bottom lip.

The fork rose between us and the moment it hit her mouth, I licked my lips, bringing my own piece up to eat.

Over and over, we took in more. Each plate was paradise and Tessa was so full by the time we were finished, I felt bad for making her continue. I couldn't get enough. I wanted to taste everything. Bask in what I'd been missing for centuries.

"One more drink." The small giggle wasn't from amusement, but from her being drunk. And her intoxication was my own. Although I wasn't feeling it as much, there was slight hesitation that kept me in a lighter mood. Hell, who was I kidding? I was once again on top of the world and loving every second of it.

"There. Can we go now?"

"Yes. But tomorrow, we try something new. Every day."

Her nod had me grabbing her hand and I stood, helping her to join me. For the first time since I'd taken her, it almost felt like things were finally falling into place. Tessa was a hell of a slave, but she could be more. We could talk, enjoy our time together. I wanted that. I wanted her like this, right here.

A couple stood before us as we weaved through and I calmly held her, waiting for them to make their way out. As we left, I didn't miss the stares coming from a group of people toward the back. The blonde girl was amongst them and I figured it to be her family. Their odd gazes sparked a level of discomfort I hadn't expected. Tessa was so focused ahead, her cheek resting on my chest, she stayed oblivious. The weight took me from my suspicions and I hugged to her tightly while I walked her through the main doors of the building.

"Marko!"

The voice had my body tensing and I turned toward it, hearing Hunter's name scream through Tessa's thoughts in a panicked repeat. Before I could focus enough to spot him, her fingers locked onto my lapels and she threw her body into mine. The fire that exploded in my upper torso was so intense, my knees locked up, even as I held her sides, trying to keep us balanced. Shock from the pain had the air leaving me. Nothing made sense as I tried to get my mind to work. The confusion had me looking down to see blood soaking through the back of the white silk shirt she wore. My heart stopped at seeing the end of a thin wooden stake protruding from her back.

"Tessa?" Hunter's voice cracked into a sob and my eyes cut up with rage, fixed on Hunter's frozen expression of horror. Ma minette's weight fell into my hold and her small cry was the only thing tearing my gaze from the man I was ready to destroy.

Chapter 13
Hunter

Thoughts. Words. Nothing would come as I watched the love of my life go limp in Marko's arms. The crossbow fell from my hand and I couldn't breathe as the vampire I had every intention of killing pulled the inch-wide stake from her back. I knew with the force, it had to have gone deep. Possibly all the way through to her chest. At the blood that dripped in a steady stream to the ground, panic and pain laced my heart.

How had she known? What had she been thinking, throwing herself in front of him? She'd seen what I had pointed at him. Yet…she protected him.

Sickness swarmed within me and I fought my way forward as he swung her legs into his arms. I couldn't speak and I was torn on what to do. How did this go so wrong? When Tom had called and informed me Tessa was at Chloe's parents' restaurant, I'd thought this was it. I'd kill him and take her back home with me. We could run off or start over somewhere else. I'd had so many high hopes, pushing away the bad possibilities, but now…

"Let me take her to the hospital." My words were strained and Marko didn't even seem to hear me as he rushed for the limo door that was opened and waiting for them. People moved around panicked, but I couldn't focus on anyone but Tessa. "Please," I pushed out, "let me take her to get help."

A roar poured from his mouth, igniting what felt like scratches to race over my skin. He spun the two of them around, panting. The evil behind his eyes had my legs coming to a stop, feet away from them.

"You. Get in the car." His voice was so deep, it was almost unrecognizable. *Demonic.*

Even as his eyes searched the area, I knew he was debating on how to kill me. Blood seeped through my shirt in so many locations and dripped from my arms from his yell alone, all I could do was shake my head and step back.

"Let me have Tessa so I can take her to get help."

"You want her, *come* get her." Fangs were visible as he spoke and I felt myself lock up. The tuning fork was going crazy inside of me, making me shake and sweat. I'd never felt it this bad before. Even from Marko. This was worse. Unreal, with the frequency it carried.

"What are you…afraid?"

"Afraid for *her*. Please. I didn't mean to hurt Tessa. It was *you* I was aiming for."

Blood dripped from Marko's forearm, splashing onto the ground from her back and my features drew in in regret. I walked closer and didn't even see him move. His hand grasped my arm and he threw me in the limo, pushing in after me.

"Home, and make it fast," he said, his voice booming.

The car took off with enough speed to jolt me back. A scream exploded from Tessa as she came to. It left the hair rising on the back of my neck and arms. I reached out involuntarily as his bloody fingers brushed back her hair.

God, what had I done?

"It's okay. Calm, ma minette, I've got you."

"Marko?"

Her scared voice drew me forward. I couldn't help but call out to her

"Tessa?"

I was slammed back into the side of the limo with such force, I had to fight for breath at the pressure holding me immobile.

"Don't talk, love. I'm going to make you all better. Just, don't move."

"I can't…breathe. Hunter is…here?"

Marko's eyes rose to mine and stayed there as he continued. "I know, I can feel how hard it is for you. And yes, I have Hunter." His nails extended as he took off his jacket and ripped open the arm of his shirt. I fell to the seat, gasping for air, trying to blink past the spots covering my vision as he lifted the invisible force.

Gasps from her lips fill the interior and her body spasmed as a louder cry rang out.

"Drink and do not fear. You do not die today, ma minette. But you," he said, looking back over at me, "you *will* die for what you've done."

"Oh—God!" Tessa thrashed in his lap, twisting from side to side. "Get it out," she screamed. "Marko!"

A hiss filled the air and his face tightened in pain as he spun her over, shredding her shirt beneath his claws.

"Holy water?" he exploded. "Is that what you soaked the stakes in?"

"It was supposed to be you!"

"If *I* die, she dies. What part of that are you not understanding?" His fingers poked around the wound and he grimaced as Tessa screamed louder. "I think a piece broke off inside of you, mon chaton. I'm going to have to…" His breaths grew heavier as he sliced open his forearm, pushing it underneath her, to her mouth. My stomach twisted in knots as she clutched his wrist, crying out loudly in pain while trying to drink.

"Fuck. Fuck. Squeeze as tight as you need to." Marko shoved his finger into the wound and Tessa jerked in his lap, screaming in agony. Nausea waved through and nervousness pushed my adrenaline to soaring heights.

"Marko, she needs to go to the hospital. She needs a surgeon or someone to open the wound. Stop prolonging this and have your driver turn us around."

Physical pain scorched over my pecs and my hand shot up to the new wounds marring my skin. I could feel their depth and it made me even more lightheaded. My shirt was covered in blood. The marks on my arms weren't too deep, but deep enough to possibly leave scars. The new ones though, were deeper. If I didn't get my own looked at soon, I might very well bleed out and lose consciousness before I could try to escape him. I didn't have vampire blood, like Tessa, to keep me going.

"I know it hurts, but I can't get to it without causing a lot worse damage. Julius will help you. I'm sure he's dealt with this sort of thing before. Just…" Marko spun her back around in his lap, pulling her close onto his chest as he rocked her sobbing form. She was crying so hard, her whole body was trembling.

"I think I taste…blood. I…"

Fingers weaved through her hair as he held her tighter. Even though the sight made me sick, I couldn't overlook what I'd witnessed tonight. Tessa hadn't been forced into that restaurant. She wasn't under any spell. They'd been smiling…happy, when they exited the doors. And I'd hated it—especially after what I read. I'd never wanted him deader. And I'd shot, never expecting her to try to save him.

"If I die—"

Marko's hand covered her mouth, cutting off her words. "You will not die."

Muffling had him removing it. "If I do—" New spasms had a sound coming from her.

"I won't let you die. I won't."

Black eyes settled on me and I moved as close to the door as I could. Stinging covered almost every inch of me like fire, yet I could barely feel it when grounded by fear from the vampire's stare. I couldn't stay here. The thought of leaving Tessa killed me, but I would really be dead if I continued to remain in this limo.

My fist clenched, waiting for the perfect opportunity. We were going too fast right now, but the car had to slow at some point and when it did, I'd bail.

"Drink more."

The healed forearm was reopened and he lowered his head, turning hers to take in the crimson already starting to race down his skin. The limo was beginning to slow and I didn't wait. My hand shot to the door handle and the fact that it was locked didn't stop me. I slammed my elbow into the window as hard as I could, repeatedly, but I didn't have time to keep trying. I grabbed the dagger, using the bottom to send glass shattering. I didn't think as I stood and dove out. Even as I tucked my body to roll, the connection of the asphalt was like getting slammed with a burning torch packing the punch of a brick wall. Air locked in my chest as I rolled and I forced myself to brace down, causing the road to tear into my palms. Brakes from the car applied, but only for the briefest moment. It turned on the intersecting road and I didn't wait to start running.

Marko would come looking for me, just as I had been for him. And when the time came, I'd be ready.

Chapter 14
Tessa

Lights blurred above and turned to darkness as Marko raced with me down the stairs. The pain increased by the second, locking me into myself just as it'd done once before. I could feel the pressure of the wood inside of me and the damage it was doing was taking its toll.

Was it melting my insides like before? Yes and no. The holy water didn't seem as effective as the blessed dagger, but the results were the same. Just at a slow, torturous pace.

Noise barcly existed in the distance and I managed to push through the wall holding in my pain and cry out as I clung tightly to Marko. I knew we'd breached the heart of the city, but all I could concentrate on was the way my body felt like it was distorting on the inside. What had Hunter been thinking? Did he know if he killed Marko, I would die? I couldn't think about it as Marko's voice exploded throughout the room.

"Julius!"

The deep echo vibrated my skin and I screamed, flailing against the tight grip holding me down. A flurry of people blurred as Marko turned and seemed to change his mind. A table was suddenly before me and he placed me on my stomach, pushing his hand into the middle of my back as he thrust his finger back into the wound. The pain was so overwhelming, I fought not to pass out.

"God dammit. You're already healing, ma minette. This is going to hurt. Just…try to bear it."

To scream would have been somewhat of a release from the agony I was in, but at what I felt, no sound would leave. The room swayed, or I did, and unconsciousness beckoned. I dug my nails into the table, barely able to keep myself from falling to the side.

Growling had my head turning and Marko was suddenly breaking his connection with my back and spinning to shred his nails down a dark skinned vampire's throat as it rushed forward. I could see more vampires moving in and my heart jumped in fear at their bared fangs.

"Get back!" A hiss brought Marie into view and I tried to focus on her as she rushed over. "Julius isn't here. The Dallas Circle arrived early. He went to meet them. What happened?" Her hands were already reaching out to me when Marko slapped them away.

"Go, Marie. Let me focus. I can barely fucking think and fight them off at the same time."

"You're not rational enough to take care of your slave. Just tell me what happened and I can help. You can hold a wall to protect us while I work on her."

My head fell into the table hard and I had no idea I had even been holding it up. Sight was fading and I felt on the verge of throwing up. The food pushed to the back of my throat and I tried swallowing past the scream from the new round of spasms.

"She took a stake for me. It had been soaked in holy water. A piece broke off inside of her."

A low curse came from Marie. "You can hold the wall without seeing. Put her under for fuck's sakes and let me help her. Do you really want her suffering?"

"Don't tell me what to do!" Marko's threatening voice broke through and one of his hands cupped my cheek while he held the other toward the growling vampires. Worry clouded his gaze as it returned to me and I knew it was bad. "Mon chaton, look deep into my eyes. I'm going to make the pain go away. You're going to get better."

If I obeyed, would I come back from this? What if I died while I was under and I never knew it was coming? Fear had me reaching for his hand. He grabbed onto it tight, bringing my fingers to his lips. The kiss was hard. Desperate. Another sign indicating how dire the situation was.

"I love you. I do," I whispered. The slave in me was afraid. Fearful to leave her Master.

"And I, you. Now, look into my eyes and let yourself calm."

I blinked hard, locking with his stare. The darkness deep within sucked me forward like a slingshot and I could hear my heart beating loudly around me. Then…nothing.

****

"Do it! Don't you dare fucking stop!"

Marko's voice jolted me from what felt like a deep sleep and my eyes shot open from the excruciating pain deep within. What looked like a wall of vampires stood against an invisible force, clawing and tearing at each other, trying to get to me. The growls and yelling were so intense, they overpowered my roaring pulse.

Sweat drenched Marko's hair and the back of his white shirt stuck to him. The yell that came from his mouth was laced with pain and I knew he was feeling what I was. Combined with trying to keep his powers strong enough to hold them all back was wearing him down.

A new round of agony surged from the pressure of Marie pushing against something inside of me. It had a scream leaving my mouth and my hands pushing against the table, right into where I'd apparently gotten sick while I was under. The thought left me cringing for only a moment before the awareness of what I was feeling came crashing back.

"Love, I'm sorry. I can't do both anymore." He glanced back to me, his features twisted with emotion I couldn't even grasp the depth of.

"Hold on, Tessa. I think I'm almost there." Marie's voice was comforting and I tried to brace myself to take what I was feeling, but it was impossible. The pain was worse and increasing by the second.

What felt like a knife sliced into my back, closer to the side. I heaved, curling my fingers into a fist. Marko's hands shook as he held it before him. My eyes tried to stay focused on what was happening to take my mind off what Marie was doing. It helped a little, but the worry over what I was seeing left the anxiety worse.

Higher, the vampires climbed each other, trying anything they could to get through. Blood drenched most of their shredded clothes and black eyes remained entranced on us as they clawed and bit at the wall. My worst nightmare was coming true and there was nothing I could do about it.

"Where's Julius?" I managed as more pressure pushed into me. "Why isn't he here yet?"

"I'm not…sure." Straining in her tone gave way with a high-pitched noise following. "Mother of God," she said, frustrated. "Tessa, I'm so sorry. I—"

"What is it?" Marko's head spun back in our direction.

"I don't think I can get to it." Marie moved over to where she was in my vision. "Tessa, it's really deep. If I go any deeper, even Marko's blood won't bring you back. It's in a very complicated place. You've already lost so much blood. And…" Her eyes rose to Marko, who was still staring at us nervously.

"Do it." My head went back to the table. I was too tired to keep fighting this. "I can't take much more. You have to get it out." Heat poured from my body and I was sure I was running a fever from the holy water boiling inside of me.

"Wait." Marko took a few steps back and vampires broke out into a sprint, falling over each other as they raced forward. Growls were followed by them tearing into each other as they fought to gain ground. The power from the force Marko threw at them sent a wave of vampires flying across the room. The new group slammed back into the wall he replaced, whining at piercing volume. "Fuck! My bedroom door won't hold them out. Not anymore than what I'm doing now. You have to make it fast, Marie. You have to…" A groan came from his mouth and his elbow jerked in from our pain, but his palm still held firmly toward the vampires.

Fingertips brushed down my cheek and Marie lowered, placing her lips against my skin. "I'm sorry."

A scream tore from my throat as her finger pushed deep, tearing muscle and what felt like something harder. Lights flashed before my eyes and I was falling again. But I wasn't the only one. Through a haze, I saw Marko crash to his knees. A mass of bloody bodies raced forward as I faded in and out of consciousness. Voices broke through, but I had no idea whose they were. The accent threw me off and the words were unrecognizable. Whether it was from my lack of awareness, or the man was speaking another language, I had no idea. And I didn't care. I barely caught Marko pushing to his feet to rip a vampire's throat out as he tried to rush past him.

The room swayed and I could hear Marie talking, but to who, I didn't know. Heat formed over my back and grew unbearable as my toes pushed against the wood. Regardless of how much I tried to flee, nothing else was working. I couldn't move. Couldn't so much as crawl or push up on my hands. I was trapped while whoever was burning me continued to increase the temperature.

"Pl-ease." The sob somehow brought my plea out and my eyes rolled. If I was going to die, I didn't want it to be like this. I'd have taken the holy water pain over what I was experiencing now.

Julius was suddenly before me, kneeling as chaos blurred around him. I knew it was the other members getting everything under control. Their blurry figures only registered a moment before he stole my attention.

"So close to death. Should you die," he said, leaning down closer, looking into my eyes, "I feel your friend would…come sooner. Yes, he's responsible for this. Yet, he'll blame it on us." He paused, seeming to read something more. "But if you happened to die and be reborn into one of us, your newborn could manipulate him. You could keep him here or kill him for us."

"No." I tried to shake my head, but it wouldn't move. The fire still burned my insides and I knew someone other than Marie was doing it.

"Oh, yes. Thing is…it's not your time. I feel that. So, there's only one other option."

The strength wouldn't come to ask. I blinked heavily, almost finding it impossible to open my lids again. Pressure eased and a hand grasped around my ribs, turning me almost to my side. A cry came out as I felt the wood break free and disappear from within. More pressure was followed by heat. I knew it was somehow healing the major damage. How, I wasn't sure. My body jolted and twitched, even though I couldn't move.

Julius looked up at someone, smiling. He stood, not bothering to tell me what he'd meant. As he stepped away, I was suddenly faced with a man I'd never seen before. He was dressed in all black. The color made his dark blue eyes glow. His features were sharp and his sandy-blond hair was longer in the front, just to the top of his cheekbones, making him looking even younger. But the age behind his stare couldn't be mistaken. I wasn't looking at a man who could have graduated high school with me. This vampire was old and his power was more than I'd felt from anyone. Even Julius.

"You must be Tessalyn Antoniette. I've heard a lot about you in the last week. I'm Sayer. It's nice to finally meet my future concubine. Seems I came at the perfect time." He pulled up his sleeve with a bloody hand and slit his wrist with one of his nails. I couldn't stop my eyes from going wide, even when I didn't have the strength. My palms pushed against the table and I tried to move away. All I managed was to fall back to the surface with how weak I was.

"Don't be afraid. I'll have you healed in no time. Besides, we share the same blood. You'll be fully recovered and feeling better than ever before the sun rises."

His arm came closer and I was ripped backward so fast, I couldn't stop the cry that escaped from the pain.

"What do you think you're doing?" Marko positioned me to lie straight before him where my face could bury into his neck. Just the feel of his arms had the fear in me easing.

"Ah, the bonded." I heard Sayer's voice growing closer from behind me as he continued. "You know how things work, Master Delacroix. Tessalyn and I are to be together when she's changed. Our blood is one. You know what that means."

Marko held me tighter as he stepped back. No words came from his mouth as he cut to the side, moving more in the direction of the new tunnel where our room was. Sickness swam through me and I cried out at the twinges jerking my body.

"You need to give her to me so I can heal her more than I already have."

Marko voice boomed from beside me. "Tessa will have *my* blood. She'll heal just fine." More, we moved.

"Not as fast as if she were to take *mine*."

The statement had Marko coming to a stop. "Maybe not yet, Black Prince. But, in time, I assure you it will. If not *more*. And I'll make myself clear right now. You will not have her. Tessa is my slave and that's the status she'll carry until our deaths. I will not consent or allow our bond to be broken and that's final. I don't care who you are."

Marko spun around to head for the room and I came face to face with Sayer. His eyes narrowed while he watched us walk away. A smirk quickly replaced the anger and I couldn't dismiss the weird feeling, as if he were hiding something. Julius was moving more to his side and my heart thumped hard in my chest. My blood was going to be the death of me, and quite literally if Sayer had his way.

Chapter 15
Marko

The Black Prince. God dammit, why couldn't it have been anyone but him? Sayer. Fuck…I could feel how bad this was going to turn out. Weird prickling stabbed my insides as I tried to hold in the nausea suddenly plaguing me over our predicament.

Green eyes stared up at me while I ran the warm rag over Tessa's nude body. I could feel her pain, her uneasiness, while I cleansed the blood from her skin. The expression she wore made me even more unable to process what it would mean to lose her. Sayer wanted what was mine. The bond she and I held should have prevented that, but them sharing the same blood changed things. He could easily win over the ties I held and replace them with his own. Not only from the power he harbored, but because her blood would be more compatible with his. Her essence wouldn't fight as hard, like it had done with mine.

I was in a losing battle and I could see the end getting closer. Desperation did strange things to even the sanest man. And I was far from stable.

"Marko, I don't want this."

My stare rose to Tessa's and the tears welling in her eyes broke my heart. God, I'd almost lost her once already tonight. Now, I would, permanently, and right in my face to where I couldn't do anything about it. She'd stay here…bonded and bound to one of the strongest vampires on earth. And she'd rule. For some reason, the last part didn't bother me as much as seeing someone I loved every day and not being able to have them. Tessa wouldn't want me once she was tied to Sayers— especially if she was turned. Nothing would matter to her but the hunt and the man whose blood gave her life. There was no out for me. Even un-bonded, I'd still love her. The fact was etched into my soul as if she'd carved her name right into what I was made of. I was hers, eternally, and there was nothing me or anyone else could do about it.

"What don't you want, ma minette?"

The trembling of her bottom lip had me swallowing past the weird nausea. My heart constricted as if it were being crushed into a thousand pieces. And although it was a mix of both of our heartache, I knew the majority of it was coming from me. I'd die trying to keep her, and maybe that was for the best. To live through the torture of seeing her love and pine for someone else would kill me.

"I don't want to belong to Sayer. I don't want to be turned. I want to stay with you, like we are now, Master and slave."

At the tear escaping, I lowered my forehead to rest on hers. "Shh, don't think about it right now. I'll…" Do what? There was nothing I could do to stop the inevitable. Sayer *would* have her. Whatever he decided wouldn't be stopped. Power was the ultimate corruption for vampires. We thrived to make it to the top. With Tessa, the Black Prince may ultimately rule. He wasn't far off now. Her blood would strength him. Her own special powers would expand his.

"Can we run?"

My head lifted in surprise. "Run?"

"Yes, so we can stay together?"

The question was absurd. I never ran, for nothing or nobody. But I couldn't deny it was half-tempting if it meant I could keep her.

"No. It's out of the question."

"Then, I'll run. I won't be changed."

The strength pouring from her had a mix of anxieties going through me. If she left, I'd lose her, too.

"You will not. You are not weak, ma minette. You will face whatever it is your life holds for you."

"To rule? I don't *want* to rule. And I sure as hell don't want Sayer."

Even as she said it, a weird twinge twisted my stomach. It held enough force to make my face tighten "You lie," I whispered. "Jesus…you lie. He…*appeals* to you." Just picking up on her inner emotions drove the vampire in me to a jealous rage. I saw the fear in Tessa's eyes. Felt her internally cower at my stare. I knew it was the blood. Just as we vampires were attracted to hers, she was being sucked in by his. The need to drown it out, to end the inner cravings altogether, had crazy thoughts beginning to take me over. If I changed her first, she could carry *my* blood. It would take her over completely. She'd be one with me. But, if I did that, I'd lose her just the same. Prey would be her only love. We didn't share the same blood so the automatic emotions wouldn't exist. I'd have to win her over. Once she saw the real me, the one who was her equal, she very well might not want anything to do with the Marko she knew. Vampires and humans thought differently when attracted to one another. It wasn't all just physical. If I didn't hold something Tessa deemed worthy or would benefit her, she'd turn her nose up. If she were as powerful as they believed she would be, even I wouldn't draw her in. Past or not, what we shared now would be nonexistent. At least for her. I was doomed. And that was even if I lived. Sayer would try to kill me if I took her from him.

"I don't like your thoughts." Her voice was low as she stared up at me with uncertainty. I brought up my walls, moving to sit beside her. My face stayed devoid of emotion as I slit my forearm, only to bring my free palm back against my belly.

"Drink. You need to heal. Unless, of course, you'd prefer to feed from the Black Prince. I'm sure Sayer wouldn't mind in the least."

Her head shook and her body spasmed again while she clutched her own stomach. Her actions mirrored mine and I suddenly couldn't breathe as I looked between us. A small cry left Tessa's mouth as fear began to etch in. Although I had my thoughts blocked, I had a feeling she was picking up on my suspicions. I didn't have to wait long before they began to come true. Tessa's eyes widened even as she gasped through the increasing pain. Black began to spread out within the green, like dark vines overgrowing the color. Shock had my lips separating. The beat of my heart increased and I slid my hand up to my chest at the power it threw off. The thumps were hard, fierce as they slammed into me. Adrenaline spiked and I gasped, pushing to my feet as a piercing scream left ma minette's throat. The power her voice had was deafening. And so strong. Her body bowed as her palms pushed into the mattress.

"Sayer." His name oozed past my lips with all the venom I felt for him. Inside, my vampire clawed its way out, and I let him as I watched my slave scream through another round of shocks to her system. God, it was already happening.

I'll kill him. God, I swear, I will. I spun around, racing from the room. The monster within me roared to life at the threat plaguing it. Tessa was mine and he'd somehow given her his blood. Probably when he was messing with her back. All he would have had to do is slice open his finger and…

The tunnels blurred in my peripheral vision for only a second before I broke into the heart of the city. I spotted him immediately, not far from the last place I saw him standing. The corner of his mouth upturned into a smile as I sprinted forward. My fangs drew down, ready to shred him to pieces for the deceit he'd pulled.

Julius' hand came up and I knew he was going to throw up a wall to try to stop me. It only made me push myself faster. My own hand was already raising to try to somehow block his power, even though I knew I wasn't capable yet.

"Bonded, you return," he said, heartily. "I was wondering how long it would be before you graced us with your presence again."

I connected with the wall hard, slamming my fist into the invisible surface not five feet away from them. The air locked in my lungs from the force, but I didn't stop trying to break through. Sounds left my throat, animalistic deep snarls, and I let them.

"Oh…you're almost not bonded anymore. I should probably just go back to calling you Master Delacroix."

"What you did..." Again, I hit into the wall, feeling it waver the slightest amount.

"What I did was begin the process of removing you and inserting me. It's amazing what a few drops of my blood will do compared to your entire bond. How is she, by the way? My…Tessa, that is? Does she heal? Does she…" he paused, smiling bigger. "Oh wait, never mind. I can already feel her. Let me show you what real power looks like." He pushed from the table he was leaning against and reached forward, crooking his finger as if he were motioning for someone.

I could feel the wildness within me as my eyes flared, only to narrow. My claws sunk into the wall as I tapped into my own powers and let them simmer and stir around. I didn't want to turn around. Didn't want to see what I already knew. One exchange on his behalf. He hadn't even bit her yet, but I knew Tessa would come at his call. Their blood was too similar for her not to react.

Shuffling in the distance had my head lowering and the anger only intensifying. Closer it got, until it was directly behind me.

"Master, please." The sob had me turning to face her. "I don't want to go to him. Please, make him stop."

Tessa threw herself into my arms before I could do or say a word. I held her as I faced Sayer. "You may call her, but look who she comes to. She doesn't want you. She never will. Tessa loves *me*. Blood may allow you to claim her, but her heart will always be mine."

A laugh echoed around us. "I don't want her *love*. I want what's running through her veins. But I do believe you offer quite the challenge. I like a good game."

"Her love isn't a game," I growled. "Besides, you won't win against her. You may find yourself in love with her, too, and then where does that leave you? She'll still love me more."

"We'll see. But just so you know…I let her go to you. Had I wanted her kneeling before me, she'd be here right now." He paused. "And that's just a few drops, Delacroix. Wait until I finalize the first exchange. She won't even care who you are. Come morning, the true Tessa may arrive, and she'll know what you two share is nothing but a lie."

I didn't doubt what he spoke was the truth. Then again, for all I knew, he was bluffing. Sure, his blood had hit her hard. It explained the nausea and twinges we both felt. And she did look a little better than before, but I could still feel how weak she was. Fuck. I needed to feed her and quick. More of my blood would help dilute his. Not that it would ever go away. I wasn't strong enough to overpower the purity. At least, *not yet*. With everything that continued to happen, my vampire was constantly being tested and was still strengthening from being in lockdown. It was only a matter of time. Time, I wasn't sure I had if Tessa saw through what I'd been doing.

"Let's get you better. You're still weak."

Tessa was wrapped in my sheet and I knew she wasn't wearing anything underneath. She wouldn't have had the right frame of mind to have gotten dressed once she got called. I was surprised she'd even been able to grab the sheet.

"Yes, please take me back. I don't want to be out here with him."

I swept her in my arms, giving one last glare to Sayer before I started heading to the room. His energy pushed against my back as a warning and had I known Julius wouldn't stop me, I'd go after him again for provoking me. He may have been strong, but that didn't mean I couldn't win. I had a few tricks up my sleeve I could count on if need be.

"You can barely stay awake." I spoke the words to her as I shut us back in the room. The way she was curled into me, it showed me just how strong our bond still was. But, for how long? It would take a few hours, maybe even a day, for the effects from what Sayer had done to show full-force. I hoped that even though he had the power to call her, it didn't go past that.

"Marko, what's happening?"

Panic laced her words as I laid her on her side. The wound on her back wasn't completely closed yet, but it wouldn't be long.

"Sayer slipped you some of his blood when he removed the wood. You know he wants to make you his concubine, ma minette, and he's not waiting around to erase what we have. He means to make that happen and fast. Probably before the week is out and he returns back to Dallas."

"So soon?" Fear engulfed her, forcing its way deep within me, too. Her hand shot out toward my arm, only to pause. Tears raced over the edges of her face faster as she shook her head.

"I never wanted this life, but I've adjusted. Now, this? In a week, I'll be one of you and I don't want it. I hate that I have no say. This isn't fair."

"Life isn't fair. And you won't remember these unimportant details when you change. To you, in your mind, it'll be the best thing that's ever happened."

Faster, her head shook. "No. I will never forget how I was forced against my will into this life. *You* did this to me."

The words were so cold, there was a hesitation in my sadness. Everything within me stopped at the hatred and the speed at which it came. As thick as it was in hcr stare, it faded almost just as fast. Our bond, it was buffering her true feelings. Sayers blood strengthening hers, was allowing it to break free. And so fucking fast. It blew my mind. I'd only just hoped this sort of thing wouldn't happen and it already was. What else would come out in the next few hours?

I was losing her and it made me angry. Fuck…losing. I didn't lose.

"I did do this to you. And I don't regret it," I said, just as unfeeling. "You're mine now, whether or not you, Sayer, Julius, Hunter, or anyone else likes it. *Mine*. And you'll stay that way for as long as I can make it possible."

My nails elongated and I broke my skin, pushing my forearm hard against her lips. Ones that stayed shut for a few seconds before she opened to take me in. The sucking was brutal. Forceful. Our anger toward each other stirred my lust when it was the last thing I should have felt in the moment.

"That's right, you know who owns you. Drink and don't you fucking stop until it's impossible for you take anymore. I want to be so thick in your veins, you know nothing but me."

"Poison."

A smile pulled at my lips. *"Your poison,"* I countered. *"And you love it."*

"I love you."

I hadn't expected the sentiment. They erased my defensiveness and left me loving her even more as I stared into her green depths. It was my blood. It was drugging her back into love with me. And I was soaking it in like the filthy supplier I was. *"I love you more."*

Tessa's sucking slowed and I felt happiness burst within her. I could have cursed myself for admitting my true feelings so boldly, but if I was losing her and she'd grow to hate me, what else did I have but these last few memories? She'd forget this anyway. The realization broke my heart even more. Which was astonishing on its own. What had happened to me? I'd changed so much in the last few hours. Where was my newborn? Sure, I had spurts of anger here and there, but it was nothing like the beginning of my change. It had to be because of the power. I was getting better at controlling it. Or it was already stopping…

No. I wouldn't consider it. That only meant I wouldn't stand a chance at saving her. The power had to return. It must be going through some sort of charging stage. When it hit again, it would come back with a punch. And more rage would rise. I'd deal with the anger if it meant keeping Tessa. Although, she might not want me after the constant ups and downs. I'd put her through hell already.

"I hear you."

My eyes rose to hers and my mind cleared. What did she think of my fears?

"I think if your evil is your ticket to save me, I'll go back to sighing and waiting for you to return, Marko."

The way she said my name, she believed me to be my old self. The one she loved. Maybe in a way I was. I still didn't have the majority of our memories together. I saw a lot of stalking, a few run-ins…me almost killing her and bringing her back to Hunter. How much more was I missing?

"Not much. You're him. At least, right now. Your eyes have barely been black tonight. It comes, but it doesn't last long."

Still, she took my blood and I could feel her fullness. Better yet, I could feel her strengthening so much more. Sayer's blood may have gotten her mobile again, but mine was doing a hell of a lot better job at healing her. *"A lot better."* As I met Tessa's stare, I knew she was thinking along the same lines I was. Sayer was powerful, yes, but truly, how much more powerful than me? I wasn't so sure it was as much as we were all made to believe.

Chapter 16
Hunter

"Holy…shit. A vampire did this to you?"

My eyes rose to Gomez, my Army friend I served with years prior. He was now stationed at Fort Hood, not too far away. He came the moment I called, just like I knew he would. It was a hesitant decision, but one I couldn't prolong anymore. I needed help and I couldn't deny it any longer.

I took in the three men he brought with him. Waters and Thatcher were familiar from my tours overseas, but I didn't know them very well. Their stares were fixated on my bare upper body. The scratches were numerous and deep, covering almost every inch from my waist up to my neck. Even over my arms and fingers. The ones on my back were just as bad, but I still hadn't been able to get a good look at them yet. The deepest ones were just over my pecs and I'd stitched those up on my own.

"Yeah. Marko did this with his mind. He's very powerful. You really wouldn't believe how much. It's mind blowing. I'm still having a hard time processing it." My head shook as I tried to wade past the shock. "He has my best friend, Tessa. I tried killing him, but I shot her by accident. I'm not even sure she's still alive. She…threw herself in front of him. I…" all I could do was continue to move my head back and forth, "I don't know what happened. When I went to the police, they acted like no one reported it. I was ready to face the consequences as long as I knew what happened, but they had no idea what I was talking about. I don't even know if she's okay."

I wiped the tears from my cheeks, unable to withhold what was killing me on the inside. "I have to find her and see for myself that she's alive. He says if he dies, she dies. I'm not sure whether that's true. He uses the term bonded, but that could mean anything. All I know is I have to get her back and somehow separate the two of them until I can figure out how to get rid of him without hurting her."

"Fuck, man. I'm sorry about your friend. I really hope she's alright." Gomez leaned more forward on the sofa, resting his forearms just short of his knees. "That vampire really fucked you up. The ones we've come into contact with haven't been that powerful. You have to be dealing with a Master Vampire. We've heard about them, but never crossed paths with one before."

I stood, unable to say sitting any longer. "I believe he is. His power is downright terrifying. I emptied a clip in him and he didn't so much as bat an eyelash. Maybe I expected that part, but it's his mind that worries me. All he has to do is look at a person and he could probably kill them."

Gomez gestured his head toward Thatcher, calling him by his first name. "Frank has heard some stories from his friends in New York. The Masters are almost impossible to kill. If you can even find them. They have a way of just…disappearing."

My lips separated. "Marko has done that almost every time he's left this house. He just vanishes and I'm never able to track him."

"Yep, definitely a Master then. The others, they're fast, but they can't vanish into thin air like the leaders can. Fuck, we're going to have our hands full with this one. I think the stakes will work, though. They have for us and we didn't even have ours soaked in holy water. If your friend Tessa really is bonded to him, he would have felt it through her. Did you notice a change in him when she got shot?"

"Yeah," I mumbled, feeling my heart drop at facing the fact that they were tied together, even though I already knew it in my heart. "He initially looked weak, now that I think about it. They almost both went down to the ground, but he came back really fast. Before I knew it, he had ahold of me and was throwing me in the back of his limo."

"Limo?" Waters, a short, thick, blond-haired man pushed from the wall. "Definitely a man with status if he was sporting one of those. The vampires we've run against are more common folk. Some even giving off the appearance of thugs and homeless people. Your guy is important amongst them. I'm going to go with Thatcher and say he's a leader. If we kill him, we might start a shit-storm with vampires we aren't yet prepared for. We need more followers. More fighters, like us."

My hand rubbed over my short hair. "Let's just focus on tonight. We won't worry about killing him yet. Not until I see how Tessa is and whether injuring him will hurt her. The only problem I see with this situation is him letting her go. I'll have to take her somewhere new. Somewhere he doesn't have entrance to."

Johnson, a tall, African-American man, raised his hand from the couch. "My wife was killed a few months back by one of those bastards. I have a house on base. No fucking way he's getting in there. Not the base, and sure as shit not my house. You can bring her there when the time comes."

The men glanced toward him, only to turn and look at me. I physically hurt for the man. Tessa wasn't my wife, but I had dreams of it being so. And him, he'd gone through the worst possible thing imaginable. "That's horrible. I'm so sorry to hear about your loss. I appreciate you wanting to help," I paused. "What you're all doing means a lot. I wouldn't have called if this wasn't dire. I almost didn't to begin with, but I can't do this alone. It might take a while to search Tessa out, but if we stay together, begin to fight these vampires as a team," my head nodded, "we can do this. We can take these motherfuckers out and make them pay for what they're doing."

Thatcher nodded while the others made sounds of agreement laced with excited. As I took in their camo attire, I knew they were down to head out. And I was ready, too.

I grabbed my black, long-sleeve shirt and winced as I pulled it over my head. The sun had already set, but I tried not to think about the difference that made. I knew the significance, but I prayed we'd all made it out of the tunnels alive.

Weight from my belt added a calming sensation and I rested my hand on the butt of my gun, just as I always did. I had everything I needed for the underground, even my crossbow, which Chloe had delivered this morning.

"Why don't you all grab some of the soaked stakes from the table. I trust those more. You never know who we're going to be dealing with and I'd rather be safe than sorry. If we do face Marko or a Master, it'll be better than regular wood."

Johnson was holding his own crossbow. It wasn't much bigger than mine, but it looked modified. Bows weren't usually my thing. I'd never once had to use one before Tessa mixed up with Marko, but I was getting better. All my training with guns made me a natural.

The men stood around the round table as I placed the bow at my back. I moved my other hand over, fingering the hilt of the dagger while I waited for them to return. God, I hoped this worked. If we could get further back and find some answers, maybe I stood a chance of getting her back safe. But how would it be possible if I didn't know my way around? I needed to stay alert and remember every detail. I needed to start taking these vampires out. The daytime would be better for that. Maybe they'd be sleeping.

"I've been underground and I know somewhat where their city is. I haven't come across it yet, but there *are* vampires down there and I expect we may kill some. This won't be easy. There's a chance some of us might not make it back out. Maybe none of us. But we won't know for sure unless we try. I'm only going to ask once. Are you all sure you want to go? There will be no judgment from me if you don't. I can't stress how dangerous this is going to be."

"I'm in," Gomez said without pause.

"Me, too," the other three men said in succession. I gave a sharp nod as I headed for the door. I flipped the porch light off before stepping outside.

"The grate that leads underground is across the street at the end of the road. We'll remain in the dark until we get in the tunnels. I'll turn on my light then."

Their silent approval led me forward and Johnson closed the door behind him. We made it down the street in complete silence. Everyone's feet were light, along with their breaths. Each of these men knew what it was to be in battle and they didn't overlook the dangers as we made our way underground. The moment the grate covered us, I pulled out my flashlight and clicked it on. My crossbow was already loaded and I fixed the light to rest on the top so it could follow my movements.

I glanced behind me, keeping my voice low as I took in all four of their stoic faces. "I've marked the tunnels and ways we need to go with chalk. I'm hoping the lines are still there. Let's stay close. Thatcher, watch our back."

As they quietly got into position behind me, I kept a slow and steady pace forward. The length didn't seem as long as it had before and I paused at the end, shining the light left and then right before I made the turn, heading in the direction I went last time.

Would the group of vampires be back there? Would the one they called Boyd be waiting to take us out?

I slowed as we rounded the corner, listening for voices or anything indicating someone was there. A dripping in the far distance had my eyebrows drawing in and I slowed even more, keeping the light down so the beam didn't shine too far ahead.

"I think it's clear."

My whisper seemed to echo louder than I expected and I felt my skin break out in goosebumps. My internal warnings were going off like crazy. Although I didn't see any vampires, I knew they were here, around us, somewhere.

As a precaution, I shined the light at the opposite end, still making sure it was clear. The darkness seemed to swallow up the beam and I couldn't fight the unnerving feeling taking me over.

"Eyes open," I mouthed.

Deeper, I walked around the long curve. A rectangular area opened up no bigger than the size of decent living area and I shined the light over the graffiti on the walls. The dark words had me moving in and I felt my eyes widen as I focused on what I was truly looking at.

"That's dried blood," Gomez whispered out behind me.

"Not all of it's old," Waters said, smearing his hand on words that looked more red than black. The crimson substance on his fingertips had all of us looking at each other. To say we were scared was an understatement. Terror had every hair on my arms standing on end as an eerie silence played out between us.

"If it's still wet…" Thatcher swallowed hard.

One minute, he was in the glow of the flashlight, the next…gone. A scream had me jerking to find him in the darkness. Feet shuffled next to me and Johnson turned on his own flashlight, illuminating the room even more. More screams echoed around and I swung my body in the direction I thought it might be coming from. The sound ricocheting in the enclosed space left all of us spinning around in circles.

"Where the fuck did he go?" Gomez's voice was shaking as he kept his bow trained ahead of him.

"There are only two entrances," I said, nudging my weapon toward the closest one. I took a step and froze at the warmth that dripped onto my arm. Instinct told me to look down at what had fallen on me, but training had my arms forcing my weapon up toward the ceiling. With the change in position, the light haloed out to give view of a vampire holding Thatcher before him. A hiss filled the space, but the deep hole in the soldier's neck was what pulled my attention first. Blood was beginning to pour out now that the vampire wasn't feeding and the fact that it looked worse than Tessa's bite had been didn't escape me.

"What the fuck!" Waters' yell had my heart exploding in rhythm, but I couldn't think past hearing the alarm he was sounding when all I could see was Thatcher's body falling down toward me. Before I could situate my bow, body weight crashed into Gomez and me, bringing us both down.

Yells echoed out again and the sound of one of the bows going off registered in the background. I pulled at Thatcher, but he didn't move. Somehow, I managed to right my bow and light, giving me the view of a scene I knew I would never forget.

Waters' frozen look of horror stayed etched in his features as blood and intestines poured from his stomach in a loud slosh against the cement. In a heavy fall, his knees hit the ground and then his body fell forward.

Bile burned my throat as panic set in. I had been so afraid of this. It was the whole reason I hadn't wanted to call anyone. Death seemed to follow me wherever I went and this time, I'd brought it on all of us.

"Moretti, let's fucking go. I got the bastard, but he ran off. Let's get out of here before more return."

Johnson called my name again, but I barely heard as my training kicked my body into action, even if my brain was a little behind.

I threw Thatcher over my shoulder, growling at Gomez to get Waters. I'd been taught not to leave anyone behind. Active duty or not, I wouldn't break the code I held in my heart.

"Faster!"

The light bounced as Johnson raced around the turn. I barely felt Thatcher's weight as we came to our tunnel. Music in the distance had my feet almost coming to a stop. Everything in me knew the city was further ahead. I'd been going the wrong way the whole time.

"Hurry up! Let's go." Johnson's voice made me pick up my speed and I turned into the entrance, racing for the grate.

I may have missed my opportunity to learn anything this time, but I knew where to go when I came back. Next time, I would be alone. And next time, I knew I'd find more answers.

Chapter 17
Tessa

Whispering surrounded me; a phantom sound I knew couldn't exist. Not here in mine and Marko's room. My eyes made jerky movements as I scanned the open space. Cement walls surrounded us, yet I could hear the voice as if it were slipping through invisible cracks.

Marko sat across the room on a black velvet chair. His powerful body leaned forward while he rested his arms on his thighs, watching and listening to what I was hearing. We didn't speak a word. We didn't have to. I knew he was just as baffled by the odd change as I was. His fear was my own while I tried to hold onto sanity. For hours, I had battled with the changes taking place in my body. I'd never felt more like my old self, yet there was someone new lurking beneath the surface. Was this person talking, her? Or was it delusions brought on by Sayer's blood? They all thought the mix would bode well with what was already in my system, but no one knew for sure. I was starting to think it was having the opposite effect. I was going crazy and I couldn't figure out how to stop it.

You want him. Just stand up and go. No one can stop you. Take the human's blood. Your thirst is undeniable. Feed. Taste.

My eyes squinted as I shook my head. I had no idea what it was talking about. I didn't thirst. Hell, I didn't feel hungry at all. And human? I would have thought Marko or Sayer, but the voice kept mentioning human, as if I were already a vampire. It didn't make sense. None of it did.

I dropped my head, covering my ears. The voice grew louder. Clearer. It was enough to cause me to jerk up and rush to my feet. Pacing wouldn't do any better. I'd been there. Walked this floor for probably miles when it first started happening.

"Make it stop," I breathed out. "Make it stop!" I wasn't talking to Marko or anyone in particular. I just needed silence. My whole body was twitchy and panicky the longer this went on.

"Ma minette, come sit on my lap."

My glare was automatic, but at Marko's worried expression, I walked over to him, curling up against him.

"His blood is driving me insane. I want it out. Take it out of me, please." My wrists shot forward even as my head lowered. "I never wanted this."

Marko's hand cupped the side of my head while his other reached for my outer bicep to draw me in closer. "It's done. Side effects range when mixing blood. This is probably just one of them. They can last for days. Let that comfort you instead of worrying about this being permanent."

"Days?"

Run. He's waiting for you. He wants you.

A yell broke past my throat and my hands tore at my hair.

"Calm, mon chaton. Don't fight it, just listen."

"To some voice telling me to go after human blood? I don't think so."

"It's quite interesting to me. I wonder whom the thirst is coming from. You, me, or is it Sayer? Maybe it's for his human lover. You never know."

My face lifted and I felt my eyebrows draw in. "These cravings could actually be coming from one of us?"

"More than likely. Just…pay attention. See what it tells you."

Although Marko tuned in, I tried to let my thoughts drift to something else. I didn't want to hear anymore. I was finished with this voice. I couldn't deny that the more it pleaded, the more I actually wanted to obey. Where would I end up if I went along with where it was ready to take me?

A yawn came from my mouth and time passed as I drifted in and out of blurry thoughts. Pictures played, but nothing came into focus. I felt as if I were floating in moments when I was sure it had to be nothing more than a dream finally giving me peace. Marko's voice pulled at my attention and I tried to focus on what he was saying.

"You're…to tell me. You go too far."

"What?" My voice sounded groggy, raw even.

Anger and surprise flashed on his face. I couldn't decipher what was happening. Something felt off within me, distant as I blinked to bring him into focus.

"Ma minette…." Marko shook his head, clearly unhappy. "You've been talking for the last three hours nonstop. Quite," he paused, "bravely."

The timeframe had me tensing up. "What?" The question exploded out as I tried to fight my way from his arms. Fear that I wasn't in control of myself was causing me to panic and I suddenly noticed my shirt was soaked in sweat.

"You don't remember any of it? You were telling me about your childhood. A lot about Hunter. Some of it quite…bold of you to say."

The anger was growing as it underlined his tone and he held on tighter as I continued trying to wiggle free. The jealousy was evident and the fog began to roll back through. Somehow, I managed to hold onto reality as I processed his question.

"He's my best friend," I breathed out. "I…love him."

"Yeah, you were sure to tell me *all* about that. But you won't love him more than you'll love me. You'll never love anyone more than me, ma minette," he said, shaking me. "No one. I won't let you. Ever. Do you hear me? I'll kill them. You love me. No one else!" Black was taking over his eyes and I made a sound at the added stress. I didn't get to fret on it long. Lips crushed into mine as he pulled me in tighter. I tried breaking away, but Marko refused to stop kissing me until I softened in his arms. This part of him I knew. The passion. The way he burned for me. God, I was suddenly on fire and I couldn't stop myself from pulling at the buttons of his shirt. They broke free at my impatience and I barely noticed as he stood and brought us to the bed.

"Sayer wants your blood, I want your body, and your fucking heart is still wrapped up in Hunter. Tell me why I put any of us through this misery? I should have killed you when I had the chance."

I broke away, glaring at the anger that suddenly surfaced within me. The black was all but there now and it wouldn't be long before the beast lurking within took over completely. I had prayed this part of him was over with, but I knew in my heart things were only about to get a million times worse. The nice Marko would be gone now and what scared me the most was how I suddenly might be, too. I'd been oblivious to everything for three hours. How was that possible? To make things worse, whatever I said had built over time, triggering this episode of Marko's vampire. What I'd admitted had to have been bad. My pulse quickened at his words about Hunter. My heart was still wrapped up in him? …I loved him, I knew that. He'd been the foundation of my life. Apparently, my sub-conscious hadn't let that part go with these new feelings for Marko? The real me was trying to tell myself something I was too bonded to see. But I already knew. Deep down, I did.

"What's the matter? You were so full of conversation just minutes ago. Too good to talk to me now?"

Fingers dug into my face as his weight settled more on top of me. "I don't know what you're talking about. I don't remember."

"Let me refresh your memory."

The waistband of my panties was pulled from my stomach as his hand pushed into them. "You're going to rule, Tessa. That's what you so clearly stated while you looked up at me as if I was beneath you. You're going to rule and concubine to Sayer or not, you'll bond a slave. The only one truly worthy to be at your side. Ringing any bells?"

The pads of his fingers rubbed over the top of my slit and I felt my legs jerk at the sensitivity.

"I never said that," I whispered. "I'd never do that to Hunter."

"You'd never do that to *me!*" he exploded. "I won't let you. I may love you, but I'll kill you just as fast if it comes down to it. I own you. You'll be mine forever. *Forever,*" he growled. "No one will see this body as I have. No one will touch it. And damn sure no one is going to fuck it."

Marko's fingers pushed into my wet entrance and I cried out as he surged deep.

"Tell me I'm wrong. Tell me you'll belong to someone else."

The hand keeping my face immobile tightened even more as he turned me to look into his dark eyes.

"Tell me, Tessa." My name was spat and I gasped as he rubbed against my G-spot.

"I'll always be yours. No one else's."

In my heart, I believed that. Or…I had. I couldn't understand the odd sense of emptiness my words seemed to carry. What was happing to me? Who was I? I didn't know anymore. I couldn't even figure out who the real Tessa was. I was so confused.

"Say it louder." The hand on my face lifted enough to slap against my cheek. "Say it where I can fucking hear you."

"I'm yours."

"No one else's?"

"No one else's," I answered.

Pressure pulled my face to his as he met me halfway. I couldn't stop from moving against his fingers while they pushed deep and kept a steady rhythm.

"I'm going to make you pay for what you said. For even having it in your mind. I'll fuck him out of you if I have to spend the rest of our days pounding him as far away as I can. Now, take it back. Tell me you don't want this position as leader and you don't want Hunter as your slave."

His dark eyes held such threat behind them that my mouth opened to obey, but nothing came out. I licked my lips, trying to ignore the lust roaring through me. But who was it for…Marko or Hunter? Both swirled around my mind, confusing me even more.

"You know I don't want it." The last was slower…almost nonexistent at the force I had to use to make the sentence even come.

Marko's face tightened and I knew he didn't believe me. His fangs came down and sliced over his arm. Blood was pouring over my lower face before I could even process what he was doing.

"Drink," he yelled. "I'll drown him out. I'll drowned all of them out!"

My lips separated, but not fast enough. He removed his fingers from my pussy, shoving them into my mouth to make me open wider. "Taste me, Tessa. Taste us both. What do you think? Am I still unworthy of you? No, you fucking love the way I taste. You love *me*."

I couldn't stop staring into his eyes as his anger increased by the second.

"Don't look at me like that. You did this. You're the responsible one. It's your blood fucking us all up. But I won't let it. I'll win because you'll be mine. You'll never rule or have a slave. Will you?"

Coughing wracked my chest as he pushed his forearm deeper into my mouth, stretching my jaw and causing me to choke. Blood filled my throat and I could even feel it in my nose. He meant to drown me in him and he was succeeding.

My teeth sunk into his flesh hard, trying to get him to stop, but it only drove him on. I could feel his hard cock grinding against me as he put more of his weight down onto my body.

"Do you feel me, ma minette? Am I consuming you like you consume me? I can't think about anyone but you. And you'll be the same way before it's over with. I won't go through this alone. I won't."

Marko spun me over to my stomach and ripped my panties down. My knees instinctively drew up underneath me and my head came up just as fast as his hand connected with my bottom.

"Don't you move from that position. I want to see what's mine. Fucking, Tessa. You drive me insane. Wanting to bring Hunter here for your lover and slave."

Whack!

"I would kill him as soon as I saw him anywhere near you. For you to even—"

Whack!

A cry came from my mouth as I blinked away the tears. "I don't remember!"

"You'll remember now, won't you?"

Whack!

His hand rubbed over the tender area from the spankings and he squeezed before moving to trace down my slit.

"Oh, yeah. You'll remember. Fuck, I'll make you, even past the change. You won't forget me or what we share. I'll leave an impact so big, our minds will be one."

His fingers rubbed along the wetness, smoothing it into my folds. "Still, you respond to me. You like pain, though, don't you, ma minette?"

The bed shifted as he took off his clothes and moved to position himself behind me. Teeth bit into my ass and I sucked in air as his fangs punctured the skin just the smallest amount. Pleasure burst through and I moaned while I gripped the comforter.

"I do," I admitted.

"Let's see how much." A tug against my hair had him pulling me up until I was on all fours. The slave in me knew to hold still. Even if there was this small part that was ready to run.

"Don't move."

Marko brushed my hair to the side and I tensed as his claws eased down the length of my back.

"You don't trust me and right now, I barely trust myself, but let's just see what happens, *Ms. Leader.*"

My brow furrowed as I glared ahead. His anger sparked mine and it wasn't smart to go rounds with him. Maybe he just wanted to get me worked up, to play on my fear as he held such deadly weapons against me.

Burning began to rake down my sensitive back and I gripped the blanket tighter, letting the sensation take me over completely. The tightness in my back relaxed the slightest amount as he worked his way up the opposite side.

"Ah…shit," I moaned, jumping. Warmth traveled down my ribs and he let out a small laugh.

"You cut me," I said, turning back to look at him. "And you did it intentionally."

"I did. And I intend to do it again. Now, face forward and stay quiet."

Yes…Marko was gone. Long gone. How had I forgotten this version of him so quickly? He was surging again, growing more powerful. What I said might have set him off, but this would have come regardless. I just helped it out.

I gritted my teeth, turning back to face the front. The spanking had me tensing in surprise.

"You once teased me with a fantasy. I was painting your body with blood. I see the memory. It's so far back that I can barely reach it, *but* I see it….and I'm going to give it to myself. Not you. What you want is irrelevant. I want it. And I'm going to cover every inch of you in red while you come all over my cock."

Another nail pushed into my back and my mouth opened in a silent cry as his fingers rubbed the warmth into my skin. It was so wrong and yet, one of the fantasies plaguing me the most. Except now, it didn't carry what it once did. I was separating from him. It left me in a weird place as I picked up my compliant, slave behavior.

"You're going to have every vampire within a one-hundred foot radius trying to bust through our door," I said quietly. "Sorry, but I think I've gone through enough. I'm too weak to bleed out that much tonight."

Marko's hand paused and I was suddenly yanked to stand on my knees. His face was mere inches from mine as he came around and leaned in. The evil that radiated had me wishing I never said anything at all.

"Let them come. I will destroy anyone who breaches our threshold. Do you doubt me?"

I knew it wasn't a question he wanted answered. There was a challenge in his tone that almost said he wished someone would try to break through the barrier. He was looking for a fight from anyone willing to step up. Even me, and I wasn't that stupid.

"You know I don't."

"Then take what I give you and stay silent, unless you're moaning or crying. Those, I like to hear."

His hand cupped my pussy and I moved into the contact robotically. I could feel how wet I was against his fingers. They glided over my shaved folds so smoothly while he rubbed my juices over my entrance.

"Pleasure and pain, mon chaton. Pleasure and pain. What comes next?"

The pleasure was already there. I knew what was coming and it appeared before I could finish the thought. The force of another spanking to my ass jolted me into him and I placed my palms on his pecs for balance.

"You take the pain I like to give you so well. You were meant for this. Meant for me."

Marko's mouth pressed into mine and I sank down on his fingers as he pushed two into my channel. My nails clawed into his chest and he broke away with a hiss, pulling back against my bottom lip.

"Sayer will try to win you over. To him, this is nothing more than a game. You're not going to give into him. You're going to show him where your loyalty lies. Now, tell me." The order was embedded in his stare and I nodded.

"My loyalty is with you. I think I've already proved that tonight."

Faster, his fingers thrust into me. "You have. You could have died to protect me and I'll never forget it. People will try to tear us apart, but we're not going to let them. We'll kill them all. We'll rule."

I swallowed hard at his words. Was this what my life was destined for? To be at Marko's side, helping him…murder his way to the top? No. This was the evil vampire talking. Not the good Marko. But where did mine begin and the new one end? Would this all fade once the power died out again? I wasn't so sure and it scared me.

"No. Shh," he said, lowering to the side of my face to whisper in my ear. "You think too much. Don't think. Feel."

Fangs bit down into my neck hard and I screamed at the surprised initial pain. Thickness from the poison entered my body and my worries floated away in the cloud of ecstasy he left me on. The caressing he was doing inside my pussy was the best feeling in the world—all I wanted to know in the moment. As he built me up, I felt my head lean against the side of his. My body was weak, but blissful. The sucking and swirl of his tongue made me tingle even more. I almost cried out when he broke away from my neck and began rubbing the flow of blood over my throat and down to my chest, but I was too wrapped up in how good it felt to make a sound.

"Just you and me, Tessa. That's all it'll be when I fight my way to the top. No concubine will be responsible for making me stronger. I'll do it on my own. We'll do it together. Me. You. Tell me you want that, too."

"God, I do."

The admission that he wouldn't take a mate or wife left the drugged slave in me giddy. Hadn't I wanted that more than anything? I didn't know anymore. I knew nothing but him in this moment.

Marko eased me to the bed, never stopping the way he was fucking me with his fingers. When his mouth latched on to my hard nipple, whatever was lurking in the shadows of my mind disappeared. I moved with his rhythm, meeting the fast pace with a fevered speed of my own.

"Take me," I begged. "I want to feel you inside of me. Please, fuck me, now."

Pressure from his palm pushed over my clit and I arched, spreading my legs wide. It was an open invitation, another silent plea for him to claim my body. The desperation I felt went past all other times and I didn't understand it. Yes, it was for Marko, but again, there was an underlining need being brought out by Sayers's blood I couldn't comprehend.

"You're so wet." He withdrew his fingers, sucking them deep into his mouth. At his moan, he brought his other hand up and pushed the tip of his nail into the fleshy part of my breast. Crimson pooled over the small incision and he moved his index finger into the blood, tracing my nipple and circling the tight nub. "So beautiful," he said through clenched teeth. "I've seen the flashes in my head, but the real thing is so much better."

The ending was barely audible as he lowered, sucking away the evidence of my life. And it didn't stop as he made a path to the wound, licking over it and heading to my neck, closing those wounds, too. With every slide of his tongue over my skin, I pushed into him even more. I didn't need to beg for his cock again for him to finally give me what I wanted.

Marko positioned himself between my legs and eased his tip into my pussy slowly, teasing my entrance. The grip my channel had on his thickness sent my arms flying around his neck as he let the head stretch me with each dip of his shaft.

Over and over, he tortured me with the pleasure. My moans turned into whimpers until they ultimately became sobs. Release was so close, yet he withheld, making me edge. I was sure I'd lose my voice from the loud, continuous pleas.

"Tell me you love me and I'll give you what you want." Marko eased in to fill me with the head of his cock again before he left me yearning for more.

"I love you. You know I do."

"No," he growled. "The bond loves me. Convince me that *you* love me."

The black was still prominent in his eyes and I battled over whether to believe this was my Marko or not. Did it matter anymore? I didn't know either one at all.

I blinked, trying to get my mind to focus. A solution didn't present itself and I felt more like zombie than anything as I stared up at him. "I'll kill him," I heard myself whisper. "I'll kill Sayer."

A gasp exploded from my mouth as Marko slammed his entire length into me. The passion behind his kiss took over my own, but I never let my words leave my head. Why had I said that? Why would I even think such a thing? Why? Because somewhere deep down, I knew it was the only way I would survive as myself. The first exchange wasn't complete yet and if I wanted to remain human, it was my only chance. It wasn't for Marko. *It was for me.* Just the thought had me tensing for the briefest moment, but I was sure he hadn't heard my thoughts.

"I knew you loved me. I fucking knew it."

The pounding was so forceful, I fought to breathe past the impact of his body. Tightly, he wrapped his arms around me and all I could do was hold on as my orgasm built from the combination of pleasure and pain. Although my body reacted, my mind was far away. I could feel myself drifting in the void. Where that was exactly, I wasn't sure.

Words whispered in my ear and I heard my moans as if I were there. Even as my release peaked and I screamed out his name, I knew it wasn't really me who was going through the motions of a woman lost in desire. This one was good, amazing with her caresses and seduction. Bolder with her words. Ones I would have never had the courage to say.

"Your cock is so big. I love to feel it inside of me. I love when you come in me even more. Come, Marko. Give me what I want."

He made a sound between a moan and a grunt as I ran my tongue over the length of his ear. When I brought it back down to trace the side of his neck, I felt him swell even more.

"Someday, I'm going to slide my fangs right here," I said lowly, nipping at his skin. "And when I do, you'll come at the sting. You'll love it as much as I love yours. Then, you'll ask me to be your concubine. With Sayer out of the way and with me as a vampire, we'll rule. You and me, together, just like you want."

His hand slammed over my mouth, but it didn't stop the warmth from shooting into my pussy. The smile that came to my face under his palm grew with every wave of his release. Somehow, I felt I had Marko under my thumb, and this new, evil part of me thrived in the revelation.

Chapter 18
Marko

Side effects. From what I'd seen of Tessa over the last twenty-four hours, she was suffering them badly. The voice had pretty much taken over her completely. It was no different than a newborn, and it was all thanks to Sayer's power. Where he stood against me was irrelevant. The combination of their blood was dynamic together. Too good. She might as well have been changed into one of us for the mindset she now held. It wouldn't last. I knew that, but for how long worried me. It left me alarmed enough to bring me out of my own darkness, if just a little.

Ever since I'd fucked her, she'd been different. I felt her change come on the moment the new personality slid into place and I couldn't deny that my vampire had been swept away by it. But outside of sex, I couldn't stand her. She wasn't my Tessa. Not the way she talked and definitely not the way she carried herself. I was back to being beneath her. Even the way she looked at me seemed to put me into place. In her mind, there was no one better than her and it was thanks to the blood mixing with hers. In truth, no one really was. Not even the Black Prince. If his blood was pure, hers was even purer. If Tessa changed, she'd be an anomaly. Someone not any of us could prepare for. It was scary. For the vampire who wanted a taste and was already enjoying what he was tasting now…it went beyond tempting. But for her to be that powerful, Sayer would have to be the one to change her, and if this new Tessa had her way, she'd kill him first. And she'd do it *for me*. It was better for her not to know what was best. I couldn't afford for her to be that strong. Not if I wanted to rule, myself. One bite with the right venom could ruin everything. I just had to make sure Sayer didn't change her before he planned to do their bonding. He could, easily. She already had his blood. All he needed now was hers and then his poison could do the trick. Where I used pleasure, he might chose to bring her over to our side instead. Fuck, I had to keep them separated. Tessa couldn't leave my side if that meant Sayer had access to her. It was too risky.

Red silk billowed out around Tessa's face as she kneeled not far away. The way her eyes cut up to me as I looked over sent my anger spiraling even more out of control. The rebellion was there, as was the…disgust? God, I wasn't sure. There were moments when this new side of her seemed to love me, and then there were moments like this. She was too good to be on the floor and she knew it.

"Tonight, we won't be able to leave after the feeding like we always do. Julius will require we socialize with the Dallas members. *You* are not to say a word. Even in my lap, I want your head down. Do you understand?"

"Why, of course, Master." The malice in her tone sent my fangs down. I stalked forward, grasping her bicep and jerking her to her feet.

"I mean it, slave. You'll obey or so help me, when we get back to this room, I'll light a fire to your ass."

Fear…it was nonexistent as she held my stare, something she should have known better than to do.

"I will do as I'm commanded."

"You better. Now, let's go."

I headed for the door, yanking it open and moving to the outside as she shut it behind her. Loud voices were already coming through from the festivities and it turned my mood even more sour. I didn't want to be here—not out in the heart of the city or underground at all. Especially with Tessa as she was. There were too many risks that came along with it.

Footsteps followed me through the tunnel and into the massive cement room. Vampires flipped around in the center in some sort of acrobatic act, getting tossed up around the fearful humans strung up in cages, ready to become their meal. I knew it was Dallas' entertainment. Two torches of fire flew through the air and I tore my gaze from the bright yet evilly painted men doing somersaults to Sayer. Julius had brought another table in that was an exact replica of the one we sat at. It was only feet away and they'd both been repositioned to face where we could see the acts. My head shook even more and I slowed to let Tessa stay as close to me as she could.

"Master Delacroix." Sayer stood from his seat as we approached. I ignored the smug smile plastered on his face as I headed to Julius. My leader was waiting to test my blood again and although I didn't want Sayer witnessing, I pushed it away and focused on the light blue eyes studying my every move.

"You're increasing." The words were low from Julius as I shrugged off my jacket and reached over, handing it to Tessa. She was already standing behind the fourth chair. The fact that her head wasn't down sent my teeth snapping together. Hell, she wasn't being compliant. Her gaze was locked on the table of concubines and if I knew anything about her expressions, she was damn well looking down on them, too.

I turned back to Julius, unable to do anything but nod past his assertion. *"Hey!"* My internal voice had Tessa turning and her glare coming to me. She hesitated before one of her eyebrows lifted and her face turned toward the floor. My eyes rose to meet Sayer's and I could have ripped the smile right from his face. This was *his* fault. She had been damn near perfect before he'd given her his blood. Now, I had a monster in my midst and despite that she was human and a woman, her mind wasn't her own. She was more like one of us than she knew.

My sleeve was pulled up and blood pooled over the wound as Julius sliced his nail down deep. As my arm was brought up to his lips, I met Sayer's stare. God, I'd be as powerful as him someday, if not more. I knew it in the deepest part of what made me, me. It may take hundreds of years, but I'd be there. And I'd rule. But not just Austin. My plans were so much bigger. *Axis.*

Claws stabbed into my forearm and the sting brought me back to my leader. His hand was locked around me in a death grip, but he didn't seem to be with us right now. He wasn't moving at all.

I licked my lips, flexing the muscle and pushing his nails in further, willing him to feel my worth. Lips were still on my skin, but he wasn't taking in my blood anymore. What had happened? Was he seeing something? Had my taste set off some sort of vision? Regardless, I projected my aura even more.

A grunt came from Julius' mouth and the grip tightened impossibly around me. The action made my vampire flare and I jerked my arm free, watching as my blood began to seep past his lips and trail down his chin. A look of pain drew in his features and he made another sound. My eyes flared and Bufar, the second chair, shifted behind his seat.

"Julius?" The tan-skinned man's head lowered as he peered into our leader's frozen face.

"Julius," I snapped. My hand gripped around his bicep and he jerked to stand straight. Sweat broke out across his forehead and he clutched to his stomach as he turned his attention to me.

"Second." The raspy word was followed by him collapsing into his chair. Bufar's head shook and a loud growl tore from his throat. He wasn't but two feet away and I knew what was coming before he even so much as moved. Fangs bared and my power exploded, surging within me. My vampire naturally took over and my hand thrust forward, gripping around Bufar's thick throat as his fangs tried to search me out.

Time seemed to slow as I stared deep into his black eyes. Flashes of his past flickered before me, a time I had never before seen or even imagined. His true age registered and although internally shocked, I couldn't stop the translucent scene playing before me.

Dark veins surfaced through his face even as I saw him huddled in the corner of some underground room. The smell of earth filled my nostrils and I knew it was nighttime. The small fire he was curled around was the only warmth and I felt so cold, so…alone. But I wasn't alone. And he suddenly knew that.

"Who is it?" Although I didn't understand his language, I knew what he was shouting. Shadows danced around the room and the human version of Bufar grabbed a wooden spear and jumped to his feet, moving further back into the room. Air rushed around the space at such a fast pace, it had him spinning, trying to search out the creature. Pitch black was all around and somehow, I knew exactly where the vampire was. I stared at the corner of the darkness and was met with completely blacked out eyes, so different than ours. They'd appeared from nowhere, but they saw me. They were…watching me…even now.

Cold began to race from the core of my powers, throughout my body. Fear didn't register, only amazement and curiosity as to who exactly I was looking at. This vampire was powerful. So much so that I wanted what they had. I want to experience…more.

I was physically forced from the vision and the cold dissipated. Weight registered before me while I continued to crush Bufar's throat. I could have stopped, but the power I'd witnessed from the vampire in the cave made me not want to. My fangs were already bared and I unleashed, letting my powers suck the life right out of him and. Right into me. Greed ruled and I was basking in it. Adrenaline had my whole body trembling and I let it engulf me. The strength was feeding me, making me stronger.

"Marko, enough." Anastasia's voice broke through, but I paid it no mind as I followed his pale, nearly lifeless body to the ground. All of these vampires had no idea what I was capable of. What I *could* be capable of. Only now was I truly tapping into what I'd become so far and I was insatiable. I had to see more. This was too easy. Too—

Heat scorched my side and instinct left my hand shooting out to put a stop to it. But I didn't just throw a wall to guard myself against the attack. I mirrored it, doubling the force as I sent Anastasia flying back, right over Dallas' table.

"Enough," Julius threatened, pushing to his feet. "You will not kill him. Not today. We have plans and he's a part of them."

Fear flashed behind the eyes of my leader, sending my mind spiraling at the possibilities. Did he fear me screwing up his plans, or that I could easily kill his second in command? Possibly kill *him*? The latter had me smiling and I let go of Bufar. The intake of air was deep as he coughed, crumbling to the floor.

"As you wish." My voice was calm, cool. I stepped back, pulling out the second chair. Tessa kept eye contact with me as she came forward. There was such fascination and hunger glittering in her depths, I wanted to pull her into me and kiss her brutally. To show her I was worthy of her blood and so much more. She'd see whom she was bonded to, and if she was ever turned, she'd be begging to become *my* concubine. Begging, yes. I'd make her grovel at my feet.

"Sit," Julius growled. "We feed."

Chairs sounded all around and I took my seat, hooking my arm around Tessa as I sunk into my seat. My gaze stared straight ahead to Sayer as I pulled down the hood and jerked her head back. Holding tightly to her hair, I bit my fangs into her neck. Tessa jumped underneath me, but I ignored her pain as I glared in his direction. My vampire was looking for a fight—a real one—and I knew he'd be the biggest challenge of all. At least, in this room.

Power-spiked warmth filled my mouth and not once did Sayer break our contact. Even as he began feeding from the blonde supplier, he met my challenge. His amusement was gone. What had he thought about my new position? Was he curious about how strong I was getting, too? Was he hesitant in his plans?

Tessa's fingers clutched my chest and I waited a few seconds before I broke away from her, not wanting to take any more than what was necessary for appearance's sake. I licked over the wounds, bringing her head to rest on the junction of my neck. Her hand settled over where mine was placed on her cheek and she led it to my own neck. I blinked past my confusion.

"Cut," she ordered. *"Let me taste you, too."*

To do that, here, if front of everyone…I couldn't think past how wrong it was.

Sayer's eyes narrowed and I let my nail grow and slice into my skin. Tessa moved, straddling my waist, and I nearly moaned as her lips latched onto the small incision. What we were doing was forbidden. An act that broke every rule there was. I was granting her, a slave so beneath the rest of us vampires and the future concubine of our guest, my blood amongst every single soul in this city. The repercussions didn't exist, didn't matter as I proved who my loyalty was to. Myself? No…*her*. God, she'd commanded and I'd obeyed. Soon, they'd try to separate us and if they had their way, she and I would go head to head for the ultimate position. The power my blood held would diminish and the true hate she harbored for me would return. My time was ticking down and I clung to every second like it was our last. Soon, it would be, and I wasn't powerful enough to do anything about it.

"You're walking a very fine line," Julius said threateningly, breaking from the supplier's neck. "You'll be lucky Sayer doesn't kill you before the week is out.

Or I don't kill *her*. If she wasn't meant to take your spot, she'd be dead in your arms right now. She's out of control. I'm half tempted to send her back with Sayer."

"You're welcome to try." I met his threat without pause. Marionette wasn't going anywhere. Not at Sayer's order and sure as hell not under Julius'.

"You're not close to standing a chance against me, Marko. Don't think you are. My reaction to your blood isn't what you assume."

Maybe it was…maybe it wasn't. I knew he'd been surprised and probably saw something due to his visions, but the lock in his limbs and the pain only told me my blood had given his one hell of a fight and he could deny it all he wanted, but I knew the truth.

"As you say. I'm not looking for a fight with you, Julius." *At least…not yet.*

There was caution as he went back to feeding and I relaxed as Tessa's lips kissed over my now healed neck. I could tell from her wiggling that she wanted me to cut myself again, but I refused. She'd made her point to whoever she'd wanted— me, Sayer, the whole fucking room. I was putting my foot down and she'd just have to get over it.

"My future concubine sings, correct?"

The Black Prince leaned back in the chair, crossing his arms over his chest as he gazed in our direction.

"She does," Julius answered. "Perhaps it's time she gave us a show. It's the least she could do," he ground out, looking over at me.

Tessa's head rose, a smile on her face as she turned toward our leader. "I'd be delighted. Will you allow me the chance to change first, or shall I sing to you all dressed as I am?"

Julius twisted his mouth and I could see his confusion in her personality. Fuck, I was confused, too. She didn't like to sing in front of people—especially this many. Yet, she appeared eager to display her talents.

"Change. Make it quick."

Tess bowed her head in a single nod and easily pushed from my lap. The sway of her hips while she walked toward the dark tunnel by herself almost had me going just so I could spank her for the scene she was causing. But I knew I wasn't meant to leave. Besides…she'd get her punishment soon enough.

Chapter 19
Hunter

Dead. Thatcher and Waters hadn't even made it to the hospital before they passed away. The night had been one of the worst in my life and even now, as I traveled back through the darkness of the underground, revenge was the only thing on my mind. I'd seen the bastard who'd killed those soldiers and I had every intention of making him pay.

Where I expected news crews and police to be swarming on the vampire attack, the men's incident was brushed under the rug. Soldiers who'd risked their life for this country treated as if they were no one. The cops told us we must have been mistaken. Animals attacked all the time and surely we'd gotten confused over the matter. It had been dark. Our imaginations had to have gotten the best of us. It made me sick and enraged. It led all three of us to the local news stations. Even there, we were told to leave. No one wanted to touch a story about a vampire attack, despite the fact that I could see their fear. Things were getting out of control and the buzz online told me I wasn't the only one fighting authorities on these matters. Question was, what did we do about it? Others might not know, but I wasn't giving up.

Voices hummed in the distance and I made a right where the tunnel branched off. My bow stayed tightly in my grasp and I kept the light I mounted on top on as I jogged through. The more the elevation dropped, the louder the talking grew. Light was ahead and I slowed. My skin was prickling in warning and I couldn't stop the fear engulfing me. This was it. I knew it in my heart, but what would I see? What would I discover?

"May I have your attention please?"

The loud voice stopped me in my tracks. My heart swelled and my eyes closed for the briefest moment as I said a prayer of thanks. There was no doubt in my mind who I was listening to and it wiped away the anger immediately. The power behind the soft tone…*Tessa.*

"I'd like to give our new guests a welcome they'll never forget. There are a lot of nationalities here so some of the songs I plan to sing will be in different languages. Some of them will be mixed with two. Let's try to have a little fun."

Confused at her strength and enthusiasm for singing, I walked forward, stopping just where the light broke into the tunnel. I could see the end of a large opened room before me. I crouched and looked up. It had to have been a good three to four stories high. And big. The distance to the other side was half the size of a football field. At least. I swallowed hard, moving forward. A group came into view and Tessa stood there in a red dress, more toward me and two smaller tables resting away from a good dozen and a half longer ones.

Fuck. My breath wouldn't come at seeing her so close to the mass of vampires. A lot had what looked to be humans sitting at their feet. The surreal feeling that swept through me was unreal. There had to be…hundreds. Maybe thousands, given I couldn't see all the way back.

My stare returned to Tessa. She and the group of musicians turned and began walking deeper into the room, right toward me. Everything in me said to hide, but I couldn't. The fact that she was alive mixed with how beautiful she looked locked me into place, keeping me entranced as she swayed her hips seductively, growing closer. As if she felt my presence, her eyes cut over, right to me. There was a hesitation in her step, but she didn't stop. Instead, she turned around, facing the large crowd before her. For a good minute, she stood silently. The appearance of deep breaths left me wondering what she was thinking. I knew she had to have seen me.

"I'm going to start off with a very special song. One that means a lot to me." Her hand rose and she reached to the side, touching a vampire's temple without so much as turning toward him. He held a violin, where others had an array of different instruments. Her actions left me confused, but I couldn't even think to question what she was doing as I stared at her in awe.

The slow draw of the violin filled the space and I watched her take a shuddering breath before she inhaled and her voice filled the space. The note cut right into my soul and it wasn't because of the power she carried. I knew this song. Once upon a time, I'd asked her to sing it for me. She'd refused then, but now…

Lyrics intertwined with the beautiful melody and I soaked in every syllable leaving her lips. If this was going to be as close to New York as we'd ever get, I wasn't missing a beat.

The increase of the tempo had her turning to face me as she began the chorus. One that left my heart so far gone, the vampires could have been rushing toward me and I would have never known. Her words didn't just seem like a message. To me, they were fact. *Future.* Where I'd only one day hoped to see the love through her performance, I never imagined how strong it would be as she sang right to me.

My heart was always yours.
A familiar beat behind closed doors.
To be the one you want.
I'll fight to get us to that point.
Love me.
Leave me.
Breathe me.

My hand reached out to the wall for balance as she turned to face the massive group again. Twisting tightened my stomach and I fought not to rush out there and steal her away. We'd never make it out alive. At least, I wouldn't. And I had to survive. Tessa loved me. I knew she did and I wouldn't stop until I had her again. The words were what I needed to hear—an assurance we'd be together again someday. Had I been looking for a sign? I knew I had, and this was it.

More singing filled the room and I watched as her voice died off and the violin continued. She turned, licking her lips, and I couldn't help but mouth, *I love you.* It slipped free without my control. Where I expected her uneasiness or possible rejection, I was floored by the smile tugging at the corner of her lips. For a minute, it didn't look like Tessa. Not the shy girl I knew. She looked…different. Confident? Too accepting? I wasn't sure what I'd been expecting but confusion hit hard at the way she was practically eating me alive with her stare. She wanted me, and not just as someone to joke around with or be her friend. She wanted my cock. She wanted me as the man who burned for her in every way. Fuck, I wanted to give it to her. Show her how I'd make our future better than our past.

I shifted on my feet, fighting my lust and the need to go to her. One last look of hunger was followed by her biting her bottom lip and turning around. I knew I was wasting time. I had to go. I'd seen what I needed to. Tessa was alive. Safe. Now, it was time to flee the dangers underground, even if I didn't want to. If she kept showing me attention, they'd become suspicious. I couldn't risk that.

My feet moved back and the hardest part was leaving while she was still in view. The moment she disappeared from my sight, I turned and kept my steps light until I knew I was far enough away. I broke out into a sprint and rushed from the tunnels. But I still wasn't safe. I put the grate down and jogged back toward Tessa's. My pace slowed at seeing a figure sitting in the darkness on the porch.

I immediately placed my hand on the hilt of the dagger as I got closer. The slim frame rose and walked toward me. The long dress she wore blew to the side in a gust of wind and I side-stepped around her, closer to the door as the brunette eyed me, warily.

"You're very well guarded, and by a beautiful protector," she said, staying a few feet back and eyeing the dagger.

"You have to be these days. You're Marie, the one who took Tessa underground with you and all your men. What are you doing here?"

Her head lowered and she crossed her arms over her chest. "I'm also the one who gave her that dagger. And I have no men anymore. Marko killed them."

I paused at the sniffle that followed her words.

"I hate him," she ground out. "I hate him and I want him dead, just as you do."

My feet carried me closer to the door and I never took my hand from the hilt of the weapon. Her words pulled me in, but I wasn't going to fall for any tricks I was sure she was full of.

"I have to know, if I kill Marko, will Tessa die?"

Marie looked up, wiping her tears away as she did so. "Yes. She will die."

I shook my head, feeling my heart drop.

"Don't fret, my friend, we're in luck."

"First off, I'm not your friend. I don't trust you and if I weren't battling whether to look at you as a creature or woman, you'd already be dead. Your kind are responsible for a lot of bad things and I plan to put an end to it."

"I know," she said, lowly. "But you have nothing to worry about from me. Not yet, anyway. You see, I have a gift. I can see the future. Since I've lost my men, it's shown me a lot. The biggest threat I see though came before, and it hasn't gone away. And you have to know. Have to be prepared."

"Prepared for what?"

She paused. "You will end up killing Tessa."

A sarcastic laugh came from my mouth. "Me, kill Tessa? No, your gift is way off. I'd never hurt her knowingly. *Ever*. I love Tessa."

"I know you do," she said, stepping forward. "And it's your love that kills her. You stab her, right in the heart. Right in front of Marko. You yell to him, 'if you can't have her, no one will'." Still, she came closer. "That is your future,

Hunter. You will kill many vampires and you will have an army behind you with the likes you can't imagine. But you will kill her, just before you are killed yourself. And you will die, by Marko's hand, no less."

Nausea plagued me and I wasn't sure why I believed this vampire. She could be lying for all I knew, but I didn't think so. Her hate for Marko...she wanted him dead, just like me.

"You may speak of what you saw, but just so you know, I would never kill her."

Even as I said it, I knew it was a lie. It was enough to make me feel even more sick. If I knew I was going to die and there was no way around it...fuck. I would kill her to save her from the life of living with him and those monsters. "How can I kill him and not kill her? You said we're in luck. What does that mean?"

Marie stopped at the first step and turned around, sitting down before me. She stared ahead, not appearing threatened by me blindly having her back. I could easily pull my dagger out and stab her. I could end her life, and a big part of me wanted to.

"There's a vampire. One of the strongest in the world. He and Tessa share blood. Sayer plans to break her and Marko's bond to place his own. They'll no longer be bonded. You can kill him then."

"Why does anyone have to bond with her? God, this shit just doesn't make sense to me." I collapsed down too, sitting on the top step, leaving a good foot between us.

"Her blood is what draws us. If Sayer bonds with her, he'll become even stronger. As will she. He plans to change her into a vampire and make her his concubine. That's wife, by the way," she said, glancing back. "*That* you can't change. It's the only way to separate her and Marko. She'll forever have vampire blood in her and you're going to have to accept that."

"Bullshit. I want her back, unbonded. How do I get that?"

A small laugh came from Marie. "You can't. It's impossible. The only way to unbond a bonded slave is through the blood of a stronger vampire. Sayer is your ticket if you want to kill Marko. Besides, you lucked out even more. He doesn't want her body. He prefers men, if you know what I mean. She can take you as her own slave, Hunter. You can both still be together. It just won't be with the white picket fence you imagine. Think it over," she said, standing. "But not for too long. You only have few hours before your life will alter. Stop looking at us as the enemy and submit to our future leader. *Her.* She loves you. More than you know. I've seen how your lives can be. And you're both very happy."

Dark hair blew back from the wind and Marie turned, walking in the direction of the grate. I couldn't breathe past what she was asking. Tessa...*their leader*? Jesus. This couldn't be how our lives were meant to turn out. Me, as her slave, just like she was to Marko? I couldn't do that. I couldn't let them change her to begin with. I didn't want her lusting for blood nonstop while I became some sort of zombie just for her. Wasn't that what she'd pretty much turned into before she was taken? All day, she'd look out the window and think about Marko. I couldn't even hold a conversation with her because she was so consumed. But...would that be so bad if it was for her? God, I was torn. There were so many things to take into account. Bonds, blood, and bitterness. What did I chose?

Chapter 20
Tessa

Pieces of conversation filtered through and I knew I was laughing at whatever Sayer and his second chair, Armand, were saying, but I had no idea what the topic of conversation was. I could feel Marko's negative energy coming from behind me as I sat on his lap. Sayer and his second had, at some point, moved their chairs away from the table to make a U-shaped area between Julius and us. I had no idea how I knew Armand's name or that he was second. I just knew, obviously discovering it while I, once again, blacked out.

My body began to tremble and I turned back to look at Marko. The fear left me breathing heavily and I searched his eyes to gauge how he was doing. From the tightness of his features, he was angry and ready to be finished with the façade we were all putting on.

"You were just phenomenal, Tessalyn. I'm amazed. Three hours and your voice was just as beautiful from start to finish. And those songs. Who knew you could speak so many languages?"

I turned back to them, even more confused. "How many did I…?"

"Four," Marko answered. "All of them being ones you know from me."

The words were spoken through gritted teeth and I shifted in his lap. The movement had him grabbing my hips to still me, almost as if he were afraid for me to get even the smallest fraction away from him.

"The sun should be up soon. I'm afraid it's time we retire. Tomorrow, you'll sing again." Sayer threw me a smile and stood. The tension in Marko immediately eased. As the vampires said their goodbyes to Julius, Marko was already rising to stand. I nearly fell from his lap. Had it not been for Armand's quick reaction, I would have.

"She's fine. Keep your hands off her," Marko snapped, jerking me to the side. His arm tightened on my bicep painfully and he began pulling me toward our hall, faster than I could keep up in the heels I was wearing. By the time we reached the door, he was all but dragging me. Anger flared and half the room disappeared as darkness swept in. I blinked past the panic of fading out again. I hit the floor hard as he literally tossed me inside. Cement burned my forearms and fear took over as I spun around to see him stalking toward me with his fangs bared.

"Who do you think you are?"

The look he was giving pinned me to the floor. My mouth opened only to close. "I don't know what you're talking about." Weak. God, I sounded so…little.

"You don't know?!"

Fabric tore as he gripped the front of the dress in his fist and lifted me, slamming me into the wall. The air rushed from my lungs, leaving behind an ache so severe, I clawed at his hands. Fingers crushed into my face brutally and he pushed into my chest harder. Tears filled my eyes at the violence and pain. I still fought to get my breath back and it came in a fire that seemed to singe my lungs. I internally fought whether I should get physical, too. I knew it would make him worse, but I wasn't raised to submit to treatment like this. Before I could decide, something changed in his face and some of the anger faded as his grip loosened.

"Oh…God. Ma minette." Marko pulled me into his arms, hugging me tightly as he stayed perfectly still. A sob left me, regardless that I'd tried to hold it in. I was so scared. Not only of him, but what kept happening to both of us. Who were we becoming? "I'm sorry. I wasn't thinking. I…can't think, and I hurt you."

He was still surging, I knew that. But slave or not, I didn't deserve to be subjected to this sort of treatment. No one did.

"Let me down, Marko. I want to go to bed."

"I'm sorry. I—"

"Please," I begged, crying harder.

Surprisingly, he obeyed, but I didn't miss the horror in his features. He knew what he'd done had crossed the line and even with as far gone as he'd been, he'd broken past his vampire to stop himself.

I went right for the closet, grabbing a long, white, silk nightgown. It was low cut, exposing the cleavage of my breasts, but it beat the alternative, which was sleeping nude. He'd made it a rule of no clothes, but I wasn't going to follow it tonight. I couldn't bear the thought of him getting anywhere near me all of a sudden. I wanted to go home. I wanted…my eyes shot up as I pulled the pins out of my hair, trying to block out my thoughts as fast as I could. *Hunter.* He'd been here. Had I sung to him? The memories were extremely fuzzy, but I was sure they were real. Had I imagined that part? Hell, I wasn't sure. Even as I thought it, my heart ached for him. He was familiarity. He was home.

I turned, meeting Marko's eyes for the briefest moment. He didn't seem as shocked anymore. Just regretful. I kept quiet as I walked to my side of the bed. He was already halfway undressed and I could hear him continuing as I pulled the covers up high on my face. Still, the tears trailed down.

"You encouraged him to take you. You openly flirted with all of them right in front of me. How do you think that makes me feel?"

I blinked past his words and somehow, I knew he was telling the truth, regardless of whether I could remember it or not. I sat up, letting the covers drop so I could meet his gaze. "How do you expect me to get close enough to kill him if he thinks I hate or dislike him? Think about it. Besides, you are out of control. The way you treat me makes me sick and I can't stand it. For someone who says they love me, you have a shitty way of showing it. Now, goodnight."

I collapsed back to the bed, blinking past the dots covering the cement wall before me. Had I just said that? I had. My pulse jumped and kept a steady rhythm as the light went out and I felt Marko climb into bed. His silence unnerved me. I wasn't sure who I was dealing with. He may have had a moment of regret, but that didn't mean he was back, just like me.

The feather pillow crushed in my grip and I breathed through the anxiety. Within minutes, Marko was snoring. More fuzziness broke in and I blinked, realizing I was standing. A small cry escaped as I brought my fist to my mouth. Pitch black surrounded me and I wasn't sure where I was in the room. Or what I was even doing. My hands reached forward as I tried to feel my way back to the bed. Cold cement from the wall had me turning around and heading in the other direction. Glimpses of light broke through. Bright light. I was squinting, blinking rapidly as I suddenly realized I was walking, but I wasn't in control. Familiar houses were before me and somehow, I felt myself sigh in relief.

Wind flared angrily and it was cold while it blew my nightgown around me. Still, I kept going, until I was walking up my stairs, as if it were the most natural thing. Tears streamed down my cheeks from the light sensitivity. How long had it been since I'd been in the sunlight? Even though it was overcast, it still hurt my eyes.

The knob caught in my hand and I realized the door was locked. I pushed up on my toes, sliding my fingers over the top covering of the porch light. The key had my alternate personality smiling and I slid it into the keyhole, turning and pushing the door open.

Silently, I shut it behind me, locking the bottom lock while I headed for the hallway. Hunter's old door was closed, but for some reason, I continued to my room. Somehow, I knew where he'd be. The bundle under the covers drew me forward until I was standing next to the mattress. Wildly, my heart slammed in my chest. Regardless of whether this was me or not, my true self knew the fear of what I was doing.

My nightgown fell to the floor, leaving me nude, just as Hunter spun around, aiming a gun right at my chest. One hard blink. Two. His lips separated and the gun lowered. I took in the scratches and stitches on his chest and somehow, I knew they were from that night with Marko. But I couldn't focus on it as I watched him.

"Tessa?" As he rubbed his eyes, I wondered whether he thought he was still dreaming. I felt like I was, but I couldn't react past what I was seeing. My hand came out and I didn't give him time to react before I pulled the covers back and eased my way in. Nervously, Hunter studied my face.

"Are you back for good?" There was a strain in his question and my head shook as I moved in closer. The heat of his body warmed the coldness covering mine and he copied my actions, moving in closer, until he was pulling me under his body.

"This isn't real," he said, lowly. "It can't be."

Even as he said it, his hand moved up my side, toward my breast.

"Kiss me and find out."

Looking out through my eyes and not being able to stop what was happening left me panicked, but not for me. For him. God, Marko was going to kill him the moment the sun went down. Was he watching now? Seeing what I was doing? Could he feel that I had no control over the situation? Or was he still dead asleep?

The questions faded as Hunter moved in. I could feel the hardness of his cock, of his body, as he slid the underside of his long length up and over my wet folds. He lowered, bringing his lips down to mine and I watched him in a different light. I saw his passion, his want of me. His love… *I love you.* He'd mouthed those words. I was almost certain of it.

Harder, he grinded into me, making me even wetter and I returned the hunger. My tongue met his as it pushed into my mouth and mint took over my senses. I blinked past the confusion.

Hunter's weight shifted while he kissed down my neck. Impatience filled me. I needed more. Something I couldn't even define. And I didn't have to wait.

His fingers rubbed over my folds and I spread my legs wide, arching while he smoothed in the wetness.

"I'm going to make it good for you this time, Tessa. I promise." Suction tugged at my neck the softest amount and I felt myself come to in a jolt of awareness. Hunter's head lifted at the harsh spasm and I swallowed hard, trying to calm the deer in the headlights look I no doubt sported.

"Hunter," I breathed out. "Oh shit."

Confusion drew in his features and my heart twisted, just as my brain did. What did I do? Who was I? What did I want? To continue would be wrong, yet I didn't want to stop. It made my dilemma even worse.

"You have to know that I didn't come here as myself. The blood in me, it's…causing me to blackout at times."

"But you're here. You came to me. That has to mean something." He paused and I heard the pain in his voice as he continued. "Do you want to stop?"

I swallowed hard, unable to turn away from his blue eyes. They were so bright in the light, almost lavender. Just like the night he returned, they pulled me in, holding me captive to a dream I thought had died off long ago. "No," I whispered, "but you have to know…Marko—"

His fingers pressed against my mouth, cutting me off. "He is not going to deter you from what you want. You let me deal with him."

Before I could continue, his lips replaced his hand. The need in the kiss brought me to life and I wrapped my arms around his neck, pressing my breasts into his chest. So close to him, I felt safe for the first time in as long as I could remember. I wanted to believe that this had all been a nightmare and I was just waking up, clutching to a life that was meant to be when Hunter returned. Maybe I'd always secretly hoped, even when I was unsure. Over the years of writing each other and talking on the phone, I'd opened myself to him as more than my best friend. We'd grown so close over those years, despite the distance between us. It was the reason I'd asked whether he wanted to move in with me as a roommate. I knew I loved him as a person, but maybe I had hoped more would transpire. The fact that I didn't get to find out for myself because Marko stole my opportunity had me holding on tighter.

"I love you, Tessa. I always have. If you only knew how long I've waited." He breathed the words against my lips, placing one last kiss before he moved down. The light touch of his lips traveled over my chest and he cupped my breast, slowly making his way to my hard nipple. Teeth gently pulled at the tight nub and I moaned as he sucked it into his mouth. The pressure sent pleasure shooting straight to my core and I pushed more into him, arching against the desire overwhelming me.

Gentle flicks teased the tip and he swirled, causing my hands to move to his shoulders. Where guilt should have been taking me over from the passing minutes, I felt nothing but my want of Hunter as he moved to my other breast. Teeth grazed over the fleshy part and I lifted my head to meet his stare as he circled just short of my nipple. My breasts were so sensitive, so full, as he gripped both of them and took his time going back and forth, lavishing them with attention. By the time he began kissing down my stomach, I was so hot and wet, I couldn't stop the constant rotating of my hips.

"Hunter, please." What I was begging for was beyond me. I was lost to his touch. And clearheaded. That's what surprised me the most. When I was with Marko, his blood kept me in a frenzy of uncontrolled lust. I loved it, but I wasn't myself. Here, right now, this was the Tessa I knew, and I hadn't felt her for so long, I was basking in every second I got to be myself. What was happening was *my* decision. Not some blood-induced poison tempting me to the forbidden. Hunter was home and I'd been homesick all along.

The covers were pushed to the end of the mattress as he settled between my legs. I suddenly felt self-consciousness and he seemed to sense it, shaking his head.

"I've waited too long for either of us to hold back. Don't leave me now." His tongue flattened over my opening and he made a path to my clit, only to move back down and push into my entrance. My head dropped and my body melted into the bed. Fingers gripped my hips as he pushed deep.

"Oh, yes." A sound came from deep within my throat and I rocked as he thrust repeatedly. The sucking against my folds changed the sensations and ecstasy was all I knew as he applied suction over my clit. My legs kicked out and I felt the orgasm surge forward as the minutes past.

The gasp that left me as his thick finger slid into my channel was followed by my screams as he thrust deep and I shattered. The pressure of his sucking increased over my clit and my whole body jerked repeatedly through the waves of my release. Tingling covered every inch of me and I relished in it as Hunter positioned himself above. The pull on the edge of his lips had me shaking my head and I couldn't fight the smile that appeared. My hand gripped the back of his neck and I pulled his mouth to mine.

Weight settled down on me and he froze as the head of his cock pushed against the outside of my pussy. "Jesus." His head dropped to the pillow next to my face and he groaned into it, only to push up. "We can't, Tessa. I don't have…if you were to…" he looked around my room. "Do you have protection in here?"

Blindly, I reached over, pulling the drawer open. I never thought I'd need a reason to have condoms stashed away, but I'd always been prepared. Maybe I hoped with him moving in, something would happen, even if I didn't want to get my hopes up. But, here we were, and this was the man I knew would always think of me first. His concern over my wellbeing made my heart swell more. Even in the heat of passion, he was always looking out for me. Always protecting me.

Hunter reached in, shredding the wrapper with his teeth. I could see his impatience. The need he had for me fueled my own and by the time he rolled the condom down his length, my hands were pulling at him. Fear was slightly there. Our first time had hurt really badly. And it wasn't just because I was a virgin. Hunter was long, a lot longer than what was deemed average, and I braced for the pain as he inched his way inside of me.

"Relax," he said, kissing me again. "I won't hurt you. I promise."

I sucked against his bottom lip, gasping as he moved even deeper. The movements were slow, giving me time to adjust until he went even further. I couldn't stop my nails from sinking into his back as he pushed through a part of my channel that hadn't been breached before. Not even by him. He'd never made it that far the first time.

"Fuck," he moaned, withdrawing and returning to the same depth. I knew he still had at least another inch or so to go and I wasn't sure whether I could take it. It didn't hurt yet, but would it if he went further? With the way my body craved his, I had to find out.

"More. Fuck me, Hunter. I want all of you." My knees drew up and we both cried out in pleasure as he surged forward, his mouth meeting mine. His hand reached down, grabbing my ass while he pushed even deeper. The grinding of his hips added pressure to the top of my slit and I held his back while I moved against his thrusts. The friction tightened my stomach and I latched onto the side of his neck, sucking with everything I had as another orgasm began to build.

"I don't want this to ever end." He lifted, breaking my contact. He pushed my legs open wide as he stared down at where we were joined. The swirl of his thumb over my clit kept a steady rhythm until I felt myself burning through the bliss. The moment felt perfect and I didn't want it to ever end either.

"Hunter." The rise in my tone had the speed increasing and I breathed out deeply as I tightened around him.

"This is what I've always wanted to see. God, you're so beautiful. Come for me again, baby. Let me see."

And I did. Lights flashed before my eyes and I screamed, thrashing my head back and forth as he flew forward and pounded his cock into me hard. It brought another orgasm bursting right over the first and my yells were muffled while he kissed my mouth. The thickening of his cock was heaven inside of me and I barely finished my release as I drank in his own sounds of pleasure.

"Oh, shit," he breathed out, rolling to his back and pulling me on top so we were still joined. All I could do was soak in the way his thick chest left me feeling small and protected, when I was anything but. God, Marko was going to kill me. He truly was.

"Stay with me. Leave with me. Fuck...marry me."

My head shot up as I stared into Hunter's eyes. Words wouldn't come. Nothing would as I tried to process what in the hell I was going to do.

"Be with me, Tessa. I love you. Don't go back. If it's a fight he wants, so be it. I know how to kill him. I can do that."

"And then I die, too." I went to move off him when he stopped me. "Hunter, I have to go back. I have more than Marko to worry about. They have plans for me. Ones I'm not sure I can get out of."

"Sayer." He closed his eyes and I felt my head cock to the side.

"How do you know about him?"

Hunter eased me off him and placed me at his side so we could look at each other. "Marie came to see me a few hours ago. She told me what you're going through. You're meant to be his wife. It'll destroy the bond you and Marko have."

"Marie?"

"Yes, she wants Marko dead for what he did to her men. She wants me to kill him."

My pulse jumped in Marko's defense. Regardless of whether our love was real, the slave in me felt the need to protect him. And in truth, a part of me did love him. I was just confused on exactly where I stood between both him and Hunter. I loved them both, and for two completely different reasons.

"I'm going to kill Sayer before he bonds me. I don't want to change, Hunter. I don't want to be one of them. Though, if I do kill him, I'm Marko's forever. I'm not sure if can do that either. I don't want that life. I don't want to be underground."

"They're priming you to rule, apparently, if what Marie says is true," he said quietly. "Could you do that, Tessa? Rule an entire vampire community?"

"Absolutely." The one word was laced with so much confidence, my eyes widened. Hunter lifted his head and I tried to calm. "I'm sorry. I'm not myself sometimes. If I changed, I wouldn't be at all. That's what scares me. How much of me would really exist anymore? I'd have nothing left of my life."

"You'd have me. I've had plenty of time to think about it and I've decided. I'll be your slave. I'll remind you every day of who you are. I'll protect you." He grabbed my hand, giving it a reassuring squeeze. "I'll love you to the end."

Chapter 21
Marko

Seven hours and forty-two minutes. That's how long I'd been awake. Dreams plagued me. Dreams I now knew were as real as if I were there with Tessa and Hunter. The mass of emotions going through me weren't even comprehensible, yet I was experiencing every single one to the full magnitude one *could* experience. And I was destroyed.

"I'm going to kill him. I'm going to—"

"You're going to sit down," Sayer snapped. "You're giving me a headache with all your threats. So Tessa's off fucking her boyfriend, so what. She loved him long before she ever loved you. Have you learned nothing in the last few hundred years of been a vampire, Marko? Humans don't lose the feelings they harbor for the living, regardless how of much we try to brainwash them into thinking otherwise with our blood."

My eyes cut over at having what I'd been doing thrown in my face. Whether he knew I was force-feeding Tessa to make her love me, or just assumed, was beyond me. I didn't care, either way. I just didn't want it thrown in my face.

"She loves me. It's your fault she's doing this. Ever since you gave her your blood, she's been a completely different person. An unruly one, at that."

"Tessalyn knows her worth. You think she'd play the compliant slave when she's meant to rule? Please."

"She's my slave! She's meant to obey *me*. Me, not you. Not some alter-ego possessing her either. She was doing perfectly fine until you ruined everything."

He laughed, growing straighter. "And I'm going to ruin it even more in about three minutes." Sayer stood, causing me to spin around toward the tunnel I knew Tessa would be arriving from. I looked over at him and moved more in her direction.

"You're not going to do anything, Sayer. When she appears, she's going back with me to face the consequences of what she's done."

The Black Prince turned his dark eyes on me, full of his vampire, and I met him with my own.

"So you can place your hands on her again? Maybe rough her up even worse this time? To the point where you critically injure her frail human body? I don't think so. You're lucky to be alive after the stunt you pulled. And don't think I don't know. I know everything."

Guilt swarmed my stomach. God, I loved her. Yet, I continued to hurt her and I couldn't stop myself from doing it. It drove me crazy, especially since I was fighting with my mind over what her status was to begin with. Sure, she might become a powerful vampire, but she wasn't yet. She was a slave. A human. And she was mine. It was a jumbled clusterfuck in my head and nothing I did to try to figure it out made sense before something altered it and screwed everything up all over again.

"She's coming with me," I bit out.

Silence drew out between us until I caught the softest whisper of footsteps. Slowly, Tessa slipped from the shadows, but she didn't put her head down and cower as I expected. She held it high while she covered the distance to the member's table. A flush from her fucking Hunter one last time still rested on her cheeks and I knew I wasn't looking at the Tessa Sayer brought out. No, this was my Tessa. The realization only broke my heart even more.

"I have a confession to make." She swallowed hard and looked between Sayer and me nervously. "But I don't think I have to tell either of you, do I?"

"We know," Sayer said, grinning. "And what you've done is perfectly normal. Acceptable, no. Normal, yes."

"I'm going to fucking kill him. You know this, don't you? I can't believe you." I stepped closer and watched as she moved a good foot away. Instead of addressing me, she turned her attention nervously to Sayer.

"I want you to…change me. I want you to do it right now. If you do this, I'll become your concubine willingly and do as you wish. But I want Hunter as my slave. He's agreed and is ready to be at my side to help me when I'm ready for him."

The floor could have fallen out from me at the betrayal of her words. What happened to killing Sayer? What happened to her wanting to remain with me? My claws extended and the devil in me raged at the agony shredding my heart.

"Done. Go to my hall, Armand will be waiting for you. I'll take care of your bonded."

Growling poured from my throat and my vision went red as Tessa stared over at me, terrified. With every side-step she made toward the tunnel, I countered it.

"Don't you dare do this. Don't you dare take another fucking step." My voice was deep, almost unrecognizable as I tried to move in closer. Sayer stayed even with us, ready to step in if he needed to. I barely caught Julius rushing from the tunnels from my peripheral vision.

"Marko, please. I—"

"Don't please me," I exploded. "You betrayed me! You…deceived me! Fucking Hunter while you're bonded to me? I loved you! Do you think I give that away freely to just anyone?" *Love you to death. Love you to death.* The familiar mantra repeated in my head. *Death. Death.* "I could kill you right now." My footsteps grew quicker, as did hers, and I saw the horror in her eyes. "I should fucking kill you right now for what you've done!"

Power slammed into me from behind and the air exploded from my lungs at the force. I used my own, pushing with everything I had as I fought to my knees. I knew it was Julius' and it wasn't strong enough to keep me down. It might have been impossible to get up and walk, but I wasn't immobile like he'd hoped to make me.

"Let her go, Marko," Julius said, getting closer. "You knew this was going to happen. He has the right."

"She's mine," I snarled, turning to face him. "Mine. No one else's."

Still, he came closer, adding more power. My hand slammed into the cement, but I refused to go down all the way. Tessa's bare feet padded against the floor and I fought with everything I had as she disappeared with Sayer into the darkness.

"Help me escort him to lockdown. I want him there until I say otherwise."

Anastasia and Natalia were a good five feet away. I felt myself lifted to stand by their combined powers and although my legs moved, I felt as though I were floating through the large room.

"Don't do this. Tessa! Tessa!" I thrashed against their hold, unleashing the true depths of my power in an explosion from my body. The boom was so loud, like a crack of thunder, causing all sound to dissipate. Ringing left me lightheaded as I fought to focus on my surroundings. The members were trying to stand, just as disoriented as me, but I didn't wait. I rushed toward the tunnel Tessa had entered, colliding with the curved side as vertigo took over. I knew it wouldn't take long to change her. One bite. One insertion of his fangs to push out the true poison he harbored. The blood he needed of hers would come from the bite. Seconds, that's all it would take. It drove me faster.

"Tessa!"

The door loomed ahead and just as I approached, my knees almost gave out. And not because of anything anyone did or how fucked up releasing that much power had left me. I suddenly realized how weak our connection was. Our link. Our…bond. It was fading. The ties holding us together were breaking one by one.

But not my love. Not the obsessive state of mind I was in concerning my former slave.

My fist slammed into the door, knocking it from the hinges. Sayer's tall body had Tessa's pinned against the wall and her nails were digging into the back of his black shirt. His arms were around her waist and I watched him untwine them from her body as he lowered her to turn around and face me. Blood was still on his chin as he met my eyes. But I couldn't see him. Couldn't see anything past the haunting look on Tessa's face. She was frozen in shock. *No.* She was frozen in fear. Little did she know, the scary parts hadn't even begun.

"Marko?" Trembling laced her tone and tears filled her eyes. A small part of my slave was still there, but she was disappearing so fast.

"God, what have you done, ma minette? What…?" My head shook, even as my heartbreak drowned out my anger and drew me closer. "Why would you do this? I love you. I do. I know my actions haven't always shown that, but I'm trying. And now this?" My voice gave out at the end and she rushed past Sayer, throwing herself into my arms. Hearing her sobs crippled me even more, despite the fact that my vampire should have hated her for betraying me.

"I'm sorry. I love Hunter, even if I love you, too. This is the only way. I know you're so angry with me, but—" Tessa stopped, pulling back and wiping her fingers over the blood escaping from her nose, right over her lip. The stream was slow but steady and her features drew in, first confused, and then panicked.

"I'm *so* angry with you, but more hurt. More…" I ripped at the bottom of my shirt, pushing the material in to catch the increasing flow. Knowing what was happening to her left me numbing just the smallest amount. "It's done. We're finished talking about it. You've just erased the past and now it's time to focus on the future. On you. What's happening to you right now is natural under these circumstances. You're going to bleed out everything that is not your or Sayer's blood. Then, his is going to combine with yours and take over, making you stronger What you're wiping away, ma minette, is *my* blood. You're bleeding me out, just as I'm doing for you. Right here," I said, patting my chest. "You won't remember me for quite some time. But when you do, I'll still love you. Even if you did deceive me." I paused. "Even when we turn into enemies, because *we will*...I'll even love you then. I hope you remember that, although I know you won't."

Her head shook and she swallowed profusely while she stepped back. Whatever she was thinking, I wasn't sure. Those precious insights were forbidden to me now. It made the loneliness I knew was resting ahead even more of a reality. The swallowing increased and I sighed, shaking my head.

"Don't hold it in, it'll only get worse. The faster you get me out of your system, the faster you can be done with this. But you'll have to excuse me, because I refuse to see you die. That'll be coming here soon and I won't witness your suicide. I don't think I could bear it. See you in a few months when they set you free."

Despite the anger that resurfaced, I couldn't stop myself from jerking her to me and forcing my tongue past her lips. Blood flooded my senses, the essence I'd loved more than life itself tinged within, the smallest amount. I took it in as if I were the one dying. Only when I felt her knees give out from her internal pain, did I pull away.

"Love you to death, Tessa. But you won't remember any of that either for a while," I said, running my finger over the ink pushing its way free from her neck. "It won't be long now. Stay strong. You're going to need to be."

I spun and pushed past Julius. His hand latched to my bicep before I could make clear of his presence.

"You're going under lockdown. That's final. If you fight me or pull another stunt like you just did, you'll be in there for even longer."

"If that's what you feel you need to do, fine."

Maybe it was for the best. I could already feel her dying and it was pushing my mind into dark places. *Places, I'd never been before.*

I let him lead me through the tunnel and back into the heart of the city. My feet planted the moment we entered the room. Hunter stood there with Marie. Although there was a smugness in her expression, it meant nothing compared to my need to tear the human apart. Why had I waited? Why hadn't I killed him when I'd had more chances than I could excuse? My procrastination and distraction had cost me my slave. Cost me the only woman I'd ever loved. And now she was his.

"Don't do it. Don't even think about. You'll be in lockdown for years if you do."

"You're dead, Hunter!" I yelled. "So fucking dead."

My threat had him stepping toward me, but he halted at Marie's grip shooting to his arm. The tug against mine had a warning escaping my throat. My stare jerked to Julius, who shook his head.

"I *will* kill him, her slave or not. So help me, I will. Maybe not today, but soon. Mark my words."

"We'll see," he said, looking back over. "The future changes by the second. Nothing is for certain anymore. We may all be surprised by these turn of events. After all, even I didn't see this happening."

Julius led me into the tunnel and darkness encompassed me, pushing into my skin like the living thing it almost was. The beat of my heart slowed and my steps faltered. I knew what I was feeling was the last of our bond dying. Of Tessa…dying. I pulled at my collar, cursing the burning that stung my eyes. My heart clenched and tightened, becoming crushed and torn against the spasms leaving hers fighting to continue. But it wouldn't. One set of beats…two…the hard thump hit again, and then, *nothing*. No second beat. No new sets.

"Fuck." The word dragged out and my breaths came out labored as I felt my legs almost give out. My steps were as broken as the walls crumbling down around me. Life suddenly didn't matter. Nothing did. *Death.* God, I wanted to die, too. I wanted to be back with her, even if I knew she'd return here and I wouldn't. Even though the bond was gone, my love for her was stronger and clearer than ever. I knew she wasn't herself when she'd left my room. Even when she'd climbed into bed with Hunter, she hadn't wanted to do it. Regardless of her former feelings for him, the blood was making her even more confused. Yes, I knew she loved him, but she could love me more.

Bars slammed behind me and the shield rippled at my back. I knew what I had to look forward to. This time, I wasn't being tortured with Tessa's blood. No, my grief would my passenger and that wasn't any better. I'd mourn the death of ma minette. The *her* that was now gone to me forever.

Perhaps it was for the best that her human life was over. That version would have never truly loved me anyway. Not like I loved her. She would have never understood what it was to be like us or why I'd treated her the way I had. Now, she would. She'd do it to her own slave. So, where did that leave me with her vampire? Would we truly be enemies when she was able to rejoin our world? How long would it take her to remember her past?

I sunk to the floor, leaning against the wall as my evil oozed through, trying to take over. The rage singed my insides and I torturously let it drag out slowly. Love. Hate. It collided in a swirl of aggressive sounds that left my lips. Words came back. Words she'd spoken. They filled the hollowness growing inside of me loud and clear.

"Someday, I hope our roles are reversed. You will feel what it is to be powerless to me. No matter what it is concerning, your pleas of mercy will go unheard. I'm going to make you suffer and I'm going to enjoy every minute of it."

"Maybe I'll become the stronger one and I'll let you serve me."

Her threats repeated continuously. They quickly became all I heard. They mingled with my madness. Tempted the Master Vampire in me to dominate her back into submission. In my dark, twisted mind, it was suddenly warping into some sick game. A new one, filled with excitement and challenge. And it was with the woman I loved. One I knew better than anyone. But this time, she'd be tougher. Smarter. Even if I had to scheme, I'd make sure I wouldn't lose. Tessa may not have met the perfect version of me yet, but the one she'd be introduced to all over again as a stranger would be what her dreams were made of. I'd seduce her. Show her why I was the one who deserved her love. I'd *make* her love me.

As for Hunter, he didn't stand a chance when it came to a fight. And that was if he even stayed around long enough for me to have permission to kill him. After he got a real glimpse of the monster his childhood love was going to become,

I had no doubt he'd run from this life. And when he decided to, I'd intercept him. It made me smile. He was in for more than he bargained for and no amount of faith was going to smooth the blow he had coming to him. And I'd be there, watching, waiting…taking what was mine.

To be continued….

Lure

Marko Delacroix #3

Alaska Angelini

Lure
Marko Delacroix #3
Alaska Angelini
Copyright © 2014 by Alaska Angelini

ISBN:

All Rights Reserved

Chapter 1
Hunter

Rumbling and what felt like a small earthquake left me sweating as I stood before Julius and Marie. The episodes happened every few minutes over a period of hours and even as Julius looked toward the hall where Marko had been taken for lockdown, I didn't have to be told what or whom it was coming from.

What had I convinced Tessa to do? How had I thought her turning into a vampire was for the best? Yes, Marko had bonded to her, and with Sayer, the Black Prince, erasing the marks, she'd have been free from Marko's spell...but how did I let this happen? We could have run. Tessa wouldn't have gone willingly, but I could have convinced her. Or taken her against her will. Fuck, I had been blinded by her admission of love. Reading it in her diary had been one thing, but when she came and crawled in bed with me...I'd been swept away. For hours, we'd talked and made love. I'd had plenty of time to go over the prophecies Marie warned me about, and at the time, having Tessa turned seemed like the best choice. But now I was regretting my decision. She didn't want this life and had tried to explain that she wouldn't be herself anymore. Yet, I told her I would remind her of who she *really* was.

With the creatures before me, I was starting to think that might not be possible. They were so cold. So...unfeeling. Shouldn't they have been even a little afraid of what was happening down the tunnel? The fucking ground was shaking because of Marko's anger. Shit, *I* was terrified, and I wasn't afraid to admit it.

"What exactly is he doing back there?"

I barely finished speaking before another rumble sent vibrations through my body. Surely someone above ground was detecting this shit? Would the government come? Or brush it under the rug like everything else concerning these monsters?

"Master Delacroix is just blowing off steam. He'll tire out soon enough."

"How soon? I've been waiting to see Tessa for..." I glanced down at my watch, "four hours, now. When can I go back? I promised her I'd be by her side through all of this."

Julius chuckled under his breath and glanced over at Marie, who threw him what looked to be an amused smile.

"You don't want to go in there. Tessa may be restrained, but I think it's best you give her a few more hours to adjust. She'll be in pain. You don't want to see her like that."

"If she's in pain, I need to be there. She has to know I didn't abandon her." Abandon? Hell, she'd made me promise I wouldn't come for her when I left her at the grate. She had insisted she'd come for me when she was ready. I couldn't do that. I'd given her my word that I'd be by her side through it all. That's exactly what I planned to do.

Julius shrugged and gestured toward the hall not far ahead. "If you'd like to go, then by all means, the decision is yours. But don't say I didn't warn you."

Marie's head shook back and forth slowly. "Hunter, I wouldn't do it. There's no rush. She won't even remember whether you're there. She'll try to kill you at the first opportunity and every one after that. You'd be safer if you stayed away from her for the next few months."

"Months? Uh-uh. I'm going."

A sigh came from Marie but I ignored it as I waited for Julius to lead the way. Instead, he continued to stare at me.

"You are aware Tessalyn Antoinette is spoken for, yes?"

"By Sayer. I know and I don't care. Tessa's mine. She's going to make me her slave. That was the agreement."

"Your agreement with her is null and void if the Black Prince doesn't agree. I'll leave the decision to him."

The need to argue was there, but I would wait for the time to come before I reacted. Julius was already walking and I was too impatient to see Tessa. I grabbed my flashlight and followed him toward the dark tunnel. I clicked the button, illuminating the pitch black space before us. Julius immediately turned around, annoyed. I didn't speak as he threw me a look and continued. There was no way I was going to be in a dark, confined space with a killer. Especially one as strong as him. I could feel his power. It left the tuning fork sensation in the pit of my stomach reverberating nonstop. Nausea was constant and I tried my best to fight it, turning my focus to the woman I loved. God, was Tessa okay? He'd mentioned pain. How much?

"Prepare yourself, human. Tessalyn won't be herself right now. She'll appear free, but I assure you, Sayer has her restrained. When we leave her alone, she'll go into chains. Under no circumstances are you to get close to her," he stressed. "You have no idea what she's capable of in this stage."

I swallowed hard as he reached out and turned the knob, pushing the door open. Light flooded into the tunnel and I quickly put up my flashlight. My breath caught as I followed him inside. The door shut, making me jump, but I couldn't turn to look at the barrier. My gaze was trapped on Tessa. Or…someone slightly resembling her. I barely recognized her beauty through the amount of blood covering her body.

Two dead women were lying to the sides of her feet and I almost couldn't believe what I was seeing. The knowledge of what she'd become was present in my mind, but seeing what she was capable of in person felt surreal.

Heavy pants left her mouth as she stood a few feet from the bottom of the bed, glaring in our direction. The darkness of her stare pinned me in place and I fought the need to run for safety. Julius said she was restrained, but it didn't look that way to me. What I saw was a threat and my body screamed to flee.

A low growl began to fill the space and razor sharp claws extended from her nails as she took a step forward, moving in a slow, predatory sway. It was as if she was trying to decide whether to dart left or right.

"You must be Hunter."

The hearty voice broke my focus. I glanced over quickly to observe a tall, blonde vampire, but went back to watching Tessa.

"That's right," I said lowly. "She can't…?" I pulled at the collar of my shirt as she cocked her head and sidestepped to the left.

"Oh, you're safe for now. She can't get past the wall I've put up. I'm Sayer, by the way." From my peripheral vision, I saw him extend his hand. I didn't even turn to face him as I brought mine out to the side for the shake. The strength from the squeeze had my head spinning to face him and I watched a grin pull at his mouth. "Now that I have your attention, you must be the new slave."

"I guess you could say that." The dark clothing made his pale skin stand out even more and I didn't dare look up to see the color of his eyes. From the quick glimpse, his features were perfect. Attractive to me, no doubt women also. Jealousy sparked, but I kept Marie's words fresh in my mind. He didn't want Tessa like that. He preferred men. Somehow, I should have feared him even more, but I couldn't think about that now. I turned, unable to take my eyes off the scene before me for long. My hand drew up and I pointed to the women on the floor. "What happened to them?"

As if I had to ask.

"Food. She has to eat and I'm not letting her feed from me. Not yet."

Julius laughed, moving in closer. "Wise decision. She'd try to rip your throat out."

"Probably worse than that." Sayer moved in closer to me and a shriek poured from Tessa's mouth as she lunged toward us, crashing into an invisible force. The action had her swinging her arms in unbelievably quick, slashing movements. I braved the few steps closer, still in disbelief.

Pain pulled in Tessa's features and a sob took over as she collapsed to her knees, screaming with incredible volume. Black hair fell forward while blood-stained fingers pushed through the long strands just past her temples. My chest ached at the heart wrenching cries that began to leave her.

"Tessa?" Two more steps and Sayer grabbed my arm, stopping me. I crouched, trying to peer into her black eyes. The whites were completely gone. The evil they cast nearly made it impossible to speak. "Tessa, baby. Look at me. I'm here for you, just like we talked about. I'm going to take care of you. I know you're hurting, but this will pass. You'll get better and then we can be together again."

My words died off as her head lifted and the evil met me head on. I was nearly mesmerized by fear, but I tore my gaze away to look down toward the crimson staining her cheeks and full lips. God, what had I done to her? This was all my fault. How many hours had she argued with me against this? So many.

"We'll get you through this. I promise."

Small hands slammed into the invisible wall not inches away, keeping their position. I brought my palm up to fit on the other side of the hard space, palm to palm. For a few seconds, neither of us moved. I stole glances at her face, gauging her expressions, and was upset to find she didn't have any. Cold. Empty. Yes, she was all of that.

"I'll be waiting for you to come back. Every day. I'll talk to you and remind you of who you are every chance I get."

"And you'll be wasting your time," Sayer said, interrupting. "She will not remember these first few weeks for probably over a year. Tomorrow, she will not remember today. In a month from now, she won't remember what she did the week before. This will go on until her fog clears. Right now, your best bet is to head to the surface and live your life to the fullest. Once Tessalyn claims you, that life will end. You will be dead to the outside world, Hunter. Best to go spend time with your family while you still can."

I looked up, unable to understand. "Why can't I go back to the top afterward? I thought vampires and humans were becoming one now?"

"Yes, but you are not just any slave. You are the slave of a future leader. Despite the fact that you'll have no urge to go when the moment comes, Tessalyn will be in need of your assistance at all times. You are not to leave her side unless she commands it. That's what slaves are, Hunter." He turned toward Julius. "You explained this to him already. I know you did. I can see it."

"He was too focused on Marko to listen." Julius eased into a chair, yawning. I knew it was almost dark, but from the looks of it, he hadn't gotten any sleep during the day. I would have guessed vampires could have gone without it, but apparently, I knew nothing.

"Marko." Sayer bared his fangs, practically snarling the name. "I can't stand him."

Julius nodded. "He's in line for the throne if Tessalyn doesn't live up to what we believe. And he'll get it. He's already damn near there. It won't be long now. He's going to surpass me, Sayer. We'd be fools to deny it."

"No," Sayer said, shaking his head. "We can't let that happen. Fuck, I don't want to have to deal with him politically. You'll just have to delay testing him. I thought after the last time, he'd already overpowered you. You damn near shredded his arm while battling his blood."

Julius glanced at me, seeming to choose his words. "He's strong. Too strong. Luckily his powers aren't like ours or he'd know just how much."

"What happens if he discovers it?" I looked between them, wishing I hadn't opened my mouth. Anger flashed on both of their faces and I felt like I'd overstepped a status I didn't even understand.

"Since I'm not worried about you running back to tell him, I'll enlighten you." Sayer grabbed my bicep, jerking me to my feet as if I weighed nothing. The instant loss of contact on the wall left me feeling hollow, as though I'd abandoned Tessa, even if she did look right through me. Before I could stop myself from meeting his eyes, it was too late. Images exploded into my mind. I couldn't understand what the strangers were arguing about, but I did recognize blood—lots of it. And they were all vampires. God, he was going to massacre them…a lot of them. They were high ranking. They were…leaders.

"Marko will ruin what we've worked for hundreds of years planning if he continues to gain ground amongst the members. I won't let that happen."

The room came back into focus and I quickly put distance between us, nearly stumbling into the wall separating Tessa and me.

"Why don't you just kill him?"

My question seemed simple enough. The looks the vampires gave me said it was anything but. There was more involved here than powers or simple murder.

"Tessalyn will be stronger. She will rule and Marko will *have* to obey whatever she commands. He may fight it, but mentally, he'll have no choice. It's better this way. Then, we'll have his gifts, too. We need them if we're going to pull this off. With him on our side, we can't fail."

I turned back to Tessa, noticing she was now rocking in position.

Was it true? Would she not remember her day-to-day life for a long time? If she was as strong as they believed, wasn't there a chance she was somewhat aware of what was going on? Sayer and Julius's certainty told me no, but the flicker of cognizance I kept catching in her black stare told me she was in more control than we thought her to be.

Chapter 2
Marko

Silence was quickly becoming my worst enemy. The lack of sound…the lack of hearing my slave's thoughts. Tessa was completely gone from me and I couldn't stand it. Had I thought myself alone before she came? It didn't even compare to the hollowness festering within me now. Even in my worst episodes of surging, when I was oblivious to how horribly I was treating her, she'd still been there. Now…nothing. It drove me crazy. I missed having Tessa's presence dwell within. It left me fuller, heavier, than the empty shell I was now.

How was she? Was the change hard for her? Was she alive? Some people didn't make it through the transition. What if she hadn't? Because of how powerful we knew she'd be, we all just assumed she'd make it just fine, but what if we were wrong? What if Tessa really was dead?

A roar poured from my mouth and I projected my power out in an explosion of pure blistering heat. An aura of orange glistened across the shield, warping the invisible force in a wave of translucence. The blowback pushed my sitting body back into the rattling wall, once again knocking the air from my lungs. The ground shook for a few seconds before finally becoming still again. Each expulsion of power left me more tired than the next, but for only one reason: I was getting stronger. Every release shook me harder and I couldn't stop the excitement as I watched the wall weaken before me. But I wouldn't be able to carry on much longer. I was mentally and physically exhausted. Sleep beckoned and I wanted nothing more than to forget about the last two days. They'd been was the worst of my life.

Had my slave really been lost to me? Had she really betrayed me by fucking that human, Hunter? By choosing him? God, she had. So why did I still love her? Why did I still want her? I hated it. Hated that she'd wrapped me around her finger as if she were the Master and I was the slave.

"Tessa!"

Rawness stung my throat and I let my head fall back against the wall as my elbow shot back to slam into the cement cell holding me prisoner. How long would Julius keep me here? If the goal was just long enough to allow me to cool off, it would be weeks. Months. Fuck, I'd never let this go. Tessa deceiving me was bad enough, but Sayer was going to pay the ultimate price. It was his fault that this had happened to begin with. Had he not slipped Tessa his blood, she would have never formed a conscience. She would have remained trapped under my rule for as long as I permitted. With the rate I had been going, I would have bled myself dry trying to poison her with my blood to make her love me. It was all I wanted, and now she'd never feel that way again. Not when she'd be bonded to Sayer and *his* concubine.

"God dammit. Tessa!"

She may not love me, but I'd always love her. Just like the tattoo that had oozed from the skin on her neck when she began changing…I'd love her to death.

Love you to death. Love you to death. The French lettering appeared in my mind. I could still see it embedded right below her pulse point. There, next to where my fangs had slid in so beautifully. Just the thought brought them down and burning singed the length of my throat. I had to get out of here. I wanted to taste her again. Taste my Tessa. Taste the new her. What would vampire ma minette taste like? Better? Not as good? I was dying to find out.

Another explosion of power burst from my body and I put everything I had into letting the force reveal the worsening of my rage. The brutal wave that crashed over me from the blowback sent my head cracking into the wall. I winced, blindly falling over to the side. Images raced before my eyes. Of her smile. Of how happy she'd been the one time I took her above ground. Before Hunter had nearly killed her with that fucking stake. Why hadn't I paid more attention to our surroundings? Why hadn't I killed him when I'd had the chance?

The good and bad between us played out as the hours flew by. I let it. I drifted between sleep and consciousness, never wanting to wake up until this stage was over with. Until I was set free. What happened then? I couldn't think about that now. I'd torture myself even more. All I knew was they were going to pay and pay dearly. Marie, that fucking bitch. She had something to do with Hunter and Tessa coming together, I just knew it. The way she'd guarded that human when he challenged me in the heart of the city…I wouldn't overlook that.

"Time to feed."

Julius's voice brought my lids open and I snapped my eyes right to his. I jumped to my feet and rushed in his direction. I wanted to see. Had to know what was happening. At the turn of his head, I growled at the missing connection. There was no telling whether I could force my way into his mind, but I was desperate to try.

"How is she?" I gripped the bars as he reached for the brunette supplier standing at his side with her head down.

"She lives," he said, nudging her toward the bars. "Now, get back. I'm going to open this door. If you try anything, you'll remain here for a lot longer than originally planned."

My jaw clenched as I obeyed. "Tell me more. Show me." I licked my lips, pacing the length of the room as he practically forced the human woman past the door. It was for a good cause—she wouldn't make it out of this room alive and she knew it.

"There's nothing to tell. She lives. She feeds, albeit, rather harshly. She's a newborn. Nothing sets her apart. Well…" he paused, "nothing but her eyes, which alone speak volumes." A smile broadened across his face and I felt myself step closer.

"What about her eyes?"

Still, I tried to connect with his stare, but he kept me closed off.

"They're black."

I sighed, shaking my head. "All newborns' eyes are. What about hers are different?"

A quiet laugh shook his chest and he glanced up. "You misunderstand. All of it is black. The entire eye."

My lips separated as Bufar's memory came back to me. In the cave he rested in, the vampire who was stalking him had pure black eyes, too. But he'd been beyond powerful. So old, he had to have been around since Time itself. And he'd seen me watching him. Even through the memory.

"How?" My question came out winded, almost silent from my shock.

"I don't know. Sayer and I were both surprised, but it speaks of things to come, I'm sure. Tessalyn Antoinette will be quite the Mistress and leader. We'll see when we start putting her through the tests. The Black Prince wants to begin as soon as possible, so I'm sure we'll get to witness it after we feed.

"Tests? What sort of tests?"

A whimper sounded from the side of the cell and I threw a glance toward the girl curled into herself against the wall. When I turned back to Julius, he was already shutting the door and stepping back.

"Just tests. See you tomorrow."

I rushed toward the bars, gripping them with every ounce of impatience and anger I harbored. "Set me free. I want to watch. I can help. I—"

"You will remain here."

"I won't kill Hunter, dammit. You have my word. Set me free."

Julius didn't pause as he continued to walk away. It left me pulling at the bars in aggravation.

"Julius! Wait!" I shuffled my feet to the far corner closest to him as he disappeared. The crying behind me became heavier and I growled, spinning around and baring my fangs. "You humans are always so weak. Do you not face your death with honor for who you serve?" I stomped in her direction, lunging and locking my arm around her waist as she tried to run around me. Dark hair swung as I jerked her to fit against my body, slamming my fangs into her neck. Thrashing was followed by screams, filling the space with exactly what I wanted to hear: utter terror. I sucked hard, relentless in my feeding. The deep draws brought me the closest I'd been to home in the last few hours and although her blood held no appeal, the beat of her heart did. I soaked in the fast rhythm, letting it soothe the monster within. Not just my vampire—the once bonded male. God, how I missed Tessa's presence of being mine. Of my blood racing through her veins, feeding me her thoughts and emotions.

As minutes went by and the speed of the woman's pulse slowed, I didn't stop. Only when I knew death beckoned, did I pull back, snapping her neck and letting her limp body fall to the cement. The dark hair fanned across the floor and I stared at it, fascinated. For seconds, I couldn't move. Could think past the wavering reality of it being *her*.

So much like my Tessa's hair: beautiful, long, and dark. Entranced, I lowered until I was lying next to her. From behind, I could almost imagine Tessa was asleep and we were back in my room. So clearly could I see her.

"We'll be together again, ma minette. I promise. And this time, you'll love me for real. You'll want me more than you ever have." I ran my fingers down the long length, picking up the end to twist around my finger. The smell wasn't right. There was no lavender or jasmine. No traces of strawberries. But I didn't need it. My memories mixed with delirium and I conjured what I wanted, letting it tempt me back to sleep. Back to her. Visions returned, but not for long.

"Help me."

My eyes snapped opened as I bolted to a sitting position. I reached up, pressing my palm against my racing heart. Had I been dreaming? My eyes darted toward the empty cells on both sides of me and then down to the dead girl I'd been curled around. She wasn't breathing. At the only possibility left, I felt myself stand. *"Ma minette?"*

Silence.

"Ma minette," I called out in my mind, more forcefully. *"If that was you, you better answer me right this minute."* I paused, swallowing hard. *"Please. God, please, tell me that was you. I miss you. I fucking love you. Talk to me. Answer me! Are you hurt? Why do you need help?"*

Back and forth, my footsteps ate up the length of the cell. It had to have been Tessa. No one would have been able to communicate with me that way. Did she still have some of my blood in her? Was it possibly strong enough to stand a chance against Sayer's? For minutes, I contemplated.

"Fuck...me," I gasped. *"Tessa! Come on, mon amour. You can do this. Feel with the pit of your stomach. Use your power to force our connection. Feel my blood. Feed it. Focus on it. Give it power and let it take you over."*

My mind was racing. If by some miracle she still held some of me inside of her after all this time, she might always have it. But what did that mean? I'd never heard of it happening, but it didn't mean it couldn't happen. If that were the case…

Chapter 3
Tessa

The hammering of multiple hearts surrounded me, beating against my skin and pulling at my ears while the three males stared at me from across the room. Two were like me...different. *Vampire.* But one wasn't. He smelled good. It was killing me not to be able to get to him. *Human.* My mind told me what he was, but I couldn't decipher why he stood out when the others didn't. Nothing made sense in my mind; it all mingled together into a realization just too big for me to grasp yet.

My fangs lowered as I kept my attention on the rise and fall of the human's chest. Nothing mattered but what was flowing through his body. I wanted him—to taste what he was made of. I was angry that at being denied. Who were they to keep me trapped here?

"Hunter, I do believe she has eyes for only you."

The human watched me, shifting on the chair not feet away while the other walked in slow strides before him. I saw the way the vampire in black looked at what belonged to me. He wanted him and I didn't like it.

"That's because Tessa knows who I am. She recognizes me."

Laughter filled the space and the blond stopped, glancing in my direction. "Yeah. As food." He turned toward me, walking closer. Instinctively, I lunged, hissing at the threat he presented. There was something about him I didn't like. Something...no matter how hard I tried, I couldn't unlock what kept wanting to come. Pain shot through my head and my lids lowered in agony.

"Are you hungry, Tessalyn? I know you're pretty much going to stay in that state, but this time, we're going to make meal time a little fun. What do you say? Want to play a game?"

A game. What did he think of me as? A child? I forced my eyes open, watching his facial features pull tight as he smiled.

"Hunter, go stand in the corner. I'm going to let her loose for a minute."

"Are you fucking crazy? She's going to try to kill me."

The blond laughed, again. "I thought she knew you. Surely, if she was aware of who you were, she wouldn't do that, would she?"

The human threw me an indecipherable look, but turned his aggression on the blond. "*She* knows who I am. It's the vampire who wants to eat me for lunch."

"Better get going or else I might not be able to get to her fast enough."

Movement had my stare jerking to the human as he stood from the chair and quickly moved further away. Panicked, I shifted on my feet. He couldn't leave. Couldn't run from me. I wanted him. He was mine. Somehow, I knew that. But for what was clouded with confusion. He spoke of me knowing him and although I didn't know what that meant, I felt it was important.

Air pushed against my skin in a small gush and while the need to burst into a sprint was there, I waited. Watching. What did this vampire expect me to do? What was he hoping to see?

Slowly, I moved in the opposite direction, pausing as the quiet vampire in the chair by the door stood. His long dark hair fell over his shoulder while he covered the distance between the blond.

Help me. Help me. Help me. What did I do? The words repeated even though I was confused as to why I needed someone to save me.

"Ma minette?"

I froze, feeling my eyes go wide at the voice that came through. My head jerked toward the sound and I scanned the room, turning in a full circle. Where was it coming from? Who had that been? His voice…sparked something. It made my skin hot. Made me…

"If that was you, you better answer me right this minute. Please. God, please, tell me that was you. I miss you. I fucking love you. Talk to me. Answer me! Are you hurt? Why do you need help?"

"What is she doing?"

The human had me spinning with such force, I couldn't think past the need to have him. I flew forward with speed that made me feel weightless. Growling broke through my throat and all I could think of was sinking my teeth into his neck. I could hear his heart. It drew me to him. Begged for me to experience how it would feel against my fangs.

"Good girl!" The blond's arms shot out, wrapping around my waist. I snapped my teeth in his direction, screaming as I began to thrash in his hold. "Did you see that, Julius? Fuck, she moves faster than I thought she would. Come on, Princess. Let's see what you're made of."

Julius opened the door and the one in black rushed down the tunnel, taking us deeper into the darkness. Another door opened and I was thrown in a large open area full of more people like me. More…vampires.

Lithe movements had them prowling around the room and their attention was on only one thing. The smell had my eyes shooting toward the ceiling. Hanging above was a cage with a human man trapped inside. Scared sounds poured from his mouth as he stared down at us, gripping tightly to the bars of his prison. Instantly, I knew I had to have him. But they wanted him, too, just not as badly. At least, that's what my mind told me. I was above them. What I wanted would supersede anyone else's needs. *I* was all that mattered. *Me.*

One by one, their attention changed. They turned to me, cocking their heads as their attention focused on my chest and then my face. I felt their threat. They wanted my blood. They wanted me as their meal. But they weren't going to get it. I'd kill them. I'd kill them all.

Eight. The number registered before I even thought to count how many there were. Dark eyes flickered and one of the vampire's lips peeled back as he snarled.

"Come on, Princess. What are you going to do? You better think quickly. You're running out of time." The voice echoed around the room, sounding like it came from some faraway place. The word *speaker* registered in my mind, but I didn't quite know what it meant. I brought my attention to the right. To a glass wall. A light flickered in the closed-off space, giving me a view of Sayer, Julius, and my human, Hunter. But I didn't get to look long.

Growls broke my focus and I stepped back, closer to the wall behind me. *Eight. Eight. Eight.*

"Tessa! Come on, mon amour. You can do this. Feel with the pit of your stomach. Use your power to force our connection. Feel my blood. Feed it. Focus on it. Give it power and let it take you over."

The voice sent me screaming and grabbing at my head again. Even though hearing the words set off pain, it didn't stop me from noticing the odd pull I had in my core. *In the pit of my stomach.* My eyes cut up as I watched two vampires move closer toward me. Thoughts vanished and the room faded out as I focused on the warmth swirling around. Power…yes. I had power. And I would not be afraid. I was someone. Someone important. Someone with status.

Lights above me flickered, but I barely noticed. Heat was growing, spreading, as threats came closer. A black mist began to creep along the walls and ceiling, rolling toward me. It ate the light as it thickened and began swallowing the interior of the room. The connection it had with my vampire was immediate. I called it closer, coaxing it to my will, even though I wasn't sure exactly what it was or what it was doing. Instinct took over and a deep sound came from my throat. The lights above began to strobe, giving flashes to the black fog suddenly pouring from my mouth.

"Phenomenal, Princess. More!"

Sayer's voice pushed my rage to a boiling point. Claws shot out from my fingertips and I pushed to the balls of my feet, slicing through one of the vampire's necks, spinning and slashing the other across the face. Blood perfumed around me and an inferno took over my mouth and throat. I screamed, racing across the room in my bloodlust and sinking my fangs into a female vampire's throat. The skin shredded as I bit down and ripped my teeth free. Flickering left everything in slow motion, calming me. Yes…I needed black. Nothingness.

Just as I reached the next, darkness took over completely, feeding my adrenaline and the need to kill even more. Here, I was home…where I was supposed to be.

Each heartbeat tickled my skin like a beacon. It led me forward, slicing through flesh and snapping bones as I fought off two who rushed at me. Blood spilled over my lips and I screamed in impatience as the warmth soaked through the white nightgown I'd been given to wear. This bad blood wasn't enough. I wanted something more. Something richer. I wanted my prize hanging above.

A high pitch wail echoed around the room with my last attack and I snarled in fury as claws raked down my side, cutting deep. The pain sent my arms straight to the vampire's hair. I dug in deep, twisting and shredding until I felt the creature's head tear from its neck. I let the head fall to the floor and pushed from the balls of my feet, jumping high and catching the end of the cage. The swinging didn't stop the inevitable. The newly formed muscles in my arms easily lifted me and I reached for the bars of the door, ripping it clean from the hinges.

Murmuring in the background registered, but I ignored it as I launched myself toward the sweet smell of the heavily muscled human cowering against the side. Screams broke from his throat as I dove forward and sank my fangs just below his pulse point. The cries vibrated my entire body, sending prickling sensations along my skin. The sudden arousal was so unexpected, I almost broke away at the odd thickness that left my fangs aching. The venom pushed into the man and the hands that had a death grip on my hips eased the smallest amount…until he was pulling me in and pushing his hard cock against what didn't belong to him. Who did he think he was? Didn't he know who I was? *Who was I?* I didn't know, but I was someone. Someone who wasn't be touched unless she gave permission.

I sucked harder, crushing the bones in one of his hands. The sob was followed by the fingers of his good hand digging into my back. I jerked free of his neck and hissed as I sent my fist right through his throat. The act just came. Not from thought or even want. Instinct. It ruled me.

"Bravo! Excellent first test. Way to make me proud."

I spun around at the voice, noticing the light had returned through the dark haze I'd created. I didn't hesitate to jump down and stalk toward the glass. Although I wanted to shatter it, I didn't. My stare connected with the blond, who I now recognized as my maker, and I raised one of my blood soaked hands, fitting my palm against the glass.

"Je ne fais pas cela pour vous. Je le fais pour moi." *I don't do this for you. I do this for me.*

The smile melted and a hardness took over his face. He shook his head, keeping eye contact with me.

"Did she just speak French?" Julius looked over at Sayer nervously. "You can speak French, can't you, Sayer?"

"No," he said lowly. "I cannot."

Chapter 4
Hunter

I wasn't sure whether to throw up or run. Both were options that sounded pretty fucking good at the moment, but I was too in shock by the vampire's revelation to do anything but stay fixated on the killer before me. Jesus. Tessa was soaked in blood. Her long, dark hair was drenched from the substance and it blotched over her face and arms, making her appear more a victim than the perpetrator. And this was only the beginning. What the fuck did they have in store for her? More tests. For what? She'd sliced and diced eight vampires and bled another human dry. She'd expelled black smoke from her goddamn mouth. What more did they need to see? It moved like a living thing and it scared the shit out of me. I didn't like it. Didn't like this. I knew I'd fear Tessa's bite, but what she'd done with controlling the light and that…smoke…fuck no. I was terrified. But what could I do? I loved her. I promised to protect her. Maybe I should have been more worried about protecting myself.

"Marko's blood. It remains." Sayer clenched his fist, squeezing it tight as he took in Tessa. "I have to kill her. I was afraid something like this would happen."

"Whoa!" Julius shook his head quickly. "You can't kill her. Why would you want to? This is great news. Think about how this will benefit *you*. You'll possibly gain some of Marko's powers. Tell me you don't want that."

"And he'll gain mine! She's nothing but a vessel for us to be joined and I will not allow it. Not to mention, she'll benefit from both of *us*. It's a fucking disaster waiting to happen. She'll be *too* strong. Dammit. I never thought I'd say that. Tessalyn will be uncontrollable. Axis can't risk it. Look at her for fuck's sake. She's a baby and she just wiped out a group of six month olds. She shouldn't even be walking or really functioning yet, but here she is."

Julius exhaled deeply. "Simple. Look at the blood she held before the change and the one who took her over. Healing this fast is a little…strange, but for her, it's to be expected. You worry over nothing. The blood will still battle each other. You're stronger. You'll eventually win and Marko's blood will be history."

"But how long will that take? Weeks, years…centuries?!"

"Weeks," Julius said, matter-of-factly. "Trust me. You have nothing to worry about. Let's watch and see what happens. We'll continue the tests and monitor her to the best of our abilities. Just don't do something rash, you may come to regret it."

Sayer pursed his lips and followed Tessa with his gaze as she walked to stand before the door. I knew she couldn't hear them talking anymore, but I had, and there was no way I'd let her change just to get killed.

"We'll see how it goes. Right now, I'm hungry and tired. " Sayer walked over, throwing open first our door, then the one Tessa stood behind. His hand lunged forward, grabbing the back of her head before she could so much as try to move. The brutality had my jaw clenching.

"Let's go, Princess. Back to the room for you."

Tessa remained quiet as Sayer began to lead her down the tunnel. The flashlight illuminated the area and I stayed in the back, keeping my distance. When Sayer turned to open the door, Tessa's head snapped in my direction. My blood went cold front the threat she threw off. I wasn't sure what to make of it. I was rattled. Not quite myself after seeing what she'd done. If the real Tessa discovered the monster she truly was, she'd be devastated. But what could I do? The question was suddenly becoming too much. She had to feed and none of us trusted her to do it from us, so what were we left with?

The floor rumbled under my feet and I gritted my teeth. *Marko.* He was still at it.

"Ca c'était quoi?" Tessa's head snapped toward the exit of the tunnel and she tugged at Sayer's arm the smallest amount.

"I can't understand you," Sayer said, loudly. "Speak English."

"I think she asked what that was," Julius answered.

Sayer snarled, glancing toward the light. "*It's* forbidden and you'll stay away from him." He went to lead her inside when the vampire in Tessa attacked, biting and clawing into his chest. The reaction had Sayer letting go and howling in anger. Then, she was gone. Faster than I could even process, Tessa's body blurred with her speed and she raced toward the heart of the city. I didn't think, couldn't, as I flew past Julius and Sayer to run after her. I didn't have to guess where she was going. I knew.

Sounds grew louder as I broke into the large room harboring all the tables and shops. A body was lying on the cement floor, blood pooling under the vampire who was groaning as he tried to roll to his side. Fabric from his shirt was shredded at the shoulder and the bone that was exposed had me cringing as I jetted past. I pointed my flashlight into the darkness filling the tunnel Marko rested in and kept going. I wasn't sure where he was located inside, but I knew it wouldn't take long for mc to find out.

The pounding of my shoes echoed and a glow at the end of the hallway pulled me faster. As I approached, I slowed, pulling out my dagger. The entrance opened up to a large room full of cells, but my focus was only on one thing.

Tessa stood in front of the bars, a low growl leaving her as she stared at a surprised, but exhausted looking Marko. His hair rested loosely on the sides of his forehead, so different than the usual combed back style he sported. The vampire stepped closer, reaching for the bars as if in a trance. I couldn't move as I watched the two of them stare at each other.

"Ma minette." The whisper had the sounds from her mouth growing louder. He licked his lips, easing one of his hands through the opening cautiously. Tessa's head whipped down to take in the hesitant movement. In a small step, she moved further away, almost appearing to study every move he made. I couldn't deny there was something there as she looked at him. It was as if she wanted to get close to him, but decided against it.

"Qui êtes-vous?"

A gasp from Marko was followed by a shuddering exhale. The smile that appeared brought his hand more toward her. "Who am I? I'm the one meant for you. Celui qui tu aime—the one who loves you. Remember that, ma minette. Don't let them tell you otherwise. They are not your friends. Their intentions are *bad*.

Sayer means you harm. Look what they've done to us. They've torn us apart. You *love* me. You want me."

"Liar!" I stomped forward, breaking Tessa's attention from Marko. My eyes flared as she screamed and began running right toward me. The laugh that exploded from Marko's throat floated in the background as my pulse beat wildly. I battled with what I should do, but I didn't get to think long. Fangs lowered and Tessa's arm pulled back as her nails elongated. Sayer blurred by me, slamming her on her back just a foot before she reached me. And I…had the dagger ready to use. *Jesus.* Would I have killed her? Frozen at the last minute and let her kill me? Fuck, I wasn't sure.

"Remember, Tessa! Tu me aimes et je te aime. Rappelez-vous!" *You love me and I love you. Remember!* The French I recalled from high school let me piece together his words, but I wasn't sure if I'd gotten them all right. With that being the only language Tessa seemed to speak, perhaps it was time I brushed up.

"You! Are a very bad girl." Sayer clamped what looked to be thick metal cuffs onto Tessa's wrists, binding them in front of her while she fought and snapped at him. My eyes rose to the rage covering Marko's face. Intelligible sounds were coming from him now too and I could clearly see he didn't like Sayer anywhere around Tessa—especially man-handling her like he was.

"Put her in here with me. Let me take care of her. She won't harm anyone here. Sayer!"

The vampire's glare cut to Marko as he stood and jerked Tessa to her feet, wrapping his bicep under her chin in a chokehold and squeezing her against him. Her arms shot up, razor sharp claws ready to do their damage, only to come to a halt as spasms shook her body and she cried out in pain. What in the hell had happened? I moved in closer, watching tears escape down her cheeks. Whatever it was she'd felt had Marko jerking against the bars frantically.

"Tessalyn will *never* have anything to do with you again. You're forbidden to get close to her."

"You are not my leader and I do not take orders from you," Marko yelled. "Besides, she came to me. Tessa wants *me*! Give her back. You'll still have your ruler, just let me have her."

Sayer's head shook as he stared in what looked to be disgust. "I see through your lies and I will not let you use her as your ladder to the top. Even if that means I take her with me until she's ready to come here and rule. You will not win, Marko. I won't let you."

A loud roar left Marko's mouth and light blinded me as what sounded like a cannon exploded, shaking the earth violently. My arm jerked up to defend my face and I almost fell from the ground shifting beneath my feet. Had it not been for the invisible shield, I knew we'd all be dead.

I followed Sayer as he back stepped toward the exit. Harder, Tessa fought, but she couldn't overpower the Master Vampire holding her. Not even close. With every rise of her hands in an attempt to cause injury or break free, a jolt had her trembling and crying out in pain.

"Let's go, my princess. Time for you to get your beauty sleep." Sayer kissed the side of her bloody forehead, narrowing his eyes at Marko before turning them around. I couldn't move as I stared between the Masters. To these two vampires,

Tessa was nothing more than a pawn in their plans to rule. She was a balance between two evils and what they failed to see through their blinding hatred was instead of turning on each other, they should have been keeping their eyes on her. She'd overpower them both. She was the one to fear.

Chapter 5
Tessa

Heat poured from my body as dark eyes bored into mine. Closer he got, moving so seductively, yet terrifying in his advance, I felt my guard come up. I feared him. Wanted him for reasons unknown to me. French poured from his mouth, coaxing my legs to spread wider. I couldn't move. Couldn't understand why my arms wouldn't reach toward him like I wanted.

"You love me," he purred in his thick accent. "And I love you. We are one."

Harder, I struggled against the bonds keeping me subdued.

"They want to keep you away from me, but we're not going to let them. Are we, kitten?"

My head shook and my legs drew in, scissoring past the lust overtaking me. "Come closer," I begged. "Lay with me."

A smiled pulled at the side of his full lips and he hesitated for only a moment before his nude body lowered to hover over mine. Dark hair fell forward, but he didn't connect with my body. Not immediately. Torturous seconds went by before his weight began to register.

"Your heart calls to me. I want to hear it slow. I want to hear it stop."

Something about the words doused my lust. He wanted to kill me? That would surely happen if my heart stopped.

Confused, I shifted beneath him.

"Ma minette, why do you look so sad? You love my bite. You love me. Love me," he demanded more forcefully. "Love me back. You're not trying hard enough."

Fingers bit into my face as his features twisted angrily. "Love me. Love me to death."

Tighter, the grip grew, until my eyes were flying open. My maker hovered above me, the same angry look on his face. My head thrashed, but he didn't ease or let go. The cuffs confining me to the bed bit tightly into my wrists as I jerked against them.

"You shouldn't be dreaming already."

Although I understood his words, the reply I wished to give was almost impossible to say. The language felt wrong. Foreign to my tongue as I tried make myself speak.

A grin began to surface and he pulled back only slightly. "You're seeing the truth though, that's what's important. Marko is not your love, Tessalyn. He wants our power. Our blood. But not you."

"Wh-o?"

Thoughts were already beginning to fade and the name didn't register. It only seemed to make the vampire happier. But there was something else behind his gaze. Something evil I didn't like. My maker...yes. He was that, but I could barely register that his name was Sayer as he continued to search my eyes.

"I speak of no one. You remember nothing. It's time for your next test."

The cuffs fell free and I rotated my wrists, reaching down to the clean gown I wore. My head immediately shot to the side where a man was asleep on the sofa. The smile Sayer sported grew and he glanced toward the human, his face darkening with an emotion that kept surfacing. *Lust.* Yes, that's what had been on his face before.

"You want him? How much?"

The response was impossible for me to get out. Instead, I eased to my feet, continuing to stare at the blond.

"I want to see you with him. I think…he may like it, too. I'll tell you what." A thick aura projected around Sayer as he raked his eyes over the sleeping man. The weight of the invisible force left me ready to attack. It was malicious, full of bad intentions, and I didn't like it. Not toward what was meant to belong to me.

Sayer's hand settled on my shoulder, causing my claws to extend in self-defense. My reaction had his other hand burying in my hair at the base of my neck roughly, locking my head still. "I am not your enemy. Get that through your head. You belong to me, Tessalyn. And if you can face that, you'll have the world at your feet. I'll give you everything you want. Even him," he said, nodding toward Hunter. "But there are conditions. A small price you have to pay. Not that I think you'll mind." The grip loosened and he moved to trail his finger around my throat, up to my bottom lip. "I want to watch the two of you together. In all ways. At times, I'll touch you, or him. Maybe more. It'll depend on my mood. That's not so bad, is it?"

My stare went back to the human and I tried to process what he meant. Nothing existed past the craving I felt for the man's blood.

"That's all I want, Tessalyn." Sayer brushed his knuckles against the side of my cheek. "We'll be one happy, little family. Me, you, and your soldier. I think I like him, too. You don't mind sharing with your future bonded, do you?"

Share? Light snores filled the space and haziness had my head hurting again. I couldn't think. Didn't want to. All I wanted was the human's blood and to go back to sleep.

"Say yes, and he'll be yours. If you deny, he'll have to leave."

My head snapped around and I felt my fangs lower.

"Careful, Princess. You don't want to get upset with me. I'm about to give you a wonderful gift. One we can both enjoy. Be a good girl and say yes."

"Y-es." The single word was all I was capable of and in my state, it required no thought. My throat was on fire, my skin tingling with anticipation. Impatience had me taking a step to the side.

"Perfect. Now, I want you to watch what I do. All it takes is a second to accomplish and it's usually the first gift vampires are capable of. I'll go first, and then I want you to try." He took a few steps closer, holding out his hand for me to stay. Curiously, I watched, trying to ignore the impulses screaming for me to take advantage of my freedom.

Casually, Sayer walked forward, so quiet on his feet that he didn't make a sound. As he leaned down toward the sofa, the human stirred, but didn't appear awake.

"Hunter." My maker's hand gripped the human's large shoulder, gently shaking. More, I moved around to see better. Hunter's eyes flew open and he froze, becoming a zombie as he stared ahead. "Piece of cake. Do you see that, Princess?

Look into his eyes. Feel the connection as you stare into his depths and catch it. It's as simple as breathing." Sayer stood, not turning away from him. "Hunter, stand."

And just like the, he did.

"Remove the rosary from around your neck and take off the belt. You won't be needing your dagger right now."

There was a hesitancy to his actions, but I watched in surprise as the necklace fell to the floor along with the belt of weapons.

"Take off your clothes and go to the bed. You're going to lie down and raise your hands over your head."

Deep inhales were followed by a panic behind the human's stare. It stirred the numbness in my mind, causing me to question why I was worrying. The man was food. My food. And Sayer was getting him even more prepared for me. What was I afraid of?

Muscle rippled across Hunter's stomach as he pulled the shirt over his head. Even with the material covering his eyes, the connection wasn't lost. The pants and boxers were removed just as fast. My lips separated as I looked down at his cock and I couldn't help but swallow hard. *Lust.* Yes, it had me, too—just as much as it had Sayer. I wanted this human. Not just his blood. I suddenly wanted his body against mine.

"You outdid yourself landing this one, Princess. I do believe we both may enjoy your slave more than you know."

Sayer stayed even with Hunter, holding his gaze as they came to the bed. Their stare didn't break until my maker had the human secure.

"There. Easy as one, two, three. Your turn."

"What the fuck!" Hunter thrashed on the bed, looking down at himself, only to rip his vision up to me. The terror he displayed left a fluttering feeling deep within and I didn't like it. It left me conflicted, unsure in my already unstable mind.

English words mixed with French in my mind as I tried to find what to say to get him to quiet down. He was making my head hurt with his yelling.

"Shh." My finger came to my mouth and I moved slowly toward him. He jerked his hips further away from me, pulling against the cuffs. My fangs were already down, already cutting into my lip, making blood coat my tongue. I somehow knew I wasn't meant to speak French, but I let the words pour out anyway. "Look into my eyes, Hunter. Let me see you."

"No," he said, shaking his head. "Don't do this, Tessa. This isn't you. You wouldn't want me at your mercy like this. You love me. You…" he trailed off, thrashing hard enough to cause the bed to move.

"I want to taste you," I continued, "but first, you're going to look at me."

Before he could move his legs further away, I flew forward, straddling him and using my hand to secure his hip. He went wild, nearly tossing me from his lap. But I held on tight, causing him to wince at my nails tearing into his skin.

"Look…at…me," I managed in English.

Hunter grew still, closing his eyes. The anger passing through me blocked my desire for him, replacing it with the need to end his life. I was tiring of his game.

"Nope. You can't kill him yet. We have plans that include him, remember?" Sayer's words had me glancing in his direction. How he knew what I was thinking was beyond me and I didn't care.

"Hunter," I managed, "look."

"Don't do this, Tessa." Even as he said it, I couldn't ignore the hardness increasing against my stomach. It washed away the anger, replacing it with something new. Something I liked.

I lowered to lie down on his chest. Light scars marred his skin and I let time drag out as I began tracing over the odd angles. The more I touched him, the hotter his skin became. But I couldn't focus on it. I felt like I'd done this before. Yet, the realization only had an odd sense of fear associated with it. How did he get these? Did I know?

Rocking beneath me had the questions disappearing. "You like this?" I whispered in French. "You like me on you, touching you?"

Hands pushed under the thin nightgown I wore and I knew it was Sayer. I couldn't stop from tensing at the initial touch of his hands just below my ass. They gripped my upper thighs, lifting until I was on my knees. As they began to move higher, they pushed the nightgown up the length of my back, until he was pulling it over my head.

"Beautiful. Now, continue."

Hunter's eyes were open, staring at my breasts. I lowered, rotating my hips so my pussy could travel down his long length. A groan had him clenching his jaw, but he didn't turn away. The sounds of my wetness filled the room and I reached up, holding against his chest as I rocked with instinct. It was everything I knew, all that I was, and I was losing myself in the moment.

"Love me," I whispered in French. Love me…was that what I was looking for? I wasn't sure. Didn't care as my arousal increased at him groaning even louder.

"Love you?" he repeated in English. "God, I do."

And just like that, his eyes came up and I had him. He was stiff under me and I knew he hadn't meant to meet my stare, but the odd tug in my eyes kept his attention on me when I knew he wanted anything but.

"Yes," Sayer said lowly. "Perfect, Tessalyn. Just don't break that hold. If you look away, you'll lose him. I want you to kiss him now. But keep your eyes open. Let his passion increase."

Pressure from my maker's hand settled on the middle of my back and he eased me forward. Just as my lips brushed against Hunter's, a voice pushed through my mind.

"Ma minette, can you hear me? Talk to me, dammit. I miss you. I can't stop thinking about you."

I blinked, confused. Had I heard this voice before? There was something familiar about it I couldn't place.

"Holy fuck!" Hunter bucked his hips and if it weren't for Sayer, I would have flown off to the side. My heart was racing, my head…thrumming in pain from the voice. I screamed, latching on to the human's hair while I dove forward, sinking my fangs into his neck. Fingers locked onto my shoulder, but Sayer didn't pull me away.

"Oh…God. Jesus." Vibrations from Hunter's words made the pain from the venom hurt even worse as it left me. I sucked his blood into me hard, pushing my pussy down on his cock while Sayer stroked my back. "No, no, no…"

"Oh, yes," my maker breathed out. "You're going to love this so much, Hunter. You're going to be on your knees, begging for our bite before this is over with."

Already, I could feel the hard muscle under my body relaxing. Hunter moaned, exposing his neck even more. As his knees drew up, he rocked his body with my rhythm.

"There we are. Let go and enjoy what my future concubine has to offer. I won't let her kill you tonight. I have so much in store for the three of us. If you thought you loved her before, you're going to love her so much more now. That measly emotion that brought you here will feel nothing compared to the devotion she's going to grant you with when your bond is in place."

Sayer's words meant nothing to me as I pulled back, licking my tongue over Hunter's wounds. Desperation had my mouth coming to his and Hunter met my lips with a hunger only I thought I was capable of having. The fluttering tickled my stomach again and I tried to push the feeling away as Sayer's hand cupped my hip, lifting me. He grabbed Hunter's cock, applying pressure as he rubbed it up and down my slit.

"Fuck, this is a nice cock. Hunter, you're going to go slow. Tessalyn is new all over again. Like a virgin. Her body has healed strong. Maybe a little too strong with how early it is, but that's okay. She can take the pain."

Hunter's lips broke from mine and I saw the dazed look in his eyes as he blinked repeatedly.

"Wait," he said, grinding against me. "This isn't right. This…"

"Damn, her venom needs to get stronger already." Sayer's hand stroked up the human's long length, slapping the head against my ass. "Tessa's going to be your Mistress, Hunter. If you want that, this is the way it will be. These are my terms."

More, Hunter's face sobered. He looked between us, shaking his head. "You want to witness what happens between us? I don't know. Watching might be one thing, but I'm not yours to touch."

"You are now."

"No—"

My mouth was back on Hunter's before he could finish. I was tired of Sayer's terms. Of his voice in general. I wanted him gone, away from me and this human who was mine.

"Tessa." Hunter broke away, breathing against my cheek. "We shouldn't. I can't do this."

My mouth quickly found his again and surprisingly, he didn't rebel. But I could feel his tension return and although he continued to slide his tongue against mine, I felt his withdrawal.

Repeatedly, I moved against him, but it wasn't the same. Hunter had lost interest and it showed in the lack of response from the one thing I wanted most. The curse behind me proved what I already knew. Hunter didn't want me.

Chapter 6
Hunter

She wasn't my Tessa. That's what I kept reminding myself the moment I felt the urge to continue. She wasn't the same person and she wasn't in control of her mind. It was like I was cheating on, yet raping, the woman I loved, and I couldn't do it. The intimacy wouldn't come until I knew Tessa was in control.

"I have very little patience for you right now, human." Sayer stood, but I refused to look at his face. His actions and demeanor were changing. Or maybe he was just letting his true colors finally show. Either way, I had a really bad feeling about the man I'd overlooked through this process. I'd been happy at the thought of having Tessa, but I never considered Sayer a threat. I was starting to think I'd made the biggest mistake of all.

Tessa rose to climb off, but Sayer jerked her by the hair to make her stop. A blur of claws slashed toward him, catching his bicep, shredding the skin and black button up shirt he was wearing.

"You think you're a match for me, Princess?" Sayer's arm went around her throat and he threw his weight forward, slamming her to the bed and covering her nude body with his. Frantically, I jerked against the cuffs. My legs were trapped under them and I couldn't get free. It was like their weight was cement, grounding me to the mattress. "I'm the one in charge here. Not you, Tessalyn. Not Julius, or anyone else in this city. Me," he growled. "And I get what I want. You're going to fuck your human or I will. Make him want you or I'll leave him little choice on my end."

My eyes widened and I couldn't believe what I was hearing.

"Il ne veut pas de moi." *He doesn't want me.*

"English," Sayer yelled, reaching back and striking her across the face. "Speak" *Whack!* "English!" *Whack!* Tessa's hands shot up as she tried to defend herself, but he was too strong.

"Get the fuck off her!" A deep yell poured from my throat as rage like I'd never felt engulfed me. Again, he reared back, just in time for the floor and walls to rattle with Marko's presence. It only had him pausing before he hit her twice as hard. The cry that left her collided with my anger and although I'd never wanted anything from Marko, I would have given my life for him to see this. To stop Sayer with his powers…if he could.

"Please, fine. Just stop. Tessa, baby, come here. Come…" Nausea threatened as his fist came back and hit her again. One minute, they were on the bed, the next, Sayer was pushing to stand and Tessa was being thrown through the air, right for the wall. The crunch as she made impact with the concrete left the room spinning for me. Her small body fell to the ground, not moving as she lay there. "Jesus," I breathed out, drawing up my feet to try to sit. "Tessa? Tessa!" Vampire or not, I couldn't take seeing violence against her.

Knocking registered on the door and Sayer panted heavily as he surged forward and threw it open. "Later," he ground out.

"Prince, Julius says it's urgent. He wants you immediately."

Sayer turned and glanced at Tessa before he nodded. "Tell him I'll be right there."

The door shut and his hand came down to run over the wounds on his arm. "Fucking bitch. You've attacked me one too many goddamn times. Get up," he said, storming over, "get the fuck up. You come from my blood. You are not weak!"

His hand shot down to grab her, but she was on him before either of us could comprehend her moving. Nails tore into his face and throat as her legs locked around his waist. A table caught the back of Sayer's legs and he fell back with Tessa still latched to him. Her lip peeled back and I saw the fangs for only a split second before she buried them in the front of his throat. Blood sprayed and trailed down his neck while he let out a gargling sound that made my skin crawl. His hands flew to the sides of her head and her screams overpowered his while he managed to unlock her jaw.

"You..." he trailed off as he managed to stand and pull her up. The cuffs fell free from my arms and gravity disappeared as I collided with the wall not a few feet away. The comforter was somehow trapped around my legs and I fought with it as I scrambled to my feet. "You'll stay locked down until I get back." His stare came to me. "If you think about setting her free, I'll tear you limb for limb while you suffer through the pain."

Tessa's body thrashed wildly as he pinned her down and got the cuffs buckled. It was like I suddenly didn't exist as he went to the closet and changed his shirt. The ragged flesh on his neck had healed before he even got Tessa restrained. I couldn't believe it.

Slowly, I eased to the side, reaching down and putting my rosary back on. It didn't take me long to slide on my clothes. My fingers connected with the dagger and I held it tightly in my grip while he cleaned the blood off him and headed for the door.

"Oh, and Hunter," he said, glancing over, throwing me a smile, "this isn't over. We're only beginning. Welcome to your new life."

The door slammed behind him and I rushed to Tessa's side. Tears and sobs were constant, even as she snapped her teeth in my direction. Blood trails flowed from both nostrils, covering her chin and neck. Tears burned my eyes while I shook my head.

"I'm sorry, baby. I'm so sorry. This is all my fault." I couldn't get past the agony in my heart. Wetness trailed down my cheeks and I wiped it away angrily. "We're going to figure out how to fix this. God, what the fuck was I thinking? You tried to warn me, but I didn't listen. I was too greedy to have you as mine, I didn't even let myself fathom this." My head lowered. "This is hell. It has to be."

Marko shaking the walls returned and Tessa looked around, sniffling, and closing her eyes.

"Si cela est l'enfer, alors je prendrai une décision. Je vais gouverner et détruire tous ceux qui se ma façon. Dead. Je les tuerai tous." *If this is hell, then I will rule. I will rule and destroy all who gets in my path. Dead. I'll kill them all.*

It took me a few seconds to piece the words together. I kept my head down, trying to make what just happened disappear from my mind. But I couldn't.

"Go…to him."

"Who?" Still, I stared down at the bed. I already knew who she was referring to and it made me even sicker.

"Help…me."

My head shook in a steady rhythm while I clenched my teeth. "He can't help us, Tessa. He's behind bars. Locked away. And for good reason. He wants to kill me."

"Go."

The order was just that: a command. And it wasn't put nicely. I stood, flexing my fists at my sides. "It's pointless."

"Go!"

Silence played out behind me and I grabbed my belt full of weapons, putting it on. The glance back only made me wish I hadn't. More tears slid down her cheeks and they had me stalking toward the door. I hated leaving her alone, but what else could I do? Sit around and wait for Sayer to return? God, I hated this fucking place. I knew no one. No one but…Marie. I swallowed hard. No, she couldn't help me.

Music poured from the heart of the city and it was all but deserted on my end. The shops in the distance were filled with people coming and going and I rushed the length of the far side of the room, slipping into Marko's tunnel. Faster, my heart raced, until I was sure it would explode. The moment I stepped into the large, open space full of cells, he eased from the floor. Neither of us said a word as I closed the majority of the distance between us.

"What's happening? Something's wrong, I can feel it. Is Tessa okay?"

I didn't dare look into his eyes. Not just because of his powers, but because I was on the verge of breaking in front of the one person I had to be strong against.

"Sayer has to go," I said lowly. "He…I don't want him around Tessa anymore."

"Hunter," he growled. "What happened?" His hand shot out between the bars to grab me, but I jumped back just in time. "Show me," he went on. "Let me see."

"He hurt her," I managed. "He…beat the fucking living shit out of her right in front of me and I couldn't do anything about it. What he wants for the three of us..." My head just kept shaking. "I can't do it. She can't. She asked me to come to you."

I glanced up for only the briefest moment, seeing the pain on his face.

"Tell me. What does he want?"

How in the hell was I supposed to divulge that? "He…wants all of us to be together. Like…"

"Sexually?" Marko rushed in.

"Yes. He trapped me with his eyes." I paused. "Cuffed me and tried to get Tessa to... Anyway, I couldn't and he got mad. Then, he and Tessa got into it. I can't see him do that to her again. Fuck, I want to kill him. I'm *going* to."

Marko's arms shot out to try to grab me again, but he went back to gripping the bars after a few seconds. "He'll kill you. Let me see, Hunter. I *have* to see. You know I love her. Let me see what happened."

"No way. I'm tired of people fucking with my head. I can't take this! I hate this place. I…" My jaw clenched shut and I took a deep breath.

"I just want to see," he said calmly. "I want him dead, too, and I don't need an excuse to kill him, but I have to see what he's done."

The deep tone of his voice made the end of the words almost impossible to make out. Deep, heavy breaths left his mouth and I braved bringing my eyes up enough to see his fangs were exposed.

"Hunter, please."

Cautiously, I stepped forward, meeting his stare. Darkness sucked me in and it felt like I was falling down a deep, dark tunnel. My fingers twitched and I could think, but I couldn't break away from the darkness. Seconds went by while Marko's exhales became louder, turning into what sounded like snarling. Fear vibrated my insides, humming down the length of my arms and legs until my body trembled at the power he was expelling.

Yelling filled the space, followed by unhuman growls. Even though Marko didn't hold me captive with his abilities, I couldn't turn away. I stayed trapped in utter terror at the veins bulging from his neck in his rage. His hands clutched tightly to the bars, jerking at them every few seconds. And then, like I was introduced to a new scene, he grew still.

"He's dead," he said calmly. A little too calmly. "Protect her as best as you can. But rest assure, Sayer will not make it out of this alive. Death will be paying him a visit when the time is right. Tell Tessa not to fear. They can't keep me in here forever."

I shifted, remembering the conversations between Sayer and Julius. "They'll try," I said lowly. "They fear you."

Marko's eyebrows drew in and I quickly looked back down to his lips.

"Go on," he urged.

My mind battled over whether I should say anymore. Marko wasn't my friend. He was the enemy just as much as Sayer was. They both wanted Tessa for their own selfish reasons. But who was the bigger threat? Right now, it wasn't Marko.

"I have to get back to Tessa before Sayer returns."

"Hunter, wait." Marko's hands moved down the bars as he tried to stay even with me. "Why do they fear me? Explain."

I stopped, grabbing my flashlight. Slowly, I looked up, only glancing into his eyes for a moment. "You're ready to rule and they know it."

Chapter 7
Marko

Reality blurred in and out, casting me into episodes of complete blackouts. My vampire was taking over and it was all due to what I'd seen in Hunter's eyes. The once bonded male I used to be was losing it. After seeing the woman I loved hit repeatedly in the face and thrown across the room so brutally, I was ready to cut my limbs off and place them through the bars just to see if I could put myself back together again on the other side. I was gone. Going insane from the rage and separation, and there was nothing I could do about it. I'd exhausted every option. I couldn't break free from this cell. It was physically impossible. So what did I do?

I didn't know.

From what I gathered, days had gone by. Maybe two. Maybe more. I wasn't sure. Only one meal had arrived from multiple leaders, but not Julius. And the members were too careful, too strong together, when placing the supplier in my cell. I was losing precious time. With every minute that passed, I feared something worse was happening, yet there was nothing I could do to stop it. Sayer was going to pay. I'd kill him if it was the last thing I did. But I couldn't yet. Not obviously, anyway. I may have been past the point of being rational, but I wasn't stupid. He was a member of Axis. They'd have me sentenced in a heartbeat if I murdered one of their own. I had to play this smart. I had to come up with a plan.

Footsteps in the distance had me coming to the bars. Was it meal time again already? The hours were getting away from me. I could barely tell if the sun was up or down, which was odd since my vampire lived on instinct in this state of mind.

Closer, they came, until Sayer appeared in the entrance. My fangs shot down and I couldn't stop the threatening sound from escaping my lips. In a leisurely pace, he strolled forward, locking his hands together in front of him. That stupid smile I'd come to hate was plastered on his face and it had me squeezing against the bars even tighter.

"I saw you had a visitor a few hours ago."

Hours? Surely, it had been longer than that?

At my silence, he continued.

"What did he tell you, Marko? What did he hope you'd do, locked away as you are?"

"I don't know what you're talking about."

Sayer's mouth twisted, but he remained still. "I know Hunter came to you. I saw it in Tessa's eyes. She told him to come and then he left."

"He didn't come here. Do you seriously think I'd have anything to do with him? Besides, he knows better. Do you forget I'm going to kill him for what he's done? For who she chose?"

A laugh filled the space. "You say that now. Good luck getting near him. He's guarded well."

I knew about the rosary and dagger, it was his shield against us, and it would work as long as he kept his eyes safe from ours. But that didn't mean he could withstand a beating or the powers we held. We just wouldn't be able to touch him physically. Not without risking injury.

"The fact that he's guarded well doesn't worry me, Sayer. What do you want? Why are you concerned that he told me something? What would he have to say? Something about you?"

"So many questions. Ones I'll answer just after you prove to me that he didn't come here."

It was my turn to laugh. "You fucking wish." I turned my back, walking deeper into the cell to collapse down and sit against the wall. I didn't want him to know what I saw. I didn't want him to suspect me as a threat at all. "If you're not going to set me free, leave. I have more important things to do than have a conversation with you."

"Like what? Continue to scheme over how you're going to get Tessa back so you can take over? It's not going to happen, Marko. Tessalyn belongs to me now, as does her pet, and I'm not going to let you kill him. It's time for you to move on."

Her pet. Yes, Sayer would see the human that way. So beneath us, just as I used to view the situation—how I still did concerning everyone but him. Hunter was different, I just wasn't exactly sure why. I hated him. Hated him with a passion. But his arrival to help Tessa had twisted something within me. Maybe it was his love for her. Even though I despised it, I knew he'd try to take care of her— especially when I couldn't.

"Nothing is set in stone yet, Sayer. Just because you changed her and Julius is going along with your bonding, doesn't mean it'll happen. She has to agree, and I don't see that happening any time soon. She's a newborn. All she wants right now is food. Not a future."

"Tessalyn will agree. She'll have to."

My chest jumped at my sarcastic laugh. "Why, because you're going to threaten to use something against her? Sounds right up any of our paths. What will it be, her human? She might still say no."

"Perhaps," he said, shrugging. "But once I complete our bond, I don't see her disagreeing with much of anything I say. Together, our blood will thrive under the marks. She'll be like putty in my hands. Besides, she and I had a deal. She wanted the change and agreed she'd become my concubine if I did it. There's no going back on her word. I won't let her."

My jaw locked as I held in what I wanted to say. His gloating about bonding her was enough to make my insides boil. The fact that she had become one of us on those terms was a verbal contract she couldn't break. Not in our world.

"No come back? No threats? What's wrong, Marko, is your blood thinning within her? Are you losing the love you two once shared? She's speaking better English, so I'm guessing that's the case. Don't worry, I'll take good care of her. I'll love her so good, she won't be able to get enough." He walked forward. "How does it feel to know you once had it all and now…nothing? I bet it hurts like hell."

I flew from the floor, crashing into the bars with every ounce of strength I possessed. My claws were inches short of reaching him and he only laughed harder.

"Do you want to know my plans for your beloved Tessalyn?" He glanced down at my outstretched fingers, taking a step closer, teasing me. "I'm going to make her my own personal whore. She'll fuck me or whomever I want on command while I watch. And she's going to love it. Especially at this stage where she runs from instinct." He licked his lips, reaching up and trailing the tip of his finger over one of my claws. "I think I may just go do that now. I haven't been with a woman in a while. Perhaps I'll fuck her while I make her human watch. Hunter will love that. Maybe I'll even make her suck his cock while I drill her tight, little ass. I can come back and let you enjoy the show after I'm done. If you'd like, of course. I know you must be bored in here all by yourself."

Had I thought I'd been mad before? My power was blistering my insides as I held his stare. For the first time, I wasn't worried about him pushing into my mind. I had confidence that he couldn't. Hunter hinted I was ready. I believed him.

"Un jour, je vais vous déchirer. Je baigne dans le sang pendant que je vous fais souffrir. Le temps est court. Votre mort sera la mien." *Someday, I'm going to rip you apart. I'll bathe in your blood while I make you suffer. The clock is ticking. Your death will be mine.*

"God, you make me sick," Sayer spat out. "Such a coward not to say what you want to my face."

I let my smile stretch across my mouth. "Coward…no. You shall see."

The pull of Sayer's cheek caught my attention. He stepped back, crossing his arms over his chest. "Was that a threat?"

"What reason do I have to threaten you? You're right, I'm losing Tessa and my bond. It hurts, but I'm okay with that. I may not like you using her as part of your sick game to get back at me, but it is what it is. I have bigger things to worry about right now. I'm starting to find the need for a new slave. One who's more obedient than she *ever* was. I'm ready to hit the streets once Julius sets me free."

"A new slave?" The disbelief was there, but I could also see something resembling relief. "I should have known it was only the bond making you love her. You're incapable of feeling anything for anyone. Or, portraying loyalty," he ground out.

"I'm only loyal to myself and my beliefs. As we all are," I said, raising an eyebrow. "Loyalty, trust, we both know those don't exist toward others in our world. We prize ourselves above all others. To deny that would make you the biggest liar there is."

Sayer grew quiet, glancing down at his feet. "You're right to an extent, but my loyalty is to Axis. Tell me, when you come to lead this city, what will you do? How will you run it? Will extreme mayhem break out under your rule? Massive slaughters because the community will not accept you, or will you change laws and make them bow at your feet the moment you walk into the room?"

My eyes rolled and I went back to lightly gripping the bars. "I will be a great leader. I do not expect anyone to bow to my feet, but they *will* respect me."

"Someday, we may see. Then again, maybe not. You still have a long way to go before either of us have to do worry about that. At the rate you're going, your enemies are piling up."

"My enemies? You mean you?"

He laughed. "Amongst others. Julius isn't too happy with you. Or any of the members, really."

"They *fear* me. As they should. But I will rule, Sayer. Don't doubt that."

His eyes scanned the surrounding as he let out a deep, slow breath. "I'm done talking about this. I have things to do. Tests to put my princess through. Try not to have too much fun in here by yourself."

Sayer turned and I felt anxiety for Tessa kick in. My brain scrambled for a way to buy her more time.

"If you want to test her, why don't you put her up against some real competition?"

His steps slowed and he turned to look back at me. "Who? You? I'm not stupid, Marko. You just want her in your clutches again."

I laughed, letting my evil bleed through. "She owes me some satisfaction for what she's done. I promise to take it easy on her. Besides, don't you want to see how she reacts around me? Maybe it'll help put your mind at ease. I'm ready to move on. Is she?"

"You're a grain of salt in the back of her mind. She can't even remember what happened hours before. Trust me, I'm not worried about her nonexistent feelings for you. You're the one I don't trust."

"What's there to lose? You're more powerful than I am. If you don't like the way things are going, you have an excuse to get what you want. I'm just curious about what my future leader is capable of."

His head shook. "I thought *you* were the future leader."

"I am. I'll be ready before she will. Or do you know something I don't?"

Sayer's mouth broke into a grin. "She might beat you to the punch. We'll see."

My fingers gripped tighter. She'd beat me because they weren't going to allow me to advance. It had my anger flaring more than it already was.

"So, are you bringing her here or not?"

"Not," Sayer said, continuing to the exit.

"And you said I was the coward. I bet her powers aren't even that strong."

Sayer's body jolted to a stop. Black eyes met mine as he spun around.

"You dare call me a coward? Me, the Black Prince? I could kill with just a whisper of your name. I'm not afraid of you Marko, and I assure you, in a few months, Tessalyn won't be either. I doubt she'd be right now. Maybe I will bring her here so she can try to kill you. After all, Axis wouldn't blame her with her status as a newborn."

"Seems like a logical enough plan to me. But I'm sorry to say, your little shadow doesn't stand a chance. Probably never will. You have such high hopes for her, but I'm going to watch her fail. And I'm going to laugh right to the throne."

Red tinted his cheeks before he spun, stomping and disappearing into the tunnel. I laughed, shaking my head as I turned and moved back to the wall. He wouldn't be stupid enough to bring her, but it felt good to put him in his place. Other than our assumptions, there was no proof Tessa would be stronger than me. The greed in me prayed I was right. Then I could rule and have her, too.

Chapter 8
Tessa

I stared at the wall ahead, refusing to look or give my attention to the human sitting on the edge of the bed. He hadn't stopped talking since Sayer left, but I barely recalled what he'd been saying. All my focus was on trying to figure out how to kill the man who'd made me. I hated him, and although the details of what happened were already fading, I couldn't let it go. He'd hurt me. Hurt me so badly, my jaw and cheekbone were crushed under the force of his blow. They were all but healed now, but I couldn't erase the pain of his brutality. It ate at my brain, causing me to scheme on how to make him experience the same kind, just a million times worse.

"I'll talk to Julius. Maybe if he knew what Sayer did or what he has planned for us, he might protect you, or…" his head shook. "What am I saying? He won't. No one will. No one but…God, I fucking hate this. We have to leave. We have to figure out how to escape him."

I knew he was talking more to himself, which was fine. I'd tired of hearing him try to figure out a situation I didn't want to change. Sure, I wanted Sayer dead, but I wasn't going anywhere. I couldn't fathom why he'd want to. This was my home. My room. I didn't want to leave it.

"I wonder if he drinks anything? I could poison his drink with holy water. Yes," he breathed out heavily, "I'll kill him that way. Or…" Hunter's head lowered. "I'm on the right track. I'll have to think this through a bit more so I can get it perfect. I'll only have one chance."

I let out a deep sigh, wishing I could turn on my side and go to sleep. I was getting tired. And hungry. I was so fucking desperate for blood.

"Humaine, me nourrir." *Human, feed me.*

The mumble of words died off and Hunter's head lifted. "Feed you? No way. You'll kill me."

I continued in French, knowing he somewhat understood what I was saying. "Your life isn't the one that matters, mine is, and I need to feed."

Seconds went by and something raced over his features. He pushed from the bed, staring down at me. "You're so damn cold. I can't stand it. I sure hope this passes because if it doesn't…."

I licked my lips, moving my body seductively. I didn't miss the way his eyebrows pulled in. "Come…here," I managed in English. "I want you." My voice practically purred with my accent. Hunter swallowed hard, watching as I arched my hips. I was still unclothed and I hadn't forgotten how hard he'd been trying not to look at my body. "Come. Lay on me. Donnez-moi votre cou et votre robinet. Je les veux." *Give me your neck and your cock. I want them.*

"Fuck, Tessa. I really wish you were in your right mind. I really do."

My jaw clenched angrily, but I spread my legs, trying my best to entice him. The door swung open, hitting the cement wall hard before Sayer halted.

"Now she wants to fuck. Perfect." He shut the door and Hunter immediately moved closer to the bed, blocking my view of my maker. My eyes narrowed as it dawned on me—the human was trying to protect me.

"Go sit," Sayer commanded.

Hunter's head shook and he grabbed the hilt of his dagger. "What are you going to do with her?"

"I said go!"

Still, Hunter didn't move.

"Don't push me, pet. I'll break you into a million pieces. Don't believe me, keep stepping up." Dark fog began to swirl along the top of the ceiling directly over the human and Hunter shifted nervously. "One," Sayer, hissed, "two."

A yell came from Hunter's mouth as his shoulders curled in and he fell to his knees. With a whoosh, his body flew through the air, slamming into the bottom of the couch.

"Stupid human."

Sayer ripped off his shirt, bringing his black eyes to mine. "Seems your test just got a lot harder. But you're going to excel. You're going to kill and I'm going to assure you're in the perfect mindset to do just that."

I bared my fangs, digging the heels of my feet into the mattress as I pushed myself higher on the bed.

"Oh, yeah. You know what's coming, don't you?"

His evil laugh filled the room and I jerked at the cuffs. No matter how hard I pulled, they didn't budge or set me free.

A loud roar filled the room and just before Hunter made it to Sayer, he hit an invisible wall, crumbling to the floor from the force. The dagger fell from his hand while he sucked in air. But he didn't stop. He rose, grabbing the weapon and slamming it into the wall wildly.

"Your pet may be a problem, Princess. Luckily, I know just how to handle him. Have you ever seen a broken slave? Oh, it's so fun to get them to that point. Hunter's going to be such an obedient fuck by the time I finish. And I mean that in every sense of the word."

Sayer's pants fell to the floor and I took in his hard cock. "Reste loin de moi." *Stay away from me.*

"English! Goddammit, how many times do I have to tell you?" He flew forward, grasping my ankle and jerking me down. Both of my legs kicked out at him, over and over, trying to get his body further away from mine. It didn't work. Sayer forced himself between my thighs, prying them apart with his palms as he positioned himself above me. My head lifted, but my fangs were useless when I couldn't reach him.

"Get off me. Get off!"

The continued French only made him angrier, but I couldn't think to try to speak English. The back of his hand connected with my cheek like an explosion and I gasped, trying to catch my breath from the shock of my bones shattering once more. Stars danced in front of my eyes, only for the next hit to come almost immediately. The room wavered and sound dissipated for the briefest moment. I could still feel my arms moving, still trying to defend myself.

Pressure pushed against the opening of my pussy and my hips tried to pivot, but the death grip he had on one of them prevented me from moving. Hunter's yelling in the background swirled and mingled with my heartbeat and the nausea turning my stomach. More, the force pushed into me, and I screamed as Sayer tore into me completely. I gagged, too paralyzed by the brutal invasion to yell anymore. His hand turned my head and he applied enough weight to hold me still while he lowered his lips just above my ear.

"You're going to kill Marko Delacroix." He withdrew, plunging into me harder. "You're going to kill him because if you don't, I will do this to you every day you continue to live. Do you hear me?" Faster, he went, moaning as he repeatedly pounded into me. Bile burned my throat and I gagged again, trying to block out his threat.

"God, you feel good, Princess. Maybe this isn't so bad after all. And I have your pet when I bore of you."

My eyes opened, connecting with Hunter's blurry face. I could barely see it past the tears blinding me. The look of horror and pain couldn't be masked. I saw it and it burned into my memory like a blowtorch, lighting the fire back within me. My hips bucked and my whole body thrashed beneath him. It wasn't enough to remove him, but it did make it harder for him to enjoy himself, and somehow, that was a small victory of its own.

"That's right, fight me. Show me what you're going to do to Marko. Let your vampire free. Let it rule you, Tessalyn!"

Hands continuously tried to pry down my face, but by some chance, I managed to slide free. My jaw snapped repeated in his direction and I caught the side of his palm, shredding it open as he jerked it away.

"Almost there, sweets. Keep fighting. Keep…" A loud moan tore from his throat and warmth shot deep inside me, causing another type of fire. The amount of stinging was enough to have me crying out from the pain. I knew he'd torn me to hell and back. I was bleeding, I could smell it, along with his cum. The two scents made a stench I couldn't stomach. I heaved, screaming at the top of my lungs the moment I caught my breath. If it was from the pain or the pure rage sweeping through every inch of my body, I wasn't sure. I was losing it. Maybe I already had. My eyes darted around in jerky movements and my heart was slamming into my chest.

"I'm going…to kill…you," I managed in my broken English. "Kill you," I said more steadily. "You're dead."

"Good luck with that." Sayer pushed from the bed, pulling his cock to each side, examining it. Crimson covered his shaft and balls. The smile that appeared only dragged me further under. As he disappeared into the closet and then the bathroom, I couldn't take my eyes off the door guarding him. Slowly, my lips separated and I stared before me, watching the black smoke pour from my mouth. The long trail hit the ceiling, billowing out and crawling along the walls. Thoughts faded as the room darkened and disappeared completely. The amount surrounding me was so thick, like a blanket comforting me and keeping me safe. I heard the door shut and a laugh broke through the smoky surroundings.

"Oh, Princess. Do you really think you can use my own gift against me?"

Like a shadow standing out against the darkness, a blur sped toward me. All I saw were fangs as my feet shot up. Before I could use my teeth as a weapon, his were sinking into my neck. He didn't drink. Didn't do anything but use his force to render me immobile. It was a warning—a show of his power. I didn't stand a chance. He could kill me now. Could have killed me before, yet he hadn't.

Sayer let go, bringing back his fist to plant it right into my mouth. Teeth fell loose against my tongue with a gush of blood and I turned, spitting them out. Within seconds, they grew back, but not without a price. The pain was crippling. A blood curdling scream left me and I was frozen. Even with the cuffs magically falling loose, I couldn't move. I was so weak. In so much pain, it was hard to get past the thought of being defeated.

"Get up." Sayer pulled me to stand, pushing a loose, white slip over my head. It came down a few inches above my knees, but it didn't hide what I saw. Cum mixed with blood ran down my legs and I squeezed them together, feeling and seeing the wetness just past the hem smear.

"You look great. Marko's going to love this," he whispered in my ear. "And this is what he's going to see right before you kill him. He's going to know you're mine. That *I'm* the one with the power to do to you whatever I want. He'll be so devastated by your appearance, his guard will be down. And you'll end him once and for all. You got that?"

Sayer jerked against my arm, pulling me toward the door. I could fight, but I didn't. He was taking me to see Marko. Somehow, I knew this person, but I couldn't put the pieces together in my mind. Everything was blurring together. I was fading again and there was only one thing I knew: I had to get to him. Had to get to Marko.

Hunter's shouts continued, but not for long. The door closed behind us and Sayer pulled me toward the tunnel at a fast pace. Blood was all I tasted and smelled, and it was my own. It left my adrenaline soaring to dangerous heights. The moment we broke into the large open room, every sound in the city pinged in my ears, spiking my need to defend myself. Musicians sang. People laughed far off in the distance, moans even broke through from somewhere, but I was pulled from the moment by a group of people coming to an abrupt stop in front of me. Their power was strong. Together, it made me pull against Sayer's grip so I could try to protect myself. Two men and two women. One with dark hair had my eyes narrowing. She stirred something in my mind, but I wasn't sure whether she was a threat.

"Oh…God," she breathed out.

"Mind your business, Marie," Sayer snapped, pushing us past them. I turned around, seeing the dark haired woman's mouth drop open as she shook her head. She spun on her heels, racing deeper into the large, open room. Darkness took over and two heartbeats in the distance had my attention snapping to the front. Light rested further down and I couldn't shake the feeling that I'd been here before.

Tighter, Sayer's arm gripped. "Remember what I told you. Kill him," he said under his breath, "or I'll rape you again the moment we get back to the room. This time, it won't be so nice or quick."

A threatening sound left me, so deep and loud, it bounced from the cement around us. But he didn't stop. Didn't even seem fazed by my reaction to his warning. We broke into the light and a dark haired man had a woman pinned against the wall of his cell. His face was buried in her neck and I watched him stiffen before he turned around, letting the woman crash to the floor. Blood stained his chin and he wiped it away, reaching down to blindly kill her before he stepped forward. Not once did he take his eyes off me. It was like I was looking at Hunter all over again during my rape. Horror. Pain.

The man I knew as Marko reached to his chest and took a few ragged breaths before turning his attention to Sayer. The hate he projected was equivalent to my own, but the expression was so fast, it didn't last. Hardness came over his features and he shook his head, beginning to laugh.

"Fuck, you did a number on her. I have to say, I'm a little shocked right now. I thought for sure you were joking. Yet, here she is, beaten to hell, covered in blood and…" His head tilted as he looked down at my legs. The fury flickered again, but was gone as his eyes rose. "Cum. I take it that's yours?"

"Of course it's mine. Tessalyn belongs to me. I can fuck her when I choose."

Slowly, Marko nodded, his mouth growing tight.

"My princess has decided she wants to fight you after all. Don't you, sweetheart?" Lips pressed against the side of my face and my claws shot down. Before I could raise my hand to attack, his fingers slid into my hair and he yanked me forward. The door to the cell slammed open and I was thrown in so low, my chest slid across the rough ground. My hand came down and I tried to push myself up, only to collapse.

There was movement next to me, followed by Marko lowering and whispering in French. "Jesus, ma minette, what has he done to you? I'm so sorry I haven't been there to protect you. My heart is breaking right now."

I sniffled past the tears burning my eyes. I didn't know this man, not really, but his sympathy hit right in my heart, stirring unfamiliar emotions.

"I'm going to kill him," I managed in our language. "I will not forget this. I…can't."

"Nor will I let you," he said angrily.

"Enough talk!" Sayer yelled. "Get up, Tessalyn. You wanted this fight, now show him what you're made of."

Sadness swept over Marko's features and his hand came out toward me. I couldn't help but flinch after everything I'd been through.

"I wish I could say I wasn't going to hurt you, but you know that isn't the case, right? I don't want to, but it's the only way I'm going to convince him I'm moving on. It's the only way they'll set me free. But, I'll never get over you. You're my heart and I'm going to show you how much I love you once I'm released. Stay strong for just a little while longer. If he's not dead by the time I'm out, I'll be the one who kills him. No one hurts what's mine and gets away with it. And you *are* mine, Tessa. Forever."

Marko's arm latched onto my bicep and he jerked me up, violently. Threatening sounds left his mouth, but I felt no fear. "Now, fight," he said in English. "And fight hard. I'm not going to take it easy on y—"

My nails ripped across his cheek, causing him to growl out in anger. His head snapped back to me and his eyes practically sparkled with approval.

"I don't…know you." I created more distance between us, shaking my head. "I don't know you!"

Whether Sayer believed my statement, I wasn't sure, but I *did* know Marko. Somehow, I did, and the vampire in me gravitated to him like nothing I'd ever experienced before. It made trying to fight him hard. I didn't want to fight. I wanted his arms around me, holding me while I breathed him in.

"You may not now, but I guarantee after this day, you won't forget me." Marko charged in my direction and my instincts flared, assessing the threat racing toward me. I dropped low in a crouching position, thrusting myself up to catch his waist and bring him to his back. Sayer's laugh filled the background, as did a clapping sound. My fangs bared and I dove toward his neck. Where I thought he'd move or try to prevent my attack…he didn't. Viciously, I bit down, jolting at the power his blood caused pooling over my tongue. Fingers embedded in my hair and I felt the low moan all the way to my toes as he held me to him. The vibrations joined with the richness of his flavor and my body softened, molding into his. For the first time since I could remember, I felt safe. I felt *at home*. My tongue swirled over his neck and his grip grew tighter.

"Not yet, ma minette, but soon," he whispered, jerking my hair and spinning me to my back. Feeling defenseless had me fighting in earnest and I wedged my feet against his hard stomach, sending him flying into the wall. Through the lust and panic, I managed to climb to my feet, just in time for him to make it back to me. My claws shot out, but he defended himself against the strikes. Blocked every fucking move I tried to make, over and over. It was almost laughable how good he truly was. He was taking it easy on me. Every move. Every action. I didn't stand a chance.

Anger began to seep in and Sayer's words repeated in my head. He was going to rape me again after this and there was nothing I could do about it.

Heat swirled in my belly and although Marko had me from behind now, I barely felt his strong hold as I tuned into myself. Darkness clouding the top of the cell projected in my mind and met me as my lids opened. The grip holding me loosened, but didn't break.

"There we go," Sayer said lowly. "Do it. Show him what you're capable of!"

Black fog billowed from my mouth, pouring out in a thick mass that began to creep around us. The darkness would keep me safe. The darkness was *me*. Only I could save myself, and somehow I took comfort in that—even if it was only temporary.

"I love you. *To death*. Remember that through your hell. Know that I'm going to be there with you soon. We'll make them pay. We'll make them *all* pay."

I wasn't focusing on Marko's words anymore. All I knew was the substance leaving me. It wasn't like before and the realization was stealing my focus. The slight twinge of an odd perfume started to coat my throat. Surviving was key. I had to protect myself because I couldn't kill the one person Sayer wanted me to. He promised to be there for me. He said he loved me. And something told me I might have feelings for him, too.

"Ma minette, what is that? What…" The hold loosened, quickly breaking away as footsteps stumbled back. Multiple voices filled the surroundings, but I could see nothing but the darkness swirling and dancing around me happily. Yes, it looked so happy. So alive as it rose and stretched out.

"Tessalyn Antoinette? Tessalyn?" A familiar voice had me turning, but I didn't know who it was. Didn't want to see as I clung to my armor. It was hiding me. Protecting me from the evil outside of it.

"Tessa?"

Another voice. *Hunter.*

I took a few steps, looking down at Marko's barely conscious body on the floor. His lids appeared heavy as he blinked up at me. There was a smile on his face. One of pride? I wasn't sure. "Soon, me and you," he whispered. One last blink and he closed his eyes for good. Whether he was pretending or really affected by my gift, I wasn't sure. His heart was still beating, I knew that. I could hear it so strongly. *Thump-thump. Thump-thump.*

In a daze, I lowered, putting all my attention on the call. And it *was* calling me in some unexplainable way. *Thump-thump.* Faster, it increased at my presence. But Marko didn't move.

My head cocked to the side and I lowered, resting my ear over where his heart was located. A coolness enveloped his skin and I placed my hand over his defined abs, letting the temperature soak into my palm. He wasn't healthy. Not in the sense that my instincts told me, but I couldn't understand what it meant. He'd been feeding, or had started when I arrived, but how often did he get to in here? Was it enough?

So many questions began to push through my mind and for the first time, they weren't about me. They were concerned over the man below me.

"What are you waiting for?" Sayer's voice boomed above me, but was overtaken by a dark haired man, moving in closer to the side. I knew him, although I couldn't remember his name. He swayed and swallowed hard, shaking his head roughly. It sent his long hair to the front of his shoulders.

"She's poisonous," he said, slurring his words. "God, my head hurts. Okay, Tessalyn, make the rest go away."

I didn't want to. I wanted the fog back. Wanted it to save me from what I knew would be happening soon.

The sound of heaving had me looking through the haze. Hunter was kneeling and gagging, holding his stomach as he braced his body up with his other hand. No words came from me, but I let go of the connection with my gift and watched it fade out. Within seconds, I was suddenly alone again. Exposed completely to the people who wanted to hurt me.

"Well, he's not dead." The vampire with long hair crouched next to us, putting his hand on Marko's chest. With a tug of his shoulder, Marko began to blink heavily.

"Of course I'm not dead, Julius." He coughed, rolling to his side. "You seriously didn't think she could kill me so easily, did you? It was the distance. She's damn toxic up close."

Sayer's jaw clenched as his glare shot to me. "Give her another few days and her powers will grow. She'd be able to kill you then. The poison will increase over time. She'll be able to do whatever she wants with it."

Marko's eyebrow rose and he pushed to stand, falling into the wall to hold himself up. "Then maybe you should bring her back in a few days. If you're brave enough."

"Maybe I will," Sayer countered.

"You going to make sure to rape her again before you do?" He turned to the dark haired vampire. "You see that, Julius? Is that what you allow to go on as our leader? A high-ranking member raping newborns?"

"Enough." Julius looked between them, but I could see his uneasiness.

"No," Marko said, shaking his head. "It is *not* enough. That blood staining the top of her dress was from the horrific beating she'd received before he brought her to me. I may be moving on from Tessa, but as second in command, I refuse to allow this sort of brutality to happen to one of our future members. Hell, future leader! She'll take the throne someday. Imagine what this is doing to her psyche. Is he trying to create a monster? One who's uncontrollable and worthless? We all know if this treatment continues she's going to slip into the wrong frame of mind. One she'll never be able to come back from. Tell me how Axis would feel about that?"

Sayer grabbed my arm, jerking me to stand. "I *am* Axis! Tessalyn will be treated however I see fit. I made her. She's mine. If I want to beat her to within an inch of her life every day, tell me, who's going to stop me? You?" He laughed. "Julius? No," he said, shaking his head. "No one tells me what to do. If you don't like how I treat Tessalyn, she and I will gladly go back to Dallas."

"No…no." Julius's hand rose and he continued looking between me and Marko. "Sayer, you may have made her, but she was a part of this community first. You know the rules. You can leave if you feel you must, but she stays. If you'd like to take it up with Axis, you can, but we all know what they're going to say. They'll need my permission for relocation and I refuse to give it. Tessalyn Antoinette stays. That was the plan from the beginning and my gift tells me that's the way it's meant to be."

A smile tugged at the corner of Marko's mouth.

"As for the…treatment of her." A wealth of emotions played across Julius's face and I could tell he was having a hard time trying to pick his words. "What happens behind closed doors is of none of our concern. Sayer knows the repercussions his actions will have on Tessalyn. For all vampires concerned, let's hope he chooses wisely how he wants to mold his future concubine."

My heart jumped as nausea and panic had me trying to pull free of Sayer's grip.

"Are you serious?" Marko shook his head at the older vampire. "You're going to allow the beatings and rape to continue? To her? To the one you're entrusting to rule in your passing? What if she ends up taking us all down? Can you seriously say that's good judgement from a leader?"

"One more word and I'll push back your next feeding for weeks. Don't test me, Marko."

"Fuck…the feeding," he yelled. "It's not right and you know it. Be our leader, not the puppet you've been to Sayer since he arrived. He owes you nothing and you have absolutely nothing to prove. She's turned. You got what you wanted.

What else could he possibly have that tempts you? Axis? Do you feel he's going to convince the elders to let you in?"

Julius narrowed his eyes and spun around, refusing to answer as he left the cell. Sayer pulled me out, letting the cell door slam behind him. Marko's eyes held mine and I didn't care if he saw the tears escape. Apparently, my leader had abandoned me to the worst hell there was and I had no idea how to survive it.

Chapter 9
Hunter

There were many times in my life where safety was nonexistent. Through the night patrols and being in a foreign country where death sometimes happened on a daily basis, the only thing that got me past the fear and uncertainty was knowing I could provide assurance and courage to the soldiers who looked up to me. But I wasn't on another tour. And the woman I loved wasn't some soldier under my command. Here, I was helpless. And, with what was happening to her, even more so.

To see your heart, your other half, endure grotesque acts of violence and rape when there was nothing you could do about it was worse than anything I could imagine witnessing. It was destroying me. No matter how much I yelled or threatened, nothing helped. It only made Sayer hurt her more. And now, he was threatening me.

As I stared at Tessa's limp body, cuffed to the bed on her stomach, I couldn't stop the stream of tears from racing down my face. Four days this had been happening. Aside from the bastard letting me loose for bathroom breaks and meals, he kept me restrained in his invisible bubble, trapped right next to the bed. He wanted me to see her pain. He wanted to break me, and he was succeeding.

"Yes! Hurt me." I could feel the craziness in my eyes as I waved him closer. Anything to get him away from her. Blood coated Tessa's sides from where his nails had repeatedly tore open her back. The tears had long dried on her face. Now, she just stared in my direction…gone—a zombie of his making. I could tell she was no longer aware of what was happening. She'd been that way for a while, only jolting or whimpering when he added new marks. But she wasn't here. I'd seen that haunted look before. My Tessa was possibly more broken than I was and I had to find a way to bring her back. To get rid of her maker and fix the damage that had been done. Looking at her blank stare, I wasn't sure that was possible.

The mattress shifted as he moved more in my direction. Although I somewhat kept my attention on Sayer, my real focus was on Tessa. Her breathing was so slow, almost nonexistent. The separation of her lips and lax features once again forced death into my mind. Faces flashed before my vision, causing my hands to clench. I fought to breathe as I was thrown back into my past. Back to holding one of the many bloody men whose lifeless eyes stared up at me.

"Do you think you'll make an obedient slave, Hunter?"

Sayer's breath was suddenly brushing against the back of my neck. I jumped, gasping as the room was before me again.

"I will be the best slave for Tessa."

"Wrong answer. For both of us," he hissed.

My eyes closed and I tried to still my pulse past the shock of the memory. Slowly, I nodded. Anything to diffuse the situation. If I could make Sayer calm, maybe he'd change his mind and leave. I knew what he intended. After all, he hadn't finished fucking Tessa. I noticed he rarely came with her. Not unless she was fighting him, and she'd learned to stop doing that relatively quickly.

"Good. Now bend over the bed."

Opening my eyes was almost impossible. When my lids lifted, I brought my gaze back to Tessa. I didn't procrastinate or put off the inevitable. I knew what would happen if I fought. He liked that too much and I wasn't going to give him the satisfaction of hurting me more than I knew he was already going to.

The top half of my body leaned over the side of the mattress and I immediately wrapped my arm around the small of Tessa's back. Blood met my forehead as I placed it against her ribs and I closed my eyes again, bracing for Sayer's invasion.

"You learn faster than I thought. Or maybe you secretly want this." His fingers stroked up the back of my thigh and my jaw clenched as they moved over the curve of my ass. For days now, he kept Tessa and I both nude. It was a sign from the beginning of how things were going to be with him here.

"I don't. Just get this over with." My words were forced, clipped, as I fought the rage shaking my body. Fear should have been there, but my hate overshadowed any other emotion. I'd never wanted to kill someone as much as Sayer. Not even Marko, and that showed me just how deep my revulsion ran. I had to find a way to end this.

Pressure circled around the entrance of my ass and my hand clutched Tessa's hip. Tighter, I hugged her. There wasn't anything I wouldn't do to protect her. If, somehow, this was the cost to prove my love and duty, it was all I had left.

"Someday you may come to enjoy what we all have. It doesn't always have to be a bad thing when the three of us share each other. Tessa will learn who to obey; you will learn, too. Once the two of you know your place, things can fall together perfectly. I can see it. It's beautiful. With Marko dead, nothing will stop Tessa and me from reaching the top."

His finger disappeared for only a moment before it was replaced. Wetness messaged directly over my entrance and my whole body tensed as his finger slowly slid inside. I couldn't stop myself from clenching around the penetration. I didn't want this, yet I knew I couldn't stop it.

I stayed quiet as he withdrew, only to surge deeper. Tessa body jerked at my increasing grip and I loosened, grunting at the pain as he slid in another finger, stretching me wide.

"When Tessa faces Marko again, there will be no hesitation. She's going to know the repercussions. She's going to finish him immediately." The anger lacing his tone only increased the brutality of his thrusts. He had no care to be gentle.

"Marko is going to kill you. *I'm* going to kill you."

Tessa's clear English had my head jerking to face her. How many times had she repeated that statement in her head to make it sound so clear?

My hand shot up to cover her mouth but she snapped her teeth in my direction, causing me to pull back.

"Is that so?" Sayer's hand stilled, but he didn't stop violating me.

"Yes. Take…hands off human…you're dead."

"Shut up, Tessa. You're only making this worse," I rushed out.

Her black eyes met mine and I wasn't able to turn away fast enough. Like gravity, I was sucked into the darkness. Where I expected her fear or anger to take over, I didn't find it. Calmness and a sense of peace settled over me. I could still hear voices, but I couldn't make out what they were saying. And I knew Sayer was still having his way with me. Yet, I felt nothing. Nothing but a sense of relief for the first time since I'd come to this underground hell. Whether time stretched out for seconds, minutes, or hours…I wasn't sure. Warmth blanketed me…coddled me, like I was a baby. And in the blackness, I was safe. Free of my duties and responsibilities.

But it didn't last long enough.

Pain jolted me from my blissful haven, so intense and sharp, the gag was automatic. My fingers dug into Tessa's hip as my body curled into itself, heaving through the agony of what was happening to me. My toes dug into the cement as I tried to scramble away, but I couldn't move.

"Say it. Say it, Princess!"

I looked up in time to see Sayer digging into the side of Tessa's face with his fingers. Blood dripped down her cheeks from his nails while he shoved her head more into the pillow. I could feel his weight over my back while he kept his cock buried inside of me.

"Say it!"

Spit sprayed out of her mouth, barely making it to the bed, her face was being pressed down so hard. I thrashed, slamming my elbow back into his ribs in quick succession. It was enough to have Sayer swaying to the side, but closer to her.

"You will say it! You are mine! You think Marko is going to protect you? Where is he now? That's right, he's locked away. And he'll stay that way forever if I have my way. You'll never see him again so you might as well let him go and start worrying about the other man you love."

My head snapped back at his pull and I locked up completely as his teeth and fangs bit into my neck. The thickness from his poison was immediate. Tessa's screams pierced the room so loud, I fought against Sayer's hold so I could cover my ears. Harder, he gripped, thrusting his cock into me wildly as he drank my blood. The pain engulfing me was easing, twisting and morphing to some sick form of arousal. I didn't want to enjoy what he was doing. I didn't want to like it…but suddenly, I did.

"I told you," he said, breaking from my neck. "Tell me you want more."

Tessa's screams continued, but I didn't care. I held her waist tighter, pressing my fingers into her skin as I stared, fascinated. An animal was taking over me from his venom. I needed more of his cock, but I needed…

Sayer reached forward, jerking Tessa's legs apart. He didn't have to tell me what to do. I was lost, gone, as I dove forward, burying my face right into her pussy and ass. I wanted to taste all of her. To fuck her in both places with my tongue while Sayer had sex with me the one way I never thought I'd want to experience.

"I knew you'd see my way, pet. Feast on what belongs to us while I take care of you."

He rested more into me, reaching around and stroking down my length. His thrusts turned slow, tortuous, making my head even fuzzier. I couldn't think or decipher anything but my cravings. And I was desperate for Tessa's cum. For his, inside of me.

Vibrations from the continued screaming made my body hum. They weren't lessoning. The steady volume buzzed in the distance: high pitched, low pitched, long, short. The vast power from behind the voice never wavered. I wasn't sure how long it went on. All I could do was suck and lick on every inch of her most private areas. But I never got what I wanted. What I longed for the most. Sadness started to etch in and with it, the pain of what was happening to me. Swelling inside my ass increased as Sayer pounded harder. Each sway forward jostled my stomach and regardless of my drugged state, I heaved again. And again. Words spoke lowly behind me, but I couldn't focus on anything but the moans beginning to pour from his mouth. Warmth pumped into me and I couldn't hold in what was dying to escape from the moment the vampire had touched me. Reality was starting to sink in. What I'd done was pushing through and mortification didn't even break the surface of the guilt starting to fester inside of me.

Still, the screams continued, even after Sayer pulled out and left me lying there limp in my own vomit.

Broken. Yes, he wanted to break me. He wanted to break her. Perhaps he'd done his job. Tessa and I were his toys, and he'd accomplished what I thought no one could ever do. Sayer shattered me. Defeated me. And I'd violated her. I was just as bad as my rapist. He wanted to show us who had the power, and it was all too clear. No one was coming to help us. We were alone.

Chapter 10
Marko

Like gravity—like the tide—Tessa's presence pulled me. I knew the moment they had her on the move. Her power was but a speck of what I was made up of, but I could feel it nonetheless. And I was hoping it was because she took in more of my blood.

Over a week and a half had gone by before I discovered what I was experiencing was her. When it registered that my sense of direction drew toward a certain location, I could imagine where she was in the underground city. Easily, I could piece together her path. But I couldn't see her and she had yet to talk to me again.

Maybe Sayer's blood had won. It was possible after what she'd displayed when she was in my cell. My powers and instincts were what was responsible for me being able to pinpoint her. Not a bond or any ties. But at least I had this. It drowned out the loneliness, gave me something to focus on while killing the hours before I found out whether I got another meal or not. And I had to try to focus. After I knew what Sayer was doing to her, it was all I had not to go insane. I longed to shred him to pieces. I couldn't think of his name without my fangs shooting down, ready to filet him alive. And I would, when the time was right.

I let the first time I'd seen Tessa replay over and over in my mind as I greedily held onto her imprint of energy. She'd spoken French to me. The beauty of the realization, and her words, were perfection. Had there not been bars between us at that moment, I would have gotten on my knees and begged her to love me. She was still new, easily moldable, but the last visit told me Sayer was already beating me to the punch—and not in a good way. What I'd spoken to Julius was the truth. Sayer could ruin her for good. If she sunk down too far, there'd be no coming back. She'd be a killer. The worst kind of vampire there was, and she'd have to be put down. There was no getting around it. She'd be ruined.

I had to figure a way out of here. Tessa needed me more than ever. I knew she fucking wanted to spend her life with me and I was going to make it happen. Just like she'd said as a human while she was under the influence of Sayer's blood—together as vampires, we'd rule. And we would. Fuck doing it on my own, I needed her. Not just her blood, but her love. And she needed mine to heal her. We'd be unstoppable once I killed the bastard. We'd be...one.

Footsteps in the distance had me rising just as Julius appeared. Feeding wasn't that far away but given the fact that a supplier wasn't with him, I knew he wasn't here for that reason. Was he thinking about what he'd done? Was his guilt eating at him? I prayed it was. I stepped closer to the bars, once again hoping his eyes would tell me something. Like any time he came to me, he refused to meet my gaze long enough to for me to discover anything.

"I've come to update you on the meetings you've missed." Julius's arms crossed over his chest and I could tell he didn't want to be here. He seemed preoccupied. He definitely wasn't worried about the meetings. What *was* he thinking about? I stepped closer, still not taking my focus off his eyes. Was Tessa still getting raped? Beaten? He had to know…

"There's a rise in the west. In the Los Angeles area, to be exact. A small group of a few hundred have come together there, somewhat like I saw in the beginning of Hunter, but their leadership is weak. They, along with a few other groups around the country, have broken into the underground cities in the area, hunting our kind. They soak their stakes in holy water. Much like Hunter did when he shot Tessalyn. It's a dangerous situation, but Axis doesn't seem too bothered by it. At least, that's what Sayer is assuring me. I don't like it. The humans catch on too quickly. They're defying law enforcement, coming together to figure out a way to rise against their government. It's unsettling to me, but I don't feel that there's a real threat yet, and I don't think there will be as long as Hunter remains here."

That couldn't have been Julius's main concern, but I went along with his words, saying the one thing I knew would spark his anger. "You think he'll stay so he can get raped by Sayer, too? I'm sure your approval of that situation will have him loving our life. I don't see him wanting to run away and kill us at all, do you?"

Light blue eyes cut up to mine and I pushed into his mind with every ounce of strength I possessed. Visions exploded before me and I locked onto our connection. As I moved my head closer, the makings of his past assaulted me. I dove in further, flying through his human years, until I was fighting through the centuries of Julius being a vampire. The deeper I got and the stronger he'd become, left me wading through memories that felt like tar. They gave off the impression of sticking to my skin and in my lungs, making it hard to breathe, but I didn't stop until I got to Tessa being changed.

Thoughts filtered through, so vast, I didn't waste my time trying to decipher them. Instead, I let the conversations and happenings transpiring around her become my sole focus. I could see her placed in a room with a group of other vampires. In Julius's awe, I watched the black fog roll through the room for the first time. One by one, she took out the vampires, revealing her bloodied with the human dead at the end. It was amazing to witness, but I needed to see more.

Days went by and I could see Julius breaking his ties with Sayer. They weren't compatible and Julius couldn't stand his personality. Less, he began to go to him, until the scene with me here in the cell. The shock Julius held for Tessa's beating and rape soaked in, confirming the dreams Julius feared. There was an uncertainty on what he should do, but his fear was for Axis, not her.

Screaming echoed in my mind and I could feel myself pacing in the darkness. I knew whose screams they were and I could feel what he knew was happening. *More rape and beatings.* For days, this continued. Screaming. More pacing on his part. Sayer always found him in the hall, trying to bullshit like nothing had just happened. My anger turned to rage, then to fury. Quicker, my pulse raced, and Julius's greed over his reasons for allowing the rapes exploded within me. Before I could hear more, the scene vanished and Julius blasted my chest with a force that sent me flying across the room. I hit the cement wall hard, groaning through the loss of air.

"How *dare* you push into my mind. You are not the leader here!" The door to the cell swung open and I held my ground as I saw the vampire in him want the fight, but the leader in him restrain. He stepped back, taking a deep breath. One thing was clear to me and it made Hunter's words more a reality than ever. With what I'd done, there was only one leader, and Julius wasn't it.

"You're slipping. Something bothers you. Tell me," I coaxed. "I am not your enemy. Not yet, and it doesn't have to be that way. I'm your second. You're supposed to trust me."

His jaw tightened as he glared. "You will never gain my trust with your plans. I know what they are and so does Sayer. You'll never make it as a member of Axis with the route you're going. We both know you'll never be powerful enough to rule the higher leaders, so where does that leave you? Dead. Think about it, Marko. One of the rulers will kill you because of your greed and you'll gain nothing."

The words were truth, but I refused to listen to them. With Tessa and her blood, I stood a chance to rule with her by my side. But was Axis what I really wanted anymore? It had always been my main focus. Now all I could think about was protecting and healing the woman I loved. What if I did go along with my plan after all of this? What if one of us died in the process of fighting our way to the top? It was all mixing around, twisting in my mind. Was it really worth it? I needed out of here, to clear my thoughts and reground myself.

"I'm ready to be free now."

My change of subject had him shaking his head. "You need more time."

"I do not!" I exploded. "I'm good *now*. I promised I wouldn't kill Hunter and I won't. You have my word. As your second, and as future leader, I promise Hunter is safe until you give the word."

The hesitation was there. If it weren't for Sayer, I knew Julius would let me go. What was it about the vampire that was swaying his decisions? It had to be Axis.

"Another week." Julius turned his back and I was on him before I could control myself. He'd allowed this to happen to Tessa. He'd hurt her just as much as Sayer by allowing it to continue. Besides…I was the leader, not *him*. And my chance to be set free was finally here.

My fangs sunk into his neck and I bit down hard, taking his blood into me for the first time. The power had my eyes widening as I sucked the delicious tonic eagerly. It was so full of everyone's knowledge, of pieces of the community that would now belong to me.

I spun him around, wrapping my arm around his back, and pinning him immobile against me. With my other hand, I jerked his hair, sinking my fangs into him again. I'd meant to quit, but I could already feeling myself growing stronger with every drink. The thrashing was forceful, but not more than I could suddenly control. Electrical currents began zapping at my core as the first tie of a bond began forming. With the amount of my blood he'd taken in the past, it was happening at a faster rate than I could process. The immediate connection was one I knew I didn't want. It wasn't the reason I was doing this and was enough to break me from the greed of taking more.

I tugged, using the leverage of his hair to control his body, pushing him to step back, off-balanced. I didn't think. Didn't wait as I dove forward and twisted his head around, breaking his neck. All I could see was Tessa's face. Her bloody, battered face. I knew Julius wasn't dead, but he would be soon. My eyes narrowed at all the repercussions filtering through, but I blocked them out, tugging and twisting as I severed his head. The broken finalization of power through our shared blood brought me to my knees and an odd heat rushed through, tingling in my veins.

For seconds, I couldn't move. Couldn't form a rational thought. Slowly, my eyes lifted and the smile of my vampire appeared, blocking all humanity. This was it. The moment I'd been waiting for. *Me.* I was the leader. No one would stop me from taking my throne. Axis was just going to have to deal with this new series of events. They'd see, I'd play their game. After all, I played a very important part and they needed my powers. They wouldn't kill me. If they did, who would lead? Bufar? He didn't have the balls or power to do what I could. And Tessa was far from ready if shit went down too soon.

I stood and walked from the cell, wiping my hands on my pants as I headed for the tunnel. As the darkness swallowed me up, I mentally called in the collectors. Let them take care of the body. It was time to clean up and show these vampires who was in charge. First person on the list, my dishonorable guest.

Chapter 11
Tessa

"Tonight will be the biggest test of them all." Sayer dropped the invisible wall restraining me and took a step forward. The need to attack was there, but something told me not to. Instinct? Perhaps. I couldn't remember why, but the voice in my mind said to be still. To wait out my time. If I didn't…there was no telling what would happen. A new sort of fear had crept in and it cloaked around him, influencing my decisions.

Hunter sat on the couch, staring at me quietly. I felt as though it was something he did a lot. Since I'd woken up hours ago, we hadn't spoken a word to each other. Maybe we knew better, maybe we didn't have to. I wasn't sure. I felt different. More alert and cautious. And he definitely gave me a different vibe than before. I just wasn't sure what exactly it was. Nothing made sense and I was so tired of waking up as a fresh slate. I was missing so much inside of me. My mind told me I kept forgetting, but it didn't allow me to see what it was hiding.

"Hey." Sayer snapped his fingers in my face, pulling my attention back to his. My eyes narrowed in anger and it caused his mouth to tighten. "When I talk, you listen. I need your full attention. Say you understand."

My eyebrow rose and I knew what he wanted, even if it was hard for me to get the words to process right. Talking English didn't feel natural and I didn't like it. "I understand."

"Good. Tonight, you face only one. You may very well die. I'm leaving it up to fate. I will not step in and neither will anyone else. If you die," he shrugged, "this wasn't meant to be."

Fear should have been there, but I felt nothing. Nothing but the need to see and taste blood. I craved it like nothing else and it didn't matter who it belonged to. "Let them try. I kill them."

"I'll," he corrected. "I'll kill them. And no, I do not think you will."

"Then you are a fool."

Hunter stiffened and it pulled my attention, but it didn't last as Sayer snarled. "You are the fool for underestimating who I put against you. And for talking to me like that. You think because you have my gift you can win or you're better than me? Not even close. You are nothing compared to me. Besides, they'll have gifts, too, Princess. Ones a hell of a lot more powerful than the amount you've tapped into."

A deep exhale left me and my hand came to my hip. "Male? Female?"

"Female."

I shrugged, feeling my attention go back to Hunter. The sadness on his face had me taking in his features. He was handsome. Very handsome. But so sad. The need he stirred in me was different. I wanted to protect him almost as much as I liked the idea of killing him—which had been on my mind since I'd woken up as much as the questions concerning his change in demeanor. Instincts to go to him had me sidestepping Sayer. His hand immediately jerked at my bicep, bringing me back in front of him.

"What did I say? Focus. Now is not the time to be distracted by Hunter. You can kill or fuck him some other time. Right now, you need to think about how you're going to win this fight."

"I tire…of this," I groaned, letting myself collapse on the end of the bed. "I win. You will see."

A frustrated sound left Sayer. He clenched his fist before my face and spun around, beginning to pace. "Where the hell is Julius? He should have been here fifteen minutes ago."

"He's dead." The words came before I realized I shouldn't have said anything. My maker probably wouldn't like me tapping into the voice constantly in my head. It wasn't always talking to me. Sometimes, I magically found it. Like a light in the darkness of what rested inside.

My head turned toward Hunter and I bit my bottom lip, spinning on my side as I studied him more. His head cocked to the side while he returned my stare. The beginning of a grin started to appear, but faded just as fast. What replaced it as his stare lowered to the ground made me stiffen. What was that…pain? Guilt? Horror? I didn't understand. Was it me? Was I the one who had hurt him?

"What did you say?" Sayer ripped me off the bed and the sound of a warning did leave me then. My nails shot down and a hiss poured from my lips as I fought to decide whether I should attack.

"I said, he's…dead. Dead. No head." I gestured, spinning my hand over my own, trying to get him to understand. I knew I was saying it right.

A knock had Sayer spinning toward the door just as it was thrust open. Hunter pushed from the wall, immediately jerking out his dagger. My pulse jumped and I swallowed hard at the man who walked in.

"Marko. What are you doing here?" Sayer's voice sounded an octave higher in pitch as he let me go. The dark haired vampire closed the door behind him, coming forward. The smile on his face had my heart thumping so hard, but I wasn't sure why. His aura threw me. Anger, as if he was ready to destroy us all was present, but that wasn't the part that gave me pause. The center of his being, his power, the piece that made him who he was, called to me. *He* called to me. It was enough to have me moving forward in a daze. Dark brown eyes cut over to me and his smile broadened, losing its menace.

"I'm making my rounds to make sure everyone's okay, of course. As leader of this community, it's something I plan to do on a regular basis. And, well, I had to come check on my *guest*. How is everything, Sayer?"

Although the question sounded almost normal, I felt the venom return toward my maker. He didn't like Sayer any more than I did and somehow, that brought a relief so massive, I almost couldn't believe it.

"Where is Julius?"

I rolled my eyes, throwing Sayer a look. "Dead, I tell you." The words twisted on my tongue and he shot me a glare.

"Tessa told you," Marko repeated. He took a step and stopped, glancing at Hunter and then back to me as he spoke in my language. "Tessa, will you tell your slave to please put the dagger down? He has nothing to fear from me. Not yet, anyway."

"He's not my slave," I replied in our language.

Marko shrugged and I shivered at the way he stared at me. It was as if we were suddenly the only two people in the room and I liked that. So much so, that I took another step. "That's good news on my end. But can you tell him for me? I would hate to have to defend myself against him. He'd die if it came down to that. You'd hate to lose him, wouldn't you?"

Hunter's stare went back and forth between me and Marko. I felt my brow furrow at his question. "I don't want to lose him. Does he look sad to you?"

"English!" Sayer's yell had my teeth clenching.

"Hunter. Please put...dagger down."

The human shook his head and something in the action pulled at my anger. He was disobeying me. *Me.* Even if I did feel sorry for him, I knew I was above him and I didn't like that he wasn't listening.

"Down." My word was filled with such authority, the dagger lowered and Hunter let his arm fall to his side. Sayer moved more toward the human, only causing Marko to get closer to me. The switch in position had my maker doubling back.

"Are you hungry, ma minette?" French, once again, filled the room at his question and I licked my lips, glancing at Sayer before answering in English.

"Yes. But," I searched for the words, "I fight to feed today."

Marko's eyes glazed over, making the brown turn black. Still, he continued. "Have you been treated well? Has he hurt you anymore?"

"Hurt?" I blinked as I tried to push into memories that wouldn't come.

"I see you don't remember. Pity, really. Your maker likes to hurt you. But I'm your friend and leader, I'm not going to let that happen anymore. I'll take care of you no matter what it concerns. I'll make him pay," he said, lowering his voice. "You know this, yes?"

"Yes." My response was so low, it was almost inaudible. Faster, my mind raced. What Marko said felt right. Sayer had to pay. But...why? I couldn't remember.

"Yes, what?" Sayer's eyebrows drew in and I glanced over at him. My vampire swiftly calculated and I stood taller, smiling.

"Yes, you...take care of me."

"Of course I do." He made his way over, hooking his arm in mine and pulling me toward the closet. The light blue shift I wore was tugged at my waist and I looked down at where his fingers held, noticing my fangs were already down. "Change while I speak to Marko alone. We have things to go over and I want you ready when I return."

Marko's voice had both of us turning in his direction.

"She won't be fighting to eat. As the new leader of this community, which she's a member of, that's an order. If she wishes to increase her skills, that's one thing, but it won't be to survive. I'm willing to make sure she lives, no matter what." He narrowed his eyes. "And I'll be monitoring everything concerning my successor from now on."

Something passed between Marko and Sayer as they held each other's stares. After a few minutes, Sayer stormed past, heading toward the door. Marko's gaze hungrily traveled down my body before he followed, taking his time. The moment the barrier shut, Hunter's movement had me zeroing in on him and it seemed to hit both of us at the same time. We were alone. Unrestrained. And no one was here to help him…or stop me if I wanted to have him or his blood. I couldn't resist getting closer.

"Tessa." His hand shot up and I took in the way he tightened his hold on the dagger. He was battling over whether to raise it. I paused, coming to a stop a few feet away.

"You…are sad? Yes?"

The surprise that lit his features turned into the same look I'd witnessed for hours. Hunter nodded and pushed from the wall, stepping closer. The smell of his skin…his blood, had me taking a step, too.

"I'm glad you can't remember. I don't want you to ever know what we've been through. I miss you, Tessa. I miss my best friend."

"Me?"

"Yes, you," he breathed out. "We love each other. God, I've loved you since we were children. And you, you've loved me too, but only recently did I know that. You never told me. If you had," his head shook, "we wouldn't be here now. We'd be married. Have children. We'd have the perfect life. I'd do anything for you. I'm here, even when I don't want to be. And fuck, I don't. I hate this place." His voice cracked and he wiped a tear from his eye just as it escaped. "But I promised to take care of you, no matter what that entailed. Someday, you'll remember for more than a few minutes at a time. Or for a day. Then, you'll see."

What exactly I'd seen was beyond me. But I didn't like him hurting. It only made me more defensive as I glanced toward the door. "Why does Marko…?" Words jumbled around my tongue and I battled with the English that didn't want to come. "He says…I love him, too. Who is he?"

Hunter's jaw tightened and a wave of heat poured from him, tempting me even more. I moaned, moving closer though my deepening breaths. Lust ruled me whether I liked it or not. And concerning him, I wasn't sure I did.

"He did this to you, Tessa. It's his fault you're a vampire. True, we made the decision, but if he hadn't bonded you against your will, you wouldn't have had to take this route. He almost killed you once. And Sayer's even worse. I want us to leave here. There has to be a way."

I got quiet, bringing my gaze to the cement floor. I didn't remember anything of Marko or even Sayer. All I had were feelings…instincts. Marko promised to help me. Protect me, even. Yet, he'd hurt me? I knew not to trust Sayer. But was Hunter telling me the entire truth? Who did I believe? I trusted no one. The only person I held to was myself.

The door swung open and Sayer stormed in, jolting to a stop as he took in how close Hunter and I were to each other.

"No…you're not safe here with her. Hunter, let's go, you're coming back to Dallas with me until I can convince Axis to overrule Tessalyn's residence here. We'll make sure it's granted in our favor. We don't need this place."

Immediately, a growl left my throat as I put myself between the two of them. Warnings were exploding in my mind, growing so thick, they blocked out everything but the need to fight. Although I wasn't sure why, I didn't dismiss the one fact I knew: Marko and Hunter both claimed Sayer had hurt me. If he could harm me, he could surely do it to Hunter. Had he already and I didn't remember? It was enough to cause me to lower my head as I let the killer within take over.

My hand rose, my fingers spreading wide as I put up my palm, facing Sayer. I wasn't sure why or what it meant, other than the fact that it grounded me, but I held steady, waiting to see if he made a move.

"I'm not going with you. No way. I'm not. I can't." The fear was thick in Hunter's voice, feeding me. His energy drew further away, as if the human was moving back toward the wall. It was a clear indication that the things locked away in my mind were worse than I even could process. I knew Hunter's energy. He held power like me. He was a strong fighter. So why wasn't he fighting now?

"I said let's go! Did you learn nothing in the last few weeks, pet? You get over here right now or so help me…" Sayer began to circle around, but I stayed even with his steps. I could see Marko edge through the door in my peripheral vision, but I paid him no notice. Every ounce of my focus was on the one man I saw as the biggest threat.

"He…stays."

Sayer glanced my way, but his eyes went right back to Hunter.

"He's coming, Princess."

"No…I don't think so," Marko said, walking closer. "He's property of Tessa. Not you, Sayer. I say he stays."

The reverberation of Sayer's voice went through the room and his eyes turned black as he pinned Marko with a glare. "They are both my property! Mine! Not yours."

"Wrong. He stays," Marko ground out.

"So you can kill him before I return? He goes with me."

Closer, Marko stepped, until he was standing but a foot away from me. "Hunter will not die at my hand. Not yet. As the leader of this community, you have my word. You can clearly show that to Axis when you meet with them."

Heavy pants left Sayer and he shifted a few steps before he lunged. Marko was in front of me before Sayer could connect with my arm. Only inches separated their faces and Marko didn't budge once as he glared down at my maker.

"Leave. Now. Or else I have every right to make sure you never leave again. And I don't mean to make you a resident here. You understand me?"

Hands gripped my waist and I let Hunter draw me back against him as he led us further away from the two vampires.

"I'll be back and when I do, I'm taking what's mine. You might as well have Tessa and Hunter packing their bags now. They won't be staying long."

"We'll see about that."

Every step Sayer took toward the door, Marko was sure to stay even with him. The moment the barrier shut, Hunter's face dropped into my neck. His deep exhale rushed out over my skin and Marko turned, eyeing him.

A deep silence lasted for seconds while no one moved. Finally, Hunter's head lifted and he spun me around, hugging me tight. It was dangerous and I knew he had to have known that, but he didn't let go or step back.

"Thank you, Marko. I…" Once again, a quietness settled around us. Hunter eased the tension in his arms and stepped back. "I couldn't leave Tessa. I couldn't…go with him."

"He hurt you, too." Marko came closer, his head cocking as he kept his attention on my human's face.

"I don't know what you're talking about. I'm fine."

Marko's head shook. "No, I don't think so. Look at me, Hunter. Show me what he did."

"Stay the fuck away from me," Hunter burst out, raising the dagger. "Stay…away."

Slowly, Marko's hands rose, as if in surrender. "If you wish. You can say you're fine, but I know you're not. Whatever he did, whatever you had to go through…he's gone now."

"But for how long? What if this Axis thing lets him take us? What if we have to leave?" The questions dispensed at a fast pace. "Tessa can't be hurt like that again. I can't watch…I can't. No." He shook his head quickly. "You have to tell me how to kill him. You have to…I…no." Words began jumbling together through his fear. My hand rose to my head at the pounding beginning to register again.

Marko extended his hand to me and I instinctively went to step forward. Hunter wrapped his arm around my stomach and lifted me off the ground against him. Thrashing came natural. The dagger was pointed out toward my leader, but I could feel its power so close to my face. The holiness made my skin crawl. It was hard to breathe in the closeness.

"Keep back from her. You're not good. You may have helped us with Sayer, but that's only because of your own agenda. You want Tessa as your own, and you'll do anything to make that happen."

"True," Marko said slowly. "I do love Tessa, but I gave Sayer my word you'd live. What are you afraid of?"

"A man can have a heartbeat, he can breathe air like everyone else, but that doesn't mean he's alive. There are ways to kill a person and continue to let him walk through life."

"I'm confused," Marko said, stepping back and sitting on the edge of the bed. "Would you like to explain?"

Hunter eased me to the ground, but didn't break our connection. I couldn't fight anymore; I was just as perplexed.

"You can try to break me like he did. You can…kill me without ending my life."

"I guess I could," Marko said, nodding. "But my focus isn't on physically hurting you, Hunter. I only want what's mine. What you stole from me."

"Stole? You stole her first!" Hunter's whole body shook with anger. "And even after that, she chose me. She wanted this for her life."

"This?" Marko asked, gesturing with his hand. "Do you seriously think she wanted this? I happen to believe this is what *you* chose and she ultimately accepted. Am I wrong?" His hands clasped between his knees as he leaned forward. Hunter didn't say a word as he continued. "You do realize when she went to you she was under a spell from Sayer's blood, much like the episodes that take her over now, right? *And,* even somewhat lucid after those blackouts, she still wasn't completely in control of her mind? Let me tell you something, Hunter. Tessa loved me, regardless of what you believe. She loved me, even when I didn't deserve her love. And I love her. I always will. I wouldn't have chosen this life for her, but what's done is done. There's still no one else for me and no one better for her. You've seen our world. You know the evil that resides in us. She is not apart from that. Tessa will never be the woman you once knew. This is the new her. She may regain her memory, but her new personality will not change. No one is a better fit for her than me. You have to know this. You have to *see* it."

Fingers pushed into my stomach and Hunter shifted. "Tessa will come back. She'll remember what we shared. She loves me."

"She loves both of us," Marko said angrily, "but she will not return to you. The day her human body died, the woman you knew died, too. I'm not saying this to you as some form of manipulation. I'm telling you this from experience. Your Tessa is dead. This one belongs to me."

"No!"

"Yes," Marko said forcefully. "*You* killed her just as much as Sayer did. Tessa is gone, Hunter. Accept it. I have. What's left is the version meant for *me.* The vampire. Not for Hunter, the human or slave. You fear being dead while alive. What do you think you'll be if she bonds you? You'll love her, yes, but do you think she'll love you as you're meant to be loved? You're a human. You're food! Just as I viewed her up until her death. Why do you think it was so hard for me to grasp? I loved her, but I knew it was wrong for my kind. It doesn't fit into our personality to love that way, Hunter. It just doesn't. I can promise you one thing. As you sit there and you hold her, she may be allowing it, but do you know the main focus in her mind? It's not the comfort or affection she's receiving from you…she wants your blood! Tell him, Tessa. Tell him what I speak is the truth."

My lips parted as I looked from Marko and then back at Hunter. The words processed and I didn't feel Hunter's pain or Marko's anger. I knew sadness existed within my human, but all that revolved around that was the worry and the question why. "Truth. I know nothing of…love. Protection…yes. But love, no. Not…for you…" I turned back to Marko to say the same for him, but nothing came. I couldn't speak. I couldn't lie.

Chapter 12
Hunter

I was lost, spiraling down some vortex of right and wrong. It was pulling at my psyche, twisting and morphing what I felt I should and shouldn't do. I couldn't deny the relief I felt with Marko free of his cell, but I wasn't naïve to the fact that he was still the enemy. He just wasn't the one raping me on a nightly basis.

With Sayer gone, I found myself sleeping like the dead. But it didn't keep me safe from the nightmares. They haunted my mind with visions of dead soldiers, ones who now looked up with Sayer's face. Suddenly, I realized they weren't dead at all. Not only did I endure the violations during consciousness, he stole my sanity in my dreams as well. I woke up sick, rushing to the restroom. And Tessa was witnessing it all. She flew forward in an attempt to sit, pulling at the cuffs like the savage creature she truly was. My flight had jolted her vampire awake and the first thing she'd tried to do was attack. I heard the growls as I slammed the door shut and I thanked God Marko had checked on her earlier and restrained her before he left.

I flushed the toilet, making my way to the sink. The toothbrush I'd been provided sat in a pale blue plastic holder and I took it out, trying to block Sayer's bared fangs from my mind as I began to brush. Nothing I did or thought could make what I'd been through go away. I was still sore. Still healing from his last rape, which was sometime in the middle of the night a few days ago. I hadn't even heard or felt him make his way to the couch where I was sleeping. I thought by regaining my rosary and dagger I'd be safe. Now I knew why he didn't mind me having them. Unaware, he easily caught me off-guard, catching me with his eyes.

I was powerless. *Prey.* Yes, that's what Tessa had once called herself, and she was right. And so was Marko, whether I wanted to admit it or not. Food. That's all I was to these vampires. And Tessa…her admitting the truth just wouldn't leave me. My faith kept me hoping she would pull through and eventually remember who she was and what we shared, but I was starting to think it was impossible. Maybe Marko was right. Maybe I had killed her the day I convinced her to change.

Tears streamed down my cheeks and I wiped them away, not caring anymore if it made me appear weak. In this moment, I was…lost.

I opened the door, watching Tessa pull against the cuffs. She wasn't herself right now, if I could say she even had a sense of self, which she really didn't—not one that stuck around anyway. It broke my heart, just like it did every day. How much of this could I endure?

"You…come."

She'd spoken more, but it was in French. I didn't have the brainpower to decipher it at the moment. I always knew when she was more vampire than anything else. She always spoke French. It was only when she spoke in English I knew she was having to actually use thoughts. She was thinking, then. Not…being what she naturally was: a cold-blooded killer.

"Go to bed, Tessa." I looked at the bedside light I'd left on because I couldn't stand to be in the dark. If I couldn't see, then Sayer might be there. I used to fear death the most. Now, it was the undead. God, he'd fucked me up. And here I thought I couldn't get any worse than I'd been from war.

Hissing sounded from behind me but I ignored it as I made my way to the couch. I grabbed the blanket, pausing before I laid back down. Slowly, I turned toward Tessa's nearly sitting frame and walked back toward her.

"You need to feed."

Her blank expression turned to confusion before she nodded. A small sense of humanity entered her, but I knew I couldn't trust it. I walked around to the other side of the bed, lowering down at the foot. She couldn't get me here. I'd be safe. As a test, I reached forward, grabbing one of the pillows. Almost faster than I could process, her head shot toward me and she missed latching onto my arm by mere inches.

"No," I snapped. "You are not allowed to do that to me. Manners, Tessa. You are not a animal." I felt like I was trying to train a pet. Yet, what I was telling her was pointless. She didn't understand right now, nor would she until time brought her back. She was hungry. Ready to feed again. When she got this bad, no one was safe. "You need blood." I sighed, glancing toward the door. "I guess I should go try to find a supplier. Not like they're going to want to come," I mumbled under my breath. "Tessa, I need you to listen to me."

Dark eyes narrowed and again, she nodded.

"I want you to try something for me. When you feed, I want you to try not to kill this one, okay? It'll probably be hard for you, but will you at least try? For me?" I needed to see if she'd try to obey. I needed…hope. Hope that she was redeemable, because at this point, I didn't think she was.

Silence. She was always so damn quiet.

A groan tried to escape as I stood and walked toward the door. I had no idea where the suppliers were held or where I had to go to find one. Sayer—or now, Marko—always took care of that.

The weight of my belt was a relief as I walked through the door and pulled out my flashlight. My feet didn't want to move through the darkness. I hated it. If I ever made it back above ground, I'd probably never sleep in the dark again. I couldn't stand that I'd come to this. I'd never been a coward. I shouldn't be now. The rapes were just something I'd have to overcome, and the only way that was going to happen was if I killed the vampire to blame.

My footsteps were soft and fast, maintaining a steady pace to the end of the hall. Sounds from the heart of the city grew louder and I put my flashlight back in my belt as I broke through to the large room. It was busier than I'd previously seen and I couldn't stop the increase in my pulse. I didn't like this place. I trusted no one.

A few heads turned my way, but the humans continued toward their tunnels. *Slaves.* I knew what they were. But they didn't scare me. It was the creatures they served that had me holding my dagger the entire time. The vampires seemed disinterested in me, but that didn't make me safe.

"You're getting braver, coming out here." Marko's voice suddenly behind me had me spinning around. I never heard him. Never even saw how he managed to slip behind me. He was wearing an expensive looking suit, like he did every time he came to our room since his release. He'd worn them before, too, but now there was just something different about him. Maybe it was his aura. He was the leader now.

He just appeared so much more…threatening. Scary—even if he was calmer than I'd ever seen him.

"Tessa needs…she's hungry." I kept my eyes on his chest, refusing to look at his face.

"So, feed her. You're still going to be her slave, correct?"

I did steal a glimpse of his face at that. "She's too far gone. She'll kill me. Call one of the suppliers. They can feed her."

A small laugh came from the vampire as he moved even closer to me. "What the hero you are. You'll sacrifice another human life for your own? I thought you had honor."

"Fuck you," I snapped. "They chose this life. To do this and feed vampires."

"So did you," Marko growled, his voice deepening. "Or did you forget why you're here? You took her from me. Now do your duty. *Feed* her."

My fist clenched and I stepped back, shaking my head. This was too much. I couldn't take it right now. "I knew you weren't going to be any better than *him*. All of you vampires are fucking evil. You'll have her kill me so you can have her yourself."

A smile came to his face and he shrugged. "Fine. You don't want to take care of her needs, I will. Gladly." Marko turned, heading toward our tunnel. I quickened my step, keeping up with his long strides.

"You did that on purpose. You wanted to gauge my reaction so you could sweep in and do the one thing you wanted most. You don't fool me. Tessa should have been fed earlier but you prolonged it for your own greedy reasons."

Marko paused and turned toward me slowly, narrowing his eyes. "You're right. I did prolong her feeding. But not for me. Not like you think. It's more than that, Hunter. I want to show you what you're getting into. Tonight, I let Tessa hunt on her own. You're going to see firsthand who she really is now. *What* she is."

"You're letting her go above ground?" My question was breathless as scenarios burst through my mind. What the fuck was he wanting? A massacre? Tessa couldn't control herself and he was going to let her loose with unsuspecting humans? She was going to kill someone. Humans above ground were different. Here, suppliers knew the risk, but up there…*my home*, they'd be unsuspecting. It really would be murder. Did he have no regard for life? Of course he didn't, he was a vampire. To him, we were nothing but a walking buffet.

"Don't do it," I said through clenched teeth. "Don't you dare fucking let her free up there. What if she kills someone's husband, wife, or kid? I will not let her be responsible for something like that. Do you know how long I served protecting this country? Protecting every person walking those streets? I can't allow you to let the woman I love go against everything I've fought for. Not to mention what that will do to *her*. When she comes to, she's already going to hate herself for what she's done."

Marko laughed, rolling his eyes. "No, she won't. You have no idea what *you've done* by allowing her to become one of us. Stupid, stupid human. She's going to have the time of her life tonight while I assess her skills and you're just going to have to get over it. It's the least I could do for not protecting her from what she's been through. As for your…honor, I can't help you there. You chose this life,

Hunter. You chose for her to live as she is. You're just going to have to accept this as part of it. Stay or go, it's irrelevant to me, but Tessa will be heading to the top."

Marko stepped in closer, lowering his voice. A softening of his tone had my anger fading and something entirely different taking over. "You need to let go of the person you used to be if you want a future here. And I'm not talking about Tessa. I'm talking in general. This is your home now, regardless of whether you want it or not. You carry many burdens. I feel your sorrow like a deadly poison seeping from your skin. It's almost unbearable. It concerns me. Would you like to show me what you've been through? Perhaps…I can try to find a way to ease your troubles, too." His hand lifted toward my shoulder and I slapped it away from me. I saw how genuine he was being and I wasn't sure how to react to it. I didn't recognize this version of Marko. This leader, who I felt deep down just wanted to offer some sort of assistance.

"Stop fucking with me. You don't want to help me. Besides, you're wrong. I'm fine. The only trouble I have is you letting Tessa murder someone tonight."

"Murder? I'd like to think of it as survival. You won't let her feed from you. Maybe you should view it in that light, too. If you can't, you're going to have a very long road ahead of you here."

Before I could say anything else, he turned, heading back to our room. His words tugged at the overwhelming conflict within. My head stayed down and I was so consumed, I didn't even bother to pull my flashlight out. What met us as we entered had me coming to an abrupt stop just behind him.

"Ma minette, how did you get free of those cuffs?" There was amusement in Marko's voice as he let a smile come to his face. The surprise Tessa held quickly melted and her expression began to mirror his own. She took one step forward and his hand rose. My lips parted in shock as she actually obeyed and waited for him to speak. "I have a surprise for you. If you want it, come to me."

Marko stayed perfectly still while Tessa looked from him to me. Although she began to come our way, her eyes never left me. I swallowed hard, too afraid to let my guard down. She'd already tried to attack me tonight, I didn't trust her not to try again. And I hated that.

"Mon chaton, look at me." Tessa stumbled over her feet and jerked to a stop, glaring at Marko. French poured from her mouth, but I understood enough to know what she was saying.

"You call me an animal? Is that what you think of me?" The hurt on her face was evident as she stared up at him.

"Not at all," he said quietly. "Mon chaton was a pet name. One you used to love. I'm just testing your memory," Marko answered. "Think about it. You're missing a lot of things, aren't you?" At her silence, he continued, "You used to like mon chaton over ma minette. You don't remember that though, and it's okay. Your past will return with time. I promise. Now, why don't you come to me and let me take you to get ready. I have a surprise for you, remember?"

Multiple expressions flashed across her face, but she started toward us again. By the time she arrived and Marko wrapped his arm over her shoulder, my lungs burned from holding my breath. I let the tension ease as they walked away and headed to the closet. I almost couldn't believe the difference in her at his arrival. His presence changed her. Maybe it was the authority he held, but I wasn't sure. And I didn't want to think about it. My suspicions were just too much to bear over what was already worrying me.

Minutes went by before they exited, but I barely noticed. My mind was racing. Marko's concern was getting to me. The need to open up and confess everything, to rid myself of the guilt and pain plaguing me, was beyond tempting. I was drowning here and maybe if I told him, I'd be able to breathe again—at least, in the moment. At this point, I was almost willing to take the small relief. It might help me to move on and focus on other things…like how the fuck I was going to continue this life without losing it.

I stood from the bottom of the bed, blinking past what I was seeing. My head shook furiously as I ripped my gaze to Marko.

"You are *not* letting her go out like that." The little red dress barely held in her cleavage. If she bent over, the whole city would be exposed to her ass and lord knew what else. Was she even wearing panties?

"Tessa picked it out. It's what she feels she needs to wear. I'm letting her take the lead. We'll be following."

"This is bullshit," I snapped. "Tessa wouldn't want this, Marko."

He crossed his arms over his chest. "This is Tessa and I assure you, this is what she wants."

I took in the flawlessness of her pale skin and pouty, crimson lips. The hue of pink tinted her cheeks and I chanced a peek at her eyes. A laugh fell free and I pointed. "How is she going to disguise those? Anyone who takes one look at her will know she's not human. Her eyes are black, or have you not noticed? She looks like a demon. She's going to scare off anyone who looks her way and when she can't feed, she'll turn into even more of a…vampire." I had almost said monster, but caught myself. I knew Marko didn't miss my meaning.

Slowly, the side of his mouth pulled back and he turned to Tessa, easing her to face him. "Look into my eyes, ma minette. Deep, deep into my eyes. As your leader, I'm going to draw you out. Your instincts will flare, but in a good way. You'll be more in control." Softer, his voice became, and she didn't hesitate to meet his gaze. *Such trust.* I couldn't stand it.

Marko leaned closer, moving in until their lips were but a fraction of an inch apart. French words were whispered between them and the air changed entirely as her body softened, gravitating more into his. Her lips separated and she licked them, reaching to grab onto the jacket of his suit. At Marko's hand rising and his fingers weaving into her long hair, I barely registered the angry sound that left me.

"You're an excellent student," he said, cupping her face. "I could teach you so much, if you'll let me."

Although Marko had switched to English, Tessa replied in French.

"Will you teach me everything? Will you…?" She bit her bottom lip, letting it pull against her teeth as she began to smile.

"Perfect," he said huskily. "You'll do great."

A smile appeared on both of their faces and hers stayed in place as she turned to me. The pale green of her eyes had me gasping and for the first time, I could almost see the old Tessa. It left me speechless as she swayed her hips and headed in my direction. Each step had her personality transitioning. She was a goddess—the definition of seduction. Worry began to pull at her features and it wrapped around my heart. My brain locked and thoughts disappeared. The need to rush toward her and do something…provide assistance, brought my hand up. I could feel the lack of control on my thoughts. It was her. She captivated me.

"Can you…help me?" Her lip trembled and tears clouded her eyes. "I'm…lost. I'm not from here. Can you help me?"

What the fuck?

I brought my widened eyes to Marko only long enough to catch his laugh. Fingertips traced down my face and she looked so scared, yet alluring, that it threw me, leaving my mind racing on what I should do. The emotions I felt from her were real. So genuine.

"I'm…lost. Please." A few seconds went by when a laugh exploded from her mouth and she patted my cheek, turning back to him. "Good? Yes?"

"Fucking excellent. Come to me. I'll walk you out. When we reach above ground, you'll appear on your own. But I'll be there every step of the way. Do as I told you here," he said, bringing his finger to her temple. "And you must remember the rules. I'm your leader. You have to obey. If you break any of them, no more going out for you for a very long time. This is for fun. Don't ruin it by losing control."

Tessa headed back toward him while I stayed rooted to the floor. As her arm looped in his and they headed for the door, it was like I suddenly didn't exist. I was no one to them. It took all I had to make myself follow. Two killers were before me and they were headed to the world I'd spent over a decade protecting. The realization tore at everything I represented—of what I stood for. Sickness swarmed in my stomach and only worsened as we headed down the tunnels and made it through a manhole placing us in downtown. Darkness engulfed us and I climbed up, glancing at the broken light from the pole looming above. *How convenient.*

Marko moved the lid back over easily and reached for Tessa, pulling her close. Her chest rose in heavy pants and she shifted nonstop in his grasp.

"Slow your breathing and pulse, ma minette. You're too excited. Calm, remember? Slow. Do everything in a leisurely pace. Tempt them. Use your beauty to lure them to where you want them. It's the name of the game. Seduce. Charm. Act lost if you must, like before with Hunter. Whatever it is that you feel from them. And you will. You're going to be able to read them like a book. Keep eye contact. You don't have to use your powers. What lies within you will be enough to have them helplessly following."

His hand lowered to press flat against her stomach. "You feel that," he said, pushing in enough to make her inhale deeply. There was lust written between them as he leaned in closer. "That heavy pull tells you who you are. *What* you are. What does it tell you?"

Tessa licked her lips, never breaking their stare. "I am…somebody. I rule. Nobody else."

Marko's eyes flickered with something, but he nodded. "You are of worth. You always have been. Now, use that. You can have anyone you want. Anyone. You are Tessalyn Antoinette, the Black Princess. You *will* rule. Right at my side. Together, this city is ours. Happy hunting. I'll be watching." He lowered, barely brushing his lips against hers. I couldn't stop my hand from thrusting forward to grip his bicep. He had to stop this. I couldn't watch what my deepest fears told me.

Even now, after everything I'd gone through, had to witness…she wouldn't be mine. It didn't matter whether I wanted her or not, it was the principle.

A growl exploded and Tessa was on me, slamming me to the ground before I saw her move. Her small body straddled mine while she applied pressure to my neck, baring her fangs inches away as she secured me.

"Shh," Marko said, lowering to the side of her face. "It's okay. He can't hurt me."

The grip loosened, filling me with oxygen, but the anger never left her eyes.

"Why does she protect you like that?" More, she let go, and I pushed her hard to the side, getting her off me as I came to stand.

"I'm her leader. She carries my blood. You reacting as you did is equivalent to doing it to her. She knows who she belongs to, Hunter. This will never change. She may remember the past someday and become angry at the things that have happened between her and me, but Tessa's love for me will never die. We were bonded once. Deep down, we always will be."

"God, I fucking hate you." I wiped the dirt from my pants and shirt, glancing over at Tessa doing the same with her dress. Still, she watched me threateningly. Wasn't I supposed to be the person for her? Wasn't she supposed to love me, too?

Marko seemed to read my mind. "You worry for naught. Watch." His hand reared back as if to hit me and I was jerked toward Tessa, who quickly put herself in front of me. She didn't attack him…but she did protect me.

"Like I said," he rushed out, "she loves us both. Only difference," he said, beginning to smile, "she'd kill you for me. I can't say she'd do the same for you."

Before I could talk, he motioned his head to her. "Go. We'll be here."

Anxiously, she looked between us, giving both of us aggravated looks before she turned and headed for the light. The closer she got, the more her hips swayed. Marko began to follow and I stayed by his side. The silence between us wasn't uncomfortable. My mind began to wander again and I hated where it always took me. I glanced in his direction, only to turn and take in Tessa.

"Sayer…raped me. A lot." Where the statement came from, I wasn't sure. I couldn't look over as we continued.

"I know," he said lowly. "I saw through Tessa's eyes. She aches for what he did to you. She may not be aware of it now, but it'll come back. When it does, she's going to…" He glanced over. "She sincerely cares for you. She really does. You know this, yes?"

"Yes."

Sweat began breaking out over my skin and I pulled at the collar of my shirt as we neared the clubs. "The things he did to Tessa…I'd sacrifice myself for her again. A million times."

Marko glanced over at me. "I won't forget what you've done. I may not like you, but I *love* her. You need not worry or fear anymore. Sayer will pay. You have my word."

"Do I? Why didn't you kill him when you had your chance?" Anger took over my words and he came to a stop on the sidewalk, keeping his focus on Tessa ahead.

"It's not that easy, Hunter. Our race is just as political as yours. Sayer holds position. The timing is key. Julius's killing, I could get away with. Being locked away as I was, I was not in the right state of mind. Anin will see that. They'll accept that. Besides, it was my time to rule. They'll know this, too. Sayer…" he turned to me, looking right in my eyes. "Sayer must meet his fate by unfortunate circumstances."

Flashes of different scenarios projected into my head and the one man who held my fate in his hands caused them. From me, to Tessa, to Marko actually committing the murder, but using one of us as an excuse. Any of us could commit the act, but it would have to be justifiable. I was human, I was the exception. Tessa was a newborn, she was an exception. Marko was not. He was free of restraint and leader of a community now.

"I see," I whispered. And I did. I knew exactly what I had to do. Marko may have not been able to walk up and try to kill Sayer, but one thing I did learn through his energy was that if I did, Marko wouldn't let me die. He'd be by my side, protecting me. He'd help me kill the Black Prince.

Chapter 14
Marko

To watch Tessa in action left my heart pounding and my blood racing. Hunter's concerns may have been focused around Sayer, but I couldn't think about that anymore. We'd deal with the bastard when the time came. As of right now, all I wanted was to watch the woman I loved unleash the predator within—one I knew was just as vicious as mine. Right now, we were the same. She was like me, thirsting and craving blood. But where she needed to experience the hunt, I longed to hunt her. To taste this new vampire version of my Tessa. *Prey.* Yes…what fun we could have.

Dark waves moved back and forth around her hips as she scanned the groups of people walking along the sidewalks. The vast energy radiating from her had my feet moving faster. My cock was getting hard from just feeling her aura. Her power was growing by the day. I almost couldn't believe how strong she was for being so young. I was hungry for her. Just as much as I ever was. No…more. Fuck yes, so much more.

"White shirt."

"What?" I glanced over at Hunter, annoyed that he'd disrupted my thoughts.

"She's eying the man in the white shirt standing across the street. See," he said, pointing to a line outside of a club.

My eyes narrowed and I brought my attention back to Tessa. Just as quickly, her head snapped further down the line. Wind blew her hair back and she looked between the two, turning her head from left to right. The decision was final at her clenching her fist. I knew it. Felt the air change as she shifted her feet in the other direction.

"But…he's not human," I said lowly. "What in the hell?"

Tessa broke to the right, jogging across the street in her stilettos. A bad feeling began to creep into me as I followed. Faster, I went, ignoring the curses leaving Hunter's mouth.

"She's going to fucking kill him right here on the street. Goddammit!" Hunter broke out into a sprint and I followed, just as fast. Aaron, one of Boyd's friends, turned, feeling her energy. The moment his stare stopped on her, his arms drew in and he burst free of the crowd, taking off at lightning speed. But Tessa was already on his heels, heading for a dark alley not a half block away.

"She knows. She saw."

"What the fuck are you talking about?" We burst through a large group just in time to see both of them disappear past the dark entrance. "He killed my friends and I had every intention of finding him. I think she knows that."

Darkness swallowed us up as we burst into the alley. Male growls rang out in the distance and my eyes quickly adjusted to see them at the end. Tessa shoes were off while she lowered, swaying in a stance, baring her fangs. Slowly, she began to circle around as he held his ground.

"Aaron." My voice echoed through the space, a warning to the creature within him. His eyes jerked up and Tessa lunged, tackling him down. Like a blur, her face dove forward. "Fuck," I ground out, moving at my true speed and leaving Hunter behind.

Within seconds, I had my arm locking around her waist. I pulled back, exposing the vampire's shredded face and neck. Blood was everywhere, even soaking into the sleeve of my jacket from the deep wound across Tessa's chest. The sounds of his feet kicking wildly were followed by his hands clawing at the massacre left of his throat. The front was completely gone, hanging loosely to the side. Anger swept through me and I brought my foot down, right over the massive hole, grinding until his head was severed. A flashlight clicked on and I watched the blood drain from Hunter's face.

"Turn it off." My voice was deep, almost unrecognizable as I let Tessa down, spinning her around to face me. Blood was smeared across her face and cheeks. Black eyes once again stared at me. "What the fuck did I tell you when we left? I said no deaths. That means vampires, too. You're in so much trouble. You're…" My teeth snapped shut as I tried to breathe through the anger. I was leader and one of my vampires had just died at the hands of a woman I was responsible for. Love or not, my mind wasn't letting me dismiss that.

I dropped my hands and Tessa surged forward. Hunter's body slammed into the ground and the smell of blood masked the air. I couldn't believe what I was seeing. As a newborn, she should have instinctually known better than to react when her leader was in the middle of reprimanding her. She should have waited for my command. It came natural to all of us, but Tessa wasn't like other newborns and I was quickly realizing what I'd missed during lockdown.

I grasped her hair, holding tightly as I lurched her to her feet. The puncture wounds were evident on Hunter's neck, but it was his side that was bleeding out.

"Fuck," Hunter gasped, holding to the slashes tightly. "I fucking told you this was a bad idea. Shit, she got me good." A ragged breath left him and I internally used my pull to summon Marie and Bufar. Sweat collected on my skin at the chaos Tessa was causing. She wasn't ready to be exposed to humans. Not even close. How had I thought her to be? Hunter loved her, but he'd been afraid for good reason. She was more vampire than anything. Her thirst for violence had my biggest fear creeping in and I prayed it wasn't true. Sayer may have ruined her. He may have…

I lowered, pushing Tessa to the ground on her stomach while I pinned her fighting form down with my knee.

"Lift your shirt, let me see."

A groan left Hunter's throat and he shook his head.

"Do it," I demanded. "You said it was bad. I can smell how strongly you're bleeding. You have to show me. You may need blood to heal."

"Fuck you," he ground out. "Never. I think I'd rather die before I let you save me that way."

"Stubborn fool." I reached forward, ripping the material of his shirt. The skin was cut open, but not to the point of being fatal—at least, not yet. If he continued losing blood at the same rate, things would go downhill fast.

Tessa's nails scraped against the asphalt as she continued trying to get to Hunter. I knew these spells for her wouldn't last long. She's was in the process of forgetting again. An hour, maybe a little more, she'd come to. It was the newborn process and one that could range in time. But if Sayer had ruined her, she'd only get worse with her increasing strength. And this need she had would never go away.

"I'm having Marie come for you. When she gets here, I'm leaving to subdue Tessa. She'll take care of you."

"Marie?" Hunter took a few deep breaths, letting his head fall to rest on the ground.

"Yes. You trust her, don't you?"

"No," he said, letting his head roll to the side. "But she'll do. Why are you being nice to me? I don't understand? I hate you, you hate me. That's how we work. You've been nothing but—"

I pushed into one of the slashes, evoking a loud grunt from Hunter. "There, feel better?"

"Fucking asshole. Goddammit. What the hell is wrong with you?"

"I'm being mean. Now, stop talking, you're making yourself bleed out even more." Tessa tried twisting herself back and forth, only making me push against her harder. "Besides," I went on, "I have my reasons, Hunter. If you think I'm starting to like you, you're wrong. I still want Tessa."

"That doesn't mean you can't like me, too. And I think you're starting to. I think in another life, we could have possibly been friends."

My head shook and I couldn't stop the sarcastic laugh from leaving me. "Are you sure you didn't hit your head when she tackled you down? You're talking nonsense. We would have tried to kill each other then, too. If you want me to prove just how much I don't like you, I'll gladly finish you off right now and rid myself of one less problem."

Hunter took a deep breath and pushed to position himself on his elbow. "You could have done that a million times already. But you haven't. Why?"

I didn't have time for this. I didn't like Hunter, yet…I didn't hate him either.

"You live because I want Tessa to love me more than she already does. She can't possibly do that with me killing her best friend, can she?"

"I suppose not." Another grunt left his mouth as he tried to stand. His weight hit the ground hard as his strength gave out and I shook my head.

"Fuck, sometimes I think dying would be so much easier than living this nightmare."

A soft cry left Tessa and I stood, bringing her up with me. I could feel Marie and Bufar close. "Embrace this beautiful nightmare. For when it ends, so will your life. This is all you have left, Hunter. You chose this path, now you have to face the consequences. Giving up is for cowards. You are not a coward. I can at least say that about you."

"You're wrong." Hunter met my eyes for only a moment before he looked back down at his wound. "I'm only strong because I have to be. For Tessa, for those soldiers. What happens when I don't have anyone left to save?"

My lips parted and even though I felt the need to speak, I wasn't sure what to say. This man was opening up to me, laying himself open and my vampire couldn't stomach it. But me…the man I used to be, felt jolted to the core. He wouldn't have Tessa forever, she'd be mine. Then, what really would happen to him? How would Tessa take that? Would she deny what I knew to be her true feelings to keep this human emotionally afloat? I couldn't see her vampire being able to, but she'd have humanity, too.

Two shadows moved through the darkness toward us and I held Tessa tighter as she squirmed in my arms. "You'll be fine. You'll adjust to whatever Tessa chooses." I couldn't continue to be near him. I lifted Tessa's feet from the ground as I headed to Marie and Bufar at a fast pace. Only once did I glance back at Hunter. Thoughts swirled, colliding with different possibilities. Only one coalesced. One I didn't even want to consider.

Serious faces met me as my number two and new number ten awaited my orders. I glanced at Marie, feeling her loyalty through and through. This was all she'd ever wanted—to be a member. Dead slaves were a distant memory of her past and I knew she was already on the hunt for more. She was thriving, still growing stronger from her grief. Something I knew she now thanked me for.

"Aaron is dead. Have the body disposed of." I swallowed hard, staring over my shoulder as Hunter once again tried to stand. "Tessa hurt him pretty badly. Give him your blood for healing. Start the process. The two of you bond."

Red lips separated as her gaze jerked to Hunter and then Tessa. "She'll kill me when she remembers her past. I...can't do that."

"Yes, you can. I'm your leader and you'll obey. Don't worry about Tessa. This is for the best. She'll come to see that. She'll see everything."

Chapter 15
Tessa

Throbbing began to register in my head and I blinked past the blurry vision of water pouring down before me. I couldn't think. Could barely breathe past the steam rising around me. A heartbeat pulled at my ears and I rubbed my eyes as I turned toward the thudding sound. Seeing Marko's arm extending out toward me made jump back. I reached toward the wall, walking my hands down the length as I tried to figure out what was happening. My mind screamed to run, even if I didn't know from what. And I couldn't see straight. The walls blurred in and out as I got to the back.

"Calm, ma minette, I'm not going to hurt you. Look, all I have is shampoo. I'm going to wash the blood from your hair."

"Blood?" I turned, glancing at his exposed palm. The white substance in the center told me he was telling the truth. But what blood? I couldn't remember anything. Where was I? Nothing made sense. I knew I was underground. I knew I was a vampire. And I knew somewhat who Marko was, but something was missing. Lots of things were gone from my memory. Wasn't I supposed to be afraid? Fear was present, but I wasn't sure why. And there was an emptiness that had me scanning the surroundings for what I was missing.

The pressure of his hand had me tensing and I let him draw me back. As his hands rubbed together and rose to my hair, I let him lather and massage the soap into my scalp. His eyes stayed on me, but I couldn't keep his stare.

"Whose...blood?"

The words were thick leaving my mouth and I closed my lids, trying to will my sight back to normal.

"Aaron, a vampire. And I'm sure some is Hunter's."

My lids shot open as flashes of my human began to register. I glanced over his shoulder, instinctually looking for the tall, dark haired man. "Did I kill him?" I shouldn't have cared, but the possibility left me feeling sick. I couldn't deny I felt a part of me growing attached. I liked him. He protected me, even if I couldn't remember from what.

Silence drew my attention to my leader and he tightened his fingers in my hair.

"He was alive when I had him taken. But you hurt him very badly. You're probably going to be angry with me, but I'm having Marie give him her blood so he'll heal. He needed it if he was going to make a speedy recovery."

"Marie?" *Did I know who that was?*

"Yes. She's my number ten. She'll take good care of him."

I grew quiet, not sure what to think. If Hunter took this vampire's blood...? Nothing came. Something would happen, but what? I didn't know and it had me pulling against Marko's fingers. He slid them free and I stepped back, washing the shampoo from my hair. As he grabbed the body soap, I instinctively ripped it from his grasp.

"I can do it." The French came natural, but it had me stuttering at the end. I wasn't supposed to speak that language. But I had. It made me pause, clashing with the fact that Marko spoke it, too. Why wasn't I supposed to speak it? I hesitated, looking back toward the door. "Where's Hunter. I want him here."

Marko's features tightened before smoothing out as he let out a deep breath. "He's with Marie. I already told you that."

"I know. But where, with this Marie?"

"In her room."

Marko took the soap from me and squeezed a good amount into his hand. I flinched at the initial touch, too sensitive to be able to take the water, and more or less the pressure of his fingers. He seemed to realize and softened the caressing of my stomach. The tingling only caused me to reach for the wall as lust began to buffer the anxiety I felt.

"When will Hunter be back?"

The motion of his hand slowed and he glanced up for only a moment. "He won't, Tessa. He's not safe with you. I have him staying with her now."

I reached down, slapping his hand off me. "He was not yours to give away. Hunter belongs to me."

Marko straightened, towering over me as he glared down. "You'll kill him. Is that what you want? If so, I'll go get him right now and we'll end his life this very moment."

My lips separated, but somehow I knew he was right. The conflict left me whimpering past the pain in my head. I turned into the wall, letting the tears of aggravation and agony seep free. I hated this. I hated not having control. The lack thereof made me hurt the human. I didn't need him, I knew that. And I'd wanted to kill him before, but now, I wasn't sure where my feelings rested. He was gone and I felt like I needed him more than ever. I was afraid for him. Hadn't he been through so much? Had I been the one to hurt him like that? Maybe it was better if he stayed away.

"Shh, don't cry, ma minette. Everything will be okay. It's these changes in you. You're hurting. Come here."

My palms pressed to the sides of my face even harder before I turned, taking in the Master before me. His outstretched arms had me rushing into them. I was scared, something I didn't think happened often. I was tired of all these episodes stealing my sanity. Even now, it wasn't all the way present. Or maybe it was. It was the emptiness in my head. The lost time. It was driving me crazy.

"There, there." His arms wrapped around me, holding tight. The smell of his cologne, of his blood mixed with the scent of his power, wrapped around me, leaving me feeling even more secure. My eyes closed and I let my weight mold to his body. Fingers wrapped around the back of my neck and his palm flattened just above the swell of my ass. The contact was heaven. I didn't feel as though the closeness happened often…if ever. It felt right, comforting, and somehow, I needed that. *I needed him.*

Slowly, I looked up, meeting his stare. My breaths deepened and my whole mood changed as my gaze lowered to his mouth. Hadn't I kissed that mouth before? I could barely recall, but something told me I had. And I wanted to do it again. I wanted to taste him while he continued to hold me.

"I smell your want for me. Say it." His voice was deep and full of need as he spoke to me in French.

"I want to kiss you. I want—"

The words were cut off as his lips crushed into mine and he lifted me, walking through the water and pinning me against the shower wall. The force nearly knocked the air from my lungs, but the worry vanished just as fast as my tongue hungrily met his. His actions sparked such need, it was all that mattered. I tightened my arms around his neck, thrusting my breasts harder into his chest. All thoughts and concerns disappeared. Nothing existed but our moment and I clung to it as tightly as I held him.

"Yes," he moaned. "I've waited so long for this. I love you. God, help me, I do." His mouth pressed back into mine and I could feel him pull frantically at his belt. I didn't hesitate to start jerking at his shirt. Material tore while our kissing grew to a fevered pitch. The concrete wall scratched against my back and I sucked in air as his fingers explored over my most private area. My pussy was so wet, so slick and swollen as he rubbed circles over the top of my slit. I broke away, moaning as he massaged back and forth quickly.

"Tell me you want me. I've waited so long. Let me hear you say it."

A cry came from my mouth at the pleasure and I moved against him, greedy for more.

"I want you."

His finger eased into my channel and I pushed down the length as I tightened my grip around his neck.

"Fuck, you're so tight." Another finger joined the first and my mouth separated in pleasure as he began to move within me. The friction had my hips rotating out of desperation and I couldn't stop my stomach from tightening through the intense arousal. I held off the need, but it almost became impossible as he flattened his hand to the top of my slit, applying pressure to my clit.

"Who knows what you like?" he asked in English.

"You," I moaned.

"That's right. I know you better than anyone ever will. That's what makes us perfect for each other. We're one. Une âme, un seul cœur." *One soul, one heart.* His fingers slid free, immediately replaced by the head of his cock. The thickness pushed at my entrance, stretching me impossibly wide as he inched inside of me. I held on tight, meeting his lips as he gripped my ass and surged in even more.

"Fuck, you feel so good. I've missed you so much."

I screamed as he plunged in all the way, grinding his hips into me as he forced his way even deeper. Ecstasy exploded and I clawed at the back of his wet shirt.

"No more prolonging this. Taste me, ma minette. Sink your fangs into me and taste what is yours."

My eyes met his and the vampire in me purred for his power. My fangs lowered and I let my fingers slide up to grip his hair. At the small jerk of my hand, his head leaned to the side and I slid my fangs home. Sweet potency washed over my tongue and the lust had my poison oozing free from my fangs. I knew it would make the experience better for him and for some reason that was important.

Within seconds, Marko was moaning deep enough to vibrate my chest. I drew hard on his vein, savoring the taste as it rushed through my body. It was too much. He was strong. So much so, I could barely take it. Tighter, I held, taking one last hard suck before I slid my tongue over the wounds.

The thrusts increased and I met his mouth again, but only for a moment before I pulled away. I reached to my neck, pulling my hair back to expose what I wanted him to take from me. Why, I wasn't sure, but it seemed right in the moment.

"God, you tempt me. I've been dying to taste you. Are you sure?"

His words had me nodding and the kiss of his lips over my sensitive skin brought my hips moving back into a frantic rhythm for more. Stinging caused me to jump, but with everything going through me, I didn't care. At the venom entering, I screamed through the orgasm that came instantly. My channel gripped his cock while he continued to thrust and drink me in. The perfection of the moment was unlike anything I could imagine. Twinges pulled at my stomach and I cried out at the uncomfortable sensations, but for the life of me, I didn't want him to stop. Even though he seemed to be experiencing it too, Marko held me tighter.

"I love you," he said, breaking away. "Listen to me and feel my words. I love you. I love you. To death, Tessa. You and me. There's no one else for either of us. *Remember* your love. I want you to see it. Feel it."

His pleas stirred nothing but my curiosity. Part of me was hesitant to push my mind through the pain; another part felt something come naturally. It warmed my chest. My heart.

"Jamais de ma vie je ne ai aimé que je te aime. Je ne suis pas l'un sans toi." *Never in my life have I loved as I love you. I'm no one without you.*

The French words had me closing my eyes. The passion and familiarity was what I needed to hear. Tingling mixed with the tremors jerking at what I was made of and another orgasm hit hard, causing me to cry out as my body betrayed my mind. Despite the pain, the two mixed and I gasped, moaning while I traced my fingers over his lips. The swelling of his cock grew while he thrust and I pulled his bottom lip back, tracing the inside with my tongue. A moan tore from Marko and he nipped at my finger.

"Be my concubine." His head pulled back and I saw the puzzlement in his eyes. He battled with the question, but I could see how much he wanted it, even if I wasn't sure exactly what it meant. Why did that term pull at my memory as if I was already one, or supposed to be?

"Marry me, Tessa. That's what I mean. Be mine, here, for all of the vampires to see. Take your place by my side. Help me rule. Let me take care of you through this tough time."

The grind of his hips slowed, leaving me foggier than ever. What we were doing felt so good. If it stayed like this, it wouldn't be so bad, would it? I could do this. And I'd have status. I'd rule. Wasn't that what I was meant to do? No, there was something else. Something I was forgetting. Hadn't I just known what it was not that long ago?

"I..."

His lips met mine and he lifted, pressing his hand to cover over my mouth as he moved faster. "I don't know where that came from. Don't answer that yet. Fuck…just…love me like I love you. That's all I want. I just want us to love each other." A sound came from his lips and he removed his hand, kissing me. I rotated more urgently and he gripped tightly around my waist, pounding his cock into me almost violently. Warmth shot deep within and I felt him jerk with wave after wave of his release.

For minutes, Marko just held me, turning me into the shower, but keeping us joined. My head rested on his neck and I closed my eyes as exhaustion and adrenaline fought against each other. His blood was racing through my veins and I suddenly realized how much I liked that. Liked…him. A lot.

"Let me wash you."

My feet lowered, but he still held the majority of my weight as he reached over and poured the body wash over my chest. In soft caresses, he smoothed the liquid over my breasts and stomach. When he reached between my legs, I held my breath, biting my bottom lip. A smile pulled at his mouth and I let mine come.

I couldn't stop the attraction that left me in awe of him. The full lips grabbed my attention and I slowly rose back to his brown eyes.

"I want to be your concubine. I want to lead."

His fingers froze on my inner thigh, only to be removed as he pulled me into his body. "I'm…honored. And probably the happiest vampire alive. You won't regret this. I promise."

Those full lips met mine and I let him finish washing and rinsing me. As he pulled the shower open, we both froze. Hunter's bloody body sat on the floor directly across from the opened bathroom door, his forearms resting on his knees as he glared toward us. The pain and hurt on his face was evident. My breath caught and I felt heaviness pull at my heart—the same heart that had just belonged to Marko.

Him. Yes…how could I have forgotten about my human?

Chapter 16
Hunter

There were no words for the amount of anger and betrayal running through me. I couldn't blame Tessa, although a part of me unwillingly did. She wasn't in her right mind and from the look on her face, she somewhat regretted what she'd done. Or did she? Fuck, I wasn't sure. What I knew for a fact was Marko didn't regret shit.

He grabbed a robe from the wall, sliding it on her and wrapping a towel around his waist as he led her right past me toward the bed. I pushed to stand, following. One of my hands went to my side while the other went to the hilt of the dagger.

"If you think of using that, I will kill you where you stand." Marko wasn't even facing me, but he sensed my actions and I couldn't stand it. Nothing was working out here. Not my relationship with Tessa and not what I felt I should have been doing to these monsters. No one was to be trusted. How I'd even let myself open up to Marko about anything was beyond me. How was I starting to like him when he continued to hurt me by manipulating Tessa?

"How could you?" I stopped at the end of the bed as he pulled back the blankets, helping Tessa climb in. Still, she stared at me, uneasily. Hurt. God, she was hurting? I was fucking dying here. She was meant to be mine. I'd gone through hell just to try to keep Sayer away from her. I was supposed to have her this way. It was the reason I convinced her of the change. But I didn't have her. *He did*. Again.

"Where's Marie?" Marko pulled the blankets up and straightened, facing me.

"Dead. I fucking killed the bitch before she could poison me with her blood. Same with the big guy. They're dead. The power of prayer is one hell of a thing. It'll stop a vampire in its tracks, making them easy targets. Want to see?"

I grabbed the rosary from my pocket, dangling it in the air as I cocked my head to the side and stepped closer. A growl poured from Marko's throat and gravity left me as I crashed into the far wall from the force he threw.

Air refused to fill my lungs, but I managed to regain my footing as I hunched over, raising the rosary back up. A groan came from my mouth and Tessa slammed her fist into Marko's arm, speaking so fast in French, I couldn't understand. I caught my breath, bringing myself to stand. My side was aflame from the gashes and I knew they were still bleeding, but the bandages were helping. Just not enough. I was lightheaded. Weak.

"She was mine," I yelled. "She was mine and you took her from me again! But I'm not leaving. I'm not running away from what belongs to me. Tessa will *not* be your concubine. I won't allow it. If I die trying to prevent it from happening, then so be it. At least I'll die knowing I gave it everything I had trying to stop her from making the biggest mistake of her life."

"Hunter." Tessa rose from the bed and Marko went to grab her arm, but she swatted his touch away. "You're hurt. I…hurt you."

I stayed quiet as I watched her features pull in.

"I hurt you…a lot and I'm sorry. I don't remember. I don't know what's happening to me."

"I know." Sounds left me again as I limped to the bed and collapsed at the end. My head went down and I couldn't stop the burning of my eyes. "He loves you. I love you. And you love us both. That's just the tip of the iceberg. Your vampire is out of control and I don't know how to handle that."

"Then allow me," Marko ground out. "I will spend the rest of my life taking care of her. I'll make her happy, I promise you."

My glare couldn't have been any more full of hate as I met his stare. "Shut…the fuck…up!"

Tessa walked between us and came to me. As I looked up, I tried to sit up straight. With my wounds, I couldn't. Nausea plagued me and stars danced before my eyes. Her small hand cupped my face and I closed my eyes, moving into the touch, regardless of being so pissed at her. Or more, that I should fear her.

"Let me heal you. Yes?" Her features twisted while I watched her search for the words. "I'll make you my slave, okay?"

A sarcastic laugh vibrated my chest and my head shook as I opened my eyes. "You want me as your slave when you've already consented to be his concubine, *despite* the fact that all hell's going to break loose when Sayer finds out? Not to mention, I never know who I'm getting with you. You're so unstable."

"Sayer?" she repeated the name while her eyes scanned the room. "Do I…know him? I do, I think."

"Jesus," I snapped my head to Marko, who was moving more toward the bottom of the bed. "Do you see what you've done? She doesn't even know who Sayer is right now and you fucked her? How is that consensual?"

Marko's lips peeled back, revealing fangs. "I assure you, it was consensual. Tessa is more herself right now than she'll ever be. You're bleeding like a stuck pig and she hasn't once tried to attack you, has she?"

I blinked hard, looking back at her. "No. She hasn't."

"Nor will she. My blood helps her. She can continue to be like this if she stays with me and keeps the regular feedings. I'm making her better. Stronger. Her English is getting clearer, too. She's growing into who she's meant to be with me."

"You just want her to continue so you can finalize the bond all over again." There was no mistaking my rage. I clenched the rosary tighter as he stared at me.

"I told you I wanted Tessa. Of course, I want to be bonded with her. And she wants it, too. I know you saw her give me her vein. Deep down, she wants *me*. Apparently, she still wants you as her slave." He paused. "I'm willing to let her keep you if that's what she chooses. But only as her friend and occasional supplier. Nothing more. I think that's a term you might find to your liking more than you want to admit—especially after what you did to her."

All I could do was project my anger at him as Tessa lowered to her knees between my legs and rested her head in my lap. I was stroking the length of her hair before I realized it. My mind was taking me back to the one thing I couldn't think about. Her screams began to echo in my ears and I could almost taste her pussy on my tongue all over again. Jesus, I'd never live that down.

"Don't listen, Hunter. I make decisions for my life. No one," she paused, meeting his eyes, "will tell me what to do. Not even…him."

I laughed, raising my eyebrow to Marko. His face may have been devoid of emotion, but I knew he was hurt…and pissed. He couldn't control her any more than Sayer. Tessa would rule. She'd show them all who their true leader was. But what would that mean for the two of us? I wasn't even sure I could be with her physically anymore. I loved her, but sexually, I couldn't even let myself go there.

"Will you be his concubine?" I brought her face up until she was looking at me. The black tint was almost gone now, revealing the green shade of her eyes below. They were so light, I couldn't help but take a few extra seconds to stare. God, she was beautiful. My question twisted my insides even more than the damage her claws had caused. I was torn on what I should do or feel.

"I think…I should. Why?" Her head shook. "I feel for him. Here." Small fingers pressed over her chest. "But…" she trailed off, obviously confused.

"You have doubt. That means you have to wait. Do not rush into a decision you're not sure of. You heard his terms. He will not share your love. Not physically, and I doubt emotionally. You will lose me if you accept his offer. It's unfair for me to be subjected to that sort of life. You know this, don't you?"

A quick nod had her agreeing. "You be my slave. He will accept *my* terms."

Marko shifted behind her. He wanted to do something, say something, but he didn't. The longer I took in her face, the more I let her words sink in. Tessa put herself over her leader. She knew what she was meant to do. It was in her blood, in her mind, even when nothing else was. She always knew. And she'd do it. I had no doubts. So was I safe giving myself to her that way? Would she love me and let me heal enough to try to love her again, like we were meant to? Or…was I doomed? *No.* I had to get over this. When she remembered what I did, surely she would understand. Sayer had given me his blood. I was drugged. Out of my mind when I'd forced my face between her legs. I had to try to have faith.

"I'll be your slave, but we should start now. While you're still somewhat stable."

Tessa rose, sitting in my lap. Marko crossing his arms over his chest had me glancing up, but more so, I could watch him from my peripheral vision. Slowly, Tessa brought up her arm, staring down at the robe as if she were trying to feel out how to go about this.

"Cut," I whispered.

"Yes," she agreed. "You first. Just in case." Shallow breaths left her as she pushed the sleeve of the robe up and stared down at her forearm. "If I…change and hurt you…" her eyes came back to meet mine, "kill me. Kill me…and leave. No looking back. No regret." She moved her finger to the side of my head. "Remember this. If I ever become too much and become a…monster…kill me. Promise. I can't…" A sniffle ended her words and I couldn't turn away from the shock of what I was seeing. If I'd been unsure of who Tessa was in the moment, her words all but erased any doubt. This was *my* Tessa. The real Tessa.

My hands went to her face and I leaned in, pressing my lips to hers. Wetness dampened my cheeks and I pulled back, wiping her tears away. "You've been so strong. I knew you were still here. You have my word. But let's focus on us. Let's start our future."

Tessa nodded, turning to Marko and switching to French. "If I change, you will stop me from hurting him."

Marko didn't say a word as he gave her a hard look. I knew he didn't like what was about to happen.

"If you do not…" the threat was clear in her eyes.

"You will what?" he said in English through clenched teeth. "You will kill me?"

"No," she said, shaking her head and continuing. "There are worse ways to hurt someone than ending their life. I'll make you suffer for an eternity. And even after that." Her French flowed faster with every word and by the time she finished, Marko's anger was finally shining prominently on his features. He'd thought he had her. That Tessa had been all his. He was wrong. He may have been able to trap her in the moment, but she would always come back to her true self. I just prayed the real Tessa would hurry up and stay for good.

"Don't threaten me, ma minette." Marko didn't have to say more. As the two kept each other's eye contact, Tessa let her nail slice down her arm. Still, she stared at him as she let it rise to me. I gripped around her wrist, keeping my eyes on Marko as I brought the blood to my lips. Metallic flavor swept over my tongue and I forced myself to swallow. When the blood hit my throat, I literally felt the life within the source rush through my system with a speed that had me gripping her tighter. My pulse spiked with the force and the need to take in more warped my mind, leaving me sucking harder. But this time was different. She was sweeter. Deliciously addicting.

I opened my mouth wider, running my tongue over the surface of the wound while she moaned. Within seconds, tightening clutched my stomach and I broke away, sucking in air. Tessa was looking at me now, her eyes already darkening with her vampire. As she began to straddle me, I let her. I wanted her on me, suddenly needed her want of me, more than I needed anything.

"My turn," she whispered.

My arm was lifted and I knew she was going to cut me, too. I jerked out of her hold, clutching the back of her neck and yanking her face into my neck. I should have been afraid, but I didn't fucking care about anything outside of what I knew she'd give me—what taunted me since Sayer sank his own weapons into me. And I didn't have to wait. Fangs didn't hesitate to pierce my skin. Death didn't even present as a possibility. All I knew was needing her bite.

"God," I breathed out, wrapping my arm around her waist and pulling her pussy closer to me. At the rotation of her hips, my hand shoved under the robe to grab her ass. Fingers laced in my hair and my head was jerked back as I was met with Marko's evil glare.

"Hands off," he growled.

"Fuck you. Sit back and take a seat. Watch me fuck her like I watched you."

Nails extended and I couldn't move as his hand blurred toward me. In slow motion, the claws got closer to my face, but I couldn't stop him. Couldn't think to react fast enough. Out of nowhere, Tessa's hand shot out, catching his wrist. She was gone from me now. Off my lap and shoving her hands into his chest as she pushed him further into the room. French filled the room and I fought to decipher the language through my fog.

"You dare try to harm what is mine?" Her hands connected over his pecs with brutal force, making him stagger back.

"*You* are mine," he corrected. "Mine! Not his. Not Sayer's. Mine!"

"Wrong. I am both of yours now. At least through one tie. Both. Accept." She shoved him again, but his feet grounded and he stayed in place. "Accept," she said more forcefully.

Her arms shot up to push him again when she drew in, crashing to her knees. I felt the spasms the moment she did. They cramped in my stomach worse than anything I'd ever experienced before. My insides twisted and pulled until I was sure I'd be sick. I could feel my side tingling and I knew her blood was healing me, but I didn't have the strength to check. I fell back on the bed and my lids heavily went down.

It was starting. I'd be Tessa now—always. Even though it gave me a sense of relief, I couldn't deny the fear associated with it. This was bigger than I could grasp and I was only just experiencing her true self breaking through her vampire. But what if what she ultimately became wasn't what I wanted? What if she fell into Marko's trap and I couldn't stop her?

I wasn't so sure of that as he snarled and looked down at her with too many emotions for me to take in. Disgust? Pain? Betrayal all over again? He slammed the door, leaving her curled on the floor. And with his absence, I prayed this was finally our beginning.

Chapter 17
Marko

A little over four months old and although Tessa still had episodes common for a newborn, she was pulling through with shocking stability. She wouldn't talk to me or acknowledge my presence since I'd refused to accept her keeping the two of us. I was back to square one concerning her and I was too stubborn to give in. I loved her, that was fact, but I couldn't let her keep both of us for her pleasure. Not for a relationship like Sayer wanted.

A slave to feed from, I could accept, but not a lover, too. That pushed the bounds of my vampire and I'd kill Hunter if I ever saw them together like that. It was best for all involved that I keep my distance—at least until she came around and saw how I'd changed. And she would, the more her vampire aged.

My eyes went to the end of the meeting table to face Marie. Hunter had only thought he killed her and Bufar when he pierced them with that damn dagger. It had taken a good three days for both to bounce back, but they'd done it, with more contempt toward the human than ever. Marie's dreams were increasing, but nothing was for sure, as they changed paths every day. The only thing certain was Sayer. He'd be back soon. Not only could she see it, but I'd gotten a message from Margo, a member of Axis, saying she was going to accompany the Master on the trip. Her interest in Tessa was no doubt piqued, as was the rest of the elders'.

"Has the outcome changed on Sayer, Marie?" I leaned forward, resting my arms on the thick oak as I took in the nine members before me.

"No," she said confidently. "Sayer won't budge, but Margo will rule in your favor. The Princess will stay."

I cringed, hating to hear her as that. But it was truth. With Sayer changing her and the title associated with him, she gained the nobility by her birth. She'd always have it, regardless of whether my blood took her over. It wasn't like anyone would ever know…unless they tasted her blood and had either mine or Sayers to compare.

"It's settled then." I continued, watching the all-too-bored faces begin to fade out in front of me. I swallowed hard, cursing the surging I'd only hoped had stopped with me taking the leadership role. "If there's nothing else, we're excused."

Marie shifted and her hand slowly rose. "There's more to my dreams. Things I don't like."

"Go on," I said, pulling at my tie.

"I'm not really sure how to put it into words, but I see lots of blood. I think something bad is going to happen. But my vision won't allow me to see what it is."

I blinked slowly. "But you said everything works out in our favor? The community will get to keep Tessa?"

"Well…yes. But, I can't shake this feeling of something bad happening."

I shrugged. "If we don't know, there's nothing we can do about it. We're just going to have to keep our eyes peeled to see if anything happens."

Silent nods had me standing and the others following. I waited until everyone was heading through the tunnel before I pulled the door closed behind me and stalked toward my room. It was Julius's old room, bigger than the one I shared with Tessa. And it was adorned with everything she'd need for when the time came for her to be mine. I hated looking at it. Hating even having done it. As I swept in and took in the red silk sheets, it only reminded me of what I didn't have. Darkness tinted my vision and I roared, grabbing a vase from the porcelain pedestal and smashing it against the wall.

I'd been so fucking close. Then Hunter had shown up, ruining everything. Even with as much as I couldn't stand it, I couldn't deny that I was softening toward him. I could have killed him at any moment, yet I hadn't. I allowed him to stay with the woman I loved. And it was all for her.

What was I doing? I didn't know anymore. I didn't know anything.

Knocking had territorial sounds leaving me and I spun around, swinging the barrier open. Hunter standing before me had my fangs lowering. I'd seen him a few times since I'd left Tessa that night, but he didn't look any happier than he did now.

"What?" My harsh tone earned me a glare, but he couldn't hide the fear pouring off him. It mixed sweetly with Tessa's blood and perfumed the air so intoxicatingly, I felt the monster within flare to life for her.

"She's gone. I woke up and Tessa's not in the room. I've looked everywhere. In the shops…tunnels…I didn't know who else to go to."

My jaw clenched and I took a deep breath, trying to calm. If it wasn't one thing within the community, it was something else. And that something usually revolved around her. I was getting frustrated. If she would have been with me, none of this would be happening.

"Didn't you restrain her?"

"For what? Tessa hasn't shown any signs of aggression in over a week. Even before, they were only mild. Growls, so forth. But she hasn't attempted to harm me once. Quite the opposite, actually."

I walked into the tunnel, slamming my door behind me. The illumination of the flashlight caused me to shake my head. I couldn't do this right now. I couldn't even control my own damn self. But I had to. I was the leader. This was my responsibility. *She* was my responsibility.

"Listen, I wouldn't have come to you if I didn't have to. Do you really think I like seeing your face?"

I spun, my hand going for his throat, only to jerk to a stop at the rosary resting on his neck. It made me hiss and forced me to take a step back. The flashlight rose and my eyes squinted at the light.

"Hunter, now is not the time to push my buttons."

"Why, because you're going through the same thing as her? Your eyes are black, Marko. More so than I've seen in a very long time. Can I expect some massive killing spree from you, too?"

A laugh left me as I continued walking. "Let's hope not," I mumbled under my breath. "The world would never be the same."

The illumination from the heart of the city had me lowering my lids even more and I came to a stop, closing my eyes and feeling for Tessa. As I opened up our connection, thoughts invaded my mind. I'd done my best to leave her alone, but just feeling her again opened the wounds caused by her decision over Hunter. When she had told me she'd be my concubine, I'd never felt happier. Then, she'd tied up with him. It was like a slap in the face with a brick. The hate I harbored for him grew to heights I couldn't ever remember feeling. I'd left, destroying everything in my path so I wouldn't kill the fucking human. Even now, I knew I could, but the time apart had made things fade. I just felt tired. Exhausted.

Music filtered through and the base I heard vibrated my insides. My eyes snapped opened and I headed for the hall leading to The Craze, our underground vampire club.

"Well, did you find her?"

Footsteps pounded behind me and I glanced over my shoulder. "Yep."

"Well? Where is she?"

I was too annoyed to answer. My head was starting to hurt and my throat burned for blood. Her blood. I wanted the next tie. I wanted to mark her twice.

A group of vampires wearing short, tight dresses stepped out of my way, cringing back at my aura. I let it pour from me with every ounce of aggression I held. Damn Tessa for interfering with my need for peace. Yet, she was my salvation. She'd make me feel better. If only I could get her under my control and back with me.

"Music. Is she at the club? The one Marie took her to a long time ago?"

"Yes," I said lowly, moving faster.

The entrance rested ahead and I stopped, pounding my fist into the heavy metal. The male vampire who worked the door took one look at me and swung it wide, letting me and Hunter stroll past. Lights flickered, red and blue, beaming and spinning around the room. The strobe resting on the dance floor had the crowd appearing to move in slow motion. I scanned the space, grasping our connection and letting it pull me deeper within the large space.

"This place is huge." Hunter moved in next to me, peering around the two-story room. I kept quiet as I eyed Boyd's gang in the back. The way one of the vampires tensed, I knew where she was. It drew me faster and sent my rage to blistering heights. I hadn't forgotten about Boyd's manipulating ways. He'd already tried to get Tessa's blood on more than one occasion and I didn't put it past him to do it again.

Laughter died as I walked up the four steps and took a left. It bought me to a sitting area nestled in the back. Perched on a black leather chair, sipping on a drink, was none other than Tessa. Four vampires rested at her feet, kneeling. She glanced at Hunter and me and continued her story without missing a beat. They looked enamored, fixated on nothing but her. The vampires who had been watching the show were already gone at my presence.

"So, I walked around the corner and all of a sudden, I heard a woman whispering. Now, mind you, this wasn't just any woman. I'd heard her whisper before."

"When you were down here. When you went to your human. She is you." I watched a dark haired vampire lean a little closer in his enthusiasm, never breaking his focus on her face.

"Correct, Dillon. You're such a good listener. It was me. But when I heard her tonight, it was different. I had control of her. So, I walked around the corner and way off in the distance, at the end of the street, was none other than…" her head tilted, "who wants to guess?"

"Me." Boyd rose higher on his knees, but his ass never left the heels of his shoes.

"Go ahead." The French accent was almost gone and I couldn't believe how good her English had gotten in such a small amount of time. I narrowed my eyes as I got closer. I knew this version of her was the true vampire resting within. It made me cautious to see what she'd done.

Tessa watched my movement, stealing glances at Hunter. Patiently, she waited as Boyd fiddled with his hands, seeming to think.

"Was it Marko? Marie? Nooo….Sayer!" he burst out.

"Wrong," she smiled. "Anyone else want to make a guess?"

The men didn't take their eyes off her and I couldn't quite grasp what was going on.

"I'll tell you." She reached over and gripped a trash bag to her left, pulling it closer to the end of the small table resting beside her. "You see, my human, Hunter, he's very important to me, as you all now know from my stories. There's nothing I wouldn't do for him. Nothing I wouldn't do for anyone who meant a great deal to me." Anger started to work its way into her tone and her features tightened as she brought the bag to rest on her lap. It covered the simple black dress she wore, exposing her pale calves.

The bag opened at her pull and I jerked my face back at the smell of blood. Humans wouldn't have detected it, but it was simple enough to pick up for a vampire. It was a few hours old and spoiled from the temperature of the surface above.

"Father Moretti, here," she said, removing his head by his hair, "tried attacking me on the street. Threatening me, saying I'd hurt my human. Me, can you believe that? I'd never do anything to harm Hunter. As will none of you."

Hunter's hand latched to my jacket and I barely caught him as his knees gave out and he almost crashed to the ground.

"Tessa doesn't know," I said lowly. "She doesn't understand."

A ragged inhale racked his chest and I managed to help him stand.

"This is a clear warning to anyone who thinks about hurting him or accusing me of the same thing. I've heard your whispers during my outings. You're not even safe from your own thoughts. Mess with what's mine and the next head in this bag will belong to one of you. Or all of you. I don't care if you're a member, a slave, or a priest. I will kill you if you get near him. Now, leave me, my human and our leader has come to join me," she said, flicking her wrist.

The men scattered to their feet and froze as they spun around, spotting me. "Go," I snarled. They didn't wait to obey as I passed them. Hunter tugged against my grip and I let him go, watching his actions cautiously.

"How could you? God, Tessa….how could you! He loved you. He…" His fingers raced through his lengthening hair and he stopped mid-stroke, pulling at it as he head lowered. "Jesus, I can't believe what you've done. I…think I'm going to be sick." Deep breaths left him as he came back up and paced back and forth. I shook my head, narrowing my eyes at Tessa. She was clearly confused. And hurt by his behavior.

"Are you allowed above ground?"

Her shrug as she stood had me snatching her by the arm and pulling her to me. "Love you or not, I will not hesitate to punish you for disobeying. I asked you a question. Answer."

"No. I am not." Her eyes left mine, moving to Hunter, and she dropped the bag to the floor. The action caused another sound to come from his lips. His hand slammed over his mouth as he raced to the side, becoming sick in a trashcan. Sadness mixed with anger on Tessa's face. I could feel her conflict. The lack of her attention left me gripping her harder to bring her back to what we were talking about.

"You're hurting me. Let go," she said, pulling.

"No…I don't think so. You are not to go above ground. *Ever.* Not until I can go with you and make sure you're stable enough."

My brain was getting fuzzier, but not to the point where I couldn't control myself. I loosened my grip, letting her jerk free. Immediately, she went to him, trying to reach out to his arm. The flinch as he scrambled away from her had her lips parting. Slowly, she brought her hand to her mouth, only to extend it out to him again.

"Aren't you happy?" she rushed out. "Hunter, look at me. I thought you said you liked my protection. You said…" Her head lowered and a small trace of anger surfaced on her face as she looked up. "I said I'd take care of you. You're going to be my slave. I wanted to..."

A look of disgust crossed his face and he continually shook his head. It left me puzzled as to what was going on between them. Something was off. Not right. Especially with their tie. Or, ties. Had they made their second mark yet?

The bass died off as another song began to play. I crossed my arms over my chest, watching the two of them. Tessa was becoming more upset, where Hunter was getting angrier by the second. I walked forward, focusing on Tessa. "I'm only going to say this once. Go above ground again and you'll force me to put you in lockdown. Now, tell me how you got past the guards? I have one at every exit. Did you kill one of them, too?"

"I might have," she said, quietly.

It only caused Hunter's jaw to clench, repeatedly.

"This is your warning," I continued. "Hunter will have to fend for himself if you get put away. He's forbidden to ever return to the top, so you'll be left to worry about whether he dies without your protection. We both know he'll try to escape and when he does, they'll kill him. They're ready, Tessa. Waiting for him to become accessible. They want their chance to taste his blood and they'll take it at the first opportunity. Do you want his death on your hands?"

I held still as Tessa's face grew serious. But Hunter's reaction worried me worse. His eyes scanned the area like a caged animal, only to lower while he moved deeper into his thoughts.

"No, I don't want that. I just want him to love me. He doesn't love me and it's making me mad. He won't even let me get near me half the time. He…" Her eyes went back to him and I couldn't stop myself from blinking past the shock. Something was definitely wrong. She sounded like me.

"Have you completed the second tie?"

Her head shook as she tried to reach for him again. Hunter stepped away from her quickly, turning to me. "I'm not ready for the second tie."

"No?" I moved in as close as I could to him, inhaling deeply. It didn't make sense. He should be going as crazy as I was to have her. Yet, he clearly didn't want to be around her. Not now, and from what Tessa said, clearly not before.

"Why would you wait this long? I thought this is what you both wanted? You were going to start your future. That's what you said," I said, getting louder with anger.

Silence had me raising my hand, questioningly. Hunter glanced at Tessa and couldn't disguise his negative reaction to her presence.

"Hunter. Answer me."

Narrowed blue eyes shot to me. "I'm just not ready, okay? I need time."

Again, he got quiet.

"Hunter, we're talking vampire bonds here. As your leader, I'm telling you to explain."

"Goddammit! I don't give a shit about talking bonds with you. My uncle, a priest, is dead! His head is in that fucking bag. Killed by the woman I..." He paused. "Who am I kidding? She hasn't been Tessa since you first forced your blood on her. She's...evil. Cruel. You all are. There may be moments, like right now, where she's trying to be...something good for me, but she's not! For once, I want to wake up without her hovering over me to rip my throat out. She does that, you know." He pulled the necklace out of his shirt. "If I didn't have the rosary on, she'd kill me. All I wanted was to be with her. Happy, like I'd always dreamed of. But this isn't the way. This...*her*," he said, gesturing angrily, "she's a...she's..."

The honesty left me speechless. Relieved, but shocked, nonetheless. Where I should have felt sorry for him, all I experienced was the greed I harbored to have her myself. It lasted until I took in the tears rolling down Tessa's face. As much as I wanted to bask in the moment, I had bigger responsibilities, ones my position made me aware of.

I pulled a pack of cigarettes from my jacket pocket, lighting one up. The inhale was deep, casting white smoke into the air at my equally forceful exhale. I took another drag, contemplating what to do about the situation. I needed to talk more with Hunter. It was too late for him to leave here. He knew too much. He'd have to stay. But what the hell was I going to do with him? He'd fight it out and try to escape. If I had him killed...Tessa would hate me forever. The longer she stared at him, the more hurt she was appearing. But it wouldn't last. That pain would turn to anger. I knew that for a fact. When it did, things wouldn't be good for him.

"We three need to talk."

"Start talking then," Hunter snapped. "It's not like I have anything else better to do down here. I could probably go to bed, but I'm sick of passing time that way. It's a nightmare either place."

"You're upset because you're grieving," I said calmly. "You need to try to look past that while we figure out what is going on right now."

Tessa walked closer to me. "Let's take this back to the room. I need the quietness. I'm getting...not good. My head." Her hand lifted as she blinked heavily. I knew she was at risk of fading out again and the more upset she became, the bigger the possibility was.

I dropped the cigarette to the floor, grinding my foot against it as I followed her and Hunter through the large room. We all stayed quiet until we were sweeping past her door and she was shutting it behind us. Hunter immediately turned his back to us. I stepped closer to Tessa as she wrung her hands and seemed to catch herself on what she wanted to say.

"What's wrong, ma minette? Something besides your bonding is bothering you. I can feel it." I kept my voice down, allowing Hunter to try to relax. Tessa opened her mouth, only to shut it. Finally, she sighed.

"I keep hearing a name in my head. It repeats and I feel its presence coming closer."

"A name?"

"I don't want to say it."

"It's Sayer," Hunter bit out. "She asked about him earlier. She still doesn't remember who he is."

Dread settled in my chest and I didn't want to think about him. He was getting closer. As her maker, she'd feel that.

"He's the one who turned you, Tessa. But you have no reason to be afraid. I won't let him hurt you. I promise."

"You can't promise her that," Hunter said, spinning around. "You can't promise that! You don't know what he's capable of. He could very well take us to Dallas with him. He'll rape us all over again. Every day, until he decides to finally put us out of our fucking miseries."

"Rape?" Tessa's eyes flared and black began to vine through the green.

"He won't hurt you," I said, turning her to make eye contact with me. "Marie can see the future. Your future is here. Margo won't remove you. You'll stay here, Tessa. You'll be safe."

Her head shook. "I don't think so."

"I promise you. Both of you will stay here. I won't let Sayer take you. You have my word."

Hunter kept his head down as he sat on the edge of the bed. "Unless he kills you first. Then we'll be doomed. We're doomed being here anyway."

"Enough," I growled. "Sayer isn't going to kill me. Now, enough with this. Let's talk about the bond. You both have one tie. Correct?"

"Yes," Tessa answered.

"Is there anything besides Hunter's...*lack of feelings* that stand out to either of you? Anything maybe you've overlooked, by chance?"

"If we overlooked it, how do we know?" The rage Hunter projected had me getting defensive. He was walking a very thin line and I didn't have the patience to deal with it right now.

"I...saw something. Of us," she said to me in a soft voice. "I see lots of things with us lately."

"You do?"

She swallowed hard, glancing at Hunter, but returning to me. "Yes. We were together. All the time. Things were...not always good."

"No," I said, shaking my head. I was going through times much like you are now."

"I know." Tessa licked her lips and stepped closer. "What I saw. It goes together with what I've noticed."

I couldn't stop my brow from furrowing at her words. She was somewhat lucid now, but I could see the darkness laced within her eyes. She wouldn't be thinking clearheaded for long.

"Hunter wears his rosary all the time."

"Yes, I've noticed. What are you trying to get at, ma minette?"

Tessa licked her lips and I could see her searching through her thoughts. "It's kind of blurry. Very hard for me to see things clearly. Why can he when I couldn't? I remember a church. And my hand…it was burning when I held Hunter's dagger."

My stare shot up as it hit me. She was right. The only time Tessa had been able to hold the rosary was when she didn't believe. But I knew Hunter believed in God very much. The relic put off power. Power that went against vampires. Yet, it wasn't burning him or making him sick. And he still had the dagger at his waist.

"I don't know," I whispered, walking closer to the bed and the human. "Maybe…" my stare went to the floor as my mind raced. Why could he? It was as if they weren't bonded at all, yet I knew the tie had completed. They'd both gone through pain. I saw it. But Hunter wasn't obsessed like me, either. What was happening between them? I could smell her in him stronger than ever. Her blood remained, but…

"Hunter, can I taste you?" I walked to the edge of the bed as his eyes cut up angrily. "I won't bite you. Just a small cut. I want to see something."

"No."

"It'll only take a moment."

"I said no."

He turned his glare on Tessa and I knew he was upset that she'd told me.

"Hunter, please." Tessa went to the other side and he looked back between us. It was the same expression he wore before. The caged animal. And maybe he was.

Chapter 18
Hunter

With Marko on one side of me and Tessa on the other, I quickly withdrew my dagger, flying off the bed. There was no way I was going to let them come near me if it meant they were after my blood. Tessa, I hadn't mind feeding via my arm, but there was no way I was letting Marko have a taste. Then he'd have power over me. I was done with having anything to do with these monsters. The last thing I wanted was for him to control me, too.

"Aren't you at all concerned why you're not more infatuated with your future Mistress? You were so ready to love her, but you don't. Not like you should. I want to see the reason."

Closer, Marko came, and I raised the dagger even higher. "She killed my uncle. I have every reason to be upset. Now, get back. It's not going to happen. If Tessa needs to be fed, I'm okay with that, but never you."

Marko's jaw tightened and he brought his hand to his head, closing his eyes. When they reopened, the black color was back.

"I don't want to have to read her thoughts to experience you. It's not the same. I have to taste you myself."

"Why does it matter?" I scooted more to the side of the room as Tessa came around.

"It's not right," he stressed. "Something is going on with one of my vampire's blood and I'm the leader. I have to get to the root of the problem. That means, I *have* to taste you. You're a part of our world now, Hunter. Like it or not, I rule this place. You obey me, and I say get the *fuck* over here." The last was so deep, it made the hair on my arms stand up. The constant fear and uneasiness was getting to me, making me even more unstable. "You can come willingly," he threatened, "or I will take it from you. Your choice."

"Try and I'll kill you."

"Stop it, both of you." Tessa eased forward and I angled my head at her as a warning not to get closer. I still loved her, but I far from trusted her. When she stopped, she was next to Marko. "Hunter, please. We're asking nicely. You have to comply."

"I don't *have* to do anything I don't want to."

"That's it." Marko started forward when Tessa grabbed his arm, but he didn't stop. He jerked out of her grasp, keeping his eye on the dagger. I held it out, breathing through the fear caused by his vampire. Warnings were shooting through me at the rate of a freight train and my legs felt weak and shaky. As he approached, I thrust it forward, right for his chest. He easily dodged the strike, rearing back and catching me across the cheek with the back of his hand. My head shot to the side at the force, but it didn't stop me from slicing lower, just at Marko's stomach area. Fabric tore and he moved back even faster. The next blow he threw at me caught my lips and I felt my teeth tear into the skin on the inside. The blood washing over my tongue sent my rage to massive heights. Back and forth, I swung the knife, going faster with my lunges and thrusts. Marko remained just a step ahead of me, but I'd already forced him across half of the room and he was running out of space. As long as we stayed like this, I stood a chance. What I feared were his mental powers. Luckily, he wasn't using them.

"Where you gonna go?" I asked, swinging my arm at him again. An evil smile was etched on his face and just as my hand went to rise again, he blurred around me, disappearing so fast, I didn't have the time to turn around. A growl sounded just behind my right ear and I felt the rosary ripped free and his fangs bite into my neck brutally. A spasm locked my body from the pain and I felt the dagger fall free. It all happened so fast. Before I could process it, he was gone, clear across to the other side of the room, back by Tessa. The satisfaction on her face tipped the scales on my sanity.

"You fucking bastard." I spun, advancing on him again. The invisible wall that came up easily held me at bay. I slammed my hand against it and turned, contemplating escape, when I ran right into another. Fuck, I was trapped. Completely fucking trapped. And not necessarily in the bubble he had me in. I was trapped in my mind…trapped here. Forever. Escaping would be impossible. I knew this in my heart and although it killed me, there was a certain numbness associated with it. This place would be the death of me. And even if I did luck out and make it above ground…I'd failed in my duty to Tessa. I killed her the same day she admitted her love for me. It was too much.

Marko's head lowered and he looked at the floor. Tessa hugged her arms over her stomach as she stared at him quietly. Minutes passed before he came back to look at me. Those minutes darkened with every second. *I darkened.*

"The two of you aren't tied. You hold Tessa's blood, but no form of a bond is there. With me and Sayer inside her…I'm not sure there ever will be. I think our strength is preventing your ties from happening."

Tessa's lips parted and pain washed over her face. Emotions collided within me and I wasn't sure whether to be upset or relieved.

"I don't understand it," Marko continued. "How you can hold her blood but there be no attachment to the fact…I don't know. And it's weaker than I imagined. You smell so strongly of her, but only because of how powerful she is. Her essence in you is fading. In time, maybe a few weeks, it might very well be gone completely. That is, if she doesn't give you anymore."

"He can't be my slave?" A sob had her lips remaining separated and the bottom one quivered as her eyes filled with tears. "But I feel for him. There has to be a tie. I…love him."

Marko brought up Tessa's arm and made a small incision before moving it to his mouth. As he tasted her, I didn't miss his grip tightening on her forearm. He licked over the wound and rose.

"I'm sorry, ma minette. There's nothing tying you to Hunter. What you feel is the vampire within you. It's the reason you killed for him tonight. The evil is forcing you to prove yourself in ways humans wouldn't do. The way they don't understand," he said, lower. "I'm sorry, Tessa."

"Sorry?" she spat. "You're not sorry. You're probably happy I'm only tied with you. You didn't want Hunter and me together. And now I can't have him as my slave! You…"

Black was entirely taking over her eyes and the poisonous fog she harbored began spinning around her feet, rolling out across the floor as it slinked over the surfaces. I stepped back into the invisible wall, but Marko didn't move. His arm lunged for her throat and he brought the other behind her head, keeping her immobile as his eyes locked with hers in a black death-glare. He looked ready to kill her, but somehow, I knew he wouldn't.

"You stand against your leader? You think you can step up to me?"

The moment his stare broke from hers, Tessa came alive, letting her claws come out and slice toward him. Marko caught her wrist, spinning her around and pinning her against his legs as he sat down. Her dress was jerked up and I felt sick as his hand came down hard, right over her ass. Once. Twice.

Whack!

The third time had a scream coming from her mouth and she thrashed even more as the fourth and fifth connected. Sobs quickly replaced the high-pitched squeal and he spun her over to sit on his lap. Green shown vibrantly in her eyes and I shook my head at him bringing her back so fast. It hurt…it broke my heart. He was the one for her. It was so clear.

"Look at me." His fingers gripped her chin, turning her to face him. She dove into his chest, hugging him tightly before she tried to break free again. The action had him hesitating for seconds before he continued. "You pull that shit again, next time, it'll be worse. Let's get things straight right now. If I was so against Hunter being your slave, would I allow him to stay here in this room with you? Would I have even let him live? I was going to let you keep him and you be my concubine. No, I wouldn't have let the two of you fuck, but that's because you're mine. I can't willingly allow that, Tessa. I'm sorry, I just can't. It's not in me to share you that way. I wish it were. I wish I could give you everything you needed to be happy, but I…can't. I love you. I won't spend every day of my life ready to massacre some human because you need more than his heart." He sat her on the bed and stood, throwing me a glance and dropping the invisible wall as he headed to the door.

Small cries still came from Tessa and I saw her angst as her hand reached for him. She truly did love Marko, whether she wanted to admit it or not. I'd seen it the night I shot her with the stake and even now in her vampire form. Not to mention, the passion that had come when she'd fucked him. I saw everything first hand. Watched as they held to each other like nothing else mattered. It brought me more into my dark thoughts as he stalked out and slammed the door behind him.

And he loved her. The grasp of what they *could* share left me sick. He could control her more than I ever could. I couldn't feed her like Marko. I couldn't even wrestle her down and stop her from killing me or someone else. *Someone like my uncle.* What was I here for aside from leading her on to something neither of us could ever have? I couldn't love her like I wanted. That was gone. Over the months of seeing her murder and connive, I didn't know who she was anymore. Even the small glimpses where I assumed it was my Tessa didn't do it for me. Mine was gone. Dead for real. Yes, I was a killer just as much as they were. This was all my fault and now I had nothing. No one but this monster before me. And she was. One of *my* creation. God, I'd tried to convince myself it would all work out, but she was evil in every way. Murdering my uncle…and then telling the story of how she did it. Bragging, yet threating more death as she held up his head for them all to see. I hadn't been proud that she'd tried to protect me that way. I'd been horrified that she felt nothing for humans—even someone who'd known her since she was a child. She had loved my uncle. And the devil in her killed him.

Cries brought me back to the room and I walked forward, picking up the dagger from the floor. I swallowed hard, knowing what I needed to do. God, it tore me to pieces, but there was no other way around it. I was done. Tessa made me give her my word and I wasn't going to break it. She had to die, and I was going to be the one to do it. I'd kill us both and end this misery once and for all. There was no way I could go on living with the act I was about to commit. I'd killed enough people. Women. Children. My PTSD was bad enough. Between the rapes and dead bodies I'd witnessed on a daily basis from my nightmares, I was finished with the images that plagued my weary mind. I couldn't face my parents or hers ever again if I did this, and it had to be done. She'd crossed too many lines. She was the one thing she didn't want to become and it was up to me to put a stop to it.

Chapter 19
Tessa

To say I didn't have feelings for my leader was a lie. I hated him as much as I yearned for him. But nothing was right. Nothing made sense. I was a puzzle, more to myself than anyone else. There were times I heard Marko's thoughts. I doubted he knew I was listening. Sometimes, I didn't even know what I tapped into until time brought everything back. It always did with him. His voice was the only thing that could pull me from the perplexing abyss of my mind and center me. It unlocked secrets within myself, flooding my vision with images of fights and amazing lovemaking. What I saw as bad in the past, I clung to now, watching with fascination at our lives. Other than telling Marko tonight, no one knew I was regaining my memory. Or how much everything was coming back. And it was…with a vengeance. I was beginning to clear and the person I was becoming was one I was embracing more by the day. I wanted my Master back. I wanted…what I couldn't have. I couldn't have both men. I knew this and Hunter's actions tonight showed me why. That's what had upset me the most. I knew what I had to do.

Pressure gripped tighter around my waist, so unlike how Hunter usually slept, which was as far away from me as he could. For days, I'd tried to get him to love me. I tried fucking hard. He couldn't. Not with the passion I was capable of. Why he was showing me any form of affection now left me trying to figure him out even more.

Thoughts weighed down his mind, I could feel it from his aura. It brought me back to the anger he harbored. I had to make things right with him, regardless of how a part of me didn't seem to see the point of it. But he at least deserved that. *Rape*. Yes…I remembered now. The gruesome memories made my stomach turn and it wasn't necessarily because of what happened to me. It was for him. He'd taken Sayer's brutality to get him away from me and I wouldn't forget it when I killed my maker.

"I'm sorry about what I did to your uncle. I…didn't know you'd be mad." I still didn't understand why he was. I'd killed for him. He should be proud. Honored. That's what I'd thought when I severed the man's head. But Marko's words were coming back. He and I weren't the same. And it was something I was learning the hard way. "I'm sorry about what happened to you with Sayer, too. I really am."

Hunter stiffened next to me, burying his face against the side of mine. "Just go to sleep, Tessa. We'll talk tomorrow."

Sadness pulled at my chest. I hated him not being happy with me. That's what kept me going for so long. I wanted to try to make things work, but they wouldn't. All he ever did was look at me like I was a bad person. Hunter was never satisfied with anything I did. I kept trying to impress him. To show him as his Mistress, I'd do anything for him. Even if all he wanted was someone to talk to, like I knew he wanted most. But every conversation had him looking at me in disgust or disbelief over something I said. I couldn't continue to witness it anymore. He was holding me back. From what, I wasn't sure. Happiness? Peace of mind? I didn't know. Regardless, I couldn't stop the ache I felt for his state of mind. What did I do about him? How did I make him better while also going after what I wanted?

My eyes darted toward the door. From the soft glow of the closet light, I could see the barrier keeping us closed off from everyone. It called to me. Told me to go through it and feel out the one person I wanted to be with. Marko was out there. Marko…

I closed my eyes, feeling for our connection. My brow drew in as his words began to filter through.

"Doesn't she see? How can she not? I'm trying so fucking hard." A sigh filled his mind and I waited quietly while he continued. *"What am I doing? Walking around a room she'll never fucking come to? She doesn't love me."*

"Yes I do."

Silence had me waiting.

"Ma minette…"

"Red silk sheets, a closet full of clothes you believe I'll never wear. You bathe in my soap. Do you miss me so much?"

A small groan echoed through my mind. *"You have no idea. Tessa, I…you know I love you. The pain I feel for not having you with me is the worst torture I've ever gone through. Such sweet torture,"* he said, trailing off.

My eyes opened and I turned more toward Hunter. His lids were down but I knew he wasn't asleep. The vibes he threw off were ones I didn't necessarily like. They made me defensive. They made me…angry. No, I couldn't do this anymore. All I was doing was wasting time. Time, I didn't have. When would I lose my memory again? The episodes were coming less and less, but they still came, regardless.

On instinct, I let my lips separate. I knew our problems were going to take a while to sort out, but I wasn't going to contemplate over them anymore tonight. I had better things. Things I'd been secretly longing for more and more.

Tingling covered my skin as I tapped into my gift. My adrenaline began to race, making my heart thump hard in my chest. Numbness coated my throat and I pushed down the strength of my poison until I felt it was right. Slowly, I let black fog ooze from my mouth. Hunter's body jolted and his eyes flew open, but he didn't move. *Couldn't* move.

"Sleep tight, my dear friend. I love you," I whispered, leaning forward and pressing my lips to his. More crept free and I let it enter his mouth. The breaths that had come out panicked were already deepening, growing leisurely in his almost sleeping state.

"We're going to make you better, Hunter. I promise. Tomorrow," I said, sliding from the bed. The long, red gown I wore was one I'd never thought to sleep in before. Why I'd chosen it tonight was a mystery. Maybe my mind knew, even before I did. Only now was I starting to see the light.

I was Tessalyn Antoinette, the Black Princess. I was going to rule, right next to the man I was meant to. The one like me.

Darkness swallowed me up as my bare feet padded through the tunnel. I'd never been to Marko's room, but I didn't have to know where to go. His heart called to me, even from as far away as we were. Our tie, our soon-to-be bond…it was all I wanted. What I knew I needed to move forward and grow stronger. And I'd do it with him. Together, we'd be one. Just like he wanted. Like I now wanted.

Music played in the distance and it sparked an odd sense of happiness. This was right. My instincts told me that and I never went against them—ever.

I broke into the heart of the city, only to turn into the next tunnel. Lyrics I had no idea I knew flowed quietly from my mouth, echoing against the cement enclosure. Each step sent my heart racing even faster and my singing somehow soothed that. I had no reason to fear, and I didn't. I thrived in this decision. So much so, my whole body was shaking.

Light flooded the space at the end and a tall, dark silhouette stepped into the tunnel. I didn't wait. I couldn't. I broke into a sprint, racing toward Marko. Toward what my clear mind said it wanted more than anything.

"Oh, Jesus," he moaned, sweeping me into his arms and crushing his lips to mine. My arms wrapped around his neck and I thrust my tongue into his mouth, moaning at all the pent up lust and passion I carried for him. Fingers gripped my back, pulling me as close as he could get me. "What are you doing, ma minette? *What are you doing?*" There was pain was in his voice as he spun me through the door, shutting it behind him. "You're trying to kill me, aren't you? You'll go back to him. You'll leave after we're finished."

My head shook as I met his mouth again. I had to taste more of him. I was desperate and I couldn't get enough. When I finally pulled back, I switched to our language. Ours, because we were right. We were each other's pair. "I've chosen. Hunter and I…it's not meant to be. We're not the same. I see that now. I choose you. We are going to do this together. That's what we agreed. It's what I want. Together, we'll rule."

His eyes held mine and a smile broke out on his face just before he kissed me again.

"We'll rule," he said, pulling back and nodding. "But what about Hunter? What do you feel I should do with him? I can't let him go, Tessa. He knows too much."

I blinked past the possibilities. I had no idea the workings of our world, but I knew what he spoke was true. Safety of our kind was ingrained in me. It ruled just as much as Marko and I would.

"He has to be happy. That's all I want."

"We'll figure it out. I promise." He fisted the red nightgown I wore, twisting it in his hand as he turned us toward the bed. He sucked my bottom lip into his mouth and I moaned, pushing into him even more. "I never thought I'd get to experience this, here. Not so soon."

I looked down at the bed. Although I'd heard him describe it in his mind before, I wasn't prepared for the beauty and elegance of what was before me. I stared in awe, almost feeling like I was in a dream as he pulled back the comforter and laid me down.

No matter what he wanted, I couldn't remain lying down. I rose to my knees, grabbing the hand holding onto his tie. Our stares held and he let me pull it free. The jacket fell to the floor at his shrug and one by one, I slid the buttons free. His pale skin drew me in and I let my mouth travel between his pecs, licking and nibbling as I moved down to trail over his defined abs. A moan vibrated his body and I let my nails push into his sides while I sank my teeth in harder.

The shirt was next to fall to the floor but I barely realized as I worked his belt free and unclasped his pants. The scent of his arousal had me pushing them down his legs and all I could do was lick my lips at the hard cock before me. To taste him…yes, I had to.

Fingers weaved through my hair, following as I lowered my head. Pre-cum beaded the thick tip and I flattened my tongue, sliding it over the smoothness.

"Oh…ma minette. Fuck." Heavy breaths left him and he tightened his hold on my hair while I circled around his thick girth, basking in the power I held. Marko may have been my leader, but here I secretly reigned. I could feel our powers against each other's and in this moment, he let me take the lead. For how long, I wasn't sure. I could remember our lovemaking when I was human. He liked to fuck me roughly. And I wanted him to. I wanted him to control me as much as I controlled him.

"Tell me you love me." I looked up, meeting his heavily lidded eyes, but I didn't stop pleasuring him. I needed to hear the words. My vampire craved it.

"I love you."

"To death?" I finished.

"Yes," he smiled. "And nothing will change that."

My stare stayed on his as I opened wide, letting his length slide over my tongue. Lower, his lids fell, but he didn't close his eyes. That meant more to me than I could have thought. Marko wouldn't turn his back on me. His feelings would never go away. I saw it in his depths, holding the truth as I took him to the back of my throat. Small sounds filled the room and I stored them away, never wanting to forget what I could bring him. I did this. Me. And it was coming from him. That made the moment perfect. His moans were flawless and more beautiful than any music I could ever remember hearing.

I pulled back, tracing the head of his cock over my lips. "Tell me again."

The smile that came dazzled me. He jerked back my hair, lowering his face to hover just above mine. "I fucking love you more than any human or vampire ever will. Even death, itself, will not separate us. I won't let it. Why, ma minette? Why won't I let it?"

It was my turn to smile. "Because together, our love will be more immortal than we are. Amour immortel."

"Let anyone try to tear us apart. I'll set the world in flames before I let Sayer or Axis take you away from me. You're consenting. You're here and telling me you love me. Tomorrow, you may forget this, but I'm going to assure you every day of this moment we're in right now. Even if I have to show you a million times." His other hand came to my face, holding me even more trapped. And I loved it. "You. Are. Mine. Say it."

"I am you. You are me…we are one."

"Then we'll make it official. Right now. I'm not letting you go again. I can't."

Marko dropped his hands and reached down, pulling up his pants. He quickly secured them before grabbing his shirt. Doubt or insecurities weren't within me. I knew what he meant. What he wanted. I stood while he buttoned the bottom half of his shirt. Dark hair fell forward, resting on the side of his forehead as he reached for his jacket. My hand went out, stopping him.

"Like this. Just as you are now. I want to remember this night laced with our passion. Your shirt," I said, trailing my finger down the exposed part of his chest. "Your hair, just this way." I reached up, touching the strands next to his right eye. "Yes…like this."

Marko pulled me into his arms, kissing me hard before he led me to the closet.

"You may be fine with me like this, but if you're going to be my concubine, you're not going in red. You…can't," he said, glancing over at me. "There are traditions, even in our world." His hand rose to settle on a white gown resting at the very front.

"This is what you are going to wear. With this," he said, moving to the next hanger.

A black silk robe hung down to the floor, the member's symbol embroidered largely in gold on the back.

"I had hoped. I…prayed you'd want this. I made sure to prepare."

My fingers rose to travel over the soft material before I pushed to my toes, gently sealing our lips. "I shall wear it then."

Knocking at the door had his head turning. "That's Marie. The other members are gathering as well. As is the rest of the community." A grin pulled at his mouth. "It's good to be leader. I've been wanting to make this call now for what feels like forever." He searched my eyes and took a deep breath. "You're so sure and I'm relieved. I promise you're making the right decision. This time, I'll be better. This time, I'll show you how much I really love you."

He stepped back, placing himself in the threshold. "I have to go and get everything organized. I'll see you out there."

I nodded, swallowing hard as he continued to retreat. I didn't want him to leave. This moment was right, but if he left, what if it disappeared?

"Smile, my soon-to-be concubine. You're going to make the most beautiful bride a leader has ever had."

The sincerity and love in his words had me obeying, but I couldn't shake the fear beginning to settle in the pit of my stomach. Maybe it was only jitters, but I wasn't so sure.

Chapter 20
Hunter

Shifting on the mattress left my body swaying even more in the dark emptiness I floated in. I tried turning to face Tessa, but I felt heavy despite being so free. My mind tugged, reminding me I had been thinking something, but for the life of me, I couldn't bring back those thoughts. I felt tired; too exhausted to try to force them to return. They weren't very good ones anyway—at least, from what I could remember.

Fabric rustled and cool air brushed down my side as the covers were pulled back. Again, I tried to open my eyes, but they refused. At this point, Tessa could just drink my blood. She'd probably kill me and I suddenly didn't care about that either.

Kill. Death.

Like a wave, the memories came flooding back. She couldn't kill me, I had to kill her first. That way, I could assure we were both dead. Then we could be together again, like we were meant to. She wouldn't be a vampire and we'd be free of this nightmare.

My hand jolted into a fist and surprisingly, my eyes fluttered open. Blond hair hanging toward me had me sobering immediately. My hand jerked up to the rosary only to realize it was gone. Marko had broken it when he'd pulled it free of my neck.

"Did you miss me, pet? I have to say, I missed you *a lot*. So much more than I thought possible."

My hands backtracked, shooting to his chest, but Sayer's strength easily pinned them down. Tessa's name exploded in my mind and I turned my head quickly, feeling my heart sink.

"Where's Tessa?"

His lip peeled back, exposing his fangs. "Probably fucking her precious Marko. But it makes this perfect for us, doesn't it? Just me, you, the entire bed to ourselves, no screams in the background. Well, not hers anyway."

A smile appeared and I bucked my hips, thrashing my body to try to break him free.

"That's not going to happen again, Sayer. No more."

"You're wrong. It'll happen every day now for as long as I allow you to live. You see, I might not have won in getting Tessa to come back with me, but I petitioned Axis on letting me keep you. And they've agreed. You're mine now, Hunter, and there's nothing you, Marko, or even Tessa, can do about it."

Fear turned my blood cold and I refused to believe this was how things were going to end.

"I'll kill you first. You're not taking me anywhere."

Sayer put both of my hands in one of his as if my struggles were nothing. It left my breaths shallow. Sweat began to collect over my skin regardless that my insides felt like ice.

"Someone forgot their place. It's okay though, I'll retrain you."

My eyes jerked to the bedside table where my belt rested. He followed my gaze, laughing.

"Not going to happen, pet. Face your fate. You're mine now." Like I was nothing, he forced me over, grasping to the gym shorts I wore and jerking them down. A fire exploded within me while I felt my muscles tear at the strength I used to try to fight my way away from him. Still, it wasn't enough.

"Perfect. Keep going. I love your determination."

Pressure landed in the middle of my back, cementing me to the mattress as I felt him jerk at his belt and pants. Tears stung my eyes and I refused to believe this was happening again. At least, this time, Tessa wouldn't have to witness my humiliation. But she wouldn't be here to buffer my pain either.

Sayer's arm wrapped around my neck in a chokehold and I went still, panting through the fury that left me trembling. But this wasn't over. My belt may have been on the table, but my dagger was with me, right here under my pillow. All I had to do was let him drop his guard and I'd finish this once and for all.

"Your smell. I can't tell you how much I missed it." Sayer's face lowered. The room tilted from my panic, but I focused on his movements, trying not to allow what was about to happen enter into my mind.

The wetness I heard as he took his free hand from his mouth to stroke down his cock was enough to make me gag. My eyes shut, trying to ignore how his bicep was tightening, cutting off my air.

"You're going to like it in Dallas. I'm going to make you my slave and you'll be the envy of every vampire and human there. I'm a God and soon, you'll see just how lucky you are. You're going to want me all the time and I'm going to fuck you everywhere. Maybe right there in front of everyone. They'll love seeing you. They'll love tasting you, too, if I allow them."

The head of dick pushed against my opening and I grunted, unable to stop myself from swinging my shoulders back and forth.

"You want it the other way? All you had to do was say so."

Once again, he rolled me over so I was on my back. My hand shot under the pillow and I left it there, being still as he stared at me.

"So, you're going to give me your blood then? To make me your slave?"

Sayer cocked his head to the side. "Is that what you want? After my bite, I thought you might want to taste me. I should have tied you to me long ago." He got quiet. "You hold Tessa's blood, but no tie. I bet her bite didn't compare to mine. Mine was phenomenal, wasn't it?"

"Yes," I forced myself to say. I flinched as he reached down, grasping my cock. My fingers touched the hilt of the dagger and I brought my hand up even more as I rocked my hips, pretending to enjoy the way he stroked me. Sayer never took his eyes off me and I knew I was probably throwing red flags. My brain scrambled and I felt even sicker as I continued. "It…did feel good," I admitted. "I hate that I liked it. But rape, beatings...Hell is waiting for you, Sayer, and I'm your one-way ticket. Did you really think I'd let you get away with what you've done? What you made me do?" I shook my head. "Tell the devil he needs to prepare for my arrival. I'll be there shortly."

Sayer laughed under his breath, dismissing my words as he positioned himself again.

"Lord Jesus, I ask in Your Holy Name..."

Sayer's body jolted above me and his eyes turned black as they shot to mine. Louder, I began the prayer, using the delay I noticed with Marie and Bufar to lung forward, thrusting the dagger right through his heart as he dove toward me. Blood dripped over my face and into my mouth as his hands shot down to try to grasp around my throat. But he didn't have the strength he did before. I broke his hold and his weight collapsed into me. I bolted out from underneath, pushing his body to the side and withdrawing the dagger, repeatedly stabbing it into where I knew his heart was. This time, I wouldn't miss.

Grunts and deep sounds filled the room and he repeatedly gasped. I didn't think as I pulled up my shorts and scrambled away, grabbing my large knife from the sheath attached to my belt.

The mattress shifted under my weight and I crawled up, moving in next to the man who'd fucked up my life more than anyone had. The side of his neck was exposed and I immediately thrust down the thick blade, piercing his skin. The loud cry quickly died and his body spasmed as I sawed through the toughness of his neck, severing his head. He wouldn't come back. He couldn't. I wasn't going to let him hurt anyone else.

Cramps sparked in my stomach so strong, for minutes, I couldn't move. I wasn't sure what was happening. I'd taken his blood when he'd hovered above me, but he was dead. Surely it had to do with that. Regardless, I couldn't think about possible repercussions. I wasn't done. I still had one more person to kill. Maybe two, and I knew just where to find her.

I removed the dagger and grabbed my gun from my belt, checking the ammunition. It had a full clip, but I'd only need one bullet. One shot for me to finally end this thing once and for all. I'd save Tessa. We'd finally be together again. We'd be happy, and she'd be free from the hell that was her life now. After all, Marie was right. If I couldn't have the Tessa I was meant for, Marko wouldn't have this version of her either. I'd make sure of it. If I had to kill him in the process, so be it. I'd be doing him a favor, too. Hell, I'd be doing the world a service. With both Sayer and Marko gone, humans might possibly stand a chance.

Blood covered my chest and I could feel it sticking to my face. If someone saw me like this...if they smelled the blood on me...

I raced to the bathroom, grabbing a towel and wetting it. Hard, I scrubbed, but I didn't have the time I needed to make sure I was completely free of the dark red substance. I had to go. To get to Tessa before someone came here first.

Slowly, I pulled the door open, not even bothering to put on a shirt or find shoes. The cool air bit into my bare limbs and feet, but I kept a fast pace toward the end of the tunnel. Loud voices and noise had me slowing until I eased to face the city head on. Masses of people were gathered around. At the head of them, with his back to me, was the male vampire I wished I could kill. My eyes scanned the surroundings, spotting Marie heading in Marko's direction, but Tessa was nowhere to be found. Quietly, I eased out, racing not ten feet away to his tunnel. I didn't stop running through the darkness until I got to where his door was. A small sliver of light was my only clue to the location and I prayed I was right. I clenched to my gun harder before I tucked it into the back of my shorts and thrust the door open.

"I'll be right there, Marie."

Tessa voice rang out weakly in the distance and I walked in, shutting the barrier behind me. A mass of white and black silk billowed out around her as she staggered from a door in the back. The paleness she'd been before didn't compare to the ghostly appearance she held now. Tessa came to an abrupt stop, separating her lips as she stared at me.

"Hunter...I..." Sadness etched into her features, but I didn't care. Didn't feel anything but justification for what I was doing.

"Wow, look at you." I clutched the dagger tighter, holding it at my side as I stepped forward. "You look beautiful. Something you want to tell me?"

She didn't have to say a word. I knew what she was doing. With the mass of people gathering, it was all too clear. And I'd come at the perfect time. *Fate.*

"I'm sorry. I..." Again, she was at a loss for words. Her hand rose to her head and she swayed a little. "I love him," she said lowly. "I see that now."

I nodded, leisurely, twisting my mouth and shrugging. "I know you do. This is for the best, I think. You and I would have never worked in this life. We're too different. Incompatible, I guess you could say."

"Yes," Tessa breathed out, heavily. "I'm so glad you see it that way. You don't know how relieved I am to hear you say that." Tessa reached up, pulling back the black silk hood, revealing beautifully decorated hair. Diamond pins glistened throughout the mass of curls sitting on top of her head. She looked every bit the Princess and ruler she was meant to be.

"Marko and I are going to make sure you're happy here. We'll take care of you. Maybe you can find a vampire who will treat you well. Who you can love and who can love you."

Her enthusiasm was so fake. So forced. She knew it was just as impossible as I did. I'd never love one of these monsters. They didn't deserve love, they deserved death.

"I'm sure everything will work out just as it should. Here, come to me. You don't look like you're feeling very well." I let my free hand rise, but her attention went to the dagger I held. Her features pulled in and she returned her stare to mine.

"Hunter...there's blood on your dagger. Did you hurt someone?"

Closer, I got, but she didn't move away. She barely looked able to stand. "Sayer. He's back. But he's not going to hurt anyone anymore. I made sure of that."

"You...killed him?" Tessa's hand shot out to the open air and her eyes rolled back as she began to fall. I knew what she was feeling was linked to his death and although fear for her safety was present way back in the distance of my mind, I didn't let myself think about it. I rushed forward, catching her just before she connected with the hard floor. Her body was limp in my arms as I lowered us both. White silk from the skirt of her wedding dress pooled around us and the fact that she was wearing one for him and never me pushed me over the edge. She was meant to be *my* wife. *My* partner and soulmate. I couldn't have the first two in this life, but I'd make the third a reality. Our souls would belong together. We'd be forever tied in a place far, far away from here.

"I made a promise to take care of you and I'm going to do that now. No more pain, Tessa. I'm going to save us. We're going to be together again. That's how much I love you." My voice cracked as I brought up the dagger. Tears raced down my cheeks and a sob escaped as I focused on her chest. The silk top was beaded with more diamonds and I hated how beautiful she looked. This could have been what she would have worn for me had Marko not came along.

Bile tried to push free, but I held it in, using the focus to force my hand down as hard as I could. The dagger pierced through the material, burying deep inside of her chest. A gasp had her eyes flying open wide, connecting right with mine.

"No, shh," I whispered, hurriedly. "Go back to sleep, baby. This is only a dream. Only a dream," I repeated. "I love you. See?" I took the gun out of the back of my shorts, flashing it before I moved further down to lay beside her. Horror masked her flawless face while I pulled her in closer to face me. My hand was trembling as I brought the barrel to my mouth. The metal was cold against my tongue and I bit into it hard to stop the chattering of my teeth. Tessa's whimpers were growing louder, but definitely weaker.

"Hu-nter...noooo." She managed a sob that shook both of our chests. One I couldn't stand to feel. I was done. We were done.

The pounding of heavy footsteps in the distance made my pulse jump. He was coming. He knew...but he wouldn't win this time. It was too late.

My eyes connected with Tessa's light green ones and flashes of friends and family began blinding me. Tessa's smile stretched across her face as she waved me closer. We were still young. Still so happy. Tears. Yes, I was crying. Further, my finger pulled back and a sound escaped me involuntarily.

"Tessa!" The echoing roar that grew closer didn't disrupt my moment.

Cold bit into my skin from the cool breeze rustling the leaves in the trees. Winter was in full swing in Austin, but we didn't care. All we wanted was to be together, and now we would. I was going to turn back time. I was going to mend this right here and now.

"Do you think we'll always be this happy, Hunter?"

Dark hair blew back from the gust of wind and I smiled, pressing my lips into Tessa's as we sat on her parent's porch swing. She was staring at me with all the love I felt for her. The green of her eyes were darker and her lips were only a light pink. Yes, she looked perfect. She was human. This was the way things were meant to be. The way things would end.

"I know we will be. Forever. I'll make sure of it. There's nothing I wouldn't do for you, Tessa."

BAM!

To be continued…

RULE

Marko Delacroix #4

BEST SELLING AUTHOR
ALASKA ANGELINI

RULE

Marko Delacroix #4

Best Selling Author
Alaska Angelini
Copyright © 2015 by Alaska Angelini

ISBN:

All Rights Reserved

Prologue
Axis Headquarters

"Breaking tonight. Riots plague the streets of Los Angeles. From what started out as a peaceful demonstration to bring awareness to the growing vampire violence within the United States and the World, turned into complete and utter chaos.

Good evening, everyone. I'm Jane Branson.

Blood fills the streets of downtown Los Angeles. Where not hours ago, a large group of gatherers held hands and chanted for peace—tonight, bodies of those protesters line the sidewalks, waiting to be identified.

It all happened shortly after sunset. Greg Mathers is here to tell us more. Greg?"

"Thank you, Jane. It wasn't a few minutes after eight o'clock when the first vampires began to take their place on the other side of the street from those demonstrators. Although they held similar signs aimed toward the unity of the two races, what no one expected was the massacre that quickly ensued.

"Reports gathered so far aim toward the vampires being the ones who initiated this latest outbreak of mayhem. We came across a witness who was at the scene where it all began. Sir, can you tell us what you saw?"

"Man, it was crazy. One minute we were standing there, doing our thing, the next, this vampire starts walking across the street, right at us. His eyes ... they ... they just started getting all dark. Like, the colored part turned black. He was staring at us all evilly, hissing, and then ... he just like ... blurred at a fast sprint. All hell broke loose. People were screaming and trying to run. I thought I was going to die."

"Can you to tell us what happened after the vampires rushed the protesters?"

"I just did. They all started attacking us. People were getting their throats ripped out—women, dudes ... even this little girl who wasn't far away from me. They just killed her—dead. Shots started going off and tear gas was thrown in and set off right in the middle of all of us. I couldn't breathe. But it didn't stop them. They kept coming. Kept..."

"I can clearly see you're getting upset. Thank you."

"Damn right I'm upset! The cops couldn't do shit. They don't die! We have to stop them before it's too late. We have to—"

"Thank you, Greg. Be careful out there."

"You just heard from our reporter and a witness, on scene. You can clearly see their emotions run high tonight. As do all of ours for the families that lost their loved ones."

"The growing debate on whether our government made the right decision to allow vampires to walk unimpeded amongst us continues, as does the death toll on both sides. While some push for the benefits the vampire race provides to our sick *and dying, others say the consequences far outweigh the medical positives of their blood."*

"Tonight, we'll discuss those benefits with Dr. Rakul Chilton, as well as get the opinion of retired Lt. Colonel Dan Rutgers on his take of these recent riots. And that leads us to our top story tonight. Will the riots in New York, Chicago, and now Los Angeles get a reaction from our silent White House, or will the whispers of a war between the two races continue to grow?"

Chapter 1
Marko

Silence was never truly devoid of sound. Even when you eliminated outside sources and got close to reaching the desired state, there were always things like the heart that still thrummed. The steady rhythm was impossible to stop, just like thoughts. The two together were the loudest of all things when you wished to make everything stop. And I did want it to cease—the beating of my aching heart, my agonizing, mournful, grieving cries that screamed to me from within for peace. *Silence.* The act wasn't for the weak. Although, I *was* weak at the moment.

I was heartbroken.

"Master Delacroix…it's time."

My head lifted, rising so I could glare at Bufar. From where I was sitting on the edge of my bed, he stood a good ten feet away. He suddenly knew it wasn't nearly far enough. The aura around me was just as toxic as the taunting voices that begged me to obliterate everything I could. To kill everyone within my reach so their loved ones could feel the crippling sensations that festered within me. Why should they get to have what I'd never feel again? It wasn't fair. None of this was.

Bufar backtracked more toward the door as I tried to rein in the need to destroy him for interrupting me. Did he not know what I was going through? Did he not care for his leader enough to grasp that I'd just lost the only woman I had ever loved? That she was dead and never coming back?

"The meeting today is cancelled," I managed. "Send me Margo."

Bufar's eyes narrowed as he gave a quick shake of his head. "I…" Another shake. "Master Delacroix, I told you yesterday, she's gone."

I blinked through the confusion. My mind wasn't right. It hadn't been since I had found Tessa on the floor with the dagger in her chest. Had Hunter's brains not been blown across my floor, there would have been no hesitation on my part to tear him to shreds for what he'd done. But they had been, and all my focus had been on my bride … still in her wedding dress. The one I'd put such care into having designed and made just for our special day.

Dead. I couldn't bring myself to believe it.

"Send me Marie."

Again he paused. "She's at Axis with Margo. There needed to be a witness to report the accident."

"Murder," I exploded, pushing to my feet. "Tessa was *murdered*, right here in our fucking room. Right there!" I pointed. "On our bonding day. She would have been my concubine. My—" I quickly stopped. Boiling was taking over my insides, teasing the power within. To unleash would have been heaven in the hell I was living. Was this what I had to bear for the rest of my life? Hundreds of years of more suffering? God, what was I going to do without her?

"Yes, Master. Murder. I apologize."

My jaw clenched as I continued to take him in like a meal. I could kill him so easily. He was my second and I could have eaten him alive. I knew it, just as I knew my power continued to grow at an alarming rate. *Especially now.*

"Tell the other members I will go to them when it is time. Do not bother me again."

"Yes, Master."

Bufar slipped out of the door at a fast pace and left me to the loud voices that reappeared in my head. I sat back down, leaning forward to stare back at the spot where Tessa had taken her last breath. I could still see it as clear as the moment it happened. I'd been crying. Me … crying. I never thought I'd see the day, but the tears had poured from my eyes in a constant stream while I prayed to a God I wasn't sure even existed.

"No." My head shook as she stared up at me with fearful eyes. *"Don't you dare say you love me as a way to say goodbye. You're not going anywhere, ma minette. I won't let you. God…"* Talking was almost impossible through the sobs that kept pushing their way free. Maybe I knew even then that no amount of my blood would save her from a wound that severe. The dagger being blessed had been her undoing. She wasn't powerful enough to survive a direct blow like that.

I'm…sorry. I…love you. I do."

I cried harder, holding her tighter in my arms. Margo was talking with Marie. About Hunter, I had assumed, but I heard nothing but each beat of Tessa's heart. I held to the rhythm like nothing else mattered. And it didn't. Her life was mine.

"Let me have her." Margo's dark brown eyes connected with mine as she knelt before us. My head shook as my arms held Tessa tighter.

"She stays where she is." I wasn't going to let her die alone, and without me holding her or communicating with her, she would be alone.

"Master Delacroix, give her to me."

Movement had me looking over her shoulder to see collectors taking Hunter's body away. I growled, snapping my focus back on Margo. *"If you're going to help save her, do it as you are now."*

"Ma-rko?" Deep breaths became rapid and broken up. My pulse jumped to a dangerous speed as desperation and panic began to set in. I recut my exposed wrist, trying to force down more blood, but it was pointless. The coughing began and then came her own blood, filling her mouth.

"Marko Delacroix!" Margo's voice echoed in my head. Her call and threat warped into one. Over and over I could hear one of the high leaders yelling my name. I wouldn't let myself think past that point. I couldn't see Tessa die again. I couldn't relive that.

Fucking Hunter. I should have known. He'd been a God damn mess when I had left them that night. The guy had just lost his uncle the priest because of Tessa. How could I have assumed he wouldn't retaliated against her? *How?* Because I thought his love wouldn't allow him. Mine wouldn't have. Then again, vampires didn't feel the same about death as humans did. Emotions were involved with the living. After hundreds of years, we rarely felt anything. Especially grief. Although … I was feeling it more than I ever had now, alive or dead.

Hunter. Hunter. I stood in my rage, walking in circles, doing my best to avoid the area where the two of them had died.

My steps faltered, only to continue in my perplexed state. I didn't like that I hadn't gotten closure. Hunter's body had been moved out so fast, it made my head spin. Not to mention my floor sanitized. They were scrubbing the area so thick with bleach and water, I could still smell the remnants days later. Days … how many days had it been? Two? Three? Fuck, I didn't even know.

I groaned, running my hands through my hair. It was probably for the best. If I had to have been left with his body in here for long, there was no telling what I would have done. Still…why did I feel off? Was I still in shock?

Burning laced my throat and I closed my eyes at the renewed surge of misery. The trigger to feed was nothing more than a reminder that I'd never taste Tessa again. Why had I let myself accept happiness in that small amount of time she'd chosen me? My dreams, my wishes, they all suddenly had been answered. I let myself imagine only feeding from each other—surviving from each other. She and I were going to be pure of other contaminants. Of other suppliers. We would have been *one* in the true sense.

Deep pants left me as both of my hands laced in my hair. I gripped tightly, suppressing the need to scream at the top of my lungs. Pain flared in my knees as I hit the ground, but I didn't care about the pain. Nothing would ever surpass the hole that was now in my heart.

Why? Was this payback for all the evil I'd done throughout the centuries? It had to have been. I had always thought that I would be rewarded for the hell I had gone through. What I neglected to see was that although I had suffered, I'd also made others endure just as much. It was a never-ending cycle, repeating in never-ending bouts of despair. And I had to learn to accept that.

Chapter 2

Far away laughter brought my eyes open. I'd been dreaming. Even as I went through the motions of watching Tessa run toward me, I knew what I was seeing wasn't real. It hadn't even happened when she was alive. Not like that. Not outside, above ground during the day. For one, we weren't human. For me to have dreamed of something as stupid as going into the sunlight to find her spoke of just how far I had fallen. And how much I'd lost my mind.

A groan came from my mouth as I turned on my side. The cement was cold against my cheek. I was getting sick, I knew that, but I didn't care. My eyes connected with where Tessa had last been and I stared ahead in a daze.

Had I really let them take her away from me?

My memory skipped over her death, refusing to let the smallest detail in, while I focused on what happened afterward. Something…

The more I tried to conjure the events, the more I blinked. Slowly, I pushed to sit. Where *had* they taken her, and why had I allowed it?

The fog was finally starting to clear as I pushed to stand. If she was dead, surely her body would be somewhere. A coffin in the memorial room? Julius would be there. All leaders and royalty had a place, and Tessa had been The Black Princess.

Why hadn't I thought of this before?

I broke from the room, trying to ignore the sweat that had my shirt sticking to me. Nausea was damn near debilitating. It was hard to run. Hard to breathe with the fire that singed the back of my throat.

Light opened up at the end of the tunnel and I staggered into the heart of the underground city, jolting to an abrupt stop at the flowers that rested along the perimeter of the large room. The sight crippled me. Had I almost convinced myself that Tessa wasn't dead? After all, I couldn't see her body. I didn't have it.

Stares turned to me and I sidestepped toward the nearest tunnel. It was Tessa's old tunnel. No, I couldn't go in there to disappear. I shouldn't be hiding for these people, *my* people, but I just couldn't face anyone yet.

"Master?"

I took a deep breath, smelling Natalia before I saw her. The power of her blood called to the killer in me. My fangs shot down and I immediately threw up a wall to block out the scent.

"Marko?"

I turned, facing her. From the widening in her eyes, I couldn't imagine what she saw. I hadn't looked at myself in days. If I appeared as sick as I felt, no doubt my skin was paler than normal and my eyes, bloodshot to hell.

"Master, we have to get you to your room. I'll call a supplier … or three."

My head shook and I took a step, only to stop. What was I doing? Tessa, yes. I scanned the heart of the city, trying to remember where the correct tunnel was. I couldn't and it left me spinning even more. This was my home so why did I feel so lost?

"I want to see Tessa. Where is she?"

Valencia approached with John, stopping next to Natalia. My head cocked to the side as I watched them look me over. I knew they were preparing for some sort of outburst or attack on my part. Did they really think me that far gone? Hell, I couldn't blame them. I didn't even know what day it was, or for how long I'd been locked away in my room. Time didn't exist in my world.

"Where's Tessa?" My voice was more demanding. More impatient as they stared.

"She's gone," Valencia said, softly.

"I know she's gone," I snapped. "Where's the memorial room? That's where she's at, isn't it?"

The three vampires looked at each other, confused. It only made me even more pissed. "Master, she's not here in the city. Margo took her to Axis. She was the last of her line. She rests in *their* memorial room, where she should."

My heart felt as though it dropped free from my chest, right into my stomach. Burning increased and I tried not to collapse from the weakness.

"I … must have forgotten that, too."

"You've lost your bonded," Valencia continued. "We know you're going through a hard time right now."

Tessa and I hadn't technically been bonded, but almost. Regardless, we were mates, and I'd always refer to her as my concubine. That's who she was, vows or not.

"You need to feed, Master. Let's go to your room and I'll allow you my vein. You need someone with strength. Humans will not do for as far gone as you are."

"No." I shook my head, wildly, at the thought. No vampire deserved to take Tessa's place. It would have to be a human. Their blood was weak. It would dilute faster, which is what I wanted. "I'll take a supplier. After…" I looked at the tunnel that held the collectors. "After I check on something."

"Down there?" Natalia was following my gaze and it was clear she knew. "You want to see the human? He's been dead for over a week."

A week. Was that all it had been? It had felt like an eternity.

"I have to see."

She gave a nod, but lifted her hand. "If you'll please allow me to call in a supplier before you do."

My lids closed slowly though my aggravation. "I am fine. I will see Hunter and then I will feed. Now, if you'll excuse me." I turned, trying to keep my posture straight while I made my way to the tunnel. The moment darkness surrounded me, my shoulders caved, but not for long. Movement headed in my direction. Two humans. They were collectors. My knowledge came from Julius' blood within me. There wasn't anyone's history in the underground city that I didn't know. Their names, ages, even their personality types filtered through and I focused on it long enough for them to pass. My claws were extended, as were my fangs. The demon inside of me went wild and it took every ounce of restraint I had to make it through the door at the end. The moment I broke through, lightheadedness slammed into me. The smell of death was so overwhelming it was sickening.

Bodies were piled in the corner. The closer I got, the more their identities began to register—suppliers, collectors, four vampires … humans who didn't belong here. But not Hunter.

My eyebrows drew in for only a moment before anger flared. Someone was taking humans from the top and bringing them underground. It wasn't allowed. Not for kills. Kills were meant to stay above. From the looks of things, someone had grown comfortable breaking the rules.

"Master Delacroix?"

I turned, eyeing the collector who stood a good distance away.

"Where's the human? The one who committed suicide."

The tall blond man glanced to the side before his lips parted. "The soldier?"

"That's right," I said, walking closer. "Where's his body?"

Confusion masked his features before he glanced to the far left at the furnace. "Sir, we burn them. The human was here, but I only saw him once. I assume he's already gone."

Gone. The word kept crawling under my skin, enraging me past the point of sanity.

"How often are the bodies burned? Once a day? A week?"

I could have easily pried into his memories … his knowledge. If I wasn't feeling so weak, perhaps I would have. Even through death hung heavily in the air, I could smell the collector's blood, teasing the vampire in me.

"Usually every other day. Sometimes three can go by before the collector on duty gets around to disposing of the bodies."

I nodded, reaching up, tempted to pull at my hair. Nothing was going as I wanted. If I could have seen Hunter, maybe a part of me might have been able to move forward. Now all I felt was more frustrated than ever. And I'd never move past this. At least not anytime soon.

"Thank you." I turned to leave, catching something glistening from the opposite side of the room. My steps faltered and I switched my route, heading toward the small reflection on the floor. The closer I got, the sicker I felt. The pure aura warned me back, but I couldn't stop. I knew what I was looking at. I knew who it belonged to.

Sitting by the exit of the room lay Hunter's rosary. Everything in me wanted to lower to pick it up, but I knew better. Normally, I could have touched it, but in my state, the relic would have burned right through my skin like acid. And probably at a faster rate. I turned, waving the collector over who was still staring at me.

"What is this doing here?" Even as I asked, I took in the barrier that blocked off the tunnel. It had a door in the middle. Anyone could come through or leave from it. Not that I thought Hunter would have been doing much walking. Not in his condition. No human could withstand a gunshot wound to the head. Not even if Tessa's blood would have still been within him. She hadn't been that strong. It would have taken… My head shook. It wasn't worth thinking about. Or perhaps my mind was grasping at straws for some form of closure or revenge. Hunter was dead. Even if by some off the wall chance he'd taken blood from someone more powerful … like Sayer … he wouldn't have survived. He couldn't have.

"Never seen it before," the collector said, picking it up.

"I have. It was the human's. Why would it be all the way over here?"

The man shrugged. "Must have fallen out when we were transferring the body."

"We? You mean to tell me you were one of the men to take him from my room?" Fury was seeping back in. Seeping back, because I couldn't remember. My attention had been on Tessa as I soaked in her last moments.

"Yes, Master. I was one of the men."

Before I could stop myself, I was lunging toward him. A hiss left my mouth, muffling as my fangs sunk into his neck. Memories and more information of who he was all barreled into me. The bright colors of days flashed and I sped through his life before the underground at astronomical speed. I could feel myself soak in who he was like a sponge, feeding me strength that normally wouldn't have done anything for me. Yet, in the moment, they were a shot of speed to my weak self. My adrenaline raced, making my pulse slam hard into my chest.

I felt the moment the human received the internal call on that horrible day. It wasn't from me, but Marie. The man instinctually grasped the connection and raced toward my room with every ounce of devotion he held for this dark, fucked up place. Footsteps pounded behind him—another collector. The moment he came through my door, I could see the scene through his eyes.

Resting on the floor not feet away, I held Tessa while Margo and Marie looked on. The collector's heart grew tight in grief. The emotion was so real in the moment that I almost pulled back and sobbed. It was Marie's words that kept me hanging on.

"But he lives."

Margo looked down at Hunter with disgust, then back to me and Tessa. Ultimately, she returned her gaze to Marie. *"His heart may still beat, but not for long. He will **not** survive. Let him die outside of this room, alone. He should never have been among us to begin with."*

The collector I was living through stepped forward at Margo's gesture. The attraction I felt for her was immediate. Her dark skin and even darker eyes called to me, promising of nightmares I'd bask in. I knew what I was feeling wasn't me, but the collector's. The headdress she wore draped gold braided stands over her forehead and he kept looking, curious about her status. I pushed through his thoughts faster, jolting to awareness as he and the other man came up and began to lift Hunter. A gasp escaped the soldier, tugging at my temper as I continued to watch a *steady* repeat of breaths.

"He smells of Sayer," Marie whispered. *"He is here, isn't he? I haven't seen him."*

"He was," Margo said just as lowly. *"I feel he's dead now. His blood ... it .... rest on the human. Such a waste. This whole situation. Aetas will not be happy."* She grew quiet, waving us collectors to hurry. I felt the impatience through the man as he struggled with the mass of Hunter's weight.

The door opened as Reggie came in with cleaning materials. Although I knew of him, I wasn't aware of his name until the collector thought of it. The tall, thin Native American held the large wooden door as we rushed away. Warmth was beginning to run onto my forearm. I didn't feel my stomach turn at the fact that it was blood. Quite the opposite.

"This bastard weighs a ton." The bald man on the other side of Hunter groaned as he shifted. I could feel myself nod, but otherwise I stayed quiet. My mind was on the dark skinned woman whose blood made me want to bow and serve. I'd become immune to the fearful sensations the vampires put off. Now all I focused on was my addiction.

Heads in the heart of the city turned toward us as we shifted through at a relatively fast pace. Whispering ensued, a hum of shocked tones, but the large crowd stayed back. Darkness once again engulfed us and my arm flexed against Hunter's back. What sounded like a groan echoed around us.

"Te-ssa?"

A growl roared through the vision, escaping through my thoughts and into the collector's. How could he speak? How could he dare to call her name after what he did? None of it made sense except that I was seeing the last moments of a dying man. One who was suffering through his end in great pain, or so I hoped.

"He's still alive?" The bald man faltered in his steps, but managed to make it inside the waste room. The door shut behind us and we lowered him to the ground next to the other pile of dead bodies.

"I'm out of here," I said, stepping back, wiping the blood on my shirt. *"My shift's over. See you tomorrow."* The concern over the human was outweighed by my hope that I could catch a glimpse of the Axis woman again. All I could think about was how rich her blood must have been.

"Wait... What am I supposed to do about him?"

I glanced down at the soldier whose reputation had made its rounds in our city. My head shook in disappointment. There was such talk about whether or not he'd last in our world. The majority hadn't thought so. Guess they'd been right.

"You heard the Axis woman. Let him die. Nothing you can do anyway, guy blew his fucking brains out. He doesn't want to be alive no more, anyway."

"Shouldn't we, I don't know, put him out of his misery?"

My loyalty pushed through, filling my chest with love for the kind who took me in. Who gave me what I needed. *"Nah ... let him suffer. Bastard deserves it. He hurt our Master."*

I pulled back, breaking from the collector's memories and neck, gasping for air. The man crumbled in my arms. I'd taken too much blood.

"Thank you," I said, breathing heavily. "Your loyalty has earned you a reward." A smile tugged at the man's lips, even though he could barely open his eyes. "I will send Demetrius. He will take care of you."

Although the old me would have dropped the man to the ground without regard for his safety, I wasn't him anymore. I was Austin's Ruler. That changed things. Changed me.

I lowered the collector to the ground, taking care to lay him down without letting his head drop to the cement. As I headed back to leave, I gave one last look to where they cremated the bodies. Hunter was dead. And he'd gone out as painfully as he could. That was enough for me.

Chapter 3

"What do we have?"

As I looked around the table at the other eight members before me, I could see their nervousness. Although another week had gone by, I hadn't gotten much better in the stability department. I wasn't sick anymore. I did more than my fair share of killing and feeding, but there was a wildness that had imbedded itself inside me. A recklessness that was beginning to spiral out of control. I'd always been one to love a fight. Now, the battle was within myself. It left my power projecting itself like a poisonous curtain, blanketing everyone within a twenty foot radius.

"Marie has sent a message." Bufar's hand was slightly shaking as he held out the fancy sealed envelope. I took it, clenching my jaw as I let my claw extend and rip through the expensive material.

Dear Master Marko Delacroix,

I am sad to inform you that I won't be returning to Austin for quite some time. Although I have held court with Master Aetas, there are still things he wishes to know. I'm not sure when I will be allowed to leave.

My deepest condolences.

Mistress Marie Bardot

P.S. My heart is broken for you. Please take strength in knowing Tessa loved you until the end.

I crumbled the paper, clenching it in my fist as pain squeezed my chest, making its way through every inch of my body. Bufar and Anastasia, the closest members to me, shifted uneasily. The need to scream or break down was there, but I couldn't let them see me like that. Somehow I managed to get myself under control.

"What else?" Irritation was in my tone. Anastasia took a deep breath before she placed her interlaced hands on the table.

"The riots are spreading throughout the states. The humans are starting to rebel worse than ever. There's talk of martial law going into effect."

"Martial law?" My eyebrow rose in surprise. "Is this decision from our people within?"

She nodded.

"Do they not know the action will start an uprising worse than the fights or attacks going on already?"

"I assume they've taken it into account."

My breath came out in a large exhale. Did they not see the power behind these mere humans? They were willing to fight for what they believed in. Their government might have thought they had a handle on things, but I'd seen what passion for a cause could do to a person. It would be a war within an already building one. Earth would be a mess. Why not allow us to continue to let things play out? Some of us would die, but more of them would. Surely they could see that?

"I will write and inquire more information on their plan." A few nods followed and I sat up straighter in my chair. "I want to talk about something else I recently discovered. Something that I'm not happy with."

Hard stares were cast my way, but I could see their underlying fear.

"Someone is bringing humans underground and killing them here. I came across four bodies. From what I learned, the bodies are burned every two to three days. That means those humans were brought down here on a regular feeding basis. Does someone want to tell me anything? I know it wasn't a commoner. They wouldn't dare disobey the rules. It had to have been someone with power. Someone who has forgotten their place. One of you."

Stares were cast around at each other.

"You know I'm going to find out. If I have to go to each of you to do so, it's only going to make the consequences worse. Out with it."

Silence stretched while I waited. Still they looked around. I could feel their walls come up. No one wanted me to see their secrets.

"Well?" Beatrice snapped. "Who was it?"

Still no one answered. My lids began to lower with each minute that passed by. The disrespect and lack of honesty was something I couldn't have.

"Let's start at the end. Zachariah, come forward." I didn't bother standing. I felt no threat from any of the members here. They were powerful, but they didn't hold a candle to what I was capable of.

The blond vampire stood. Long hair was tied back, barely reaching past his shoulders. Light green eyes stayed on mine as he approached. The moment he got next to my chair, he knecled, keeping the contact. Visions gave way as I pushed into his mind. The vampire jumped, clutching to the table as I rushed through his memories—hard. Aside from some rapes here and there, nothing.

"John."

The dark skinned man shook his head, stiffly. My eyes widened in surprise. I felt myself slowly rise. I was ready for a fight. Ready to tear someone to pieces and his response was triggering my need. "Are you disobeying a direct order from your leader?"

"John," Demetrius hissed. "Go to him."

Again the man refused.

"Aright." My voice was calm as I eased the chair back enough to make it around the table. The man rose and tried to sidestep away, but I held him locked with my gaze. I was already pushing through, already seeing the beginning of his life unfold before me. By the time I made it to him, he was vampire. The time fast-forwarded even faster, until it was but a blur before me. Regardless, I knew everything I was barely seeing. The information was pouring into my mind, registering with extreme clarity.

"Master, you scared me. I didn't see you there."

One of the collectors skirted away, ducking around the far side of equipment as John tossed a human body to the pile. It wasn't one of the ones I'd seen before. Internally, I shook my head. When John began to turn away, my stomach dropped at his vision settling on Hunter. Amongst the pile, Hunter rested on the far side. He was in a different location from where I'd seen him before. Further away, at the very back.

Closer, John moved, cocking his head as the essence of Sayer wafted through. It turned my stomach the moment it had become clear to the vampire I held hypnotized.

"Holy ... shit." He said, pausing in his advance.

Hunter groaned and his head turned the opposite way. Something told me it was the following day after the attack …. and Hunter wasn't dead. No, he looked … *better*. Healing.

John turned, taking big steps back toward the furnace area where the collector had went to hide.

"You! Come out."

There was dread in the way the man shuffled forward.

"The human in the back, the one who killed the princess, were you aware he was still alive?"

"No, Master, I just got here."

John glanced back at Hunter, only to return to the collector. *"Well, he is. Take care of him first thing. I don't want this getting out."* With one last look, the vampire headed for the door.

I broke away, shaking him with everything I had as he came back from the fugue.

"You kept information from me?" I roared. "You knew he lived and you didn't kill him? You left it up to a collector?" So many questions were pouring from me as heat blistered my insides. I had to find this man who was given the order. I had to see Hunter thrown into the flames myself. Sayer's blood within him was obviously enough to prevent him from dying completely. With time…

Hands gripped tightly to my clutched grip and I nearly latched onto his throat. The need to choke him until his windpipe gave way under my hands was almost unstoppable. My mind screamed the word, *no*.

"You better hope the human was killed, or so help me." I drew John closer. "Lockdown will pale in comparison to the hell I'll put you through."

I let go, spinning for the door. "Meeting is over. Bufar, Anastasia, please escort Master John to his cell."

I didn't turn to look behind me. I rushed through the door and kept my composure all the way to the waste room. Talking ceased as I broke through and four men straightened at my arrival. I scanned over their faces, pointing to the one I saw John talking to you.

"You. Come here."

Hesitancy had his steps starting out slow, but he picked them up, not meeting my gaze. When he finally came to rest before me I snapped my fingers. His stare cut up and I didn't say anything as I pushed into his memories, wading through them as though they were nothing. Time passed and I slowed as he watched John begin to leave the room. The roll of his eyes as the door shut had my stomach turning. The man shook his head and headed further into the back. Resting next to some pipes lay a bottle of liquor. He took the bottle, unscrewing the lid, and gulped down the fiery alcohol. It burned my insides and I quickly realized he wasn't going to obey John. I sped up time, going through hours of him sitting there, drinking his sobriety away. Finally, he stood, walking back to the front. Voices rang out with laughter following. He walked toward it, coming to an abrupt stop as he went to glance toward Hunter and realized he was gone. Panic flared and he rushed to the bodies, pulling them to the sides as he searched.

"Where's the soldier?" he asked, throwing the other two collectors a glance. "The soldier?"

"Yes," he exploded. "The soldier. Did you put him in the furnace?"

The two gave each other confused glances and shook their heads. "You're the one on duty, why would we do that?"

"Oh, God." He raced for the exit, his adrenaline crashing as the door came open in his hand. It was unlocked. Something I knew from his thoughts wasn't normal. Wasn't allowed.

The barrier came flying open and he grabbed a flashlight from the shelf along the wall, sprinting through the darkness. The tunnel didn't go far. The ending appeared and he looked up, coming face to face with the removed grate.

I broke from his thoughts, roaring as I brought my claws down over the side of his face. Once I started, I couldn't stop. Blood …. murder, it ruled me. Skin shredded beneath my blows and I grabbed to his neck, holding to his hair with my other had as I tore his head from his shoulders.

The room came back into focus and the collectors were bowed, cowering as I headed for the exit. The sun was still up, blocking my possibility to go to the outside world. If I had thought myself uncontrollable before, it didn't compare to the frenzy that rested within now. A bloodbath waited ahead. There was no stopping the carnage that my vampire wished to release, and I'd let him. Hunter couldn't hide from me. I'd burn Austin to the ground before I let him disappear somewhere in the cracks.

Chapter 4
Hunter

It was laughable that I'd awake here on earth when I had every intention of being sent to hell. Was this God's way of making me pay for my sins? I knew it was. Why would he send me to a fiery world full of demons when there were more than enough roaming the streets here? *This* was hell, and I'd be forced to roam amongst them the rest of my days.

My arms crossed my chest, hugging the black hoodie to me tighter as I sat in a fetal positon. My thighs pressed into my forearms, pushing them into me harder. The sadness welled within and tears escaped as I went over the scene for the millionth time. I had killed my best friend. Murdered the woman I loved. True, she wasn't the real Tessa, but weren't there moments when I could almost feel the old her?

I tried not to think about her calling my name after I slid the dagger into her heart. Her voice, the one I'd fallen in love with, haunted me. I could hear her calling to me in the dead of night. Even in the light of day. *"Hunter…don't."* It was always there. Always, pleading to me. It lit the fuse to my anger even more. The defensive part of me roared to the forefront as I tried to convince myself that it wasn't really her. That what I had done was for the best. And it was. I knew that, even if my mind wouldn't let me believe it.

Trash blew around the dim alley, pulling my attention from the daze I'd been in. Soon, it would be dark. I was unprotected and I didn't care. Maybe someone would kill me for good this time. I had no wish to live. No drive to try to connect with anyone in this forsaken place. I was done and resentful that I had somehow lived. That I continued to. It had to be vampire blood. It was in me and I couldn't stand it.

Weak and disoriented, I had stumbled into the light for the first time in months. *Alive.* Even trying to bleed myself out later that night hadn't worked. It just set me back a few more days. Now, more than two weeks later, I was stronger, healed completely, and past the point of suicide. I was adjusting to the depression. Letting it process. For days I nearly drowned in it, but I was numbing out. I could be killed, or not. Whether I lived or died didn't matter. Something would eventually happen. So what did I do in the meantime? The answer wouldn't come and I had no urgency to make it.

A sigh left me as I leaned my hood-covered head against the wall. The longer hair was gone. One couldn't walk around with only half a head of hair. The back where the damage had been from the gun, healed—bald. Now I looked like I did during my military years and I didn't so much like that either.

Groups of people walked past the alley, heading toward the restaurants. My stomach growled at the thought, reminding me that I hadn't eaten in days. The realization had the side of my lip lifting in distaste. The appeal wasn't there. I only craved one thing and I wouldn't even let myself think about my rapist. Even with as much as I hated Sayer, an odd addiction for more of his blood tugged at my core. It was pointless, he was dead, not that I would have given into the yearning. *Fuck, I hated my life.*

I pushed to my feet, keeping my head down as I turned onto the street. I had a few dollars left from the man I'd robbed, but the amount wouldn't last after today. The majority of my cash rested in my bank account, but I was dead to this world. I wouldn't touch a dime of it. What I had on me would have to hold me over until I came to a decision on what I was going to do next.

The scent of food wafted through the air and I sidestepped groups waiting to go into the crowded places. I couldn't afford anything from there. Not even close.

I broke around the corner, turning toward the fast food restaurant that I knew was a few blocks away. Shouting and chants had me slowing as I approached the next block. People, as far as the eye could see, crowded the street. Height gave me advantage, but I couldn't see the source of what everyone found intriguing. I scanned further, squinting to read a sign someone was waving around. Only one word was noticeable enough for me to read. *Vampire.*

My heart jumped in rhythm and I began to try to push through the mob. Inexplicably, people began to step back, away from me, staring as if I were some sort of monster. I caught their curiosity and fear before I looked more toward the front. One by one they turned, before I could even get to them. My feet slowed. God, was something wrong with me and I just couldn't see it?

Whispering began and I forced myself to continue. A voice grew louder, yelling as it spoke to the crowd. The closer I got, the more I recognized it. Faster, I went, almost running by the time I entered the small park.

"Allowing these vampires into our society was the biggest mistake our government has ever made. As a soldier with the US Army, I'm putting my foot down and saying, no more. We have to stand together. We have to—"

Johnson stopped speaking as his eyes followed the parting sea of people and he settled on me.

"God… Holy shit!" He stepped down from the small podium where he stood on, rushing toward me. He stopped short as if he hit a wall. My eyebrows drew in and I closed the distance. Although Johnson tensed, he didn't step back.

"What the hell is going on here?" I asked, looking around. "Where's Gomez?"

"No, man, what the hell is going on with you? Where have you been? We thought you were dead."

I shook my head, not knowing what to say. People were beginning to step closer. It made me uneasy. "We need to talk."

"Damn right we do," he mumbled. "You got vampire blood in you. Strong fucking blood. I feel the fear, just like with them." He stepped back, climbing on the podium long enough to announce another man who immediately began to stir up the people watching. When he came back to me, he led me deeper into the park, away from the crowd. "Now tell me what the fuck happened to you? Did you find your girl?"

I bit my lip, feeling what only could be described as a knife through my heart. It was too ironic given that's what she had probably felt, but worse.

"It's a long story. Where's Gomez?" I asked again.

"Dead. Vampires got him during a hunt outside of Fort Hood." He gave me a sad look. "I'm sorry for your loss. I know the two of you were close."

My head dropped and I couldn't stop the sorrow I felt for my friend.

"Where you staying?" he continued. "Not at the other house. I've been back more times than I can count. Already has new renters staying there."

I nodded, remembering the couple I saw walking from the front door when I'd tried to return to get my things.

"I … don't have a place. I've been sleeping a few streets away in an alley there."

"Fuck," he said, letting the word drag out. "You'll come back to my place. You'll stay with me."

I immediately rejected the idea, shaking my head. "I'm sorry, I can't do that."

"Sure you can. Why not? You worried about that vampire finding you? The one whose blood you carry?"

"No," I whispered. "I killed him."

"Then come with me."

I took a few steps back. "Can't. Death follows me wherever I go. Unless you're looking to die, I'd suggest you stay away."

I turned to leave when he made it to my side. "I'm not taking no for an answer. I want you to come. You can help us."

"Do what? Kill vampires? No, thanks. I've done my fair share. I'm finished."

"Moretti." His hand grasped to the arm of my hoodie as I began to walk away and I didn't think as I lunged out, slamming him over and down. The strength and speed I held had my eyes going wide. Johnson's mouth opened while he tried to get oxygen from the impact. I dove down, pulling him to stand as I tried to calm his panic.

"I'm sorry. Breathe. Just …. fuck."

A deep inhale sounded, followed by another.

"I'm sorry. See, you have to stay away from me."

Johnson's hand shot up, even as he fought to breathe. "We need you, Moretti. Did you see yourself? You're like one them, but you can come out in the light. We could use you. With that kind of speed and strength you can find your girl. We can save her."

The enthusiasm in his voice made me flex my jaw repeatedly. "No."

"Don't you want to find her?"

"I *did* find her! I found her and I made her turn into a vampire so we could be together. She wasn't herself anymore. She was like them and she tried to warn me. She…" A frustrated, desperate sound left my lips. "I fucking had to kill her. She told me to. She said if she got too…" A sob was next, breaking through my numbness as I walked backward. "She's dead, just like everyone who gets close. Stay away, before you're next."

I gave him my back, walking toward the restaurant at a fast pace. I heard his footsteps before I knew I should have. My fists tightened and I pushed from my feet into a fast run. But it wasn't just fast, it was humanly impossible. It was as though my feet were barely touching the ground as I blurred past everyone. My pulse spiked and my mind raced. I might actually stand a chance against those bastards. Like ,,, really stand a chance in a fight without a weapon.

I slowed, already blocks away. I took the long way around at a normal pace, not even winded as I came to a stop outside the double doors. My appetite wasn't there, but I went forward, ordering a hamburger. As I sat in the corner and ate, I took in everything. People stayed a good distance away, displaying what I used to feel when confronted with one of those creatures. They didn't even seem to recognize they were doing it. Aside from a few giving me weird looks, they went on their way. A smile pulled at my lips and I couldn't deny that I wanted to test out my skills.

Darkness was coming quickly. While I stared out of the window, I plotted what I should do. Where I should go. There was only place I knew vampires would be for sure and I had every intention of heading there. No weapons. No stakes. Just me. If I was meant to live for some reason I couldn't understand, then it was God's will. But if I died … I'd go out with one hell of a fight.

Chapter 5
Marko

The large number of vampires before me looked on in eagerness as I walked the length of the large room. They kneeled, awaiting my instruction. I could feel their excitement. We all craved the hunt and I had no doubts the rumor of Hunter's escape had made its way around the city.

"As most of you are aware, my concubine was murdered on the day we were meant to take vows. She was murdered by a human named Hunter Moretti. The soldier not only has to pay for his crimes against Princess Tessalyn, but also for his escape from our world. He was prohibited to go back to the top and he disobeyed. Until he's located, you will give search. If he is found, you are *forbidden* to kill him. That's my job. Now who here isn't aware of who Hunter is?"

I was prepared to show them, but no one raised their hand. Everyone knew who the bastard was.

"Good. I want this city torn apart. You are not to return until you either have him or the sun is threatening to rise. Do I make myself clear?"

Nodding had me gesturing with my hand. The two dozen vampires left in swift strides and I dropped back, but followed. Hunter would be mine soon enough. If he was in Austin, I'd find him.

Darkness engulfed me as I headed into the tunnel. The vampires were already long gone, no doubt breaking out into their true speed to make it to the exits as fast as they could. This would be a game for them. For me, this was more. This was pure, hot revenge. I'd make him suffer for as long as it took for me to get over this pain of losing ma minette. If that took years, decades, so be it. He was going to see what the definition of what love truly was. What he felt for her wouldn't compare to the devotion and worship that I surrounded her with in my mind. The focal point in his core was his God, but Tessa was mine. She was everything to me … and I'd prove it.

Moonlight shone down through the grate above and I climbed up the ladder, pushing it free, and taking in the familiar street. I hadn't been back here since Tessa had run away, and Julius and I had found her. Seeing her neighborhood again made me feel sick. If I went into her home, would it still smell like her? The question drew me forward. The closer I got, the more grief engulfed me. I stopped in front of the driveway where a new vehicle was parked. Someone had moved in which meant I was fucked from going inside. They'd have to invite me in. Temptation was there, but I wasn't sure I could bear it. The amount of longing I had for the female I was meant for was killing me. If it wasn't for my status, I probably wouldn't have gotten out of bed at all. Let me die too. As long as I could be with her again. Maybe that's why I was out here, knowing the radicals that were trying to hunt down our kind.

I strolled past the house, watching a light flip on. It was Hunter's old room. I paused, seeing the silhouette of a woman. I could tell she had short hair, but reality blurred with my instability and I quickly found myself headed to the front door. I knocked harder than I had intended. A middle-aged man answered, slightly overweight.

"Can I ... help you?"

His fear clouded around me and I watched as an older woman peeked around the corner and took a few steps into the living area.

"I'm sorry. I was looking for my friend who lived here a few months back. Her name was Tessa." My voice gave out and I had to stop the tears from blinding me. Fuck, I could still smell her. Lavender with a hint of jasmine. It was right there, trying to lure me in. "I'm afraid we left on upsetting terms. I was hoping she was still here so I could ... get her back."

The man shook his head. "We've lived here for two months. I'm sorry, I wish I knew how to help you."

"It's quite alright," I said, stepping back and pushing my hands in my pockets. "Have a good night." I turned, heading for the sidewalk before I broke down completely. This wasn't what a leader was supposed to do. We were meant to be strong. Ruthless. Tessa was my only weakness and I would have given anything to get her back.

"Sir?"

I turned, looking over my shoulder.

"I hope you find her."

A sad smiled pulled at my lips. "I'm afraid that's impossible now."

He frowned. "Sometimes the answer is the most obvious. Often times, we just don't see it until we step back and assess the situation. Maybe you're forgetting something important. Think on it. I have faith you'll find her."

"Thank you." I turned, heading toward the church. He wanted me to assess the situation. There was nothing to assess. Hunter had stabbed her through the heart and she had died. What more was there for me to think over? Tessa was dead. I had seen it happen. I'd ... I blinked, still not able to conjure the scene my memory seemed to lock away. I knew in my head she was dead. I felt my mind telling me so, but no matter how hard I tried, I couldn't actually see it.

Aggravation had me jogging across the street. The church made my skin crawl. I couldn't even look at the cathedral without seeing Tessa. It's where I first spotted her. That hair, twirling in the wind as it blew around her. *And her smell.* Fuck, it was still with me from her house... It was as though she'd embedded herself in my lungs, teasing and torturing me with each breath I took. Figured Tessa would do something like that. She wouldn't want me to forget her and I had no intention of doing so.

Music from the downtown clubs registered. I turned right, heading toward them. Although I didn't think Hunter would be here, I needed to feed. It was almost an impossible task to even think about, but if I didn't try to get rid of Tessa's scent, I was going to lose the restraint I held to. It wasn't safe to bask in the sweet fragrance for too long. I needed to drown her out while I was so exposed. If not, I'd not only lose my leadership, but probably my life. I could wipe out this entire city in mere hours if I used my powers. No one here stood a chance. And Axis wouldn't stand for a massacre of that proportion.

Axis...

Something tugged at my brain, but I pushed it away as I zeroed in on the cluster of young people in front of me. Mostly they consisted of college aged kids, but a few were younger, trying to sneak into the clubs. A handful were in their thirties and forties, but I couldn't focus enough to read them. My mind kept getting foggy. It was enough to have my feet coming to a stop.

Axis. What about them kept messing with me? My head shook as I let what I knew of them slide through. Aetas led us all. He was the oldest vampire alive. Margo was the third oldest. *Margo.* Her visit had been so brief. So…

The more I thought about it, the more it felt as though I was watching a movie of her time there. Everything was distorted. Had my grief disassociated me so much? I couldn't even remember her departure. How long had I been sitting on the bed? A week? How or when had I gotten there from the floor? I wasn't even sure. The last thing I could remember was holding Tessa and Margo was yelling at me to hand Tessa over, but I wouldn't.

Marko Delacroix!

My body jerked at hearing the memory of her shout. It was the last thing that was clear. Everything else was a haze.

I shook my head, trying to clear the night from my mind. For some reason I didn't want to remember. Pushing too far felt toxic to my system. It made me sick. And too sad. Yes. I was fucking bleeding on the inside without Tessa.

"Jesus." A girl walking past jumped a few feet away, throwing me a weird glare. It was my aura. *I* was the one toxic. My killer was ready to get to work and here I was, taking a trip down one fucked-up memory lane.

I continued toward the clubs, searching out women who appeared to be by themselves, but they didn't have appeal. I couldn't bring myself to take a female. I caught myself eying men. They were plentiful enough. The majority of them were waiting to get in. I zeroed in on a short, brown haired guy in his early twenties. His eyes scanned the line, stopping to come up and connect with mine. I locked our stares, smiling as I internally called him forward.

Like an enamored zombie, he obeyed, following me as I walked backward toward the closest alley. I stepped into the darkness, jerking him into me the moment he emerged into the shadows. My fangs sunk in deep. Images of his life began to pour in as a gasp came from his mouth. Hands pushed against my shoulders, but I ignored everything as I drank. His sighs and whimpers echoed around us and I slammed him into the wall, covering his mouth with my hand. I took enough to sate my thirst and not a drop more. I couldn't bear to put more into me than needed for my survival. As my tongue slid over his neck to conceal the wounds, I didn't think twice before breaking his neck and letting him fall to the ground.

Movement in the far distance had my head jerking in the direction. The darkness was easy enough to see through, but nothing stuck out as unusual. Regardless, I headed toward where I'd seen it. Light haloed a good ways away from the adjoining street. The closer I got, the more I eyed the dumpster toward the end. Just as I got within feet of it, a vampire emerged, wiping his mouth. I looked down at the dead human girl, returning my glare to him.

"Master. I didn't know you were there."

"That's a problem. You should always be aware when you're feeding. I could have been anyone."

The young vampire wasn't one I had sent out looking for Hunter. He probably had no idea what was really going on at all.

I stepped closer, wiping the blood from his mouth with my thumb. "I want to show you something. A human I'm looking for. I want you to keep your eyes peeled for him. Do you understand?"

"Yes, Master." *Frank Williams.* My mind registered his information as I stepped in to close the distance between us. He was scared. I could feel him shaking as I held to his arm. I could easily kill him and he knew it.

My eyes penetrated into his and I let Hunter's face and voice break into his mind. I pushed back into his brain, hard, making sure if he ever heard the man's tone that he'd recognize it. Just as fast as I planted the information there, I blinked, breaking the connection. "He killed Princess Tessalyn. She was to be my concubine. You know that, though, don't you."

"Yes."

I nodded. "I want this human found. If you spot him, you give me the call. You know how to do that?"

The pull on my core had me throwing him a slight grin. "Good. Do that and I will know you've done right by me. If he appears armed, which he might, do not get close. Not until you warn me. I don't want him dead. His death is mine."

"I won't kill him," he said, quietly.

"That's what I want to hear. Now watch yourself. Times are getting dangerous. Vampire hunters are no longer a myth we dismiss. They exist and they're growing by the day. They want our kind gone and they'll do whatever they can to achieve it. Watch your back."

I left it at that, giving him one last look before I headed into the light of the adjoining street. More clubs rested along the strip, but I turned left, away from it all. Now that I gotten what I needed to focus, my mission was only one thing—finding Hunter.

Chapter 6
Tessa

My lids were impossibly heavy as I tried to open them. A blurry figure moved in closer and I tried to take a deep breath, but it was barely there. I had no strength. The need to defend myself was there, but as I tried to get my arm to lift, the most I could do was feel my finger twitch against the sheet.

"Don't move, Tessa. You're okay."

The woman's voice put me at ease. *Marie.* She'd been here for me from the beginning. I wasn't sure how I knew her, but I knew I did.

My throat was dry and burning as I tried to open my lips to speak. She seemed to know what I needed. My head was lifted and I felt cold metal settled on my bottom lip. I somehow managed to open my mouth the smallest amount. Warmth ran over my tongue and I almost chocked on the first swallow. As I forced it down, coughing had my eyes flaring open for the briefest moment. There were two more people in the room. The awareness triggered my vampire and instinct kicked in. My lids lifted higher and the bedroom I was in began to come in clear.

"You heal, but very slowly."

A man eased from the chair and walked to the end of the bed. A crown sat atop his short brown hair and he looked young. Too young to hold the amount of power he did. It was inconceivable to me how one could be so strong. But he was. I could feel the energy roll from him in suffocating waves. They were so thick it made it even harder to breathe.

"Wh … ere…" My throat was so raw I could barely speak. Marie brought the cup back to my lips and I took another drink. And then another. Just the small amount of blood made me feel a lot better than I had when I'd awoken.

"Where are you?" He glanced at the blonde woman who still stood in the back. "You're at Axis Headquarters, where you'll stay until you heal. You are the last of The Black line. We can't afford to lose you."

"Then you should give her your blood," the woman behind him said quietly. "Or allow me."

The male vampire turned, giving her a look I couldn't see. It was enough to silence her.

"We do not mix blood," he said, giving me his attention again. "The blood you carry is strong enough. To mix another with what you carry would be a disaster. Two donors is bad enough. Three would kill you for sure. It doesn't matter how strong we are. It can't be done."

The woman crossed her arms over her chest and I took in her tiara. Were the man and woman king and queen? I didn't feel as though they were together as a couple.

"I…" I blinked, trying to remember why I was here. There was something way in the back, but I couldn't remember. I turned, taking in Marie's face, studying her features.

"You look beautiful, Princess. Such a beautiful bride."

Bride? She was smiling … and I was… Memories rushed back so fast and hard that I gasped, clutching to my chest as agony flared in my heart. Not just from the heartbreak of what transpired that day, but because of the injury I could still feel. Together they were overwhelming.

"Calm," the man said, walking around the bed. His jaw was tight as he went back to looking at the woman. "I thought Margo scrubbed her memories?"

"She said she did," the woman whispered. "I'll … go get her."

A flare of cream silk followed her as she ran off.

"I'm okay," I said, wiping the tear that escaped. "I am. Don't make me forget. Don't…" Words were getting harder to speak. "Where's Marko?" I glanced up at Marie. "I want Marko. Where's Marko?" Panic was beginning to edge into my tone. Even though I tried to hide the anxiety, it was inescapable.

"Master Delacroix is fine." The man assured. "He's in Austin taking care of his duties."

That's right. He was leader now. Yes … I was remembering …. everything. My human life. How we had met. My time of change. It was all coming back at such a fast rate that I was trembling at the overload of knowledge. The rate of my pulse was beating at such a speed that I had to lay my head back down to try to slow it, not that it made a difference.

Marko! Marko, please. Help me. I want to come home!

I used our connection, closing my eyes as I prayed he'd hear me. With how weak I was, I wasn't sure it would work.

"Marie, I want to talk to him. Can I call him?"

Her eyes were wide as she looked between me and the man. He shook his head and the door burst open as the blonde and another woman came rushing in. Pearls rested along the dark skinned woman's shoulders and she wore a gold, flat band on her head that dipped braided strands over her forehead.

"It's impossible," she said, rushing up angrily.

"I assure you it is not. Tessalyn would like to go home. Back to *Marko*. I hear her thoughts."

Dark eyes settled on me, fearful, as she shook her head. Margo bowed before the young man before moving around him to make it to Marie's side.

"Princess Tessalyn, look into my eyes. I'm going to make you feel better. I'll help you relax."

My head shook and I squeezed my lids shut. "I don't want to forget. I just want to sleep. Please, I'm fine. Leave me."

Finger's settled over my cheek and she turned my head to face in her direction, but I forced my lids tighter.

"Marko! Marko, please! Come get me!"

"Tessa, open your eyes." Pressure tried to separate my lids, but I began to thrash, trying to dislodge the touch.

"Please," Marie, begged. "She'll be okay. Please, don't upset her worse."

Silence followed her, ending with a voice in my head. *"Tessa? Oh … God. Tessa? I have to be losing my mind."*

"Marko!" I put everything I had into screaming his name. Light broke through and I thrashed more, feeling a hand settle on my other side, holding me down.

"I'm fucking losing it. Jesus Christ. Tessa, why are you doing this to me? You speak and I hear you, but you're dead. Fuck, I miss you. I wish this was real.

A gasp exploded from my mouth and my eyes flew open at the pain that exploded on my inner elbow from the slice of fangs. Just as I took in what the man had done, Margo pulled my face over, tapping into my stare. Heaviness began to take over my body and I felt the fight leave me as I relaxed into the fluffy mattress. The man immediately lifted. He'd done what he needed and now I was going to disappear again.

"You will remember nothing. Sleep, Princess. Sleep and heal. You still have a ways to go."

Remember nothing.

I blinked heavy, feeling a zap in my mind. My body jolted as my lids flared opened. "No! Marko!"

Margo's gaze shot to the man next to me who growled.

"Impossible," she breathed out. "She can't fight my gift. She's nowhere near powerful enough!" More anger was laced in her tone and she lunged for me, trying to bring my stare back to her. I slapped at her hand, ready to attempt to try to use my own gift. If it weren't for the threatening sound that came from the man, I wasn't sure what would have happened between us.

"Not impossible," he said, moving closer toward me. "She's stronger than we thought. Her blood," he said, lowly. There was a seductive drawl in his tone. "She's growing at a rapid pace. Right now she's more mind than body. Her physical strength hasn't caught up, but it will. When it does…"

His fingers gripped my chin, making me look at him. When my eyes came to his I was nothing but a shell. My soul was sucked from my body and I was pulled deep into his depths. It was as though he had captured me and taken me to live inside of him. I was him and he was me …. my creator, more than Sayer had ever been. He was foundation. He was the first, and yet …. not. I didn't understand. His information poured into me. His name, *Aetas*, which meant time. He had no last name, no record of birth. The vampire just *was*. Space, power, love, hate, energy, emotion—I was in awe of the multitude of his being and what it meant. Resting within him, I felt no pain or weakness. Just bliss. Freedom.

Surging energy surrounded me in the black void, brushing along my skin and coaxing me to give myself over to it even more. I was floating in the nothingness. The tingling was pleasure-inducing and I never wanted to leave. Nothing else existed in this moment except for the sensations and my own power swirling within. I could feel him tap into it, tugging and playing with the darkness as he let it combine with his. And I let him. I didn't feel threatened with the way he was dissecting my gift. His curiosity and happiness at what he was discovering made me giddy. It made me feel important.

And then I suddenly felt it, clouding around the edges of the blissful bubble I resided in.

Evil. Devil. My mind locked and the heaven I was a part of was overclouded. I didn't fear Aetas. I feared the magnitude of *who* he was. He might not be the actual devil, but he was equivalent to what I viewed true evil as.

The essence of who he was perfumed around us as he stayed focused. I put all of my attention into cracking what it was. At first I couldn't quite understand why I could see my fog before me, but nothing from him. I could feel his gift, but I couldn't see it. As his focused energy came to me, I knew. A spell spun around my energy, so powerful I almost couldn't deny giving myself over to it. *His gift, or at least one of them.* It wasn't a substance or an actual force like my fog. He was mentally strong—mentally persuasive. He could become everything I had ever wanted. Everything *anyone* wanted. Whatever it was a person desired, they would see it within him at first glance. Like love at first sight. He was the answer to all of their problems. Love, protection, money … they would know he was the solution. But it was an illusion. None of what registered in the minds of his victims was real. Not the comfort of his presence, or the beauty of his face that caused a woman's heart to soften. He was the opposite of what he portrayed. He was malicious. *Real* evil. And here I was, the true me, trapped inside of a place I might never be able to escape from again. He could hold me here if he wanted. I knew he could.

Even as I soaked in the vastness of the situation, I couldn't stop the obsessiveness that began to tug at my mind. No one was like me. I was different. Aetas wanted me. Our gifts played well together and I could still feel his pleasure at seeing that. He wanted me. Me. *Wanted* me. Just me…. It repeated over and over until I was shaking my head and screaming. I couldn't escape the mantra that was continuous.

"Shh, don't fight it, Princess. Don't you want to love me? Don't you want me to love you? We could be happy, together. You'd have the ultimate position at my side."

The void that was him, enveloped me, hugging with the right amount of strength to make me feel safe and secure. *Needed.* Yes, he needed me. And he was handsome. *Everything I'd always wanted. Dreamed of….* No! I loved Marko. This was a trick, a test, and I couldn't fall into it. Nothing about this was real.

"I want to go home. Send me home right now." Panic had me nearly screaming the words. I wasn't sure how long I could stay unaffected by the temptation he was drowning me in. He was beyond strong and somehow I knew he wasn't even really trying.

"Hmm." The tingling covering my body increased until I was vibrating perfectly in all the right places. I moaned, arching through the ecstasy he was pleasuring me with. Deep pants left my lips and I tried to turn and move away into the nothingness, but I wasn't sure which way was up or down or to the side. The pitch black surrounding me was so disorienting.

"Send me home. Marko will heal me. He'll make me better."

A laughed echoed all around. *"Always so focused on Marko. Will he heal you? You have such faith in Master Delacroix. I don't. His intentions for our race are not honorable. Greed rules him."*

"Ruled," I corrected. *"He's changing, and it's because of me. We love each other."*

"You think you do. I can see the memories that make you believe what you say to be fact. I see everything," he said slowly. *"His … love. His adoration for you. It doesn't mean he will not change when your honeymooning period comes to an end."*

"I will not let him tease the idea that he can rule over you. We know our place. You have my word."

What felt like hours went by as I floated in the silence. *"Watch what you say, Princess. Your word could be your death."*

"Marko will not try to take over." I swallowed hard. *"I will not let him. He'll have to kill me first."*

"And you have faith that he loves you more than his own greed?"

"I do."

Again he got quiet.

"I can see your Marko sleeping. Even now, he dreams of you."

My heartbeat all but stopped. When I caught my breath, it began to increase, fluttering around me like a living thing that made up the void. *"Will you show me? Will you teach me how to see him like you do?"*

"I can show you, but your request comes with a price."

"A price? What kind of price?"

"That I cannot tell you. First you must make the decision whether or not it's worth the cost."

Marko was worth any cost to me. *"I want to see him."*

"If that's what you wish."

Color began to warp all around me and I gasped, suddenly seeing our old room. Aetas was suddenly at my side, but I barely gave him my focus. Marko lay in bed on his side, with his arm thrown over the pillow where I would have slept. His features were drawn in and I could see the distress in his expression.

"Feel." Aetas said, quietly. *"Feel what he feels in this moment."*

His hand came down between me and where Marko was lying. Aching engulfed me, so crippling it nearly brought me to my knees. Tears began to stream down my face at his pain.

"I want to learn this," I said, looking back at my true leader. *"I want you to teach me, I beg you."*

He stayed quiet as he studied me. I frowned, moving closer to Marko. When I got to the bed, I pulled up the white nightgown I wore and climbed up next to him. Marko turned in his sleep, only to roll in a complete circle. His hand reached right through me, trying to grasp at something, as if he knew I was there. I lowered to the pillow, crying harder. I'd never forget his pain.

My hand came up and I settled my palm over his cheek. At the shuddering breath, I turned back to Aetas. *"Can he feel me?"*

"Subconsciously, yes. He'll feel your energy. The two of your share marks."

"Energy. That word keeps coming to me. How is this possible?"

"Anything is possible. The mind is an amazing thing. Even humans can come to this realm. Researchers do tests on this all the time. Out of body, astral plane. This is child's play, Princess. Watch."

Aetas stepped closer, letting his hand hover over Marko. I nearly screamed as he began to lift the shape of a figure out of his body.

"Like I said, child's play. Humans can't summon, but I can. And you could, too, if you grew strong enough." His eyes narrowed. *"I find it interesting that you'd pick this path to learn, when your black fog is such an amazing gift."*

"I wish to learn them both." I turned back to him. *"I never want Marko and I to be separated again."*

"You're not separated. He's dreaming of you, as we speak. That's a connection, whether you see it or not. The way he is with you." He paused, seeming to choose his words. *"What the two of you share doesn't happen often. Trust me. I know. I'm not saying that's a good thing, though."*

My bottom lip pushed out the smallest amount and I dismissed the last of it. Marko was dreaming of me. It may have been a connection to Aetas, but not for me. And not for Marko. We didn't feel happiness right now. To him, I was nothing but a dream. A memory so powerful that the footprints of my soul had embedded permanently into his scarred heart. I was a lovely illusion, dead and gone. That's all that was left of me for him and I couldn't stand it.

Slowly, I lowered back down, gazing into his face. I couldn't help but lean closer and kiss his lips. In this form, I felt his power surging through his body as he slept. It was stronger than I remembered. Enough so that it left my lips vibrating from the contact. I ran my tongue over the hum and moved in again, separating them as I tapped into my core. There was something there. A tug, just like when I wanted to summon my fog. Instead of breathing out, I sucked in. Marko's essence, his power, was in my grasp and somehow I knew I could take it. And I wanted to. I wanted him within me.

Like a rubber band I felt the link between us stretch while I took in more. Marko's eyes shot open and I was face to face with his startled gaze. A roar filled the surroundings and I was pulled from the room so fast that I literally felt my body snap into the mattress as I was thrown back *into my body.*

"You!" Aetas glared at me with his slightly glowing eyes. He turned to the others in the room. He didn't have to say anything for them to go running for the door. It shut quietly behind them and he turned back to me. Anger I'd never been faced with before bore into me as he hovered inches from my face. Already I could feel how much stronger I'd become. And it was all thanks to Marko.

"Was that not allowed?" I whispered.

His hand latched to my throat. He didn't squeeze, but breathing wasn't easy, either. "I gave you a gift and you took advantage of it. I could kill you for that." He tightened his squeeze for only a moment.

"You wanted me stronger. It … worked."

"He wasn't to wake," he exploded. "His brain wasn't in the right state. Marko could have seen you! You lack the knowledge of what you've done. Of what the brain is capable of."

My lips separated and I pushed back, wincing as I came to a sitting position. He let me go, but he didn't stop giving me the evil look.

"Marko will believe it was a dream. He thinks I'm dead. No one can come back from the dead."

Aetas slowly shook his head. "That's where you are wrong, Princess Tessalyn. You *were* dead. If not for me, you wouldn't be here."

"You gave me your blood?" I asked, confused.

"No. My remedy came from here," he said, pointing to his head. "This is more powerful than any life source that keeps your body alive. This tells your organs to start again. To not shut down. For your heart to continue to beat, and for your blood to race through your veins faster, to clot, and begin the healing process."

I let out a shaky breath. "If that method is so powerful, why am I still so weak?"

Anger appeared again. "Because I gave you life, nothing more. You should be thankful I went that far."

"I am thankful. You have no idea how much." I grasped to the comforter trying to calm myself. "Why did you do it? Why save me?"

Aetas let his features relax as he continued to calm. "With Sayer dead, you must carry the line. You hold great power within yourself that will grow to heights even I can't predict. It's risky, but I'm willing to let it play out. I think you have potential. *Great* potential."

I lowered my gaze, processing his words. I knew what I held, but I couldn't begin to imagine what that meant. Especially coming from someone as powerful as him.

"How long will I have to stay?" I was far from well, but I also knew I could heal better with Marko. I had to get back to him. We'd only just began to connect. After everything we had been through, all I wanted was to finally be able to live our lives as it should be.

"Until I say. You will get better and we will assess your skills. There are things I can teach you. It's an honor you shouldn't refuse," he said, narrowing his eyes at me.

Somehow I knew what he spoke was true. I *should* be honored. I *should* be grateful. Although I longed for Marko, I'd be stupid to walk away from this opportunity. Stupider to refuse him. I was trapped here until I proved myself and he set me free. With his talk of the mind and the true strength behind it … mine was already coming up with ideas that I knew I shouldn't be considering.

Chapter 7
Hunter

I blurred through the shadows, feeling the wind whip past me at my speed. The vampire I chased turned to look over his shoulder and I didn't miss his confusion or fear. I was gaining on him … and thriving from our tables being turned. I wasn't the one afraid for once. It was *him*, running from *me*.

The top half of my body leaned even more forward as I put everything I had into closing the distance. Just when I got within reach, I dove forward, tackling him down to the ground. Without a weapon, there was no quick kill, but I didn't want it to be fast. I wanted a fight, and over the last three days, I'd gotten my fair share. The first night, I'd almost been killed, but I quickly learned their speed. All it took was some getting used to. Once that happened, I was a natural. And a target. Sayer's blood called to them like a fucking drug. One catch of my scent or aura and they couldn't help but race toward me, blind with bloodlust. It was their mistake, and my gain. But this one had been different. He was stronger. He had managed to snap out of his crazed state, long enough to see the light. I was going to try to hurt him and he knew it. He had taken off the moment he slipped free of my grasp. Now, I was going to end this once and for all.

We hit the ground hard, rolling over and over from our speed. My hands and feet pushed into the earth, slowing me enough to find stability and go back at him. The vampire scrambled to lift, but I was already tackling him to the ground again.

A grunt came from my mouth as his claws extended and slashed toward me. They caught the edge of my side, but not deep. I pinned his arms under my knees. He was strong, almost throwing me off, but I was stronger.

I reared back, slamming my fist into his face. Once. Twice. I didn't stop, letting all of my anger and rage pour into each hit. Blood began to seep from the vampire's mouth and nose and would have from my knuckles, had I not invested in gloves. I couldn't afford for them to taste my blood. Then they'd be powerful like me. At least, that's what I assumed, and it was too risky.

A hiss poured from the vampire as he tried to squirm out from me, but I'd had enough training throughout my career to know how to subdue him.

Harder, I connected, feeling his bones cave beneath the impact. It only led to the blows turning more severe. What I was doing wasn't going to kill him, but I wasn't in it for the kill. Not yet. What I was doing was way more personal. Way more stupid. Maybe I was trying to make a statement. To prove to them that I wasn't the weak human they all thought me to be. Or … maybe it was something within myself I was trying to prove. I'd taken the cowards' way out, killing Tessa and trying with myself. Perhaps…No. I wouldn't think about her or try to analyze myself. These fuckers deserved it and the moment I got more stakes and holy water, I'd start the real hunting. But not with Johnson or anyone else. I would do this alone.

Teeth broke under my fist and I smiled as the vampire's fang fell free. I threw my next right into his temple with excruciating force. The creature's head rolled to the side and I stood, bringing my boot down to stomp on his face. What felt like a freight train slammed into my side, knocking the air from my lungs. We hit hard and my hands flew up in defense. They locked on the jawline of a female vampire who was intent on shredding me to pieces with her fangs. As her arm drew back, I spun us around only have a moment of hesitation before I connected with her cheek. She wasn't a real woman. She was a monster. Just like Tessa had been.

Loud cries came from her mouth in between hits and it fucked with my head even more. The thrill suddenly wasn't there anymore. It was too close to what I'd done. Even though I had every intention of hurting this vampire, she was still a female … still like the woman I had once loved.

My fingers latched to her hair and I twisted her head, breaking her neck. I heaved, crawling backwards to get away from them. The other vampire was already slapping his hands against the ground. He was healing. Fuck, I had to get out of here.

A loud cry in the distance traveled through the trees and I jumped to my feet, heading away from it. Everything within me said it was another vampire, coming for me. I had to lose it.

Downtown was on my right. I ran as hard as I could in the direction, rushing past a couple of random people who were leaving and entering the park. I didn't slow until I came to one of the major intersections. The building where I was staying was only a few blocks down. If I could make it to the rooftop, I'd be safe.

A shout from behind me had me glancing back. Fangs flashed as the vampire yelled something. I didn't wait. I rushed into the street, barely missing the car that zoomed by. The hoodie swayed back and forth with my speed and I was almost completely across when I slid to a stop. Bufar stood on the other side—waiting. I could see Marko racing in our direction. Time practically stopped as he and I connected stares.

Beep! Beeeeeep!

Headlights blinded me and I jumped as a car came skidding to a stop. The hood clipped my feet and my shoulder slid, hitting the windshield hard. Glass broke and crunched underneath my weight, but I didn't stay there long. I rolled, racing right at into oncoming traffic. Cars swerved, honking, and I didn't try to hide my true speed. I let go and gave it everything I had. Marko was still coming toward me. I could feel his presence keeping up. Possibly getting closer.

"Hunter!" The roar literally cut into my skin. The gashes he inflicted covered my face, neck and chest and stung like fire, but I didn't stop. Couldn't. He'd kill me for taking the vampire version of Tessa away from him. I didn't want to die just yet, if at all anymore.

I broke to the right, glad the cars were far enough behind that I didn't have to dodge them. As I looked over my shoulder, Marko was a good half block away. A smile lifted my lips. *I was faster.* The fact had me feeling lighter. People moved out of my way as I went down another block, turning left, going down a few blocks and then making a right. I zigzagged back and forth until I was sure he was lost in the maze. When I rounded back to the alley that led to my building, I kept my eyes peeled. The fire escape was high and there was no way I could reach the ladder. I climbed to the top of the dumpster, jumping to catch the railing, then pulled myself up. I took the stairs at a fast pace until I made it to the top. Rocks were loose under my feet as I ran to the edge, peering over. There was no sign of Marko that I could see, but I wasn't going to stop watching. I'd keep my guard up for the rest of the night. It was clear he was after me. That he'd figured out I was alive, and I knew he wasn't going to give up until he killed me.

It was time to invest in weapons.

Warmth ran from under my eye, down over my cheek. I wiped the blood away, glancing down long enough to take in the damage to my clothes. Fuck, he'd cut the shit out of me, again. I knew what he was capable of and I had no doubt I was going to have new scars to go with the old ones. Or would I? I pulled off the ripped hoodie, taking in the numerous gashes. As I scanned the area, looking for a vampire to arrive, I noticed after several minutes they were already healing. The bleeding was beginning to stop even from the deepest ones. A laugh escaped and I shook my head in disbelief. Sayer had put me through hell, but if anything good came from the situation it was the power he gave me. *Fate.* I was meant to end the race who had ruined my life. To stop them before they got even more out of control. It's what I felt in my soul. So how did I do that? I couldn't on my own. But … Johnson? His followers? The military?

My head shook as I rubbed my hand over the stubble beginning to grow back. No. I couldn't get involved with anyone else. They'd die if I did. But wouldn't they anyway if they pursued these vampires without me? It was going to happen whether I joined them or not. The call to rise was loud and clear, and if I could help, they'd stand a better chance. I was a hell of a soldier. A fucking leader. I could do this and they'd follow me. I knew in my heart they would.

I ducked, peering over the edge as Marko and Bufar broke around the corner on the opposite side of the street, studying the area as they kept a fast pace. The light illuminated them enough for me to see how much of a mission they were on. They wanted me dead, and badly.

My lids narrowed as I took in the evil getting closer. Yes. Perhaps it was time I stepped up to finish this once and for all. If I didn't, we'd surely fall to their darkness. Then what, become mindless slaves as they destroyed everything we stood for in this country? In this world? Fuck, no. I had fought way too hard for our freedom for it all to have been in vain. And so had everyone else who had, or was currently serving.

Marko came to an abrupt stop, spinning in a circle. I lowered even more, watching as he growled and slammed his palm into the brick building he was standing next to. His anger was my pleasure.

"Keep walking, motherfucker." I gripped to the brick and froze as Marko's head lifted. He appeared to be taking deep breaths. I pulled back, looking down at my blood-covered chest. Fuck! He could probably smell me. Or Sayer.

I grabbed the hoodie, squatting as I jerked it over my head. It wouldn't do much for covering the scent, but it was better than nothing.

Slowly, I rose, feeling my blood turn cold. I lifted even more, jerking my gaze from one end of the street to the other. He was gone. I hated not knowing which way he'd gone. Was he at the fire escape? Had he found me?

The panic had me rushing over there as quietly as I could. The closer I got to the metal ladder, the faster my pulse increased. I stopped at the edge, listening.

Voices brought my lids down. I knew, being on the fourth floor, my hearing shouldn't have been as clear as it was, but it was another gift.

"He has to be here somewhere," Marko growled. "He couldn't have just disappeared into thin air. He's a fucking human."

"With Sayer's blood," Bufar added.

"Not for long. He'll be bled out completely by the time I get done with him. Hunter's going to wish for the day he never crossed my path. He'll pay for what he did to Tessa. I'm going to…" Marko's voice trailed off while I waited. Nausea twisted my stomach at hearing her name come out of his mouth. She'd always been mine, but not anymore. Tessa was Marko's, and had died ready to bond herself to him forever. Him, *not me*.

A bang in the distance had me tensing. Footsteps scattered from the alley, moving back toward the main road. I lifted enough to see them pause as they glanced to where a man was loading his car.

"Let's go look down here," Marko said, moving further away.

I lowered, leaning back against the building. My heart was still racing. I knew if I had to go against Marko right now, I'd lose. Paired with Bufar, I was goner for sure. It was time I armed myself and got within protected walls. Fort Hood was waiting, and come morning, I'd be on my way.

Chapter 8
Marko

If it weren't for the sun, I would have never of given up my search for Hunter. Every night we came closer and this time I had almost had him. It wouldn't be long now. To see the strength and speed I had only heard about from my vampires was shocking. Their memories hadn't been enough. Sure, I could see his rage through their eyes as he destroyed them with his bare hands, but for him to run from me … and escape. There were no words for that.

I collapsed to my bed, rubbing my hand down my face from the exhaustion plaguing me. The anger was taking its toll. As was the lack of sleep. Even when I was unconscious, I never truly rested. Tessa haunted my dreams. Last nights had been the most real, by far.

My fingers came up to my lips, tracing over the surface. I could almost still feel her kissing me. It had been so tangible. The moment I opened my eyes and saw her slightly glowing form, I could have sworn she was really there. One minute she was before me, the next, gone. With one blink, she had disappeared. For hours I had laid there trying to decide if what I saw was real. And I felt as though it was, but that only meant one thing. I didn't discount ghosts. They were energy, as were our gifts, but I wasn't sure that's what I had seen. Then again … perhaps she was still with me in some spirit form.

I sighed, stripping down, and headed for the shower. Throughout the whole routine, I kept seeing her—long, flowing hair, white nightgown, pale skin. Yes, she'd been so pale. Almost sickly looking now that I thought about it. The realization was enough to have my brow furrowing. If she was a ghost, wouldn't she be as she appeared when she had died? Even in death she hadn't looked so poorly. Not like in my dream, with dark circles under her eyes as though she was physically ill.

My head continued to shake as I got out and wrapped a towel around my waist. The moment I made it to the bed and laid down, I found myself turning to face where she'd been. If she was a ghost, would she come back? Was it crazy that I wanted to talk out loud in hopes that she could hear me? Fuck, I was seriously in need of some help. I missed her so much that I was grasping at straws. *A ghost.* It was almost laughable. I'd known many vampires who had died and not one person ever mentioned them coming back from the dead to haunt anyone.

I yawned, feeling my fangs extend as I began to close my mouth. Although I'd fed plenty in the last few days, it didn't compare to what I'd tasted within my Tessa. Her flavor was incomparable to the weak human blood I took in now. I yearned to taste her once again. Just the thought had my cock getting hard.

A groan came from my mouth as I stripped the towel from my waist and pulled back the blankets, climbing under. The need for release was getting harder to ignore, but it was pointless. I didn't want to do anything to appease the torture. I wanted *her*. Not some fantasy. Besides, I wasn't to the point of thinking about what we had shared. It hurt too much to go there. I was barely surviving as it was. My duties and the hunt for the human who killed her were all that was keeping me going. To even think about how she tasted or how her pussy gripped so perfectly around my cock killed me.

My eyes closed and I tossed and turned, trying to get comfortable.

"I never got to show you how much I loved you, ma minette. There were so many things I wanted to see you do." I reached over, grabbing what would have been her pillow and holding to it as I stared at the wall in a daze. All I saw was her. The expression she held when she chose me. I'd always remember that smile. The want she had of me.

"See me do? Like what?"

My heart felt as though it dropped through the bed and I could see my fingers turn white as I stared at them.

"I'm going fucking crazy."

"Perhaps," she said, slowly. *"But let's tease the idea that I'm in my room and you are in yours and we're just having a regular conversation."*

I flew from the bed, racing to the closet. My suits hung in a row, but I didn't grab one. I reached to the top, pulling a pair of silk pajama pants down and an undershirt, practically tearing them on. *"Are you there, ma minette?"* I didn't care for her answer. I had to see for myself, even if I did know it was impossible.

"I miss you," she said, quietly. *"There's never a moment when you're not on my mind."*

The door swung, hitting the wall hard as I raced through the darkness. *"Keep talking, ma minette. Keep talking. Don't stop now."*

"I really shouldn't," she practically whispered.

"Shouldn't?" I broke into the heart of the city, making the next right. It didn't take me long to make it to her door. I jerked to a stop, reaching for the knob. My hand paused just before it touched and I wasn't sure if I could do it. If she wasn't there…. No, I knew she wouldn't be.

The metal was cold to the touch and I turned, pushing the barrier open. The room was darker than the tunnel, but I could still see inside.

"If you're a ghost, let me see you. Come to me so I know I'm not losing my mind."

Silence met me as I stepped in, shutting the door behind me. Light filled the room at the flip of my finger and I felt my heart break all over again. The bed resting in the far back and the chairs and sofa were also empty. Minutes went by as I continued to scan the room. Hoping. Wishing.

Fuck. I could still smell her. The scent had my eyes burning with tears all over again.

My knees gave out and I collapsed to the cement. As if hell, itself, was pulling me down, my head lowered until it was resting on the floor. My insides … my chest … how could losing someone hurt so fucking much? I felt like I was the one dying. The aching went beyond any physical pain I had ever experienced. The sensation wasn't just an impression from my loss. Loneliness, sorrow, anguish, despair, they all pushed into the pain, weighing down not only my heart, but my entire body. I never wanted to move again. I didn't feel as though I had the strength to even lift. Only one person in the world had the power to destroy me, and it was her. Had anyone ever wanted me to suffer, they would have done what Hunter had.

She was my life and he'd taken it from me the moment he thrust that dagger into her chest.

"*Please,*" her sobbing voice said, breaking through. "*I can't bear it.*"

She couldn't bear it? I couldn't fucking bear it. "*Let me see you. I have to see you. Are you here? Can you see me?*"

"*No, I cannot.*"

I lifted enough to look around the room, searching for something I knew wasn't there. *Her.* As I pushed to my feet, my head shook. I couldn't believe I was carrying on a conversation with a phantom voice in my head. It wasn't her. It couldn't be. It was me. All me. My brain just had to have been trying to cope with my grief. "*So where are you, then? Are you a ghost?*"

Nothing. I turned around, flipping the light off behind me and heading back to my room. The moment I shut the door, my shoulders caved and I walked over, letting myself fall back on the bed.

"*I saw Hunter today. I'm going to kill him, Tessa. I'm going to make his last days ones he never forgets.*"

"*Hunter! He's alive?*"

My eyes narrowed as I slowly sat up. Why would *my* mind say or react that way?

"*Tessa ... where are you?*"

Anger was beginning to take over my sadness. My pulse was causing my whole body to shake. Something wasn't right. Something was off about what was happening.

"*I'm dead, Marko. You know that.*"

"*Are you?*"

Hesitation. "*Tell me about Hunter.*"

"*No... Ma minette, is this really you?*" More minutes went by and the only thing I heard was my increasing breaths. I was getting pissed and I wasn't sure why. Again, I tried to tap into her death. Still, I couldn't see it. Why was that? Had I really blocked it out?

My mind went back to Margo. She'd left without even saying goodbye. Or ... she had and I didn't remember that either. But why wouldn't I? Yes, I was in shock. I couldn't remember what happened days afterward, but that couldn't be normal. There was no way I would have let her leave with Tessa, and she had. Why didn't I stop her? Why couldn't I even remember what happened after Tessa's death?

Internally, I pulled Bufar to me. While I waited, I kept going over everything. It wasn't adding up and it was starting to get under my skin.

A knock at the door had me pushing from the bed to stand. "Enter."

The wooden barrier opened and he stepped in, shutting it behind him. It was clear he'd been asleep.

"I need to speak with you about the time right after Tessa's death. What happened? Why didn't Margo say goodbye and why did I let her take Tessa?"

Bufar's eyes narrowed and his head shook, confused. "Master ... you held a ceremony for Princess Tessalyn the day after they left. You ... helped Margo load the ... body in their SUV. You were badly upset. Are you telling me you don't remember any of it?"

I flexed my jaw, letting the red hot rage seep back into my veins. "I did not do any of that."

"You did, Master. The whole city was at the ceremony. You can ask any one of them. They'll tell you."

My lids lowered while the denial reigned. "I did *not*." When my stare came back to Bufar, he was closer to the door. "You were by Julius's side for decades. What do you know of Margo? I get nothing when I tap into my mind. If Julius knew anything, his memories have been wiped, right along with mine."

"Marko." Bufar looked around the room as if there were something hiding in the air. "If what happened to you was a result of something she did, there's a reason. I think you should let it go. This is Axis we're talking about here."

"You're saying I should accept that Tessa is dead when she may very well be alive?" My voice was nearly at a yell by the time I finished.

"Yes," he said, steadily.

This wasn't happening.

"You never told me what Margo's gift was. What is it, Bufar?"

A paleness tinted his lightly tanned skin and he kept looking around the room. "Is this an order?"

"Yes it's a fucking order," I snapped. "I'm ordering you to tell me right this very moment."

A swift nod was followed by his stepping closer. Even his voice lowered. "She can reprogram the mind. Like … what you mentioned. She can wipe memories and make you go through a lifetime as nothing more than a … zombie. She … scares me."

"Jesus!" I spun in a circle, not sure whether to get dressed and go to Axis or wait for word from them. I'd never been to their cathedral. I probably wouldn't be allowed admittance, even if I did have the address. Not anyone could just show up. It was forbidden. Especially for a leader like myself. I had to send a request and even then it could be denied.

"You're sure about her gift?"

"Yes, Master. I've … seen her do it before. Forty or so years ago, but I know what I saw."

I glanced behind me, throwing him a look. "What in the hell are you looking for?"

"*Him*," Bufar hissed.

"Him?" Even as I said it, I knew. "Aetas?"

Another nod. "If Margo did reprogram you to think she's dead, and Tessa is indeed alive, there has to be a reason they haven't gotten in touch with you to let you know. The decision would ultimately be up to him. The question is, why doesn't he want you to know?"

My fists drew in and tightened. "You think he means to keep her there?"

Buffar shrugged. "She's the Black Princess. Her gifts might be beneficial."

"They could be just as beneficial here," I argued. "What would be the difference between her being here or there?"

"With what's going on in the world, combined with what Hunter did…" Bufar trailed off, but I knew what he meant. There, she'd be safer. Protected against the worst threat imaginable. No one would be able to find her if Aetas didn't want them to. Not even me.

"*Tessa.*" Even as I called her name, I didn't expect her to answer. Perhaps I was blowing this all out of proportion and I really had blocked it out from shock. No. It was *too* coincidental. But if that were in fact true, ma minettte was *alive*. And if she was alive, I'd see her again someday. That gave me hope. Something I thought I'd never feel again.

Chapter 9
Tessa

The longer I stayed confined to bed, the more my vampire grew restless. Aggravation was seeping in, as was anger. Not toward Aetas or Marie, who were constantly hovering, but at Hunter for doing this to me. Hadn't I tried to show him how much I cared? I'd shed blood for him and he didn't even see the significance of what that meant. And now he lived when I was barely able to walk around for more than a few minutes at a time without getting weak. I couldn't stand how long it was taking for me to get my health back. Vampires were meant to heal almost instantly. My make-up told me that, but weeks had gone by. It was unacceptable, not to mention embarrassing. I was in the presence of the greatest vampires in the world and I couldn't even hold a conversation for more than a few hours without dozing off.

That was just the beginning of my problems. If I didn't get better and start my lessons, it would be forever before I got back to Marko. I couldn't have that.

Hunter. This was all his fault.

I threw back the covers, easing from the bed once again. The half hour rest was enough. I couldn't continue to stay locked away in here. I wanted to get this over with. To start these lessons once and for all.

"Princess, you shouldn't be up yet."

Even as Marie said it, her head was down.

"I need clothes. I want to leave this room."

Her eyes cut up and she glanced to the door nervously. She didn't want to be here anymore than I did. It was as though she was in a constant state of fear being in the presence of these leaders. I didn't feel her unease, even if I did understand why she felt threatened. We were the weakest ones here. No one was to be trusted. The only thing that kept me from not falling into Marie's position was because I knew I'd surpass the majority of strongest. I was *someone*. The entitlement had always been there from the moment I was changed. Being under this roof versus the underground city made no difference. I knew my place and it was amongst these vampires.

"Aetas wants you to stay in the room."

I barely heard her as I forced my heavy legs to move toward the closet. They didn't want to follow the simple order to walk and it was just another thing that made me want to scream. Why was this so hard?

"I'm going whether you help me or not." I was breathing heavily by the time I pulled the closet door open. Lightheadedness had me pausing. Marie's hand settled on my bicep causing me to look up at her.

"Come and sit, Princess. Let me get your clothes."

I let her lead me to the edge of the bed. When she returned with a red dress and a pale pink one, I met her eyes. She was clearly unhappy with the choices, but she placed them down anyway.

"Stand, let me help you dress."

When I rose, our bodies were but inches apart. Her hands settled on the tie on my chest and she pulled the string loose. The material eased from my shoulders and pooled at my feet as her small push

"Look at me, Marie."

Still, her head was down. It was unlike the woman who'd once been full of life. I could remember our meeting. Our beginning. We were both different now. I'd been the cause of her bondeds' death. She had wanted to help me, and Marko made her pay the ultimate price for doing so.

Marie met my gaze, but wouldn't hold it. After a minute of me not saying anything, she finally came back to me.

"I'm sorry," I said, lowly. "I truly am."

Tears came to her eyes. "I'm not sorry. I can always get new slaves. Besides, I'm stronger now. Our paths were meant to play out this way." She grabbed the red dress, sliding it over my head.

"I don't like this path," I said, placing my arms through the long, silk sleeves. "Look at me, I can't even dress myself. I'm so … dependent."

"You're already tiring. I can see the circles coming back. Let me get you another drink."

My mouth twisted at the thought of the weak blood they kept feeding me. It wasn't nearly powerful enough to make me better.

"I can tell you don't like it," she said, pouring me a glass. "Not that I blame you. I tried it the other day. I wonder why they won't grant you your own supplier. They did with me."

"You were given a supplier?" There was a longing in my voice as I watched her turn around and hand me the glass.

"Yes, his name is Dustin." A blush flooded her cheeks. "He's very cute. And tasty." As Marie said it, she turned me, tightening the back of my dress. I took a drink, cringing at the thick blood. It was cold now and not at all easy to swallow.

I moved to the side, placing the cup down. "Lucky. There's nothing I'd give to taste…" I turned, cocking my head. Confusion swept over her features as I tapped into the smell of her skin. "A vampire," I finished. "You. You'll feed me."

"Oh, no, we can't," she rushed out, stepping back. "Aetas said we couldn't mix blood with you. One more—"

"Of them," I finished for her. "Their blood will battle mine. Yours won't." I stepped closer as she moved more to the side. I could see her fear and it had my vampire instincts flaring. "You can heal me."

"But … Marko. He'll kill me."

My head shook as I sidestepped to cut her off. Desperation had me stronger and in predator mode. I was ready to catch the smallest mistake on her part and attack.

"Marko will thank you. He wants me back. I'll never get home if I don't do as Aetas wants. And he wants me to learn. I need you, Marie."

"I can't…'

Lust. It ruled her fear. The scent hit me hard as I grew closer.

"And if I don't give you a choice?"

"You're not thinking straight. Don't do this, Tessa. I don't want to hurt you."

Marie was physically stronger, but I had something she didn't, and I knew how to use it.

Dark fog began to cloud the edges of the ceiling, rolling toward the two of us. Panic left her eyes darting around in jerky movements. To get to the door, she'd have to pass me, and I could smell her fear. It mixed with the increasing arousal. Whether she wanted to admit it or not, she wanted my bite.

"Tessa, you have to stop."

The room began to disappear in the thick substance. I opened my mouth, letting my poison, my lure, seep from me in waves of black smoke. Marie let out a sound and she broke to run around, only to turn at the last minute and dive over the bed. Before she could rise, I was throwing myself on top of her.

My fingers laced on the sides of her head and she arched underneath. I didn't hesitate to lock my lips on hers. Heat ignited in my core while I started to drug her enough to help her relax. Muffled sounds vibrated my mouth and she rolled us over, still trying to fight. It had me clinging to her tighter.

"You want this, now lower to me. Let me taste you." Seduction may have taken over my tone, but I was focused on only one thing. Her blood. I needed it and nothing was going to stop me from getting it.

"He'll kill me," she said, slurring at the end.

"No one will touch you," I purred.

A whimper filled the space between us and I let myself relax as she obeyed. The softening of her body was followed by her molding into me. Marie dropped her head, exposing her pale neck. I brushed back her dark hair, already feeling my fangs push down. A bang sounded and I lunged forward, sinking through her skin. Warmth filled my mouth and I sucked in hard, greedily taking her into me.

Power exploded over my taste buds, rushing through my system. Her grip on my shoulders increased and she moaned as my eyes widened from the effects. Movement through the fog had me wrapping my legs around her body, holding tightly.

"Princess?"

The voice got closer. I pulled at the darkness, making it thicker around us to conceal what I was doing. Vibrations tingled across my skin and the need to scream was almost unbearable. It'd been too long since I had good blood, it was shocking my system.

"Princess Tessalyn?' The voice was more demanding. More so, laced with impatience. I broke away, licking over the wounds. Marie panted and I pulled her up, sitting her on the edge of the bed as I lifted my hand, waving away the fog. It cleared enough for me to see the blonde who'd been here before.

"Can I help you?"

A suspicious glare was sent my way and I raised an eyebrow, waiting.

"Aetas wishes to see you. He'll be here shortly."

I glanced at Marie's flushed face and shook my head. "There's no need. I was just on my way out. I'll go and see him."

The blonde's lips parted and she appeared to go blank. Maybe my bluntness wasn't allowed or heard of here, but I wasn't staying in this room for a moment longer.

"Just tell me where he is. I'll find him."

"No." She drew out the word. "You should stay and wait. If you leave, he will be upset. You don't want that." Before she could finished, the door opened and he walked in. I wanted to groan. His visits usually lasted hours and I couldn't stand to think of staying here that long.

The blonde spared me a glance before she rushed past him and left. Anger was clear in his expression as he stared at me. Instead of speaking, he turned to Marie.

"Your presence has been greatly beneficial for Princess Tessalyn's healing, but I do believe she's not in need of your services anymore. If you'll head down the stairs, Margo will be waiting for you. She'll escort you out."

My mouth dropped open and I quickly shut it as I put myself between them. "I want her to stay."

Marie stood from the bed and I put my arm back so she couldn't walk past. Aetas' silence had her ducking beneath me and rushing to the door.

"I want her to stay. Please. I need her with me."

The door shut, but he never took his eyes off of me. "Lesson number one. Be solely dependent upon yourself."

My jaw tightened in anger. I was already shaking from Marie's blood. The combination wasn't good for my temper. It was hard enough to control as it was. My vampire was still so new. It ruled me more than I did.

"Is lesson number two more mind stuff? I want to see Marko again."

"Was speaking to him not enough for you?"

The threat in his tone had me looking down. "I didn't tell him I was alive. I never answered him."

"You didn't have to," he said, stepping forward. "He suspects enough. He sent a request this morning to see me. I denied it."

"He wanted to see you? And you said no?"

Sadness had me tearing up while I took in his stoic expression.

"I have nothing to say to him. Besides, I'm busy with you. He will have to wait."

The answer was exactly the reason why I knew I needed to hurry and heal. If I could learn, I could leave.

"What do you want me to do? Just show me and I'll do it."

A laugh left him and he grabbed my arm roughly, pulling me to the end of the bed. I hit the mattress hard at his push. It had been so unexpected that my palms shot up to defend myself.

"Calm, I don't want you that way. Even if I did, I wouldn't have to take it. You'd give yourself to me willingly and never look back."

My head shook. "You're wrong."

"You think so?' Aetas' smiled, but it was full of challenge. "Close your eyes. Don't look at me. When you choose me, I don't want there to be any blame that I somehow messed with your mind. You're going to pick me all on your own.

My lids lowered and a few seconds went by. The silence drew out and I blinked up at the ceiling. Was he going to do anything or not? I sat up, looking around the empty room. A knock sounded at the door and I rolled my eyes at his game.

"Come in." I stood, crossing my arms over my chest. One fell free almost immediately as I used the other to push against my racing heart. Breath wouldn't come as I stared into the face I longed to see the most. Dark eyes met mine as he shut the door and I was torn on whether I was dreaming or not.

"Jesus ... it's true. You're alive."

Tears streamed down my cheek as I shook my head wildly. "Impossible. This isn't real."

Marko didn't listen as he raced in my direction. He gripped around my waist, pulling me into his body. It was so real that I started to wonder if Aetas had really left and Marko had come for me. He would if he suspected I was alive, wouldn't he?

My eyes stayed open, watching him as I battled whether this was an illusion. He felt real. He smelled real.

"Wait,' I breathed out.

"I've waited long enough. God, I've missed you so much. I thought I lost you." More he kissed, lying me on the bed as he pinned me under his large frame. I found myself kissing him back as the hardness of his cock rubbed against me, continuously.

Pressure gripped one of my wrists, holding it above my head, and he jerked up the side of my dress. "I can't believe I have you again." His fingers made a path up my thigh and I couldn't help but rock against him.

"I'm going to take you home and we're going to be happy. I'll never let anyone hurt you again."

I paused, looking up into his face as he hovered above. Fingers rubbed the length of my wet slit and I cried out as he torturously eased one inside of me. Impatience had me gripping into his suit jacket and pulling him closer. Anything to get more.

"You want me? You want me to fuck you? Let me hear you say it."

"Yes. Don't stop," I begged. "Please."

"You're so hot and ready. You…"

He tensed the smallest amount and something swept across his features that I couldn't quite decipher. Regret? Confusion? It pulled me from the moment enough that I let the scene play out. This wasn't the way things would play out if Marko truly found me, would it? My head slowly shook as I began to wiggle against him.

"Aetas … if this is you…"

I could tell something was happening. Something not right. Marko's finger withdrew, only to push in deeper. He bit his bottom lip, withdrawing from me as he brought his other hand up to place against my mouth. Slowly, his head lowered until his forehead was pressed against mine.

"Too tempting. Too much. Fuck." Marko panted and I nearly screamed as the colors of his face began to warp. Aetas was suddenly before me and I couldn't get over the horror I felt.

"You…You…" My words came out muffled against his palm.

"Shh," he said, wiping the sweat from his face. "Marko is stronger than I thought. His thoughts aren't right. They're so much darker than I expected."

I sat up as he walked back a few steps.

"I can't believe what you just did."

"You said I couldn't make you choose me. You did."

"You! Not him. Of course I would react that way to Marko."

Aetas didn't seem to be listening as he paced. Worry began to cloud the violation I felt. His reaction to Marko wasn't good. It left me worrying for his safety.

"You mentioned his thoughts weren't right. Are you saying you were truly him?"

"I drank your blood. *His* blood," he said, cutting his eyes up. "It was easy to take his form. What I didn't prepare for was how much his blood had won over you, or his personality. His … feelings for you. They overshadowed mine which is rare. The depth of hatred and destruction goes beyond what I've felt in a long time. Not to mention … the amount of his love. His want."

"You didn't want to stop."

Aetas glanced at me, but went back to staring at the ground. "No. I reacted the way he would have. I haven't felt…" He started to walk abruptly to the door when he stopped and turned back toward me. "Lie down."

My head shook and I spun to the edge of the bed, only to freeze up as he was suddenly blocking my path. How had he done that? Just appeared? "Lay down," he said, pushing my shoulder to the mattress. "I want to see something."

Colors were already changing in his face and his features were morphing back to Marko's. I tried to scramble away, but he held tighter. I was suddenly pulled to the top of the bed while Aetas moved in to cover his body with mine. God, he looked just like Marko. He was Marko, even if he truly wasn't. It was so disorienting.

"Yes, this is better," he said, closing his eyes and breathing me in deep. "Now, love me and then do something to anger me. I want to see how deep his powers run. I can't do that unless I'm affected by what triggers me the most. That would be you."

"Love you?"

"That's right," he said, lowering. "Love me, ma minette. Kiss me and tell me how much you miss me. Give yourself to me completely. Let me feel your devotion and loyalty to only me."

Pressure from his hand gripped my hip as he pushed harder between my legs. This wasn't right. It may have been Marko before me, but Aetas wasn't him.

"I … can't. Get off. There has to be a different way."

"You can," he growled. "And you will, or this is the only version of Marko you'll ever see again."

Vampires. It didn't matter how nice they were at times, their motives were their own. How was I so quick to forget that none of us were good?

"It's not that easy. I know you're not him. Besides, I don't like you lying on me like this. You have no right."

A smile tugged at his mouth. "But I do. Here, let me help you forget what you can't accept. Let me be everything you've always wanted. Let me be him, for real."

Marko/Aetas dove forward embedding his fangs in my neck. My scream was loud, dying out as an all too familiar poison pushed into me. But this one was different. More powerful than I could remember. Whether it was Aetas' bite or Marko's new one, I wasn't sure. All I was certain of was the sensory overload that had me moaning and clawing into his back while he pushed his hard cock against me.

"There you are," he moaned into my mind. *"You love my bite, don't you?"*

Tugs on my vein were pronounced—greedy as he reached behind my back and pulled at the laces that held my dress together. When his hand came up to pull the material off of my shoulders, I tensed … but didn't fight. I was past the point.

"Marko." Pleas poured free from deep within and I rocked impatiently as he lowered the dress on my chest even more. When my breasts burst free of the silk, there was no hesitation on his part. Marko's tongue swirled around my hard nipple and he sucked it into his mouth. When his teeth tugged at the tip, I gasped, turning my head to the side. White curtains registered in my mind, throwing me off.

Marko didn't have curtains. I held to the thought, trying my hardest to ground myself. Somewhere in my brain, I knew things weren't right.

A gentle caress traced up my thigh, pulling my dress higher. Marko's attention went to my other breast while he fondled and teased. Faster, I moved against him, desperate.

"More. God, give me more."

"You want me to fuck you? Beg me, ma minette. Beg me and I'll give you anything you desire. All you have to do is say the words. Say them. Fuck, just … love me. Talk to me. Talk more."

"Yes," another voice said, breaking through. Another… Marko. *"Please. Let us hear more. I just love listening to someone pretend to be me as they manipulate and attempt to fuck what's mine."*

The anger from the real Marko had both of us frozen as we stared at each other. Heat poured from my body and I couldn't stop the shaking of my head. Aetas didn't change to himself as he stayed in place, now, pinning me down. I wanted to run. To flee and get away from him and this place.

"Tessa, speak. Who's with you? Is it Aetas?"

I stared at our leader, torn.

"You gave your word to back me, Princess. Do you think Marko stands a chance if he tries to overthrow me? If you do, by all means, tell him it's me and I'm keeping you against your will. He can show up and attempt to rescue you." He paused. "But if you love him and you want him to *live*, you'll close off your mind and hike up your skirt a little higher."

I bared my fangs, feeling my gift boil inside of me as it worked its way toward my throat to get free. Flashes of Sayer's multiple rapes became all too real. I couldn't go through something like that again.

"That's it. Get mad, *mon chaton*."

"Tessa! Answer right now. Who has you? Who is doing this to you?"

Fog left my mouth in a constantly flow of darkness, so thick and toxic it was impenetrable. But Aetas had been ready. The shield he held around him blocked the substance from breaking though his walls. The laughter that left him only increased the sudden rage within. I tapped into my core, searching for something I didn't even know. His words filtered through, speeding through my thoughts. *I took your blood. Marko's blood.* If I had Marko's blood and we were tied, surely I held his gifts, too?

An odd emotion flashed over Marko's face as Aetas thought something. Whether he was reading my thoughts or not, I didn't have time to think about. I reached from within, projecting the burning sensation outward from my body with everything I had. Marko flew back at the energy burst, slamming into the far wall as a sound resembling thunder exploded around me. A translucent shield rippled along the room as it shook, holding in the energy. The blowback shook everything around me like a massive earthquake. Sound dissipated and my ears popped painfully. Seconds went by before the rocking finally stopped.

"Oh … God." I rose to my knees, placing my hand over my heart as I took in the damage around me. Did I kill our leader?

The door burst opened and I jumped at the banging the force caused. Margo, the blonde, and a tall, thin man with muscular arms came rushing through. They took one look at Aetas' true form crumbled on the floor and lowered defensively in stance. Their fangs came down while threatening sounds filled the room. Closer, they came, assessing me as they neared. The burning was still there. It singed my core, wanting to be released again.

"She's a traitor," the blonde said, snarling. "She has to pay for what she's done."

My head shook, but I couldn't deny my actions. I'd meant to hurt Aetas. *To kill him.*

The male broke from the two females and moved in from the side. I rose to my feet, slowly, holding my palms toward the two directions where they stood. I had no idea what exactly I was going to do, but the action meant something.

"Lessons," Aetas groaned, pushing to rise. "She's of no threat."

We all spun to look in his direction as he smoothed down the dark shirt he was wearing. His eyes came to me and my head lowered in both fear and conflict. A part of me still wanted to fight because of what he'd tried to do, but my vampire seemed to know her place. Especially after what I did. He *was* my leader, regardless of what he'd done. The submission was there instinctively. And I was lucky. He could very well kill me for attacking him.

"No threat?" The blonde yelled. "Her power rocked the entire building. You were … down." There was a shock in her statement, as if she couldn't believe what she was witnessing.

Aetas only had eyes for me as he seem to stalk in my direction. My fear increased while I soaked in his every move.

"Down … but not dead. *Not even close.* Leave us. We're far from finished."

Chapter 10
Marko

Even Marie arriving couldn't stop my wrath for long. As she kneeled before me, nothing more than a zombie, it fed the fury harbored within. I read her memories, taking in each one she carried from Axis Headquarters. At least the ones she still had. I wasn't sure what was real or what was planted. I didn't trust anyone concerning Tessa anymore.

"Hurry, we have to get her to Aetas."

Margo and I ran behind a vampire who held Tessa's lifeless body in his arms. I knew she was dead. I'd had seen her truly pass through Marie's eyes not long after they'd left the city. Over an hour they traveled and each minute Tessa was dead, felt like forever.

A dim light and what sounded like the news filled the cathedral as they practically flew through. They were going so fast, Marie could barely keep up. A tall man stood at the end, before a throne, waiting. He knew we were coming.

"Master Aetas, Your Highness." Margo slid to her knees, bowing her head as I lowered, hitting my knees hard. Anxiousness had me shaking. I was afraid of the power before me.

"The Black Princess." He came forward and I felt myself get closer to the marble floor. *"How long?"*

"Fifty-three minutes."

"Too long," he growled. *"I cannot save her after her body's been shut down for that length of time. She's dead. How did this happen? Show me."*

Margo stood, letting her head rise. Actas' hand was around her throat, pulling her toward him before Marie could prepare myself. My eyes went back to face the floor, not able to stomach being here. I wasn't strong enough for this. The mantra kept repeating in my head.

"The human." Aetas let go, pulling my arm and jerking me from the ground. I didn't want to look into his eyes, but I had little choice. I knew he wished to see what I held. And I allowed him. My eyes lifted and I was gone. Nothing existed in that time. Nothing but darkness. When I came to, loud shouting appeared somewhere in the distance and I was alone. Completely. Then … nothing. Nothing but the ride back to the underground city.

"No! I refuse to believe that."

I let go of Marie's connection watching as she, too, coward in my presence. Something had happened to her while she was there. Something that had left its mark.

"Bufar, take Marie to her room and then return. Check to see if there's word from Aetas yet on whether he'll meet me."

"Got it right here," Anastasia said, sweeping into the room.

I rushed forward, taking the envelope from her. Breaking the seal had my pulse pounding. I took out the note, unfolding it as I walked to the far corner of the room.

Dear Master Delacroix,

I was surprised to receive your request to meet. I am aware what you wish to discuss, but I must tell you, you will coming for naught.

Princess Tessalyn arrived too far gone. She had been dead for quite some time and although my powers are great, there was no way I was able to save her. I'm sorry for your loss. You were spared the pain of witnessing this and should be grateful for what Mistress Margo gifted you with. I fear in your unstable condition that you wouldn't have been able to take the actual loss.

As for the human who goes by the name Hunter, I am aware of his escape. I am leaving his capture and punishment up to you. Temporarily. You have four weeks to find and seek justice for his crime against your betrothed. If you can do this, his punishment will be up to you. If you fail to find him in the allotted time, his acts toward The Black Princess become a royal crime and enforcers will be send to handle the situation.

-Master Aetas

I clutched to the letter, barely able to contain the need to destroy everything in sight. His intentions weren't good. Tessa wasn't dead. She couldn't be after what I had heard not an hour ago. He was pretending to be me for one reason or another and I was going to find out why. No one else could have done what I'd heard. No one. The task was impossible. Only he would have had the power to become someone else. So why? Why be me, get in her head, and try to seduce her? It didn't make sense. Had he wanted to fuck Tessa, he would have just done it. No one would have stopped him. No one would have believed her allegations, or if they did, care that she had made them. He was our ruler. He couldn't be overthrown. Not unless…

My head shook and I roared as I threw the letter.

Tessa. Talk to me right now.

How many times had I ordered her to speak? Too many, and she wouldn't. Or couldn't. I wasn't sure. One thing I knew was Aetas hadn't expected me to hear them. Or maybe hadn't thought about it. Either way, he fucked himself because now I knew what was happening. If he thought he was keeping me from finding headquarters, he was sorely mistaken.

"I'm leaving," I said, turning to Anastasia. "I'm going to Axis. Bufar is to rule in my stead. I want the teams to go out and scour above for Hunter. If he's found, put him in lockdown. No one is to touch him."

I headed for the door as she cried out, reaching for me. "Don't do it. Stay. If she's alive like you believe, he'll release her on his own time. Marko, you can't afford to make more enemies there."

My jaw tightened and Anastasia came up short of touching me.

"Please," she begged. "Just wait this out."

"I can't. I'm going. If I'm not back in a few days … Bufar will know what to do."

I left the meeting room, walking through the tunnel at a fast pace. The driver was already expecting me. I'd sent him the orders to be ready the moment I'd come to the decision in my head. As I entered the heart of the city, heads spun in my direction. The band quieted their somber tunes, but didn't stop playing them completely as I walked past. Maybe the song was fitting. I might be going right to my death, if I could find this place at all.

The stairs stretched out before me and I took three at a time until I reached the top. I didn't have to open the thick metal door, the servant was already waiting for me as I rushed through.

"Lionel is awaiting your arrival, Master." He rushed ahead, opening the front door. The limo driver stood stiffly at the back door, staring ahead. I went to climb inside when screaming had my head whipping around. Marie was clawing at Beatrice, fighting to get to me.

"Marie." I waved Beatrice off as Marie crashed into my chest. "Calm," I said, soothingly. What is it?"

A sob tore from her throat while she clutched to my jacket. "I don't … know. I … don't go." She wasn't making sense. I lifted her face, staring into her depths, trying to will more of her missing time away, but nothing came.

"Shh. Talk to me. Tell me what you feel."

Marie wiped the tears from her face as she tried to gain her composure. "I don't want you to go. I fear that if you go, you won't come back. Tessa wouldn't want me to let you go."

I narrowed my eyes, gripping her face so she couldn't turn away. "You say Tessa wouldn't want me to go. Do you know if she's alive?"

Marie's brow furrowed and she shook her head. "I don't … think so. I see her dead."

"Don't think," I said, quietly, meeting her eyes. My power swirled and I used it to try to open up more of her mind. "Listen to me. Clear your thoughts and just speak. No thinking. No trying to remember. Let the words just come for themselves." I kept the contact, feeling her pulse slow under my spell. "Is Tessalyn alive?"

A few seconds went by. "Yes," she answered in a monotone voice.

My breath caught and I held to her biceps tighter. "Is Aetas hurting her?"

"I don't know. I don't think so. He … saved her. He … wants her to heal. To learn."

"Learn," I repeated. "Is she well?"

"No," Marie breathed out raggedly. "She … fed from me. I couldn't stop her. She attacked me even … when I said you would … kill me."

I clenched my jaw. Yes, it made me angry, but I would have let Tessa feed from Marie a million times over her feeding from Aetas or anyone else.

"Do not fear for your life, Marie. I am not angry with you. Did your blood make her better?"

"Yes. She was so sick… She was barely surviving before she fed from me."

Relief had me nodding. "Good. I'm glad you were able to help her. That makes me feel better. Is there anything else? Did anyone hurt you while you were there?"

Tears raced down her cheeks. "Y…es."

"Name," I ground out.

Marie's lips parted and I could see in her eyes that she didn't want to say it. I left her little choice as I pushed into her mind deeper.

"Gina."

I searched for the missing memories of what happened, but they were gone. Too far locked away for me to get to. I shouldn't have been able to extract as much as I had, but the fact was, I could do it. I was so much more powerful than I had realized. I made her clear her thoughts again and told her to speak. "What did she do?"

"She made Margo stop me from getting in the car. She … hit me. She said I was an embarrassment to our kind for not subduing a sick weakling like the Princess. I didn't want to hurt Tessa. I…"

"No more." I broke the contact, turning her and pushing her toward the door. "Go rest, Marie. I'll be back soon."

She cried harder as she turned back to face me. "Don't go."

I climbed in the car, pulling the door shut before the driver could. There was no way I wasn't going to go after Tessa. As for this Gina, it was against the code to treat visitors with such disrespect. I'd be sure to make that clear when I arrived.

Chapter 11
Hunter

Fort Hood had never been my home. Although I'd visited the Army base before, I had never been stationed there. It was bigger than I remembered. And busier. As I walked along the sidewalk toward housing, I wasn't sure where I was going. Johnson had said he lived here, but aside from the fact that I knew he drove a black truck, I had no idea where it was. And I didn't have a telephone number. Finding him was going to impossible. The only thing that gave me confidence as I watched the sun set lower in the sky was the fact that I couldn't see vampires working their way inside of here. Sure, they might be able to sneak on, but they wouldn't stand a chance against the number of soldiers ready to destroy them.

If I needed any idea of how great the rise was to battle them, all it took was the large manmade sign on the gate that said *No Vampires Allowed*. Government or not, our military wasn't standing for a breach on their base.

A car passed by and I glanced at the white sedan as I rounded a turn, taking me deeper into the neighborhood. It seemed to stretch out forever. Red trucks, white ones, but even with as common as black was, I had yet to see one.

A kid cried out in the distance and I stiffened. The round of laughter that followed had me shaking my head. I was on edge. A part of me didn't want to be here. I sure hoped I knew what I was doing.

"Silvia, I told you, it'll be fine." A man in tactical gear stomped from the porch area of a house, heading past one of the two cars in the driveway. His wife's dark hair flew out from behind her as she chased after him. My feet faltered at the familiar face. He seemed to notice me at the exact time.

"Moretti. No fucking way."

Romano laughed as he headed my way, embracing me before pulling back.

"Long time no see," I laughed. "Last time I saw you, you were arriving in Afghanistan."

"And you were leaving," he said. "How have you been? I thought you got out."

"I did," I said, pushing my hands in my pockets. "I'm actually looking for a Sgt. Johnson. Big guy, he drives a black truck."

Romano's head turned and he peered down the street. "Shit, man. I have no idea. Do you know how many Johnsons I've run into throughout the years?"

I looked down at the strap around his chest, holding the bow. "Probably a lot. Say, where you going all geared up?"

He glanced toward his wife and turned back to me, frowning. "Me and some of the guys head out to clean up the underground here. Fucking vampires. We're starting to make some headway. The ones we haven't gotten are clearing out. Probably heading toward the city."

"That's why I'm here. Johnson's been rallying in Austin. I'm coming to stay with him for a while to help out."

"Oh … *that* Johnson. He's got a white truck now, man. Four houses down. Come with me, we'll ride out with him."

Romano turned, giving his wife a peck on the cheek before heading back toward me. I could see her unease. I understood it. She had every right to fear for her husband's life. I knew better than anyone what they were capable of.

"Be careful," she called out to us as we began to walk away.

"Always," he answered over his shoulder.

I planted my feet and it took a few steps before he realized I wasn't by his side. I pressed my lips together as he faced me. It wasn't usually my place to say anything, but after what had happened, I couldn't keep my mouth shut. She was still standing there. Watching.

"What's up? You change your mind?"

"No," I said, taking in her sad expression. "But I'm not going anywhere until you go back and give your wife a real kiss and hug. Is this the way you want her to remember you if shit goes down? Come on, she deserves better than that. Who's stuck by your side through everything?"

Something flashed behind his eyes and he peered over to her. "You're right. Guess I just don't want her to worry. We've been through so much already."

"Yes, we all have. I've seen too much death, lately. Make this right. Every time you leave the house, give her something to remember you by."

I barely finished before Romano was jogging toward his house. I turned my back, not able to witness their emotion. Instead, I focused on the white truck I had already passed. It wasn't seconds later Johnson emerged from his house with another man. They were talking. As if he felt me, he stopped the conversation and looked in my direction. A smile came to his face and I shrugged, heading his way. It didn't take long for Romano to catch back up.

"Moretti. Didn't think I'd ever see you again. Glad you proved me wrong."

I sighed, taking in the three men who surrounded me. "I figured we're all out for the same thing. If I can help contribute, I'll do so."

"Oh … *you* will," Johnson said. "You're going to help us out more than you know. Your skills. Fucking phenomenal. I can still feel you."

I glanced nervously at the Romano and the other soldier I'd never met before.

"What is that?" Romano asked. "It's … like them. I felt it before I saw you. I thought I was imagining it."

Johnson gestured to his truck. "Well talk about it on the way. Let's load up."

The guys went to the back doors so I climbed in the front. Johnson didn't speak until he reversed and started heading down the street. "So how'd you get here?"

I shifted in the seat, not proud of what I had to do. "I stole a car. Dumped it off base."

"Jesus," he whispered. "Gotta do what you gotta do, I guess."

"Yep." I swallowed hard, not really wanting to go into why I was here, but I knew it was coming. I could feel the energy from the men behind me getting restless. "Vampire blood," I said, turning around. "That's what you feel. I was searching for my … best friend. She was taken by a Master. I found her and went underground with her. They kept me there for months, refusing to let me leave.

Her…" I let out a deep breath. "Her maker did some really fucked up shit to us. I ended up having to kill both of them before I escaped."

Romano's eyes flared and I watched as his mind worked. He was thinking, and he knew enough about me to put the pieces together.

"We're not talking about—"

"Tessa," I said, cutting him off. "Yes."

"But, you were going to come back to marry her. It's the whole reason you were getting out. Fuck, man, I'm sorry."

Pain lanced my heart and I tried to push the images away. "It had to happen. Once she changed, she wasn't the same. And she couldn't escape them. She made me promise. I went through with it."

"What's up with that?" the stranger asked, nodding to my head. I didn't have to read his mind to know what he was talking about. My hair might have been growing back, but not where I wanted it to the most. Not yet. Maybe never.

Nausea had me pausing. "That would be where I blew my brains out after I killed her. The vampire's blood prevented the one thing I wanted the most. It wasn't meant to be so here I am."

Silence left sweat pouring from me. Johnson glanced in my direction before he took a left. "I don't blame you. Crossed my mind on more than one occasion when I lost my wife to vampires. If I would have had to kill her, I would have done the same thing."

"Same here," Romano said, reaching forward and grasping my shoulder. "We got you. Never doubt that."

"I never have."

Johnson pulled into a base's movie theater and I followed as they climbed out. When we entered, my feet halted. The place was filled with soldiers. Some were in uniform, others weren't. Men and women, all ages. They grew quiet as we came in. Johnson led us to the front and I crossed my arms before me, clutching to one of my wrists as he began to speak.

"Thanks for coming, everyone. Before we go into what we've learned, I'd like to introduce to you a veteran and a good friend of mine. This is former Sergeant First Class, Hunter Moretti. He's done multiple tours in Afghanistan. He's a damn good leader and he's going to be one of our greatest assets. He knows more about the vampire community than any of us can begin to imagine. He's spent the last few months as a captive to the underground and he's managed to escape, but not without a price. He lost someone dear to him too, just like the majority of us in here. He was also the one with me and Gomez when we lost Thatcher and Waters. He's dependable and exactly who we're looking for. Let's give him a welcome and get down to business."

Whispers and something short of cheers echoed through the large space as I gave a nod. Johnson turned to a table set up next to the screen. There were a few papers resting on the top. He grabbed one, scanning over the contents.

"We lost two more soldiers?" He scanned the crowd, stopping on a man in the second row, toward the end. "What happened, Artega?"

The man stood. Even in his posture, I could see his grief. The weight had his shoulders sagging. He wasn't taking the losses easy.

"A vampire came up in the rear at a fork in the tunnels. Munez must have not seen it in time. It got him and Kepler before we could take it out with the stakes."

Artega sat back down and whispering ensued for only a moment before Johnson began scanning the crowd again.

"What do we have on ideas to make this easier? Hanson?"

A tall soldier on the first row looked up from his own paper. "We're still looking into a few things. We have the soakers, loaded with holy water, the stakes, and even a few flame throwers but due to the size of the tunnels, it makes it hard for us to use anything with real power."

A sigh left Johnson and I couldn't help but speak up. "What about thermal? It would read their heat signatures. If we could get some down there, we'd be able to see a lot better than with just the headlamps or a flashlight. They may not register to the temperature we would, but they'll come close enough."

"Thermal," Johnson repeated. "Yes, Hanson, you hear that. Get us some thermal."

"You're using night vision, right?" I asked.

"Well." Johnson twisted his mouth. "We use our own equipment. Some of the scopes on the guns have it, but not everyone can afford it right now."

I glanced around at the crowd. "We'll go out to businesses and ask for donations. We'll set up a drive. Whatever we have to do. People will help. They'll support us."

Johnson smiled, nodding. "What else do you suggest?"

Already, he was looking up to me. It was only a matter of time before they all saw I was meant to lead. And I would.

"Physical training. We've all been through it. It's time we work our hardest and step it up. These vampires are strong and fast. We have to be able to physically fight if it comes to that. Not all have special powers or gifts. At best, they're faster, stronger, and they can climb walls. If we can eliminate them before they get to us, great. If not, you have to learn to break necks. It'll incapacitate them long enough for someone to make the kill. Do not make the mistake in thinking that it will kill them. The only way a vampire can die is by decapitation or a direct hit to their heart. Even a Master can die if you stab them in the heart with a holy relic. I know. I've killed two this way."

Well, Tessa may not have been a Master, but she would have been. And she was just as strong with her gifts. It wouldn't have been long. And her blood made her stronger than a normal vampire. She counted.

"You're telling me you've killed two Masters?" A man rose from the back row. "That's impossible."

"I assure you it is not. I killed him and paid a price for it. His blood got in my mouth. A lot of it. I can never get rid of it. Made someday it will fade, but with the vampire's status, I doubt it will in my lifetime."

"Status, what do you mean?"

I squeezed tighter to my wrist. "He went by the title, The Black Prince. His name was Sayer. He was a member of the most elite vampire circle there is, Axis. Ten members are all that fill this circle and they are the strongest vampires in the world. He … attacked me for reasons I will not disclose. During our fight, I managed to stab him in the heart repeatedly with a dagger that was blessed by my uncle, a priest. It worked. I decapitated him afterward. I wasn't going to take chances. If you're faced with a Master and manage to pierce his heart, I suggest you do it, too. Their healing strength is amazing. No bullet will do the job. A stake, a knife … it has to break the skin. Bless everything you can. Carry a rosary or cross. Prayer will stop them in their tracks. It's also a time saver if you need a few seconds to attack."

Wide eyes stared at me. I glanced at Johnson, taking a step back. "My best advice—find God. You'll need to if you decide to continue this."

Chapter 12
Tessa

"More!"

Heat raced from the core of my stomach and through my limbs as I let the power explode from my body. Sweat was drenching the red dress I wore and the more Aetas tested me, the weaker I was becoming. I wasn't ready for this. I'd barely just got out of bed. If it weren't for Marie's blood, I would have been on death's doorstep.

The walls and floor shook around me as Marko's gift rippled the shield around us. Aetas was protected from the blast, but I could see the toll it was taking on him, too. He was sweating, absorbing the force I continually let free.

"Perfect. Each time you do this, you grow stronger. Already you've made progress. It's phenomenal, really. The talent you have could bring you right here to the top. Right under me if you kept this up. There'd be nothing you couldn't do, Princess."

"I don't want to be at the top. I want to go home," I said, angrily. "You wanted me to learn. I'm learning."

"You've learned nothing," he said, exploding. "You feel so confident in your abilities? Take me into your gaze. Show me what you can do."

He came forward at a swift pace, stopping before me. I could barely stand, more or less try the mind tricks he was so good at.

"Do it. Show me what you got. Make it quick or else I'll take you back into mine. That's a dangerous place for you to go if you want to be true to your precious Marko."

The threat had my eyes rising to his. I pushed into his mind, immediately feeling a wall block me. He was trying to make it impossible for me to enter, but I refused to give up so easily. Darkness began to seep in and I could feel a slight give. Powerful or not, Aetas had cracks in his armor. All I had to do was find a spot big enough for me to squeeze through and I'd have him.

"Come on, Princess. I don't have all night."

His words were far away, echoing in the distance. The harder I pushed, the more ground I lost. I tried to let myself relax. The need to become one with the void teased my thoughts. I wasn't sure if it was him slipping the idea in my mind or if it was me, but something within the knowledge clicked. Instead of keeping my energy focused toward a certain point, I let it expand. I could begin to feel myself ooze forward, slipping and sliding through as I grew larger. It was a scary sensation, but one I didn't balk from. If Aetas reversed our roles, he could use his authority again. I couldn't have that.

"You have two min—"

Like light in the darkness, I surged over his wall, falling right into his mind like a bottomless pit. It was the opposite of what I was supposed to be doing. I was meant to bring him into my mind. To control him that way, but this was better. Here I'd have unlimited knowledge. Here ... for the smallest moment ... I'd rule.

Images began to pour their way through, categorized in time. Time … yes … the void was the beginning. I could feel myself in it. Feel myself born as light blinded me. Years bombarded my brain. Centuries. I'd always been a vampire. Always known nothing but the dark.

As my gifts grew and the population within my kind expanded, I learned. I prospered. Nothing was out of reach. Nothing too hard. Boredom came. Loneliness. So many centuries and nothing I had to look forward to. *War.* It was always there. Always a game we came back to. One we relied on to kill time. We'd done this before on multiple occasions. We could do it again. Humans were stupid. We could always make them forget about our existence. Our myth would continue after our fun and we'd count down the decades before we geared up again. But this time was different. This time there was more media access. More technology. We could still cover up who we were after the bloodshed and population control, but did I want to? I was tired of this game. Tired of how everything was a never-ending cycle of the same old shit.

Aetas' thoughts continued, but I searched for more. More secrets. More information on his gifts. They were there, within me now, but I couldn't get a good read on how to use them. Just more imagines and sensations. They were my guide. My knowledge.

Energy raced up my mass causing me to internally claw to Aetas' mind in surprise. A pull snapped me from the void so hard that I stumbled back into the bed, falling over the corner of the mattress. Trembling shook my entire body as the realization hit me. The call wasn't from my leader. It was from Marko and he was close by. He was using our ties as a rope to lure me back to him. And I couldn't deny the order. I would react whether my mind wanted to or not.

"You…" Aetas dove, covering me with his weight as he grasped my neck. "How did you do that? What made you think you had the right!"

There was a murderous glint in his eyes. Training or not, I had overstepped my bounds. Saw into what our nature really was. *War.* It would always be there and he would never allow us to win. We weren't meant to. He knew what I had from the beginning. If we took over, we'd destroy this planet. The thing was, he was teetering on the brink of allowing it to happen. He was just as unstable as he claimed Marko to be.

"I made a mistake by thinking you had limits. You're more dangerous than I thought at this stage." His fingers eased on my neck, but still held firm. I saw the conflict in his eyes. He may have been threatened by my strength, but it enticed him. Greed. Even Aetas harbored it.

The pull yanked harder on my being and I fought to get myself loose from my leader. Through the daze, he hadn't noticed Marko's presence. I watched as the awareness had his gaze jerking to the curtains. A deep sound escaped his lips and he held tighter to my neck.

"The two of you are beginning to pose quite the problem."

"Let me go, then," I tried saying.

Tighter he choked me. My lips began going numb, along with my limbs. I hadn't seen much of this side of Aetas, but the longer I was here, the more I was starting to see that he wasn't above any of the other vampires I'd met. We were all cruel. All focused on our own needs. To hell with anyone else.

"You'll stay here. I'll deal with this once and for all."

"No, please." Everything within me wanted to attack him. To fight to escape. I couldn't. Not if I wanted to live. I would be nothing more than a fugitive. A vampire on the run. And they were good enough to find me. Besides, I was putting Marko in danger. Maybe it was best for him to think me dead. He would be safer. His pain I could soothe when I left here.

My eyes closed as the tears escaped. I could feel myself closing off. Become just as numb on the inside as parts of me were on the outside. Aetas seemed to feel my submission to the situation. His grip eased and his lips brushed over my cheek.

"Let me take this urge," he said, lifting enough to place his palm over my belly. "I will feel his call for you."

The connection from Marko snapped, making me cry out in agony. It shattered my heart the moment the need disappeared.

"Oh yes, he's on a mission. I'm going to enjoy this. It won't take me long."

Couldn't he just leave me be, tonight? I couldn't take anymore. I was beyond exhausted and hurt. I just wanted to lie in bed and have one good night of crying myself to sleep. *Alone.*

Aetas stood just as a panicked knock sounded at the door. The smile he threw me as he reached for the knob had a sickening feeling engulfing me. To him, I was nothing but a new toy. Something to fuck with until he grew bored of me, too. But how long would that be? I was breaking through his walls, physically and mentally. I didn't think that was a good thing. Perhaps I should have played the fool and pretended to be weak.

It was too late now.

The barrier shut and I stood, gripping to my stomach. The emptiness within had more tears sliding down my cheeks. I wanted Marko. I wanted to go home. What if Aetas hurt him? I didn't trust my leader. He had nothing to lose and he obviously didn't like Marko.

My vampire had me heading to the door. The protectiveness I felt had my pulse jumping in a frantic rhythm. I closed my eyes as I grabbed the door knob, searching through the knowledge I had gained from breaking into Aetas' mind. Warmth sunk into my palm from the energy imprint he had left behind and I was immediately looking through his eyes.

"Oh my God," I whispered.

A smile came, even through my fear. What I had done may have come with consequences, but I wouldn't regret breaching his trust. If I had insight into my leader, it left me a step ahead. He couldn't lie to me and that put me at ease.

Vampires slipped into the nooks and shadows as he passed. As *I* passed. We were one in the moment and he didn't even have a clue. There was anger surging through him, just as there was excitement to put Marko in his place. This was my house and no one came here without my consent. But he had, and now I would kick him out, probably weeping and begging for my mercy. Begging for *her*.

The emotions that surrounded him as he thought of me were confusing. He wasn't sure what to think. As much as he wanted to mentor me, to have someone to trust in, his make-up made it almost impossible. He wanted to hurt me, both physically and mentally. He craved twisting my impressionable ways with his own. Corruption was deeply buried within and if he could make me squirm, it'd feed his boredom. If he ruined me and Marko, even better. I deserved to be here amongst the best of our kind. And I'd be closer living here. He wanted me close. I could see him wanting to slip inside my room at random moments. It wasn't too sexual yet, but it was there. As it was with all of our kind. It was just a part of who we were.

"Tessa!"

Marko's yell echoed through the large space. He was being restrained at the front door, I could feel information feed through me from the vampires who served Axis. The fact that Marko had even made it through left them begging my forgiveness.

I bounded down the steps, seeing the scene come into view.

Two vampires clutched to his shoulders, holding him down to his knees. Dark hair was falling over his forehead, messily. He'd been fighting them and not with his gift. No … he wouldn't dare do that here. It made the joy within flare even more. He knew his place, even in his most desperate state of mind.

"Aetas! I know you have her. Give me Tessa."

I slowed as I approached, soaking in the anguish he held within. His power was a physical force against my skin. It was heavy as I let it feed me information on just how advanced he was in person.

"You got my letter. I've already told you, Tessa is dead."

"No," he said, shaking his head. "She's not. I heard her. She's alive. Our connection led me here."

I laughed, crossing his arms over his chest. "Of course it did. She's in the memorial room. Her spirit is strong. You will always feel it."

"She's not dead!"

I lowered, scanning over Marko's face as I pretended to think. "I see you're more grief-stricken then I assumed. Would you like to visit her tomb? Perhaps you will accept this and be at ease."

Marko made an agonizing sound and his head dropped, sending more dark hair falling forward. "She's not dead. She's not. I feel her here. I feel her alive."

"She will always be alive, Master Delacroix. We all are energy, alive or dead. You just have to accept that she's not going to be coming back to you in this life."

"No." The growl was deep. Marko thrashed his shoulders causing the two men holding him fight for footing. The bottomless sadness that began to fill me had Aetas' vision fading. I was slipping in my own impatience to leave the room. The battle to ease his suffering played out in my mind. What was better? Did I allow him to suffer until I got free, or disobey Aetas and put Marko at ease with my stay here? If I raced downstairs and exposed myself, my leader may never let me leave. But at least Marko would know I was alive. The biggest question was, would he fight to bring me home, or could I convince him to wait for me, no matter how long it took?

I didn't know.

I eased the door open, focusing more on Aetas' energy. He was still staring down at Marko. Still trying to figure out how to hurt him and prove a point. I knew I should stop and go back to the room, but my feet wouldn't stop going forward. God, what was I doing? Aetas could very well kill us both. Maybe when I got closer to the stairs, I'd come to my senses.

Aetas, let me speak with him. I will stay and do whatever you say. Please.

The words left me before I even considered whether I could talk to my leader. I should have known I could. He heard almost everything. As I watched his vision jerk up, it was clear he had.

"You left your room. Go back there now. I will deal with you when I return."

"You want me to stay. Marko will never be at peace or leave you alone until you let me do this. Allow me to send him home."

"Princess!"

"No!" I shouted back to him. *"Allow me this!"*

Aggravation roared through his head. He wanted to fight me, but he knew I was on the verge of shutting him out completely. He couldn't afford to lose me. My blood was too strong. Too vital if something unforseen were to happen and he needed me to help protect our kind.

"Allow me. Please. You will have me at your disposal for as long as you need. But do not cheat me this opportunity to say goodbye to the man I love." I didn't have to threaten what would happen if he didn't. It was evident in my tone.

"Rise," Aetas yelled, angrily. *"Rise, Master Delacroix and tell your beloved goodbye."*

Marko's head snapped up and confusion filled his features as he slowly pushed to his feet. I didn't wait for Aetas to say anymore. I sprinted for the stairs, taking them as fast as I could. Marko jerked from the grasp that held him and raced past Aetas, toward me. My heart was pounding so fast that the ache was returning, but I didn't care.

"Tessa!"

I kept my eyes on Marko, barely even seeing where I stepped. When I got to the bottom, he had already covered the distance, sweeping me in his arms.

"God, I knew you were alive." The grip in which he held me was so crushing that I fought to breathe. He seemed to catch himself as he pulled back, pressing his lips into mine. "I was so lost without you. I…" Again he kissed me. I held around his neck, taking in his scent, trying my best to memorize everything about the smell, even though I already had.

"I've been lost, too. I've miss you so much."

The sob couldn't be contained as I locked myself to him tighter.

"Look at me, ma minette. Let me see you. You don't look well."

I didn't want to pull back and leave him. If I could close my eyes, perhaps I could convince myself this was just a dream. Maybe I'd be back in his arms the night we were meant to become bound. I could kill Hunter before he killed me and reverse this horrible path.

Fingers buried in my hair and I let Marko ease me out of his neck. His brown eyes searched my face for so long, I couldn't help but wonder what was going through his mind. I couldn't read it and I knew why. He didn't want Aetas hearing, but I doubted what he was doing was working. Aetas heard almost everything.

"You're not well."

My head shook. I knew I wasn't. I was growing weaker by the minute. Marie's blood had lasted for a while, but not long enough with what our leader was having me do.

"I'll take care of you when we leave here. I'll make you better."

Again, my head shook. "I'm not going, Marko. I … have to stay for a little longer."

"Stay? To learn?" he asked, quietly.

"Yes. Aetas is making me stronger.

"No, he's making you weaker. Look at you. You're sick. You need to be resting and taking in my blood. You need to heal."

I wanted to peer around Marko to see what Aetas was doing, but thought against it. Instead, I placed my hands on his cheeks, letting him feel the energy of how much stronger I'd already become. His wide eyes rose to mine and my new knowledge of Aetas pushed through his depths, flashing before his vision. My journey of being here followed. My leader wouldn't be able to pick it up. Marko was too high in rank to let our information slip though. As long as we didn't speak internally, we'd be safe.

"Shh," I breathed out, under my breath. "You have to give me time," I whispered. "You have to leave me until I'm ready to be released. Will you wait for me?"

"I can't leave you," he said, pained. "I can't…"

"You can," I assured. "You see I'm here. I'm yours. All I need is your word that you'll be ready for me when I'm finished."

Marko's arms came around me tightly, hugging me close. "I would wait a million years if it meant you'd become mine all over again."

"You just might have to," Aetas ground out as he walked around to the side of us. "You interfere with what I wish for her to learn. You were a problem before, but you're an even bigger problem now."

Marko turned, glaring in his direction. Heat, so intense it was almost unbearable, penetrated into my chest from his anger. I reached up, bringing his attention back to me.

"I will learn fast. You will see me soon."

The furious heat dissipated as he gazed into my eyes. "I believe in you. When you return I will be honored to announce our newest member, and my concubine. You've come so far. You hold great power, ma minette. I'm proud of you. What you've been through would break most, but not you." He glanced at Aetas, bringing his focus back to me. "I will wait for you. For as long as it takes."

I'm not sure what I expected, but it wasn't that Marko would take to this so easily. He was thinking something and although I wanted to know, I knew better than to take another chance at seeing with Aetas watching. I had faith that I'd see soon enough. And I would. With the knowledge that came from Aetas, Marko and I could see each other sooner than I imagined.

"Tell the Princess goodbye, Master Delacroix. She has more lessons to learn."

The glint in Aetas' stare made me feel sick. I was going to pay for what I'd done. It was etched so deeply in the way he looked at me, I was afraid to know what it was.

Marko gripped the back of my neck, pulling me into his throat. I wrapped my arms around him pretending to give him a hug. What he wanted was clear and if I was already going to be in trouble, I might as well be strong enough to face my punishment.

My fangs lowered and I bit down, brutally, needing more blood than a small puncture would allow. Fingers tightened on my neck and I didn't think as I let my claw extend to slice into my wrist. Blindly, I jerked my arm before me and Marko found it almost instantly. His lips locked on the wound, taking me into him as I sucked him in with everything I had. Shooting pains, exploded in my stomach.

The final mark. The last tie to bond us together forever.

An inferno flared, shooting through my body so intense that my lips broke suction. The intensity was like I'd never felt before. A scream tore from my throat and I was suddenly being pulled back and held against a body. It took me a moment to realize Marko was standing a few feet away. Aetas, he had me.

"Get out!" His voice left my skin vibrating even more. I screamed again, feeling my body bow in his arms. The fire was growing, feeding me in all the right places. My heart expanded, only to draw back in with such force that the thump in my ears was like a cannon. Marko was holding to his stomach, staggering backwards as he kept his stare on me. He didn't want to leave. I could see that. Aetas' order would have pushed him to the door whether he wanted it or not.

"Out!" He yelled again.

The blaze grew in my stomach as I twisted roughly through the pain. Marko was so strong. So amazingly potent that having us linked together completely was excruciating. More of his powers were becoming mine, and mine, his. It was a shock to my weak system, just as Marie's blood had been. But Marko's station make it ungraspable.

"Breathe," Aetas yelled at me. "Do you know what you've done, Master Delacroix? You could very well kill her for sure! Her heart wasn't ready for this. Why do you think I've been feeding her weak blood? Why do you think I've kept you away!"

My feet slid out from under me and I realized I couldn't feel them anymore. My whole body seemed to be disappearing. If it wasn't for Aetas' grip, I'd be on the floor.

"We have to stop this. We have to…" Aetas lowered me to the ground and I could see his true fear. He wasn't pretending or over-exaggerating like I had thought he'd been doing. Something was seriously not right.

"Okay…" His hands rose to my cheeks while he blinked repeatedly. He had no idea what he was going to do and I could read into it too easily.

Movement settled next to me and Aetas' head shot up. "What the hell are you still doing here? I said leave."

"The devil himself couldn't keep me away. If Tessa's in trouble, I'm going to be here until she's better. Do you seriously think I'd depart thinking there's a chance she might die … again?"

"You will both pay for what you've done."

"Do what you have to, but first focus on her or I will."

My feet were able to plant and I pushed against the floor, sliding through the round of electrical currents that attacked my internal system. Deep breaths were leaving me and I couldn't slow my pulse from hammering wildly. The expansion was so hard and fast that I almost could feel the wound in my heart tear back open. I thought I had been healed … I was wrong.

"The two of you stop fighting. Put me to sleep." I choked out the words. "Knock me out!"

The men looked at each other, but Marko reacted first. He locked with my eyes and I was sucked into darkness. Into the heaven within him. It was peace … serenity, and it wouldn't last. Hell would be waiting when I awoke. Aetas would make sure of it.

Chapter 13
Marko

The pain in my chest wasn't my own. My heart was beating so fast that I felt like I could run the distance from here to the underground city and not break a sweat. And Tessa was feeling the same thing whether she was unconscious or not. My eyes kept darting around wildly and my lungs were sucking in air every few seconds. The vast amount of power my bonded held was too shocking for me to grasp. I knew someday she'd be one of the strongest in the world, but to feel it within myself, even I couldn't hold both of our strengths, combined. She hadn't surpassed me yet, but she wasn't far off. The fact that she had come so far so fast had me afraid for her. Not just because of her heart, but because of what our leader wanted. What were his motives?

"You can barely hold yourself together." Aetas snapped at me. "Look at you. You're a fucking wreck."

I glanced at Tessa, glad I had gotten her under before she had a chance to see me. "You did this. It's your fault. Had you not pushed her too hard, too fast, I wouldn't have felt the need to try to save her. The bond... I hadn't expected her to do that, but I couldn't deny her, either. Never."

"You're stupid in your love-stricken state, Master Delacroix. Who is the real leader, here? *Me.* There's a reason for that. I know what is best for her. Had you left this situation alone and continued to focus on your human, I could have healed her and sent her home to you in amazing shape. She would have been ready to rule. Now you might have ruined everything."

Footsteps pounded across the large room as members rushed forward. I could feel their power emanate as they grew closer. One wasn't even as strong as me, barely as strong as Tessa, and my bonded was only beginning to tap into herself. Jesus. She was going to be in trouble. She couldn't handle what Aetas had unlocked inside of her. Now with the added abilities she'd just received from me, she was going to be worse. Too supreme for her own good. Maybe for all of ours. And her personality would change because of it. That was a given. If she had felt entitled before, it wasn't going to compare after the blood combined completely.

"Master Aetas." Margo and three other vampires came to a stop before us. They looked at me nervously as I stared them down.

"Draw a cold bath in the Princess's room," Aetas said, lifting her. "Get her a Valium and a large glass of water."

"Valium? Have you lost your mind? She's a vampire. It won't last five minutes in her system."

Cold eyes cut toward me. "The initial shock of her waking is what I'm trying to calm. Anxiety will kick in the moment she becomes aware and I don't know about you, but I'm not ready for the wrath that will follow. Her heart can't handle any more excitement."

Maybe he had a point, but I couldn't see what difference it would make. Tessa didn't have short fits. When she was angry or upset, she could go for hours. Days, even. At least she had me. Surely, that would help with the side effects.

Aetas started up the stairs and the moment I began to follow, he threw me a look. I didn't stop and I wasn't leaving until I made sure Tessa was alright. Regardless that he was the leader, she had rights. Now that we were bonded, I had a say in what they were. Our kind worked as a system. Aetas might have had a hand up over the laws, but he still had to follow them.

A hall stretched out on both sides and we turned right. He walked at a fast pace, turning into one of the rooms toward the end. Her scent engulfed me the moment we walked in. If I wouldn't have been so hyped up on our bond, it would have calmed me. As it was, I couldn't stop fidgeting.

"There we go," he said, quietly, laying her on top of the blankets. He turned her on her side, jerking the lacing free in one hard yank. The moment he reached to pull down her dress, I couldn't stop the growl that left me.

"I can take it from here. I think you've done enough. You're not me," I said, staring right into his eyes.

A smile tugged at his lips and he raised an eyebrow, taking a step out of the way. "Go ahead, your time here is limited, anyway."

My head cocked to the side and I stopped myself from speaking. I didn't have to say words for him to know he was pushing me further than he wanted to. I didn't care who he was, I wasn't going to back down, concerning Tessa. Not as her ruler, and sure as hell not as her new mate.

Bonded. Yes … we were finally getting where we needed to be.

I stepped forward, taking his place. The water was already running and I turned as a blonde woman stepped from the adjoining restroom.

"Mistress Gina, set the Princess out a nightgown. She'll be confined to bed for at least twenty-four hours. I want her as comfortable as possible."

"Gina," I repeated. I straightened as she paused to look at me. "I do believe I owe you something."

The blonde took a step back at my advance and I didn't care if she was male or female. I reared back, slapping her across the face. She gasped and jerked her palm to her cheek.

"If you ever raise your hand to one of mine again, you will face *me*. I don't care that you're a member here. Marie was a guest under this roof and you treated her horribly. I will not forget that."

Margo paused at the door, looking between me and Aetas. "How did he know that? How did you know that?" she said, walking at a brisk pace in my direction.

"I know things," I said, coldly. "You all-mighty vampires think you're untouchable. Truth is, you're not as good as you think. Your gifts have flaws. Ones I have no problem deciphering. Let that tell you something. Politics or not, I know where I deserve to be."

I turned, sweeping Tessa into my arms. My gaze stopped on Aetas. "You should stop holding this grudge against me and maybe think about bringing me in. Tessa belongs to me and together, we're one hell of an asset. You trying to get her alone will only weaken what you're attempting to accomplish. If you want her to be the best, let me be by her side. She'll flourish."

There was no point waiting for an answer. I didn't expect one.

"Pill." I held out my hand and Margo cautiously came forward, handing over the tablet. I shut myself in the restroom, slowly undressing Tessa. The sound of the water had her stirring and I separated her lips, pushing the pill through and rubbing her throat until she swallowed.

"Ma minette." I leaned against the counter top and caressed her face, waiting. Aetas was right in assuming she'd come to in hysterics. It was natural. What I didn't expect when she opened her eyes was for them to be completely black like when she was a newborn. "Slow breaths, love. It's just me and you."

A large intake had her chest rising. Aside from her obeying, she stayed eerily quiet and still. It was either a good sign or a disastrous one.

"I'm going to give you a bath. It's going to make you feel better. I want you to prepare yourself though, it's going to be very cold."

I eased to stand, making sure my movements were slow. Anything could set her off. The last thing I wanted when she held so much power was to defend myself against it. I could throw a shield all day long, but the action took its toll. And who was to say she wouldn't make her way through. This new Tessa was pretty damn strong and the more she used her gifts, the fiercer they would become.

Slowly, I lowered, easing to my knees as I let her hover over the full tub.

"Remember. It's cold. This is best for you. It's going to slow your blood-flow."

Tessa's hand dropped lifelessly to the side, sliding into the water. I felt myself tense as I waited for some sort of reaction. Still nothing. I let my arms begin to lower, jerking to a stop as the water began to boil beneath us. I jumped to my feet, pulling her hand up to inspect for any damage. It wasn't so much as red.

"Shit," I breathed out. My eyes went back to the steaming water. I couldn't believe what I was seeing. She shouldn't be able to affect the temperature. I didn't hold that gift and neither did she… But Tessa had showed me things. Things she taken from Aetas when she had breached his mind. It had my pulse racing even more. This wasn't good. She shouldn't have been able to get in his head to begin with.

I leaned over, pushing down the knob to drain the water. As I stood back up, Tessa still stared at the ceiling, more in a comatose state than anything.

"Ma minette, can you speak to me? Can you tell me if you're alright?"
Silence.

I waited for the water to drain and turned the cold back on, refilling the tub. I had to slow down this process. The cold would stall the effects. It would bring her back, slowly, but surely.

"Let's try this again. Don't heat the water, okay? Cold." I said the word as I began easing her down. The frigid iciness soaked into my jacket and I paused in holding to her, waiting to see if I needed to lift. I wasn't going to chance her getting burned if she increased the temperature again. When seconds went by and she didn't respond, I sat her down. In a quick pace, I stripped my jacket off. Tessa's eyes were still black. Still empty of anything. As time went by, I kept my stare locked, waiting to see some type of change.

Get me out.

The voice was robotic in my head. Almost devoid of tone. It was enough to have me pause as I processed it. The delay mixed with my refusing thoughts. I didn't want her to get out. She needed to slow her blood. To be brought out of this state.

Within the mere seconds it took to gather my thoughts to speak, they were cut off by water exploding from the tub. The shock wave that surrounded the freezing liquid sent me flying back against the far wall. The door blew from its hinges, sliding into the bedroom. And the invisible force didn't stop. I stayed glued to the wall as I watched Tessa stand from the tub. The anger she held radiated off of her in an aura so powerful I couldn't do anything but stare as she headed past me through the door.

Aetas and Margo stood a few feet away. He was yelling at the female, telling her to prepare. It took every ounce of force I possessed just to get to my feet.

"Tessa!" My hand reached for her, breaking through some form of thick shield that surrounded her nude frame. Black eyes shot to me and she turned her head. *Evil.* The killer she was put all of its attention not to my physical self, but to the real me, within. For the first time, I feared her. What she wanted to take wasn't just my life. She wanted my soul. The essence of who I was and I knew where she'd gotten the knowledge to do that.

"Come to me," I said, cautiously. "Let me hold you. I'll take care of you."

Some sort of awareness flickered in her black gaze. She was coming to. She was going to be okay.

"Gina, stop! Go back outside!"

Margo's voice had Tessa's head snapping to the side … and suddenly she was gone. My heart stopped in that moment. Nothing I'd ever seen in all of my years could have prepared me for witnessing an actual disappearance of a vampire. Masters could make themselves invisible all we wanted, but that's not what had happened. I would have still seen her, felt her. Tessa was gone.

"No," Aetas said under his breath. "No!"

I ran my hand through my hair trying to suppress the shiver that raced down my spine. My clothes were soaked, but it wasn't because of that. My eyes searched the room in panicked movements as I searched for some type of difference in the atmosphere. I wasn't sure if she was still here or if she'd gone somewhere else.

"Do you see what you've done?" Aetas asked, advancing toward me. "Do you see what you've created?"

"Me? It's your fault," I exploded. "Had you protected your mind better, she wouldn't have learned this from you."

A strangled sound had both of our heads whipping around to Margo. She was stiff, rigid, as her fingers twitched and her eyes rolled back. A sickening sensation rushed through me while I watched with dread.

"Jesus," Aetas said under his breath. "She's absorbing. She's…"

"What?" I yelled. "She's what?"

He raced to Margo, placing his hand over her eyes. I could *feel* his strength as he used his powers. An energy filled the room so thick that I fought to breathe. From out nowhere, Tessa's body appeared hovering, only to drop, crumbling to the ground. I rushed to her side, watching as she gasped, repeatedly. Her eyes were closed as if she were sleeping.

"Actas." A cry sounded through the room and he caught Margo's body as it began to fall. Sobs left her and he immediately began to escort her to the door where Gina watched fearfully. *She had witnessed it all.*

"Take Margo to her room to rest. Have her feed. I'll check in shortly."

His voice was almost hollow sounding and I didn't miss it as he dismissed the two females. When he came to kneel before me, on the other side of Tessa, I could read his shock.

"She's an absorber. A snatcher. She reads and steals." He lowered his gaze, staring into her face. "It could have been a one-time occurrence due to her condition, but I'm not so sure."

"Are you saying she just did to Margo what she did to you?"

"Took in my knowledge…?" His eyes cut up to me. "Yes."

There were no words as I let my stare drop. "What are you going to do?"

To say I didn't know there were consequences were ridiculous. Tessa was unstable. A danger to our race if she decided to be. And I had felt her ability to steal who I was, even if Aetas didn't. Tessa could have killed me from the inside if she have chosen to do so.

"There are many things I could do about her imprinting Margo's gift, but only one I care to." He licked his lips as he watched her and a smile pulled at the side of his mouth. "I'm going to take it as my own."

Chapter 14
Hunter

During my life, I had been covered in blood more times than I could count. Tonight was no exception. As we emerged from the underground tunnels surrounding Fort Hood, I took one look at myself in the dim light from the street light above and shook my head. My shirt was drenched, as were places on my black cargo pants. Johnson emerged from the manhole, laughing as he stared me up and down.

"You are one crazy son of bitch, Moretti. I can't believe you took on those bastards with your bare hands."

I shrugged as I helped him out. "When you have nothing to lose, death holds no fear. The only thing that scares me is not making a difference in this world before I breathe my last breath."

Johnson slapped my shoulder, turning to help more soldiers from our exit. "You made a hell of a change here, tonight. I don't think we've ever had a kill count that high before."

"Y'all already pretty much have the area secure. The hard part will come when we get to the underground city. We're talking hundreds, maybe even thousands of vampires and slaves. They'll stick together. The humans will die trying to protect their masters. It's going to be one hell of a battle."

Childers placed the manhole cover back on and I turned to follow Johnson toward his truck. Romano and Andrews rode with others so it was just the two of us as we separated from the group. Traffic was at a steady pace through the town of Killeen, but no one seemed to care what we were doing. Maybe they were used to it.

"How long do you think before we head to Austin?" I couldn't help but ask. I couldn't lie and say I didn't feel fear at going back again. I did. Where once my nightmares revolved around the battlefield, now they were all about the underground city.

"Probably a few more weeks. I want to get in all the new equipment before we take on a place that big. We'll need more soldiers. More volunteers with some sort of training. The last thing I want is another massacre down there. I wish I would have known what we were up against when we lost Thatcher and Waters. Hell man, I didn't have a clue back then."

"That makes two of us," I breathed out.

I reached for the passenger door, pausing as I went to open it. Long, dark hair blew back from a pair of pale shoulders and I felt myself take steps to the front of the truck. The woman was so close to the size of Tessa that I had to blink past the confusion. Even the hair was around the same length.

"Hey!" I yelled trying to get her to turn around.

"What's up, you know her?"

Johnson's voice barely registered as I began to walk at a fast pace in her direction. I knew I had to be losing my mind, but I couldn't shake a weird feeling that made me physically feel sick.

The woman stopped, keeping her back to me. She was right on the corner of the road. Was she looking for something? Someone?

"Hey!" I called out again, beginning to jog across the busy street. Her long, white dress billowed out behind her, so unfitting for the urban surroundings that it had me going even faster. Darkness began to engulf the woman's small frame as she rounded the turn. I pushed myself, breaking around the corner…to nothing. Not a person was in sight. Slowly, I stopped, rubbing my hand over the top of my head. "I'm fucking losing it."

I turned to go back to the truck, jolting as I came face to face with black glaring eyes. Tessa was there one minute, gone the next. *Just like a ghost.*

In fast steps, I stumbled back, hearing laughter echo off the walls. Johnson was suddenly before me, talking, but I couldn't make out his words through the mocking sound.

"Do you hear that? Did you see her?"

Deep pants left my mouth while I continued to spin in a circle.

"Calm man, I don't see anyone. Maybe the woman went into one of the…" He stopped as he looked around. There were no business or doors on this side of the street.

"She was here. She … disappeared before my very eyes."

"Shit like this happens to me all the time," Johnson said, uncertainly. "PTSD, it has to be. Let's go home."

I jumped back as his arm lifted out toward me. "But you saw her, too."

Glowing skin flashed in the far distance and I let my hand come to push against my heart as she swayed her hips, heading toward me. Like there was a bad connection, she disappeared, only to flicker and reappear closer. Her features where hard, enraged, as she kept my stare. But all I heard was the laughter. It taunted me. Teased and ridiculed my failed attempt to kill her. Even dead, she was determined to not let me forget.

"I'm watching you. You're going to pay, Hunter."

"No." My head shook as I stepped closer to the brick wall. "You're dead. I killed you. You're dead!"

"Am I?" Tessa flashed right before me, baring her fangs before she disappeared, again. I jumped back, hitting the wall. Johnson grabbed my bicep, pulling me toward the road as I stared at the now empty street in shock.

"She's dead," I repeated. "I killed her. She's dead."

"I know, man. Come on, you need rest and some water. You're probably dehydrated. Let's get you home and in bed."

"You didn't see her?"

"No," he whispered. "Only the woman on the street when you first took off after her."

I stayed quiet as we loaded up. It wasn't until Johnson began driving that I could bear to look at him. "She was there. I saw her. I saw Tessa."

"I'm still here," she said, flashing before my vision. I gripped to the door, trying to tell myself these images were all in my head. Guilt. It was fucking with me. What I did to her was necessary. Tessa had been out of control.

"I believe you," Johnson said, glancing over, concerned.

"He thinks you're losing your mind. That you're going crazy."

"Maybe I am," I whispered.

"What's that?" Johnson kept taking peeks at me as he turned to head toward the base.

"Nothing," I mumbled. "You're right. I need rest. I haven't been sleeping much."

Not a mile went by before we were pulling up to the guards. I stayed in a daze, waiting for her return. Waiting for Tessa to catch me off guard. When we pulled into the driveway, I was finally able to somewhat relax.

"Let's eat. I'm starving. I know you have to be, too. You like leftover spaghetti?"

"My last name is Moretti, what do you think?" I raised an eyebrow, following him in as he laughed.

When he unlocked the door and we walked inside, I took in all the pictures of him and his wife. Pain shot through my chest and I averted my eyes, not able to look at them for long.

Johnson walked in the kitchen, flipping on the light. As he began to take the Tupperware out, he handed me a beer. I had never felt more in need of one. I cracked the top of the can, savoring the taste as I took a huge swallows.

"Back there on the street... " I began.

"Don't even," he said, pulling out two plates. "You don't have to explain nothing. You've been through some heavy shit. It's going to be tough for a few months. Don't hesitate to talk to me if you need to," he said, glancing over. "We take care of ours. You know that."

I nodded, taking another drink. "She … killed my uncle. The priest I mentioned, earlier. It was the final straw. He was a part of her life since childhood. I knew after that Tessa couldn't be saved. The worse part, she said she did it for me. To prove her loyalty or something." I took a shuddering breath. "She was so different. At times, I was more afraid of her than I've ever been scared of anything. Other times, I thought maybe I was catching glimpses of the woman I had fallen in love with. The decision didn't come easy. It fucking destroyed me."

Johnson popped a plate in the microwave, turning to lean against the counter. "You made the right choice."

"Yeah," I said, lowering my head. "After everything, she still went back to him—the vampire who had taken her. She fucking chose him over me. She was going to get married that night. The dress. She looked beautiful. Like a dream with all of those diamonds in her hair. I … hated her for it in the moment."

The beeping of the microwave caused me to look up. The sadness on Johnson's face had me stiffening. I wasn't in my right mind. I was babbling. Maybe it needed to come out, but I didn't want to talk about it. Yet, I was.

"You did what you had to." He handed over the plate and I took it, walking to the small table he had in the corner.

"I suppose. If I wouldn't have, Lord knows what she would be capable of. She was meant to rule." I glanced up to him as he put his plate in the microwave.

"Rule? Rule what? Austin?"

My head nodded. "Austin… Maybe the world. Hell, I don't know. She holds the same blood I do, but it's mixed with Marko's. That's the Master Vampire who took her. He rules the city now. The combination of the two strains of blood would have put her above him, right into Axis."

Johnson's eyes were big as he blinked past my confession. "Holy shit. That's just … crazy. It's good you killed her. If she would have gotten into her true powers before you had your chance, you might not have succeeded in stopping her."

"Yeah." My head lowered and I stared at my plate as I began to eat. I couldn't imagine what Tessa would have been capable of if she grew to her true strength. It was too scary to think about. Marko was terrifying enough, but if she would have surpassed him, how developed would her gifts have become?

Johnson sat across from me and we ate in silence. When we finished and cleaned our plates, he walked me to a back bedroom, decorated in a pale yellow and white.

"Your room."

A grin tugged at my lips. "Thank you. I appreciate this more than you know."

"Hey, anything for a fellow soldier. You'd do the same for me."

"I would," I said, walking forward. "And someday I'll pay you back. I promise."

"Let's kill the motherfuckers responsible for ruining our lives. That's repayment enough." He pointed across the hall. "Shower's in there. I'll get you some of my clothes. We're close enough to the same size."

"I appreciate it."

He spun, disappearing back down the hall. I reached for the belt around my waist, unfastening it and placing my weapons on the bed. An uneasiness crept over the back of my neck and I spun around, seeing nothing.

"Pick up the gun, Hunter. Let me see you eat that barrel again. Do it. Come with me for real this time."

"Uh-uh." My teeth clenched and I squeezed my lids shut, reaching to place my fingers over my forehead.

"It's only fair. You promised you would take care of me. You said you loved me. You lied! Murderer!"

My fingers twitched and I groaned deeply under my breath. When I opened my eyes, the gun was out of the holster, lying on the bed before me. I couldn't breathe while scanning the bedroom. Fuck, I was seriously losing my mind.

"Here you go."

Johnson's voice had me jumping. I turned, taking the workout shorts and Army shirt he held out.

"Thanks."

"You bet. Get some rest. I have to head in early, but make yourself at home. There's some restaurants on base if you want to check them out while I'm gone. I'll leave some money on the bar."

My head shook, but he put up his hand, stopping me. He turned, leaving, and I clutched to the clothes tighter. I was going to owe him so much and if the only thing he wanted me to do was kill vampires, I was more than happy to do my part.

Chapter 15
Tessa

Pounding thrummed in my head, pulling me from the deepest sleep I could ever remember. I wasn't ready to wake up. There was something I had to do. Something … I couldn't remember. I felt groggy. Hungover, as I turned to my side. When my hand brushed against a bare arm, Marko's name registered. My eyes flew open and I had to fight to remember him even arriving. Yes, he'd come for me. And we were bonded, now. The realization was enough to make me forget about the headache.

I bit my lip, snuggling in closer. Even asleep, his arm came to pull me in the rest of the way. With my face against his chest, I breathed in his intoxicating scent. Was Aetas letting him stay with me? What had happened after we exchanged blood? I couldn't remember past the pain. Marko had put me to sleep and then … nothing.

"Je t'aime."

I told him I loved him in French. It was a part of who I was now. It was all I wanted to remember of who Tessalyn Antoinette Kennedy was. She was a vampire, born and meant for a French aristocrat, who loved her just as much as she loved him. There was no human life. No reminders of everything we'd gone through. Bonded, we were new, again. Just Tessa and Marko, rulers of Austin's underground city.

"I love you, more." Marko answered back in our language, holding me tighter. "You're awake. How do you feel?"

"Hungover. My head hurts and my body aches."

"It's to be expected after last night." His lids fluttered open. "And your heart?"

I tuned into my body, smiling. "Stronger than ever."

"Perfect."

My thigh eased between his and Marko moaned as I pulled my nightgown to my hips and rubbed my pussy along his leg.

"You're not ready," he said, already lowering his lips to mine in a light brush.

"I am. Feel." I grasped his hand, sliding it under the low collar to place over my heart. "Do you feel how fast and strong it beats? I *am* ready."

Pressure pushed against my slit as his leg drew up. I couldn't help but arch as my clit pulsed for more.

"You want me," I said, breaching the lining of his pants to grasp his hard cock.

"That's an understatement. You have no idea how badly I want you."

Marko rolled me to my back, pulling the nightgown over my head. Clumsily, my fingers worked the clasp free. We both made incoherent sounds as I unzipped his pants and his cock fell free from the restraint. With a firm grip, I stroked the thick length, moving impatiently as I waited for him to get into position.

"Are you sure you can take me?"

His chest dipped as his mouth hungrily found mine. I could feel my nails extend the smallest amount as I held to his back with my other hand, trying to get him to drop his hips even more.

"I can take all of you. If you'll just..." I wiggled, while he pinned me down with more of his weight. A small chuckle left him and he buried his face in my neck. The warmth of his breath had my eyes closing. I gasped as his fingers began to massage the length of my folds.

"You're so wet, ma minette. Maybe I'll taste you first and see how well you do before we go too far."

The thought was torture for all the right reasons. I wanted to feel his face buried in my pussy, but I longed to have him deep inside of me, too. I was impatient and it was showing.

Marko lifted, kissing his way from my neck, to one of my breasts. Suction tugged against my nipple as he drew me into his mouth. With the path he made around the outside of my entrance, I couldn't help but whimper.

"Marko, please."

"We've only just begun. Don't tell me you're ready for me to stop already?"

"Stop? No." I pressed into his shoulder, but he couldn't resist teasing my other nipple before he lowered toward my waist and sucked against my skin.

"*Yes.*" My head lifted while I watched him bite down, only to continue on. One of his fingers breached my opening and I cried out as he eased the length in at a slow pace. I rocked, trying to get him to go faster.

Marko's eyes shot up and I stilled at the silent command. Deeper, he pushed, spreading me wide as he added another digit to join the first. In slow circles his thumb teased over the sensitive nub. My legs braced against the mattress as intense heat formed at the contact.

"More." The thrusts had continuous sounds leaving me and I could barely speak through the need. The scruff on his cheek rubbed against my inner thigh and I made a deep groan as he turned and pricked the skin with one of his fangs. Pleasure burst through and I nearly screamed at the shock of how intense it was. Blood beaded over the skin and his tongue licked over the wound, closing it, only to break it open, again. My pulse was pounding so hard that I could feel it throughout my entire body.

Crimson began to flow from my thigh and his tongue flattened over the stream.

"I wonder if your cum will taste as sweet as I remember? I bet it will."

I blinked past his thoughts, too clouded with desire. Marko's tongue replaced the contact over my clit and I cried out as he flicked the tip in a fast pace. I knew I was getting louder, but I couldn't contain the bliss he was giving me. Faster, I moved, so close to release as he began slamming his fingers into me.

"You like that." He sucked the top of my slit into his mouth. With the accompanying pressure against my G-spot, I felt myself spasm and explode in release. My orgasm sent waves of ecstasy crashing over me. The room spun, yet it was the last thing I was thinking about. Marko's fingers withdrew almost immediately and I clutched to his hair, rocking my hips as he pushed his tongue into my entrance. The passion he held while he took his time reveling in my release had

me building all over again. When he lifted, he looked fierce, possessive, and ready to eat me alive.

His pants were thrown across the room as he stripped down and his arm looped around my waist, pulling me on top of him. I lifted, grasping his cock. For the smallest moment, I locked up. Something was pushing through and I wasn't sure what it was. As I stared into his depths, Marko's arm lifted and he clutched to my hair, wrapping it around his fist. He was trapping me and I knew it, but for the life of me I couldn't help but push past his wall. His life unfolded in a movie that was on hyper-speed. I felt myself relax as I took in his memories. The content I didn't care about. It was him that I had to make sure of. When I got to him meeting me, I pulled away, not caring to see more. It was Marko; that's all that mattered.

Slowly, I eased down, letting his thick length stretch me. A tug on my hair had me lowering and I met his lips, yelling into his mouth as he surged forward.

"Fuck, you feel so good. I knew you would."

I squirmed, trying to rise so I could look at his eyes again. Tighter, he held, plunging into me deeper.

"Marko?"

"If that's what you wish."

My arms shot down, trying to wedge between his so I could unlock his hold and wrestle myself free. I was flipped to my back so fast that I didn't think to brace my leg to try to prevent it. Aetas was suddenly before me, pinning me down with more than just his weight. The air seemed to move in, enveloping me with an invisible blanket and I screamed at the top of my lungs. Faster, he thrust, covering my mouth with one of his palms.

"Shh, don't fight it."

Marko was suddenly over me, again. A confused expression covered his face and I wasn't weighed down anymore. He was fucking me, slowly, passionately. For the briefest moment I questioned if I'd invented the entire thing in my head. Had Aetas been before me at all?

"I love you," he said, lowering to cover his body to mine. Marko went to kiss me and I quickly turned away, pressing into his chest to get him off.

"You have to stop. I…"

There was no fight on his end as I separated us and moved to the other side of the bed.

"What's wrong? Did I do something?" Pain flashed and I felt my heart break. Somehow I knew I was looking at the real Marko, but I wasn't sure what the hell was happening.

"I'm sorry. I…" Confusion had me sliding off the mattress to grab my nightgown. I quickly put it on, wiping the tear that slid down my cheek. I hated not being in control of my mind.

Marko stood, walking around to pull me in his arms. "Talk to me. Why are you so upset? Did I hurt you?" His palm came to fit over my heart and I shook my head, furiously. Anger was starting to sink in, but not at him.

"I … heard … saw, Aetas. I thought he was you for a moment. I got confused."

Marko's jaw tightened and he wrapped his arms around me tightly, kissing the top of my head. "We'll be out of here soon. I'm going to stay a few days and hopefully in that time he'll release you."

"If he doesn't?"

Marko broke away, grabbing his pants and sliding them on. I could see the battle on his face. He'd betray Aetas if it came to me and I couldn't allow that. Not if I wanted to prevent an all-out war between our kind. I had seen the way the members reacted when they thought I had hurt our leader. They were ready to kill me or lock me away. They'd be faithful to him even after his death. We'd never win. Even if me or Marko rose enough to beat him, there was no guarantee we'd be able to lead.

My fingers came up to press against Marko's lips as he separated them to say something. I shook my head, cutting him off.

"I leave when I can. However long it takes. You will wait for me and I will wait for you."

The rage within him only seemed to increase.

"Don't think it," I whispered. "It's a suicide mission. Let it go."

"I don't work like that, ma minette. I can't just let something go, concerning you. You're mine. Not his to toy with."

"You've lost me once. Do you want to lose me, again? That's what will happen if you do not stop this. I gave my word. You and I will deal. After this, we will never come back and we'll be happy. Together. *Alive.*"

A small growl left him as he pulled me back into his arms. "I hate this. I hate you being here."

I hated it more, but I couldn't say that. I'd do my time, no matter what that entailed, and then I'd be free. Once that happened, I could focus back on what was important. On revenge.

My body stiffened as images flooded in. Ones I wasn't sure were memories or delusions of my bond.

Hunter. Yes...

Chapter 16
Marko

My cock was aching, my head spinning, and I had never wanted to destroy Aetas as much as I did in this moment. What he had done to Tessa over the time she'd been here pushed the boundaries of my mated vampire. I wanted to kill him. Annihilate him so there was nothing left when I finished. Whether or not he was fucking with her now, I wasn't sure, but I was already past the point of dealing with his shit.

Rigidness straightened her frame and I pulled my head back, looking down. "You okay? What's wrong?" I tried to keep my tone smooth, but it was anything but.

"I…" She stepped back, out of my embrace, and begin to pace. "I think I may have gone to Hunter last night."

My eyes widened in disbelief. "What do you mean, you went to him?" Jealousy and anger flickered, but I pushed it away.

"He's … killing vampires…I think."

"Not killing, just beating them," I stated. "Unless something happened while I was gone. I think Bufar would have warned me if something had gone down."

Tessa blinked rapidly and I could tell she was far away, not even seeing the room.

"He wasn't there. He was in another town. An … Army base. He was surrounded by soldiers and they were raiding the underground there."

Heaviness pulled at my insides and I let her words process. "I guess it's possible. Fort Hood isn't too far away. The vampires we reject go further away from the city. I'm sure there are some in Killeen. They're probably all over the outskirts of Austin." I walked closer. "What else happened?"

A coldness came to Tessa's face as she peered at me. "He believes me to be a ghost. That, or he thinks he's going crazy. I … taunted him. Told him he was going to pay. I tried to convince him to blow his brains out, again."

I couldn't stop the shock from showing. My lips parted and words disappeared. I wasn't sure what to say. Tessa had loved Hunter. Apparently that was over now. Her vampire would want vengeance for the betrayal, and to her, that's exactly what Hunter had done by physically hurting her. Trying to kill her.

The old Tessa was gone.

"How did he respond to you?"

"As one would expect a human to respond. He got emotional. Scared."

"I don't blame him," I said, quietly, still keeping her stare. "You can be very terrifying, ma minette. And *cruel* when you choose to be. I can only imagine how he felt when faced with the woman he loved … and killed."

Tessa's mouth tightened. "You don't kill someone you love. Hunter doesn't know what love is. *I* killed for him. Did he appreciate it? No."

"Am I detecting bitterness on your part?"

"Of course I'm bitter," she said, crossing her arms over her chest. "It wasn't easy killing the priest. He could have been the end to me if he had gotten closer with any of those relics he had on him. After all I did, for Hunter to end my life, it makes me angry. I *was* dead," she growled. "He killed me and now he's going to pay."

My head nodded, slowly. "I agree that he has to die for what he's done. I've already been looking for him and almost had him once. He's not the same person you knew though, Tessa. He carries Sayer's blood. He's stronger and faster. He won't be easy to catch."

"Wrong," she said, glancing at the door as a knock sounded. "I found him once. I'll do it again."

"Do what?" Aetas said, walking in.

"You have to ask?" Tessa snapped. "You're already in my head. You know very well what I was talking about. You see *everything*, or am I wrong?"

Aetas' eyebrows rose and he glanced at me indifferently before coming closer. "I happen to have a lot on my mind. I can't be stalking your thoughts every moment of the day."

"That's not what you said before," Tessa mumbled, under her breath.

"As it is," Aetas continued, "I did happen to catch Hunter's name when I walked in so I'm not entirely unaware of the conversation."

Tessa threw me a look as if to say she didn't believe him.

"Did you have fun, last night, Princess?"

"Fun? When? With Hunter?"

He nodded.

"I guess. I don't really remember it all too clearly. It was more like a hazy dream when I think back on it. Was it real? Did I really find him?"

"You did."

"Wait," I said, glancing between them. "How do you know this? Is it because you saw it through her, or another reason?"

Cockiness shone through the smile that came to his face. "I know because I was there following her. It's the reason I'm here. She has something that belongs to me and I'm ready to collect."

Tessa took a step back. "You stay away from me. I don't have anything you need."

"He's does," I said, quietly. "You took something last night that doesn't belong to you. For your best interest, I believe you should let him have it."

What the hell was I saying? Tessa stood a better chance against Aetas if she ever had to protect herself. I shouldn't be letting her lose Margo's gift. If I wasn't concerned about her mental stability, I would have fought to allow her to keep it, but I did fear. It was too much with how strong she was already becoming.

Tessa looked at me, hurt, as if I'd handed her to the wolves, and I couldn't stand it. I walked over, trying to assure her with my eyes that everything was going to be okay.

"You entered Margo's body last night, ma minette. You stole her knowledge without her consent. You can't do that. Now Aetas has to strip your mind of what doesn't belong of you."

Her head shook furiously. "I didn't do that."

"You did," Aetas said, getting closer. "Now come to me. I'll make this quick."

"I…" Dark hair swayed at her denial. "No, you'll take everything from me, I'm sorry, I can't allow you to do that. I have to find Hunter. I can't do that without your knowledge."

"It wasn't yours to take," Aetas exploded. "Now step forward. You don't want me to come after you."

"You want it," Tessa growled, surging forward. "Take it, then. *If* you can."

Aetas' fingers locked on her face as he towered over her. I lunged forward, hitting a mental wall. The need to go crazy, wild, to break it down with my powers burned my stomach. *Not yet.* I carefully watched as he locked eyes with my mate.

"You do realize what you're doing is against our laws, don't you? Do you know what I could do to you?" He kept his voice low. Almost seductive. It had my breaths coming out heavier as I watched him press his body into hers.

"I need those powers."

"Is revenge so important to you that you'd risk banishment? Imprisonment?" My blood turned cold as I listened. He wouldn't dare…

"I won those powers fair and square. I got into your mind when I shouldn't have. That deserves a reward."

"A reward?" Still Aetas stared. Still, I knew he was trying to break into her mind. "You want a reward? You knew better. You went against what I told you. Instead of bringing me into your mind, you pushed your way into mine. Tell me why I shouldn't kill you for doing something so bold."

Tessa grew quiet as she gazed up. For the briefest moment, I quit breathing.

"You can't kill your future second. We both know that's what I am. Who will rule in your passing and stand any chance of preserving what we are if it's not me? You need me and I need these gifts. Face it, we need each other. If you want Margo's gift as your own, go take it from her yourself."

Rumbling shook the floor as Aetas' eyes began to glow. One minute he was there … the next, gone. Just like Tessa. Boiling heat shot through me and I threw everything I could into the wall that kept me separated from them. The wall warped, shining bright colors within the translucence. For a moment I thought it would give way. The blow-back sent me slamming back against the back wall. The room wavered before me and I tried to blink the lightheadedness away, but I could barely see straight. Tessa was stiff. Almost beginning to bow as I continuously tried to make her come in clearly.

I pushed to my feet, side-stepping as I fought for balance. It wasn't until I got closer to the wall that shielded them that I realized she was levitating a good inch off the ground. My feet stumbled, not able to believe what I was seeing. This wasn't right. Wasn't natural within our kind. Tessa and Aetas were on a completely different level. So similar, yet so different. One thing was clear. Tessa would surpass me by far and while I shouldn't have been surprised, I was. She was already close to my strength in ways, in others, past me … and she was only just beginning to live her life as a vampire. In enough time, she could very well pass Aetas, himself.

A scream pierced the room, making the hair on my neck stand on end. Tessa's body jerked and fell back, dangling, limp.

"Aetas!" I hit the shield, feeding my powers again. Getting ready to try impossibly harder. "Aetas!"

A form appeared, barely visible to my heightened sight. Within seconds it grew into a solid body. Aetas brought his arms out, catching Tessa as she fell at his silent command.

"Still so much to learn," he said, soothingly. "But you're already so open. There's such potential in you."

"Aetas!"

I hit the wall again and watched as he ignored me, heading to the bed to lay her down. As if captivated, he crawled over her body, moving in beside her. His head dropped to his raised fist and he continued to stare down.

"Aetas! God dammit, let me out of here!"

Nothing. It was though he actually didn't hear me. There was emptiness in his stare while he gazed down. I didn't understand it anymore that I understood what had just happened. What I did know was that I didn't like it. He'd already overstepped his bounds more than once. What would happen after I left Tessa here? The thought was sickening. Deep down, I knew. The question was, what did I do about it?

"I haven't had to use my real powers in a very long time. I forgot what all I was capable of. You push me. Test me. You're not afraid," he said, even quieter. "How about we start the morning over? You be you, I'll be me, and we'll continue where we left off. Just me and you."

My brow furrowed as I pushed my palm against the invisible wall, walking down as far as it would allow me. The color and features began to transition in his face and I had to blink past what I was seeing. Half awe, half horror had me shaking my head. When faced with myself, in person, I was too stunned to move.

"It's time to wake," he said, pulling her closer to his bare chest. *My* chest...

I pushed the tips of my finger into the wall. The calm evil that began to creep in had me watching. Seething. Barely even moving as I waited to see how far he would take this. To be so bold in front of me … something didn't seem right. I didn't know Aetas personally, but from what I recalled, he was closed off. Hard to everyone. No caring. No emotion. Now he had feelings. He had mine.

French words began to fill the room as he wooed her awake. Sweet endearments that I wouldn't have thought to say. Not because I wouldn't have meant them, but because I was always so impatient to have her that I didn't slow down and take the time to consider what she might have needed to hear.

"You're so beautiful when you sleep. I never thought I'd get to wake up to having you by my side, again. Open your eyes, ma minette, I want you to look at me. See only me as I see only you."

Tessa made a groaning sound and tried to roll to her back, but he held her firmly, putting even more of his body on top of hers.

"Marko?" Her voice was pained. It had me pushing into the wall even more. What the fuck had he done to her?

"I'm right here, love. I'm going to make you feel better. You want me to make you well, yes?" His grip moved to her hip, sliding to her ribs as he hovered over her still somewhat unconscious body.

"No," she said, pushing her hands into my chest. "I want you to get off of me."

I tensed, just as Aetas did.

"You want me off of you?"

Tessa's eyes cracked open and she reared back, slapping him. Slapping … *me*. Panic had me looking between them. Why would she react that way to me? It didn't make sense.

"Ma minette…?"

"Don't you dare go there. Get off before I make you."

Aetas slowly rose to his knees. He was just as perplexed as I was. Tessa grabbed the blankets, pulling them over her as she turned her back to him. Sobs began to shake her small frame and I hit against the wall, still unable to speak through the confusion. I knew she wouldn't hear me. Aetas might, but he didn't care.

"What's the matter?" he coaxed. "Let me help you. Let—"

The covers were thrown back and she sprang to sit up. Disheveled hair haloed out around her and her red rimmed eyes glared. "Help me? You want to help? Leave me. You've done enough."

Aetas … *me*, looked torn between hurt and annoyed.

"On your way out, be sure to become your true self so your members don't get confused on who you truly are, *Aetas*."

Our leader's jaw tensed.

"I feel you now," she hissed. "It like acid in my brain. You're there so deep that I see right through these masks you wear. Your game is over. You will not get what you need from me that way. Not ever again." Tessa rose to her knees, clearly wanting a fight. One she'd lose if she continued to provoke him. "Change," she yelled. "Turn to yourself, you do not deserve to be him."

Aetas' lids lowered threateningly. "I might caution against that, Princess. As myself, you will not be saved from the love I feel for you right now. To that form, you're becoming quite the threat. Do you really *want* to see how I handle those? Do you *want* to see the real me?"

"Enough!" I slammed my hand into the wall, then was taken off guard as Aetas' hand shoved out in my direction and I flew back. The force was nothing short of being punched in the stomach by the most powerful man in the world. Air left me and I hit the wall, fighting to breathe as I landed.

"I'll take the real you over this version any day."

"So be it," he ground out. "Welcome to Axis, Princess Tessalyn. Welcome to hell—a world of nightmares. A place you could have never imagined existing. You say you're my future second. Get ready to prove it."

One minute I was fighting to stand, the next …. falling from the cement ceiling in the heart of the city. I was gone from her. Unable to protect the woman I loved from the one person who held our fate. And I'd never find my way back. Aetas would make sure of that. Tessa was on her own and there was nothing I could do about it.

Chapter 17
Hunter

Through the darkness I stalked, lost from the mission the soldiers behind me held fast to. I broke from the group, eyeing the vampire crawling along the ceiling of the tunnel through the night vision. *Even if I didn't need it.*

Closer, he got, thinking he had us at his mercy. He was so wrong. I longed for his blood. Craved to drink it and take the substance into me. The need was increasing and it was driving me insane. I would never stoop so low as to be like one of them.

Let it warp my mind and make me even more suicidal. I didn't care. The need to constantly kill was all I could think of. It ruled me, just like Sayer's essence within my body. I was numbing out to food, water … even my thoughts were dark. Where light had never been an issue, I found myself squinting in the brightness. Even though sunglasses. It warmed my skin more than it should have and that only told me one thing. Sayer's blood was somehow taking over. Getting stronger within me. I didn't understand it, but I didn't care either. Nothing mattered but exterminating the race that ruined my life.

"Moretti," someone growled.

I went faster, beginning to jog toward the creature. He seemed to notice something wasn't right. He began to crawl away, trying to escape what he knew was coming. It only drove me at speeds no human should have seen me move at. I headed up the side of the tunnel, springing from my feet as I flew in his direction. The vampire tried to get away, but I grasped his leg, jerking him down as we rolled along the concrete. Blood perfumed the air, a mixture from us both. It had my mouth watering, even as I drew my fist back to connect with his face.

I won't be like them.

Repeatedly, I tried to convince myself. Each strike to the vampire's head was harder than the last. It bounced from the concrete in sickening thuds, making my adrenaline spike even more. I reached back, grabbing the large knife from my belt as I threw one more punch with my other hand. The first slice through his neck sent a release through me. A combination of victory and disappointment. I was glad he was going to die, but sad that he didn't give me a better fight. That this would be over. He was one of the last who remained and had given us a hell of a search to begin with. This would end soon. At least until we made it to the city. The impending fight was one I was looking forward to, more by the day. Would Marko be waiting? I could almost guarantee it. He was smart. He'd give me the fight I needed. Possibly the death I longed for.

Tessa.

I sawed through the vampire's neck, severing his head.

It'd been over a week since I had seen her ghostly apparition. I didn't expect her to come back. She'd never been there to begin with. It had all been me. My mind, guilting me over what I had done. I should have been with the old her in heaven or hell. Wherever she resided. We were meant to be together as our old selves. I was starting to think that would never happen. Not while Sayer's blood left me a supreme species in my race. I healed at an incredible rate. My body was thriving in this state. But not entirely. I needed blood. My instincts told me that What happened if I kept prolonging the inevitable?

"Moretti. He's dead, man."

I let my fingers unweave from his long hair and stood. The aroma of the crimson essence I was covered in left my nerves skittering all over the place. A tightening was taking over my throat. Tingling for what it wanted coating it.

"I'm done for tonight." I couldn't look at Johnson as I walked past. Or any of them as they parted to let me through. I was different than them in every way and I never felt more so as I headed toward the exit at a fast pace. Their whispers brushed over my exposed forearms, ones that were getting bulkier just like every other part of me, and it was no thanks to any training. All I did was hunt and sleep. I needed to forget everything. I was only happy when I was killing vampires and awake, I was haunted by images and thoughts that I wanted to forget.

Light shone from above. I took off the night vision, letting it dangle around my neck as I surged up the ladder and pushed the manhole cover free. Where it should have been a great effort, it felt almost weightless. I broke into the town, breathing in deep as the humid air hung thickly around me. There wasn't so much as a breeze. My shirt was soaking wet from the combination of sweat and blood. I could barely take in the discoloration of my arms from where I'd killed the vampire. Knowing I was covered with blood tortured me.

"You okay?" Johnson's head appeared through the hole and I glanced down nodding. Quickly, I wiped my arms on my pants to get rid of the evidence.

"I'm good. Just needed a break. We've been down there for a few hours. We're about done. Maybe one more raid and I think the underground will be safe. I don't…" I stopped. I couldn't tell him I didn't physically feel their presence anymore. I didn't want him to know how they almost called to me. Like family.

Footsteps approached and he slapped my shoulder. "You've done great here. Each night we kill more than we ever have. And it's all thanks to you. We haven't lost a soldier on our team since you arrived. For that, we're all grateful."

I nodded, staying quiet. I couldn't help but let my gaze drift to where I'd seen Tessa's ghost. It was pointless to even wonder if I would see her again. I wouldn't and I was glad. For days her voice taunted me. I was just barely able to look at my gun again.

"It's still early. Some of the guys mentioned having a drink at a local bar and grill, you feel like going?"

A part of me felt obligated, but I couldn't force myself to try to be social. I'd never been, but I was even more distant now.

"I think I'll just walk to base and head home to get some sleep. You should go and have fun."

Uncertainly masked his features and I forced a grin. "I'll be okay, really. Go. I'll see you tomorrow."

I was already stepping back as he nodded. "Wipe the blood from your face before you go past the gate guard. They'll know what's up, but we wouldn't want to scare the wives that might be passing through."

On instinct I brought my shoulder up, using my shirt to rub any remnants away. He gave the okay and I turned, giving a small wave. I didn't look back as I headed toward the base. It wasn't but a mile away. Cars passed and I got lost in my thoughts. In the cage of vicious memories I was trapped in, I didn't even realize when I passed the area where Tessa had been. My past assaulted me with the bite of a million bullets, blowing me into scattered pieces.

Why couldn't I have died? Moments I felt as though I was meant to destroy what had broken me down, but then there were these lows. They suffocated the will from me. I hated this. I had no one. No family. No loved one that I could look at a future with, and I didn't want one anymore. The old Tessa had been my soulmate. That soul was gone now, waiting for me until the time came where I finished God's work. He'd saved me for a reason, I just had to keep reminding myself of that.

"Hey man, you need a ride?"

I glanced toward a car holding two men who were waiting in line to get on base.

"No, I'm good. Thanks."

I continued to walk, pausing as they called out again.

"Say, you wouldn't happen to be Moretti, would you? Sergeant First Class Moretti?"

My feet came to a stop as I gave them my full attention. "Who wants to know?"

"I knew it," the passenger said, nudging the driver.

"Sir, everyone's talking about you. Is it true you kill vampires with your bare hands?"

A sigh left my mouth and I took a step back. "Y'all have a good night. Stay safe."

A knot formed in the pit of my stomach and I turned heading toward the entrance. It was already happening. Word was already getting around. It didn't surprise me, but I wasn't proud of it, either. I did what I needed to. The anger had to be released in some way. It worked.

"Moretti." The guard gestured with his head for me to enter.

"Private. Have a great night. Keep up the good work."

This life was all I had known for so long. Even being inactive, it still felt natural to enter the environment. And I'd left this all for her. For a chance that went to shit. Fuck, I was cursed.

The light behind me faded and I cut across a dark field, headed for Johnson's. The weight of the seclusion made the itch return. Unease flared and the need to turn around and head below to the tunnels once again pulled at me. I had to stop thinking about her. If I didn't, my mood would head even further south and that wasn't a good thing. Just the thought made her presence seem so real. I looked over my shoulder, half expecting her to be there. Following me.

"Come on, Moretti," I whispered. "Keep walking. Don't do this."

My pace increased and the field stretched out even further. I glanced behind me again, noticing I was about halfway. Movement in the shadows to my left had my gaze narrowing. No one was there, I could see even though I shouldn't have been able to. Still, something had been different, hadn't it?

My attention focused ahead, even as I paid attention to my peripheral vision. Again, something blurred to stay even with me. I licked my lips, coming to a stop.

"Alright, come out. Let me see you."

I wasn't playing these fucking games. And even if I was imagining things, no one would see how bat-shit crazy I must have appeared.

A good minute went by as I faced where I had thought I'd seen something. My head shook and the moment I went to turn to leave, the air picked up around me. Leaves blew, rustling in the distance and a form began to take shape. My breath caught at the size. It didn't appear to be Tessa, but I wasn't sure as it grew closer.

"What do you want?"

My hand came to the hilt of my knife as I waited. Clearer it became, rising to around my height as a man took shape. I had to blink repeatedly to search my mind to see if I knew this person. This … ghost. What the hell was happening to me?

"Who are you?"

An unnerving grin came to his face as he stared me up and down. Fuck … he was solid now. And a vampire. I knew that in my core. For so long I'd become immune to the fear, but there was no mistaking the way I was affected.

"I'm your leader. My name is Aetas."

"My leader?" I repeated, nervously laughing. "I don't fucking think so."

"I say you don't have a choice in the way you think. I am the answer to every question you may have. And I say I'm your leader. You've killed enough of your own kind. You've had your revenge on Sayer. It's time you stop and take your place."

The hard thump in my chest was followed by my pulse increasing. "What do you know about Sayer?"

"I know it's his blood you carry. I know he raped you multiple times while he made Tessa watch. I know everything. Like I said, I'm your leader."

Sweat poured down my face at my life being so exposed out loud.

"You will let me turn you and you will take his place when you're able." His hand shot up as my mouth opened. "And before you try to deny me, take into account that, one, I don't need your permission. And two, I'm the most powerful vampire in the world. What do you think that will say about you?" At my pause he continued. "You want revenge on Marko Delacroix? Think about this, Hunter. Infused with my blood, you will succeed me. The world could be in your hands. You're a natural born leader. I need someone like you in my passing. You'd have complete control."

Temptation flared, along with nausea. I took a deep breath.

"You'd be stupid to pass up this opportunity. It's this, or death. Marko is looking for you. He will find you and he will kill you. I know this to be fact. You will die and we will still exist. You can't kill us all. Even if we do retreat back into hiding, we will grow, again. We will flourish, just like we always do. This is never-ending. These wars have been happening for centuries. This is just another that will end with the same result. Do you think me such a bad leader that I would kill off the only source of our food by taking over completely? Population control on both ends, and we once again become myth. It's how this works, so push your fears away. Let's merge our blood. Let's get you to where you belong."

Everything inside of me said I couldn't outrun this vampire. And I sure couldn't fight him off. My legs were shaking so badly that I could barely stand.

"And if I refuse?"

Aetas' grin returned and he shrugged. "I could take you anyway. Force my blood on you. I'd break you down until you obeyed. But really, do you want to have to go that route? I think you enjoy leading. I'm offering you an entire city. And, I'm offering you to show up Marko. He wouldn't stand a chance if I mix mine and Sayer's blood."

"What's your deal with Marko?" Suspicion was creeping in. Something wasn't right with his proposal. Even though I knew I wouldn't take it, I needed to know his motives.

The young vampire studied me as he seemed to think. "Do you want to see something?"

"Depends," I said, stepping back.

"Tough." His palm surged toward my chest and my hand shot up defensively, but it was useless. My lungs locked up, preventing me from breathing. I was immediately sucked into a dark nothingness. It was an endless mass of pitch black and I spinning in the realm with no way to control what I was doing. My arms waved out and I yelled, fighting for stability. A light appeared in the distance and I was slingshotted toward it like a vacuum. The blinding sensation had my arms lifting to my eyes. Suddenly my feet hit a hard surface and an arm was gripping my bicep, bringing it back down.

"Open your eyes."

Hesitantly I lowered the other, stiffening as I realized I was in a bedroom. A very nice, elegant one. A form was hidden under the blankets and I glanced up at him before turning back to it.

"Who is that? Where am I?"

My voice had the body stirring.

"Why don't you go see for yourself?"

His hand dropped and my feet felt heavy as I edged around the side of the bed. A small hand peeking from the top of the covers had me slowing. I swallowed hard, reaching forward and gently tugging back the comforter. Dark hair followed the length of the forearm that was resting on it and I gasped, moving it down further.

"Oh … God." Heavy pants left me. I already knew and yet I couldn't believe what I was seeing.

"She was dead when they finally got her to me. I brought her back to life. You could have her again. Your vampire could win her over. The power will be like an aphrodisiac to her. With the love you both once shared, it will lure her in like candy to a baby. She'll love you and only you. Marko will be nothing but a name of the past."

The covers dropped below her chin as I stared in awe. How had I forgotten her beauty? Asleep, she almost looked like the old Tessa. There was a healthier glow to her now. More so than the last time I'd seen her. She was so pale, then. So…

Flashes came back of her holding my uncle's head. Bragging about what she'd done. I stumbled back, shaking my head. If Tessa was alive, then she *had* been the one who had come to me. She'd tried to get me to kill myself again. *Evil.*

"I don't want this. Take me back or I'll find my own way."

My voice had Tessa flying to a sitting position. Her eyes scanned the room, right past me as if she didn't see me standing there.

"Aetas?" She rose, still staring around the room. "I know you're here, I can feel you. What did I say? Get out! You can't be spying on me. I thought we already talked about this."

The younger vampire's eyebrow rose as he looked at me. "I said I wasn't leaving you a choice. You killed one of my members and you're going to replace him. You're going to continue his line with Tessa."

"Like hell I am," I yelled. "You'll have to kill me first. Or ... perhaps I'll help take care of it for you." I grabbed the knife, stabbing it through my chest before he could make it to me. The pain had me crumbling to the ground, and then through it as I was snapped back into my body so fast that I woke up on the ground of the field, gasping. My hands shot to my chest, devoid of any injury. "Jesus," I cried out, scrambling to my feet. As I scanned the area, I didn't wait to see if anyone would make themselves known. I put everything I had into running and didn't stop until I burst through Johnson's front door.

Delusion. Hallucination. I didn't think so. It was too real. Too ... frightening. And I couldn't allow it to happen. If Aetas had plans for me to come to their side, he had another thing coming. I'd kill him or myself first. Either way, it wasn't a bad thing.

Chapter 18
Tessa

I couldn't stop fuming as Aetas appeared at the foot of my bed with a smile on his face. He looked as though he knew something I didn't. As if he had a secret. It pissed me off even more. We had left on bad terms the night before after his little lesson on reading minds had turned into him twisting mine. Again. He was suddenly on me, trying to get me to willingly kiss him. I couldn't stand another moment of being close to him. He was getting scarier. Meaner. Regardless that I knew how bad this was turning out, I couldn't back down from him. If I did, he'd walk all over me. He'd try to make me break my bonds to Marko and I wasn't willing to risk it. To him this may have been a game, but this was my life. My future.

"You said you would knock."

"I forgot," he said, blandly. "Time to get up. You have lessons to learn."

Was it nighttime already? I dreaded having to wake. At least when I was asleep, I could go to Marko. I wasn't strong enough to wake him or get him to hear me, but I could be at my old home. There was a comfort in that.

"Can I at least get dressed?"

"By all means," he said, gesturing to the closet. "No one is stopping you."

My eyes closed in annoyance as I tried to ground myself. I walked over, grabbing the first dress I came into contact with—a dark blue velvet one with long sleeves. When I headed for the bathroom door, the knob locked just as I went to turn it. I threw him a glare and it went loose in my palm.

"Hurry, I have meetings in a few hours and I want to get to this as soon as possible."

I didn't answer as I shut myself in. As I went through my morning ritual, I couldn't help but stretch out the time as much as I could. A sickening feeling was making me hesitant. When I opened the door, Gina was walking away from Aetas. She slipped out of the door, quietly shutting it behind her.

"About time. What the hell were you doing in there?"

"Getting dressed." I kept my voice low, watching his every move as he began circle around.

"To lead you will have to know how to deal with situations that may at first appear to be beyond your control. You'll have to look out for our kind, but not above what is best for the outside world." He stopped just behind me. I turned, not able to stand that I couldn't see him. I didn't trust him at my back. Apparently, that was the point. Aetas spun me back around to stare at the wall.

A few seconds went by and my skin prickled at the goosebumps that raced over my limbs. My breathing became heavier as defensiveness sank in.

"Do you agree that our race is in need of a true leader? One who can separate himself from the corruption within?"

My head cocked to the side.

"Yes."

"Do you think that is you?"

I licked my lips, assessing his question. Every scenario possible entered my mind and I knew the truth. "Yes. I will not balk under pressure. I will do what is right. What is best for our kind."

"I don't think that's true," he whispered just behind my ear. "I think if your precious Marko decides he wants to rule, you will let him. He could lead us to destruction. He could be the death of us and I believe you'd let him."

I spun around, narrowing my eyes. We were but inches away from each other.

"You're wrong. I know what this responsibility includes and I know Marko. He's an amazing leader. He takes his duties very seriously and the last thing he would do is put any of us in jeopardy. But I would not forget who leads. He may be by my side, but it is I who rules. *Me*."

The hard lines in Aetas' face eased and he shrugged, stepping back. "Perhaps you could if something were to ever happen to me. Then again, maybe I have other plans."

"Other plans? What do you mean?"

My leader turned his back on me and walked over toward the covered windows. "In time it will be revealed."

I followed behind, my jaw tightening as I got closer. I didn't like this sound of this. Something wasn't sitting right with how he was acting. The vibe he was projecting left me antsy.

"Are you saying there's someone you think will be a stronger leader than I will? I assure you that's not possible."

He slowly turned. "One thing you will come to learn is that nothing is as it appears. Vampires grow more powerful by the century. You may not be qualified for the position when your time comes."

"You're wrong. I will grow as they do. Nothing will stop me from standing where you are someday. I was meant for this. There has been nothing clearer to me. From my rebirth I've known this."

"We all do," he ground out. "Every single vampire feels entitled to my throne. Every one. Your blood makes you the exception."

"Exactly. So then who would be better suited, than me? I'm the last."

"Are you?" He stepped closer, staring into my eyes. I quickly averted my gaze to the black button-up shirt covering his chest. My mind raced as I tried to figure out the puzzle he was weaving around me.

Movement stopped just before me and I braved a quick look up.

"Do you think you'll always love Marko? Do you think time will not come between the two of you? Things happen. New vampires come to join us."

There wasn't hesitation as my head shook. "My love for Marko will not be broken. Not by time, distance, or someone new."

"What about Marko? Do you not worry another's blood will appeal more than yours?"

"He loves me," I said, angrily. "Is this one of my tests or do you have a point in asking these questions? They're meaningless."

"Perhaps not. Your *test* might prove that. I'm going to give you a glimpse of something you never considered. *Temptation.* Do you think you'll be able to resist? I'm not so sure you can."

I clenched my teeth together. The need to argue was there, but I kept in the worst. "You're wasting your time with these games. Teach me something else. Show me how to travel like I did when my vampire took me over. I've tried continuously and I can't do it again. I want to learn that." I couldn't do it because he stole my knowledge. I wanted it back. I longed to find Hunter again. To make him pay for what he'd done.

"You learn what I teach you. Everything is a lesson. Until you see that, you'll remain."

My internal groan didn't escape his notice. His eyebrow rose and I stood straighter, trying to ignore the disapproving look. Aetas was growing tired of my personality. We were clashing left and right and it was only a matter of time before he showed his true colors at all times. With the glimpses I'd seen already, I was hoping to escape here before that happened.

"Let's take a seat." He gestured to two chairs angled toward each other on the far side of the room. I walked over, watching as he pulled the chair to the middle of the floor, facing forward. "Now put yours in front of mine. This will be fun."

I doubted it, but I obeyed, moving the chair to rest a good two feet from his. He quickly pulled it closer and sat down, gesturing for me to follow. Reluctance had me moving at a slow speed. When I lowered to the chair, he immediately grabbed my hands, pushing our knees together.

"Sit straight, but let your mind relax. You're going to looking into my eyes and we'll go from there."

Right. I knew where this was headed. Temptation, he'd said. Nervousness rushed through, but I focused on the grip of his fingers over my palms. My stare rose … and darkness was all I knew. Colors swirled, warping my thoughts—my mind. Suddenly, I knew nothing but who I was and that I was in some strange large room. It reminded me of a place I'd been to before, but different. Large amounts of people were gathered, sitting at tables and feeding. If it weren't for the assurance of myself, I would have felt awkward.

Heads turned in my direction as I left the darkness at the edge of the room and headed toward a table that sat further away from the rest. Something within me said I belonged there. The wide back of a vampire broadened, and leisurely, he turned, coming to stand as I approached. The shock of seeing his handsome face brought me to a standstill as we stared. Both of us seemed … close, and yet not. I'd never seen this man before that I could recall. Yet, it was like I'd known him forever. And I was conflicted on how to feel. I was lured in by his large body and handsome, rugged looks, but there was a nagging at the back of my mind that I couldn't put my finger on.

"Princess. Please, come join us."

A chair was available to his left side and I managed to get myself to move forward, despite that I couldn't break my gaze for long. I was intrigued. Almost hypnotized by how his aura called to me.

"We haven't officially met, but I feel as though we have." He paused as I came to the chair, extending his hand. The touch of the contact as my fingers slid over his had my pulse accelerating. His eyes cut up from where he was staring at our joined grip and I knew he could hear my heartbeat. A wickedness flashed behind his gaze … hot, red lust. It left my emotions deadening to everything but what my body responded too. *Him.*

"I'm Master Moretti, but you can call me Hunter. I've looked forward to this day for quite some time. They didn't lie about your beauty."

Heat flashed over my skin. *Hunter. Hunter.* Did I know that name?

The combination of appeal and confusion left me speechless. As he led my hand to his mouth, everything vanished but us. Full lips pushed into my knuckles, only for him to turn my wrist to face up so he could connect there, too. Yes … I was so hot. So … drawn to this vampire.

In a small tug, he drew me in close, lowering to the side of my face. I was positively trembling at his nearness. He was powerful. *More than me.*

"I can't wait to taste you, Tessa. I can't wait to make you mine."

I blinked through the words and was able to withdraw from the spell I was under. "No," I whispered, stepping back. My head turned and I took in the strange faces who watched us. I didn't know these people. I didn't belong here. This wasn't right. "No," I repeated, louder. "I … don't know you. I…" I spun, taking in the walls. Taking in the seating arrangements. It was all too familiar. But, not.

My feet stumbled back even more and the urge to run was there. A voice rang out in the background causing me to jump and I turned to the far end of the room. A group of people emerged and my heart thudded faster as a couple emerged, surrounded by what looked to me like high ranking people. A man with dark hair walked with purpose. Power. He was flanked by a woman who I swear I knew.

"Master Delacroix, so nice of you to join us on our bonding day." Hunter may have tried to sound welcoming, but the malice in his tone didn't escape me. He walked forward to meet the Master—the man whose stare left me feeling desperate—and shook his hand, bringing his gaze to the woman. "Your concubine grows more beautiful by the year. Marie," he said, bringing her hand up to his lips. "It's a pleasure for the two of you to join us."

My head shook as I stared between the two of them. This wasn't right. This wasn't happening.

Master Delacroix's stare never left me as he came to stand a few feet away. There was a hardness in his expression. A … hatred. Was it for me or the situation?

"Princess Tessalyn." His head bowed the smallest amount and I felt my lips separate as I took another step back.

"It's a pleasure to meet you at last," Marie said, joining his side. "We've heard so much about you. It's like I already know you. I think we'll all become very great friends."

My eyes darted to Hunter who had a warm smile on his face. As he rounded the two and came to my side, I wasn't sure what to do. Where did I go? I didn't want to be here.

"Please excuse my future concubine." Hunter placed his arm over my shoulders. "I'm afraid she's still adjusting to her new environment. It has to be hard going from a place like Axis, to the underground. Headquarters is all she's ever known. The difference will probably take some getting used to."

The excuse sounded not at all believable, but was it? What was Axis? Is that where I had been?

"Completely understandable," Master Delacroix said, eyeing me warily. "From what I hear, she was mostly kept in solitude. The shock of so many people must be quite straining."

"Yes," Marie agreed. "Princess, would you like me to take you to your room? If that's alright," she said, looking at Hunter. "Maybe she could use a friend? Another woman?" Her voice drew the Master's attention. He leaned in, kissing her head and pulling her in closer to him. The sight nearly took my breath away. It had my claws coming out and my fangs pushing into my bottom lips. Anger swirled and I felt my control slip.

Fingers gripped tighter on my bicep and I glanced up at Hunter's curious expression. *That face...* I loved it as much as I hated it. The odd sensation left the rage building. The more they looked at me, the more I felt the need to retaliate. None of this was right. My vampire felt threatened and even though I wasn't sure why, I didn't care. The need to attack Master Delacroix was there as much as I felt compelled to destroy the one I was meant for.

"Let go of me," I hissed, pulling away from Hunter. "You all just stay away."

"Princess?" Hunter shook his head, baffled by my outburst.

"It's okay," the Master said. His fingers grew tighter around Marie and I took in every flex of his fingers.

I bared my fangs, eyeing him as I began to pace in front of the couple. "It is not okay," I exploded. None of this is the way it should be. And *you*," I said, pointing and yelling. "You ... traitor! You ... betrayed me. You..." I had no idea what I was accusing him of, but I couldn't stop.

A gasp came from Marie and the pain was evident, even if I sensed she wasn't sure what I meant either.

"I beg your pardon?" The Master's own anger shone through and a man stepped closer to Marie taking her a few steps back as his arm eased her in the vampire's direction.

"Marko?" she whispered.

"Marko," I burst out. "Yes. Marko, that's your name. You're a traitor! You lie." More, I paced, sidestepping Hunter as he reached for me.

"I apologize. It's clear the Princess isn't well right now." Hunter lunged and grabbed ahold of me. He threw me a furious glance, squeezing me tight. The look brought my claws down even more. Thoughts were gone and the threat he made evident sent me tapping into the one thing that would kill me in a room full of vampires more powerful that myself. But I didn't care. I knew I meant for something different than this.

Heat bubbled inside of my stomach as I kept Hunter's stare.

"Release me."

"Or what?" He did, but moved in closer, forcing me to take a step back with some invisible shield. Repeated steps bought me further away from Marko and I couldn't stand it. I wasn't done getting my point across. He'd lied to me. About what, I couldn't remember, but maybe if I could continue it would come back.

"Get out of my way."

"No … I don't think so. You need to feed and rest. I'm going to make you better."

There was a hunger in his fixated gaze that I didn't like. I knew he meant for me to feed from him, but I couldn't. Not because his blood didn't call to me, it did, but this wasn't over. It couldn't end like this. If Hunter got me in the room, he might never let me come out again. Not while Marko was here.

"Wait," I breathed out. "Just." I lunged to the side, not able to make it past the wall, but I could see the Master still staring in my direction. My mind searched through the fog, desperate for something to come. I'd been enraged at the betrayal I had felt, but now that I was going to be separated, I couldn't imagine being away from him. "Don't let him lock me away," I begged Marko. "Please. Help me. Marie!" I yelled, turning to her and slamming my hands against the wall. Suddenly, anything was better than being alone with Hunter. He was stronger than me. I couldn't forget that.

"Marko?" Confusion filled the female vampire's expression and I could see she was just as torn as he appeared to be.

"To the room," Hunter said, his voice growing angrier.

"Take me home. I want to go home! Please."

"You are home." Hunter was suddenly through the wall and grabbing my arm. He spoke to the others. "Feed. I'll return as soon as I can." As he pulled me toward a tunnel not far away, I couldn't stop looking back at the two vampires who seemed to make my heart hurt. They stared, but they didn't move forward.

Darkness engulfed me and no matter how hard I pulled to break the hold, I couldn't. Even the heat within my core wasn't reachable, when it should have been.

A door opened at Hunter's push and he spun us into the room, shutting the barrier. I was pulled to the bed so fast and slammed against it that he was on me before I could turn to try to scramble away.

"I'm disappointed in you, Princess, but I can't blame you, entirely. This is a shock for you. I shouldn't have allowed you out so soon. Let me put you at ease."

"No." My body try to struggle free, but he was pinning me with more than his weight. From the neck down, I couldn't move. The invisible force kept me unable from defending myself.

Hunter's actions became slower. He lifted his hands from my wrists, tracing his fingers up my forearms before reaching my shoulders. When they got to my neck, he angled my face away. Warm aim came out in a rush over my ear and he rocked his body against mine. "The way you make me feel … I can't explain it. I want you as much as I long to hurt you. Why do you think that is? Do you feel that way too?"

I did, but I couldn't answer.

"Perhaps time will show us what way we'll lean more toward. Or maybe, we'll stay in this limbo. Love and hate. It could make for an interesting bonding."

One of his hands lowered and he pulled up my dress, running his hand higher on my thigh. Another rock of his hips had a moan leaving my mouth, but it wasn't entirely from pleasure. I felt on the edge of bursting into tears. This wasn't right. I couldn't get over that. I was so lost and confused.

Fire exploded in my neck and my mouth flew open at the pain from his brutal bite. Fangs embedded in my neck and his venom pushed thickly into my system. Pain warped into pleasure, but for the life of me I couldn't stop the tears that raced over the bridge of my nose. I wanted to be mad. I wanted to kill him for feeding from me without my permission. But it was beyond that.

Vibrations hummed in my throat from his continuous sounds. Over and over he tugged at my vein greedily, grinding his hard cock along my pussy. When his hand moved from my hip to his pants, my panicked gasps grew louder.

"No. No."

The weak denials were ignored as he broke from my throat. Blood was smeared over his chin and Hunter was drunk on my essence. He didn't appear to even see me as he ripped at his clothes in a fevered state. When he was nude, he threw up my dress, burying his face between my legs. Still, I couldn't move. I couldn't fight. Why was this familiar? Why did I feel like he and I had been here before?

Pressure from the tip of his tongue pushed into my entrance and I cried out, conflicted on the ecstasy that my body forced me to feel. Hunter's eyes shot up to mine and he pushed deeper, using his fingers to rub over my clit as he tried to slow his impatience. But he couldn't. I could see his fight and it was evident in how fast he was trying to build me up. The sad thing was, it was working. I was losing myself in the hunger he was displaying.

"Hunter?"

"That's right. Let yourself go." He sucked against the side of one of my folds, moving up to apply the same pleasure to the sensitive nub he was torturing with his touch. He dipped down, thrusting back into my channel before I knew he couldn't take it anymore. Hunter's broad shoulders lifted and he crawled on top of me, rubbing his long length over my slit. When the tip nudged into my entrance, I somehow managed to move my head back and forth, but not from my own doing. He was the one allowing the freedom.

"Fuck," he moaned, inching himself inside of me. He lowered, trying to brush his lips over mine, but I couldn't get accustomed to how it felt. To it being *him*. "This is right," he said, lowly. "It was always supposed to be this way."

A cry began to leave my mouth, fading out as I sucked in air at the depth he reached.

"No." The word repeated over and over as I clawed through the fog that refused to let me make sense of what was happening. More I looked into his face, pulling the strings of my memories until I was sure they would snap. Blurry images flickered, not making sense, and I held to one. One that turned my blood cold. Hunter, looming over me. There was pain, so much so that I knew it was killing me. "Off," I managed.

"Never." His lips pressed into mine and I bit against the full flesh, feeling blood gush into my mouth as the skin tore at my jerk. A laugh filled my head making me freeze.

"If you wanted to taste me, all you had to do was say so." Hunter's arm rose and he sliced his fang over the skin. The wound was forced into my mouth and once again my head was trapped. As his lip healed before my eyes, all I could do was scream. Even as he drowned me in his blood, he continued to use his nail to keep the wound deep.

Weight over my mouth made my jaw ache while he continued to thrust. My choking had his arm pulling back and a smile came to his face as he let his arm drag over my face, covering me more in the crimson substance. I could feel is coat my cheek as warmth overflowed from my mouth. More flashes blinded me, but not of Hunter … of Marko. He'd forced his blood on me before. I could see his determined face so clearly. He loved me, wanted me, as much as he seemed to be out of his mind in that moment. And I wasn't a vampire, but human. Yes. None of this was as it seemed.

The panic that swirled within had my powers so incredibly hot that I screamed through the pain. I had to release it or surely it would burn me from the inside out.

Louder the laughter surrounded me and Hunter's blurry body went in and out as I pushed back into a dark void somewhere within me. I didn't want to be there anymore. I couldn't.

Screams were still leaving me as my body jolted through a weird popping sensation. I was sucked down a tunnel so fast that it didn't make sense as I fell into my body and instinctually kicked back. The chair I was sitting in rocked and I threw myself forward to stop myself from tumbling back. Aetas' outraged glare met me the moment I settled and somehow I knew I'd done something wrong. Something I shouldn't have been able to do.

The memories of his *test* came back and all I manage was to shake at the fury that I felt. Sickness flooded me and I could still taste and smell Hunter's blood in my mouth and nose.

"He is us, you … and me. *Sayer.* You're going to turn him. You're going to try to have him take my place."

Aetas didn't answer, but with the silence, he didn't have to.

Chapter 19
Marko

Loud sirens filled the background not far from the gates of Fort Hood. The smile on my face couldn't have stretched any wider as I strolled the streets of the military housing. After Aetas refused to allow me admittance into Headquarters by making it impossible for me to find, rage sent me on the path to destruction. The group of vampires I got together was enough to overwhelm the tunnels of the small town. The massacre I orchestrated was no doubt just finding its way to officials, but I didn't get the result I wanted. Hunter hadn't been present and for that, he'd pay even worse.

My claws embedded even more into the scalp of the head I held and I slowed at seeing Hunter's silhouette step from the front door, onto the porch. Concern masked his features and he pulled a white shirt over his head as he stared toward the large, protective wall across the field. My arm reared back and I launched the head right at him. I was only two houses down, but at my movement, his head snapped in my direction. It gave him just enough time to catch the dark shape that was crashing into his chest.

I didn't wait for him to process what was happening. I was already running, flying across the grass right in his direction. A sound tore from his mouth and his hands jerked back, dropping the head. Recognition of his roommate, his friend, registered for only a moment before his eyes shot up to mine and he stumbled back, racing for the front door. He was fast. So fast, that I still couldn't believe that he was breaking past the threshold just as I was stepping onto the cement square pad of the porch.

"Hunter!" Electrical heat surged the length of my limbs and I expelled the sensation, not even shielding my face as it burst from me. Glass blew from the windows and screen door. The shockwave from the impact was like a rubber band effect and my ears popped as I began to pace. I needed inside, or him to come outside. The repercussions didn't matter. Nothing did but ending this once and for all. I knew I had to be careful. He could very well kill me, but my status wouldn't let me believe he was good enough to succeed.

Fragments of brick broke off toward me as the loud pops of a gun exploded through the air. Pieces hit my shoulder, tearing through the long sleeve white shirt I wore. It was already untucked and half way unbuttoned. I was mess, not only in appearance from relishing in killing the handful of soldiers, but also in my frame of mind. I longed for the blood of my mate and who better to get a taste of it than from shredding Hunter's throat. It'd be the closest I would ever get to her until she returned. Regardless that I'd taken her over, it would still be close enough.

"Have you learned nothing?" I roared, stepping closer. My voice was almost inaudible it was so deep. My vampire was taking me over completely and there wasn't a single part of me that wanted to stop my monster. I'd blow this house straight from the foundation if it meant getting to Hunter.

"Come out, here. Fight me, human. Show me what you're made of. Let me taste you." I bared my fangs, racing forward to crash into the invisible barrier that protected the house. More shots rang out and my body jerked at the force of the bullets. Clinking echoed on the ground as the flattened pieces of metals oozed from the surface of my skin, bouncing at my feet.

"You want me, motherfucker?" A whiz broke through the air and Hunter appeared around the edge of the wall just as a stake flew in my direction. My reflex flared and I reached out, plucking the wood from the air as it went to the right of my shoulder. Smoke poured from my hand and the burn was excruciating. It only fed the anger as I snapped the length in half and let it fall to the ground. Hunter's eyes narrowed, determined, as he pulled the trigger of the bow again …. and again.

The wood fell inches in front of my feet as it hit my own protected wall. A laugh poured from my mouth and I reached deep inside to the core of my powers. The house began to rattle until I had it shaking violently around him.

"Come out, or else you'll be buried in what remains of this place. Your choice."

Sirens still cried out in the distance, but new ones were coming closer. They were from the base. If I didn't hurry, I'd have more to deal with than Axis. Sure, I wanted to get Aetas' attention, but not because of what I was doing. We had laws, ones I was already breaking by using my powers so openly. Our leader would have every right to lock me away until he saw fit, and that was the last thing I needed.

"You always were a coward," I yelled, jolting the house even harder. "Come out!"

"Fuck you! You'll see me soon enough, on my terms. Not yours."

Hunter held out to the wall for stability and my head jerked around in time to see a car hauling ass around the turn. "I'll be waiting … and watching you. You'll have to leave here at some point. When you do, I will find you. And I will kill you."

"She lives," Hunter exploded. "I saw Tessa. She lives."

The shaking stopped in my shock. "How do you know that?" His silence had me yelling louder. "How do you know that?"

"Him," he mouthed, almost silently. "He showed me. I'll kill you all. I'll kill her, again!"

I crashed into the wall with every ounce of my strength trying to claw my way through. "I'll end your life first. I promise you that."

Tires squealed in the background and I threw up my personal protectant, turning invisible. Hunter's jaw clenched, but he didn't move closer. He knew I was still here, regardless whether or not he could see me. It was the military police I didn't want to deal with.

"I am going to put one of those stakes through your heart for what you did to Johnson," Hunter said in a lower voice. "You watch and see. I'll take care of you, then Tessa, then Aetas. That's his name, isn't it? That's what Tessa called him. I'll find all of you and I'll end this once and for all."

If it wasn't for Tessa being alive, I would have leveled the house. With her, I had something to live for, but if she were truly dead, I would have let Aetas kill me over what I'd have to do to kill Hunter. No one threatened the woman I loved and got away with it. Especially after what he did. He would try again, this I knew for fact. But Hunter *would* pay. If I had to stay until just before sunrise, I'd stalk his every move until I had my chance.

I stepped out of the way as the police officer gripped his gun and stopped short of Johnson's head.

"Moretti, what the fuck is going on? Someone was here. I saw him." There was a fear in the officer's tone as he looked at Hunter.

"Vampire," he said through clenched teeth. "That *vampire* is a Master and he's still here. You just can't see him. Please," he paused. "Rios, come inside. But only you," he said louder. "No one else is allowed past this door."

My lids lowered in anger as the man rushed passed me, into the house. He looked over his shoulder, clearly shaking, and it took everything I had not to attack. The smell of his fear fed the creature in me and made him even more impatient for blood. Two more cars pulled up as the men stood in the doorway.

"Johnson was leading the men tonight. I'm afraid something very bad has happened underground. You need to make some calls and get some soldiers in those tunnels. Not civilian cops, *soldiers*. I also need you to…" he paused looking in the vicinity of my direction. When he lowered and whispered something in the man's ear, I clenched my fists. My heart was racing so fast and hard that I couldn't hear shit. I saw nothing but Hunter's throat. I was going to tear it to shreds and bathe in his blood.

Two other soldiers walked toward the door and my fingers twitched as Hunter relayed the story to them too. Their anger and emotional status was evident. One soldier wiped continuous tears as he stared at Johnson's head. More people were arriving but I didn't move as they began closing the roads off. Their unease at my presence had many looking around. Watching the area with caution and they needed to. The more time that went by the harder it was to restrain myself.

A tug on my insides had my eyes closing. It was a call. One from Marie. I could feel her vampire in need. It made me even more enraged. I didn't want to leave to see what she needed. If Hunter came out of that house, I wanted to destroy him. I couldn't do that if I wasn't here. Instead, I used my powers as leader to push into her mind. It wasn't what a leader should do. I should have been present in the city I ran, but I couldn't think of something more important than destroying the threat that would surely arrive in my own tunnels if I didn't stop it now.

"What is it, Marie?"

There was a hesitant surprise before she answered. *"Humans. They've pushed past the west entrance. Twenty of so of them. And they were equipped with those holy water stakes. We took care of them, but there were more that escaped. We lost four of our kind and two slaves."* An internal cry sounded. *"It's starting. I dreamed this. I told you in the meeting it wouldn't be long."*

"Fuck!" I paced the small distance of the porch, glaring at Hunter. *"I'll be there soon. Have Anastasia and Beatrice stay close to where they got in. Get Bufar to put up a wall preventing any more from entering. I'll be there shortly."*

I cut off the connection, watching one of the soldiers jerk to a standstill not a few feet away. He spun around in a circle, scanning the surroundings in a panic.

"Sergeant? I don't like this." Although he addressed another soldier next to him, I could tell he was just speaking out of apprehension. Sweat was dripping down his face while he continued to survey the area.

"Just keep your eyes open," the man whispered. "I don't fucking like this either. I can't stand that these bastards can hide so openly. It's not right."

Hunter was gone now, deeper in the house an I turned my attention back to my prey. Would he come out again while it was dark? I didn't think so. Even if he did, he'd be prepared, right along with the other men flocking around him. Time. I might have had plenty of it, but I didn't feel that way. My impatience wanted to nip this in the bud *now*.

I forced myself to take a step back. Each foot further away made each one harder to accept. My eyes scanned the structure of the house, and I wasn't able to stop myself from what I knew I needed to do. I couldn't leave so easily. And maybe I'd get lucky. Besides, it wasn't like anyone could see me right now. They couldn't blame me if they didn't have evidence.

A smile pulled the corner of my lips and I closed my eyes letting the fire within build. At the ground shaking beneath my feet, my lids opened. I let the heat explode from me in a blistering gust. Bricks, wood, more glass all burst into thick debris, spinning in slow motion before me. Off in the distance, yells broke through the haze in my mind, but I couldn't stop watching the beauty of my devastation.

Pieces flew through the air as the front of the home cratered in, blowing back at the invisible wave of force. Already I was walking closer, right through the ruin. Waiting ... praying.

What I did didn't put a dent in what I could have done, but it was enough to get my point across. Just not enough to draw Hunter out. Dazed, he pushed rubble off, crawling out from a partially broken bookcase. Heavy pants left him and where I thought I'd pick up fear, there was nothing but wrath. Even though I wasn't visible, he seemed to look right at my face.

"Come on. Step off of that foundation." I moved to the yard, ready, already in stance to attack if he felt brave enough. A groan at his feet didn't break the focus he seemed to have on me as he followed my movements.

"Get ready, Marko. You want a war, I'll give you a fucking war! You don't stand a chance against what I have planned for your city. You think your powers will save you, but I have something stronger on my side. It's called Faith. Something you'll never have. God wouldn't have let me live if he didn't plan for me to beat you. And I will. Your life is in my hands and it's only a matter of time before I take it. So stay here for the rest of the night if you wish, but remember one thing. This is two-sided. You have to sleep at some point, and when you do, I'll be the one to wake you."

I dropped my shield, baring my fangs. My hand rose as I let his threat sink in. "I look forward to killing you. Before I leave, tonight…" Pain slammed through my limbs as I let my powers once against leave me in a heated rush. The wave sent Hunter's body flying back. Again, I unleashed, and again, watching the house buckle and collapse in a large cloud of dust. Shots rang from the far side and I turned, glaring at one of the soldiers as a bullet burned into my arm unexpectedly. I turned invisible, racing in his direction as he continued to pull the trigger, missing me. When my body slammed into his, his back hit the ground hard, breaking through a foot of the earth. I didn't wait. Couldn't see through the haze of my need to kill. My fangs buried in the side of his neck and I sucked against his vein, greedily, teasing myself before I jerked up and snapped his neck. My eyes scanned the neighborhood and I was done being restrained by rules.

These humans were going to see that they couldn't cross a vampire and get away with it. I'd abolish them all. It was what we were meant for. No one stood a chance. This wasn't a fairytale where vampires came out and coexisted with humans. That would *never* happen. They were food—our life source. With the way things were going in every country, the world was already starting to see the truth. *War* … yes. We were ready.

Chapter 20
Hunter

The tears wouldn't come no matter how much pain registered in my heart. Losing Johnson, losing the team I'd come to know here at Fort Hood, deadened me on the inside. I was numb, lost in my own personal purgatory of despair. Waking up, covered in bricks and pieces of sheetrock left me confused for only the mere seconds it took for me to regain the memory of what Marko had done. He was gone. I knew that as much as I breathed. But the devastation he'd left behind gave a clear statement on where he and I stood. With the sun, came the ruin and death.

The only ones who lived outside of Johnson's home were the wives who stood in the distance sobbing at the fear they were no doubt plagued with. They were obviously in shock, too afraid to come close. Some, no doubt, already dealing with the news of their dead husbands. Now they were staring at the truth of what we were up against.

It was no secret what caused this. Of what we were facing. *Death*—on both sides. I'd lead the massacre of one race just to put extinction to another. There was no room left for emotion. It was just as dead as I was.

"Up soldier." My foot nudged against the leg of a man I didn't know. He stirred, reaching for his head. A large gash was on his forehead, but from the look of it, it had stopped bleeding long before. The dried, dark substance disappeared into his stained, blond hair and I tried not to stare at it. Just the acknowledgment would bring the cravings and need to kill.

"Come on," I said, pulling him to his feet. "We have soldiers to help."

But it wasn't the truth. They were already being rescued by the others who had come to our aid. Personnel was swarming the area, their hands full by not only us, but the others. The neighborhood that surrounded me looked like a battlefield. *One I'd seen before, overseas.* Houses were leveled around me, a stray piece of frame sticking out if the structure had been lucky.

Marko did his job. He was proving a point to me of just how strong he really was. This was child's play to what he was capable of and we both knew it. I'd been lucky last night that I had been trapped under the rubble and not blasted right into the yard.

"Hunter Moretti?"

The voice boomed through the eerie silence, but I wasn't intimated by the authority the tone held like I would have been in the past. No one ruled me anymore.

I turned, eying an officer in dress uniform. He was highly decorated. My hand clenched and I had to remind myself that I was a civilian now. I wasn't a soldier in their eyes so there was no reason for me to salute.

"I'm Moretti." I went to step over a picture of Johnson and his wife and stopped, picking it up. His eyes scanned the length of my body as if he were assessing me, but I barely noticed as I went back and forth to him and the picture.

"You need to come with me. We have a few questions to ask you."

I glanced back down at the picture, running my thumb over the cracked glass. "Questions? Concerning what? This, or the entire fucked-up situation our world faces?"

I couldn't deny that I had little trust for the higher-ups in government. Especially since they were the ones who got us into this mess to begin with. There was corruption in the White House and Pentagon. I would have bet my life on it.

"We can talk about it when we get to Headquarters. You have vital information we could use."

"Ask and I'll tell you whatever you want to know. I'm not going anywhere."

The older man glanced toward the road where three men stood watching. My lips pressed together and I let my eyes cut back over to him. If he was trying to intimidate me, he was failing.

"Mr. Moretti, I don't think you understand. You *have* to come with me."

Even as he talked, I was already stepping back, scanning the debris for my bow. I managed to get my belt on while I was going over a plan with the soldiers. That had been just before Marko struck. My bow couldn't have gone too far.

I threw a large piece of wall out of my way, pushing over a shattered curio cabinet that had been against the far wall, by the door.

"Mr. Moretti." Annoyance was heavy in his tone, but I ignored him as I moved deeper into where the dining room had been. Sweat dripped down from my face and I wiped it away, kicking a bulk of chalky remains. The end of my bow had me reaching down and sighing in relief. A throat clearing in the background was lost as I scooped up a pile of stakes scattered further back.

"Your weapons are useless. I'm afraid you won't be taking them where we're going. If you'd like, I can have one of the men hold them for you. When we're finished you can have them back."

A laugh poured from my mouth and I slowly turned to face him, glancing at his rank. "No disrespect, Colonel, but I know you heard me the first time. I'm not going anywhere with you. And you sure as fuck aren't getting your hands on my bow."

"I'm afraid you don't have a choice, son. You're coming, whether you like it or not."

This was not how I saw this playing out. I'd have to run, again, and without an army to support me. At least for now. But where did that put me? Marko found me once, he could easily do it again.

I looked up at the sun. It had to still be early. A little after six, I suspected. It hadn't been light for long. That gave me a good part of the day to run and set up … but where? I had nowhere left to go.

"We all have a choice," I said, lowly. "What some of us don't have is the guts to make the right one." I took a step, putting me closer. "I'm leaving. If I were you, I wouldn't try to stop me."

I kept going, walking around the Colonel and heading out onto the yard. I kept the three men in my peripheral vision, watching their every movement. If I could just get off of base without any trouble, I'd stand a chance.

"Moretti."

The threat was evident. It was now or never and I couldn't see how I was going to get out of this. It was daylight. I couldn't hide in the shadows, hoping to escape them. At least ... not up here.

A manhole rested ahead. I took the five steps, bending down and pulling it free. I wasn't sure how the ones under the base were laid out. Johnson had told me they were sealed off, separate from the rest in town. How, I wasn't sure, but I had a feeling I'd find out soon enough.

Darkness engulfed me as I dropped a good fifteen feet. Yelling was erupting above ground, but faded as I took off running through the large tunnel. My eyes adjusted almost immediately and although I knew I couldn't see as good as a vampire, I could see well enough to lead me through the passages.

Water splashed under my feet, echoing through the enclosed space the further I got back. Voices called out in the far distance and I took a right, then a left, immersing myself deeper, yet closer toward town. A slight hum along my skin had my eyebrows pulling in. I was made to believe vampires were clear of the base, but I knew what I felt and I didn't like it. The fear that it could be Marko had me jerking my bow from my back and pushing one of the stakes home.

An abrupt ending had me rushing back a few feet to take a new path. Faster, I went, becoming in tune with the vibrations that were increasing by the second. Whatever, or whoever was in here with me, was right in my direction and I prayed the creature was somewhere asleep and wouldn't pose a threat. When the tunnel branched off in a Y, I knew I wasn't going to be that lucky. Scratching in the distance had me slowing as I surveyed the circumference.

"Master said I'd get my chance with you. I didn't imagine he meant this soon."

From out of the pitch black was a vampire I knew all too well. One who had stayed out of my way throughout my time in the underground city, but I knew him well. *Boyd.*

"Tessa's not here to save you now. Not that she would after what you did. I could kill you for that, alone. Such rich blood and you had to ruin it. But that's okay. I can smell her in you. Even better."

I moved closer, ignoring the threat my mind perceived. My blood was richer than his. There was a confidence and even a cockiness at knowing that. It was what all vampires felt. I had been with them long enough to know how they worked and despite the hate I harbored, I was taking on more of their characteristics by the day.

"You want my blood? I'm right here," I said, putting my bow behind my back. "I'm not going anywhere. Come get you a taste."

Boyd's fangs were drawn. One step. Two. As he became clearer, so did something else. He wasn't alone. I scanned the shadows, making out at least three more vampires.

This wasn't good. Two I could do, but I'd never tried four. Somehow the human in me couldn't process how it'd be possible. The vampire in me wanted the fight. Yearned for their blood. My mouth watered and I couldn't stop the moan that came. Yes, I wanted this. I wanted to taste them as I tore them apart.

"Let's go," I purred. "Let's do this."

God, I was begging. Dying for them ... for a lifestyle that wasn't my own. It increased the need, feeding the adrenaline until I found myself becoming the instigator. I lunged forward, juking to one side as I surged a few more feet toward the group. They were stopped now, confused on my actions. But one thing was clear. They wanted me as much as I wanted them and nothing was going to stop the clash of monsters we all had buried within.

"He's crazy," one of them stated. "Let's get him."

But they wouldn't attack first. I would. And I did, rushing along the side of the tunnel with a speed that clearly caught Boyd off-guard. My fist came down, crunching onto his cheek as I barreled myself over him, right on top of another vampire. My bicep wrapped around his throat while my legs locked around his waist. We fell to the cement hard, but it gave me the leverage I needed to use my strength to twisted and tear at the connection of his throat. Bones snapped under my violent jerks and skin tore as I gave one more hard tug, severing his head. Warmth gushed over my arms and I had to stop my eyes from rolling at the ecstasy of it. I didn't have time to bask in what I wanted. Claws were already tearing into my back, breaking open my skin.

"He's mine!" A growl poured from Boyd as he pushed one of the other vampires out of the way, but it was the one closer to me that attacked first. He threw his weight on top of me, diving for my neck. The strength behind his determination was surprising, but not something I couldn't overpower.

With a push from the side, I managed to roll us, placing me on top. Boyd made it to my back before I could do any damage. Fingers gripped my shoulder, the claws at the tips, biting in painfully. I grabbed Boyd's wrist, flinging him over me with all of my strength. Before I could think of what to do next, a force hit, sending the top of my body closer to the vampire I was pinning down. Teeth bit into my chest and I couldn't keep in the scream that tore its way from my throat. I could feel my skin shred from the jolting reaction. The wound would heal, but not before I perfumed the room with more of an aphrodisiac for all of us.

"Yes." A hiss from the vampire under me grew in depth and I could feel him becoming stronger. The panic had me breaking his neck, but I knew he wouldn't be out for long. Not with my blood inside of him. Fuck, what had I been thinking? I needed to get on my feet. Put more distance between all of us that way I could pick them off instead of getting jumped by all of them at one time. But how?

I pushed to my feet, bracing as Boyd threw himself back at me. The other vampire was already coming, too, following in Boyd's footsteps as he tried pinning me against the curved wall. I used the leverage to launch us forward, but his claws were starting to hook into my back, keeping us stuck together. The fear within me unexplainably spiked and I could feel his vampire surge.

"I'm going to relish in tasting you," Boyd said, bringing his face closer to my neck. "You're going to make me stronger. You're going to—"

My bite had the vampire's body going rigid. I may have not had fangs, but the strength of my jaw, combined with all of my teeth left me tearing through his thick skin. Blood poured into my mouth, sweet, hot and thick. The frenzy it brought had me locking and squeezing around him with everything I had.

"Boyd?" The other vampire stopped, mid-run, sliding to a stop as he watched on in disbelief. And perhaps what I was doing wasn't normal. Humans didn't feed from vampires. But I wasn't human anymore. I was a killer like them.

"Boyd?"

A grunt had my teeth tingling and I wasn't sure why Boyd wasn't fighting me. *Or why he was throwing off more power than I had felt from him before.* I bit harder, tearing into his skin to bring more blood flow, and he let me. His submission had my arms easing when I knew I shouldn't have trusted him not to attack. I was too fixated on the taste, of the power he was feeding me. It was like nothing I had ever experienced before. Not even with Tessa. Something was happening. Something I couldn't even begin to fathom.

Movement on the floor registered and seconds later, the vampire with the broken neck stood. His steps were slow, forced as he staggered next to the other. "What is that?" he asked the vampire in a scratchy voice.

"I'm not sure." There was awe, yet fear, in their tones. What were they feeling? Sensing, that I wasn't? Something was off, I knew that. Still I couldn't stop immediately. It took a good minute for the confusion to sink in enough to allow me to break the suction.

Embarrassment and shame quickly registered and I shoved Boyd away from me as if he were the devil, himself. The need to heave was there, but for the life of me I couldn't waste what I'd just basked in. What I wanted more of even as I took slow steps back.

"Boyd?" One of the vampires circled his rigid frame, staring into the vampire's blank stare as he seemed to watch my every twitch.

"What's wrong with him?" I asked, nervously. "Why is he just standing there?"

Both vampires snapped their heads in my direction and where I thought they were going to attack, they didn't. They were genuinely afraid of something.

"It's … not right. He's, not right. It's like…" The vampire sniffed, stepping back a few feet, growling lower the further he got away.

"What?" I exclaimed. "What the fuck is going on?"

The vampire with the broken neck didn't have to get close to Boyd to start retreating. I couldn't believe my eyes as he lowered to the ground too, sinking to his knees as the vibe of power increased around us.

"That's not Boyd," the first vampire said, lowly. "That's not Boyd…"

Chapter 21
Tessa

"You're free to go."

The words had to have repeated in my head a million times. As I stood in the now empty room that had been my residence for weeks, I couldn't believe that Aetas was just going to let me leave. I knew why, but I still couldn't process it. Was he really going to turn Hunter to lead us all? I couldn't believe that. I didn't want to. Just the thought that I would have to coexist with the man who had tried to end my life sent my vampire into a rage I couldn't get over.

Free to go.

The statement had come over a day ago and I was still here. Still in a panic and daze from what it meant. My mind was torn. What if somehow Aetas did erase my memory and change my path and Marko's? What if he tried to get me to be with the one man I couldn't fathom myself being bound to? The action could happen at any time. Could I prevent it? *No.* Not if Aetas was determined. Although I had outsmarted and overpowered certain aspects of what had happened in my lessons, he was stronger than what he displayed. To him, I wasn't a threat yet. I was still growing … learning. For him to unleash entirely, I was afraid of the outcome of what he could truly do. It was the reason I should go. And the reason I should stay and try to convince him to let me kill Hunter. But was there really any convincing him? Aetas ruled. He could do whatever he wanted. And he would in the end. I knew this in my heart. His decision was made and the only one who could stop it was Hunter, himself.

I took a deep breath, shaking my head as I walked in a quick pace to the door. Gina was standing outside, waiting for me. My request to see Aetas was denied not an hour ago and she informed me she wouldn't leave until I was ready to go.

Silence followed us as we headed for the stairs and made our way to the large double doors. *This was it.* I'd leave and give this one to fate. Marko needed me anyway. War was coming. I'd known this for a while now. Even as Marko's slave. Now that my memories were back, I could feel the threat from the outside world. It didn't help that every time I left the room, the sound of a television played the current news. It blasted through the cathedral as a constant reminder to all that lived here. It was an annoyance to my vampire. A buzzing that I felt was beneath me to even waste my time listing to. But now, as I walked through the main room, I took in the fears of the reporter on martial law. Of vampire attacks and the rise against us. It had my feet slowing.

"Princess?"

Gina paused at my side, nervously, as did Margo, who had met us when we stepped from the stairs. They both gave me puzzled looks while I soaked in the report that began on the Fort Hood massacre. One they were blaming on us.

"I don't think I can leave until Aetas speaks with me."

Margo shook her head, taking a step ahead to usher us further along. "I told you, he's in a meeting. He's asked to not be disturbed. If you wish to have further contact with him in the future, you can send a request."

A request. Yes, I was just another vampire now. No one of importance anymore.

"He's been in the meeting since last night. I don't mind waiting until he's finished."

"I'm sorry, Princess. Once he denies a request, that's the end of it. He doesn't wish to see you over your concerns. And he knows what they entail."

Right. Of course he did. I had no say. No opinion that mattered.

I bit my bottom lip, glancing around the massive room. Doors were everywhere, leading to who knew where. Were they bedrooms? Offices? Feeding chambers? I had no idea and suddenly I hated that I'd been confined into one small space. This place held mysteries I wanted to explore. Answers I longed to discover. This could have been my home. I could have ruled, but somehow throughout my lessons, I had failed. Now Hunter would lead us and I'd be damned if I stood with him. Not as a member and sure as hell not as his mate. What that spoke was volumes. I gave my word to Aetas that I would wouldn't rise against him with Marko. That I wouldn't let the man I loved start a war amongst us. I wasn't so sure about that anymore.

"I need a white dress. And a crown. *My* crown," I said staring between them. "I won't leave until I have them. If I'm to go home, I will do it with honorable standing."

"You sure you don't read minds, too? I was just about to take you there." Something flashed over Gina's face, but she stepped back, spinning to head to one of the doors to the left.

"Two weeks," Margo mouthed, watching Gina go.

"Two weeks?"

"The request. Put it in in two weeks." She stepped closer, keeping her tone barely audible. "Aetas is making a mistake. Dehlia can see the outcome. She's told me, told him, but he refuses to listen. Two weeks, resubmit and seek his council. Do not bring your mate. Come alone and I will stand at your side." Her eyes rose to mine. "In the meantime … *rule*. Take Master Delacroix's position and show Aetas what you're capable of. It's still not too late to stop this, but I fear if we prolong much longer, it just might be."

I nodded, feeling adrenaline race at the thought of dethroning Marko. He wouldn't stand for it. It didn't matter who I was. But I did have the right. I had the power and the blood-status. As for the physical strength … the thought that it would come to that left me sick.

The door opened and Gina waved me in her direction. I stood straighter, embracing who I was meant to be. If Aetas needed to see a ruler, I'd show him what it meant to lead. "Prepare me a guard," I whispered to Margo. "Aetas mentioned enforcers. The stronger, the better."

Her nod had me turning and heading toward the door Gina stood in. I took deep breaths, pushing my thoughts away as I headed inside the large room. I didn't trust her to not try to read my fears. With as powerful as she was, I didn't doubt she would at least try. Until I knew where she stood, I couldn't trust anyone.

Three white dresses were laid across a large bed. I swallowed, licking my lips as I looked at them. *Tradition.* This would be the last time I ever wore white. The color made my think of the past. I could almost imagine the silky material of each one covered in dark crimson.

Two were elaborately decorated in diamonds. The third was just white silk, low on the shoulders with long sleeves. I pointed, not speaking a word as I pulled at the laces of the dark green dress I wore. I stepped free, glancing down at the black flats still on my feet.

"Shoes are in the closet," Gina said, gesturing to the far side of the room. "There's also an array of crowns. You'll know which one to take."

I slid off the flats, walking nude to the closet. Where once I would have been self-conscious, I felt nothing now. Nothing, but who I was, dragged me forward.

Light flooded the space and the closet was even bigger than the bedroom. Shoes lined the back wall, where fancy dresses hung to the left. They were covered in plastic, but somehow their beauty still shone through. As I took in the entire right side, glass cases, housing crowns of different sizes and stature, filled the length. Some were plain gold bands that looked to rest on the forehead, much like the one Margo wore. Others were filled with gems and diamonds that were meant to sit high on ones' head. There were tiaras, wreaths that twisted and turned, filled with branches of jewels. Where some were what was to be expected of royalty, others were black and jagged in their appearance. Eerie and fitting of who we were.

The more I walked along, the faster my heart raced. There was a calling … an internal ache, I couldn't understand as I inspected them. Gina's words came back and I suddenly understood what she had meant. I had no choice in this matter, my vampire did. *My blood.* Thousands, maybe even millions of years of who I was was searching and seeking out my worth. My path…

Footsteps had me coming to a stop and my hair tickled my waist as I looked over my shoulder to take in Gina's expression. She looked just as nervous as I felt. And she had reason to be. This was more than it appeared. My crown would define me, *but what would that mean*?

I turned back scanning over the cases. My eyes stopped on a platinum band with rubies, only to move three more crowns down to one of a darker color. The charcoal grey had my pulse increasing until the beat slammed into my chest with unbelievable force. There was no diamonds, no gems or clusters of shiny, fancy decorations. It was a crown with pointy ends. A symbol of a leader. But it wasn't for show or prestige. It was of glory and death. For fighting while signifying who you were. And it was *mine*.

My hands were shaking as I lifted the lid of the glass case. The moment my fingers touched the smooth surface, my powers surged, hugging my insides in a glorious sense of self. But it was anything but happy. It was my evil, my darkness, thriving in its own silent battle cry. I was ready to lead. To project who I was not only from the inside, but now in appearance too. My city had no idea what to expect, but they'd see soon enough. Everyone would know who I was and they'd fear me.

I lifted, placing the crown on my head, surprised when it slid perfectly into place. It was meant for me. A part of my makeup. Perfect for every aspect of what my life would stand for.

I turned, watching true, unadulterated fear lace Gina's eyes as she sank to her knees. Regardless whether she was one of the strongest vampires or not, I was going to be more. I'd always been, and her expression confirmed it. They all had reason to bow. Every single one of them. I *could* rule. I could take Aetas' spot when the time came, but not with Hunter being turned. Suddenly, I knew I couldn't allow that to happen. No matter the cost.

Gina stood, her head still slightly lowered as I approached. We walked silently to the bed where my chosen dress sat away from the others. Her hands were trembling as she removed the plastic and took the gown off the hanger.

"I will notify Aetas of your … choice. I'm not sure if Margo told you to resubmit your request but I advise you do so. One week," she breathed out, uneasily.

I stepped into the dress, allowing her to pull it up and adjust the laces. I blinked past her words. "Margo told me two weeks."

I gasped as she jerked at the laces hard, securing them, and spinning me to face her.

"One week is the earliest. Resubmit and he will not be able to deny you. Not now," she rushed out. Her eyes rose to the crown and she immediately took a step back. It was followed by more steps until she was spinning for the closet to grab a pair of white flats. I could tell she wanted to escape me and I wondered why.

Gina once again sunk to her knees, placing them on the ground before me.

"Mistress Gina?" The address asked every question I wished to know. When she rose, she fiddled with her dress nervously.

"Darkness means to lead. The lighter the color, the further away from power one wishes to truly be. Your vampire picked the darkest. It picked *his* crown."

"His?" Confusion had me glancing at my reflection in the mirror. To deny that I was growing even more powerful from my appearance was a lie. I was, and I knew it had to do with what was now decorating my head. Whether it was feeding who I was just by being connected to me, or it held remnants of the previous owner's energy, I wasn't sure.

"Aetas," she hissed. "It was his centuries ago. Before he chose another. You're following in his footsteps. Dehlia would say it's a sign of what she's seen. She'll stand with us to state your case, although I feel as though she's your biggest support." Gina's mouth clamped shut, only for her to lower her voice. "Not here. I will accompany you and Margo to your city."

I nodded, allowing her to lead and open the door. When I walked through, Margo and another female vampire's heads jerked from the group of men they were speaking to. The red haired woman's arm locked onto Margo's bicep and she took gasping breaths.

"I saw this," she said, loudly. "I told you."

Margo reached up, leading the woman closer to me. Her expression was fearful, yet almost in awe.

"You must be Dehlia," I said, stopping before them.

"Yes. I…" She threw a glance to Margo and then Gina before she turned back to me. "It was the gold crown with the rubies or this one. I saw the contemplation in my dream. You weren't sure which one you were going to choose, but you reached for the throne. You reach for this one. You wish to lead us?"

I scanned the women's faces, so young, so vulnerable in the moment. But they were anything but weak, and ancient. They were the best. The strongest of our kind and they'd back me. I could tell they wanted to.

"I was meant for this. I *will* rule."

"Not if Aetas has his way," Dehlia said, looking over her shoulder as if someone was there. "You know what he wishes to do?"

"I do, and I'm sorry, but I can't allow the human to take my spot. He tried to kill me. That alone warrants his death. Aetas cannot overlook that. There are rules, laws, aren't there?"

The women grew quiet, telling me all I needed to know. I clenched my fists knowing the time to talk about a solution wasn't now. Not under this roof.

I moved my attention to the group of men standing a little ways off. *My guard. My protectors.*

I may have not needed them when it came down to defending myself, but their presence was exactly what I *did* need. It showed my true status. They were there to prove a point and I'd need the impact if I was going to stake my claim where it belonged. Over the city … over Marko.

Chapter 22
Marko

The cloud of fear perfuming the vicinity around me as I paced a small section of the heart of the city was something I was getting used to when dealing with the vampires under my leadership. Cort and Ronny constantly shifted on their feet as their story poured from them in a gush of stumbling words.

"Slow down," I bit out. "What do you mean Boyd took the human? And what's this about drinking blood?"

Cort ran his fingers through his short hair as he tried to catch his breath. "We wanted to come back last night, but it was impossible. It was too close to sunrise for us to make it by the time Boyd, or the man, left."

"Stop right there." My hand rose and I glanced at the table of members who were still in the middle of their feeding. Although they were occupied, I knew they were listening to every word that was spoken.

"Hunter. He came through the tunnels under the base like you suspected. He killed Abbot and he was giving us a hell of a fight. Even broke Ronny's neck. Well, Boyd got to him before I could and out of nowhere, Hunter bit his neck. He was feeding, like one of us. That's when I noticed something wasn't right. Boyd's scent changed and it was like it wasn't him at all, even if it did look like him. He just stood there, letting Hunter drink his blood. That's when shit started to get … weird."

I blinked past the words. I knew Hunter held Sayer's blood. Of course, he'd crave the substance, even if he wasn't one of us.

"Hunter started yelling, screaming, like he was in pain. He started to go crazy, throwing himself in the wall with all of his strength. Boyd just started laughing. He was…" Cort swallowed hard. "No disrespect Master, but the power Boyd had, it was like nothing I've ever felt before. It … scared me. I…"

Sweat was beginning to bead on my skin. *Aetas*. Had it been him? There wasn't too many more vampires who was more powerful than I was.

"What happened next?" My hand gripped tighter to the back of my chair.

"Boyd…" Ronny threw a look to Cort, but continued. "He started speaking some sort of language we've never heard before. It was as though Hunter understood. Like, he was following orders to whatever he was saying. He stop being aggressive to himself and stood at attention. Like a soldier. Boyd would say something and he'd react with some sort of movement. It was like he was being programmed or something. I don't know. We kept quiet and in the background until they left."

"And their leaving!" Cort's eyes were wide. "They just disappeared into thin air. Just, gone. Humans can't do that. Not even with a master at their side. It wasn't right. Nothing about what went down last night was normal."

"You may go," I bit out. "Don't speak of this again or you won't have a tongue left when I get done with you."

The vampires went rigid before they nodded and practically ran away. I pulled out my chair, glancing at the worried faces of my members. "Meeting after we finish." My words were quiet, but I knew they heard. I sat back down, staring ahead in a daze. My mind was running a million miles a minute. Hunter did mention Aetas showing him Tessa. That meant he had his sights set on Hunter, but what were his intentions?

My jaw clenched. I didn't understand any of this. Aetas had said I had time to take care of Hunter on my own, but he hadn't given me that. It made me shake my head, pissed. Was he letting Tessa get her revenge? If that was the case, I could be okay with that. She deserved to see him suffer, but damn, I wished I could see it too.

"Master." Anastasia's eyes shot up to the ceiling. "We have guests. Unexpected ones."

My hands pushed against the table as I rose. "Who is it? Do you know?"

"They're coming through the house. I'm … not sure. Such power," she said, letting out a deep breath. "Margo." Even though I knew she couldn't see what was before her, her eyes jetted back and forth, wildly. "So many. I…" She swallowed hard, blinking rapidly to bring her attention back to me. "It's a group. Margo for sure, but a few are member worthy. One in particular holds a different sort of power. She's to be watched very carefully. Her entitlement. It's great. So much so," she said, shuddering. "I can't read her."

Anastasia didn't have to say another word. My bond pulled, tugging at me internally. My chair flew out as I jumped to my feet and I couldn't stop the excitement that surged through. The beat of my heart was positively thrumming in my chest.

"She's back," I whispered. "My mate is who you feel, Anastasia. That's Princess Tessalyn. She's come home."

Slowly, the members rose. The shock and fear on their face made my vampire thrive. It made me proud. The need to rush toward the stairs all but killed me. Although I wanted to, I held my place at the head of the table, waiting. Watching. What greeted me wasn't what I expected.

A mass of men, eight to be exact, poured from the stairs, two at a time. They halted, separating to allow Tessa to get in between them. Black eyes of the enforcers took in everything. They were in their vampire form, never allowed to escape their monsters while they did as instructed. Usually they were meant to take out threats in specific cases, but here, they played more of a role. They were guarding royalty. From what, I wondered? Tessa wasn't in danger here.

Vampires and slaves cowered as the guards flanked Tessa, Margo, and Gina. Although I was confused by the other members' arrival, I only had eyes for my beautiful mate. She'd left me here in a white gown. Now she was back wearing another. Could it mean what I hoped it would?

I broke from the table, heading to the center of the room to meet her. A smile came to her face and I could see the impatience. She wanted to run, and fuck if I didn't want to either. Was she here for good?

"Princess Tessalyn." I grabbed the hand she extended, bowing the top half of my body as I placed a kiss on her knuckles. The scent of her skin nearly made me moan. I couldn't stop myself from flipping her hand over and placing my lips against her wrist, too. The pointed end of a dagger pushed into my throat and I stiffened.

"He's not a threat," she said, sternly.

The blade disappeared and I rose, glaring at the vampire to her left. His dark skin and darker eyes left him looking more menacing than I had thought when I'd first taken a glimpse.

"I'm sorry," she whispered, smiling. "They're a little overprotective. That's a good thing."

"Yes," I said, reaching for her hand. "Better protective than not enough so." I glanced at Margo and Gina, feeling the leader in me snap into action. "Please, let us get another table. Had I been expecting you, I would have made it formal. Have you fed?"

"Yes," Margo said. "We wish to speak with you alone. Then we will go."

I clenched tighter to Tessa's hand, going to lead them to the back, when she planted her feet.

"Talking can wait. I do believe we were disturbed during a very special day. If it's alright with you, I think I'd like to pick up where we left off. I mean, everyone's already here."

My smile couldn't have gotten any bigger. I searched her eyes, nodding through the happiness I felt. "I'd be honored."

"Margo." Tessa turned toward her and I didn't miss the unspoken words they seemed to somehow communicate. It had me looking between them curiously. Had they gotten so close since the last time I saw them? And there was something else. *Power.* Yes, Tessa had soared in strength since we'd been separated. Maybe even surpassing me. It had me looking over her again as if she were a stranger. My eyes stopped at the crown on her head and I felt my fingers break from hers.

"Who gave you that?" I whispered.

The underlining of anger, I couldn't hide. There was something about the energy that came from her crown I didn't like.

"No one gave it to me. I chose it. It belongs to me."

I swallowed past the need to pry or argue. Fuck, I'd just gotten her back. The last thing I needed to do was pick a fight. I just wanted what was best for her. This new entourage, the new crown, it was going to take some getting used to. The crown I might be able to deal with, but the enforcers… Maybe they'd leave once she settled in. Even though I thought it, I wasn't so sure. Something was different. I tried not to think about it as I blocked it away.

I turned to the room, knowing they felt the call I was emitting. It was one of pride. One of finalization. It was time Tessa and I made it official and nothing was going to stop us this time.

Margo took her place in front of us, grasping Tessa's hands as she leaned forward, whispering in her ear. As she nodded, Gina moved up to her side. My finger laced with Tessa's the moment she broke free of the Axis member. She faced me, letting happiness shine through her eyes.

"We gather here tonight in a moment of joining. In a beginning that marks not only a great new era, but an alliance between two people that will undoubtedly go down in history.

"The Black Princess and Master Delacroix share a special kind of love. One that doesn't happen to our kind often. It is in these times that we see the true depth of devotion. Through pain has emerged a bond so true that I can say without regret that this union is meant to be. With that..." Margo turned to me. "Master Marko Delacroix, do you as leader of Austin, take Princess Tessalyn Kennedy as your concubine? As your one and only mate, for as long as she lives?"

The grin on Tessa's face wiped away any worry or questions I may have had. She was beautiful. The only one I would ever love or take vows with.

"I do," I said, squeezing her hands.

The smile grew as she kept her stare locked to mine.

"Princess Tessalyn, do you as the new leader of Austin, take Master Marko Delacroix as your mate for as long as he shall live?

The smile melted from her face and it took me a moment to make sense of Margo's words. A gasp and whispering filled the room and I couldn't break from Tessa's apologetic expression. *New leader?* As in, she'd just taken my throne?

"I do," she said, lowly.

"Excellent," Margo said, loudly. "We have a joining. You may kiss your concubine, Master Delacroix."

My jaw clenched and I had to stop the rage that was screaming in my head. My hands cupped Tessa's cheeks firmly and I didn't leave her eyes as I brought my lips down to brush against hers. It wasn't the kiss I had dreamed about. Or the joining. I had been conned. Duped, right at the altar, in front of every single vampire I had ruled over.

Tessa's hands locked onto my wrists and she held to them tightly as I drew back. She knew I was pissed. What made it worse was her reaction. She was ready, as if I was going to try to fight her for the position over the city. For her to think me capable after how much I'd confessed to loving her ... it blew my mind.

"The meeting room," I ground out.

I clutched to one of Tessa's wrists and jerked her toward the tunnel so fast that I left the enforcers racing to catch up. The moment we were inside the room, I spun her around cupping her face one again.

"What is the meaning of this? To turn what was supposed to be the happiest day of our lives into a God damn spectacle of besting me in front of the city...? What were you thinking?"

"I didn't know," she rushed out. "I mean, I knew it was going to happen, but I never thought..." Tessa trailed off, jerking her face out of my touch to look at Margo. "Did you have to do that right then and there?"

Margo had barely made it to the room before she was hit with the question. "Yes. It was best to get it into the open as soon as possible. Princess Tessalyn rules this city now. It had to come out with her arrival."

"You don't even know if she's stronger than me," I burst out. "You can't just hand her over the city because you feel she deserves the right."

"It depends how one measures strength. She may not be able to physically outmatch you, but she's stronger," Margo said, matter of factly. "This is *her* city. It is your responsibility as her bonded mate and former leader to make sure she learns to rule correctly. Besides, after what you did to the Army Base, you're lucky you're not behind bars."

I stood straighter, shrugging. "No one can prove it was me."

"Aetas knows," Margo snapped. "If he wasn't preoccupied with the one person you failed to kill, you'd be locked away for abusing your powers."

My mouth turned dry at the thought of Hunter. "He has him, then?"

"Yes," Margo hissed. "And the outcome will not be good unless your new concubine can somehow put an end to what he plans to do."

My attention went back to Tessa and I could see the worry on her face. "What does he plan to do?"

Tessa's hands rose to my face and I watched as her lids closed. I was hit with flashes so hard and fast that it took my breath away. The vivid colors, the walls that rose around me, it placed me in a room I'd only seen once. *Dallas underground.*

A musky scent filled my nostrils and if Tessa would have wiped my mind to make me forget who I was, I would have really thought I was standing in the heart of the city with Hunter not feet away. He was poised in the leader's seat, as if he ruled Dallas. The sight alone surprised me, but what began to play out was even more shocking.

Tessa walked forward, obviously confused. She didn't appear to know where she was, or even *who* Hunter was as she came to a stop next to him. Their words played out and the moment he mentioned tasting her, I tried to lunge forward, after him. I couldn't. This was a memory of hers. Or a vision. Either way, I couldn't interfere. Upon seeing myself with Marie … mated … there were no words. My gut twisted and ached at the scene that was going down. By the time Tessa got to the rape she had to endure at Hunter's hands, I couldn't contain myself anymore. My body was spasming with fury, trying my best to escape what was in front of me.

The walls crumbled and I stumbled back, soaked in sweat. It dripped from my hair, running down my face as I looked between the faces of the people who now surrounded me.

"He can't do that," I breathed out, heavily. "Aetas can't do that."

"No, he can't," Tessa said, coming back over to me. "Not legally, anyway. Hunter tried to kill me. Aetas is breaking laws by not putting Hunter to death. I know they're his laws, but there has to be something I can do. There has to be."

"And if he goes through with this plan?" I looked between Tessa and the other members. They wouldn't turn on our true leader. They may have wanted Tessa to out-rule Hunter, but they wouldn't do anything to help her beside what they were doing now. If Aetas chose Hunter, they'd follow, just like they always did. It was the reason I harbored such hatred for Axis. It was their way, or no way—laws be dammed.

"Don't answer that," I said, pulling Tessa into my chest so I could hold her. "This is our wedding day. None of that matters right now. We'll have plenty of time to go over everything in the following days. Tonight, let's focus on me and you."

I kissed her forehead, turning my attention to Margo and Gina. I had hoped they'd catch the hint, but Margo didn't seem finished.

"Tessa is to resubmit a request to meet with Aetas in one week. She's to make it urgent and immediate. Dehlia is already going to inform him of her choice," she said, gesturing to the crown. "It was his. Tessa's vampire has chosen his path. She's meant to rule. Aetas cannot deny what this means."

I swallowed hard, once again, taking in what sat on Tessa's head. "And what if he does?"

"I don't know," Margo whispered. "That crown was retired, but the significance is clear. Their paths are the same. She could have chosen any, but she chose his. He has to honor that. It shows she's the right choice, just as Dehlia has tried to convince him. He refuses to believe because of you. He thinks Princess Tessalyn will bend under your pressure. That you'll rule in her favor. I happen to think she's stronger than that. I think," she said stepping closer, "that you're just the person she needs to support her through the trails of leading us. Am I wrong, or right?"

My arms held to Tessa tighter, letting everything we'd been through play out. I knew the truth in my heart. As I knew what I was going to say was fact. "No one will ever support her more than me. If she's meant to rule, *no one* is going to stop her."

Chapter 23
Hunter

Sometimes love and hate were so close in depth that deciphering what you were feeling was impossible. I hated Aetas more than I hated anymore. More than Tessa for killing my uncle. More than Marko and his undying love for her. Even more than Sayer after he'd raped me repeatedly. Aetas was worse. He made me relive it all, over and over, until I knew the exact color of each fiber of threads that made up the blankets I'd stared at when Sayer violated me. To the rich smell of Tessa's skin as I buried my face against her bare waist and held to her through the unbearable pain.

He tortured my psych, pushing to boundaries no human was capable of enduring without going crazy. And maybe I had, days ago. Now, I was nothing but a body. I was what he wanted me to be. Completely empty. Completely emotionless. A blank slate. For that, I may have loved him.

Love. Hate. The two were mingled and had transitioned into a torturous relief. But it didn't come without a price.

I still wasn't where he wanted me. I couldn't willingly say I wanted to become his predecessor and rule after his passing. *If* he ever did pass. I knew enough of who he was to know he'd lived thousands upon thousands of years, if not more, and I didn't expect him to kick the bucket in my lifetime. But even though I couldn't say, it didn't mean he wouldn't turn me anyway. He was just having fun playing with me like some toy. All he wanted me to do was admit the appeal. I just couldn't do it. I didn't want this life. I didn't want Tessa, and revenge against Marko wasn't worth the cost of eternal hell. And that's what this would be. Forced to face centuries of run-ins with those two, all the while having to lead my own vampire city… No thank you. I didn't want that.

The only thing that held my interest even the slightest amount was what ran through Aetas' veins. He'd fed me enough of his blood to last a lifetime. Each drink was like a shot of heroin-based candy to my brain and speed-based ecstasy to my cock. I loved it. Ate that shit up like it was going to expire if I didn't drink fast enough. And even now as I watched him lick his lips and think about what he'd do next, all my attention kept going back to was his exposed wrist. The one he loved to cut and tease me with. God … I was fucked if I ever made it out of here. I was addicted, and he was making sure I stayed that way.

"What if I let you kill Marko before I turned you? Would you want it, then?"

My eyes jerked up and I shook my head. "No. I'd pick Tessa to kill over Marko. It's her I wish to put at peace. Marko deserves worse than a simple death."

"Hmm. We'll, I can't give you the princess. I need her alive. But Marko, I'd let you keep for a few days. You could have your fun before I changed you. How about then?"

My eyes rolled and happened to stop right at his wrist again. "No." My voice was monotone from the constant repetition. "I told you, I'm not letting you change me."

"Wrong. You have no control if I wish to change you. What you're doing is answering my questions. We're bargaining in a way. I'll give you something. In return, you accept that this is the way your life is now. It's a win-win."

"If you're going to change me regardless, what difference does it make? What's the point of bargaining?"

"Because it's fun," Aetas stressed. "And because I need you a certain way."

I could tell he was losing his patience. Maybe he thought I would break already. Little did he know, I would never admit to wanting this life. I'd kill myself first. After the last time when I'd stabbed my heart in Tessa's room, I thought he would understand that. He wanted me to accept. That would never happen.

Knocking had Aetas' lids closing. When they opened I could see a light burning in their depths. His anger was worse than I'd imagined, but I wasn't afraid. What was there for me to fear? The emotion didn't exist within me anymore. He'd either kill me or turn me. If that happened, I'd just either kill myself, or continue to kill them.

Aetas turned, heading to the door. I glanced around the large room he had me in, taking in the desks and books. It looked like a library, yet not. There was a bed not far away from where I stood, but I didn't feel as though this was his bedroom. Possibly a study, but nothing about this place made sense.

The wooden curved board I rested against hugged my body, almost giving the impression that I was lying down. There were no restraints. No ties that kept me captive. Aetas didn't need them. His energy made sure I didn't escape. And I never got tired of standing.

"Master," a woman whispered. "I beg to speak to you. I've requested now for days. I have vital information that you must know."

Red hair waved down past pale shoulders and the woman looked terrified to even be in his presence. A black dress hugged to her curves, exposing the cleavage of fairly small breasts. Even though I didn't feel myself attracted to her, there was some odd pull as he waved her in. Brown eyes shot in my direction, but I didn't feel as though she saw me.

"What is so important that you felt the need to knock on my door after I told you I would come to you?"

A shiver had her hands cupping her biceps while she hugged herself.

"It's Princess Tessalyn—"

"I denied her request," he snapped. "I said I did not want to speak with her. What is so hard to understand about that?"

"Master," she breathed out. "It's not her request I wish to speak to you about. She left two days ago. It's her choice in crowns that I must speak to you about."

Aetas tensed the smallest amount and shrugged as he stared at her impatiently. "Well … what about it?" His hand came up. "Let me guess. She chose Sayer's line. No," he immediately corrected himself. "She wouldn't do that."

"No," the female breathed out.

Aetas' lids lowered and I could see him actually start to think. I felt the seriousness in my body as his blood began to surge. "I can't see it. Why can't I see her choice? That makes absolutely no sense."

At his roaring at the end, Dehlia jumped. "You can't see her choice because you're blocked."

"Blocked? By who?"

"You. Master … she chose your crown. The one you retired. It … protects her as it did with you."

"What?" The yell was so loud that even I jumped. "The crown didn't protect me. *I* protected me. The damn thing just has my impression. It shields her because I shielded myself." He growled, walking over and grabbing a glass of some sort of dark liquid. His back was to us and I could see how stiff he was.

"You know what this means," she said lowly. "It is *her*. She must be the one to lead us."

Aetas spun around, pinning her with a glare. "I will not hand my kingdom over to Master Delacroix. And that's exactly what will happen if she rules. She will bow because of her love and he will destroy you all." He shook his head. "I refuse. I've seen her love. I know … how they feel for each other. It's not going to happen."

"You're jealous," I said lowly. "I feel your conflict. You don't even know that's what it is, but you," I paused, trying to assess the strange emotions within me. "You long for something you will never have."

Aetas' head whipped to me, but the woman seemed to not have heard.

"Master, I beg you. Meet with her. Princess Tessalyn will not bend to Master Delacroix. She's stronger than that. You'll see it if you just look into her again."

"I've already *seen* into her. She always submits to him. It is only he who makes her weak. Now leave me."

Tears flood the woman's eyes and they angrily came to me. My pulse jumped and I was sure she was aware of my presence, whether she could see me or not.

"As you wish." She turned, rushing for the door. A sniffle followed and I couldn't get over the fact that there was something about her that was different.

Aetas growled, stalking toward me. "I am *not* jealous. That's ridiculous. Petty and juvenile. Do you know who I am?"

"Yes. But no one is immune to emotion."

"You know nothing. Your mortal brain can't begin to comprehend the significance of the situation. I need a true leader. You can be that."

"No." I shook my head. "If anything, all I want to do is watch you all die. I'll destroy what you've worked so hard to build up. I'll do it intentionally."

The vampire's blood boiled inside of me, reaching degrees that had me thrashing against the invisible force that held me still.

"You will not want to destroy what you become a part of. Your vampire will not have that desire."

"You so sure about that? Are you willing to take the risk?"

Fingers bit into my face and Aetas' enraged eyes met mine. I knew where this was headed. We were about to go right back into my past where he could once again torture me. When his hand flatted against my stomach, I gasped and nearly heaved at the soul-tugging feeling that took my breath away. Tighter, he clutched, jerking against the one thing that made me, me.

"Maybe they're right. Perhaps I am just wasting my time with you."

A yell was ripped from my throat at the rubber band feeling that stretched out my core. I tried thrashing so I could break myself away from his unexplainable hold, but escaping was impossible.

"You're not tempted by power, love, or greed. What about pain?"

Heat scorched my insides at his anger and the pull grew even more intense. Lightheadedness had my head rolling to the side, but my screams never ceased. He was tearing me apart from the inside-out. He had my soul in his clutches and it didn't matter whether I wanted him to have it or not. Something told me he could take it if he wanted. He could kill me with the disconnection and he was so close to achieving the unimaginable.

"Do it," I yelled. "Take me from this nightmare and end this once and for all. Anywhere has to be better than the hell this place has become." A sob left me for the first in as long as I could remember and all I wanted to do was escape the life I'd been forced into. To flee this world for another. I wanted to forget everything. To simple not exist a moment longer.

"Death will not be your savior, only acceptance. Take this gift, Hunter. Accept what I want to give you and everything will stop. You can be happy again. You can have whatever you want. Just say the words. Tell me yes."

The seductive tone in which he spoke tempted me, promised me a release from the pain. But I refused to believe it. I'd seen their life. Seen what it would do to a person who was changed. That wasn't me and it wouldn't ever be.

"Never."

Where I thought the pain couldn't get any worse, it did. My screams increased and his stare sucked me into the dark void he'd taken me so many times before. *My own personal hell.*

Chapter 24
Tessa

Lips kissing down my spine pulled me from a deep sleep, bringing a smile to my face as the memories of the last two days and nights replayed in my mind. Happiness was something I'd only caught glimpses of since I'd been turned, but if my new life had anything to say about my future with Marko, I'd gladly take it.

We were in heaven. A dream that promised a blissful existence so long as it stayed the way it was now. Of course, we hadn't left our room since our vows. We were given two days of uninterrupted honeymooning, but one I knew would end tonight. Then, I'd take my role as the new leader, and everything would change.

Marko and I hadn't spoken one word about what would happen now. Maybe we didn't want to know. Maybe we didn't want to imagine the ups and downs we both knew were coming.

"You want me." His voice purred as he lowered, letting his tongue swirl over my lower back before he sucked against my skin. Fingers wedged between my thighs, separating my legs while he began to rub over my wet slit.

A moan left me as I arched through the contact. "Only you," I managed, finally opening my eyes. In my peripheral I could see his dark hair falling over his forehead as he watched where he touched. I spread my legs wider. The sounds that left him sent satisfaction wrapping itself around me. My vampire loved pleasing him, just as much as she loved teasing him. To see his obsessive need went beyond right. It's what I longed for more than anything.

I yawned, closing my legs and rolling to my back. The look on Marko's face almost had me laughing. The tightness of his features went lax and his eyebrows drew in, determined, as he pulled me more in front of him and spread my legs once again.

"Stay." He licked his lips, moving his fingers back to my pussy as he explored the distance between my opening and my clit. In slow circles he built me up, applying just the right amount of pressure to the sensitive nub, only to make a path back down to nudge into my channel. I rocked, clutching to the sheet as he slid one digit inside of me. "Fuck, you're so wet." Another finger followed, stretching me as he eased in deep. Just as my orgasm began to come, my legs shot up to close and I pushed to sit. Marko's eyes flared and once against I was pulled to lie down.

"I think someone forgot how to follow orders. You may rule this city, but that doesn't mean you lead in our room."

Again, he pushed my legs open, gripping to my inner thighs to drive his point home. My stare rose to his and uneasiness set in at the reality of what waited outside of our room.

"Don't speak of that right now." My hand rose and he lowered enough for me to grab the back of his neck. "Kiss me. Make me forget everything but us."

"A leader never forgets what is outside of his walls," he said, lowering more of his weight on me. "It is something you will have to accept, ma minette. These vampires need you at all times. And someday, it'll be our entire race. Our future will be far from easy. You do understand this, yes?"

I nodded, swallowing past the concentration on his face. He was reading me. Trying to see if I had what it took to be that strong. I never broke our gaze as I let him inside of me to witness my desire. When he pulled back from his hypnotic daze, he took a deep breath.

"God, you've come so far. It's actually quite scary if you want me to be truthful." He dipped down pressing his lips into mine. "But you'll be a great leader. You want it." He paused. "You'll teach me what you learned?"

I laughed, pulling his mouth back to mine. "Later. Tell me more about how much you love me."

"You mean, show you how much I love you. I would be happy to."

His tongue pushed into my mouth, massaging into mine, while he rubbed his hard cock against the outside of my pussy. My arms wrapped around his neck pulling his closer.

"Marko." I moaned into him, wiggling to try to get him to make love to me like he had the numerous times already. I couldn't get enough.

"I've never loved my name more than when it falls from your lips during these moments."

Thickness stretched me and my breath caught as he inched his way inside. My legs locked around his waist and I cried out as he surged the remaining distance. In slow thrusts he withdrew, only to plunge even harder. The tease of his chest against my nipples only made them tighter and my breasts ached, causing me to thrust them into the muscles that flexed with his movements. Every inch of my body was screaming for more, and my voice was echoing those screams.

"Faster," I begged. "You're holding back. Give me more."

"You get more when I'm ready."

Marko lifted, spinning me to my stomach. His arm wrapped around my waist, lifting me to my knees. When I started to rise, he pushed my head to the mattress, keeping a firm hold as he began to fill me again.

"You want me?"

I screamed as he slammed into me.

"Yes," I cried out, adding pressure to his hand as my head tried to lift. A slap to the side of my ass had me biting my lower lip. Since I'd been turned, everything had been passion-induced fucking or making love. But we had shared something once that I was dying to delve back into and Marko seemed to pick up on that as he spanked me again. Harder. And then harder.

Fingers weaved into my hair, keeping my face to the mattress, but angling my head back. Swift, deep thrusts became almost brutal. Pain raced through my scalp and I could feel myself on the edge of an orgasm so powerful that it was almost impossible to control. When claws raked down my back, almost breaking the skin, I screamed through the spasms that tore themselves free.

"You didn't have permission to come, did you?"

Another spanking had my pussy clenching around his cock. My whole body jolted from the twitching of my limbs.

"God, more." I pushed back, only to suck in air as he squeezed the side of my ass, letting his nails break the skin at my hip. Stinging left my gasps coming out loud. The scent of blood flooded the room with a sweet fragrance and I could smell my power intoxicate the atmosphere. *Intoxicate us.* The need to cry out again for him to do more was there, but he was already beginning to fuck me so hard, I didn't think the words could leave me. I could barely breathe, more or less speak from the jarring thrusts.

A loud groan filled the room and Marko pulled me up by my hair, placing me on all fours. His chest molded to my back while he went even deeper. Still, he held to my hair, controlling me.

"It's laughable if you really think about it," he said, nuzzling into the side of my face. "You may someday rule the world, but here you'll always be my slave. I'll have you trained to my every sick, twisted desire and you'll love every minute of it. Won't you?" he asked, giving my hair a tug.

"Yes. Show me everything."

"Everything? You so sure about that?"

I was past the point of caring what he meant. Every part of me craved every hidden secret within him. I wanted it all, no matter how dark it was. For so long, my human self had hid things I only dared to fantasize about. Now that the fear was gone, I was dying to push the limits on the forbidden.

"Whatever you've dared to dream, I want it."

Marko's arm locked around my throat in a choke hold and he brought me to my knees, growling low in his throat as he cut off my oxygen almost entirely. "Ma minette, what a dangerous path you wish to walk. It's not safe to hold hands with the devil. Are you sure? There's no going back. It's all or nothing." He withdrew his cock, inching back into me slowly. I knew I didn't need air to live, but the uncomfortableness left my hands coming to his arms in a slow building orgasmic panic. *Submission, fear…* Not only did my vampire need the balance of not being in control in my personal life, but the real me craved the treatment.

"I'm yours … however you want." The words were almost impossible to get out as I held tighter. For seconds he did nothing but cut off my air supply while he used my body. Tears poured down my cheeks and air came in a gush. I sucked in a greedy gulp just in time for his fangs to tear into the side of my neck. It wasn't the bite of a lover, but of a predator. I screamed, feeling myself being pushed into the mattress. Moaning vibrated my neck and his thrusts became slow, passionate as he reached around, playing with my clit. My vampire went from defensive to unabashedly in love all over again.

The tugs on my veins had my lids growing heavy with bliss. Just when I began to enjoy it too much, Marko bit down harder, giving me that slice of pain I needed. The stinging mixed with the need in my core and I could feel the impending release building to unimaginable heights. Venom oozed into me and I cried out at the delay I didn't think was coming.

"There, there. Now your treat." His tongue licked over the wounds, closing them. Pleasure shot through me with such force that I teetered on the brink of the drugged orgasm. "I want this new beginning to be what you've always wanted. What *both of us* have longed for." More of his weight settled as he continued to thrust. "No matter what happens outside of this room, it's trivial. Let the world be on fire around us. None of that makes a difference. As long as we're together, ma minette, that's all I want."

Arms wrapped around me, holding tightly just above my breasts. Even through one side of my face was buried in the mattress and my hair was nearly blinding me, I had never felt so aware of the room around me. Tingling from Marko's breath gave me goosebumps and the energy in the air fluctuated, making my brain pick up on every little detail of not only us, but the entire city. My mind was so open I didn't have to physically see to witness the ongoing events. And it had been like this since I'd taken rule here. With Margo's words and Marko's blood, the realization of who I was had never been clearer. And there was peace in that. Peace within myself where Marko and I were headed.

"That's it," he whispered, going faster. "You're so close. I can feel your pussy tightening around me. Let my poison take your over, love. Come for me. Give yourself to me."

And I did. My face turned more into the mattress and I cried out, arching as his cock grew heavy inside of me. Trembling left me jolting through the forceful release and it was only prolonged as Marko's cum shot deep and hot.

"Fuck," he said, rolling us over while he still pumped into me. My legs were spread with my feet firmly on the mattress, and I was facing the ceiling, lying with my back against his chest. When he slowed, I buried my face in his neck, content to keep him in me forever. I never wanted to leave this moment, but I knew I would have to. And soon.

Comfortable silence filled the room while he held me. Minutes went by, drawn out as I breathed him in. The exotic scent had me smiling.

"You're in a good mood."

"I think I have you to thank for that."

He chuckled, rolling me to the bed. As he hovered over me, on his side, I reached up, running my fingers through the hair that fell forward. It was so much like the scene before our first bounding ceremony. My hand froze and my stomach dropped.

"No," he said, shaking his head. "We don't think about that night. It didn't happen. I didn't lose you and you didn't die."

"But I did," I whispered. "Hunter killed me. Now it's our turn to return the favor. Aetas might have him under his wing, but he can't hide there forever. We'll all meet again, and when we do, he'll be finished for good."

I wiggled free, standing from the bed to head to the shower. Marko was right behind me the moment I walked through the entrance.

"If anyone is going to kill him it will be me. You have no idea what I went through when I thought you were dead. Hell, I was dead, too."

"I know." I turned on the shower, spinning around to face him. "I saw you. I heard you. I lived your pain. It destroyed me not being able to do anything about it."

Marko's hands gripped my biceps gently as he lowered his head down closer to mine. "Then you know that it is I who must do this."

My head shook and I could think of more than a couple of reasons why I had every right, too. He'd violated me with Sayer. He'd betrayed me and disrespected me. The bastard had driven a dagger through my chest. And even as I thought it, my human tried to give excuses. Ones that my vampire saw as unforgiveable.

"Maybe neither of us will have the chance," I said, climbing in the shower. "Maybe Aetas will see the light and end this for us once and for all."

Chapter 25
Marko

To say I wasn't upset by being dethroned by my concubine was far from the truth. I'd spent my vampire life dreaming of nothing but reaching the top and not long after I'd gotten my own city, she'd come in and taken it right out from under me. I knew Tessa didn't know what Margo planned on doing, but it still pissed me off that it'd gone down that way. I couldn't even think about it without reacting negatively.

As I led her out of our room and was faced with her guard, reality sunk in. Our honeymoon period had been more than I could have dreamed of, but it was over, and the city needed its leader. It needed *her* and I was meant to just sink back into the shadows as if the citizens here hadn't taken to my rule so well. It upset me and left me in a sour mood. Tessa immediately felt it and I could have cursed myself for making it more stressful for her.

"Remember what I told you," I said, leaning in as we walked.

Before I could go further, the strength of her power surged, weighing against not only me, but her guard. Their presence forged with hers leave a suffocating cloud around us. It was meant to show the community who was in charge and there was no doubt in my mind that they'd believe she ruled. I could hardly fathom the toxicity, myself. It had me studying her through the darkness. Was this really the Tessa I had stalked that night outside of the church? My blood slave that I'd abused and ravaged when I got the whim?

The smile she flashed at me said it was. The crown and confident air that blanketed around us was what left me questioning it. She was so different.

Light radiated ahead and I slowed our pace, coming to a stop just feet away. "I love you," I whispered. "You've got this. I'll be at your side if you have any questions."

Something flashed on Tessa's face and my brow creased in concern.

"I love you, too. I…" She glanced toward the heart of the city and shook her head.

"Shh. There's nothing to worry about. Your fears are mine now, remember?"

White teeth flashed at her smile and she took a deep breath. "You're right. Everything will turn out fine."

Although I didn't know exactly what was on her mind, I didn't try to force my way in to find out. Tessa would inform me if it bothered her too much.

We headed toward the light and she never missed a beat as we entered the heart of the city. Talking died out and I gripped to her bicep tighter as I led us to the member's table. Eight were present, minus John, who was still in lockdown. The anxiety as we approached was all too clear. Weary glances were thrown Tessa's way and I had to remind myself that barely anyone had seen her since she was turned. When they had, it was usually because Tessa was getting herself into trouble.

A loud blast sounded from the corner and Tessa's power flared to asphyxiating heights at the announcement of her arrival. It had been so long since I had heard the formal horn that I had to swallow past the spike of my own pulse.

My arm dropped from hers and I pulled out the leader's chair, giving her one last look before I stepped off to the side. The action felt alien. As if this was all wrong. I was the male, the one who should have been the one who ruled … but I didn't, and I never would again.

"Thank you, Master Delacroix." Tessa's hands lowered and her palms pressed against the table. When her lids closed, I found myself scanning the faces of not only the members, but of the surrounding tables. If I hadn't been able to read her actions, I would have been as lost as everyone else. But because I could, I felt even more panicked at her approach. Where most leaders tested blood, Tessa was reading their energy.

"Marie." Completely blacked out eyes met us as Tessa's lids fluttered opened. Marie was so stiff and that I felt sorry for her as she looked toward me questioningly. "Come forward."

Tears shone as she focused on her new leader and obeyed. The moment she made it to Tessa's side, she lowered to her knees, waiting for what we all knew was coming. With Tessa leading, I'd move down in rank, as would everyone. That left her going back to the ranks of the commoners.

"Stand."

The command was soft, but did the job as Marie rose tall before her.

"Do you accept my rule?"

Wide eyes shot to Tessa's face, only to lower submissively. "I do, Princess."

"Then you're willingly accepting your dismissal from this table?"

The tears spilled over and Marie nodded. "I am."

"I'm not," Tessa said, loudly.

Gasps came from a few of the tables and I felt my own expression of shock surface. *Tessa couldn't do that.* She couldn't increase the number of members to eleven. It had never been that way. It was against our laws.

"I'm sorry?" Marie shook her head confused. "I … don't deserve to be here."

"You're wrong." Tessa grabbed Marie's hands, moving in closer so the vampire had to look into her eyes. "I see so deep inside of you right now that I am convinced this is right. You're going to be a vital to not only me, but everyone in this room. But I don't merely want you at this table. I want more. I want your vow."

Shifting further down the table had my eyes going toward Demetrius, who was staring at them threateningly. The expression alone had my claws pushing out.

"What sort of vow?" Marie asked, softly.

"One of loyalty. *One for life.* I want you as my secretary. My own personal lady-in-waiting, so to speak. I want you as my number three."

A roar echoed through the large room. "You can't do that!" Demetrius yelled. "That's not fair."

"She has the right to do as she wishes," I countered. "Plenty of leaders do the same thing."

"But the vampires they move up aren't members, they're slaves. She can't just skip a number ten to the number three spot because she fancies a fortune teller to do her bidding. It doesn't work that way."

Tessa's hand came to rest on Marie's shoulder while she eased the vampire back. Longer, my claws extended. The need to move in her way, to take care of Demetrius myself almost had me flying over the table to get in front of her, but I couldn't. Tessa had to lead, and to do that, she'd have to fight her own battles. She had to prove herself.

Silence once again became unbearable as Tessa stopped before Demetrius, eying him up and down. She didn't say a word. It left the male vampire shifting uneasily in her presence. He looked at her, and then at me, before starting with his attitude once again.

"What are you doing?" he snapped.

"Waiting for you to say it to my face. I'm right here. Why don't you tell me I can't make her my number three. I'd like to hear you say it."

"You can't—"

Black fog blew in a fast stream from Tessa's mouth, right into his, causing him to choke on his words.

"I'm sorry, I couldn't hear you. Would you like to try to say it again?"

Demetrius began coughing, grabbing at his throat while his face turned a deep shade of red. Fear had some of the other members moving behind their chairs as they looked on in horror. Crimson began running down Demetrius's neck as he started clawing at his flesh.

"I still can't hear you," Tessa said, louder. "Maybe you really didn't have anything to say at all. Is that it?"

Wide brown eyes shot to her in desperation while he nodded furiously.

"I thought so," she said, smiling. "I knew I must have misheard you. Here, let me fix this." Her claws shot out and the fake sympathetic look melted as she glared and jerked his face toward hers. "If you ever so much as doubt my actions again, there will be no second chances. What I do, I do for this city. Marie has a gift. One you'll be thankful for when her prediction saves your life. War is coming. Let's hope you're smart enough to survive it."

Tessa's lips crushed into his and blood poured from their chins, dripping onto the table in a constant trickle. My vampire went crazy at the sight. I knew what they were sharing was far from intimate, quite the opposite, but I could barely keep in place.

"Now apologize to Marie." Tessa wiped her chin, stepping back.

"I'm … sorry, Mistress."

Marie's fist clenched over her chest as she nodded.

"Good. Now that we have that settled, we can continue." Tessa jerked up her sleeve and headed back to the throne. "For the next week you will no longer feed from the servants. You will take my vein and my vein only. Is that understood, Mistress?"

Marie once again nodded while Tessa took her place. She sat down and we all slowly followed. Even Marie, who kneeled on the floor next to her side. The gesture to feed was given and Tessa's attention went to her arm as she pulled the sleeve up higher. I watched, curiously, reaching for the arm of the servant before me.

"A week should be more than enough," Tessa said, lowly, "My blood is strong and continues to grow by the day. You do understand we will share a tie from my previous … feeding of you, yes?"

Her French accent rang out as she studied Marie's face.

"I do, Princess."

"And you're okay with that?"

"I am."

Tessa glanced at me, almost a silent request for my approval—as her mate. I didn't like the thought of her holding a tie with another person, but I trusted her instincts and it would be good for Marie to grow stronger.

I gave a quick nod.

"Feed." Tessa let her arm dangle to the side as her free hand came to weave in the human woman's hair before her. I noticed her fingers tightened at Marie's bite and she only paused for a moment before she moved in and fed, herself. I held to the servant's arm, watching Tessa's every expression as I let my fangs sink into the bend of blond girl's elbow.

A good minute went by and when ma minette lifted, her eyes were back to a light green. She closed them almost immediately, clenching her jaw as she took deep breaths. I knew she could feel the pain from the first mark, but she didn't so much as budge. Marie was another story. Her cry was loud, pulling attention in her direction as she lowered her head and made continuous sounds. Her shoulders tensed and she reached up, gripping to the arm of the throne as the currents and power took over.

"Slow your pulse," Tessa said, soothingly. "Roll with it and don't fight the currents. It'll only be worse."

Marie's eyes peeked over the edge of the chair. Her pupils were dilated so wide, her eyes almost looked as black as Tessa's had been.

"Too … much."

"It's not more than you can handle," Tessa snapped. "You're stronger than you know. What the body can endure is only as much as the mind tells us. Strengthen your mind and your body will follow. Accept this. No more fear, Marie. Fear shows of weak leadership and I will not have it."

Tessa's eyes shot to me and I could read her impatience. Her determination to build us all up stronger. She shifted in her chair, and I could tell she was getting antsy. But we were far from over. There was the meeting, the reports, and the most important thing, the calls to the surrounding leaders. I was curious to see how they took to her. It could be a great partnership or impending doom. They wouldn't be able to feel her power over the phone. All they had was word of mouth, and if rumors of Sayer had made its round, which I was sure they had, leaders just might want to put Tessa to the test. It was a test they would lose. That could be even worse. Not just for her … but for me as her protector and mate.

Chapter 26
Hunter

Whispering in the distance pulled me from the blackness surrounding me. I knew somehow I'd been sleeping, but for how long or where I was, I didn't have a clue. My brain felt like mush and my body ached as if I'd been beaten repeatedly.

The voices grew louder and no matter how hard I tried, I couldn't open my lids. I didn't see the point anyway. I didn't want to be awake. Not here, wherever I was. I couldn't remember exactly where I'd come from. Or how I got here. Now that I was thinking about it, I really couldn't remember anything at all. Not even my name. Who was I? I knew the truth was hidden somewhere deep within and it'd come back. There wasn't a rush to force the information. I was too tired. Too … hungry.

"I don't know about this," a woman whispered. "If Aetas finds us in here, it'll be the death of us."

"He won't find us. He sleeps. I have Cataline and Harmon watching his chambers. They will inform me the moment he so much as stirs."

"This isn't right," the first woman pled. "I have a bad feeling."

A small growl filled the room and I listened curiously, almost seeing their movements even though darkness surrounded me.

"Push them away, then. You've seen the paths. We have no choice. We have to kill him."

Something inside of me snapped to attention. Tingling raced down my skin and heat began to blister inside of me. Although my breathing never changed, I felt as though I was panting inside. What were these woman thinking? They couldn't seriously be wanting to hurt me? Didn't they know who I was?

"What if Aetas changes his mind? The Princess put in the request this morning. He'll see her. He'll choose to listen. He always does what is in our best interest. You know he goes through these weird cycles, but our leader always does what's right. Always."

"Dehlia, you saw him tear her letter up at the meeting. He's gone too far this time. What we're doing will help. We'll make the decision for him, then he'll have to go along with the Princess."

Silence lasted for a few seconds before light footsteps grew closer.

"Wait," Dehlia said, out of breath. "Just … wait a moment."

"What for?" the other woman asked, irritated. "Let's do this and get the hell out."

More silence. Then a gasp. "Look at him," Dehlia whispered. "Look at his skin."

Rushing footsteps.

"No … Oh … no. No," the other woman said, dragging it out.

"Let's go," Dehlia said, panicked. "It's too late. We have to prolong this. If we interfere now, my vision comes true. I don't want to die." Sniffling sounded and

I could tell the woman was stressed. From the moment I had heard her voice, she appeared beyond control of herself.

What sounded like metal scraping against something had blood coating my tongue. The warmth ignited a burning deep in my throat and I felt my fingers twitch. My body was beginning to come alive and break through the internal pain that held me locked into place.

"No one is going to die," the other woman said angrily. "No one but him. Hurry up. You pierce his heart and I'll cut off his head. We'll leave and I'll wipe this room clean of memories. Aetas will never know. Tessalyn's the only one who's been able to break through my gift."

"Marko found his way around it," Dehlia whispered. "What if Aetas does, too, this time?"

"Enough."

The footsteps grew to what sounded like only a foot from me. Seconds went by while I tried to fight myself through the darkness. My death would come any moment now, but something … *someone* inside of me wasn't ready to leave. He was ready for a fight. Ready to murder these two women who threated his purpose. His life.

"On the count of three. We'll do it at the same time."

"Alright," Dehlia managed through the sob.

"One….. two…."

Light broke through and my lids flew open. Wide brown eyes were haloed by waves of red hair and the female gasped, dropping the dagger she held. Wet heat was already enveloping my hand and I glanced down to where my fist was through her chest. I gripped to her heart, flexing my fingers. I squeezed tighter and she cried out, but I didn't stop. I crushed the beating muscle, feeling it ooze between my fingers.

A swift blur had my other hand catching the wrist of a woman I didn't recognize. Her dark skin was in complete contrast to my paleness and fear rolled from her as I stepped from the wood that had been curled around me. Dehlia's body fell to my feet as I withdrew from her chest. I stepped closer, towering over the other female's thin frame, forcing her back with another step.

"Look into my eyes," she said in a trembling voice. "I'm going to make you better. I'm going to save you."

Words wouldn't come, but they didn't need to. I was already lunging forward, embedding my fangs into the side of her neck. Blood flooded my mouth at the brutality of my bite and I wrapped around her fighting form, pinning her to me. Cries and screams filled the room and out of nowhere a blast seemed to shake my insides. I knew it wasn't a weapon, but a call. A cry for help to anyone that would come. I wasn't sure how I knew, but I wasn't going to stick around and find out. I let the female fall to the ground, screaming as I raced for the door. Two men were already forcing their way through, but there was no stopping me. My claws tore them open as I burst past and practically flew down the long hallway.

"Hey! Get him!"

Double doors became visible as I slid into a huge room. There was a grand staircase and multiple places to run, but there was only one direction I needed to go, and that was out of this place. Warnings were shooting through me and everyone I saw was someone I knew I needed to kill. We might have been the same, but we weren't. *I was different.* I wasn't like them.

"Gina!"

Three men raced from the far end of the room with their fangs exposed. The one in the middle pointed to me, but looked up to the second story. As I glanced back, a blonde woman was jumping the rail, her focus on me entirely. The threat was obvious and somehow she made it to me before I could reach the middle of the room. Her impact sent me flying toward the door with her still wrapped around me.

"The Princess is going to thank me for killing you," she said, growling and biting into the front of my neck. Nails tore into my face and strength I didn't even know I possessed came barreling through as I pried her jaw open and threw her almost halfway across the room. The men were almost on me. I barely managed to stand and make it to the door before their weight knocked me through the barrier, right onto the porch. Cement tore into my exposed arms. Where I expected them to be on me at any moment, they didn't step through the threshold.

Smoke poured from my skin and I suddenly knew why. Although I couldn't see the sun, it wasn't entirely down yet. Instinct flared and I knew I couldn't be out during the day. Fire raced over my chest and I jumped to my feet, barely able to open my eyes as I scanned the nothingness around me. Fields for as far as the eye could see. Where the fuck was I? Where was I supposed to be?

The blonde vampire pushed her way through and a smile pulled at her lips, exposing her pointed fangs. We kept eye contact for only the briefest moment. She looked me up and down. I was only wearing a pair of jeans and it was the only part that wasn't burning excruciatingly.

"Do yourself a favor and start walking. Do us *all* a favor and kill yourself. You're not welcome in our world. No one will accept you. You're better off dead."

The door slammed and I blinked past the hatred they all had for me. Although it affected the monster within, something deeper inside didn't care. I didn't want to be amongst them, either. Hadn't I had the instinct to kill from the moment the voices had awoken me? *Yes.* They were going to pay for ever thinking they didn't need me.

To be continued….

REIGN

Marko Delacroix #5

BEST SELLING AUTHOR
ALASKA ANGELINI

REIGN

Marko Delacroix #5

Best Selling Author
Alaska Angelini
Copyright © 2016 by Alaska Angelini

ISBN:

All Rights Reserved

Dedication

To Dee and Nadine. You both supported Marko long before *Prey* ever came close to being published. The encouragement you gave when others thought it was a bad idea for me to take this route with my writing meant so much to me. Thank you for being there through the betas of each book, and for falling just as much in love with Marko as I did.

To my street team AKA Alaska's Sexy Subs. You ladies ROCK!! Thank you for all the promotions, for blasting each Marko cover on every post asking for them, and for voting and nominating. Your love for Marko means so much for me.

And a special thanks to Nicole Johnson. Your love for the Marko series never once escaped my notice. <3

Prologue
Axis Headquarters—Aetas

Stories were plentiful for our kind. The origins of how we came to be had been speculated on for as long as I could remember. It was once said that we were demons, reborn into this realm to corrupt the souls of weak mortals. To seduce the good and the noble. We'd change their path and take over not only the dark realms of existence, but spread our evil to walk amongst the living.

The debate was never-ending and not worth the time to think about. There was no evidence, nor would there ever be of our birth. Love, hate---kindness and cruelty. We, vampires, had it all. Our actions were our own and the way I chose to rule would never be altered by fear of a higher power. God, the devil, neither existed that I was aware of. To me, I was both, and I challenged a power so great to stand against me. I controlled the fate of not only our kind, but of the world. I let them live or die—no one else. Me. It was all because of me. I was the ultimate ruler, the perfect balance. I was not pure of heart, nor was I opposed to the torturing of souls.

"It is no secret why I gather you here tonight. One of our own is missing. A vampire of blood so powerful that his newborn status makes it imperative that he is returned to me as soon as possible. The threat he poses could change this world forever."

I stepped from my throne in the cathedral, scanning over the hundreds of eyes who stared up at me. Amongst the front, were what remained of my members. Behind them in rows on each side of the aisle, the rulers of our kind.

My hand rose, and with it, the door to the holding chamber opened. Footsteps of the enforcers pounded against the silent room in a steady cadence. Whimpering and cries immediately echoed along the walls as they pulled Margo and Gina into the opened space. They tugged at the heavy shackles that kept their hands restrained behind their backs. In sliding motions, their feet fought to gain footing against the marble floors.

Whispering began to buzz throughout the room as they were carried down the aisle.

"Please. Pl-ease." Margo's eyes searched the crowd as both of the men on her side drug her closer. "He's going to kill us all. You know I speak the truth. Please!" Her voice got louder as she neared. When her head jerked to a stop, her eyes flared. "Princess Tessalyn! Please, I beg of you!"

A large hand settled on the Black Princess's shoulder while she tightened her jaw repeatedly. She was here to bear witness to the sentencing of my former allies, as they all were. It still didn't stop Marko, her mate, from feeling Tessalyn's internal need to do something at the call for help.

"Our leader's intentions are not honorable," Margo said, louder. "Dehlia saw it before her death! She saw Aetas leading us into a war we cannot win! Do not bring the vampire they call Hunter back to Headquarters. Do not give Aetas the tool that will destroy us! Kill the newborn! Kill Hunter!"

I collected the energy around Margo with my mind, jerking her out of the enforcers' arms to slide the ten feet that remained between us. Before she could gasp through the shock of what I'd done, I spun her around to face the room.

"Betray me if you must," I warned everyone, loudly. "But know that if you do, your fate will rest in my hands. I assure you that's not a place you want to be." I tore her head free of her body in one hard tug, lifting it for all to see. The flat band representing her status still rested on her forehead and blood dripped to the floor as I held tightly to her hair. My eyes stopped first on Marko Delacroix, and then the Black Princess, Tessalyn Delacroix. Tessalyn stood along the aisle on second row and Marko held rank beside her.

"Status, bloodline, none of that will save you if you cross my path. The new Black Prince, Hunter Moretti, will be returned to me. Anyone who tries to stop that by attempting to harm him will feel my wrath."

I tossed Margo's head off to the side and Gina's cries were growing as she thrashed her shoulders back and forth in an attempt to break free. She was thrust in my direction at my nod and I spun her, wrapping one of my arms around her waist to make her face the crowd. I moved my lips in next to her ear while I went back to Princess Tesslyn's narrowed eyes. I couldn't deny my want of her. It ran just as deep as my desire to destroy her because of her love for Marko. They had something I never allowed myself and I couldn't stand that she was being wasted on him. The taste I'd experienced of their passion while Tessa was staying here still stuck with me. *It haunted me.* For the first time since I had put my plan in motion, I began to question the path I had picked.

As I kept the connection, anger sunk its hooks deeper. I wanted to push into her mind. To be able to whisper to Gina and have Tessalyn hear me as if I were speaking directly to her. It was impossible with her wearing my old crown. The protection I cloaked myself in against this very thing had carried over and now even I couldn't break through. Tessalyn would be protected against any gift thrown her way and I doubted she even knew it.

"Do you admit that when you closed my creation out into the sunlight that you were aware of who he was?"

Gina's shoulders sunk in and I awaited her pleas of forgiveness.

"Yes, Aetas."

"You knew I made him and that he was Hunter Moretti?"

She swallowed hard, her breathing picking up pace. "I did," she said, shakily.

"Are you also aware that he held the former Black Prince's blood within his veins?"

Gina grew still, only for a sob to cause her body to shake. She knew what I was implying.

"I did, Master."

"So you admit to betraying your own kind and trying to murder royalty?"

"He's an abomination," Gina exclaimed, loudly. "He's going to end up killing us all, just like *you* are with your choice. There's only one who is meant to lead! Princess!" The call for Tessalyn was the only plea that came from Gina. It drove my hands up to snap Gina's neck. I twisted, giving one last forceful jerk to put an end to her life. The warmth coating my hands had me snarling.

I dropped Gina's decapitated body and my glare met Tessalyn's head-on. She was angry, ready to fight just as much as I was. But the timing wasn't right, and my fight wasn't with her. *War* It was coming. Not only to the humans, but first, with ourselves.

Chapter 1
Marko

"Let's get the fuck out of here before I do something I shouldn't."

My claws were descending the more I watched Aetas focus on Tessa. His hate toward her was obvious and it only seemed to be growing. It left me on guard—in a protective mode so strong that it was almost impossible for me not to act on.

"Yes," Tessa breathed out. "I want to leave. I wish we wouldn't have had to come in the first place."

Her fingers wrapped along my lower bicep and she stepped into the aisle, giving me room to move around her. People were already departing. They appeared just as impatient as we were to escape the presence of our leader. But they didn't have reason to fear him in the moment. Tessa and I on the hand, did.

I moved around her, leading us toward the exit at a brisk walk. Stares were being cast our way. They pushed against me heavily from all sides and I ignored the need to see who was looking.

"Princess Tessalyn Delacroix!"

Aetas' booming voice had my jaw and fists clenching. I came to a stop, regardless that I didn't want to. Slowly, we turned around. Tessa's grip on my arm was so tight that it had my pulse slamming into my chest. Rarely did she get anxious anymore. Feeling the nervousness from her now pulled out the mate in me, causing him to crash into me wildly while he begged to be set free.

"Marie warned me about this. He'll want to seek council."

My eyes cut over to her, regardless that we were communicating mentally. *"You didn't tell me that. He's been denying you for weeks."*

Aetas stood at the beginning of the aisle, closer than his previous place by the throne. He still appeared angry, yet there was an underlining of anxiousness. Almost as if he couldn't keep in one place. He didn't want her to leave. That was clear.

"Why now?"

"I'm not sure exactly." Tessa tugged on my arm and I began to lead her back to him. The closer we got, the deeper Aetas' breathing became. Warmth swirled in core, my powers surging as we neared.

I brought us to a stop a few feet away and we both bowed our heads as custom.

"I want my crown back." The bitterness that fell from his lips accompanied with the volume had the vampires closest to us pausing to look over. Tessa's head slowly rose and her arm dropped from me as she stood taller.

"I'm sorry, Your Highness, but I'm afraid that's impossible. The crown has already chosen me. I can't simply return it."

"Of course you can. Take it off and hand it over."

Tessa's head cocked to the side the slightest amount. A laugh sounded in my mind regardless that her face was devoid of any expression.

"He can't read my thoughts and he can't stand it."

Was that what it was? If I didn't know better, I would have just assumed he was picking a fight.

"Master," Tessa began, calmly. "We both know I can't do that. Besides, it goes against your own law. Are you saying you're doing away with it now?"

Aetas let out a growl. "Of course not."

Casually, Tessa's hands went behind her back while she looked up through her lashes. "I'll tell you what. I'll give it back on one condition."

"What's that?" A flicker of unease came across Aetas' young features.

"Trade me. Your crown for mine. It's the only one I want besides my own."

Rage registered. "Absurd! This is *my* crown. Besides, you're not worthy enough to wear it."

Silence played out as I looked between the two of them.

"If you say so, Your Highness. Then you see why I can't give it back. Is that all? I really need to be returning to my city."

"That is not all," he ground out. "You requested council. I'm ready to meet with you now."

"Are you? But I received your response just last night. If I remember correctly, I believe it said, and I quote…*there's nothing you have to say worth listening to.* Truth be told, I really guess there's not. What is done, is done. I was trying to prevent this exact thing, but it's impossible now. Hunter is changed and he's on the loose. Our fate is yet to be seen. In the meantime, I wish to focus on my city. The attacks continue to increase and it requires all of my attention right now."

Aetas glanced at me, but went back to staring at her.

"More so than increasing your skills?"

I stiffened at his words. Tessa appeared calm, but I could feel her pulse hammering away in her chest. With the blood we shared, there was little I missed when it came to her moods or her body's natural reactions.

"Are you offering to start teaching me again—to prepare me to rule in your passing?"

"I'm not *dying*," Aetas snapped. "I may live for thousands of more years. Longer than you." He sighed. "But I have considered teaching you again. You're powerful, that's not in question, but you're too young to be ruling a city. You haven't lived as a vampire long enough to know what is best to make decisions for a community. You need more experience. Let…Master Delacroix take over for you for now. You can have your old room back. You can start your lessons again."

Tessa's energy spiked and I wasn't sure what to think about it. Did the lessons appeal? I knew for most vampires, they'd jump at the opportunity to grow stronger, and she would, working with Aetas. It made me feel sick. I couldn't lose her again. To be separate after we'd bonded and gotten so much closer…the thought was inconceivable.

"What about Hunter? What happens with him?"

There was hesitation as he stared at her.

"I find him—he comes back. He can join you in discovering your gifts."

Tessa's lips pressed together. "I'm honored by your offer, but I must decline at this time. I wish to stay with my husband and run my city. I believe I am more than capable, and our laws state that power rules over years of existence. And you're right. You could be our leader for thousands of more years. We have plenty of time for lessons. If you'll excuse us."

Tessa bowed and I suppressed my smile as I mirrored the gesture. Aetas didn't speak as we turned and headed for the door. Again, eyes were on us as we made our way down the aisle. By the time we were sliding into the limo, I could barely contain my need to kiss her. The door shut and I pulled her into my arms.

"I can't believe you just did that. You know you pissed him off, yes?"

A laugh drifted between us as I was already moving in to press my lips against hers. At the sweep of our tongues, she moaned, wrapping her arms around my neck.

"I may have angered him, but he went too far. First, trying to take my crown. Then, trying to get me to take lessons with Hunter. As if I could do either of those. I'd kill Hunter, or at least try to. He knows that."

I couldn't resist kissing her again. "He does. But he can't help but give you a hard time. He's Aetas. He thinks he can control every aspect of our lives."

The limo started moving. My hand settled across the back of Tessa's neck while I drew her in to deepen our kiss. Strands were escaping from the intricately mass of woven curls pinned at the back of her head. The tickling mingled with the butterflies that still fluttered in my stomach from her nearness.

"I want to taste you," I whispered, going back to duel with her tongue. "I don't want to wait until tonight."

"Don't let me stop you."

The voice had both me and Tessa's heads turning to look further down the seat. Aetas sat there with a devious smile on his face. The threatening sound that left me was unstoppable.

"Were we not finished talking?" Tessa eased from my lap, but sat against the side of my leg, staying close.

"You walk a very thin line with me, Princess." Anger once again seeped into his tone. "I offered you a gift and you denied my teachings, dismissing yourself from my presence. Do you not give regard to who I am? What you did is not done amongst vampires of *any* rank," he roared.

Tessa's head lowered, but her eyes didn't leave him. "You do not need anything from me, Aetas. You've made that quite clear over the last few weeks. Your mind is set on Hunter—a human who killed me because of his hate for our kind. You turned him, despite the fact that he should have paid for his crimes. Instead of dying like our laws state, you gave him what should have been granted to me," she said, getting louder. "Now you come back after I've settled in my city and you want me to leave my people and my husband to battle it out with Hunter, if and when, you find him? I don't think so."

"Marko is your mate, not your husband. You are not human anymore."

Tessa's back stiffened and I could feel her need to explode in argument. Her temper was rising, igniting my own.

"Mate, husband, whatever you wish to call it, *he is mine*, regardless. I find it astonishing that out of everything I just said to you, *that* is what you respond with."

Aetas' hand flicked through the air. "The rest is something I already know. It doesn't deserve a response. It's done. Hunter will benefit us. He's a leader."

"He's a murderer! He hates us and kills us off, and he will do it again. You think he will lead us, but he will not. He will pick us off one by one until we are no more. Mark my words," Tessa said, leaning her upper body in his direction. "Hunter will not be one with us. His intentions will be that of when he was human. He poses a grave threat, Master. If you listen to anything I say at all, please hear me when I tell you, I *know* him. Hunter Moretti is a danger to all of us. He will come with everything he has. *Marie Bardot has seen it.*" She paused. "If you were smart, you'd be getting the other cities prepared for him and the humans he'll win over. War is on us, *Your Highness*. Our survival will depend on you. I'm willing to die for my people. The only question is—*Are you?*"

Chapter 2
Tessa

At Marko's hand tightening on my hip, I knew I was going too far with my rant against our leader. But I couldn't help it. For weeks I had waited to try to convince Aetas of Hunter. Of why he should choose me. It was all for nothing. He turned Hunter anyway, and now he was going to learn his mistake the hard way. Maybe at the price of each and every one of us.

"You question whether I will keep you all safe?"

I swallowed hard knowing if I admitted to his question, he could very well twist my words and call me a traitor. Marko picked up on my worries and his grip tightened again as a warning.

"I worry that you put too much trust into a man you hardly know. You speak of his blood and how strong he'll be. With the personality I know Hunter to have, it has me afraid for those who might not be able to overpower him if the need arises."

"Hmm." Aetas crossed his arms over his chest. "You're saying his passion will lead him one way. I say his love will lead him another. We could argue over this all night, but the decision is still mine."

"Yes … it is." I glanced back at Marko before I braved the next question. "Will you kill him if he shows signs of rising against us?"

Aetas smiled. "Do you think I'm such a poor leader? Of course I will."

Something was underlined in his tone and my brow furrowed as I tried to detect what it was. Was he lying, or telling the truth? I wasn't sure, but I couldn't help but go on.

"Will you let me kill him?"

"My brave princess." A laugh left Aetas and it appeared genuine. "And what would I do if Hunter ended up killing you? Your Marko would be heartbroken and blame me for even more than he already does."

Low sounds vibrated against me and I placed my hand on Marko's knee.

"If Hunter kills me, I don't deserve to rule. I want to be the one to end this. I deserve that."

"Perhaps you'll get your fight, Princess, but I'm not so sure. Hunter is lost. He's a newborn, confused on where he's supposed to be. Once I get him back, he'll be monitored and begin to feel safe. After he comes out of his newborn haze, I'll groom him and he'll begin his lessons. When he's ready, he will go to Dallas, where he'll take over Sayer's old position. You may see him as an enemy for a while, but time has a way of erasing the past. Ask your Marko. He knows what I speak is the truth."

"I'll never forget what he did to Tessa. Ever." Marko's deep tone left the hair on my arms standing on end.

"I was speaking of your feelings about the princess's third. It wasn't always good between you and Mistress Bardot."

"No, it was not. I wouldn't say it's good now, either. More, tolerable, if anything. Tessa has a connection with Marie and I'm not going to tell her she shouldn't. She knows what she's doing."

"You both will get over this anger you have for Hunter. You'll see."

My blood boiled at the thought of Hunter amongst our society. I'd have to associate with him. I'd have to forget the past and what he did. Or, at least try. In truth, he could be a completely different person. I knew how one could change when they were turned. If he was like me, if he wanted this life…what would that mean? We used to be best friends. As impossible as it seemed, could that somehow be salvable? I knew why he had tried to kill me and I still had enough humanity within me to understand it. But my vampire didn't want to. She wanted revenge.

"There's no point in arguing over this. Aetas, are we being honored with a visit from you, or are you planning to poof back to headquarters?"

Marko's anger grew at my question.

"I do think I'll be your guest for a while. You say you're ready to rule and I'm curious to see you in action. Perhaps you'll prove me wrong."

"Oh." I blinked rapidly through the shock. I hadn't expected him to take me up on the offer. "Well, of course. You're welcome to stay for as long as you'd like. I do have to warn you, we're going to be pretty full in the next week."

"Yes," Aetas smiled. "I know. Introductions with your fellow rulers. I look forward to watching you squirm in their presence."

"Tessa doesn't get intimidated," Marko snapped. "Besides, she has nothing to fear. I'll be by her side the entire time."

"I don't doubt that for a minute. Marko, tell me," Aetas asked, curiously. "How do you expect your mate to come into her own if you're always…hovering?"

"Marko doesn't hover. And he doesn't hold me back. We learn from each other. Even though I'm not at headquarters, it doesn't mean I'm not learning, Aetas."

A smile stretched across his face, but it wasn't the nice kind. It had manipulation written all over it. "I'd love to see these lessons between the two of you. Can you show me something right now?"

I glanced back at Marko, unsure. He held as much apprehension as I did.

"Oh, come on. I want to see. After all, you say you want to rule and Marko is by your side. What do the two of you bring to the table as a couple? What makes you more deserving than Hunter?"

He was antagonizing me and I knew it, but I couldn't resist.

"Hunter will have my gift. That's a given. But where he'll have mine, he'll also have your persuasion. It's handy in getting what he wants, but with my blood mixed with Marko's, I bring a lot more in the form of physical power."

"Show me." There was challenge in Aetas' demand and I was confident enough to prove myself to him.

"We haven't mastered it yet on our own, but together…" I looked back at Marko and he nodded. My palms lifted, cupping as I placed my wrists together to make an arch. Black fog began to surface from my palms, growing until it circled and spun around in the shape of a basketball. Marko's hand settled on my shoulder and he leaned in until his face was next to mine. When his other hand rose and his finger touched the smoke, orange and blue glowing fire swirled around the contents, heating my palms.

"Fascinating." Aetas eyes were wide as he stared into the glowing orb. Slowly, his gaze came to mine and I quickly dropped my hand, making it disappear.

"Just stuff like that," I said, quickly. "We're still perfecting it."

Aetas' stare went from me to Marko. Something indiscernible was within his depths and I longed to know what it was.

"You'll show me more during my visit. Have you developed your own skills or just the combination of both of your powers?"

I wanted to smile. I'd come so far since the last he'd seen me in action.

Again, my hand rose. The black fog oozed from the tips of my fingers and he gasped as my skin began to fade into nothingness. My hand was disappearing and it was all too easy.

"You've become one with your gift ... already?"

Heat surged through me and I closed my eyes letting my energy spread throughout the interior of the back of the limo. I knew my form was gone from sight. As I opened myself up to see, all the remained of me was a black haze of smoke. I was nowhere, and yet, everywhere. The hum in the atmosphere tingled over me and I let my power surge. Wine glasses from the bar rattled in the distance and I felt glass from the liquor burst at my power. I quickly drew it in, pulling myself together to sit back on the seat next to Marko. The amazement Aetas held made me proud, but it didn't last as I became uncomfortable at just how mesmerized he was.

"You've succeeded my expectations for such a young age. I thought perhaps this level was possible, but never so soon."

"I want to rule. I was meant for this."

He brought his hand to his mouth as he grew quiet. Minutes stretched out as I waited for him to say something. *Anything.* I could tell he was thinking. That was obvious as he grew dazed.

"Two ties with Marie Bardot, correct?"

I shook my head in my confusion. "No. We have one tie. Why? What does Marie have to do with this?"

"I don't want you taking in anymore of her blood. Hers will dilute yours. Feed her to get her stronger, if that's your plan, but do not contaminate yourself anymore. I want to see something. I…" Aetas blinked back his concentration and glanced over. "We will discuss this at another time. We're arriving."

Lights from the surrounding mansions had me nodding. I hadn't realized we were already home. The car pulled into the large circular driveway and the moment the door opened, the servant fell to his knees at Aetas' presence. It didn't stop our leader from getting out. He pretended he didn't see the human as he stood outside and waited for us to join him.

"Welcome home, Princess, Master … Your Highness."

Silence followed all of us as Marko led me in through the mansion first and walked us into the stairwell that descended to the underground city. Music drifted through the darkness and grew louder as we approached the light that came from the bottom of the stairs. When the royal horn blasted, signaling my arrival, the activity below died down. I stepped into the large open room, watching the mass of vampires and slaves fall to the ground at Aetas' figure stepping in behind us. I didn't doubt most had never seen him before, but they wouldn't have had to know who he was. The crown and his powerful energy said everything.

"Thank you for the warm welcome. You may rise."

His voice was like silk, caressing and enticing the minds of the residents. Women gazed over enamored, while even most of the men took notice to his good looks. It was shocking how their eyes followed us adoringly through the large room. They worshipped him immediately. It showed me just how deep his gift ran on those of lower status.

"Are you hungry, Master? I'm afraid the city has already fed, but I can provide you a supplier if you'd like."

Marko kept us moving to our tunnel. The guest member's room was a few doors down from ours and I had no doubt he wanted to get rid of Aetas as soon as possible.

"I don't drink from suppliers."

I turned to look at him just as the pitch black from the entrance swallowed us whole.

"Who do you feed from, then, if not suppliers?"

We came to a stop and Marko swung the bedroom door open, flipping on the light. Aetas' eyes raked over my body and I couldn't stop myself from stepping back, right into Marko.

"That's right, Princess. I only feed from the best. Since no one of my circle is here, that would be you."

"I fucking knew he was up to something."

Marko's angry words rushed through my head and the ruler in me battled the bonded. Technically, strongest or not, I didn't have to let him feed. I was someone's concubine. That took me out of the equation. But I led this city. And I did so because Aetas hadn't forced me out. I owed him, in a sense, and I couldn't ignore that.

"You may feed from my wrist. Marko stays."

"I don't do the wrist. Neck, and he stays."

"Inside of the elbow," Marko said between clenched teeth. "That's it." His fangs were already down and there was a wildness in his eyes I knew all too well. Aetas was pushing him and he was probably doing it intentionally.

"Fine. *For now.*"

He walked past us, unbuttoning the top of his black shirt. When he sat down on the edge of the bed, I had to force myself forward. Marko didn't leave the door. He held to the wooden barrier like a lifeline. As if it would keep him chained into place through the protectiveness and rage he was feeling.

I looked down at the black lace sleeve knowing I couldn't pull it up. I sat next to him, gripping the thin material and ripping it free just above the bend of my elbow. I kept my eyes on Marko as I lifted. Aetas' firm grip latched onto my forearm and I tried to control my quick breaths as he brought it up. The slice of his fangs breaking through my skin had my lids lowering the smallest amount. Deep draws on my veins had his hold tightening. A minute passed, and then two. When he broke away, a moan followed.

"Definitely stronger since the last time." He let go and I stood, meeting Marko's stare for only a moment before my attention went back to him.

"I'm glad to hear it. We will be retiring now. Marie will be of assistance to you if you need anything. I'll see you tomorrow."

My steps were quick as I headed for the door.

"Princess Tessalyn."

I looked over my shoulder. "Yes, Your Highness?"

"I suspect Hunter will come here. It's the real reason behind my visit. This is the closest city and he'll be pulled to the power of this place. He'll come."

"Can you not call him or figure out his location?"

Aetas' face turned hard. "No. It's my blood. Just like the crown you wear, it blocks me completely. I can't search him out. I don't even know if he lives. I feel…nothing concerning him. If I wouldn't have picked up on this before he was cast out, I would have assumed he was dead. Maybe he is."

"Is that not a reason to fear him even more? He can't be monitored. He can plot our deaths and you'd never know it."

"So could you." Aetas quirked his eyebrow. "The difference between you and Hunter is you're mated. You're twice the threat. *Especially* since it's Marko you're bonded to. After what I saw tonight, you're lucky I'm not dragging you off to headquarters as we speak."

"But…*You asked to see*. I trusted you enough to show you. Why would I do that if I were a threat?"

"We're not the real threat," Marko said, reaching for my hand. "And he knows it. He's just trying to get the distraction off of Hunter because he knows how unstable he's going to be when he surfaces. Deep down, Aetas knows what he's done by turning the bastard. The question is—why he went through with it begin with?"

Chapter 3
Hunter

Blood dripped from my chin as I let the female's dead body fall to the ground. *Four humans tonight.* The thirst was unquenchable. There was nothing I could do to ease the burning in my throat. The more I fed, the worse it seemed to get, but I couldn't stop it. Nor could I slow the adrenaline that left me shaking and anxious. I had no idea where I was. My mind said I was close to where I needed to be, but nothing looked familiar. I was walking in circles, confused on what to do next.

Screams had me blinking past the fog and I turned, taking in the long line of people staring at me in horror. What were they doing, being so loud? It caused the monster in me to explode. I snarled, lunging for another female to shut her up. My head was hurting and she was making it worse. She was …

I shoved my fingers in her mouth, grasping her jaw and jerking with everything I had. Blood perfumed the air, spraying out and easing the hammering within, but more people were yelling and pointing at me.

BAM! BAM! BAM!

Pain cut into my skin and I looked down at the trickle of blood beginning to ooze from my chest. When my eyes cut up, a man in a black uniform grabbed the device on his shoulder, yelling into it. I took off at a fast run right for him. More stinging sliced through my back and legs.

These things…these humans, they were trying to hurt me. *Me!* I didn't understand why. They were food, yet they were coming after me knowing that I could kill them?

"Hunter Moretti. You! Hey!"

My claws raked down the uniformed man's face only seconds before my fangs shredded down the front of his throat. The yelling was getting louder.

"Hunter! Hey!"

I snapped my head to the side, ready to keep fighting when I noticed something about the male was different. He wasn't human. He was like me. I wanted to take ease in that, but something wouldn't let me and in the moment, I couldn't remember why.

""Hunter! That's right buddy. It's me. It's Boyd. You recognize me?"

I hissed as he stepped closer.

"It's okay, put the cop down and let's get out of here before the shit hits the fan. I know someone who's looking for you."

The dead human hit the ground as I released my fingers from his dark shirt. More popping sounded and the pain followed. Loud sounds were getting closer. I couldn't take it.

"Hunter! Let's go!"

Boyd. Did I know this man like me? Something told me I did, but I couldn't get a read on whether that was a good or a bad thing.

Slowly, I walked forward while he waved his hand.

"That's it. Come on, we have to get you underground. Everyone will be happy to see you."

Everyone? Where people looking for me?

My pace picked up as his did. We were suddenly running and the high-pitched noises were growing closer. I easily caught up, studying the smile on his face as we turned onto the next block. Church bells chimed while we approached and I felt myself move away from the holy ground. Did I know that place? Yes, there was a distinct feeling associated with the area, but my mind told me it was bad. I needed to keep going. There was a pull ahead, coaxing me home.

"I can't believe I found you. Marko is going to be so fucking happy."

"Marko?" I repeated the name, coming to an abrupt stop. My mind raced, testing the sound and emotions surrounding with the name. I didn't like it. Not at all.

"Tessa," Boyd said, gesturing his head for me to keep following.

"Tessa?" Tessa…Tessa…now she I might have liked. Or not. Fuck, I didn't know.

Blue and red lights brightened the darkness behind us. Combined with the squealing of tires, I couldn't help but be side-tracked. My instincts told me to stop whatever was happening, but the array of high-pitched tones were too grating to my ears. It made me want to gag through the pounding that surfaced.

"Shit! Let's go!"

Boyd's hand locked on my wrist and there were no thoughts as I launched myself right for him. To my surprise, he quickly dodge me, jumping out of the way.

"I'd love to fight you, Hunter, but now's not the time." His hand waved me forward while he took fast steps backwards. I felt myself being lured in his direction. When Boyd began to jog, he turned to the side, keeping the pace steady. Faster, he went. And like a robot, I followed.

"Stop! Put your hands in the air and get on the ground."

At the booming voice, I glanced over my shoulder. Boyd's tap on my shoulder had me lunging for him again, but he kept out of reach, running even faster.

"That's it. Ignore the cops, they're not allowed to come where we're going."

Where *were* we going?

The scenery became new again and everything went blank as I felt myself slow and look around.

"Hunter, no, no, over here. If you look around, things will be become even more confusing. You need to listen to me. You're a vampire now. Your mind is trying to cope with the new blood. It's shutting down, right? It's hard to remember anything?"

Still we were moving forward. My lips opened and an answer was on the tip of my tongue when a house had me stopping again. A hard slam against my chest told me I had finally made it. This was where I was supposed to be.

"Fuck," Boyd breathed out. "No, we're not going there. You don't live there anymore."

I was already turning, heading toward the door. Each step sent my pulse skittering even faster.

"Dammit. Hunter, I said you don't live there anymore."

He blurred in front of me with his speed, pushing his hands against my chest in quick movements meant to distract me. But I wasn't going to fall for that again. I stayed focused, determined as I swung my arm at him and headed up the steps. As I reached for the door and turned the knob, I felt it—an invisible barrier. It brushed over my fingertips, triggering my brain.

"See, this isn't your home. The house has new tenants. Come on, we have to go."

A jerk pulled at my arm and I roared through the rage that was building.

"Get on the ground!"

I turned to see multiple men in black uniforms surrounding the yard. A smile came to Boyd's face as he stepped closer to me.

"Well this is going to be fun. You feeling hungry?"

Hungry? Yes, my throat. The fire was still there. Still growing. I was so weak. That's what kept registering. I needed something more.

Boyd's fangs lowered and I stared at them mesmerized for a moment. I knew he'd been like me, but to see him have what I did…it brought out the need to kill even more.

Slowly, I step forward. Boyd let me take the lead, but kept his steps even with mine. Pain from the explosions stung my arm and my vision wavered through the anger. I was suddenly running. Suddenly being showered with needle-type sensations. I could see Boyd in my peripheral. We attacked at the same time, diving for the closest humans.

Blood flooded my mouth as I bit into side of the man's neck, but I didn't waste my time feeding. I clamped my jaw down, ripping his flesh while I fought to end his life.

BAM! BAM!

The shots were still coming. They hit me all over, even as I felt myself heal almost instantly. I moved from one to next, staying in tune with Boyd as he did the same thing. He was laughing—loving what we were doing. His pale skin was beginning to be covered in crimson. It was smeared on his cheeks and chin and the more he killed, the more he rubbed his face over the wounds. I repeated the action, feeling the evil within me flare at the enhanced sense of smell. It engulfed me, feeding the need. For the first time, I felt as one with who I was.

"Let's get the hell out of here!" Boyd dropped the last dead officer, letting out an exhilarated yell as he waved me to follow. There was no hesitation this time. I ran behind him, leaving the place I was so sure was my home for another that was suddenly calling me forward.

We got to the end of the road and slowed as he approached a grate. An odd tug pulled at my stomach, reaching so deep inside of me that I barely heard the words Boyd was exchanging with the vampire inside. It was heated for only a moment before Boyd tapped me.

"Holy shit. Let's go, buddy. I hear your maker has arrived. This is turning out better than I could have dreamed."

My maker?

Darkness surrounded me as I lowered within, and the tug at my core got harder, luring me deeper into the tunnels. What secrets were lurking ahead? What was the feeling … that *power* tempting me forward? I wasn't sure, but I suddenly needed it.

Heat singed my lungs with every inhale and the wetness on my face was beginning to get sticky as it dried. With the tightness that accompanied the sensation, I opened my mouth repeatedly. Movement to my side had me stiffening and almost attacking. The vampire at the door froze, hissing as I continued on. The fear I had detected had my eyes narrowing for the briefest moment, but I wasn't able to give it much thought as light from ahead caught my attention.

I knew this place, even if I couldn't remember it. The constant déjà vu left my mind spinning and defensive walls rising. Something was off…something I couldn't quite figure out. If it wasn't for the tempting aura, I would have run. But I suddenly had to have it—no matter the cost.

Chapter 4
Marko

Deep gasps drew me out of a deep sleep. My pulse was racing and it was hard to breathe. My eyes flew open and I immediately reached out to Tessa's sitting frame. Dark hair haloed around her in a mass of loose curls. From the glow of the closet light, she was paler than usual. It drove me up to her side while I reached for her.

"What's wrong, love? What is it?"

The covers flew back as she sprung from the bed, grabbing her robe. "He's here. Hunter is in the city."

"What?!" The deep vibrations of my growl filled the room. I was right behind her, racing to the closet to grab my pants. Rage was all I knew. I wanted to kill him. No, I was *going* to kill him. The urge was undeniable. Vampire or not, he had shown me pain I'd never recover from. I'd almost lost Tessa because of him and I couldn't forgive him for that.

"You have to get Aetas and let him know." She raced for the door, a mass of black silk flying behind at her speed.

"Don't you dare—"

She was already gone, leaving me trying to button my pants as I burst through the door after her.

"Tessa!"

"Get Aetas," she yelled, from the darkness. "We don't know what we're dealing with."

Fire burned into my stomach as I slowed enough to pound into his door. When I threw it open, I noticed the light was on and he was awake, reaching for his shirt.

"Tessa says Hunter is here. She went to collect him." I didn't tell him to hurry as I left the door open and started running again. I didn't even want him to know. What I wanted was to get to the bastard who could very well end up trying to kill Tessa all over again.

The lights from the heart of the city shone before me and I broke into the large room just in time to see Tessa coming to a stop in front of Boyd and Hunter. Blood covered his face and he had his head slightly cocked to the side, staring at her captivated. When I saw a smile pull at the side of his mouth, I didn't slow. I ran faster, hissing as my fangs shot down. His hand rose toward her cheek and my vision flashed red. *MINE!* The word repeated obsessively in my head. He paused, mid-way, jerking his attention to me, baring his own fangs as he shoved her out of the way and broke into a sprint, right for me.

"Marko, no!"

Tessa voice was but an echo, deep within the reaches of my mind. I was too far gone. Too impatient to spill his blood after everything he'd done to us.

My claws grew and I pushed from the balls of my feet diving for him, just as he did for me. The force from the invisible wall knocked the air from my lungs. I fell to the ground coughing as Tessa collapsed to her knees in pain. Her hand was still raised, but I could tell my power against her shield had taken its toll. Seeing what I'd done left my heart sinking.

"I said enough!" She was wheezing as she struggled to her feet. "No more, Marko! Our battle is not with him. Not yet." She eyed him wearily as she came up to stand between us. Hunter still tore into the wall. Still tried to get to me.

"Very well done, Princess. I'm surprised by your resolve."

Aetas' voice had me turning to glare in his direction. The tone had deepened along the ending and I knew why. He was looking at me skeptically and he had every right to.

"I rule this city and I take my alliance with you very seriously," she said, coldly. "What did you expect, for me to attack him as well?"

Aetas shrugged, but kept his attention on Hunter. "I wasn't sure, but your loyalty will not be forgotten. As for Master Delacroix's…" His eyes flickered back to me. "I guess I'm not surprised. He always has done his own thing. That's the problem with your mate, Princess. He is what keeps you from taking my place. This is a good example as any for you to understand my questioning of your ability. You may do what is right, but Marko doesn't. He cares for nothing but his own greed. This will harm you in the end. It could be the difference between being a great leader, or having your people turn against you. I don't want to put you in that position. I'd be grooming you for your own murder if I did."

When Tessa glanced at me but kept silent, the anger only intensified. But not at Aetas or her—at myself. The truth was like a knife in the heart, and the pain was all for her.

"Let's get Hunter into a room. People are staring. They've seen enough."

There was defeat in Tessa's tone and I knew she understood Aetas' point of view. She wasn't arguing. Wasn't fighting to try to prove him wrong anymore. Her energy was so withdrawn from me that I couldn't read it.

"Hunter." Tessa voice was calm but disassociated as she stepped closer to him. His eyes pulled from me and he gave her his attention. "I'm going to drop the wall between us. Do you think you can walk with me calmly to your new room?"

"Wait, before you do, let me in." Aetas stepped closer. "He needs my blood. It will calm him and make him able to communicate. Afterward, he can stay in my room. There's no need to separate the two of us. He can't hurt me."

"As you wish," she said, slightly bowing her head. Her hand waved and Aetas stepped in close to Hunter. The newborn's eyes studied his every move. The moment Aetas slit into his wrist, Hunter didn't hesitate. He grabbed our leader's arm and fed from it like a starving man. Minutes went by before he stopped and Aetas nodded to Tessa.

"Hunter, would you follow me?"

His eyes shot to me and he growled, reaching over and lacing his fingers through hers. Tessa's eyes widened and she grew rigid.

Now is not the time to fight, Marko. Calm. He doesn't know who I am. He doesn't know what he's done.

Pants left my mouth while I tried to control the blood-red rage that kept tinting my vision. *Let's get him the fuck in that room. I can't see him anymore. I can't see* ***this***.

Tessa began walking, leading him forward as Aetas smiled and followed. Me, I couldn't do shit but stand there, seething. There was no debating what I could so clearly see. Tessa was a better leader than I was. I'd known it for a while, but her actions in the heat of the moment proved it. I knew the amount of anger she harbored for Hunter and yet, she was able to overlook it and go as far as to let him hold her hand so he would be comforted enough to obey. If it had been up to me, Hunter would have been dead. And I would have followed in his footsteps because Aetas would have killed me, making the woman I love a widow. The reality doused the immediate need of revenge. Tessa deserved better from me. I had probably embarrassed her due to my actions.

No, I had. The whole city had witnessed my outburst—my slip of control.

"You did well," I said, addressing Boyd. "We'll speak tomorrow. You deserve compensation for bringing Hunter to us."

"Thank you, Master."

He nodded, rushing away. I turned back to the tunnels, witnessing Aetas disappear into the darkness. I slowly walked in their direction, keeping my distance. My mind raced while I recalled Hunter's appearance. His once tanned skin was gone, replaced by a paleness that marked what we were. The color of his eyes were nearly nonexistent. They had faded in with the white, barely standing out with their light blueish-gray shade. It had looked eerie, even as I ran toward him. I'd never once been afraid of Hunter, but I couldn't deny there was a tinge of something that irked me the wrong way. It left me cautious, when before I wouldn't have been.

I slowed as I approached the door, listening to the words that were being spoken inside.

"Thank you, again, Princess. I can't tell you how surprised I am with your behavior. I'm impressed. You have to know that."

There was a pause before Tessa began. "Thank you, Your Highness. It means a lot to hear that coming from you. If you'll excuse me now, I'll give the two of you privacy. Should I make arrangements for your departure back to headquarters, tomorrow? Or…" Footsteps. "Will you be disappearing back?"

Aetas laughed. "I can take it from here. You've done enough. Hunter and I will be leaving soon. Probably before the sun rises."

"Wait." Hunter's voice was deep as it broke the silence.

"Hunter, you have to let go of me. Aetas…."

The stirring of anger and impatience from Tessa had me cracking the door to look in. What I saw nearly broke every ounce of control I held. Hunter stood behind her, his arms wrapped over her breasts as he held her arms locked down. He appeared panicked as his eyes stayed fixed on Aetas.

"Hunter…let go of Princess Tessalyn. I've already told you. You have nothing to fear with me. I am your maker. I promise to take care of you."

His head shook, stiffly.

Aetas sighed. "I can feel your dilemma, Hunter, but you can't stay. You have lessons to learn. This is not your home."

"Then she goes."

Tessa tried shrugging out of his hold, but his grip only tightened. She glared at Aetas before turning to look up at Hunter.

"I cannot go, and you *cannot* stay. I have a city to run. I rule here, Hunter. You must go with Aetas to prepare to run your own."

"I'm staying."

"You know not what you say." Tessa jerked against his hold. "You're newborn. You don't know the significance of the path you've been given. You have to go."

Tessa was spun around while he gripped to her forearms. His eyes studied her while he gazed down into her face.

"We stay together. We have to stay together. My mind is telling me that."

Dark hair swung loosely as Tessa shook her head. "Absolutely not! Do you know what you've—?"

"Don't," Aetas warned. "Not yet."

Tessa turned her head to look back at him. "Then get him off of me. I can only be so patient."

"Hunter," Aetas said, angrier. "Princess Tessalyn is mated to Master Delacroix. She does not belong to you. You cannot stay together, nor can you treat her as you are. You have to let her go."

"No! Stop telling me what to do. I don't understand this, but I know what I feel."

He angled them to the side and the wood splintered under my grasp. Aetas glanced over at me for the first time and sighed.

"There's love between the two of us," Hunter whispered, still staring at her. "I don't know how I know you, but you love me. I know you do. Help me. I don't know what's happening."

"Loved," Tessa snapped. "And it was a long time ago. Before this life." She lifted her hands in between his hold, settling them on his cheeks. Her face softened and it had my pulse going even faster. "Listen to me. You're scared, but you have to trust me. I need you to go with Aetas. Come tomorrow, you won't remember this, or even me. And that's for the best. This conversation won't come back to you for months, but when it does, I want you to remember how you are right now. *How you feel.* We don't have to be enemies, and this life doesn't have to be bad for you."

Hunter's brow drew in. "We're not enemies. I could never hate you. I love you. I do."

Tears slid down Tessa's cheeks and her fingers gripped to his face harder as she drew his lips to hers. I couldn't breathe. Couldn't even contain the need to kill everything in my path. The room rocked and I could barely process the moment when Hunter's big body hit the ground.

Tessa sobbed, spinning to Aetas with a fury that matched my own. Her body was trembling as she pointed her shaky finger toward our leader. "Is that how you plan to control him? By mere words? *You have no idea what you have done!* Get him out of my city. Get him out right now before it's too late."

Chapter 5
Tessa

"Tessa, please. You have to stop blocking your mind and either let me in or talk with me."

I glanced at Marko from the mirror of my vanity. He was sitting on the edge of the bed, resting his palms just above his knees. His head was slightly bowed and I knew he wanted to talk, I just wasn't sure what to say.

Seeing Hunter again—as a vampire, no less. My duty was all I had known in the moment. It kept me from killing my enemy. It kept me from acting rash. *It saved him.* But did it save me? With my panic of intercepting him in the heart of the city, I hadn't been protected. My crown was exactly where it was now, beside the bed. I felt Hunter's power, his persuasion, he received from Aetas.

He was a newborn, but already it was there, confusing the thoughts in my head with what I knew were lies. *"We're not enemies. I could never hate you. I love you. I do."* As he'd spoken the words, I could almost believe myself still in love with him. My heart fluttered and my skin heated. But it wasn't me, it was him. He was trying to force the emotions into me, even though I doubted he knew what he was doing. His gift was bad news if he chose to use it wrong—use it against me.

"I said I'm sorry a dozen times."

I blinked past the thoughts, turning on the bench seat to look into Marko's face. "You couldn't help yourself. I don't blame you."

"*But you do*," he stressed. "I saw it in your eyes, ma minette. It hurt you to hear Aetas say you would never lead because of me. And you believed him."

I glanced down at his hands, leaning forward to take his into my own.

"Only time will tell who is meant to lead. Perhaps it is Hunter. It's likely he will be stronger. After all, he has Aetas' blood. And he didn't appear violent. Not more so than any newborn. He's actually extremely well composed for being so young. Better than I was, that's for sure."

"Did you not hear the carnage he left behind in Austin? We're talking mass deaths of police officers. Not to mention the citizens he killed before that. Were you even listening to Marie when she came to the room to report the news?"

God, I hadn't. Not really. My mind was so jumbled.

"Marko." My lips opened to speak when I stopped and stood, reaching for my crown to put on. I couldn't risk Aetas spying on me or pushing into my head. With the crown on, he wouldn't be able to do that.

I returned to the bench, grabbing back for his hands.

"I have to be honest with you. Hunter scares me. His powers … I felt them. They affected me."

Seriousness drew his features tight and he squeezed my hands. "Did they? *Show me.*"

I nodded, looking up to meet Marko's eyes. Colors swirled and I drew him into my memories, back to the moment Hunter looked deep into my gaze. His words, they tugged at something within and I could feel what almost appeared to be my soul, sucked in his direction. The tingling, the needs…

My head jerked to the side, breaking our connection. I couldn't look at Marko as guilt swarmed me.

"Oh, love." His finger's slid against my cheek, bringing me back to him. "We both know what you experienced was him, not you. Don't blame yourself. You were an open door in those moments and now we know you'll just have to be more careful in the future."

A tear escaped and I quickly wiped it away.

"I'm so confused. I still feel his pull. I hate him. But…"

"But nothing. The two of you never had time to adjust to either role, vampire or slave. There's no going back now. He is one of us. You and I are going to have to accept that. Tonight, I made a terrible mistake. One that opened my eyes. I'm so worried about losing you that I realized the only way that's going to happen is if I carry on recklessly. I'm my own worst enemy, I've known it for years, but only after seeing Aetas hurt you with his words, did I really see the truth. I really am sorry for my actions. They were deplorable for my status as not only a member, but as the mate to the ruler of the city—to you. It won't happen again."

I brought Marko's hand to my lips, kissing over his knuckles. "Had the roles been reversed, it would have been me attacking him. This position I carry, it changes us. It's like a living thing all on its own, altering our decisions in the moment. I don't know how I withheld. Even now, I don't know how I'm sitting here when Hunter is right down the hall."

"Is he still here? I figured Aetas would be gone by now."

I tuned into the energy of the city, feeling Aetas' power above everything. Hunter's wasn't very strong at all, but more so than most of the commoners.

"They're still here and I believe they'll be for a while longer. I made a mistake by getting so emotional and ordering Aetas to leave. He'll stay at least another day to prove to me that he makes the rules. I fear, longer. Margo was right when she took me into her confidence. Aetas grows bored and his sadistic tendencies know no bounds. I'm afraid of what will happen if he chooses to play some sort of sick game between the three of us."

"A game?"

"Like before, when he pretended to be you. He's in need of something and I have no idea what it is or if he can even get what he seeks. Maybe Hunter will be distraction enough. But what if he's not?"

Marko leaned forward, pulling me into his lap, only to spin us around to lie on the bed. He took my crown, leaning over me to put it back on the table. "You look too far into the future. Maybe we'll wake up and they'll be gone."

A knock at our door had my eyebrow rising. "Or not," I said, replacing my crown and standing. Information began pouring in from Marie and I closed my eyes soaking it in. Humans were beginning to make their way toward the entrances of the city. I could feel their presence in thick clusters of intense energy. My lids flew open and I let my power as ruler explode from me to add an extra seal around us. The air rushed out like an electrical shockwave causing Marko to fly from the bed.

"What is it?"

"Humans. They're outside. I think they're cops. I'm not sure. I have to get dressed."

"Who was at the door?"

"Marie. She's gone now, gathering the members."

I rushed into the closet, ripping down a deep blue silk gown. As I changed, Marko was beside me, quickly dressing himself. Another knock sounded and I growled as I reached behind, jerking the laces of the corseted top.

"My shoes." I scanned the area, sliding them on and rushing for the wooden barrier. Aetas and Hunter had anger mixing with the adrenaline.

"You sealed the city? Why?"

I glanced back at Marko, whose lip was pulled back in distaste.

"Humans. They're at the entrances. I'm headed to the main gate to see if they're a threat. I believe its police officers from Hunter's earlier massacre, but I'm not for certain."

Aetas laughed under his breath. "Do you not have faith in your members, Princess? Do you not find them capable of handling this simple task? Say the humans are hostile. You could die, and it'd be over nothing."

"Nothing?" My head shook in disbelief. "You call dying for my people, nothing? The event doesn't matter—big or small—riot or perimeter check. All due respect, Your Highness, but I think you miss the concept of being a leader. Everyone wants to rule. Few are willing to sacrifice themselves to prove it. Excuse me," I said, stepping around them. "You can go back to your room. Everything will be okay. You have my word that I will protect you while you stay here. *However* long that is."

Marko was right behind me as he swept passed and made it to my side. I didn't turn back to Aetas or Hunter as I focused on the energy and began giving my orders to my mate.

"You're to go with Bufar and Beatrice. Take the north and east entrance. I'll take Anastasia, Marie, and Demetruis. We'll check the south and west entrances. When I know what this is about, I will tell you. Do not speak to the humans and do not let them see you. I don't want our presence to make things worse."

"Got it," he breathed out, reaching over and squeezing my hand.

Footsteps pounded up from behind. I looked over my shoulder through the darkness to see Hunter getting closer. "Go back to your room." After he continued to followed, I couldn't help but jerk to a stop as I faced forward. "Aetas!"

"He said I could go."

My eyes flared and I spun around, searching out my leader.

"I can keep you safe," he whispered, stepping closer to grab my hands.

"You did this by killing all those people," I bit out. "Besides, I assure you I don't need your help. Aetas!"

Out of darkest reaches of the tunnel, he appeared, approaching at a leisurely pace. His hands were in his pockets and he took his time to get to us. "Yes, Princess?" There was seduction in his tone. A longing deep within the furthest reaches. My body tingled to life and I almost couldn't believe his persuasion made it through my crown. It was enough to give me pause.

"Take Hunter back to the room. I don't have time to babysit some newborn."

"He's fine. Look at him. My blood does him well. It helps curb the cravings."

My jaw clenched and I glanced over at Marko. I could tell it wasn't easy for him to remain quiet.

"I ask *very nicely* ... take him back to the room." Seconds went by with no response. "Take him to the room!" I yelled, ripping my hand free from Hunter's grasp. I began stepping back to put space between us, but it wasn't enough for everything I was feeling. I was already leaving—running from not only that strange tugging inside of me from both of them, but toward the war that I knew was beginning.

Chapter 6
Hunter

Pacing did nothing to stop the indiscernible need to fight. It was always there, edging along my being. No matter how hard I tried to get the urges under control, I couldn't stop myself from lashing out to my maker. I hated him. Hated him for reasons I couldn't grasp yet. The rage made it impossible to speak out loud at times. It was so different around the princess. I could beg her with words, but I couldn't even barely say two of them to the man who made me. I had so many questions and they wouldn't stop coming.

My eyes cut across the room as I projected my voice into his mind. It was something that had come from the beginning…from me. How I knew to do it, I wasn't sure, but I had heard his relief as he tried to coax me closer to him. This vampire wanted me to trust him. To open myself to him even more.

It wasn't going to happen.

"Why doesn't she want my help? Does she not think me capable of protecting her? I can fight. I can kill anyone who goes up against me."

"You have a lot to learn," Aetas said out loud, sitting on the edge of the bed. "In your mind you feel you are able, but that's because you have very powerful blood. Your gifts are not apparent to you as of yet. Did you know you had gifts? The princess was using hers almost from her birth. The images I saw from your blood, you have yet to tap into yours fully."

"I don't need gifts to prove my worth."

He laughed, feeding the fire within.

"Oh, but you are wrong. Your gifts *are* your worth. They're a blessing and can protect you when brute strength cannot."

"I don't care for them. Tell me why the princess doesn't like me? What is she hiding? What did I do to her?"

A sigh filled the room.

"It's pointless telling you now. You will wake up tomorrow and what happened today will be forgotten."

"I thought you said you saw images from my blood. You must not be very good, then, because my memory is just fine. I may be a blank slate and get confused to where I am at times, but what has happened to me has not been forgotten."

Aetas' eyes narrowed. "You treading water right now due to your attitude and you don't even know it. You're about to learn a very quick lesson. First, tell me what you mean. What has happened to you?"

Flashes blinded me of my awakening. They were almost impossible to grasp because of the underlining fog. The details were vague, but the gist of that day came back to me. A part of me didn't want to remember and I'd done well about blocking them out, but if I wanted to learn from this, *learn about her,* I had to be honest.

"My first memory is of two women. They were going to kill me. That didn't happen. I was locked outside of a huge house. The sun was burning my skin and I had nowhere to go. I ran...for what seemed like forever. Pieces of my flesh were falling off by the time I came across some type of shelter. A barn, I think. My mind says barn." I tried to buffer the smell, but even now I could almost taste the burning scent. *"I remained there until it was dark and I made my way to the lights in the distance. It took hours...There was so much movement when I arrived. So many sights and smells. Everything was familiar, yet I couldn't remember how I knew the place. There was an abandoned house along the outskirts that I stayed in for a few days. I was cautious to go out too much, but the hunger got undeniably worse. Finally, I braved my way deeper into the city. By that time I was beyond help. I had gone crazy with bloodlust. That's when the vampire found me. Boyd."*

"Your mind didn't show me those memories. I don't believe it," he breathed out. "Remembering should be impossible, even for you."

"Apparently not. What I don't know is my life before that moment. Tell me about the princess. Why does she hate me?"

Aetas slowly stood, still appearing dazed as he came closer. "This can't be happening. It's impossible. What does this mean for the future?"

"My future is not in question, my past is. I already know what lies ahead. Tell me what came before I was turned."

"Are you speaking in riddles with me? What do you mean, you know what lies ahead?"

I had to stop myself from baring my fangs. *"I make the future. I take whatever route I choose. No one will stop that. Not even you."*

Aetas laughed, glaring at the same time. "You want to know who you were before you were turned?"

"I do."

"Alright. I'll tell you. You were her best friend when you were both humans. The princess loved you very dearly, but she never told you of her feelings. And neither did you. Not until it was too late. It's a tragic story, in truth. You had dreams of coming back from the Army to make her fall in love with you, when in fact, the entire time, she already was."

"As fate would have it, when you finally did return, it was the same night Marko Delacroix came across her. He forced his blood upon Tessalyn and ultimately made her his blood slave. You once attempted to kill him, but you shot her instead. Sayer, her maker, saved her, but upon doing so he secretly gave her his blood to start the process of their bonding. Before he could finalize the act, she ran to you and confessed her love."

"You both had an amazing day together. One would think that's where the happily-ever-after ended, but that's not the case. Tessa had to come back here and you both knew it. So the two of you decided on a path to stay together. One that would break her ties with Marko, and one that would allow you full access into her life—you would become *her* blood slave."

I step forward, searching for the memories he spoke of, but they were nowhere to be found.

"Was I her slave? Were Tessa and I able to stay together?"

He frowned. "Well…yes, for a while. You see, when a human is turned into one of us, their mind's change. Tessa changed. What the two of you went through during her newborn stage was more than most vampires or humans could come back from. Sayer raped the both of you repeatedly. During that time, the two of you drifted apart. Tessa tried to make you love her Hunter, but you couldn't see that with your human mind. She killed for you, and yet you saw her as a monster. It was little things like this that drove her into Marko's arms. It also had you stabbing her through the heart with a blessed dagger. You killed her, Prince, and then you shoved a gun in your mouth and you pulled the trigger. It was only because of Sayer's blood that you didn't die."

"But he's dead, right? This, Sayer?" Just the mention of his name had my pulse pounding into my chest. I couldn't stomach the thought of him. It brought out the killer in me. Made him almost impossible to get control of.

"He is. You killed him."

"Good." I breathed out. *"What happened, then?"*

"You dedicated your life to killing our kind. To killing Marko and each and every one of us. I came to you once and I showed you Tessa still lived. You tried to kill yourself again, but you weren't able to through the state I had you in. You hated us. All the while, you never knew what it was to be a vampire." He came closer. "Do you hate us still?"

My head went to shake, but stopped. *"I…did. When the women tried to kill me and I was locked outside. I hated you all. But when I was lost and I saw Boyd, something changed. It only grew when I saw Tessa. I wanted to be here. I want her."*

"You wanted nothing but to kill her before you were turned. And the same for her. She wants you dead, Prince. Her vampire can't help but plot revenge for what you did. I can see her struggles. She is even tempered where you are not. You are like Marko in that way. You're both quick to react. If Tessalyn were free of both of you there would be no doubt in my mind that she would take my place. As it is, the plans I have set doesn't quite put her in that position. Tessa will stay mated to Marko."

"No. That won't do. She can leave with us. She can be mine."

Aetas' eyebrows rose. "I do believe I make the rules here, and no, she will not. Tessa will run this city for quite a while longer and you will come with me and focus on your lessons."

"You can't make me go with you."

"I am your leader and your maker! I can do whatever I want with you." Aetas was gone so fast that I couldn't process his disappearance before he was before me with his hand locked around my throat. "Never forget who holds your life in their hands, Prince. I gave you my blood. I can very well drain you of every last drop you hold."

My hands shot up trying my hardest to pull against his grasp, but it was too strong. He wasn't even straining and yet I couldn't break free. Survival had my mind going. Heat surfaced in the pit of my stomach and I pulled at it, searching for something I didn't even know.

"That's it," he whispered. "Show me what you're made of." His palm slammed against my stomach and I screamed through the blaze that ignited. I could feel him tugging against some sort of invisible thread that seemed to be linking me to who I was. The fire moved up behind my eyes and I growled through the inferno.

"There's your vampire. Black eyes, just like Tessa. You're so much alike when you're pushed to your limits. Do it, Hunter. Unleash what is inside of you."

Dark smoke began to drift between us, swirling through the air as it thickened. Was that coming from me? From my opened mouth? It rose higher, spanning across the ceiling, crawling over the surface as if it were alive.

"Yes! More."

The greed was evident in Aetas' tone. I tried to yell again as he pulled against what I was made of, jerking the connection tightly. In a burst, I let the rage burst free from me. Black smoke poured out so thick that I could barely see him anymore. My body was shaking from the force I used to try to make him stop. I couldn't breathe through his tight grasp and I wanted him dead. I wanted to hurt him the worst way possible.

My eyes went back to the smoke and I drew it in around him, imagining it as a physical power to push him away. Aetas swayed, but held his ground. Just at the realization of what I was doing, I pictured it being stronger. Impossibly so. I pulled the darkness back, launching it toward his body with everything I had. One minute he was there, the next—gone. And not just from where he had stood before me….but from the room.

I searched the area, panicked as I coughed. My throat was so tight. So raw, from not only the choking, but from the smoke.

"I'm not impressed,"Aetas said, re-appearing feet away with his hands crossed over his chest. "You're brute force and no brains. Tessa blows you away with her abilities, even from the very beginning. Maybe I'm making the wrong choice. If it wouldn't ruin her, I'd kill both you and Marko and be done with this once and for all. *She's* the real leader. I thought you stood a chance, but you're not as smart. You're passionate, yes, but that will not make up for instinct. God dammit!"

Aetas paced as we glared at each other.

"You'll rule Dallas upon the rebuild. You can rule, that's not the problem. But I don't think you'll have it in you to lead our kind. You're going to have a lot to prove to me in our lessons to convince me otherwise."

"What if I don't want your lessons?"

An evil smile stretched across his face and I braced myself for him to come at me again. "You don't have a choice. I'm starting them right now. Lesson number one, Hunter." Aetas' hand rose and he looked up at the cement ceiling. "Time to stir things up from above. You need to see what your competition is capable of. How far do you think the princess will go to protect her people when she really has to fight to survive? Is she willing to *sacrifice* herself like she said?"

Chapter 7
Marko

The multiple thrum of pulses from outside had me frowning as I stopped just short of the east entrance. It was the same at the north. There were humans outside of both and from the complete silence, I didn't doubt these were professionals. They were calm, collected, unlike the impatient rebels that tried to attack on occasion.

My head tilted back even more and I took the smallest step forward to peer into the light coming down from the grate above. I knew the only reason they hadn't acted out yet was because of the intense uneasiness they were feeling from Tessa's shield. It would have instilled a fear so great that it would have been impossible for them to act upon. Maybe one or two would try to brave coming down, but I doubted they'd do it if they weren't being accompanied by their team.

"Let's head back," I whispered to Beatrice and Bufar. "We can meet up with the rest of the members."

I gave a quick point to the guard who stayed hidden deeper in the shadows at our presence. At my signal, he headed to the side of the tunnel to go back to sitting watch.

"They're debating to leave." I kept my voice low as the members followed me back toward the heart of the city. "What they feel, they're not prepared to face. I don't think we have anything to worry about."

"All clear. Headed back."

Tessa's voice came into my mind just as I expected it to. I could already feel her energy begin to move closer.

"The number of potential attacks are increasing." Beatrice's face was devoid of emotion, but I could detect her anxiety. "It's only a matter of time before the humans grow immune to the sensations they feel and breach our walls. Once they do, it'll become constant. They'll keep returning, trying to kill us in our sleep."

I smiled, only for it to melt immediately. A rush of power cut right through me and with it, the shield to our city disappeared. I jerked to a stop, scanning the darkness.

"What was that?" Bufar breathed out, heavily. "Did the princess drop her protection?"

"No." I turned to face the entrance we'd just left. *Aetas.* It had to have been him. But…why? "Beatrice, head back to stand with the guard. Bufar, go to the north entrance. Be ready to fight. I have to protect the princess."

All three of us took off running. Tessa's words came pushing back into my head, feeding my need to go faster.

They're coming! Ready yourself!"

Doors flew open on my sides as vampires began to peer out of their rooms. "Get inside! If a human opens your door, kill them," I yelled.

My claws were already down, my fangs cutting into my lip as I neared the light of the heart of the city. Sounds were still coming from the room and I slowed as I broke into the large space. Marie was ushering Tessa in, but my concubine was obviously not happy about it.

"Come, we can get you into the bedroom. You can stay there until this passes."

Panic had me sliding to a stop to reach for her. I didn't mind the fight, but I wanted her safe. The mate in me was worried. The member in me stilled as she threw me a look.

"Do my words means nothing to any of you? Are you all not listening to what I say?" Black began to take over her green color and the whites were quickly disappearing as she pointed one of her claws toward me. "I may not be at the entrance, but I will not cower away in a room until this passes. We fight. *I fight.* If you want to join me, take your position at my side. But do not for one second think about stopping me."

The biggest battle of my life played out before me as the bonded male wanted to throw Tessa over his shoulder and spank her ass for not listening. Her second in command had me scowling and stepping to her side.

"Then we fight."

Tessa didn't appear to hear me as her lids closed and her arms came out. "They're breaching all entrances." Her head jerked the smallest amount to the side and I knew she was in tune with the city—with the energy, the sounds. Seconds went by as she grew quiet. Then a good minute. Two.

"Wait…" Her eyes snapped open and she immediately looked to the far left of the room. It was the tunnel that held lockdown, but there were openings that led to the outside. "They're not alone," she whispered. "The officers…they're being joined by more. *Rebels.* They're coming, too. They're pouring in. They've been waiting. They knew …"

"Marko." Marie moved closer to Tessa's left side and I stepped up on the opposite to be even with her. Our ruler wasn't here in the moment. She was too deep into her mind, watching what was happening.

"Anastasia," Tessa said, lifting her index finger, "Beatrice, Demetrius…John is still locked down…"

My eyes darted to Marie whose claws were lowering at Tessa's headcount.

"Bufar….no. No!" A sound equivalent to growl poured from her. "Bufar is dead. He's…" Her hand came out before her. "They're going into the rooms. They're killing us…"

Dark hair flared out as Tessa spun and her blacked out eyes met mine. Dark smoke began to lift from her body and span across the floor in all directions.

"Both of you take cover in one of the shops and wait for my order. They're on their way here. Only when I say, do you both come out. From there we'll finish them off."

Her words barely reached my sense of hearing before her body evaporated toward the ceiling. Marie was already running, already obeying. Just as I went to turn, I caught Aetas' energy. I couldn't see him, but I knew he and Hunter were here. *They were watching.*

Rage sparked and it took everything I had not to storm in their direction. Instead, I put my back to them, racing for the front of the city where all the shops were lined. Marie headed into George's and I followed. But my mind wasn't on waiting for our enemies to arrive. No, the real threat was already here, assessing and testing us. This was *his* fault. I knew he was the cause of Tessa's shield-failure. Why, was the question.

"I can't believe Bufar is dead," Marie breathed out as I settled down in front of the glass, next to her. "I wasn't expecting that."

I glanced over, moving my attention to the peer into the dimly lit room. "I just left him. I almost can't believe it, myself, but I know what Tessa saw was true. There's a lot of humans within our walls."

"We have a lot of vampires, though. They'll come to join us in the fight. I know this. I've seen it."

My head whipped back over to her. "You saw this happening?"

She nodded. "Moments before I came to your door. But…I didn't see Bufar dying. In my dream, it was Anastasia."

"How bad is it going to be?"

Marie frowned. "We will win. But at a cost."

"What cost?"

Yelling erupted in the distance and I could feel the humans growing closer. They were coming at alarming speed which told me they were rushing past the doors that held our kind.

"Tessa will be okay, won't she?"

Marie shifted, but kept her focus ahead. "I would die before I let anything happen to our leader. If I feared she would be killed, I wouldn't be here right now. I'd be out there with her."

"Then what is the cost?"

"I'm not sure," she whispered. "It was a feeling. The vision didn't provide the answer."

I frowned, moving my attention to the dark layer hovering just below the ceiling. Footsteps echoed loudly from all directions and I watched as men in tactical gear burst into the heart of the city from three different tunnels. Others, who I knew were rogue fighters, quickly joined them. As seconds passed, they moved in toward the center, training their weapons to the different entrances. They were cautious, inching in and taking their time. I licked my lips, feeling energy move in from the tunnel closest to us. But they were headed toward the center, too, only glancing in our directions as they scanned the large area.

"Shit. What is this place?" One of the civilians mumbled the question, but it was loud enough for me to hear the fear deep within his words. Closer, they gathered, weaving around the tables as they stayed close together. I glanced at Marie, bringing myself back to take in the swirl of Tessa's energy. Faster, it was rotating, growing darker and thicker as her anger increased. The intensity made it almost impossible to sit still. I wanted to be out there with her. I wanted to do what came natural to my vampire.

"The leader has to be here somewhere. We made it in. Now I think we should pick a tunnel and start our search. If we can kill the one in charge, the rest will be easy."

Deep tones were beginning to push against my throat. I held steady, flattening my hands against the cold floor to ground my need to attack. But I didn't have to focus on controlling myself for long. The men began to notice the air fluctuate. What started as a gust grew faster, whipping around them with such brutality some held to the tables and each other, crouching low against the force. I rose, higher, in awe of Tessa's strength. She'd never gone this far before and I wasn't sure what to expect with the fury she held over her dead followers.

Shots began to go off, echoing loudly throughout the room as some of the men began to yell. The dark smoke drew in, funneling down in the middle of the group, revealing first Tessa's feet, working its way up until her crown was visible and she was once again whole. The curls that hung down her back and shoulders were just as wild as the expression in her light green eyes. *Green*…she was still in control of her vampire which surprised me.

Tessa began to turn in a slow circle, staring down each one. "You wished to find the leader of this city?" her voice boomed. "Well, here I am. What are you waiting for?" Her arms slowly rose up from here sides and her lids closed while her head drew back. I couldn't help but jump to my feet. The explosion of round after round penetrated the air. Marie clasped to my wrist, trying to keep me still. Harder she tugged as I uncontrollably kept stepping toward the door.

Bullets and stakes hung in the air, hovering just outside of the invisible shield. Vampires were emerging from the tunnels, watching, waiting, just as I was. Seconds went by, and then minutes as the shots eventually ceased. Silence was broken by the clinks of metal and wood falling to the cement floor. Tessa's deep laughing echoed against the walls and her eyes opened. Dark smoke began to seep past her lips as her laughter grew. When I caught the blacks of her eyes, I took a deep breath. The men shot to their feet and turned to run, but hit a barrier they couldn't see. They were trapped and so was anyone else who wanted in.

Wind began to increase in the bubble until the haze lifted to the top, hovering above their heads. Like a flash, the darkness gathered and Tessa shot through one of the men's lips. His arms went crazy, dropping the gun as a red hue began to tint his face. Darker, it became, while he tore into his throat. One second he was fighting against her invisible threat, the next his body exploded out in all directions, replaced with her own. Blood covered her dress and face, matting in her hair. Tessa reared back, slicing through one of the men's cheeks before diving for his neck. Screams increased and suddenly the humans were falling over each other as the wall gave way. Tessa tossed the officer over, looking right at me, using our bond to pull me closer. My body hummed, going crazy for her. Her powers or what she was doing didn't scare me, they turned me on more than I could believe.

"These men spilled the blood of our kind. They *owe* me theirs. Make your ruler happy. Kill them!"

Vampires poured through the tunnels, snarling and baring their fangs as they headed toward the humans. They were searching for a way out, juking to the side as they looked desperately for somewhere to go. But there was nowhere. The vampires were gaining ground, becoming more animalist the closer they got to the mens' fearful scent.

I stalked forward, breaking my stare from Tessa's as I zeroed in on an officer holding a jagged knife. His breaths were coming out in heavy pants and he was swinging it at a group of vampires that were circling around him. At my energy burst, they paused, glancing over at me. My strides never slowed as I broke through them and deflected his blow. My grip tightened around his neck and I lifted his feet off the floor. I tapped into Tessa's powers, letting it mix with my own. Heat blazed in my stomach and her hand shoot up to aim toward me. I let the dark smoke mix with my fire until the bright fog was leaving my mouth, into his. Overkill— definitely. But to strengthen our gift, we needed to use them, and I wasn't going to pass up the opportunity. Especially with Aetas watching. He needed to see. He had to know that together, Tessa and I were worthy. I'd show him there was no better choice than my concubine. She'd get what she deserved. I'd make sure of it.

Chapter 8
Tessa

"Go! Search the tunnels. The humans still in our city cannot escape. I want them dead!"

My order sent vampires scattering from our main room, thirsty to quench the burn embedded in their throats. Blood hung thickly in the air and it was worse for me being soaked in the substance.

As I turned to see crimson pouring from the officer's mouth Marko held, I couldn't take it anymore. The rest my people could finish this on their own. We were safe from the majority of the threat. Men were dying with every breath I took and I needed my mate. He seemed to sense that as he dropped the body, walking toward me at a brisk pace. I didn't think as I threw myself in his arms and jumped up to straddle his waist.

"Take me to our room." I barely got the words out as I crushed my lips into his. I craved the roughness I knew his touch could bring. I needed it after the victory and death of my enemies.

Marko's tongue slid hungrily against mine and his fingers dug into my lower back making me break our connection to gasp.

"First, Aetas. He's here. He's been watching the entire time."

I blinked past the lust associated with my brutality. "Of course he is."

Marko lowered me and I gripped just above his elbow as he led me toward our tunnel. Aetas was leaned just outside of it, with Hunter at his side. The glare Hunter held had my own lids lowering. I was still ready to fight. To kill. I had barely tapped into a quarter of what I knew I was capable of and I was dying to test my skills at a much grander scale. Hunter wasn't it. Not yet.

"Bravo." Aetas' clapped, sarcastically. "But just as boring as Hunter. I've already seen you do that. I was hoping to catch something new. Something … worthy of a leader. Marko on the other hand impressed me. Perhaps I should train him."

I suppressed the need to hiss and snarl at him. My vampire was out of control. I could already feel the darkness covering my vision. She was ready to provoke if need be, and that's exactly what she was doing to Aetas.

"What should I have done, turned this room to an inferno? A death bomb with a shock wave of poison to wipe them all out in one single blow? What sort of leader would I have been if I would have done that? I would have kept all the fun to myself. My people need the challenge and hunt. It does them good. They can only be contained so much. They rarely get to go out now as it is. It's not safe for our kind on the streets."

"Surely you could have thought of something a little more creative than what you just did."

My eyes flickered over to Hunter's. His jaw was set tight and he was staring at me. Slowly, I cocked my head to the side, reading his energy.

"You need to feed again. You wish you could have joined my people in their fight when they came to protect me."

Pale blue eyes cut over to Aetas before he nodded. "Yes, Princess."

"Aetas told you no?"

Again, he nodded, but kept quiet. Pressure pushed against my back and I turned, watching Marie approached with her head down. I could feel her anger at Hunter.

"Princess, I wish to make rounds and gather up the members if it is alright with you. I think after tonight we should have shifts. We can plan them and take it from here if you wish to give your blessing."

Her eyes lifted, flicking with anger as they went from Hunter to me.

"I approve. Come to me if anything else happens."

She nodded, spinning to hurry away from us.

"Who is that?" Hunter asked quietly.

"No one worthy enough for you to bother with." Aetas pushed from the wall. "Time to feed you again."

Hardness tightened Hunter's features and I stepped back, giving my own greeting of goodbye to Aetas. When I turned to follow Marko toward the tunnel, my body jolted. I was ripped back so fast that before I could process the movement, fire burned into the side of my neck. I gasped through the sting and poison that pushed its way into my vein.

Marko's roar internally and throughout the large room deafened me to anything else. My wide eyes were locked on his face and his expression was of rage that I'd never seen before. He was beating against the shield, but it wasn't me who had placed it. A buzzing began to register just as my body exploded to life with lust. Still, Hunter fed from me, biting down viciously as he held my arms pinned.

"Let her go!" Aetas yelled. "Do you know what you have done? Marko could kill you right now and he'd have every right. *I* could kill you," he growled, lifting his hand to face his palm toward us. "She. Is. Not. Yours!"

Aetas' eyes were getting darker as his gaze stayed on Hunter.

"You will let go of her right now or so help me, you're going to regret it."

Already Hunter's bite was easing, but his hold wasn't. He turned, putting his back to the wall as he kept his arms tightly around me. My shoulders twisted, rocking to try to break his hold. Regardless that his bite turned me on, it didn't have nearly the power Marko's did. After the initial shock, my blood quickly put a stop to his poison.

"Hunter," I whispered. "You have to stop. You're hurting me. You don't want to hurt me, do you?"

His grip loosened, but not fast enough. Aetas' energy spiked to unbelievable heights and I watched as his face turn emotionless. He looked like nothing but a shell before me, and it only took a few seconds for me to piece it all together. That's exactly what he was. He had Hunter locked within his own mind, just as Aetas had done with me on more than one occasion.

Hunter's body was rigid, but I easily pried his arms off enough for me to break free of them. Marko's eyes were wild as he pressed his hands into the barrier between us. He looked on the verge of some sort of breakdown—torn between fear and fury.

"I'm okay." My hand lifted to try to calm him, but he rammed his fist repeatedly into the wall while he tore into it with his nails. When a yell escaped his mouth, I somehow managed to catch his gaze with mine. *"I'm alright. Breathe."*

"I'm trying not to kill him, ma minette. I'm trying so hard for you, but I cannot bear this. What he did ... I want ..." He paused, throwing his shoulder into the shield once again. *"I've never wanted to hurt someone as much as I want to hurt him. He has to go. He has to leave here right now, or forgive me, but I do not think I can resist these urges he brings out in me."*

"You will resist," I hissed within my mind. *"You have to. If something happens to you, we're both dead. Do you understand me?"*

I looked over my shoulder, taking in my leader and Hunter. I could kill them right now. I could …

No. I would not think such things. If I killed Aetas, the main members would rise against me. I'd be charged and sentenced to death. But if he hurt Marko, did I have a choice?

"Resist," I repeated. *"Go to the room and I will meet you there. Do not argue with me and obey your Mistress. Obey your leader."*

Marko's lids lowered and he exposed his fangs for only seconds before the roar followed. Nearly black eyes turned darker as he flexed his jaw and pointed. *"Do not order me to do that."*

"I just did. Go."

The panic only worsened in his stare. Marko slammed against the wall once more before he took a step back. At the gesture of my head, he distanced himself even more, but he didn't leave. He stood, hovering, appearing light on his feet as he paced back and forth. He was ready to spring forward. Ready to attack once the wall fell.

"Get your ass in the room, Marko!" My loud yell tore his eyes from Hunter, to come back to me, but they didn't stay. He wasn't listening. The fact that he wasn't internally forced to obey told me just how close our powers were equal to each other. Moments like this, where he peaked in his protectiveness … he only grew in strength.

I switched over to French as I tried to get his attention. "You once told me there was nothing you wouldn't do for me. That the only reason your heart beat was because of me. Do you remember that?"

In jerky movements, Marko's stare returned.

"You also took vows. You swore your alliance to me. Do you withdraw from your statement? Am I no longer your ruler?"

"Ma minette, you speak of what I can't control." His tone was almost unrecognizable. "I cannot leave you here. It is impossible for me to act on. Order, or not, you are my mate—my concubine. That—" A pained expression drew in his features. "That son of a bitch took something that was mine. He hurt you, again! I felt it! He goes too far and he has to pay. He has to learn right now that you are off limits to him. He has to learn from *me*." The last came out so loud that the floor shook with his anger. The long pointed tips of his fangs were cutting into his lip and he did nothing to wipe away the blood that was trailing down his chin.

A scream broke through the shield, so loud that it made my hands fly to my ears. I spun, just in time to see Hunter crumble to his knees. A haunting expression clouded his stare as he looked up at Aetas, but it faded just as fast. He sprung, lunging toward our leader with his claws extended. My vampire instinct had me thrusting my body forward and grasping his wrist just as Aetas latched to his face and twisted his neck, breaking it. The action and thud of the body sent my hand flying to my stomach from the instant nausea.

"He has so much to learn." Silence. "I offer my most sincere apologies." Aetas turned to face both me and Marko. "I thought he was more stable than he is. I was wrong. I ask that you please forgive my misjudgment. You won't have to worry about it again."

Marko was still seething. Still appearing threatening as he began to walk closer. "Let her out. Let her out right now!"

The shield rippled and Marko stalked forward, wrapping his arm around my waist and pulling my back to fit against his chest as he held on.

"Master Delacroix, I know what happened was—"

"You don't know," Marko exploded. "You don't know because you've never bonded. You've never loved anyone but *yourself*." His hand lifted and Marko pointed at Hunter's lifeless body. "By your law, I have every right to kill him. I could finish this right now."

Aetas glanced at me and his jaw clenched.

"I do not want him to die."

"That's not how it works," Marko said, holding me tighter. "His life is mine. He dies if I say."

"Yes…But surely there is something you want more than revenge? You know how we play this game."

The thudding in Marko's chest was so powerful that my own instantly matched it. Thoughts pushed in and I could feel peace edging within, calming the swift beats. Hunter—dead. My vampire took pleasure at the revenge that would come.

Aetas glanced down at Hunter. "Perhaps you'd like to spare him in exchange for something more, something very important to you? Maybe a chance to be ruler of this city again?"

I gasped, glaring at Aetas. "Marko would never—"

"Not good enough." Marko said, cutting me off. "What he has done cannot be forgiven for something so *petty*. Give me what I am owed. Give it to me and I will let him live."

"W-what?" My face turned up to Marko and I couldn't stop my lips from separating in shock. Vampires were beginning to crowd in, and I wasn't the only one noticing. Aetas scanned the room before he turned back to Marko.

"You want to be one of my members." There was a coldness in Aetas tone. A disgust he couldn't hide no matter how hard he tried.

"Never," Marko spat. "I want rank. Higher than your creation will ever have. Everyone knows Hunter will only ever be a prince. The Black King and Queen locked their titles in, even after death. They can't be touched. I want to be a king of my own line. *I deserve it*. You're aware of how powerful I am. You can grant me the status. You can make it official right now, in front of this entire city. I will take nothing less. King or death for Hunter. Your choice."

Aetas stare cut over to me and I could almost hear his silent words of, *I told you so*. Pain shot through my chest and I couldn't believe what I was witnessing. Marko was choosing to be royalty, rather than ending the life of the man who had tried to kill me? Betrayal had never sliced so deep.

Nearly silent steps brought Aetas closer. His gaze bore into me and I couldn't stop the stinging burn of my eyes while I glared up at him. There was no emotion present that I could detect. Not until his lids drifted down the slightest amount and slowly rose to Marko.

"You want to be a king? So be it. The night of your guests' arrival there will be a coronation. It'll be what your dreams are made of." He lowered his voice as his top lip pulled back to expose his fangs. "It'll be a night you'll never forget."

Chapter 9
Hunter

"Wake the fuck up."

Pain flared across my cheek causing my eyes to snap open. I took a deep breath, memories flooding me of the pain I'd experienced as my creator snapped my neck like a twig. I should have been dead, but my mind told me instantly that something so small wouldn't end my life.

An enraged expression was being cast my way and I slowly pushed to sit on the bed I was lying on. The need to attack again, to kill Aetas, was all I knew. Somehow I managed to control myself as I reined in my emotions.

"What you did to the princess ..."

He trailed off. His breaths were coming out heavy as he began to pace. Not once did his stare leave me.

"How do you feel?" He goaded. "Can you feel her in you? Does her blood comfort you? Does it fucking make you want more?"

The last came out loud and threatening as I sifted through the sensations within. I *could* feel her presence, and I did want more. Her flavor had been heaven. The sweetness of her power was intoxicating—addicting.

"Answer me, Prince. Was breaking the law worth the small sample you experienced? Did you know because of your stupid actions, Master Delacroix will be a king? A title I swore I'd never give him?"

Aetas lunged toward me and I sprung from the bed to put my face only an inch from his. We were both panting. Both ready to go at each other's throats. Darkness crept into my mind and I suddenly got flashes of the tortuous mindfuck he'd put me through before he'd broken my neck. His power was so much greater than mine. He could have killed me in that black abyss. Somehow I knew that.

"Let him be king," I said in a raspy tone. "A king does not define greatness, his actions do. Besides, the higher the title, the harder he will fall when he fails in what he wants." I bit my bottom lip, bumping Aetas' shoulder as I walked around him. "When he loses everything, including his queen, tell me how great he will be then?"

"You're *so sure* Tessalyn is what you want." He laughed and I turned around to meet his narrowed stare. "But your own greed and stupidity make you blind to the truth. She will never be yours, Hunter. Not with the hate she harbors for what you did."

"You're wrong. She will overlook our past. My change is a new start for both of us, and I plan to show her that."

Aetas' head lowered and his eyes were cut up as he moved in closer. "It's going to be hard showing her when I plan to not let you see her. Do you hear me? You are forbidden to get near the princess. At least until your lessons are over. That could be years. Decades, even."

My fangs shot down into my lip, stinging and drawing forth the essence of my blood. Of *his* blood. Heat burned my eyes as I projected every ounce of hate I felt toward my maker. Tingling raced over my skin and what appeared to be dark shadows against the walls grew and moved toward me. My stare went to Aetas as he laughed under his breath. Was this one of his tricks, or something more? I couldn't help but feel these dark silhouettes were real.

"I have some mending to do. You will remain here. If you try to leave …" Aetas smile grew. "Well, you're welcomed to try, but I wouldn't recommend it. My enforcers are the best in the world. They'd love nothing more than twist your body like a pretzel. Disobey my orders and who you are is of little consequence. They'll eat you alive."

In quick strides, he left, slamming the door behind him. I turned in a circle, watching the dark misted figures began to turn into smoke. It spun around me slowly and I hissed, ready to fight. As fast as it began, it stopped, becoming a single form. The black morphed with color and my mouth separated as the princess was suddenly before me.

"You're not real," I breathed out.

"Am I not?"

I glanced at the door, only to return to her light green eyes. "Aetas …"

"Doesn't know all of my tricks." A smile grew and she stared me up and down as she began to walk around me. I turned, following her movements. Her blood in my veins heated and made weird tugging sensations. I knew she was doing it, but why, I wasn't sure.

"I didn't meant to hurt you."

"Don't lie to yourself, Hunter, it makes you look like a fool. You didn't care if you hurt me in that moment. You wanted my blood and you would have done anything to get it. Admit it."

My brow furrowed as I watched her come to a stop. "You're right. I wanted it, just as I do now."

"Too bad. My blood does not belong to you. But yours." Tessa stepped in, reaching up to place her palm against my cheek. "I do believe that yours will be beneficial to me."

"You want to feed from me? Why? How will it be beneficial?"

Her hand slid down the side of my throat and her fingers stopped over my pulse point. For seconds she remained quiet, just watching my face. My cock hardened and I licked my lips as I fought the urge to push her on the bed and fuck her as hard as I could. There was no room for passion, just raw, bloody lust.

"You and I are going to have a secret no one can know about, Prince. Not Aetas, and not Marko. In our world, there's no one you can trust." Tears came to her eyes. "It's an ugly truth. A heartbreaking one."

Tessa's hand slammed into the middle of my stomach and I gasped as she grabbed to what Aetas had—my core. Fire blazed on my insides and I grasped her wrist, holding securely, trying to pull it away.

But I couldn't.

"I'm going to make you stronger," she whispered. "And in turn, your blood is going to come alive inside of me. It's going to grow and tie. We'll always be connected, dear friend. Even if we hate each other in the end."

Her hand gripped to the back of my neck and I moaned through the pleasurable sting that came from the tearing of my skin. Powerful venom sent a shock to my heart and the adrenaline had me wrapping around her waist to pull her into me.

"Yes," I moaned. "God, yes."

Deep sucks were all I felt as I spun us around and crashed back onto the bed to let her straddle me. My fingers dug into her hips as she continually tugged at my very soul.

"Pain shouldn't feel this good. I want to stay in this beautiful hell forever. This moment," I managed. "With you."

I was growing weaker by the minute. The room was beginning to spin with the amount of blood she was draining from me, but I didn't care. It wasn't until the aching warmth in my core began to vibrate and zap that I blinked through the haze. Tessa's tongue licked over the wounds and she broke away, inhaling deeply as blood raced down her chin.

"Perfect. So good."

She was practically purring as she lowered the top half of her body. Her breasts pushed into my chest and she cupped to each side of my face as she came down even more. When her lips brushed against mine, I hungrily awaited more.

"I don't have much time. Stay strong, but *get* stronger. The more powerful you become, the closer we'll be. The more you'll feel me. Even far away, we'll be able to talk to each other. Would you like that?"

Her finger traced over my lips while I nodded.

"Good. I want that, too. But in the meantime, I need you to ease up on the possessive, *she's mine* attitude. I am not yours Hunter. Not like that. But that doesn't mean we can't share other things. We can still be close," she said, lowering her voice. "But let's not let them know that."

"Alright." My agreement was nearly nonexistent. The twinges were getting more intense. Tessa flinched, but grinned as she pressed her lips softly into mine.

"I have to go. For the next few hours, rest your eyes and put all of your focus into our connection. Let it grow. Then try to speak to me here," she said, pushing her finger into my temple. I will do the same. And remember...not a word."

Tessa's body faded and within seconds the black smoke was swirling and disappearing into the far wall. I let out a loud groan, adjusting my cock as the aching only grew worse. Jesus, that bite. My body was still tingling with her venom, and my heart, it was racing, or had it grown a life of its own? Fuck, each slam threatened to break through the skin.

The door opened and I didn't even bother sitting up. Aetas stopped before me, scanning the room.

"What it is?" The deep tone that left me had me clearing my throat. Aetas' head turned toward me and he tilted it to the side as his lids dropped, suspiciously.

"What happened?"

"I'm not sure what you mean. I'm just laying here."

He moved in closer. When his hand reached for me, I bared my fangs. It didn't stop him from pushing my face to the side to expose the side of my neck that Tessa had fed from.

"What is this?" The mattress dipped under my shoulder as Aetas pushed into it. "Blood?" My head was jerked back toward him. "Who fed from you?"

"No one."

Pain burned over my cheek as the back of his hand connected. "Don't lie to me! I'll give you one more chance to tell me the truth. If you fail to do so, I go back inside your head and find out for myself. We both know how that's going to play out."

My lips tugged to the side at the half ass smile I threw him. "I've always loved a good battle, but you won't find the answers you seek. I've already forgotten. I remember nothing. *Nothing.*"

Chapter 10
Marko

For days Tessa avoided me. She barely spoke. She wouldn't even really look at me. I started to apologize for what I had done, but I couldn't find the words that explained my reasons for sparring Hunter's life.

I'd acted spontaneously, going with my instincts instead of what was morally right. But I had my reasons, and they seemed justifiable in my mind. Still, I couldn't make them sound good enough in an explanation so I avoided one. I just wasn't sure how much longer I could hold out. We weren't okay. We were drifting from each other and I couldn't stand it.

"Ma minette." I caught the endings of a smile as she turned around. Damn not being able to read her mind. It was driving me crazy. "What are you thinking about?"

"Nothing. Did you need something?"

The coldness in her tone had me pushing from the wall. I walked toward the closet as she continued scanning through the dresses.

"We need to talk. What happened—"

"Is done," she said, cutting me off. "You made the decision you felt was best for you. I don't want to talk about it."

"Not just for me," I stressed. "For *us*."

A smile reappeared, but not a nice one. "Right. I see how a higher title benefits me so much more than the one I carry already does."

"It does benefit you. And it benefits me. Do you know how many queen and kings still live? None besides Aetas," I growled. "That puts us above everyone. The title you carry is shared with a few, but you will be a queen now. No one can ever take that away from you. No one."

Tessa's head shook as she pulled out a deep red, silk gown. "I care not for titles, Marko. What I wanted was revenge. Although …" she trailed off, something flashing over her features before she walked passed.

"Although, what? Revenge can still come. I took that into account when I made my request. Hunter can still die."

Her head shook as she dropped her robe. "I've changed my mind for the time being."

"What?" I walked to put myself in front of her. "What do you mean, you've changed your mind? Hunter *is* going to die, Tessa. He has to for everything he's done."

"Enough. The time has come and gone. He lives and he will continue to."

My hand locked around her throat, drawing her to me. The red dress caught on her hip before pooling on the floor. "You forget who you're talking to, ma minette. I say when it is time to end a conversation. Never you. Not here" I said, tightening my hold.

"You think you can stop me," she said, switching to French. "Let me see you try."

We'd done this before. The fight was real and one we both relished in. No gifts. Pure force—and hardcore fucking to end it off.

My fingers tightened on her throat as I slammed her onto the bed, throwing my weight on top of her. I could barely settle before her thighs locked around my waist and she used my momentum to flip us to where she was on top. Her claws sliced deep into my cheek and the pain left my vampire surging to the forefront.

"Oh, you did it now." I threw my weight to the side, rolling us, again, as I grabbed to pin her arms down. No matter how strong Tessa was, she was no match for me. Her shoulders thrashed back and forth and I pulled her wrists higher above her head to lock in one of mine. "Apologize."

"I will not. You deserved more for your betrayal."

I growled, using my free hand to grip her face so she'd have to look at me. Blood dripped just to the side of us from my wound, but I had no intention of making it stop. Tessa would be covered in me before this was over with.

"Apologize."

She made sounds as she fought harder. I reached down cupping her breast and pushing my fingers into the flesh. As my thumb brushed against her nipple, her breaths turned heavier.

Leisurely, I worked my way in until I was rolling the hard nub between my fingers. When she still didn't speak, I pinched, drawing out a cry from her.

"Say the words, ma minette. I did this for us whether you see it or not. You will always be higher ranking than Hunter. You will rule," I said, dropping my voice.

"Will I? Or will you, King Marko Delacroix?"

My teeth clenched and my lips brutally crushed into hers. I didn't want to know what she meant by that. I didn't want to reach within the depths of my mind and flirt with my own longing need to take my place on the throne. That was over. I wouldn't think of it. I couldn't.

"Say it," I said, breaking away. "Last chance."

The second of silence was enough. I flipped her over, bringing my hand down hard over her ass.

"Say it!"

"More."

Whack! "I do this for you." *Whack!* "Can't you see that?" *Whack!* "It's all for you. *Whack!* "Everything." *Whack!* "For." *Whack!* "You!"

Sobs exploded from Tessa and I blinked past the sudden anger that had nothing to do with my vampire.

Was this for her? Suddenly, I wasn't so sure anymore. There had been a moment when I decided…

"I love you," I said, pulling her to her knees, positioning myself behind her. "You know I love you."

"I know." She sobbed again as I jerked at my belt and ripped my pants open. My cock was so hard. So fucking thick that it was aching worse than it had in months.

My fingers dipped down and I couldn't contain the possessive rumble that left me. Tessa's pussy was so wet. So swollen and ready for me. Heat enveloped my digits as I eased two inside of her channel. The way she stretched to fit me was almost too much for me to handle. How long had it been since we'd made love, fucked, anything? Shit, I couldn't remember. Days, but too fucking many for me to care to think about.

Blood dripped along her back and I rubbed it over her skin as I deepened my fingers. Small moans were beginning to fill the room and I withdrew, letting her juices coat my mouth as I sucked her into me. Tenderness could come later. Her energy told me she needed the hardcore pounding of my cock just as much as I needed to give it.

"You're going to apologize," I said, rubbing my tip along her entrance. When I eased inside, I let her adjust just enough for me to surge forward. A cry echoed along the walls and I didn't stop slamming into her.

My hands held to her hips, drawing her back, just in time for me to thrust into her roughly again.

"You love me. You know I do what is right by you, now tell me."

Dark hair swayed and I grabbed it, jerking her head back as I buried myself inside of her and held still. The spanking had her pussy clenching around me like a vice.

"I …"

Whack!

"You're what?"

"I'm…"

Whack!

"Sorry! I'm sorry. I should trust in your decisions. Even if I don't understand the motives."

Peace settled within and I pulled back, slowing my pace as I began to thrust again.

"You really should. What I do, I do for us." *Lie.* The internal whisper was my own voice. No one else's. I tried to push it away, but I couldn't ignore the guilt that was beginning to surface in the pit of my stomach. I shouldn't have been surprised. After all, I knew who I *really* was. Had I thought loving Tessa could change my make-up—my DNA? I'd always been afraid this part of me would return.

"Marko?" The passion in her voice had me letting go of her hair and pushing her to the mattress to lie on her stomach. I stayed inside of her, still fucking. Still taking what was mine.

"I love you."

I whispered the words against her ear, wedging my hand under her hip to play with her clit. Within seconds, Tessa was shaking with spasms and rocking against me. With as built up as I was, I knew I couldn't hold back anymore. My fangs shot down and I went for her neck, biting and pushing in my poison just in time to have another orgasm follow the first for her. The jerky movements beneath me had her pussy clenching and my own release was automatic. But it wouldn't have been had it only been a second later. Something foreign, something different, hit me hard. My vampire grew defensive, sucking against her vein harder as I tried to detect what it was that was off.

"Marko, you're hurting me." The words were breathy, barely decipherable with the way my pulse was roaring in my ears. "Marko?"

Tessa's top half of her body jerked, but I was already wrapping my arms around her, holding her still. Memories came, flashes of the last few weeks, but nothing that I could place as different.

"You're hurting me!" The French broke through the foggy rage and I eased on her neck, somehow managing to break away. "T'es un salaud. What were you thinking?" she asked in English.

"I'm a bastard? What the fuck is that in your blood?" I spun her over, pinning her underneath me as she tried to scramble away. "What is it?" Not what … who? I could feel the tinge of it being a vampire. "You tainted our bond by bringing in someone else? Whose blood did you drink? Who did you bite!" My hand locked around her throat, and for the first time since I'd found my love for Tessa, my vampire was overpowering it. Just like before her change, when she was my slave.

"You go too far," she wheezed out, slamming her energy into me. The force sent me flying back, but I barely landed before I was already rushing back toward her. What I was going to do, I wasn't sure. I didn't get a chance to find out before I ran right into her shield. The impact only fed the anger.

"Whose? Who is it? Are you fucking them, too? Are you giving away what is supposed to be mine?"

My fist slammed into the invisible force and I moved back with it as it extended and Tessa climbed from the bed, reaching for her red dress. It only had me grabbing my jeans and putting them on angrily.

Without a word, she went to the restroom and slammed the door. The water turned on and the dismissal sent me over the edge. Heat seared into my being and for the first time, I put everything I had into destroying her protective barrier. The wall rippled and gave way the exact moment I heard her cry out.

And I was running again. Right for the bathroom door. It flew open at my push and I froze, feeling every emotion I harbored, vanish.

"Tessa? Oh my God, Tessa."

I rushed to her unconscious body, falling to my knees and pulling her into my arms. Blood oozed from the large gash on her forehead, but it wasn't the cut that was my concern.

"Jesus. Breathe, ma minette. Come on."

My head lowered and I pressed my lips into hers, blowing oxygen into her. A loud crash in the distance barely registered as I slapped against her face and tried again.

"Breathe, Goddammit!"

More breaths.

A loud gasp filled the room and her eyes flew open, wide.

"I'm sorry. Please. I'm sorry. I didn't mean to hurt you like that. I only wanted in. I wanted …"

Fuck, I didn't know what I would have done in my rage.

"You have to let go," she groaned, trying to break free.

"No, I want to hold you. I'm sorry."

"She said let go."

The threatening tone had my eyes narrowing. I looked over my shoulder in time to see Aetas lay his hand on Hunter's shoulder. I jerked the robe down from the hook and covered Tessa's body.

"I don't believe I heard a knock, nor did I invite you into my private chambers."

Aetas pushed Hunter behind him, only to step closer. "When I experience pain from a vampire linked to me, I don't need permission to enter. Now, *move*."

"She's *my* concubine," I said, standing and lifting Tessa in my arms. "That overrules everything—rank, ties, bonds, links, royal blood. The princess is mine eternally. The day she said those vows was the day you no longer had authority over what happens behind closed doors. This is a private matter and it doesn't concern you. Now leave so I can make sure she's okay."

"I'm fine. Just put me in bed."

A tear escaped, regardless that she wasn't outwardly crying. I'd hurt her, badly. Just how much, I wasn't sure. She was still blocking me. Where she was mentally strong, my physical strength far outweighed hers. I never knew the extent until now. I'd never allowed myself to find out.

"I said leave." I didn't wait for them to obey before I pushed past them and headed for the bed. The moment I laid her down, her body jolted. "Talk to me, ma minette. Let me feel."

"Marko?" The sob tore my heart to pieces. "I'm sorry. I was so mad at you."

"No, shh. I know you were, but this isn't your fault, it's mine. Open yourself. I have to see how bad this is."

My knees buckled as fiery agony shot through my insides like a firestorm. The core of my stomach was blistering to the point that I could barely stand. If I wouldn't have been leaning on the bed, I would have collapsed.

"Oh, shit. Shit. Here." I went to cut my wrist when Aetas threw me to the side.

"If it is your powers that hurt her, your blood will only intensify her pain."

"I said this wasn't your problem!"

Nearly black eyes shot to me and Aetas' anger had me slowing in my advance. Plenty of times I had seen him mad, but not like this.

"One more word from you and I take back your title. One word."

"I am not the ruler" Tessa said, reaching for Aetas' hand. "I have failed."

"Because you neglect to learn," he said, calmly, turning his attention back to her. Such care was in his eyes as he looked at her. It had my stomach turning as he continued. "But I will teach you, and you will be stronger than any vampire to walk this earth, besides myself. I promise you that."

My eyebrows drew in, and my gaze went to Hunter, who was limping to the other side of the bed. He was in pain, too, but where I clutched to my stomach, he was favoring his right leg. *Aetas and his damn lessons.*

"How does this feel? Is the heat cooling?"

"Yes. Thank you, Master. It's a lot better."

Tessa sniffled, placing her hand on top of our leaders that was hovering just over her midsection. He turned his palm over, squeezing her fingers.

"I'm glad I could help, but you were right, Princess. Just as I was when I told you before. You're not physically ready. Especially now that Marko has weakened you. I'm sorry, but I can't let you continue to rule. With the others coming, we both know it would not be in your best interest. Yes, Marko may be by your side, but we both know a ruler cannot depend on others. They have to be able to save themselves."

Tessa gave a stiff nod, turning her head away from me as another tear escaped.

"What do you mean, I weakened her?"

I swallowed hard, trembling through the overwhelming fear and sickness that swarmed me.

"Come." Aetas waved me over, nearly crushing my wrist as he grabbed on and jerked me to her side. The need to fight against his hold was there, but he was already putting my palm over her stomach. "Become in tune with the princess. Feel."

The pain in my stomach returned to a dull burn, but that wasn't what had my breath hitching. There was a something within the layers of pain. A hollowness that I couldn't quite understand.

"She's damaged, Marko. Her shield may have been up, but she wasn't protecting herself or prepared for such a savage attack. Your power went beyond the physical force she was casting. You hit the source—where her powers come from. And you did so to an extent that she might possibly forever be weakened. I'm not saying that over time she still won't be more powerful than you or anyone else, but we'll never know how strong she could have been."

"No," I said under my breath. "Tessa?"

She was still facing away from me, and still open. I could feel her pain. The betrayal she harbored left the nausea I was experiencing even worse. What was I doing? She'd done nothing but try to be fair to everyone and rule as one should, yet, here I was, hurting her at almost every opportunity.

"I'm sorry," I whispered. "Had I known, I would have never …"

"But you did," Aetas cut in, flinging my hand over to the side. "Did you do it on purpose? Does your greed run so deep?"

"Stop it," Tessa shouted, facing us. "He did not mean to hurt me like that. What's done is done. *All of it*. Marko will rule. I will heal. And then I will restart my lessons."

My eyes widened as I looked down at her. "You're leaving? You're going back with Aetas?"

Emotions, pain, it all vanished, leaving me cold and alone in its departure as Tessa closed herself off. Light green eyes met mine, clouded with more tears. But they didn't fall. She held them in as she nodded. "This is for the best. Some time apart would do us good."

"But …" My head shook, confused. "I know an apology doesn't fix what I've done, but to leave? Tessa, think about this. Remember how it was before when you were with Aetas. Don't leave me. I can make you better. *I* can help you heal."

Something flickered behind her eyes as she stared up at me. What it was, I wasn't sure. But I felt she knew something she wasn't telling me.

"This is for the best. You don't understand right now, but I need you to trust in me. I love you, Marko. Never doubt that."

Tessa's words pushed into my head and the need to ask her whose blood she carried within our own was there, but I couldn't do it. Tessa would never betray me. I knew that in my heart, so what were her reasons? What did she know that I didn't?

Chapter 11
Tessa

"All rise!"

Seduction and lust swirled through the room at Aetas' booming voice. Even for as loud and demanding as it was, the appeal sucked everyone in like a light in the midst of a dark dungeon. We all adored him, needed him as he pushed back the cloak from his shoulder and grabbed the crown. I was strong enough to know what I was feeling was an illusion he was casting upon us all, but I couldn't stop the emotions, nonetheless.

"For the guests here tonight, for the members of this city—we gather here for the coronation of a new king. For the beginning of something that could be truly phenomenal. A new blood line. A new ancestral chart to go down in our history. Master Marko Delacroix's powers have gone far beyond expectation. The gifts he holds makes him unique. His pairing with Princess Tessalyn Delacroix have been a good match to these powers. I've seen them. I've felt them. Since it's been centuries since our last coronation, the laws have been updated accordingly in the best interests of the times."

Aetas' eyes lowered to Marko. "Do you solemnly swear and promise your loyalty to me, your leader, the one who bestows this title upon you?"

"I solemnly swear and promise." Marko answered.

"And do you solemnly swear and promise with this title to make the best judgement according to the laws I have governed to our kind?"

"I solemnly swear and promise."

Aetas stepped from the high members at his sides and came closer to Marko. "Do you solemnly swear and promise to relinquish all rights to this crown and to your title if betray your vows."

"Relinquish?" Confusion masked Marko's face.

"That's right. New law," Aetas said, firmly. "If you betray me, your title means nothing. You will lose it, whether it be your death, or mine."

Marko's hands jerked at his tie and he let it fall to the floor. "I solemnly swear and promise." The jacket followed and he unbuttoned his white shirt, dropping it to the ground as he stared up at our leader and extended his arms out to the sides. It was a sign of surrender, of loyalty to the death.

Aetas' claw shot down. "So be it." His arm rose and he cut across Marko's forehead. Blood ran down his face, racing over the bridge of his nose and eyes. He didn't so much as flinch as Aetas moved to his chest and began to cut an intricately shaped symbol I'd never seen before. I knew it was a crest, and a new one. One that would be Marko's and mine. The swirls and jagged lines made my pulse race faster. Both Aetas' and Marko's powers combined, growing and making it hard to breathe. With as close as I was, standing the arms' length away, my body was trembling at the vibrations.

"Since your powers are merged with the Black Princess, I do believe we have Black Fire. Turn around and show your gift to our curious onlookers. Show them black fire, *by yourself.* If you can show them what I witnessed during my arrival, I will crown you."

My eyes widened at Aetas words. Marko couldn't do that by himself. It was our merged gift. Yes, he held both powers, as I did, but he'd never tried alone. Not that I was aware of, anyway. And it all started with my gift. With my black smoke.

Marko licked his lips, swallowing hard as his eyes locked with mine. Slowly, he turned to face the large room. Vampires looked on in fascination, waiting for what I knew would never come. My heart was breaking, regardless that I had been upset at this outcome. But I knew how much Marko had wanted this. And now he was going to lose it before it ever happened. Right into front of everyone—rulers and commoners. Aetas had done this on purpose. As a lesson for his greed.

A deep exhale left Marko as his hands rose to cup in front of him. Concentration took over his features and he stared into the emptiness within. In quick movements, I gazed between him and the smug expression on Aetas' face. The look our leader cast me had me throwing him a glare as I turned back to Marko.

Sweat was mixing with the blood as seconds passed. His brow was creased and a slight tremble took over him as he drew his hands in closer. Darkness flickered within his palm. It faded in and out, disappearing as if it never existed. He shook his head, his features turning hard as his eyes shut through the anger I could see appearing. When his lids opened, an odd expression appeared and he dropped his arms.

Black took over his eyes and smoke seeped from his full lips, swirling as it crept into the air before him. His hands rose again, circling around the increasing fog. A smile burst on to my face as he molded it and pushed his own gift inside. Bright blue flared within the black, followed by orange and yellows. It came alive inside the darkness, pushing the smoke out to grow in size. Larger it became, until it was bigger than his own towering frame.

Aetas' lips parted as he took steps forward. The shock was written all over and there was no hiding it. But he wasn't the only one. His members gathered closer, their eyes filling with amazement and something I knew all too well. *Fear.* What Marko was displaying was something that had never been done before. Something that was going to change things forever. It was our beginning, both his and mine. If he could do it, someday, I would be able to, too.

The large weapon Marko held withdrew, disappearing into his palm. Anger reappeared as he spun toward Aetas. "I believe that was satisfactory of a king?"

Aetas straightened, waving his fingers to the members behind him. A woman with short brown hair rushed forward, bearing the satin pillow that held the crown. Aetas didn't turn around as she came to a stop at his side, lowering to her knees. Instead, his hand rose, and with it, the crown levitated, rising between him and Marko.

"King, Marko Delacroix. The Black Fire King."

Marko and Aetas kept their eyes locked as the dark crown, so similar to mine, came to rest on my husband's head. The shockwave that rushed through me and the others was like nothing I had felt before. We all fell to our knees, not only as a sign of respect, but because our vampires didn't have a choice.

"Long live the king!"

The shout came from somewhere in the crowd, and the mantra quickly began to echo around us. Marko's bloodstained body turned to face the room and I slowly rose at the upward flicker of his hands.

"Long live the king," he repeated. "And long live my queen." He turned and held his hand out to me. A smile stretched across my face and I walked forward, so proud of what he had proven to them all. I knew his powers were great, but what he had shown was far beyond what I thought him capable of. He deserved this—to rule, and to be king.

I came to stop at his side, smiling bigger as he brought my hand up to his lips. When he pulled me in and wrapped his arm around my waist, the crowd exploded with shouts and clapping. Our city was thriving, and so much happier than I had seen them in a long time. What Marko was given wasn't just a title, but an honor. It spoke for not only him, but for every one of us. Our city would be set apart from the rest. Feared by the other leaders, but craved by the commoners who would no doubt want to become part of something so grand. We would give the appeal of greatness. Of protection from a king. The only king aside from Aetas.

"Let the festivities begin!"

Aetas' voice once again rang out and the sounds of the tables mingled with the remaining cheering. Marko turned us to face Aetas and his members, who held steady behind our leader. Even Hunter had moved in from the spot he'd taken up at the very back of them.

"This is a day to celebrate," Aetas said, coming in to wrap his arm around Marko's free one. As he began to lead us to the large table where our own members usually sat, he lowered his voice. "We have had issues in our past, but I'm no fool. You are a king, Marko. You have been blessed with not only your true gift, but with falling in love with the princess. The merge of the two of your powers couldn't have been any more perfect. That you have been able to control both as you have, shows exceptional strength, worthy of the title you carry. I want to give you a gift to express this new beginning for the two of us."

"A gift?"

Marko glanced over. I felt his suspicion, but I felt my own as well. This didn't seem like Aetas. Was he truly wanting to put aside their past?

"That's right. Tonight you feed from me. And I will feed from you."

Marko jolted us to a stop. "You want to tie with me?"

A smile stretched across Aetas' face and he narrowed his eyes at me before turning back to Marko. My blood turned cold. He knew … and he was doing just as I had. He was keeping his friends close, but his enemies closer. Where I used Hunter's innocence to tie so he could never turn on me or our kind, Aetas was using my exact plan, only with Marko. And he wouldn't need more than one exchange to know Marko's true intentions, whatever they were. He was too powerful for that.

"We tie in front of everyone. They'll see our loyalty to each other. They will know my support of you."

Marko, let out a deep breath, but nodded. "I will tie with you, if that's alright with my queen, of course."

"Queen Tessalyn?"

Aetas' eyebrow rose as the smile turned to a smirk. I looked between the two of them, glancing over at Hunter before bringing my focus back to the two men who were awaiting my answer.

"I think it would be an honor to tie with our leader."

"Excellent." Aetas led us forward again and I couldn't stop the sickening feeling that was taking over. "This is going to be a great alliance between the four of us," Aetas continued. "You and I will tie, and the queen and Hunter will do the same. All four of us will come together and the three of you will dominate our world. It is a great partnership."

"Wait." Marko's pulled his arm free of our leader as we stopped at the table. "Tessa and Hunter?"

"Of course," Aetas said, firmly. "Hunter is my only creation. He is part of me. He will most certainly rise to the top when his powers develop. That is fact. In time, the three of you may be my top members at headquarters. For all of us to be close is essential, wouldn't you agree?"

Marko's stare left Aetas to settle on Hunter. The hatred was evident on both sides as the men locked eyes.

"It's time to forget the past and move forward. You are king, and Tessalyn, you're queen. I've explained that to Hunter and it may be hard for him to understand now, but as he grows older, he will come to accept this and find his own concubine. Then there will be no more feuds. No more jealousy. We can make this work."

Still, Marko kept his sights on Hunter. I cleared my throat, turning to Aetas. "You talk as if we are not in a war. As if behind these walls, the humans aren't planning another attack on our city. Are you saying you will stop this impending battle? Will we all go back into hiding and forgotten from human minds?"

The members around us stopped talking, turning their attention to our leader. It was enough to even have Marko and Hunter focused on Aetas.

"We will not speak of such things during Marko's celebration. Besides, we have plenty of time before we have to worry about war."

"Do we?" Marie closed in at my side. "Do we have time, Your Highness? I don't feel as though we do. The very fabric of human society is unraveling and if we close our eyes to it, I'm afraid it may be a mistake on our part. If you ask me, we're already there."

"Someone's suddenly become brave." Aetas' head cocked to the side as he peered into Marie's lowering face. Her eyes darted up through her lashes, but she wouldn't meet his stare.

"I'm sorry if I spoke out of turn."

"No, no," he whispered, reaching to bring her face back up. You're close to the king and queen. They trust you. Perhaps there's a reason."

Marie glanced over at me.

"She is to be trusted. Her visions are very powerful and their accuracy is usually dead on."

"Are they? I am in need of someone new."

Aetas' voice was almost silent as he whispered the words. Alarm flashed over Marie's features, but she straightened and met his gaze head on. For seconds they were silent and I knew Aetas had breached her walls and was breaking through her memories and predictions. When he blinked and turned to me, I barely caught Marie's falling form.

"I'm impressed, even if she is a bit … delayed. I'm sorry to take her, but it is vital she move to headquarters and associate herself with my members. To prepare."

"Prepare?"

Aetas nodded. "Her gift is only given to a few and she needs to strengthen it. Right now she's the strongest alive. It's best if I keep it that way. She'll become part of my circle."

The shock hit me hard, but Marie, harder. Her hand clutched to my bicep as she tried to stay steady on her feet.

"I'm … honored. I …" Her eyes flickered to me and I quickly shook my head, reading her thoughts from our tie.

"You will not apologize or worry for leaving us." I smiled, brushing back the dark curl that had escaped the pins holding her hair back. "You're going to show them who you are, and you're going to wow them with your gift. This was meant to happen, Marie. This is your path."

I leaned forward, pressing my lips against her cheek.

"It wouldn't be if it weren't for you. You," she said, lowering her voice, "are destined for great things, but you know that."

"I believe we all do," Aetas said, cutting in. "Let's sit, shall we. Everyone that is, but our queen. She will be our first entertainment for the night."

The slight grin on my face fell. "I'm not sure I understand."

"You will sing for your king. For all of us. I do believe you know how."

"But … I don't sing anymore. I mean, not since my change."

"A waste. Please, let us hear you."

Chairs slid out as everyone began taking their place. My pulse was pounding and I wasn't sure why. The passion I held dear to me was gone   as dead as the human version of me.

Marko paused just outside of one of the chairs at the head of the table. Two were positioned next to each other and I knew the other was Aetas'.

"I'd love to," I forced out.

As I walked to the far back of the room, I took deep breaths to push away the sudden anxiety. I could do this. I'd done it a million times before. The only thing different was my lack of joy at the thought of using my voice. Had I lost myself so much? The reality left my steps slower.

I had. I wasn't even sure who I was anymore. Ruler—not the ruler. I was weak now.

The vermin were already waiting as I approached. My hand had a slight tremble to it as I rose, pushing my fingertip into the violinist's temple. "I want this played slow. Make it beautiful." I moved to the next, taking my turn as I gave them clips of the song I wished to sing. The lyrics were half French, half English. But the violin was more important than any of the words of love and loyalty. They spoke a language of their own. Played the right way, the tune had the ability to lure and capture all who focused in on the sound. And I wanted that. I wanted the vampires and other rulers to remember this night. To remember a king who was going to be so great that they told the story of this night to anyone who would listen. *King Marko Delacroix. The Black Fire King.*

Chapter 12
Hunter

The first note of the violin drew in everyone's attention. Everyone but mine. Although the need to take in the princess was there, the overwhelming hatred I felt for Marko was outweighing it. *A king.* He wanted something I would never have and he got it. He had everything—the woman I wanted, a higher title, and now a tie with our leader? It wasn't fair. I may have disliked Aetas, but my vampire knew what Marko's entitlements meant. He'd be more powerful than I would. I couldn't stand it.

"Do you know this song?" Aetas was leaned in toward Marko as they both kept their attention on Tessa.

"I don't believe so. It's beautiful though."

"Indeed," Aetas' whispered, leaning in closer. His eyes closed and he inhaled Marko deeply.

My fangs thickened in my mouth as they battled with whether to come down or not. My maker was desperate to taste Marko. Why? I didn't understand it. I didn't understand *anything*. It drove me crazy. What was so good about him? His power? His taste? The queen fed from him, too, and she obviously liked it.

"Are you opposed to completely bonding?"

Marko blinked heavily, turning to face Aetas. "You want to bond with me?"

Aetas rotated in his chair, frowning before he leaned back in. "I do."

"Why would you want to do that?"

The violin continued as our leader went through multiple expressions. "I'm feeling your energy and the power you project even when you're calm. I think the match would be a good one—you and I. You have some of Black King's blood in you from Tessa, you have yours. Combine those with mine and that's one hell of a combination for both of us."

"You hate me. Why be completely bonded? That puts me in your mind and you in mine. It makes us equal, minus your experience and age. Who's to say even one tie will work? Your blood is probably so strong that it'll cancel mine out. Perhaps you weren't meant to bond to anyone."

A grin pulled at Aetas' lips. "Only one way to find out. I happen to think your blood stands a chance. Mine might even welcome it. I've never tried to bond before."

"You know what that'll mean for me and Tessa if you and I bond." Marko's brow furrowed, but I knew nothing else as the queen's voice broke through the nearly silent room. The power behind the soft tone carried and echoed against the walls, tugging at some internal trigger in my mind. Flashes began to blind me. Ones I'd never seen before. It was of me and Tessa. We were human …and I was sitting in what I knew was a church, listening to her sing. I was in just as much awe as I felt now. I was in love. So deeply in love with her.

From my peripheral, Aetas leaned forward, watching just as Marko was doing now. The violin drew out, matching the pitch of her voice. The two together were one, and yet, two completely different life forces. My heart was increasing in rhythm. Of an anticipation I couldn't even begin to decipher.

The lyrics switched to French and even though I could only decipher a few of the words the queen was saying, I pieced the meaning together as if I spoke the language fluently. I was being given a promise with her verses. She was singing of something so great that it was undeniable to question whether or not it was going to come true.

Praise was whispered throughout the lands.
The pain of time slipped through his hands.
His blood-stained sword, his name and word.
His tale, his legend, would be heard.

Marko's hands flattened on the table, drawing my attention as he slowly stood. He was entranced. Hypnotized, just like the rest of us as Tessa let the violin finish.

"Thank you. For our king," she said, bowing.

Marko was already walking toward her at a fast pace. The deep kiss he presented her with had blood filling my mouth. I rolled my eyes to Aetas, who was staring ahead at them just as love-struck of their presence as every other sap in this place.

"How much longer?" I ground out. "I need to feed."

Annoyance followed his gaze as he turned to me. "Soon. You will learn to control your cravings. And cheer up." He threw me grin. "You get to feed from the queen. With as much power that's going to be going through this room, anything could happen. Can you feel it, Prince? Can you feel the electricity in the air?" He waved his hand as a manipulative expression surfaced. Heat blasted over my skin and my cock grew hard. "I forgot how coronations could be. So much excitement with the entertainment. So much sex and lust."

The anger fizzled out and I held in the moan as I whipped my focus to the queen.

"Remember what I said earlier. Remember to ask permission, my prince." He winked at me as Marko and Tessa started walking over.

A group of men were collecting in the middle of the large room and human women were pushed in their direction. They were nude, covering themselves as they wildly looked around and let out squeaks of fear.

"Beautiful song," Aetas rang out as Marko and Tessa took their seat. The queen was directly across from me, and Marko took his seat next to our leader. "I've never heard that one before. Where did you learn it?"

A blush came to Tessa's cheeks. Her chest was rising in a rapid rhythm and I couldn't tear my eyes away from the cleavage spilling free of the low cut evening gown she wore. The white lace underneath the corset did little to conceal the exposed portion of her breasts.

"Church, believe it or not. It wasn't a song we sung during service, but one an older women in the choir knew. We spent weeks after practice perfecting it."

"I'd say so. It was magical. Very," Aetas hand rose and his finger shook as he searched for what he wanted to say.

"Enchanting?" I offered.

"Yes," He said, pointing toward me. "Thank you, Prince. Enchanting, indeed, yet, I'm not sure there's a word to really describe the magnitude."

Tessa threw me a smile and went back to him. "It's the violin. It wraps itself around the lyrics and gives the effect."

Aetas shook his head. "No, I'm pretty sure they both did their job, but it was you—your voice interlaced with them. The whole thing was breathtaking."

"Thank you, again." Tessa's cheeks grew even redder and she peeked over to Marko.

"You know I loved it," he said, as if reading her mind. "You couldn't have picked a more meaningful song." He tapped over his heart and lifted her hand to kiss along her knuckles. When his teeth nipped at the ends, my fingers gripped to the edge of the table for stability. He wanted her, right here and right now, and so did I.

Screams and laughter erupted in the background, mixing with conversation to the right of me. It was all too much for the burning that was taking over my throat. Not to mention my cock. I was so fucking hard. How was I hard when all I wanted to do was tear the king apart?

"I think its time."

Marko turned to look at Aetas and tightened his jaw, nodding.

"Queen, you will feed from the prince, and he from you. We bond and make this official. We start something amazing."

Tessa's mouth opened, only to close. She met Marko's eyes and seconds passed before he nodded. Whether they were internally communicating or not was beyond me. I didn't care as I watched her stand and walk around the table. I pushed out the chair, giving her room to take her position on my lap. Her weight settled and Marko's negative energy had me glancing up. He didn't speak, but he didn't have to. The threat was clear. If I did anything to hurt her, he'd act out on what he really wanted to do.

A weird heat hit me again and I shook my head trying to figure out what it was. Fuck, I couldn't breathe, and my skin. It was tingling all over.

"Prince." Tessa's hand slid over the length of my cheek as she lowered to sit on my right leg. "Look at me," she purred. "See only me."

Moans erupted somewhere in the distance and my maker's words came barreling back. Anything was possible. *Sex.* Yes, people were having sex right here in front of everyone. The screams, the laughter, they fed the bloodlust that was taking over all of us. With our leader present, the atmosphere was being fed with his power. With Marko and Tessa's power. Not to mention all the other leaders. But that heat?

"Look at you? But I've only ever seen you." Where my words came, I had no idea. Tessa's eyebrows drew in and she brought her face closer to mine, staring deeply into my eyes.

"You haven't remembered on your own yet. How do you know this?"

My fingers circled around her wrist and I leaned more into her touch. "The heart doesn't need to be reminded of what the mind fails to remember."

Her lids closed and she lowered her head. Her face rubbed against the side of mine, before she lowered even more. Breath brushed along my ear and I shivered.

"You were my best friend. I loved you, but I love another now."

"Can't you love us both?"

Fingers sunk into my short hair and Tessa jerked my head to the side. Pain flared in my neck followed by the most pleasurable dose of ecstasy I had ever felt. Deep breaths left me as the monster inside went crazy to have her. Aetas' words kept me from tearing her clothes off. *Remember to ask permission.*

My eyes darted over to Marko, who held just as much of a pained expression on his face. We were both torn. Both in the best hell we could ever be in. Aetas bite…his poison…I hadn't felt it yet. Not the same kind that Tessa was using, but I knew our leader was using it on Marko now. There was too much confliction, too much lust tightening his face. And he was sweating, just like I was.

"Please."

Tessa's suction increased and I knew I wasn't talking to her. I kept my stare on Marko. I was begging. Pleading for his permission. It was the only way and I hated it.

"Anything," I managed. "Name it."

A growl left Marko, but he could barely bare his fangs at me. His body was beginning to tremble.

"Jesus," I moaned. Was having her right here and now worth my death? I suddenly wasn't so sure. It might be. To have her once and die happy? Yes, I could live with that.

"Fuck!" Marko's voice rumbled as his hand slammed down on the table and his nails dug into the thick wood. Soft laughter was shaking Aetas' chest, but he didn't break from Marko's neck.

What felt like a wave of heat blasted through me, again, and the tingling covering my skin got a hundred times more intense. Louder laughter rang out wildly in the distance and Tessa was suddenly spinning on my lap, moaning as she pushed her breasts into my chest. The wave … it was like a drug, intoxicating everyone around us. *Aetas.* He was doing this intentionally. He was the one controlling it.

"No more." Marko panted, squinting as more sweat trickled down his face. "Aetas."

Our leader's hand locked on Marko's face holding him still as he continued to feed. I knew the moment my maker pushed more venom into him. Marko's shoulders thrashed, but he couldn't break away. Aetas' hand traced down his neck, lowering even more to his chest. Tessa's rocking against my hard cock made me lose focus. My eyes closed and I was suddenly pushing my hands up her dress to rest them on her smooth thighs. Tightly, I squeezed, trying to stop myself from going further.

"Marko." I clamped my teeth together. "King."

"Shut up, Hunter!" Marko voice was so pained I was barely able to make out his words.

"Then say yes. Say yes!"

The growling grew louder until it stopped. My eyes flew open, widening as I watched Marko pull in Aetas' bloody face. When their lips connected my mind went blank.

"I don't know whether to kiss you or hit you." Marko broke away, his eyes glazed as he stood, only to fall back to his chair.

"This is only the beginning. I suggest you not hit. Kiss … you're welcome to do it again."

Tessa broke from my neck, gasping and rubbing her face along the blood still oozing from the puncture wounds.

"What have you done," Marko slurred. "What are you doing to us?"

"I'm making it a night you never forget. No one here is going to judge. Look around you."

Lightheadedness overtook me as I glanced behind me to see what he was talking about. The room had become one large orgy. So much flesh and blood. Everyone was drunk on power. On Aetas' power.

"Bite me," Tessa moaned, moving against me. Do it, Hunter."

"Wait." Marko staggered to his feet and I had no idea how he was managing. Everything was swaying, or I was. My body was so alive that every part of me was screaming to be touched. Hell, I was still up the queen's dress, growing closer to her ass, and I couldn't stop.

The table rocked as Marko stumbled into it. When he got before us, his glare eased. "Spin her over."

I obeyed, not sure why he wanted me to.

"Marko." Tessa reached for him, moving her ass along my cock as she did so.

"That's right, ma minette. I'm going to fuck you right here on top of Hunter. You want that?" He smiled, diving in to kiss her. As he did so, I felt her other hand pulling at the button of my pants.

"Yes. Fuck me. I want to feel both of you come. I want …"

"Both of us?" Marko's head reared back, but he didn't' stop himself from unbuttoning his own pants.

"Both of you."

Another force swept through the room again and Marko's lip lifted in distaste for only a moment before he turned her onto one of my legs and ripped the material of her dress. A cry came from my mouth and I couldn't stop from wrapping my hand around her thigh to spread her legs wider for him.

"That's it," Marko moaned. "Perfect."

He lowered and his thick length plunged into her. She screamed as she scrambled to get my cock free. My arm was cradled around her shoulder, but I couldn't get a good enough angle to bite.

"Yes. God, yes. Fuck." Tessa's moans increased as she began to stroke up and down my cock. My legs shot out and I tightened my features as I tried to adjust to the overwhelming pleasure.

"You like that, baby?" Marko's face was so close to me. He was so near and he wasn't trying to tear my throat out, and neither was I. God, we were so far gone.

"Not like this," I groaned. "Flip her on her knees so she can rest on my thighs. Fuck her from behind."

When Marko kept thrusting, I knew he wasn't hearing me. He knew nothing but her.

"Master Delacroix, King," I said, louder.

Aetas was suddenly next to me. "Let me help." He reached over, tracing his finger down Marko's cheek. The action was enough to have the king jerking his head to look over. The anger left the moment he registered our leader. Aetas eased Marko up, turning to fix Tessa the way I had suggested.

"Fuck her while you taste me, King." Our leader's hand settled on my shoulder as he pulled the collar of his shirt open. Marko didn't have to be told twice. He surged back into Tessa, holding at her waist as he dove forward to our leader's waiting frame.

"Bite me, Hunter. Taste me. Give me everything you have."

My precum had Tessa's hand gliding down my length at the perfect speed. My hips thrust forward while I tore at the silk covering her breasts. The weight filling my palm had me burying my face in her neck.

"Ahhh," Tessa cried out as my fangs slid into her. "Yes. More. *More*."

The poison leaving me was a relief. Almost an orgasm on its own. But the blood … I'd never get used to the addicting taste or power. It had me moving under her, faster. Thrusting into her palm as I craved more. To feel the heat of her pussy around me, I would have done anything.

Loud sounds were coming from Marko while he still fed and slammed into Tessa almost violently. I tightened on her nipple and her body shook with spasms. The orgasm turned her blood sweeter, more intoxicating as I drank it down. I couldn't get my fill fast enough. Each swallow was different. Better than the last.

Aetas hand tightened against me, but I barely felt it as I tried to control the need to come. Tessa's strokes were too good. Mixed with her increasing scent and taste, I was in a realm of consciousness I never knew existed. This went beyond heaven. Beyond words or even a state of being.

"You want to come so badly, my king," Aetas groaned. "Fuck, so do I. Your poison is good. So fucking good." He breathed out, heavily. "I want it as my own. God, I do."

I felt Tessa's arm being pulled up and I knew it was Aetas. Her fumbling with his belt was an afterthought. Another blast hit us and we all tore at each other worse than before. I broke from Tessa's neck, crushing my lips into hers. The hunger that was returned was what my dreams were made of. My hands slid up to her face and I didn't have to urge her lower. She moved on her own accord. Her lips encased the tip of my cock, so hot, so unbelievably wet as she ran her tongue around the head.

Her arm moved as she slid down Aetas' long length and I felt my eyes roll. With the amount of pleasure, everything was blurring together, like flashes or clips of a movie. I knew I was here and I knew what we were doing was happening, but it almost felt like I was someone else.

"This is too good," Aetas mumbled. "Too good. Fuck."

Tessa's head plunged down, and the suction she applied drew me deeper into her sweet mouth. My hand shot out and I grabbed Aetas' thigh as some sort of anchor. Marko was breaking away, trying to breathe as he still fucked Tessa. His eyes were rolling, too, and if it weren't for him holding onto Aetas and Tessa, I was sure he would have fallen over.

"Open your eyes, King. Look at me." Aetas lifted Marko's face, pressing his lips into Marko's before his head was lifted all the way. The passion, the hunger, both of them had it as Marko's pace increased, again. Tessa's hand was even going faster along Aetas' length. She lifted, taking me deeper, stoking me at the same speed as him.

"You love this." Aetas went back for another kiss, teasing Marko as he waiting. "This is who we are. This is in the core of each and every one of us. Do you feel it?" Aetas slammed us with another wave. "People have called it our glamour. They think it only revolves around eye contact, or a mysterious sexual appeal. I tell you, there is so much more. Each gift we harbor. Everything that makes us who we are, if it were tapped into to the fullest, tapped into like I have done, can you imagine? No one looks past these little things. That is what makes them ordinary. We, the four of us, we are not like them. We are so much more. Our power together. Yours and mine." Aetas kissed him again. "Tessalyn's and Hunter's. We will discover things never imagined."

A loud yell echoed through the room as Aetas dove back for Marko's throat. Blood sprayed across my face as Aetas violently slit to his own wrist. He was shoving the wound in Marko's mouth, forcing his blood back on the king. It wasn't seconds before Marko's orgasm hit him. He was clawing at Aetas arm, even as he held our leader's wrist to his mouth. Tessa pulled at me and there was no cost, no repercussions, as I gripped her thighs and eased her down my cock.

Her arms locked around my neck and I hugged around her hard, pulling her down until she rested at my base. The gasp sounded loud in my ear and I used my weakened strength to start moving her against me.

"What are we doing?" she mumbled. "I can't think. There's too much pleasure."

"Don't think," I said, finding her lips. "Kiss me. Taste me. *Fucking have me*."

Her tongue slipped into my mouth while she rotated her hips. Faster we went, so full of passion that I wasn't thinking. Tessa clutched to me tighter and when she began to scream from her release, I didn't hold back. I didn't prolong what may never happen again.

Come shot from my cock, repeatedly, and I growled through the intensity. One minute Tessa was wrapped around me, breathing hard. The next, gone. Marko had her in his arms, looking back at us panicked as he fled the room.

Chapter 13
Marko

For two days Tessa and I stayed secluded. We were like zombies, lost in our thoughts, and unable to speak more than two words to each other. I wasn't sure whether I should be mad at her, or myself. Fuck, we'd both done things … things we couldn't resist at the time. Things we would have never done had we been in control of our actions.

A knock sounded at the door and both of our heads snapped to look at each other. Dread flashed on our faces before I forced myself to stand. "It's Demetrius."

She nodded, sadness coming to her face. I knew it was because she didn't have the power to rule anymore. I'd ruined that for her by injuring her. I would have gotten it back, anyway, but the guilt over what I had done was still there. And then there was still her secret. It made my anger surface once again. I flung the barrier open, faced with Demetrius' pale features. His nervousness was apparent as he avoided my stare.

"Master … King, I have a request from Aetas. He wishes to meet with you and the queen at your earliest convenience."

"He's still here?" Tessa stood and I nodded. Of course he was. I felt his every move. His ever pace, back and forth in his room. With how close he was, our connection was only stronger. So why didn't he just tell me himself?

"Ten minutes."

He bowed, turning away. I shut the door, leaning against it as I tried to push the memories away. God, I'd kissed him. Kissed him with every intention of fucking him. I would have if I wouldn't have had Tessa as a distraction. The mindfuck that brought sent me spinning. It wasn't the fact that it was a man that left me baffled. It was Aetas! I hated him. Despised him. Or, I had. Now I wasn't so sure. That made everything worse.

"Marko." Tessa wrung her hands as she came forward. "I have to tell you something. That day. The one where you hit me with your powers." Her head lowered, only to raise with determination. "You tasted something in me."

"Yes. But not something, ma minette. Some *one*."

She nodded. "After you refused to kill Hunter, I had a plan. One that I thought would be perfect. I wasn't sure I wanted him dead, but I didn't trust him either. I … tied us. One mark. No sex. Not until," she flinched, slicing her hand down as if she could erase the images she was seeing. "The night of your coronation was the first time. The only time."

"Wait. You're telling me you went behind my back and tied with a man that I hate. That I want to kill. All because of what? You didn't trust me when I said I'd take care of it!"

"You didn't take care of it. Besides, I don't want him dead anymore. My main objective was to be tied enough to watch him. To know if he ever changed and decided to attack us. I wanted to prepare for his betrayal. I thought if we connected like that then he'd have second thoughts when the time came. Or … I don't know. It was right at the time, but it was pointless. Aetas had us tie anyway. Now we hold two ties."

"Just as me and Aetas." I cursed, walking in a circle as I tried to lift the fog that kept my brain so confused. "You're forgiven. Never lie or do something like that behind my back again."

Tessa frowned. "I won't." She stepped closer. "Do you think they want more from us? Do you think they're calling us back to—"

"No," I rushed in. "No." The denial, my denial, left me repeating the word.

"Can you read his mind? Maybe you can see what he wants?"

My head shook. "He's too powerful. I can only get random words scattered throughout. Nothing that makes sense."

"What about Hunter?" I asked.

"Hold on." Her eyes scanned the floor, but I knew she wasn't seeing the cement before her. "He." She stopped and looked up, growing tense.

"He what?"

"He's just excited to see me. That's what his thoughts revolve around."

I rolled my eyes, reaching over and sliding on my jacket. "Of course. And here I am, about to lose you to *them*—Hunter *and* Aetas. I can't believe you offered yourself up for more lessons. You can't take that back, ma minette."

"I know," she said, pained. "That was before. Before …" Her words trailed off and I walked forward, pulling her into my arms. "We can't keep talking about this. We have to focus on the future. About what lies ahead. You've dealt with Aetas before. You're stronger than you were, then."

"Did you not see what he did to all of us? To a room full of thousands of vampires? I am but one, Marko. He hides the extent of his powers well," she said, looking up at me. "I have so much to learn. If I don't go, I'll never stand a chance against him or anyone of his caliber. I have to. I have to prepare for Hunter. To see his powers and what he's capable of."

"And so you will. Every few days I will come to see you. Or you, me. Whatever is allowed." She nodded while I led her to the door. "Things have been rocky the last few days, but you know I love you, yes?"

"Yes. And I love you. This is nothing we can't get passed. Our love is stronger than this."

I kissed her lips, leading her over the threshold. The tunnel was dark and I couldn't stop the bad feeling in the pit of my stomach. Before I could knock on Aetas' door, he opened it, gesturing for us to enter. My skin tingled at his nearness and I tried to ignore how I felt the air thicken around us.

Hunter was sitting in a chair toward the back of the room, his hands clasped, his head down, but those eyes. They ate Tessa alive, begging for things I wouldn't let myself think on. *Tessa.* What had she done by secretly tying herself to Hunter? Had Aetas known? Is that why he tied himself to me? What were the reasons? None of this made sense. The questions ate at me as I glanced down to see Tessa's indecipherable stare aimed at her former best friend.

My poor Tessa. *She lived in a hell of her own creation. She was the queen and I was the demons that fed her fiery depths.* Maybe this was my fault. Maybe I should have gotten it over with and killed him instead of sparing his life for a crown. Oddly, I wasn't so sure I wanted him dead either.

Aetas' presence behind me had me turning and putting my back against the wall.

"I see the two of you are having a hard time accepting the events that happened during your coronation. I have to admit, I'm a little surprised how it played out, myself." Aetas walked past to sit on the edge of the bed. "I got a little carried away."

"A little?" One of my eyebrow's rose and he twisted his mouth.

"Okay, maybe a lot, but what harm came from it? We were all enjoying ourselves, were we not?"

I shifted uncomfortably, as did Tessa.

"What are your true intentions for these ties?"

"I've already told you. I'm letting go of the past and looking toward our futures."

"That's bullshit. I feel you, remember? You're up to something."

Aetas smiled, half amused, the other half filled with that of a darker nature. "Is it so wrong to want to be bonded with such power? You have amazing gifts, Marko. I can't help but be jealous of them. If that means my greed matches your own, then so be it."

"Bond?" Shock filled Tessa's tone. "I thought we were talking ties. To bond to Marko, that would mean …"

Deviousness crept into Aetas' eyes. "My bond would erase your own. I'm aware of that. But you're his concubine. Is that not bond, enough?"

My jaw tightened. "You can't break mine and Tessa bond. My leader or not, I cannot consent to that."

Aetas pushed from the bed, looking between me and Tessa. "You could have the world at your fingertips, Marko. *King*. Does that not appeal?"

Of course it did, but my greed didn't outweigh my connection to Tessa. I'd fought for it when I thought it was out of reach. I had died inside when I thought I lost her. To throw that away for more power, it wasn't worth it.

"Appeal, why yes. But I'm afraid I must decline."

Aetas' face turned hard. "Then I'm afraid you leave me no choice."

Tessa was ripped from my side so fast that by the time I turned to reach for her, Aetas was already on me. Hunter was pulling her further away, locking her arms to her sides as she screamed and kicked. Fire sliced into my neck and as I searched for my powers, they were nowhere to be found. The wall I hit was not one of my own, but one of Aetas'.

"No!" An explosion shook the room and in what looked like slow motion, Tessa was running toward me. Hunter was right behind, tackling her down to the ground so she lay on her stomach. His head shot down and she cried out from his bite. Blood sprayed across the floor as he sliced his wrist. The events were so unreal and in sync that when he shoved his wrist under her mouth, it was as though he did it to mine. But it wasn't his. It was Aetas' and his blood was pouring into my mouth. My head couldn't shake. I couldn't bite down to tear into his flesh. We rolled and the blood was choking me as he attempted to drown me in it.

"Now, *you and I* are one," he whispered in my ear. "If I die, *you die*. You'll never take my thrown, Marko Delacroix. Never!"

Sounds left me and the truth had me feeling sick. I gagged as more blood forced its way down my throat. The electrical currents that followed zapped me with the force of God, himself. A roar left me and my body convulsed, jerking violently as his essence and power decimated my bond with Tessa. The hollowness that followed was like nothing I'd ever felt before. What replaced love was something so dark, so unexplainably vile, my mind couldn't grasp it. Even in the worst times of my life—human or vampire—never had I been filled with such hatred. Such need to destroy. And it was coming from Aetas' blood.

Tessa's echoing sobs faded out. My body was still thrashing. Bowing. Yes, I felt as if I were twisting every way but the right way. Acid was crashing through my veins in a wild flood of fire. I could feel every pathway that weaved throughout my form bulging with my leader's strength.

"Fuck, God." His voice broke through and he was crumbling down next to me, laughing crazily as he pulled me in closer to his side. Arms wrapped around me, one behind my head, the other around my side, cradling me like a lover. His lips pressed into mine and we both jolted at the new rounds of agony merging us together.

"I have to be truthful, Marko Delacroix. I do believe a part of me has fallen in love with you. I want to be you. I want to take over your life—your wife."

A guggling was coming from my throat as I tried to get words to form.

"Hunter and I will pick up where we left off at the coronation. With them bonded, and you locked away, feeding me your powers, no one has to know that I'm not you. They all saw us tie. If they sense me it would only make sense since you carry my blood." Again he laughed. "The leader everyone knows is about to die, my king, and the world is going to fall to the ground around us. There will be chaos in the streets with which the world has never known. And only when it is all over with and we're hanging on by a thread, will I rise again. After all, there has to be a hero in this story. Who better than the villain our people believe I have become?"

I managed to suck in a breath as ice began to accumulate in the pit of my stomach. My core rippled and Aetas face began to change, wavering with a darker tone. My features took shape and his fangs shot down. I could see my hand on his chest. The pigment was lightening, changing color as I began to take over his appearance.

"No," I breathed out. "N—"

"Shhh. Now you will sleep. Sleep, my king. You will not awake until you are entombed in my final resting place, but do not fear, I will make it so you do not perish. After all, I wouldn't want to hurt myself."

"Tess….Te…"

Darkness was pulling me under. In my mind I was screaming. Crying out and begging for someone, for anything to happen, to stop this. It was pointless. Something was happening to me and there was nothing I could do about it. I was going to be just as dead as Aetas would appear to our kind. And the world … it was doomed.

Chapter 14
Tessa

Before I could force out another scream, Hunter was scrambling off of me, staring around the room wildly. He blinked as if he were confused. With the newly formed bond we had, I felt his thoughts barrel into me out of nowhere.

God, where am I? What happened? The room registered and he stopped, looking down at me. *Jesus, did I do that to her? Aetas.*

His head whipped over and mine followed. Marko was scrambling to his feet, stumbling away from Aetas' unconscious body. Or …

The energy had me clawing my way to stand.

"Oh my God!" I couldn't stop the scream that left me as I rushed to Aetas' body. Regardless of what he had planned, breaking our bonds and replacing them with others, he was my leader. The loyalty my vampire felt for him could not be mistaken. "Aetas." I turned his head back and forth and reached down searching for a pulse. All I could hear was the heavy thudding of my own. Panic was setting in. And grief. I couldn't stop the overwhelming emotions that were causing the anxiety. They were so out of place and yet, they felt right. "Aetas, please. No, no."

My head jerked to Marko as a sob escaped. "What happened?"

His eyes were wide while he took deep breaths. "I don't know. We were bonding and I felt it go through and then … he stopped breathing. He just, stopped moving."

"That can't be right. You should be dead if that's the case."

"I don't know," he repeated. "I don't know what happened."

"Aetas!" My hands were shaking his lifeless body. As I brought my claw up to cut through my wrist, I noticed how bad I was trembling.

"Don't." Marko's arm wrapped around my waist, pulling me away.

"Don't save our leader? Are you fucking insane?" I thrashed, breaking free to spin on him. "Without him we are *nothing*. Do you not see? Our world as we know it is doomed. He didn't prepare me good enough yet, and Hunter is far from ready. We need him, Marko."

Dark hair fell over his forehead as he pulled me in. "He is dead, ma minette. Giving him your blood will not bring him back. We have to do this rationally. We have to contact the members of the high circle. They will know what to do."

The door crashed in before I could so much as say a word. Faces I recognized, others I didn't, came rushing in. The horror they held was all too clear. *Aetas was dead.*

"I was just about to put out the call."

"What happened? A woman I recognized came forward. She had short hair and I knew her from the coronation. She had been the one holding the crown. She was Aetas' second. Shit …

"Look into my eyes, I will show you." Marko walked forward and she met him half way. When she gasped, I couldn't stop my hand from pressing to my stomach. This wasn't right. Aetas … he couldn't be dead.

"Impossible."

Marko's hands rose at a loss. "I don't know what happened."

The woman's covered her mouth and she crooked her finger, calling over three others. They took turns looking into her stare. Their faces grew paler as they broke away.

"What does this mean?" I swallowed hard, wiping away the tears that were still coming. All I wanted to do was rush to Aetas' side. To hold him and break down. Why?

"We hold a ceremony. There will be a new coronation. I will lead."

"You?" One of the men stepped closer, his face full of anger. "Just because you were his second doesn't mean you lead."

"Of course it does. Aetas is *dead*. I was in line to take his place. I lead."

Arguing started between the members, growing louder as they became more aggressive. Out of nowhere, something inside of me snapped.

"Do you disrespect your former leader so much! This is not the time to argue like adolescents. He's not even cold and you sit here bickering over who will lead? You should be ashamed of yourselves. I am ashamed at which one of you will lead us. None of you will come close to filling his shoes. You are *weak*. Do you hear me?" I yelled louder. "Weak!"

My body was vibrating at the power that was coursing through me. My vision was black from my vampire and I wanted to fight. I wanted to tear these pathetic excuses for vampires apart. They were not real leaders, and not much stronger than I was, if at all.

"Enough." Marko's low voice whispered next to my ear and his arm wrapping around my waist did little to calm me. "Please," he said louder. "Excuse her. You can clearly see she is upset over our leader's death. But she is right. Now is not the time to argue. I'm sure you can all come up with his replacement later. Now, if you'll excuse us. I need to calm the queen. We'll be going back to our room. Please, feel free to relay any messages you have for me to Demetrius."

Marko turned me, leading me to the door when he stopped. "Hunter, come."

"Come? To our room?"

An array of different emotions passed over his face as Hunter came closer, looking just as confused as I felt.

"The two of you are bonded, love. Let's just say that right now is not the time to fight over what has happened. Let's all just go to the room and we can discuss what we're going to do. I don't know about you," Marko said, switching to French, "but I don't want to let him out of my sight."

"Right." I nodded, glancing at Hunter as Marko opened the door and we headed down the dark hallway. The entire length, I couldn't believe the turn of events. Aetas … dead. How was any of this possible? And death from bonding?

As Marko shut us in, I narrowed my eyes, really looking at him. "Is your blood so strong that it could have killed him?"

"No." His head shook. "It had to be a negative reaction or something. It doesn't make any more sense to me than it does to you."

Hunter was taking deep breaths, rubbing his hand over his head as he started to pace the far end of the room. I focused on Marko, trying to push away the pull to the man who confused me the most.

"Negative reaction? I'm not so sure. I mean, we're talking about Aetas, here. Most powerful vampire known to man. He's done things that no living *thing* could ever do. Man, vampire … only a God. Maybe deep down I believed him to be truly immortal. How many others has he primed to take his place? Marko, something is not right, I feel it in my soul. Aetas can't be dead. He can't. I refuse to believe it."

A pain expression turned into one of sympathy. "Ma minette, he was just a vampire. Just like any of us. He could not escape death. It would have found him at some point. Today just happened to be that day."

My head shook, my mind still not able to consider the possibility.

"Come here, let me hold you. I haven't seen you this upset before."

I sighed, walking forward, and wrapping my arms around his waist. The lack of sensation had me stiffening. *Our bond.* Tears streamed down my face and a sob couldn't be held in.

"What is it?" He lifted my chin and all I could do was hold on tighter.

"Bite me. Let's exchange blood and rebond. Aetas is gone. You can bond with me again."

The tenderness on Marko's face hardened into what looked like uncertainty. "We have to give it time. His blood is still in me. It might not work yet. Let's wait a few weeks."

"Do you not want mine tainting his?"

I couldn't help but be offended. Marko would have drained me every single day trying to strengthen our connection, wouldn't he have?

"Tainting his? Don't be ridiculous. If you want inside of me, I'll be more than happy to feed from you. I just think it's too soon to work. Would you like to try? Would it make you happy?"

My hands slid down his back as I put distance between our bodies. "No. Later." I let my hands drop as I stepped out of his arms. I suddenly felt so cold. So alone, and I couldn't figure out why. I wanted Aetas back. I felt lost. Fear of the future had never been a concern. I thought I had had time to prove myself. Now, the leader I was once feared, yet looked up to, was gone. And with his departure, I felt as though I were roaming through a room of unfamiliar strangers.

Well, that wasn't true. Hunter didn't seem that different. The appeal for him was there. But I couldn't go to him like I wanted with Marko standing just feet away. Or at all. I was married. Devoted to the king. *My king.* Why did that feel wrong to think? It had to be the missing bond.

"You're very conflicted right now. I can see it. Tell me what troubles you?"

My eyes rose and I went from Marko, over to look at Hunter.

"Yes. Now I see. Hunter, come here."

I jerked my head to Marko, frightened for what he planned to do. Now that Aetas was dead, he could kill Hunter.

I backed away, putting myself between the two of them. Hunter went to step around me, but I put out my arm, making him stay behind. It had Marko's eyebrows raising. And then he did it. A smile pulled at the side of his face, throwing everything off even more.

"Do you plan to end his life?" My hand eased down, grasping Hunter's. I had no idea what I was doing, but I couldn't let him die. My heart … I could feel him in it again. Bond, no-bond—he had always existed within. Whether it was from betrayal or love, it was like Aetas had said, the two emotions stemmed from the same thing. Hunter was a part of me and my vampire was claiming him as her own. Just as I had done once before.

Marko clasped his hands, narrowing his eyes as he began to walk around us. "I could kill him. A large part of me wants to. Aetas," he nearly growled. "He may have saved your life, Hunter. Oddly enough in the moment, I … *feel* something for you. In truth, I really don't mind this," he said, gesturing to us. "I know I should. I should be ripping him to shreds right now. But I don't want to."

An exhale left Hunter and he wrapped his arms around me from behind. All I could do was stare at Marko in shock as I numbly placed my hand over Hunters crossed arms.

"Why don't the two of you lie down and rest. You've been through a lot today. I have to go take care of some things with the high members. I'll be back in a few hours. Don't wait up for me."

The emptiness inside only grew as I watched Marko walk out of the door. The tears returned. A mourning so great branched its way through my heart and all I could think to do was turn and hold to Hunter as I broke down and cried for reasons I didn't even know.

Chapter 15
Hunter

I stayed focused on Tessa as she tossed and turned in her sleep. My mind wouldn't stop spinning. Nothing about our meeting had gone as Aetas said it would. He said we were going to talk. That maybe there was a way he could convince Marko to accept me, concerning Tessa. We did share a past and two ties. He said with them now sharing one as well that Marko could possibly be open to it.

They'd arrived ... and nothing. We were all together and the next thing I knew pain was shooting through my insides and I was springing to my feet. *Tessa.* God, I'd been on her. Bit her and somehow bonded with her and I couldn't even remember it. I knew my wrist had been cut. It was barely healed when I came to. I'd forced my blood on her for the last tie and I wasn't sure how to feel about that. I hated the action, but I didn't regret the outcome. I loved her. That was obvious. But...then I saw Aetas. How was he dead? He once told me if he died, so would I. And Marko was alive. They'd bonded! From everything I was taught so far, it seemed impossible.

Another sob shook Tessa as she rolled back toward me. She'd been crying since Marko left. It was another thing bothering me. Was she so close to Aetas? She was loyal to him. That I knew in my heart, but to be so devastated? Perhaps it was the future she was so worried about?

"Shh. Everything's going to be okay. I promise." Softly, I stoked back her hair in a slow rhythm and she quieted. When I stopped, her features drew in all over again. I couldn't stand being on guard from doing what I wanted to. Here I was in her and Marko's bed and all I wanted to do was hold her. Should I? I fucking wanted to. But what would Marko do if he walked in and saw us in such an intimate position?

Aetas always told me to ask permission. He was very direct with how I should act around Marko. The king could kill me and Aetas wasn't here to save my ass anymore. I had to be more cautious and learn better control. Tessa may have been bonded to me, but that didn't mean she would stay that way.

A soft knock was followed by the door opening. My head lifted and Marie jerked to a stop at seeing me lying next to Tessa. My finger shot to my lips to warn her to be quiet. As I eased off the mattress, Tessa rolled over, sniffling.

"Marko knows I'm here ... like this." I kept my voice low so I wouldn't wake Tessa.

"I would hope so or else you're a dead man. *Again.*"

"Ah. The suicide. Aetas told me about it. Good one. Can I help you with something?"

She let out a breath, clearly uncomfortable around me. "I came to check on the queen. She's upset. Is she okay?"

"Not really. I think she has bad dreams. I'm not sure." I tried to read Marie as she worriedly watched over the queen. "You feel her from the tie the two of you have?"

Marie nodded. "She's extremely upset. It leaves me unsettled. I worry for her. Especially since I'm not sure why she is so distressed. I can't … figure out the reason. Such grief, but I don't understand. Nothing makes sense right now."

"Your dreams," I breathed out. "What do you dream? What does the future say for us now?"

Marie's features drew in. "I …" She got quiet. "How odd you ask that. I don't know anything, anymore. Not with Tessa and not of tomorrow. My visions, they're changing. Something is happening, but I don't know what it is. Everything is so dark. It's like I'm not myself. The same dream has come now for days, but I can decipher it. It's the reason I haven't said anything. Either something's going to happen, or something already has. I'm so confused. This one is different. The air is so suffocation and stale. I fight to break free, but it's like I can't. I'm in something."

"In something? You or someone else? Or all of us?"

Marie rolled her eyes. "*I don't know.* It can mean anything, but Marko and Tessa are who my dreams mainly revolve around. Or you, I guess. I dream of you quiet often."

"You do? What happens to me?"

Marie took a step back, twisting her black dress in her hands. "I don't like talking about this to you."

"Why? I'm not going to do anything. I'm not the bad guy, here. I wish everyone would stop thinking I was."

She took a deep breath. "Today you're not. Or maybe at all. It's so hard to believe your good since you've always been bad. Your future changes more than anyone's. I used to dream that you were the end of us. You lead a war of humans to kill us, then it was a war of vampires, then a mix of both. Just the last few days it's warped once again. You …" Marie reached up, pressing her fingers against her temple. "I don't know. The night of the coronation, your path altered yet again. It's always changing. It baffles me to the point of madness."

"What did you see this time?" I stressed. "Do you see Tessa and I together? Are we happy? Marie? Is she going to be okay?"

My voice grew louder and she jerked her arm away from me as I reached for it. The slap had me gritting my teeth.

"Don't touch me. *Never* touch me. You once stabbed me through the chest with a holy dagger. I don't trust you."

"I did that?" Even as I asked, visions blinded me. My breath caught and I weeded through the emotions my human self felt in that moment. I was so desperate. So afraid of this world. I hated it. The need to kill vampires was there, but it faded the moment the pictures disappeared. "I did do that. I'm sorry."

Her lids were lowered skeptically as she watched me. "Yeah … well, yeah." She mumbled the words, dropping her wrinkled dress to hug around her waist.

"Tell me what you saw of me. Please."

Marie glanced to Tessa and an uneasy sound left her. "I'm not one to judge on mates or bonded, but," her stare returned to me. "You've bonded her, haven't you?"

"I have."

"You're bonded. That's what I dreamed of, but I didn't dare believe it. What followed ... what I saw ,,,"

My head shook. "What is it?"

"Nothing. You're bonded. But." Her lips pressed together. "Marko is ... something is different. I can feel it, but I can't see it. Marko and Tessa love each other. Their love is like nothing else. I don't know what it means for me to see you with Tessa. Maybe the three of you are meant to be together, I just don't know yet. The darkness. It all blurs, and I'm not breathing well."

I frowned, turning as Tessa rolled back to where I was. "Go back to Marko. What do you mean he's different? Is it a bad different, or is it good? Will he accept me and Tessa?"

Marie went to open her mouth when the door opened. Marko came to an abrupt stop at seeing us.

"Marie, what brings you here?"

She shifted uncomfortably, glancing over at me before addressing him.

"I came to check on the queen. She's distressed. It woke me from a deep sleep."

"Ah." He walked forward, removing his suit's jacket to place on the back of a red velvet chair. "No worries. I'm back now. I'll calm her. Go back to your room and get some rest. I'm holding a meeting at sunset tomorrow. Aetas has passed, I'm sure you've heard. Tessa, Hunter, and I will be going to the ceremony in a few days so I want to make plans for the city to be on guard in case anything happens while we're away."

Marie's mouth opened, only to close. "No. That can't be right." Her head snapped to me. "Why did you not tell me?"

"About Aetas? I thought you knew."

"I was not aware of his passing. He's ... not dead. I would have known. I would have known," she repeated. She grew quiet, moving her sights to Marko, only to drop them to the ground. "How did I not know? Why was I not made aware or woken up? My dreams, that's why they're changing." Her hand pressed to her stomach while she swallowed convulsively. "What does this mean for us? What are we to become?"

Marko's brow creased and he went to place his hand on her shoulder. The moment it touched, she scrambled backward as if he'd burned her.

"Marie?"

The color drained from her face while she began to side-step to the door.

"Marie." Marko's voice was deeper. "What is it?"

"N-nothing. Nothing, Your Highness. I ... must go. I'm suddenly not so well. My sincerest apologies for Aetas."

With that, she rushed for the door, closing it quietly behind her. Marko's eyes were narrowed as he continued to stare at the barrier.

"Odd." He turned to me, unbuttoning his shirt. "How is my queen?"

Marie's words came back to me. "Distressed. She continues to cry."

"Tessa seemed to take Aetas' passing rather hard, wouldn't you agree?"

I nodded, hesitant on how I should act. Marko *did* seem different. So much more easygoing than before. Where was his anger toward me? His hate?

"I'm tired. Have you slept at all?"

"No. Tessa doesn't calm unless I soothe her."

Marko's lips pulled back on the side and I wasn't sure if it was from anger or something else.

"Soothe her? How?" He stepped closer. "Do you kiss her? Hold her? How do you soothe my queen?"

I didn't break eye contact as I stood taller. "Aetas made sure I treaded very light around you. I did nothing but stroke her hair. I didn't hold her or kiss her. Not that I didn't want to."

Marko's smile grew and he turned, walking to the bed. I stayed in place, not sure what to do as he continued to undress.

"Are you coming, or are you going to sleep on the floor?"

"You mean you're okay with me being with the two of you in your bed?"

Annoyance flickered on his face as he let his pants drop. "*You're* her bonded. You have almost every right to her that I do. But remember who she's legally tied to. *Me.* If I want her, I can take her just as you do. We share her in a sense, but she's still mine. You still have to ask."

"What happened to you?"

I couldn't move. Could barely speak at how flabbergasted I felt.

"Aetas blood, I suppose. It isn't such a bad thing. Who knows, maybe this will work out for the best. Tessa gets her best friend and lover back, and I get to keep her too. I don't mind sharing with you. For now."

Chapter 16
Marko

The City of the Dead. I'd seen the underground tombs beneath Headquarters before, but never once had I thought I'd be here so soon. A part of me knew I'd make it to the status to be put to rest in this place, but not like this. Never still alive, trapped inside Aetas' memorial. And I knew that's where I was. The energy around me told me my location, and surrounded by darkness, it was a hard truth to deny.

The City was miles wide, housing thousands upon thousands of past members and enforcers who'd made it as high as Headquarters. Some lasted days in their position, others decades, even centuries. Only once had I walked through the large, opened space, taking in the elaborate, yet gothic memorials. But even then, I hadn't scratch the surface on covering the distance of how big this place was.

The passing of Bercolot had been hard on me at the time. He was a dear friend, a member in our city, before getting recruited as an enforcer. He lasted all of four months before he was killed by a rogue vampire. I went to his ceremony with a heavy heart, but I didn't neglect to take in the one place vampires whispered about. Or the place I longed to make a mark in. Each monument told of status, and wasn't that what I had always dreamed of? It was my biggest fault. A curse, just as The City of the Dead was. The place was a ghost story to our kind. For all of its beauty, it held dark secrets.

It was told that when a vampire of worthy status passed, his greed—even in death—caused him to take over the life of the strongest vampire present during the ceremony. Some said it wasn't greed at all that caused him or her to do this, but a sacrifice to our leader to once again return to walk amongst us. A transitioning in bodies, so to speak.

The entire story was shit. I didn't believe in ghosts coming back from the dead, nor did I think it was possible. But if I wanted to be honest with myself, being turned into Aetas and locked in a casket in the middle of a large, marble monument sort of fit the bill. The sacrifice was real, for here I was.

The entire situation was starting to make my skin crawl. The energy here was different. *Intense.* It was as if, even though I was secluded in a pitch black box, I wasn't alone. Clicking kept echoing from somewhere near me, and a slight hum was constantly present. I knew the sounds were connected, and were more-than-likely the machine keeping me alive, but what about the whispering voices that woke me from my dreams?

Insanity. And this was only the beginning.

"Dammit!" I tried to thrash for what had to be the thousandth time since I'd awoken in darkness days ago. It took forever to remember what had happened to me, or where I even was, but when the tightness on the side of my neck made itself know at my struggles, everything came back in a rush of memories. *Aetas.*

He was going to pay for what he had done. There was no way I was going to let him live my life and bring down our kind. As for what he was doing with Tessa,

I couldn't bear to think about it. The sickness that plagued me at the thought only made my mental state worse. I was panicked. Losing my mind to the point of here phantom voices. Years, possibly decades, or longer, I could be confined here … no, I couldn't survive that. Not mentally.

"Aetas! Aetas, let me out!"

As for Hunter, his role to me was as clear as day. I'd seen through Aetas' blood that Hunter hadn't been in control of himself. Nor did he know Aetas' plan. What was uncertain during the attack, was now obvious. And things were only becoming sharper in my mind. I may have been locked away, but my tie with Aetas was supplying me with information as if I were there, witnessing it all. I felt all three of them. Tessa's heartbreak at losing me, even if she didn't know it was me who was gone, and Hunter's growing love for her. *His protectiveness.*

They were all close. So close, I felt as though I'd see them if this heavy marble top was lifted off of me. There was only one reason for them to be at Headquarters—the ceremony. Grieving, for a leader that was determined to kill us all.

Chapter 15
Aetas

It wasn't every day you got to witness your own funeral. The forlorn expressions, the ones of relief and eagerness, left an internal smile permanently etched within me. *Fools.* They were so clueless to what I had planned. They wouldn't know what was hitting them until it was too late. Even now my plan was in motion and the distraction I was waiting for as I sat on the first row with Tessa and Hunter was just moments away.

"King Aetas will forever be remembered. He was our foundation. Our security and hope through times where we fought to survive. He took us from the bottom, to the top. We've come so far and it is all thanks to him."

"As we sit here today, rulers and members of a vampire society greater than ever, we mourn a leader who can never be replaced. He was fearless. Brave in the face of what most of us would cower to. The centuries that I have served alongside him has been a great honor."

Fantaza looked up through thick lashes, brushing back the short strands that fell into her eyes, continuing.

"Today we will not speak of the future, but of the past. I would like to tell you all a story of my first meeting with Aetas." Her lips pursed and she took a ragged breath, wiping away what I knew to be fake tears. The female had no heart. Hadn't, even before she was turned. It was the reason I chose her.

"The year was thirteen-forty-eight. I was but twenty-one, in human years, but far from a child. Times were not as they were now. To live as I did was an accomplishment of its own. But in Florence, where I had been born and raised, we suffered something far worse than any food shortage, or attack of our persons."

"The Black Plague hit my home, hard. People were dying everywhere you turned. Bodies were littering the streets. My mother was the first to be taken. Then my seven brothers and sisters. I woke up just at sunset, feeling death approaching. It was only a matter of time."

"I remember stumbling through the streets, bumping into the structures I was using to support myself. At that point I had accepted my life was over. I welcomed the end. I was merely passing time, taking in the sights I'd come to love and hate throughout my years."

Her head dropped toward the podium. "That's when he and Percival came to me. Child, Aetas said. Do you not fear death so much?"

"All I could do was stare up at the most handsome man I'd ever seen."

Fantaza smiled as her head lifted. "I thought he was an angel or a God, come to take me home. Somehow I managed to finally speak."

"I fear nothing, I told him. Death is but my home. Death has always been my home."

"Then I will make it so, he had said." The smile faded. "Percival took me then, biting me right in front of Aetas as he watched. It was right there on the dark streets of Florence, amongst the dead bodies and stench of illness. I can still remember the sounds of my screams as Aetas took me from Pecival and held my dirty, frail frame in his strong arms, whispering about how he had given me a new life. One I could be proud of. He had always been a God to me. Even in those terrifying moments, he kept me strong. His death … it will forever leave a piece of me missing. My only hope is—"

Footsteps pounded in the back of the room, echoing throughout the large space like thunder rumbling through the sudden silence. The multiple enforcers were paired in two, swallowing the aisles with their large, black-clothed frames.

"What is this?" Fantaza hissed.

Whispering erupted, followed by the rustle of fabric as vampires shifted in their seats.

"Fantaza Rossi, Hector Yubara, Rochester Phillips, Jackson Bastrop, step forward."

Fantaza, along with the other high members addressed threw glances at each other. The men on the other side of the aisle stood from their seats, but didn't walk forward as instructed. Enforcers circled around from all sides, their black eyes focused—their arms rising to outstretch in front of them, ready to fight.

"What's this about? I demand an explanation for interrupting our leader's ceremony. You should be ashamed of yourselves!"

"Marko?" Tessa leaned over, grabbing my hand as I pulled us to our feet.

"It's okay, ma minette."

I tried to hold in the smile as I felt the high member's power flare. Their faces were filled with worry.

"Under the orders of King Aetas, set date, four days ago, you are all under arrest for treason, sentenced to immediate death."

"Treason!" Fantaza flew around the podium, skidding to a stop and jerking her palm up to face the enforcers who were edging in. "Aetas would never charge us with treason! This is a mistake. This is not true!"

The main enforcer lifted a paper to face her. "The orders he sent to Master William Mason was discovered, hidden in your room. His signature is right here, for all to see."

Long red hair swayed along the enforcer's back as he made a slow circle, displaying the evidence to the crowd.

"It's forged. It's not real," Fantaza yelled. "Someone planted it. Someone …" she scanned the remaining members along the first row on the other side of us. "It was *you*, wasn't it, Maribel. You did this! You've always been jealous of me."

Maribel flew from her chair, baring her fangs as one of the enforcers rushed in to grab her.

"You dare accuse *me*? I bet the paper is true! I bet you and the others accused killed Aetas!"

Gasps reined through the room as she spit in Fantaza's direction.

"How dare you!"

Chaos broke out as Fantaza rushed toward Maribel. Enforcers crowded in, tackling down Hector, Rochester, and Jackson as they tried to push through the vampires and rows behind them. The air began to swirl, electrifying as Fantaza's powers stirred with in her. At the screaming, I knew the enforcers were slicing through their necks to remove their heads.

Vampires were crowding through, anxious to see the carnage of our royalty being decapitated. I didn't move. Didn't do anything but wrap my arms around Tessa and pull her closer into me as she held to her stomach, groaning in pain. I wanted to smile. To bask in this moment of what I knew she was feeling, but not saying.

Had the member's betrayed me? Committed treason? Of course they did. But only in their minds. They were all guilty. Every single one in this room. At one time or another, they had wanted my throne. Dreamt of it. Relished in the fantasies of taking it. It was enough for me. I had wanted blood. To shake the very foundation of what we were, and I had accomplished that. But I was far from over and Tessa was feeling it firsthand.

More enforcers rushed in, whispering amongst their partners as the news spread. When the lead enforcer, Colin, nodded, I was ready for the news. My heart was racing from the excitement.

He walked to the front, brushing back the red strands that were becoming loose from his ponytail.

"We have just had news. The cities are under attack."

"The cities? Which ones?" Mistress Belle Lamore of Reno pushed through the second row behind us to come to a stop in the aisle.

Colin's shoulders drew back. "All of them, Mistress. Humans have paired up with some of the rogue vampires we've been trying to track down. Their plan was orchestrated flawlessly. They all attacked at the same time, hitting every major city, in every state. We have put a shield around the perimeter of Headquarters as precaution. It is as we feared. War is upon us. War is here."

"Oh God," Tessa breathed out, twisting from my grasp. "We have to go. We can still get back in time. We can help our city."

She was already trying to move around me. Her fear perfumed the air and I locked around her waist, pulling her back.

"Did you not hear him? They have set up a perimeter, ma minette. We cannot leave." I closed my eyes, shaking my head. "I feel it now. It's already too late. They're already all dead."

"What?" She jerked against me, still making sounds of pain. "What do you mean, all dead? Who's all dead?" The shrill tone was on the verge of hysteria. Tessa was fighting harder, desperate to break free of my hold. She knew, whether she wanted to admit it to herself or not.

"The majority of our city. Some live. They have fleeing, but … Demetrius, Anastasia." I opened my eyes to look into hers. "Marie. All of our members. They're all dead."

"No," she gasped, slamming her fist against my chest. "No! How did you not know? How did you not feel our city's need? We could have left in time. We could have saved them. You should have felt the threat. I would have felt it, Marko!"

"Calm. We'll figure something out." Hunter stepped closer and his hand reached for her, only to retreat at my stare. His face was pained at his mate's anguish.

"Take her and do not let her go. Someone has to take control of this mess." I eased Tessa into his hold, stalking toward the podium, just in front of my throne. Enforcers' gazes snapped to me, cautious as my energy exploded to heights I knew they hadn't felt before. Even as leader, I rarely had to display my position, but here, in front of them all, I'd take what was already mine. Just as someone else—as The Black Fire King.

Eyes followed me as I took a step up. As I moved behind the podium, the enforcers grew closer. They watched, not sure what to do, or what to think of my power.

"From here on out, all of you will answer to me, King Marko Delacroix— you're new leader. If there are any objections, feel free to speak out. But know that if you do, you better be prepared to defend your rejection."

Maribel pushed around the enforcer who had previous held her. Her eyes were narrowed and her steps turned hesitant the closer to got. "You try to take what is rightful not yours? I am next in line! Not you. You aren't even apart of Axis. Aetas would have never allowed you to tarnish our table, nor would he approve of this atrocious claim you're trying to stake."

"That sounds like an objection to me," I said smiling.

My hand rose and my energy shot through the internal shield she used to protect her gifts. As I grasped around her core, she held to her stomach, cutting her gaze up to mine in horror. A cry fell from her lips as I projected Marko's fire to inflame her stomach. The black smoke still in me from Tessa and Marko's mixed blood ignited, and the fire I placed within her left the thick black substance pouring from her mouth as she let out a blood curdling scream. The heat bubbled and blistered her skin as it worked its way up her chest and throat. She was clawing at her herself, spinning in circle through her agonizing death.

"Anyone else object?"

A blue ball of light exploded against my shield, followed by multiple colors and forces of random vampires throughout the crowd. I laughed, reaching for the energy of the instigator of the attack. The ruler of New Mexico's body slid inches away from my feet and I jumped down, flipping him over as the enforcers held their ground just feet away. When my hands rose, his body lifted until he was levitating just below my face. The black fog rolled from my opened mouth, crawling over his face, and down his throat. The toxic poison only increased as I covered him in it. Skin began to melt down his face, revealing the muscle and bone underneath. I thrived in my new powers. Twisting them and trying everything I could to learn more about the way they worked.

Blood and chunks of his form flew toward the crowd as I blasted the body with all the strength inside of me.

"Is that all you are capable of, rulers? Is this what we have come to? Weak, pathetic powers? You all are *nothing* without me! I asked once again. Is there any more of you who object to me ruling?" My fangs were down, ready to bleed them all dry. Tessa's energy neared and my eyes shot over to her inquisitive, terrorized stare. I immediately composed myself. I had to get control. I had to stop acting like myself and be more like Marko.

"I see the decision is final. I am your new leader. Cross me again and you'll be charged with treason and dealt with accordingly." I turned my attention to the enforcers. "Your orders come from me now. Get these vampires out of here. Let them leave and go back to what is left of their cities, and then lockdown the grounds. After that, everyone who takes residence here is not to leave. I'm sure you know what to do. Aetas had trust in you. I do as well."

"Thank you," Colin said, bowing. "We'll carry out your orders, Your Highness."

I forced the anger to fade from my face as I turned to Tessa. She was staring at me like a stranger. Like she didn't know me at all. I had to make this right.

"It had to be done," I said, softening my tone. "There would have been a bloodbath here if I wouldn't have stepped up. Everyone wants the throne, but we all know who it belongs to rightfully. It's mine," I whispered. "I'm the strongest here."

Tears came to her eyes and she nodded, slowly. When I held out my arms to her, she blinked rapidly.

"Ma minette, come."

The pause had me clenching my jaw as I battled these new emotions. I had to convince her better. To play Marko's part. I didn't want to push her away. Not after I'd waited so long. I just wasn't sure how to act, yet.

Tessa eased into my arms, stiffening as I wrapped around her. The crowd was thinning out as the members rushed to get away from me. Their fear excited me, but was vital. They needed to be cautious, to respect me, and not think they had a chance to rise against my rule.

"You must be exhausted. Let us go to our new room and lie down. I will hold you. Feed you," I purred, nuzzling the side of her head.

"It has been days," she said, weakly. "I just don't feel the need to feed at the moment. I wish to see Aetas."

My head drew back. "You want to go to The City of the Dead?"

"Yes. Alone."

She stepped back, a tear sliding down her cheek as she turned away from me. The black lace dress she wore trailed the floor behind her, the train, swooshing with the sway of her hips. My old crown sat on her head and the black curls held back by pins cascaded down her back. The elegance, the bravery, she was every bit the queen she was titled.

And now she was mine. Here, in the place she was meant for.

Chapter 16
Tessa

Silence met me as I stepped off the glass elevator that opened up to the large underground city. As I'd ridden down, I couldn't stop the awe and sorrow at the sights. What I was faced with was nothing short of breathtaking. The tall statues littered throughout, the designs carved into the elegant monuments—the large steeple in the center. I knew that's where Aetas was. He'd be in the best, and from what I could see as I lowered through the tall drop, it was beautifully done in white marble.

I lifted the bottom of my dress as I followed the wide, stone path that led me through the center. The walk was going to be long, but I didn't care. My mind was racing, bombarded with so many questions that I didn't even know where to begin. It was as though I were walking through a thick fog that was swallowing me whole.

How could this have happened? How could Marko have not known of our city's fall?

Perhaps his mind was closed off. The events that had taken place during the ceremony were enough to distract anyone, but I would have felt it. I would have never of turned my attention away from what I was meant to protect. It wasn't in my nature when I had led. My instinct had solely focused on what was mine.

My clicking heels merged with the thudding of my pulse and I let my emotion to the man I was mated to by vows filter through. Maybe my retreat from him was due to our broken bond. It was quite possible. After all, where Marko once filled my thoughts, Hunter was now there. *His* emotions, and *his* need of me, overpowered everything.

Even now, I could feel his worry. He wanted to speak to me. The pressure of his concern weighed against my mind. But he didn't speak. He gave me distance, even though he didn't want to. It had me embracing the idea of him even more. When I needed to be soothed, he was the one doing it. When I needed to talk, it was him coming to me. Not Marko. At least, not like he used to. He was becoming a stranger, and yet oddly familiar in another way. It made no sense, but nothing did right now.

My head rose and I watched Aetas' memorial grow closer. My heart was beginning to race. Sweat was starting to cover my skin, despite that it was cold down here. The hum of energy to this place was downright exhilarating. It made the hair on my arms stand on end. I felt alone and yet surrounded by power.

Black marble aligned the path. Small towers of previous enforcers were on both sides of me and still in death, I could feel their protective nature. It had my lids dropping the slightest amount as I let my own aura flare out.

I was with them, and they with me. I respected them. We were all one here, and I opened myself to them completely as a sign of my loyalty and praise for what they have sacrificed during their life. They had kept us safe. Kept us on track in a world full of greed and violence. But that was no more. The lives of us, vampires, were spiraling out of control and if Marko didn't make the right choices … we were in serious trouble.

I continued on, my mind going back to my grief. As I neared Aetas' temple, I slowed, taking in the grandeur of the large structure. The door to the front was black metal and didn't hold a door handle. There was no way to get in, and I didn't think my powers would work. The energy around it was like a life force of its own. I was trembling as I stopped at the bench just feet away of the entrance. My legs nearly gave out as I collapsed to sit down.

"Aetas."

Just saying his name brought tears. My heart ached to a magnitude that I had never felt before. I clutched to my hands as I let the new droplets fall to my lap.

"Aetas, we are lost. I am lost. You do not know what you have done by leaving us. Or maybe you do. We are in so much trouble," I sobbed. "We need you back. I … need you. Marko, he's not the same since he took your blood. He is a stranger to me. What were you doing attacking us like that? I should *hate* you. I should despise you for all that you did, but look at me. I mourn you like I would a lover. Like a best friend. My h-heart—"

Sobs tore from me as I slid from the bench to rest on my knees. My head bowed and harder I cried. When my palms flattened on the dirt, I broke through the surface with my claws.

"Why have you done this to us? *To me?* You weren't supposed to die. You made me promises. *You broke them.* I demand you to come back! I …"

Harder I dug into the dirt. Words were gone. All I could do was cry as my heart pined for a man who had continuously put me through hell. But not just him. All three men had hurt me at one point or another. Now I was uncertain of what to do. I knew in their own way, Aetas, Marko, and Hunter had loved me. And in *my* own way, perhaps I loved all of them as well?

Aetas. My feelings toward him were a mystery to me. How had I never seen it before? He hadn't been all bad. There were times when I softened toward him— the moments when he praised me or healed me. There was a look he'd give. One that pulled at something within. What did that say about me? Who the hell was I to allow myself to connect with three different men like that? I was broken in so many places that I just didn't know anymore. The word lost kept coming. Was it for me or all vampires in general? Both?

"**Jeremiah 50:6**" My voice cracked but I forced the prayer to come, regardless that it scalded my throat. "My people hath been lost sheep: their shepherds have caused them to go astray, they have turned them away on the mountains: they have gone from mountain to hill, they have forgotten their resting place."

"Where do I rest within this mess you have created, Aetas? What do I do to find myself? Where do any of us go? What is my purpose anymore? Tell me." My lip pulled back in anger at the barrage of questions. "You will not tell me because you refused to be strong enough to stay and face what you did. But I don't need you to show me the way. I will tell you my path. If all I am cannot be saved, I relinquish this soul to the devil who loved me most. The devil," I spat. "Not the men in my life who do his deeds. He's the one who lured me to this point. *To you, Marko, and now this new Hunter.*"

I paused. "Maybe you are Satan, and maybe I'm already in hell."

I swept back the curl that was sticking to my wet face and stood. In three strides, I made it to the door, slamming my fist against the metal. "I hate how this has played out! Perhaps I shouldn't have held such loyalty to you, but I did, and now I pay the price. We all do. But no more. You're dead, and I will have faith for no one except myself from now on. If Marko strays …"

I pressed my fingers into the cold door, hitting it once again for all the anger that was surfacing. "I am a fool for no man. I am a warrior and I will learn to lead in case the time comes when I have to. You will regret the day you pushed me away for another. This is all your fault Aetas. You failed by making the wrong choice, but I will fix it for you. I will become the leader you doubted me to be. When my fears prove right, it will be my reign. And I will be ready."

Chapter 17
Hunter

"Wait!"

My voice carried through the large opened room I had once ran through to escape this place. I hated being within these walls, but my concern over my location faded as I rushed toward Marko and the men in black who were leaving his side.

They froze, turning to look at me as I slid to a stop in front of them. Tessa's need of revenge over the humans was my own. Her pain was mine, and all I knew was pleasing and avenging her in the moment.

"I want to go. I want to fight."

Marko laughed and I glanced at him before turning my attention back to the man with long red hair. He was their leader, I could feel his power.

"You are not trained. You're but a baby."

I growled, getting in his face. "I've been a killer since I was legally old enough to own a gun. I've taken both human and vampire lives. I know what I'm doing."

"I'm well aware of who you are Prince Hunter Moretti. I know everything about you, but I'm saying you're not ready. Besides, Aetas had plans for you that didn't involve being on the front lines. Your path is not that of an enforcer. You are to lead Dallas."

"I make my own path and I'm telling you I want to *fight*."

"Colin." Marko eyes went from him to me. "If The Black Prince wishes to fight, who are we to deny him? Will it not make him a better leader when he takes his place as a ruler?"

The man's face turned hard.

"Your Highness, he is not equipped to keep up with us. It's not like we're driving to get there."

Marko's eyes narrowed. "Are you so weak that you can't take him with you?"

Colin stiffened. "I am not weak."

"Then stop making excuses. I'm ordering you to take him. Teach him. He is yours now. We will both train him in the ways of our world."

"Yes, Master."

Although there was rage present, Colin bowed, turning to rush away. "Thank you." I threw the words at Marko, running to catch up with the lead enforcer. Tessa's emotions were flaring, going from sad to angry. It twisted my stomach, feeding my adrenaline. "You won't regret this," I said, catching up. "I can fight. I'll show you."

Pressure gripped around my wrist. "Let's go!" The order was directed at the awaiting men. One minute we were headed toward the front doors, the next, darkness. The shock hit hard and gravity became nonexistent for only seconds before my feet hit ground. My knees buckled and I tried to catch my breath as I was jerked to stand. "Try to keep up."

The tunnel I was in lost the blur as my eyes focused. The familiar smell registered and I suddenly knew where I was—in our underground city—in Austin. But I didn't get to think on it for long.

Enforcers took off running, rushing through the tunnel. They faded in and out, becoming almost nonexistent shadows with their speed. And Colin and I were trailing behind them. The sight triggered my vampire, feeding the challenge he needed as I became in tune with my own powers. My legs began moving faster. So fast that I could barely feel them.

We turned left, and then right, jerking to a stop only when we were feet from the light that brought us to the great room.

"I speak to them here," Colin said, tapping my temple. "To be an enforcer, you must tie with me. They will never speak out loud to anyone outside of their circle. Never, unless addressed, and only to one person."

"The leader," I whispered.

"Correct. We are ghosts. We do not exist to anyone but the people we kill, protect, or serve. Even then, they rarely see us. Do you understand what you could be getting yourself into? If you take this route, you have an oath you will follow. An oath you will die by while you serve."

"I understand. But the choice is not mine to make alone."

"You are bonded, I feel it, and that makes you unqualified, but our king makes the rules so it is his decision. We will talk on it later. Stay behind me. You are here to watch and learn. Nothing else tonight."

My jaw flexed, but I gave a stiff nod.

More silence. There was no signals, no hand gestures. One by one, the enforcers vanished into thin air. Colin grabbed my wrist and all color faded from my vision. We were running again, right into the heart of the city. A large group of men stood surrounding a huge mountain of bodies in the center. My heart dropped as we raced closer. Something within told me the humans wouldn't see us. With the change in my sight, it was a clear indicator that we'd done exactly as the enforcers had who had stood before me and Colin. But in this black and white, I could see them now as clear as day. They weren't invisible to me anymore.

They took their positions behind the men, waiting for Colin's orders. We came to a stop behind a human in all black tactical gear and my pulse was exploding with anticipation. They couldn't see us. We were right on them, and they didn't have a clue.

"Hunter? Hunter, where you are?"

Tessa's voice broke through and I went rigid. I could feel heat igniting in my core and I didn't understand it. It was as though I was tapping into my powers, like I was ready to use them, but I wasn't doing it. She was. Jesus, was she searching me out?

Colin's eyebrow rose at me and I tried to slow my breaths as the blaze within grew.

"Tessa, you have to stop. Give me a minute."

"Marko says you've gone with the enforcers. Where are you? Are you in the city?"

At the fast pace of her words, my head shook. *"I'll be back soon."*

Lava boiled within me and my knees buckled, hitting the ground hard as an unexplainable thickness pushed through me. It forced my lips open and I gagged as black smoke began pouring from my mouth.

Colin's grip nearly snapped my wrist as he held to me. Whether it was a warning or out of panic, I wasn't sure, but it wasn't coming from me. Not intentionally.

Darkness gathered above, only to drop before me, collecting as Tessa began to take shape.

"What the hell is that?"

The human's voice had Colin ripping me to my feet. The smoke lightened to what I knew was color I couldn't see because of my invisible state. I reared forward, my only need to protect her. She had her back to them and they were all watching with their weapons trained on her.

"Tessa, no!"

Colin's grasp broke at my force and Tessa spun, throwing her hands up just as shots rang out toward her. Bullets fell to the ground, but from the jerking of her body and the pain throughout my chest, I knew she hadn't been fast enough. Her body swayed, but she righted herself, staring down.

"Queen!" Colin yelled.

Bullet's continued to fall to the ground and she looked over her shoulder, glaring as I came up to her. The tips of her fangs were exposed and she slowly spun, pointing.

"You, show yourself."

Colin appeared, his head angled down as he walked forward at a fast pace. Just as he approached, he kneeled. "Your Highness."

"The king gave you orders to come to this city?"

"He did."

"Stand." Tessa voice was deeper than normal as she began to walk around her shield that trapped the humans. Murder was written in her blackening eyes while she took in the men who had killed our kind. And then the mountain of bodies. Her pain was my own as her fists clenched repeatedly and she tried to catch her breath.

"Tell me," she continued. "What do you call a ruler who does not protect or rule his city?"

Colin's eyebrows drew in as he rose to his feet. "I'm not sure, my queen."

"Dead," she said, flatly. "A ruler that does not protect what is his must be dead because he would never turn his back on his people." Tessa pointed to our dead. "My Marie is in there and I want her back. I was told she has passed. She is close, but she still lives. I'm dropping this wall. I want everyone killed but the one who hurt her. He is mine. Find him and bring him to me."

"Yes, Your Highness."

Tessa dropped the wall and tears came to her eyes as she threw herself into my arms. Her voice pushed into my head as I held to her tightly. *"My dear friend. I do believe we may be in trouble."*

"What do you mean?"

A sniffle left her and she drew back, wiping the tears away. "*I don't know, but I feel it. Marko wouldn't do this. He would have tried to avenge his city. He was one of the best leaders I knew. He loved his people. This new Marko.*" Her lids lowered the smallest amount with her thoughts. "*Something is not right. Aetas' blood was not a good match with his. I fear ... he may never return to the person he was before. I see him, but I don't know him. Why do I feel this way? It's not just our broken bond, it's his actions. His behavior. It is as though he has died with his change.*"

"*No. He's not dead. You have pulled back from him, too. Maybe the two of you need to try to reconnect. Maybe your love will bring him back?*" What the fuck was I saying? Was I trying to help her win Marko over? I was. I feared who he was becoming too, and I couldn't push the worry away. This new Marko wasn't good. I could feel his evil. Tessa was the only one who could stop him from making the wrong decisions.

"*Perhaps you're right.*" Her hand came up to stroke my face, but Colin's voice had her spinning around.

"I believe this is who you're looking for, my queen."

Tessa rushed over, glancing at the man, but ran to the pile of dead vampires. "Hold him," she yelled. "Marie?" Her eyes scanned over the bodies while her palm hovered before her. She took a few steps, only to back-track and start throwing bodies out of the way. I rushed to her side, helping her sort through our dead.

"She's here. I can feel," Tessa breathed out. "She's barely alive. Her energy is almost gone from me."

The ends of dark hair had me throwing a male vampire behind me. At the soft groan, I moved faster.

"Got her." I rolled an older woman over and cringed at the blood smearing her pale face. It was coming from her mouth and nose and her eyes were closed. I reached forward, pulling her into my arms. "Come on, Marie."

Tessa was glued to my side, already cutting her wrist as I eased Marie to the cement floor.

"My qu—een?"

"I'm here. I'm here. Shh, don't talk. Just open your mouth for me. I'm going to make you better."

Soft sounds of pain followed Marie as she slowly shook her head. "I'm … gone."

"Nonsense," Tessa snapped. "What did I tell you about that? You are not weak. You will fight. You will not leave me."

Blood was soaked through Marie's dress. The large gash in the material across her chest told me someone had used a blade. The skin had begun to heal, but not nearly fast enough from whatever had been used on her. Her heart … I took in where the cut had been. Fuck, her heart was damaged.

"Here. Open." The order had Marie obeying, but the coughing at Tessa's blood was automatic. Crimson sprayed from her lips and she heaved, crying out as she gasped for breath.

"Look," she whispered, trying to pull Tessa closer. "You have…to see."

An aggravated sound left the queen, but she wrapped her hands around Marie's face leaning in to peer into her eyes. Seconds went by while Marie's pained features only grew tighter. When her body jolted and went limp, Tessa's fingers tightened.

"No. No! Marie. Marie!"

My throat constricted at the words that had to come. "She's gone, Tessa."

"No." The fast flicker of Tessa's eyes told me that her mind was racing, trying to sort through this new tragedy and whatever she'd just seen.

"Tessa?"

"No." She leaned over, placing her lips against Marie's. French poured from her mouth and a good minute went by while Tessa held and talked to the vampire's lifeless body. Tears stained her cheeks when she finally took a deep breath and looked up to me.

"I'm sorry. I know it makes no difference, but Marie loved you. I could tell that when she came to see you."

"See me?"

"Yes, the night of Aetas' death. She felt your distress. She was worried about you."

A sniffle had her wiping more tears. "I loved her, too." Tessa stood, turning her sight on the human who was already cowering. The men he had accompanied were dead, laying sprawled across the floor where the enforcers had left them.

"You killed my friend."

"I …"

The man's words died off and he scanned the room in panic.

"I could return the gesture, right this second, if I wanted. You would be dead so fast you wouldn't even know it until your body hit the floor. But I don't want it to be that easy. I want you to suffer like I do." Her claws extended just the smallest amount. "And I suffer, human. So great your measly, little heart and mind wouldn't be able to bear or comprehend it. Do you know what it is to lose someone you love?"

Pause had him shaking his head.

"Lucky you. Let me show you."

Tessa hand locked on his chin and his eyes shot up to hers. Trembling immediately began to shake his limbs.

"Do you feel my pain? Do you feel what it is to suffer? See what I have seen. Feel the anguish and physical agony I have had to undergo. Live it with me, if only for this moment."

Saliva foamed at the man's mouth while his face turned red.

"The pain of my change was like nothing I'd ever experienced before. But that was only the beginning. Raped, raped, raped. How about that. Can you feel the burning? The way my body was ripped and torn at the intrusions? How about the knife piercing my heart? Can you feel that? Now lose your best friend as he kills himself in front of you. Almost die, yourself." Her fingers inched up as she held more secure. "Now lose someone you love. Who do you love? Can you see them? How shall we end their life so you will understand my pain?"

"Pl..ease. Please, no. Don't kill her."

"Can you not bear it anymore?" Her hand came back, slapping him across the face and breaking their eye contact. "Neither can I." She glanced up at Colin. "Let him go. He's going to fight me. No gifts, no weapons. Nothing fancy." At

Colin's pause, she growled. "That's an order! Let him go and don't interfere no matter what."

Colin's fingers slowly unwrapped from his arm. I swallowed as I debated on arguing. Killing with her gifts were one thing. Hand to hand combat was another. I couldn't take the thought of her getting hit.

"If you want to live, you have to beat me. I give you my word, if you win, you can leave this room without fear of being killed. No one will touch you."

The man didn't so much as look our way. His arm reared back, swinging right for Tessa's face. The connection to her cheek had her head jerking to the side at the impact. The sight was enough to make my vision flicker red. I was moving … fast, and my fangs were down.

A hand grabbed to my arm, but I was still pulling, focused solely on the man who was hitting her again. And again.

"The queen gave us an order. We are not to disobey," Colin yelled in my ear.

Words wouldn't come as Tessa's face lifted. He swung and she did nothing to defend herself. She was letting him beat her. Letting him pound into her features.

"Let. Go."

"This is nothing for her. She could crush his skull with her bare hands. What she is doing is for her, not him. We stay back."

"What is going on here!"

Marko's voice roared through the room like a cannon. Colin's grip tightened on me the smallest amount, only to drop completely as Marko's eyes went right to us, then to Tessa. Blood poured from her nose and mouth, and her eye was already swelling shut.

"Ma minette, what are you doing?" The pain and sincerity in our new leader's tone had my stomach twisting with jealousy.

"This man killed Marie. He will pay."

"He? Look at you. He is not hurting here, you are." He walked up, angling her so he could see the damage. "You want him to pay? I will make him suffer the worst death imaginable. I can do that for you. I would do anything for you."

"Would you?" Tessa tone softened toward the end. "I don't feel that from you anymore."

"I'm adjusting to this new me, but I am still the same. I'm sorry if I've made you feel that way. I love you," he said, pulling her into his body. "I love you more than anything. Let me take you home and show you."

Marko dropped his arms and lunged to the human so fast that he was but a blur. In one yank, he ripped the man's head free of his shoulders. Blood shot across Marko's angry face and some emotion I couldn't quite decipher flooded Tessa. She looked angry, yet … transfixed by Marko's action.

"Home," he repeated, tossing the head to the cement ground. "It's time to focus on us. *Just us*."

Chapter 18
Marko

Every breath, every constriction of every swallow, was a like a lighter being held to my throat. Aetas may have been keeping me alive through some machine, but it wasn't the same for my vampire. The need to bite and suck was ingrained in who I was. It was a necessity for the monster within. Every minute that passed where I didn't soothe the torture only triggered the insanity even more. My body was in a constant state of unsettlement. My legs slid from side to side the inches they were allowed and my fists repeatedly clenched. And my jaw … it kept the motion that needed to come. It open and bit down in reflex, repeatedly. The only thing that kept me holding on was Tessa.

"I will be a fool for no man. I am a warrior …"

Our love was true. Hearing her words as she broke down outside of the door had given me a hope so great that it kept me hanging on. Aetas couldn't be me. He could hold my appearance, he could pretend by his actions, by mine and Tessa's souls were intertwined so deeply that no matter where I was, she'd be drawn back to me. And maybe she thought she was spilling her worries to our leader, but in truth, it was me she was speaking to. Her despair *was for me*. For our missing bond and for the absence of my true self. She was mourning the loss of the one she was meant for. And me, I was grieving as well.

A loud grunt left my lips and my jaw snapped together. The ache caused my body to convulse against the restraining surfaces that kept me trapped. How long had I technically been dead? A month? Longer? Time didn't exist. The gaps in reality came whether I was awake or asleep. My mind was shutting down, breaking from the torment brought on by the hum of the machine and the silence that accompanied every passing second.

"Ae-tas." My weak voice had me reaching within to scream his name louder—clearer. "Aetas!"

How many times had I yelled that name? For how many days now?

Minutes went by and again I began the yelling. Light blinded me and for a moment I thought I had finally crossed over. The shock of my death quickly faded as a snarl tore through the room. Tears stung my eyes at the sensitivity and I blinked repeated, trying to see through the blur that had taken over my sight. No matter how many times I tried to make my vision come in clear, the face before me, my face, wouldn't sharpen to my regular sight.

"You wake me from a most pleasurable sleep. Why are you so weak?"

My mouth opened, only to snap shut again. Blurry brown eyes narrowed down at me and what I was sure was concern flashed on my features—Aetas' new features.

"This isn't right," he whispered, messing with the tube on the side of the throat. "The blood is too weak for you. Impossible. You cannot be growing so strong already."

I tried lifting my arm, but only managed a few inches before it fell again. Yes, I was so weak.

Warmth began to swarm in my core and I felt the powers that had been absent for so long, begin to return. The enclosed casket cut me off from my true self, somehow, but now … like this, I was returning. *More hope.* It had the anxieties easing. If I could be free of this enclosed space, I would eventually get better. I wasn't doomed like I had assumed I might if I ever got free.

"Here. Drink." Aetas cut into his wrist, placing it against my mouth. Ravishingly, I sunk my fangs into his skin. He winced, groaning as I greedily swallowed him down. The blood was like a breath of fresh air. The correction to my sight was almost immediate. And I was moving, drawing my knees toward my chest as I moaned through the simple pleasure of being able to do so.

"The queen is able to sleep, again," Aetas said, smiling. "She's starting to take to me. Her arms hold me at night and she sleeps with her face in my neck. Even though I tried, I could never imagine how that felt. The small things, they are so much greater than most know. Her bond is to Hunter, and he holds her from the other side, but she always turns to me. *Me,* Marko."

I wanted to argue, to say something to wipe that expression off of his face, but I couldn't. My hunger left me glued to his wrist.

"Her sadness is still present, but even it fades. Time has a way of doing that. Of changing things." His eyes moved down to stare mindlessly at the ground as he continued. "I thought I had loved her before, but I knew nothing. It's strange how fast the emotion grows. A little time passes and I look back now," his head did a quick shake, "the difference is almost shocking. *Love.* It does things to us. Opens places inside, both good and bad." His gaze returned to me. "I feel myself getting jealous of my creation. I thought myself incapable, yet Hunter's presence is beginning to wear on me. I don't understand it. I need him for my future plans, yet I plot ways to kill him anyway."

All I could do was watch as I focused on the heat building within. I still wasn't strong enough to overpower him and escape, and I wasn't about to risk it. But if I could let it grow. If he came back to feed me more … maybe eventually …

"I was so sure of my plan. There were no questions, just actions. This love for Tessa, it's starting to affect my judgement. The moment I gave myself to her mentally, something happened. And it grows. She's all I can think about. I want her in ways I can't even begin to describe." He glared. "And that brings me back to Hunter. To his growing love of her."

My eyebrows drew in and Aetas jerked him arm back. I took deep breaths, relishing in the burn that was no longer present in my throat.

"What will you do?"

He grabbed the heavy marble. Panic had my arm shooting out, but he easily pushed me back down. "What I always do—whatever I want."

Chapter 19
Aetas

The bedroom appeared before me as I felt myself materialize. Hunter was wrapped around the back of Tessa, kissing her neck. Small sounds left her in her sleep and her hips arched as consciousness beckoned. Jealousy swept through my veins as I stared ahead, watching her lips part. The covers rose as Hunter's hand slid up from her waist to stop chest-level. I could see his fingers moving, no doubt caressing her breasts. Teasing her nipples.

My energy flared and his head lifted. When his eyes met mine, he grew still. "*Leave* us."

The volume of my voice had Tessa's eyes fluttering open. Hunter only paused for a moment before his features tightened and he threw back the covers, leaving the bed. He reached over, grabbing a pair of jeans and pushed his legs through angrily. He didn't say a word as he left the button undone and stalked from the room. When the door slammed shut, I turned my attention back to Tessa. She was trying to get a read on me, but I didn't allow her the chance as I began to remove my clothes.

For nearly a week, I let her adjust to this new me I was suddenly becoming. I took things slow, gave her attention and affection without crossing the line and rushing her. But I couldn't wait anymore. I wanted her to the point that it was driving me crazy. Marko's need of her was my own and I was impatient to sate this passion that was stronger than any amount of hate I currently harbored.

"I dreamt of you." Her words were husky as I pulled back the satin and climbed in the bed with her.

"Was it a good dream?"

My hands were already pulling her closer, bringing her underneath me. She didn't get a chance to speak as my lips massaged into hers.

I moaned, slipping my tongue in deep to taste her. Silk slid between my fingers while I gripped to her thick hair. Fuck, I was falling…falling for her hard. The tug I gave had her breaking away in a gasp.

"It was good. I found you. You were missing."

"Missing? But I'm right here." I kissed her again, sliding my hard cock against the wetness of her pussy. Tessa's hands gripped into my back, squeezing my flesh as I continued a slow rhythm against her folds. "Don't you feel me? Can you not see how far I have come after this last week?" I changed to French. It felt natural. Right, with us. "Do you not see my love for you? It grows so fast and strong."

"I do," she answered in our language. "I wasn't sure it was still there, but it's coming back. You're returning to me just as Hunter said you would."

"No more talk of him. Kiss me."

Tightness met my cock as I nudged into her entrance. The warmth drove me deeper until I felt her stretch around me. Blood tinged my mouth. The pleasure was more than I was prepared for. I paused, withdrawing, only to plunge forward through my greed to have more.

Stinging sliced into my back as Tessa's nails dug into my skin. My hips rotated and I thrust, moaning through the victory of finally being inside of her. Finally having her like I had longed for since she'd come to me, dead from Hunter's dagger. Her powers and beauty had entranced me then, but as they grew, so did my obsession to include her in my plans. But I never saw this happening. How could I? I had never felt real love before.

"Marko." She was moving against me faster, kissing along my neck as I relished in her scent and energy. They were peaking. Already, she was so close to an orgasm. *From me.*

I pushed into her deeper, testing her energy with my own. I wanted to make this good for her. Better than Marko ever had.

Cautiously, I merged our powers, easing mine into her as I continued to keep a leisurely pace. Deep breaths filled the room as she clutched to me and I felt her body throw off a wave of heat. I kept the pulses light, hoping she was too far gone to notice. It would resemble what I did the night of the coronation and if she caught on to that, I wasn't sure how she would react.

"Faster," she moaned. "Harder."

"You don't need that, you need *me*."

I drove down, letting my fangs break through her skin with just enough bite to have her sucking in air. Venom oozed from my fangs and her response to the potency of my poison was automatic. Screams tore from her throat and her back tried to bow under my weight.

Sweet blood pooled into my mouth, hardening my cock so much that it ached with the most pleasurable agony. The screams were still coming as her body spasmed through the waves of release. I soaked them into my brain, nestling them in securely for the future. I wanted to remember everything about this moment. *Our moment.*

"So strong," she breathed out. "So … good."

A smile wanted to come. Instead, I let a little more flow from me. She clawed across my back, moving wildly beneath me.

"Oh yes. Yes."

My thrusts increased and within seconds she was screaming and thrashing through the orgasm again. I broke away, licking over her neck as I pushed the top half of my body up. I grabbed her ankles widening her legs so I could watch where we were joined. My pulse thumped hard in my chest and I couldn't breathe through the sight.

Too many dreams. Too many fantasies. But this was real. My plan concerning Tessa's part had really worked. I had her, and Marko was out of the picture for good.

My eyes shot up to hers. Her lids were heavy from passion and her full lips were separated as she took deep breaths from her mouth.

"So beautiful. You love me, yes? Tell me, ma minette. Let me hear you say it."

Dark lashes fluttered as her arms lifted to press on the headboard. Her back arched and I groaned loudly as she pushed down to sink to the base of my cock.

"I love you." Her hips rotated while I kept still, watching her fuck me. Watching her use the sway of her hips to guide her pussy up and down my length. "I love you," she repeated again, circling her hips again, "I love you."

Faster, she moved, pushing from the headboard with ever rotation. And me … I was frozen with captivation. With this new love I was drowning in. Even *I* couldn't have imagined this. It left me wanting to do something for her. Something so grand that it forced her to love me more.

"I want to taste you. I want us to be bonded again. You are missing from me. I can't bear it any longer, Marko."

The pain that swept over her face didn't compare to the sudden shattering of my own. Bond. Yes, to be truly bonded. Then we'd be in love forever. She'd be mine for real.

But it was impossible. I was tied to Marko. Her blood wasn't strong enough to overpower his. Especially now that he'd strengthen from our connection. The longer he and I were linked, the more we were doomed to stay that way.

I leaned forward, trying not to be hesitant as I lowered my weight back over her. Our special time was about to be ruined. She'd taste how much Aetas' blood had taken over Marko's. Or that's what she would assume since she was really tasting me to begin with. Still, I dreaded what was about to happen. We wouldn't tie, and she'd be devastated all over again. And me, I'd be upset as well.

Tessa's hands on my neck drew me down for a kiss. The soft brush of her lips had my lids lowering with longing.

"Your turn to tell me that you love me."

I met her eyes, caught unaware as I detected suspicion within her depths.

"I love you," I breathed out. "I do love you," I assured.

"I believe you. " She drew me down again, adding more pressure this time with her kiss. When she worked her way across my cheek and ran her tongue over my neck, I relaxed and waited for her bite, but it didn't come. "That's why I am going to ask this of you, my love" she whispered in my ear. "Bring our people back to headquarters. Stop the war now and let us go back into hiding. Make the humans forget about us. You can do it. I *know* you can."

Fangs sung into my neck painfully and I winced as I locked up on top of her. Did she know? Did Tessa suspect?

The draws on my vein were slow—calculated. As if she were reading and studying everything there was about what made up my blood. The need to growl, to stop her because of my guilt was there, but she'd only be more suspicious if I did. Instead, I slammed my cock into her. Once I started, I didn't stop. Her poison was stronger than I expected. It was growing and it egged me on, causing me to pound into her with brute force. She broke from my neck gasping and I took the opportunity to crush into her mouth. She didn't know the truth, and even if she did suspect, I would win her over. She would love me in the end. I knew she would, because I was Marko, and deep down, I knew that's where her heart was.

Chapter 20
Tessa

Sweat dripped down my face as I gathered my powers and projected it toward the shield Marko held up across the room. We'd been going at it for hours now, and not just the lessons. We had literally been arguing the entire time.

He refused to bring our people back. He said we were okay. That the fighting between us and the humans would calm now that they'd had their victory. He told me to trust him. *Trust him.* I trusted no one anymore. I would show him what was expected of me. I would play the game of loving queen trying to mend her broken ties with her mate. But inside, I was seething. Impatient and enraged at his decision.

"Again."

A yell filled the room as I took my anger out on his shield. A shield I didn't seem to affect, whatsoever. *Aetas.* His blood had turned my Marko more into him than anything. I hated him. So then why did I long to go back to The City of the Dead?

"Again."

I spun on Marko, trying to catch my breath. "I am finished."

"You are not. You must get stronger." He paused. "Do you want to bond with me, again? If so, you must heal the damage that has been done. The only way is to exercise your gifts. This is therapy, ma minette. Now continue."

My lips pressed shut as I reached inside of me and put everything I had toward the invisible force. The slightest glimmer surfaced along the wall and I cast him a quick glance. His eyes narrowed and he nodded.

"You peaked. That's as strong as you're going to get with that skill. Try something different. When you begin, only focus on the warmth in your core. Try to force as much of your powers through as you can."

I turned my back to him, facing the shield, again. I hated how much like Aetas he was. When Marko and I tested our skills, we never singled each other out. We did everything together—merged our gifts. Apparently we didn't anymore.

A bead of sweat ran down my temple and I wiped it away. My eyes closed and darkness engulfed me for only a moment before Marko's face flashed before my eyes. It wasn't of him now, but of when I rushed to his cell. At the time I had just turned into a vampire and I didn't remember him, but the expression he held. The fascination merged with pain. It had my heart becoming heavy. It was almost as if he were a different person than the one who held onto those bars so long ago.

When he reached for me …

On instinct, I felt my hand lift. I hadn't went to him then, but now, I wanted to.

To turn back time. Yes. I would suffer through Sayer's rapes all over again to go back and change things. I would have been more careful around Hunter. Protected his human emotions better so he wouldn't have ever tried to kill me. I would have never of met Aetas. Marko would be the same. We could have been happy, and Hunter, perhaps the three of us could have come together somehow.

I opened my lids knowing I was deluding myself. It wouldn't have turned out that way. Not with Hunter anyway. I was who I was. A killer, and I liked shedding blood. Vampire lives weren't meant to merge with humans. Not as friends, only as food and foe. Fuck, we needed to get our people back.

Black fog swirled around my palm, waiting. For what I wasn't sure. I was open, but I didn't have anything in particular that I wanted to do. Everything I had learned to this point I already had perfected. And I couldn't do what Marko had done. Although his blood was still thickly in me, our bond was broken … and wasn't returning anytime soon.

Tears resurfaced. Aetas. His blood was so strong in Marko that I knew it could be years, decades even, before it faded enough for me to rebond to my mate. What if we didn't make it that long?

I turned, taking in my mate's questioning expression. The fog swirled between us in my hand and once again I was in limbo. Nothing new came. I was missing something, but what was it?

My lips parted as Hunter entered my mind. I'd been so focused on Marko's gifts that I didn't even take into account what I'd inherited from bonding to Hunter. He had Aetas' blood. I now had Aetas' blood in me as well.

I looked back at the fog, smiling as I began to make it thicken and grow like a curtain around me. Outside of my space, I could feel Marko's curiosity. His energy was surging and I let my own work its way toward him. When I didn't get stopped, I continued, trying my best to stay undetected as I pushed into his unprepared mind. I didn't make it far before I hit a subconscious wall.

Persuasion. It was Aetas' gift. Could I use it differently that what was expected?

Harder, I pushed, until I hit the surface of something. I wanted to find the moment where Marko thought me most beautiful so I could use it to my advantage. Instead, I came across a barrage of images of myself that didn't exist. Fantasies? Dreams?

Baffled, I grasped one, clinging to it in confusion. As much as I wanted to think over it, I didn't have time if I wanted to attempt my plan. I studied the detail, willing it to become me. Aetas had talked of object materialization before. I could do this. I knew I could. It was no different than disappearing and reappearing somewhere else. Instead of it being me, I would materialize objects to fit what I wanted.

A deep breath left me as tingling raced over my skin. For minutes I stayed in deep concentration, envisioning nothing but the black see-through gown. It was different than any I'd ever worn before. Lace covered and concealed my most intimate areas, but the rest was sheer, leaving my skin visible under the dark, thin material. The deep slits up each thigh left it floating out around me when I walked. It went beyond sexy and had a low cut top that left my shoulders exposed. My hair was piled high on my head, fitting within my crown. What was so different than my usual self was the dark make-up I wore. The eyeliner and shadows around the green color of my eyes left them glowing as I walked toward him. The memory was looping. I was just walking, showing how much I wanted him as I neared.

"Ma minette?"

My eyes opened, leaving me with view of the dark smoke hiding me. The coolness from the swirling raced over my exposed neck and I couldn't stop the smile from coming as I glanced down at the black dress.

"What are you doing? I know you're there, but I can't see you."

The fog sunk into my skin, fading from the surroundings as I began to walk through the curtain, just as I saw in the clip. Marko's eyes flashed with lust, but he shook his head. There was shock there, and something else. Something so much deeper that he wasn't meaning to reveal.

"How did you see that? How?" He swallowed hard, beginning to circle around me. "Answer me! Were you in my mind?"

My eyes cut over to the side to look at him and my suspicion heightened as his fear turned to anger.

"Is there a reason I shouldn't be? You've never cared before."

"You wanted in mind, so you just, what, took this image of yourself and materialized it?" Marko stepped in, spinning me to face him. "Talk to me." He gave me a shake, gripping to my shoulders tightly as he glared at me.

"That's exactly what happened. I saw the image and I chose to become it."

My eyes scanned his as I willed the persuasion to return. Almost immediately Marko's features softened.

"I just wanted to look good for you. I wanted you to want me. Instead you're acting like I did something wrong. You're being mean to me. I can't believe you'd yell and shake me for doing something you asked me to." Tears welled and I could almost laugh at how real the actions appeared. I was pouting, looking up at him through my lashes as his eyebrows drew in regretfully.

"I'm sorry. You're right. I told you to learn and I shouldn't be angry with you. You have every right to be in my mind. I guess it's Aetas blood that is making me defensive. I'm sure he didn't like people in his mind. Please, forgive me."

His arms pulled me into his body and I couldn't stop the smile from greeting me in the mirror I face.

"Do I look pretty? Do you love me like this?" I pulled back pushing my persuasion through his stare even more.

"You have to ask me that?" Marko's hand cupped my cheek as he learned in, kissing me. His other grabbed my ass, pulling my body into his. "You have no idea how many times I've imagined you like this. So exposed, and yet concealed in all the right pleases."

The lamp on the table behind me rocked as he pushed the back of my thighs against it. The next thing I knew, he reached out and cleared it with his hand.

I'm going to fuck you like this. It's not a dream anymore. You made this real and now I will have it."

"I would have done this a long time ago had I of known."

I was lifted to sit on the table. The sheer material fell over and between my legs at the slits. Marko growled, gripping my waist as he lowered and pulled me down to kiss on my thighs. When he looked up into my face, there was a yearning there. A longing I didn't quite recognize. It was as though he was looking at me for the first time. *Love.* Yes, he loved me. I knew that, but why was this different than before?

Knocking had him standing. A threatening sound rumbled his throat, filling the space. "It's Colin. There's a problem. I have to take care of this. Just …" His hand rose even as he walked and threw open the door. Whispering erupted and he looked over his shoulder, still staring, longingly. When he finally turned, he was so angry that it left me concerned. "It might be a little bit. I can't fucking believe of all times, I have to leave you now. Perhaps I should tell them to handle it on their own."

"No," I rushed out. "I'm fine. Go ahead. I'll keep this on. I'll be waiting for you."

A smile stretched across his face, but it was just as fake as mine. He threw me one more look, scowling before he shut the door behind him. My grin instantly melted away. I turned, facing the mirror once again. Before I could so much as try to figure out why Marko suddenly liked this look, the door swung open. Hunter jolted to a stop as his gaze met mine in the mirror.

"Wow. My queen." His head bowed. "I'm sorry, I …thought the training room was empty."

"No you didn't," I said, turning to face him. "You can't lie to me, Hunter. We're bonded, remember? And I'm stronger and more experienced than you."

His mouth twisted. "I've miss you. I wanted to see you. Marko, I don't think he wants me around you anymore. He keeps pushing me away. I don't understand. He encouraged me to get close to you. Now, all he does is order me to leave."

"Encouraged you?"

Hunter nodded. "After he was first turned. He said I had almost just as much right over you as he did because I was your bonded now. He was just yours, legally. Something like that. Anyway, it's starting to piss me off. You *are* my mate, dammit." He walked closer. "And I can't stand being away from you. You're all I can think about. Do you think of me?"

"All the time," I admitted.

A frown came to his face. "This is so unfair. I want to kiss you. I wanted to hold you, and I can't. He'll kill me if I do. I know this. It's written in the looks he gives me. He's waiting for me to cross the line. He wants an excuse."

"He can't kill you, Hunter. If he did, he'd kill me. Besides." I headed toward the door. "I wouldn't let him hurt you."

My hand extended toward him and Hunter walked over to take it. I tried not to think about how wrong this was. Not because he wasn't my legal mate, but because I truly had forgiven him and it was too baffling for my vampire to understand. The truth was, I longed for him. *I loved him, again.* The bond was making sure of that.

"Where are we going?"

"The City of the Dead. I wish to speak with Aetas."

Chapter 21
Hunter

I couldn't hide the awe as I followed Tessa through the City. We'd been silent up to this point, but as I saw the memorials for the fallen enforcers I couldn't help but stop and show my respect.

"This place is amazing. So much energy. *So much history.*"

Tessa's hands clasped as she gave a nod. "Yes. And it'll only get more intense as we get closer to Aetas. His power radiates even after death."

My hand trailed over the black marble and I couldn't help but frown as I turned and began walking again.

"What it is?" Tessa asked, lowly. "Something upsets you."

I threw her a glance and took in the large tower ahead. It had to been three stories high. A steeple protruded from the white cathedral top and it looked more like a church to me than anything else.

"I'm torn on what I should do. I've been giving thought to joining the enforcers. I'm just not sure if I should."

"It's a very dangerous profession in our field." Her low tone didn't hide what I knew she meant.

"Yes. It's the reason I think I'm going to have to pass. If I die, well, we both know what will happen, then. I do believe Marko would make me suffer even after my death if I were to take you away from him."

Tessa's face turned stoic as she stared ahead. Our pace increased at whatever she was thinking. "Maybe. Although I'm not so sure."

"What do you mean?"

"He's different now, but you know that. He's very self-centered."

I laughed, not able to help it. I'd gotten to know him well enough before his bond with Aetas, but I was remembering more from my past.

"Hasn't he always been?"

Tessa's gaze shot to me. "Not like this. He loved me once."

"He loves you still."

"Not like before." She threw me a look. "He also loved his people once, too, but this Marko let them die. I will never forgive him for that. Ever."

My brow creased as old memories came back. "He *was* a different leader before. I remember that. He has changed a lot since then. It's almost like …" I trailed off, not wanting to go there.

"Like what?"

She stopped in front of the pathway that led to Aetas' memorial, but I continued on, making her follow as she waited for me to speak. I wasn't sure I should tell her my fears. Although, she could probably discover them herself if she only pushed into my mind like I knew she could.

I came to a halt outside of the door, amazed that it was almost impossible to stay so close.

"It's almost like Marko." I paused. "Like he and Aetas are one in the same. Does that make sense?"

Tessa's lips parted while she nodded. "I feel the same, I've tasted his blood, Hunter. He is more Aetas than Marko. In time I suppose it will fade, but what if it doesn't? What if Marko is doomed to keep Aetas' personality traits? I feel like." She lowered her head. "I feel as though I am married to a stranger. Making love to a stranger. He's so different in that regard than Marko was. Marko took care to …" She stopped. "You don't wish to hear this. I'm sorry."

"No, please. I grabbed her hand, pulling her closer to me. "I want to know everything you're thinking. Everything that happens that I can't be a part of. I know that sounds odd, but you have no idea how hard it is for me not to be with you. If I can't physically, I wish to be in these ways."

My hand was lifted and I couldn't stop my pulse from racing. She flipped it over, kissing my palm. "You were always a great friend. Sometimes I wonder if maybe there wasn't meant to be more between us."

"It will never happen being mated to Marko. Aetas told me those vows are unbreakable until death. Unless agreed by both, but I don't see Marko giving you to me."

"No," she breathed out. "He will not."

"What were you saying before? How is he different now when the two of you are together?"

Tessa's arm extended and she put her palm against the large metal door. "He used to take such care with me. Pleasure me for hours before we made love. Now, he's so eager, so impatient. He takes me almost immediately. It's as though there's more lust than passion. I don't really understand his change. And this," she said, waving her hand over her appearance. "This is what I materialized from his mind. This is how he saw me when he wanted me. Marko never liked me wearing heavy make-up. He once refused to leave the room until I took it off. He always said I was more beautiful natural than painted up. Is it Aetas' desires he feels now? Aetas' lust? I don't know."

The last was almost silent as she moved in closer to focus on the door.

"Hunter, I don't know if I can continue to hide my true feelings for this new version. He doesn't listen to me when I suggest he get our people to come here for safety. He's acting recklessly."

She bit her bottom lip looking around. Instantly, words pushed into my mind.

"If he doesn't start helping our people soon." She left the rest open and I felt my stomach drop at what I knew she meant.

"I will fight with you. I will support your rule."

Tessa's eyes closed and she reached, grabbing my shirt and pulling me to her. I wrapped my arms around her tightly, kissing the top of her head. When she dropped her head back to look at me, I couldn't stop myself from moving in. My lips brushed over hers, barely existent in my hesitation from what I was doing.

"I'm sorry."

"Sorry? You're not sorry. You want more."

"Fuck, I do. I want you so bad I can taste it. Taste you … everywhere." I pinned her against the door, pushing my thigh between her legs. "I remember what you taste like, Tessa. I dream of it. I dream of our first time after my return. We made love for hours. We couldn't get enough of each other."

Tighter, she gripped to me. "Don't remind me of that right now. I try not to think of you that way. It only makes things harder."

"Because you want me, too?" At her silence, I moved to her throat, sucking against her skin. "You do. I know you do. You love me. And you loved fucking me during the coronation. Do you not think about that day, either?"

"No. I can't. It's safer that way."

Tessa's hand pressed against my chest and I growled, pulling back from her throat.

"This is unfair and we both know it. Safer? Yes, I suppose it is, but what about what we want? You can't stand this new Marko. You talk of the forbidden if he goes much further, but you won't take me when I give myself to you so freely? Why must it always be like this? We're so close, Tessa. We're both vampires now, and we're bonded for fucks' sake, and I still can't have you. I can't stand this. Maybe for once I'll accept the risk and finally take what I want. Just like I should have taken you a long time ago."

Tessa's eyes widened. "You don't mean that."

"And if I do? If I take you so you can be with me away from here?"

Pressure pushed against my chest until I gave in and stepped away, releasing her. I could see the temptation in her pained expression. She blinked, repeatedly, and turned to face the door. Her hand rose back to the metal.

"I can't leave, Hunter, no matter how much I want to. I see possibility with being outside of these walls. A chance to save our people. But … I can't leave. I can't …"

"What is it about this place that draws you here? I've seen you come down to this city multiple times. Is this what you waste your time doing? Standing outside of the door to a leader who ruined our lives?"

Tessa spun on me with so much anger, I wasn't prepared for it.

"Do not speak of him that way. Aetas may have made mistakes, but he looked out for our kind. He did what he felt was best for us. That's more than I can say for our new leader."

"Agreed," I said, cautiously. "But Aetas wasn't as good as you make him out to be. I'm sorry Tessa, I don't understand this emotion you have toward him."

The anger disappeared and her shoulders sagged. "Truthfully, neither do I. I think that's why I'm here."

I scanned the building, taking in the metal door that had no sign of an entrance.

"What do you say we find out? Should we go in and ask him?"

"We can't go in there."

My eyebrow rose. "Why can't we?"

"Because," she exclaimed. "For one, there's no way in. Two, it's sacred."

"Sacred?"

Tessa's lips pressed together and she glanced back at the door. "I don't know why I fear to go in. Do you think you can find a way inside?"

A mischievous smile came to my face and it wasn't long before she mirrored it.

"I can try. I'll be a little surprised if I can't. Here, watch out."

She stepped out of my way as I approached the door. She hadn't exaggerated on the energy. The power it held gave off vibes that made me almost want to change my mind. I pressed my palm against the door as she had done and immediately felt myself break into a sweat.

"What's in there? Or … what is guarding this place that doesn't want us to go in?"

Tessa licked her lips, raising her hand to put next to mine.

"I don't know. I've wondered the same thing. Some has to be Aetas' energy, but the aura is off. Something or someone doesn't want anyone inside. It feels wrong to me, almost threatening. But I can't help but feel drawn back. I long to be here, Hunter, and I don't know why."

My hand dropped. "If that is your wish, I will get you inside. Maybe not today, but I promise I won't stop until I find a way."

Her head cocked to the side and something was going through her mind, but I wasn't sure what it was.

"If you can get me in, maybe this feeling will go away. Maybe then I will be at peace."

"Then what?"

She glanced back at the door. "If I have no reason to stay from the outcome, and Marko does not show improvement," she turned back to me, pausing. "I will leave with you and we will do what we must to save our kind."

I had Tessa in my arms before I could help myself. My lips crushed into hers for only seconds before I placed her off to the side and charged at the door with all of my strength. Hitting the metal was like falling multiple stories and landing on the pavement. I grabbed my shoulder, blinking past the stars in my vision.

"That isn't regular metal or I would have gone right through it."

Tessa took a deep breath. "I could have told you that. Are you okay?"

"Yeah. Just took me by surprise is all." I immediately stepped back, scanning the front. *No windows.* "Stay here." I took off at a fast pace, moving around to the side of the marble building. My eyes ate up every inch as I looked for any sort of opening I could come across. The back was solid as was the other side. As I met Tessa back in the front my teeth clenched in aggravation. If I could ease her mind, we could leave here. We could be together. Alone and away from this new Marko. "The door is the only way in."

"Then it is impossible."

"No. Nothing is impossible. They put the body inside. If they got in, so can we."

Tessa glanced around the surroundings. With cautious steps, she moved even with the door, putting a good few feet between them. "Steady yourself. I have a feeling we're about to get hit with one hell of a shockwave."

"You think it's protected by a shield?"

Worry came to Tessa's features. "Yes. My concern is, whose?"

"Don't. Not yet. We'll save that for last. What about our gift? Can we turn to smoke and try to slip through the crack in the door? Or materialize ourselves inside?"

"Not the materialization. We've never been in there. You can only materialize yourself into a place you're familiar with. Our fog …we could try, but if there's a shield, we'll be blocked."

"Dammit." A small sound left me. "Let's try to slip in, then."

Smoke began to pour from underneath Tessa's dress and I tried to focus, but my gift still didn't come easily. A good minute went by while Tessa appeared as a dark smoke around me. Finally, my hands began to fade. Once it began, I was gone within seconds.

We both pushed toward the door, our essence merging as we filled the entire surface of the barrier. I could feel a tug against my energy and I let it lead to the very top. The pressure we hit was all the conformation that was needed. There was a shield, but amazingly Tessa's strength was able to push into it. The force stuck to us tightly, swallow us whole as we penetrated through. The snap that popped against my energy was like being hit with bullet. The pain took my breath away and I went to pull back on instinct, but Tessa wouldn't let me. She surged forward and I was suddenly falling, hitting the marble floor with a hard thud.

Darkness poured around me and Tessa was standing over me, pulling me up.

"Hurry, we won't have much time," she rushed out.

Panicked for her safety, I scanned the dim surroundings. It was dark, but a glow toward the center of the room gave me enough light to see that the room was almost completely empty. There was two things present—a marble rectangle the size of a body, and a weird machine that had a red flashing light.

"Aetas?" I was already running forward, as was she. We arrived at what had to be the casket at the same time. Our hands settled on the lid and we looked at each other. Tessa's face was full of fear and I knew I had to have been displaying the same emotion. My mind was screaming that this was wrong, but I had to put my mate at ease.

"I have to see," she whispered

We both pushed at the same time, easing the heavy marble up. Tessa's breath hitched and my own got caught in my throat. A cry filled the space and she gripped to my arm.

"Oh, God. Help us. Help us all."

Chapter 22
Marko

Tessa's voice stirred me from a deep sleep, lifting me from the darkness, into such a place of light that I could have cried. And she was crying. Looking at me as she sobbed. Just as she began to come into focus, the lid was slammed shut and I was back in the dark. It all happened so fast that I wasn't sure if I was still dreaming.

"Tessa? Tessa!" My voice roared as I thrashed harder than I ever had. "Tessa!"

I knew she wouldn't hear me. I'd screamed at the top of my lungs when I'd heard her on her visits, and never once had she gave me the impression she'd heard my desperate calls. There was something about this place I was in. I could hear, but not be heard. It was Aetas' doing, I knew that. But if Tessa had been there, she'd seen me. She'd come back for me. Or … did I still look like Aetas?

The thought set me into a panic. What if I looked like him and she hadn't seen my eyes open before the lid was shut? What if …?

"What do you think you're doing in here?"

My voice roaring through the room had me quieting.

"I had to see Aetas." Tessa voice was shaky but stern as she answered back. "He calls to me. I can't help myself." She paused. "May I open it again? I didn't get a chance to see him before you closed the lid."

"Are you crazy?" My voice was moving, which told me Aetas was. "You want to see the dead body of our leader? Did you not see him that night? He was dead on the floor before all of us. What is there left to see?"

"I don't know," Tessa said, her voice breaking. "Marko, please help me. I do not know what is wrong with me." She sniffled and fast clicking from heels echoed around.

"Shh. Don't cry, ma minette. I know his passing has been hard on you, but this grief will pass. You just have to focus on other things and stop coming here. This place will not ease the pain you feel inside."

"I know," she said quietly. "I don't know why I do this to myself. It just hurts so much." Clicking grew closer to me and my heart raced even faster. "I have to admit something to you, Marko. I'm afraid you might be upset, though, if I do."

"What? Is it Hunter? Has he done something to you?"

"Me?" Hunter's voice boomed through the room. "Why do you always rush to blame me?"

"Leave." The demand had footsteps pounding against the floor in their departure.

"It is not, Hunter," Tessa said, calmly. "It's about Aetas."

"Oh … What about him?"

Tessa's presence was so thick around me that I knew she had to be right at the casket. I lifted my head, touching the hard surface above, trying any way I could to get closer to her.

"I think somewhere along the way I fell in love with him. It's the only explanation for the heartbreak I feel. I long for him, Marko. My heart is breaking when I'm not here."

"But … what about me?"

"You know I love you," she rushed out, angrily. "All I am saying is that I think I love him as well. He was cruel at times and he did things he shouldn't have, but he was a great leader. And he believed in me. He wanted me to be the best I could be. That *meant* something to me."

"I was giving you lessons earlier," he said, defensively. "And I love you. I love you more than he could have *ever* loved you. Besides," he said, dropping his anger. "Aetas is dead. Perhaps wherever he is, he's hearing you and you're making him happy by saying such things."

Silence filled the room for only a few seconds before Tessa responded.

"You make fun of me."

"I do no such thing. Maybe he does hear you, who am I to say? I don't know what happens when one dies." Footsteps. "Tessa, come here."

Fabric sounded and I knew he had her in his arms. A growl tore from me as I once again tried to twist my body. "You're clearly upset," he continued. "Let me take you back to the room. Let us pick up where we left off before I had to leave for my meeting."

"No! Tessa!"

"You want to cheer me up?"

He laughed. "I'm going to do more than that. I'm going to have you screaming my name again, begging me for more of what only I can give you." He moaned, letting out a deep breath. "Fuck the room," he said, huskily. "I don't want to wait."

"Not here. Not in Aetas' memorial. Have respect."

"Have respect for a man who didn't respect me? I care not for his feelings or his memory—Fuck, you're so wet."

Tessa soft voice let out a deep tone and I could tell she was beginning to struggle. "Marko, I said not here."

"Look at me. Look into my eyes and tell me you don't want me."

"I don't want you." She grunted. "Not here."

A small chuckle had the hair on my arms rising. It wasn't nice. If anything, it was full of sadistic intentions. I knew the sound all too well.

"Still not strong enough to escape my stare. You should have known better, but your temper makes you susceptible. That's alright. You'll learn in time. Now, we're going to start this conversation over with. Hunter has left. Your anger is gone and you're happy to see me. I'm holding and touching you, and you want me." He got quiet and Tessa's breathing got heavier. "Spread your legs wider …yes … good girl."

A loud crack sounded and I blinked through the rage that sickened me.

"Next time you want to try to twist my mind, make sure you're not sloppy about it. My core may be damaged, but my mind is far from weak."

Clicking faded and the yell that followed left my forehead slamming against the marble. It hadn't been good. Aetas had been enraged, and he was going after her. What that meant, I wasn't sure, but I knew if Tessa kept this up, it was only going to be a matter of time before he hurt her too.

Chapter 23
Aetas

"Stop right now!"

My voice carried through the City of the Dead as I yelled for Tessa. My heart was racing. Not just from her almost seeing Marko lying in the place I was supposed to, but because she'd withstood my powers and busted me. Fuck, she was getting stronger. It appeared my blood was a better match for her than Marko's. Paired with more of her own from Hunter, she was healing and growing at a much faster pace than I had prepared for. Even during her practice, she was stronger than she knew. First breaking through my mind, then through the shield I had around the memorial ... If I didn't put a stop to this fast, she was going to discover what was really going on.

"Don't you walk away from me," I snapped, catching up to her. When I spun her to face me, she penned me with a look I'd seen before—directed at me. *The real me*. Hate. Yes, she was starting to suspect. I'd have to try harder.

"Give me a chance to explain." The anger was gone now, replaced with sadness. "I keep messing this up. My behavior is appalling. I don't know what I was thinking. When I'm around you ... I can't think of anything but wanting you. I want you. Nothing I do fills the cravings. I'm desperate for your love."

"I would have given myself to you had you taken me back to our room. I tell you a part of me love's Aetas and because of your hate of him, you decide to make yourself feel better by fucking me in a place where people show their respect? That's sick," she said, turning back to walk the path. I kept even, trying to force the anger away.

"You're right. I'm sorry. Forgive me."

Her eyes cut to me and she crossed her arms over her chest, losing some of the repulsion she harbored. "Don't do something like that again. If I say no, I mean it."

"Of course."

Hunter was further ahead, leaning against a monument for one of the enforcers. My lips couldn't help but peel back, angrily. Tessa stopped, again, and I could have cursed myself when I took in the expression she had aimed at me.

"I'm jealous. He has something I don't think I will for a very long time." I was quick to admit my mistake before she had a chance to say anything. I reached, gently pulling her into my arms. "All I want is to bond with you. For us to be one and lead together. Nothing is turning out like I had hoped. And this blood. Tessa, I'm afraid of what it's doing to me. I know I'm not the same. I see the way you look at me. I can't stand it. I just want you to love me again. Like before. *I miss us*."

Her forehead came to rest on my chest while I held to the back of her neck. Hunter watched, but I couldn't look at him for long. The more I did, the angrier I was becoming. Marko's blood was fucking with me. His jealousy and short temper was mine now. It was ruining my plan. I was losing her and I wasn't sure what I could do to stop it from happening. I tried to get into her mind, but I failed every time. If I could just force her to believe. If I could make her love me …

"You're getting cool. You need to feed. Let's go to our room. We'll hold each other. Nothing more. You have my word."

She nodded against me, only lifting her head when I went to turn her so we could start walking. When we got even with Hunter, Tessa glanced in his direction. He only had eyes for her. I had a feeling they were speaking, but I couldn't get into either of their heads. Not Hunter's, and sure as hell not Tessa's since she was wearing my crown. My strength was my curse. With my blood in both, it guarded them, just like I protected myself.

Her eyes. I had to find a way in. Without the crown.

"Maybe we should go somewhere. I could take you out for a dinner or maybe you'd like to take a trip to the South Wing? I could give you a tour. Show you the museum there."

The elevator doors shut and Tessa looked over at me. Tears clouded her eyes and the realization had me pausing from pressing the button. She reached over, doing it for me as I tried to think of a way of fixing my slip. Would she know I hadn't explored the area since my return? That only Aetas would have known about that part of headquarters?

"What is it? You're upset."

"No, you're right, I'm just tired. I have a lot on my mind."

I stepped in closer, glancing toward the city below on instinct. Tessa's hand quickly cupped my face, turning me back to her.

"You'd take me somewhere after how mean and distant I've been toward you?"

"Of course." My voice softened as I pulled her in closer. "It's not just you, it's both of us. We're under a lot of stress. But I can make it better. I can fix us. Do you want to go out? To … be with me."

"What about the humans? The attacks?"

I laughed, lowering to brush my lips over hers. "I think I can take care of you."

"You've said that before. I almost died."

Flashes of Hunter shooting her with the dagger and Sayer saving her life hit me.

"I wasn't on guard that night like I should have been. I was too swept away by the love I was beginning to feel for you. I give you my word, if we leave, nothing will escape my notice. I will protect you with my life."

Tessa leaned in, pulling my head down to meet hers. It didn't take long for our kiss to get heated. And just like every time I got a taste of her passion, I couldn't control the urges to have her. What had I done by betraying my vow of celibacy? I was becoming a monster. If I wasn't fucking her, I was thinking about it.

The door opened and Tessa's broke away, pulling my hand as she led me down the hall. I planted my feet, tugging her into me. Before I could stop myself, I was shoving us both into the wall. My hands were on her ass and I had her straddling my hips.

Seeing her dressed like this for me. Tasting her and smelling her scent, I was swept away.

"Room," she whispered against my lips. "I don't want anyone to see us like this."

Before she could finish, we were falling to the bed. I ground my hard cock into her, ripping into the lace covering her chest. The black material tore in my grasp and her breasts swayed at the force. A deep inhale left her as I messaged the flesh, pinching at her nipple.

"Do you see how much I want you? God, I can't get enough." I lowered and sucked the hard nub into my mouth as she removed her crown. Tessa held to it as she arched, moaning. My teeth grazed over her sensitive skin and I moved to her inner breast, letting my fang pierce the skin. The shot of venom had her screaming out and she let go of the crown and reached for me, rocking her hips.

"Aetas." She moaned and my head shot up in shock. Tessa's lashes fluttered and then her lips parted as she gasped.

"I'm sorry," she rushed out. "I'm sorry. I didn't mean it."

My heart exploded as confliction kept me frozen. She didn't know it was me, but she wanted it to be. She wanted *me*? I thought she had been going to the temple because of her pull to Marko, but could she have really been mourning *my* loss? Everything she'd said pointed that way, but I hadn't been able to make myself believe it was true.

I lifted, still not sure what to do. If I exposed myself, it could ruin everything. It wasn't the time.

"Marko, please. Don't be mad at me."

Mad? I was dying to confess. To tear my clothes off and show her just how much her mistake had meant to me.

"We're going to pretend that didn't happen." I shrugged my jacket off, tearing into my shirt. I tried to pretend to be upset, but I wasn't sure how well I was doing. When I lowered my weight back to her, Tessa stared up into my eyes. She was searching for something.

"Forgive me?"

I tapped into Marko's blood, trying to feel what he would do if he were in my position. For the life of me, I couldn't focus enough to know. My fingers buried into her hair and I tugged back, painfully. Tears rolled down the sides of her face and I dove for her neck. It was time to make her forget this. To have her focused on only one thing—what I could give her.

Chapter 24
Tessa

Forgive me, forgive me, forgive me.

The mantra stayed looping through my mind as I tried not to be sick. Even the poison in my veins couldn't erase what I knew. This wasn't my Marko. My Marko was trapped in Aetas' memorial, looking close to death, himself. Jesus. Shit. Jesus. I was going to be sick.

"Too much," I managed through convulsive swallowing.

Marko's face rose, but I knew who was looking back at me. *Aetas.* How had I missed it? So many times he had tried this same thing, and I had always known it was him. I hadn't this time. It had to be because he and Marko now shared the same blood.

"What?"

The top half of my body shot up and I flew out from under him as I ran to the restroom. Dark hair fell loose from the pins as I leaned over the toilet, heaving. I jumped as a hand settled on the middle of my back.

"What's wrong? What happened?"

The touch had me gagging again, but nothing was coming.

I took a deep breath, feeling the tears spill down my cheeks as I stood and walked over, clutching to the counter. Mascara was streaking down my face. I looked up meeting Aetas' gaze through Marko's eyes.

"I haven't fed. I think your bite was too much."

"Of course. I don't know what I was thinking. You're trembling. Come," he said, leading me out to the bed. "Sit on my lap and feed."

For the life of me, I didn't want to. I could have used the excuse his blood was too strong for my upset stomach, but that would mean I would have to feed from Hunter. That was impossible.

Aetas stopped at the bed and pulled me down to his thigh. I glanced up to Marko's face and tried to convince myself that it was my husband, the man I loved. It was the only way I was going to keep getting through this.

"Bite, ma minette. Your shaking is getting worse."

My hand rose to the side of his neck. Slowly, I leaned in, easing my fangs into his skin. Blood trickled into my mouth, increasing as I bit down even more. Hands gripped just above my hips, turning me to straddle his lap. My eyes instantly closed. There was going to be no way around this. If I wanted Marko taken somewhere safe, I had to keep Aetas happy and occupied so he wouldn't go back and check on the real Marko. I had to buy Hunter time. *If he could even get in ... or out.* What if Aetas became aware Hunter was trying? No, I couldn't think of it. I had to keep our evil leader's mind far away from anything having to do with Hunter or Marko. It was the only way.

"That feels so good."

Fingers wove in my hair, pushing through until the remaining pins fell loose. When he gripped and pushed me more into him, I bit down harder. I kept my poison as light as I could without him knowing I was intentionally doing it. His hand was on my ass, pulling me closer to his cock and the urge to break down was there again, but I couldn't. I had a part to play, and I'd be damned if I was going to screw it up. My mens' safety depended on it.

My hips rotated and the adrenaline from his power increased my pulse. Aetas met my movements, tearing the black lace panties. With a final jerk, he tossed them, moving in to undo his belt.

"Better, isn't it? I bet you feel so good with my blood in you. Wait until I'm filling you with my cum. You like that."

I had told him that.

I breathed in deeply through my nose, willing the nausea away. Aetas leaned back, maneuvering to remove his slacks. When I was lifted, I braced myself.

Pressure from the head of his cock pressed against my opening and I hated the wetness that was waiting for him. With how strong his blood was, it was a natural aphrodisiac. Whether my mind liked it or not, my body responded.

"Fuck, I've been waiting for this all day. Suck harder for me, ma minette. Show me how much you want me."

I obeyed, drinking in more of him as he held to my hips, inching into and stretching me with my mate's thick length. How would this ever be the same for me and Marko? After Aetas … how was I ever going to look at my mate without remembering what I was doing? How was he going to look at me? I should have known, yet I betrayed him. *I was betraying him now.*

"Enough drinking, kiss me. I want to taste me on your tongue. I want to know that I'm the one you're choosing."

The thought of the single intimate act destroyed me worse than having him fuck my body. It was too connected, too loving. I didn't love Aetas. I knew that now. I didn't love him the slightest. It was Marko. It was always Marko.

My jaw extended and I licked over the wounds, leaning back. His kiss was immediate, full of hunger. *Full of a lust.* It was almost impossible to make myself portray a woman who was in the heat of passion.

"Tell me you love me," he said, in between kisses. "Tell me you want only me."

"I. I—love you. And you know it is only you I want."

If it wouldn't have been for the increasing thrusts, I wasn't sure I would have gotten away with my stuttering. Jesus, how many times had I told Aetas those words? How many times had I tried to force myself to believe them? Perhaps deep down I knew it wasn't Marko. Why hadn't I listened to that tiny voice that said so? I was going to leave this version of Marko, yes, but even then it was for our kind's best interest. Not because I ever let myself think that Aetas still lived.

"Bend over, I want to see your ass as I fuck you."

I was spun over so fast it gave me vertigo. My mind wasn't here, and that was fine with me. Marko's survival left me making sounds, left me going through the motions, but I was far, far, deep into my mind, searching out my link with Hunter.

Satin scrunched between my fingers as I gripped to the comforter. I immediately buried the majority of my face in the fabric. Darkness soothed me and I gripped to my tie with my mate, feeling Hunter's location out. He was still close. Still here somewhere. *Fuck.*

"I could look at this all day—the way you're so tight around me." He moaned, clutching hard to the sides of my ass.

"Fuck me, harder. Fuck me."

The huskiness of my voice amazed me. How I could fit the role so easily, it made me relieved and sick all at the same time. If this could just be over with.

Aetas slammed into me, rocking us forward. I gripped tighter to the darkness, covering my face more while my other hand pushed between my legs. When my fingertips brushed against his sac, I let my touch caress over his sensitive skin with ever sway of his thrust.

"Tessalyn."

"You like that?"

"Yes. Don't stop."

The strain in his tone was a relief. I traced my fingers back and forth, moving toward the back of his sac. Anything to bring on pleasure so he would finish and go to sleep. Luckily, it didn't take long.

"Okay, you have to stop."

"I thought you wanted to come in me. I want you to. Come in me, Marko."

"But you haven't—"

A loud groan left him and wave after wave I met his thrust, making sounds. When he pulled out and kissed me, all I felt was relief.

"I'm taking a shower. You going to wait for me in bed?" I already knew the answer, but I asked, trying to keep things routine.

"Hurry."

He was already climbing under the covers, already yawning.

I hurried to the bathroom, shutting the door behind me. The moment I turned on the water, I couldn't wash Aetas from me fast enough. The dress lay on the floor in pieces and I never wanted to see one like it again.

Soap perfumed the air as I sped through the routine. By the time I dried off, I knew only a few short minutes had gone by, but I heard what I was waiting for— snoring. I left the water running, materializing a dark maroon dress to cover my body.

And I was gone.

Chapter 25
Hunter

It didn't matter what I did, I was fucked. Breaking through the shield, materializing inside … I couldn't do any of it and I couldn't stand it. Wasn't I supposed to be this big, powerful vampire? Why were my gifts so hard to strengthen? Compared to Tessa, I was a weakling. She could destroy me if she chose to. What if something happened to her? How was I supposed to protect her? I couldn't even do the one thing she asked, and that was rescue Marko.

More I paced, glaring at the door like it was Aetas, himself.

How did he do it? How did he turn into Marko? And how did we miss it?

I never suspected. I thought Marko was different, but it never crossed my mind he was my maker. Shouldn't I have known? And what happened to his plans for me? Aetas suddenly hated me. It was almost as if he was Marko. Or at least turning into him.

"You didn't have luck?"

Tessa was still see-through, rushing toward me, only feet away. Her slippers turned solid as she did and the sound of her footsteps were nearly nonexistent in the surrounding silence.

"I can't. I'm so sorry, I've tried everything."

"Do not be sorry. You will grow stronger. You have to listen to me, Hunter. I'm going to materialize inside of the memorial and then materialize Marko and I over to our underground city. Then I will come back and get you. You have to take Marko somewhere no one will ever find him. He's weak now. He has to have time to grow stronger. *To fight.* I want to come, but I have to stay behind to make sure of Aetas' moves. When the time is right, I will find you from our link. It will be the same way I came to you when you were with the enforcers. They will be looking for you. You have to stay out of sight as much as possible."

Before I could say anything, Tessa was gone. She wanted me to take Marko to safety, but a place didn't come to mind. I didn't remember all of my past and from what I could recall, everyone I knew was human … and dead. Fuck! I had to think of something. I failed on getting Marko out, I couldn't fail at this.

Seconds stretched out, and then a minute. An eternity seemed to pass as I scanned the grounds, looking for any movement or shadows. When Tessa reappeared, she had my hand before she was completely visible. And then we were gone, in a void of blackness. Within seconds my feet were touching the floor of an all too familiar room. Their old room.

"He's so weak." She was already pulling me toward the bed, but my vision was still blurry. I blinked, bringing Marko's pale face and beard into focus.

"Tessa? Tessa?"

His eyes were rolling and his lips were cracked. His mouth opened only for his teeth to snap shut. The action had Tessa whimpering as she leaned in.

"Take my blood. Take as much as you need. I'm sorry," she sobbed. "I didn't know."

Stiff fingers trembled as he put them on the sides of her face. Fear had me moving in closer. I didn't trust him not to hurt her in his state. His eyes were black—all vampire. There was a darkness radiating from him. One that appeared more killer than loving husband. And his eyes. They were so haunted.

"I'm going to kill him."

His jaw bit down again, clamping shut with a click of his teeth.

"We'll talk over that later. First you have to get well. Feed."

Marko didn't need another invitation. He jerked her forward, igniting a scream as he savagely bit into her neck. Tessa's hand slammed into my stomach as I reared forward. Although she wanted me to stay back, she fisted my shirt through the pain of his bite. The brutality burned its way up my own neck, leave a scorching sensation stinging along my skin. Minutes passed. Then more. When Tessa's knees gave out, I held her up by the waist, using my palm on the middle of her back to keep up with her pulse.

"Marko, you have to stop."

I didn't bother to hide my panic as I counted the beats. Her heart was slowing the more he drained her.

"Marko!"

A growl echoed through the room as he let go, pulling her more into his arms. Regardless, that he had more strength, I still held around her waist. Tessa could barely move. Her body was limp as she sniffled through the soft cries.

"How long?"

I glanced up to Marko's black eyes. He was still vampire. Still unstable.

"Over a month and a half. Closer to two, I guess."

"It felt like years. Like an eternity of darkness. Three times he fed me. Three. And only then did I see light. I thought I had missed that sweet glow during my first century, but now, I don't think I'll ever look at the dark the same again. It's crazy," he said, hugging to Tessa tighter. "A vampire who's afraid of the dark. Never would I have believed such a thing."

What was I supposed to say to that? Nothing. I didn't think it required an answer. I could understand his new fear, even if I couldn't quite feel the emotion.

"Let her drink from me. She needs to replenish."

Marko's eyes snapped up, only for him to blink away whatever was in his mind. His features immediately loosened from the tense expression he'd had. The black lightened, turning to brown as he took deep breaths.

"Feed her here. I don't want to let go of her. I can't."

Closer, I moved in. When Tessa's head slid to the middle of Marko's chest to move in closer to me, I slit my wrist, putting it up to her mouth. The softness of her lips caressed my skin as she sucked. The action had my body reacting and I braved a stare at Marko, knowing all too well he could feel my battle. He was powerful now. So much more than he had ever been. It scared me. We had been enemies for so long that I worried how he was going to take all of this. Especially given me and Tessa's new bond.

"I didn't know what I was doing when I attacked her that night. You probably don't believe me, but I have to be honest with you. I would never hurt Tessa or force her into something she didn't want."

Emotions left him while he swept back her hair. Still Tessa took in more of my blood. "I know you had no control over yourself that night, Hunter. Aetas' blood told me the truth. Have you been with my concubine since I was away?"

The question had Tessa pausing. It rocked me so much that I paused before I shook my head. "No. Not that I didn't want to be. Aetas … well, you, I thought, wouldn't allow me. At first he seemed able enough, but things changed after the first night at headquarters."

"I don't have to ask you how Aetas was to my wife. I got to hear firsthand after you left earlier."

"After I left?" My brow drew in as I turned my attention to Tessa. She didn't break away from my wrist as she stared ahead like a zombie.

"He was going to rape her right there so I could hear. He tried to force the idea of her wanting him into her mind, but Tessa overpowered his control. She left then, but what happened after is a mystery. Concubine, why don't you tell me what happened?"

The threat for revenge laced every single word he spoke. Tessa's lips once again paused. I could feel her fear—her hesitation. Cautiously, she rose to sit, appearing paler than before I gave her my blood. She glanced at me, and then to him. When her voice came out monotone, it turned my stomach even more.

"I did what I had to do to try to keep you safe. I sent Hunter to rescue you, but he couldn't get in. I didn't know that until Aetas fell asleep and I went back. I had to distract him. I …"

Tessa swallowed hard, appearing as if she were going to be sick. Her hand came to her mouth and she tried to push from Marko, but he held to her, not allowing her to go. With each breath he took, I could see his anger grow.

"But it wasn't the first time, was it?"

Even though Tessa lay back on his chest at his pull, her red-rimmed eyes stayed on me. Her heartache and sickness was my own. Had I of known what she was doing—what was happening …

"No. I thought he was you until I saw you in the memorial. *I didn't know.*"

"Every day? A handful of times? Did he kiss you and touch you like me?"

Tessa flew to a sitting position, surprisingly breaking Marko's hold.

"Do not ask me those questions. Do you see my devastation? Do you know how I feel? You do not! I mourned your loss every day, whether I knew it was you dead, or not. I mourned," she cried. "I begged for something I didn't even know I needed. Aetas—you. Dammit Marko! Look past the surface and into what this means. Aetas has killed our city. Our members and our residents are dead. Marie is dead! She died in my arms, showing me something only now I understand. Darkness. Darkness and being trapped. But I had no idea it was you she was showing me. It matters not, now. The fact is I was too late to save her. Too late because you—Aetas, would not come to give aid to our people. Every major city has been attacked. Our kind is dwindling in numbers and our leader is making it appear that *you* are the one letting us fall. Marko, he's not going to stop until all but a selected few live. Then, what? What is going to happen after that?"

"It's not going to get that far. He's dead, he just doesn't know it yet."

"Marko." I edged closer, not sure how much I should say with the condition he was in. "We have to think rationally. You can't kill Aetas. The two of you are bonded now. If he dies, so do you. If he gets hurt, so do you."

His jaw tightened even more as he pushed to sit up. When he tried to move from the bed, Tessa was reaching to keep him in place.

"I cannot lie down, ma minette. I cannot be still. I have to walk. I need more light."

Her worried gaze came to me as she stood and let him move to the edge of the bed. Her anxiety flared and she bit her bottom lip. Back and forth her eyes scanned the floor, as if she were in deep thought.

"*I have to go.* Aetas is stirring, I can feel his energy. Hunter, remember what I told you."

Marko's face shot toward her. "You think I'm letting you go back?"

"I have to." Her voice broke as Marko's towering body stood and loomed over her. "I have to stay until I know how Aetas takes to your disappearance. I have to discover exactly what he plans to do with our kind."

Marko was on her before either me or Tessa saw him move. One of his arms was locked around her waist while the other filled the gap under her chin. He held to her as though he was afraid she would disappear at any moment. His expression was half crazed, half terrorized. "You will not go back to him. I will not lose you again."

"Let go of her, Marko. You're scaring her."

He backed away, each step a struggle as he used his strength more for his arms, than his legs. His back crashed into the wall and he slid down it at a fast pace, bringing Tessa to the ground with him. Still he stayed wrapped around her.

"You can't leave." His face fitted against the side of hers as his words softened toward the end. "I won't let you leave. I'm sorry for the questions. I'm sorry. I am not angry for what you have done. I am angry at him."

"It won't be for long. We need this information, Marko. Someone has to keep tabs on Aetas. I'm the only one he trusts."

"Loves," Marko corrected angrily. "You're the only one he loves, and it's all my fault. He has taken what I hold for you and twisted it as his own. You don't know how deep my devotion is to you, ma minette. Never has a heart loved so fierce. Never a beat thrummed so strong. I know you feel my love. You came to me without being bonded. We are meant to be."

Her head tilted back while she stared up at his face. When their lips connected, I saw true love. One that nearly took my breath away.

They pulled back at the same time, staring into each other's eyes lost in world of their own. At my shift, Marko's eyes rose to me.

"I feel your heartache as if it were my own. I'm sorry, Hunter. I truly am."

All I could do was shrug. What did he expect me to say, that it was okay? It wasn't. I was undeserving for reasons I didn't even know. Fate had turned its back on me, making it clear that I would be destined to love a woman who would never return my feelings.

"Oh, but she does," Marko whispered, lowering his lids the slightest amount as he seemed to gaze into my very soul. "And this has gone on for far too long. The three of us keep getting pulled together for reasons I cannot contest anymore. It is time we stop fighting each other and come together … as one. As it almost was when Tessa was going to take you as her slave. I accepted it then, but my selfishness wouldn't allow me let the two of you be more. I have gotten us to this point. While I was entombed, I did nothing but think through these hard times. Isolation does one of two things—it destroys you, or it forces you to face the truth of the demons you're at war with. I can't deny what my heart tells me. If I ignore this love the two of you have, it will destroy the three of us. It almost has so many times. Think about it. Look at the pain we've all had to suffer. If only we would have come together from the beginning, perhaps our lives would be different now. Maybe not for the better where equality is concerned, but there would have been peace. *Happiness*. Don't you think?"

"I think we've all played our role in this path. No one person is at fault for what has happened. But if you mean what you say." I glanced from him to Tessa, who was now looking at me. "If she will have me as more than a friend. If she can feel more—"

Tessa pushed to her feet, looking between us. "Marko, do you mean that? Or … are you saying you don't mind if Hunter and I are together for feeding purposes and friends? Speak clear. I do not think I can bear misunderstanding you. What exactly are you referring to?"

The rapid pulse that took me over wasn't my own, but Tessa's. It had me taking in the smallest emotion etching into her face. I knew she had hinted to feeling something, and I wanted to hope, to speculate, but I just couldn't allow myself.

"I have you. You have me. Perhaps there was meant to be more to us than just you and I. What else can I do?" His voice strained. "The two of you are bonded. You love him. He loves you. It was there long before I came. I … will never be able to bond you again, ma minette. I know this and it *kills* me. But we have our love, and it is stronger than ever. I feel that here," he said, tapping over his heart. "It has to be this way. It may be the only chance we have at beating Aetas. Together, the three of us may be strong enough."

Marko's expression was full of sadness as his head dropped to look at the ground. Tessa leaned down to bring him back to her.

"I know how hard this is for you. I've tried denying it to myself, too, but you are right. I can't escape the truth any more than you. I love him. I always have. For you to give us this ..." She paused, confliction, yet eagerness present. "Maybe this was the way it was meant to be. I do not know, but I can't deny how much I want to see." She paused. "Thank you."

"Do not thank me, ma minette. Not yet. I know our path, but adjusting to it will be the hard part."

Tessa nodded and kissed his cheek. When she turned to face me, neither of us moved. I wasn't sure what to say. All I wanted to do was pull her into my arms. To thank Marko, myself, but I knew it wasn't the time. *Adjust.* Yes, they'd have to do that. But I was more than ready. I'd been patient up until this point. I could wait until they were ready. However long that took.

Chapter 26
Marko

Didn't they say admitting to a problem was the first step? I'd been in denial for so long that it was so easy to try to slip back into, but the truth couldn't be avoided anymore. What I said to Tessa was the truth. If I didn't face the fact that her and Hunter were meant to be in each other's lives, we were destined to fail. And not just against Aetas, but to each other. My vows to Tessa would be for nothing. She'd come to hate me. Her bond to Hunter was only going to grow throughout time and the love she felt now would pale in comparison to the depths it would reach over the years. I couldn't keep them separate. Not if I wanted to keep her. I loved her too much to do that to either of us.

Hunter. My stare rose to him. I never thought I'd feel anything for the overprotective bastard. Thanks to Aetas blood, to the bond as his maker, I couldn't help the softening I had toward the man who had been my enemy for so long. Jealousy was there, but not nearly as much as it had been before. It was the difference between me and Aetas. I thought my greed had been strong, but his was worse. His love for Tessa was purely connection based. Mine was real. I cared about what she wanted—what she needed. And that allowed me to accept Hunter. It wasn't easy, but my heart told me it would get better over time.

"Let me help you up."

Hunter's eyes left Tessa and he walked toward me. The vampire in me wanted to snap at him. I wasn't weak, dammit. But … I was. I hadn't walked in so long that the muscles in my legs were pretty much useless. They'd heal a lot faster than a human's, but in the meantime, I was going to have to depend on him for the little things.

"Thank you." My arm wrapped around his shoulders while he pulled me to stand. When he started to slowly walk us to the bed, I planted my feet. His eyes met mine and as I held the contact, I pushed deep into his depths. A barrage of emotions hit me—all love and longing. For those moments, his pain was my own.

I broke away, shaking my head and patting against the heavy muscle covering his chest. "I hate you," I said, glancing up as he sat me down. There was a pause in his reactions before a smile edged onto his face.

"I hate you, too. I doubt it will ever go away, but I've seen stranger things."

Tessa pacing stole my attention. "You're not going back, ma minette. I may not be able to read your mind, but I know you. That's all you're thinking about right now."

"If I don't go back, we will be trying to survive blind. At least this way the two of you have a chance. If I keep Aetas distracted, he will send the enforcers. You can both hide until your powers grow and you strengthen. If I don't go … he will come, and he *will* find us. In that case, we're as good as dead. At least me and Hunter. He can't kill you, but he can entomb you again."

Trembling wracked my body at the thought and there was no way I could control it. "If you go back and you're there when he discovers the truth, he will torture, rape, and try to beat the information out of you. Let him entomb me if it means keeping you safe. You're not going."

"You can't stop me," she yelled. "I'm going, and you're going to get stronger. I will come to you when I'm able. Get as far away from here as you can."

I dove to my feet, stumbling and falling as Hunter tried to lung for her. But it was too late. Tessa was gone, back to the one person I hated more than life itself.

"Goddammit!" I slammed my fist against the cement, struggling to push myself up. Hunter had me on the bed before I could summon the strength to get my legs to work. "Your bonded is going to be the death of me," I growled. "Most stubborn women I've ever met. She doesn't listen to orders for shit."

"Tell me about it." Anger was thickly laced in Hunter's voice. "But she's right. We don't stand a chance if Aetas finds you Marko. And we need you alive. This is worse than you can imagine. We have to leave here and find a safe place for you, *now*."

I glared, cocking my head to the side. "It may be bad out there, but you do not know his instability. I feel it deep within. Tessa is going to get hurt if she's not careful. I feel it within my bones. This will not be good for her."

"Tessa will leave if it gets bad. I know her. She's not stupid. She'll escape. "And if she can't?"

"She will. But we can't debate on that now. We have to go."

I pushed away my fears, trying to convince myself that he was right. Tessa was smart. She'd know if she had to leave, and Hunter would be able to detect if she was in trouble. I had to rely on that. "Let me guess, you're going to carry me out of here like a child?"

Hunter shrugged, giving me an apologetic look. "You know a better way?"

"Fuck me. I hate this. I swear, when I'm better, I'm going to …" I broke off, not sure what the hell I was going to do. Aetas would pay, I'd make sure of it. How, was the mystery. I wanted him to go through more hell than I had. I wanted him to suffer to the extreme.

"Before we leave, do you have any ideas where we're going to go, because truthfully, I'm at a loss?"

My jaw tightened and I gave a hard shake. "No. We'll need a car though because I am too weak to use powers. We'll have to decide when we're on the road."

Hunter pulled me into his arms and I had to take deep breaths to calm myself. This wasn't right. I wasn't meant to be so dependent on someone. Especially him.

"We don't have time for you to try to walk," he said under his breath. "I know this has to be hard for you, but I promise not to tease you too much when you get better.

"One word," I threatened.

Hunter stayed silent as he eased the door open, poking his head out. The skin on my arms prickled as I tuned into the energy. The inside of the city felt empty, eerie as we broke into the darkness. Complete silence was something I'd never heard within our walls. There was always a hum of voices, or the strings of a musical instrument playing. Now, nothing. Anger made tears burn into my eyes. *I had been king.* The vampires had trusted me to take care of them, and in their eyes before death, I had failed. Jesus. I couldn't take the emotions that slammed into me.

Hunter glanced down and I knew he could feel my aura. The sadness was overwhelming me. I was the strongest vampire besides Aetas and I was no stronger than a human child.

"It's not your fault. Everyone will know what happened. I will make sure of it. I know we haven't gotten along, but that didn't take away from me noticing what a good leader you were. You'll get that back. You rule over all of us, and then we'll be safe."

My brow creased as I looked up at him. "Me? Why not you? Don't you feel the need to take Aetas' spot?"

Hunter laughed under his breath, pausing to look around the intersecting tunnel. "Hell no. I just want …"

"Tessa." I clenched my jaw and he stayed silent leading us further away from the city. "Of course she's all you're thinking about. Your bond is strong. Pure. You were connected before your transitions. Yours will be stronger than mine and hers ever was. That doesn't mean she'll love you more than me. Just, differently."

"I know my place." Hunter glanced down at me, keeping his pace fast regardless of my weight and size. "The two of you love each other. You're her mate. Her husband," he breathed out. "I'm just happy to have any part of her after what I've done."

I didn't respond. I wasn't sure what to say.

Light shone from ahead and Hunter slowed, jerking to a stop almost immediately. "There's humans," he whispered. "I feel them. I think they're guarding the exits. We should have went through the house part. I bet they would have given us a car."

My head shook. "No. Humans will be there, too. They had to have discovered the door. We'll just have to take these out and try to get into Austin before we're discovered. It's not hard anymore to notice our kind. They have to be able to feel the difference. My energy will definitely stand out. I don't think I can conceal myself yet. Tessa's blood is strong and she did wonders, but the amount I need is greater than ever. It's a double-edged sword."

"Alright." Hunter stayed light on his feet, lowering me to the ground as he stared at the grate above. "Give me little bit. I'll be back to get you. Don't run off anywhere."

"Bastard."

The small laugh that left him had a smile coming to my face. I hated that I couldn't hide it. Fuck, I was softening more toward him.

Cautious steps led Hunter up the ladder and I pushed myself to stand as he neared the top. The sudden anxiety for his safety became my primary focus. If anything happened to him, Tessa would suffer as well. And I didn't want Hunter to get hurt. Not because he was my only savior in the godforsaken mess, but because I was generally concerned for his well-being.

One more step up. Two. His face was inches from the top when he pushed from the front of his feet and shot up through the grate. Shots were almost immediate and they drove me forward on shaky, weak legs. My hands held to the bars like a lifeline while shouts grew from above. When I heard a scream, I force my unwilling body to react faster. To climb those fucking stairs and see if he was alright.

Waves of fearful energy rushed over me and I struggled, lifting my leg the next foot between the gaps. Sweat was beginning to coat my skin and a grunt echoed around me as I used the strength from my arms to keep myself from falling completely.

Tessa's powers for me were already fading. At this rate, I wasn't sure how much I'd have to drink to be sated. Whether it would always be like this, I wasn't sure. Maybe I just needed to sate the vampire within and let him get used to the frequent feedings again.

"There. Right there!"

A human voice rang out from above, followed by more screams. Then, more. By the time I neared the top, I wasn't sure how many more people Hunter had killed. The yells kept coming and he obviously had to be the one evoking them … which meant he was alive.

"Where did he go? Fuck! Jack?"

My head lifted, only for my eyes to widen as far as they could go. Men in an array of different uniforms were scattered around the field. Two Army tanks were present, along with multiple police cars. I could see where they'd been parked further down, guarding the other entrance as well. Jesus. We were fucked. Had the war broken out so badly in the last two months I had been trapped away? Yes … my city was dead, and Austin was under lockdown.

A blur of color raced from the darkness, right into the spotlighted area. One second a crouched man was positioned by the cruiser, the next he was being shredded down the face and chest by Hunter's claws. More siren's sounded and I couldn't stop myself from easing from the tunnel, onto my stomach. Backup would be here any minute. We had to make a run for it. Time was of the essence if we were going to cscape.

With the last of my strength, I projected my status. Hunter was so fluid in his movements that he was doubling back for me as if it were part of his attack. More shots rang out and I held my hand toward the sound, groaning as my muscles and bones literally ached in agony.

"Let's get the fuck out of here." Hunter barely stopped as he swept me into his arms and took off running at full speed. He headed around the cop cars, right for the city. I didn't question his actions or where he was taking us. For the first time, I put my trust in his decisions. I let him lead.

Chapter 27
Aetas

Even upon waking, Tessa's breaths were the first thing I was aware of. They were slow. Deep. She was asleep. The picture in my head of her face had my love swelling and growing to heights I never imagined could exist. The warmth engulfing my chest had me blindly reaching to pull her closer.

As my hand connected, and her scent grew stronger at my pull, I couldn't resist staying closed off from her for another second. My eyes fluttered open and long, dark waves were suddenly visible. They were scattered above her on the pillow, weaving a tangled web of mass black over the light fabric. The sight was no different than what she was doing to me—standing out in a void of darkness. Although here it was opposite. She was the dark, in a world of light.

"I missed you." I wrapped myself around her and she instantly turned, burying her face in my chest, content to let me hold on.

"You were only sleeping. Surely, you didn't miss me so much."

"But I did. I miss you more than you know when we're not together. And we weren't tonight. I don't think I dreamed at all. I must have been more tired than I thought."

She yawned, snuggling into me more. "You've been tired a lot lately. Maybe the good rest is what you needed."

I frowned, knowing all too well it wasn't that. Marko needed to feed again. He was making me weak. Could he go a few more days? Perhaps he could. But did I want him to? That was the question. I didn't like to feel weak and I had never felt so off since I'd placed the bond on him.

"Maybe you're right." My voice was low as I closed my eyes and tuned into Tessa's pulse. It was on the fast side, but not enough for concern. I reached down, spinning her to straddle me as I rolled to my back. "Feed, ma minette. I want to feel your fangs in me."

There was hesitation as she lowered to my neck. I reached over, pulling back her hair as her nose moved up and down the side of my throat. The grin was immediate and erased everything in my mind. When her fangs finally broke through my skin it pure heaven. My fingers dug into her back and ass while my hard cock slid against the silk nightgown that was wedge between her legs.

"What did I tell you about wearing these? I want to feel you. These damn things only get in the way."

I pulled the gown to her hips as she continued sucking against me. Heat met my cock and wetness came as I rubbed against her. But something was off. She felt tense in my arms. Or was it me, overanalyzing her every move? She'd felt this way before, but she was still responding. She still wanted me.

The thoughts vanished as she bit down harder, drawing more of my essence free. With every move of my hips, her arousal increased. I shifted, lifting her as I eased my cock into her entrance. A sound vibrated along my skin. Whether it was pleasurable or not, I wasn't sure. I didn't care. I locked my arms around her tighter and plunged deep. The act had Tessa's mouth breaking from my neck. She tried thrashing in my arms but we'd been here before. I'd seen her and Marko's memories. She liked it rough and I knew that must have been the mood she was in.

"Wait, stop." She wiggled more, kicking out her legs as she tried to separate us. I laughed under my breath, spinning her over to her back and biting into her brutally. Her body jolted in pain and she cried out, fighting harder. Venom oozed from my fangs and I doused her with the maximum amount I could release at one time. Something I'd never done with her before. I wasn't in the mood for their rough play. I just wanted her my way.

Almost immediately her body softened. She wasn't going wild with lust like only a normal amount would produce. No, she was floating now. In heaven and blissfully drugged on my power.

"How does that feel? Better?"

I worked the nightgown down from her arms, exposing her breasts as I pumped into her at a leisurely pace. Her head turned back and forth and her hand rose, only to fall back to the bed. As her eyes rolled, I lowered, cupping her breast while I moved my lips in next to her ear. "I think you're beautiful when you're high off of me. That feeling you're experiencing right now, that's the way I feel about you all the time. You're everywhere within me. You take me over until I know nothing but you."

A whimper left her lips and I paused. For someone who was supposed to be enjoying herself, she wasn't giving me that impression.

"Relax. Feel me. You're so fucking wet. When you come, you're going to love it."

Tessa's mouth opened and she sucked in a deep breath. A moan slipped free and a grin came to my face. I gripped under knee, spreading her legs wider as I rotated my hips, thrusting.

"M-Mar—"

"Shh," I said, pushing deep. "You're thinking too much. You'll ruin it. Be still and let me make love to you."

Pleasure rushed through me while I took in her body. Everything about my queen was perfect. Everything.

Tessa's head turned to the opposite side and her fist clenched. I grabbed her wrist as her arm swung out to the side. Small sounds were beginning to leave her and I went faster, knowing her body had to be reacting to the impending orgasm.

"Fuck. That's it, love. Come all over my cock. I know you want to."

The strain was evident in my tone as I watched her breasts sway at my force. Her nipples were so tight. I didn't hesitate to reach forward and roll one of the hard tips between my fingers. The pressure I applied had her trying to move again. Her restrained hand pushed against mine, but with my weight being held up solely by that arm, I barely even felt her.

"You're tightening around me. How does it feel? Is your heart racing? Is it the best feeling you've ever experienced?"

My excitement had me going faster. I let go of her hand, putting mine out to the sides of her as I let my cock slam into her. I was already getting so close and I knew her orgasm was going to set me off. It almost always did. This was still so new. So fucking good.

"O-off."

"I'm about to get you off. Come."

Tessa's palm pressed against my chest, only to fall to her own. Her head was shaking again, getting quicker in the movements.

"No."

The word was but a whisper, but I heard it perfectly clear. Anger rushed through me at her stubbornness and I went harder. "Come."

"Mon Dieu."

"Oh, God, indeed. Now let go, ma minette."

Her screams filled the room before I could even finish talking.

Like someone had flipped a switch within her, Tessa's eyes flew open and her body thrashed through the spasms. I could tell she was still weak as her fingers gripped into my biceps, but I was too wrapped up in my own release. Her pussy clenching around me made cum shoot from my cock without pause. I was lost again. Deaf to the French words that poured from her mouth like acid. They were angry, I knew that, but I couldn't decipher what they meant. Not initially.

"I hate you. I hate you! You rape now, is that it? Get off!"

Her fists pounded into my chest. The impact was nothing. A brush against my muscle for all the damage she was trying to do.

"Rape? I don't think your orgasm would accuse what I've done, rape. You loved it."

She hit me again, this time harder. My drug was wearing off and so was my patience. Tears were close to spilling from her eyes and it pissed me off. How could she say I'd raped her after what we just shared?

"Off."

"I. Will. Not." My teeth ground together at the challenge in her eyes. "You say I rape you, perhaps I will show you the difference. That way next time you don't get so confused."

"You wouldn't dare," she hissed.

"You doubt me?"

Her lids lowered in rage. "Do you love me?"

Silence stretched between us and I pushed from her body, too conflicted by my racing thoughts. I did love her. More than anything, but she'd hurt me by calling what we shared rape. All I wanted was for the sex to be the best she had ever had. Now this? I wasn't used to the pain that came with this emotion.

"You ask me if I love you. What about you loving me? Does one accuse a person of such a crime when they have powerful feelings for them? Do you not love me? Is that it?"

Tessa crawled to the edge of the bed, forcing her legs over the side. Her body shook as she stood on wobbly legs. "You're a fool to ask that question, Marko Delacroix. Would I be here if I didn't?"

"Where else would you go? Maybe here is all you have left? And you seem to like headquarters."

Dark hair swung over her shoulder as she spun to face me. One king size bed separated us, but it wasn't going to keep either of us at a safe distance if this fight escalated.

"You think I want to be here? I want my city back. I want to go home. One that is gone because of you! Aetas wouldn't have allowed for something like that to happen if he ran a city." The last was said under her breath as she stumbled to grab her robe. Red flashed before my vision and I flew, scrambling over the bed as I tackled her down. In that moment, I was Marko, feeding from his hate of me as she hit the floor and I pinned her with my body. The room faded and so did my thoughts. Back and forth they came and went until I barely could recall what I was doing or saying.

"You dare compare me to him?" I gave her a good shake as I bared my fangs and surged back to her throat. I bit hard, raking my claws down her arms as she screamed and thrashed underneath me. The scent of blood perfumed the room, igniting the crazed vampire within me. I couldn't think. I knew nothing but the crash of hatred and jealousy that was rocking my insides.

"Stop! Stop!"

Flesh shredded beneath our fighting limbs. The screams were getting louder, grating my ears as she kicked and hit at me. She was so slippery that it was hard for me to get a good grip, but I kept trying. Kept grabbing and trying to restrain her.

My poison left me again, leaving an ache behind so intense that I couldn't help but jerk away from her neck. The crimson that met me as I slowly rose to my knees was enough to break through the evil haze. Tessa was covered in blood. Deep slices were opened revealing the damaged muscle below. I blinked hard, not believing what I was seeing. For seconds, I couldn't move. She was unconscious from my venom … and still bleeding out.

"Jesus. Fuck." A deep growl exploded through the room as my hands shot to my head. I was spinning. Falling into a place I'd never been before. Who was I? I didn't know anymore. She said Aetas, as if I were her savior, but that wasn't me. But I wasn't Marko either. I was some creation I'd made by mixing our blood. A monster, in love with a woman who I felt couldn't love me as much as I loved her. One who would come to hate me. Nothing I did was right. I couldn't control myself in this form, but would I ever be able to again? I wasn't sure. I couldn't un-mix the blood. What was done was done.

My fingers locked in my hair as I tugged through the anxieties. All I could do was stare down fascinated and terrorized at Tessa's mutilated body while she bled all over my floor. What was I going to do? How was I going to fix this?

Was there even a way to?

My eyes rose to the mirror as I took in Marko's face—one I hated and loved. It was too soon to change back into me. My plan wasn't nearly as far as I wanted, but how much longer would I have a choice before I lost my mind completely?

Chapter 28
Tessa

I awoke from the darkness, crying out through the sting that had jolted me awake. Grogginess made it hard to open my eyes, but somehow my lids stayed open long enough to see Marko's hand drawing back, holding a bloody rag.

Memories filtered through and my head fell to the side as I let them sink in. Aetas was losing it. He was more unstable than ever. I couldn't begin to know what was going through his mind, or even how to understand it. Had he always been this way and I never knew? Sure, he'd done some bad things to me over the time I had known him, but to go this far? Marko had been right. Love, it ruled him. But not as his true self, as a twisted version of Marko. Did he even consider himself Aetas anymore? I had hoped to test it by throwing in my jab, but I hadn't expected that reaction. Quite the opposite.

"I never thought you'd hurt me like this. How could you?"

I sobbed for the separation of my men. For this hell I was living so they could be safe. I didn't regret my decision. I'd stay as long as needed, but seeing the man I love act in a terrifying way wasn't sitting right with my mind.

"I'm sorry isn't good enough. I wasn't thinking. I can't think," he said pained. "This blood in me, it's ruining everything."

I forced my eyes open to see him watching me as he lifted the rag out of the bowl and brought it back to my chest. Drops fell into the wounds and my body convulsed through the electrifying shock that brought agony.

"Why haven't you healed me? I am too weak to do it myself."

"My dear queen." His lips twisted and I let out a cry as he patted over me. "Perhaps I do not want to heal you yet. I know I should, but I want to see what I've done for just a little longer."

"See what you've done? You want me to be in pain while you soak in your mistake?"

The bite against his bottom lip eased as he moved more toward the side of my breast. "I think it's beautiful."

My mind went blank. Words, thoughts, everything was gone as I stared at him in horror.

"When I first saw you, I was disgusted with my actions. Shocked … but then came awe. I was afraid. I love you," he said, moving his hand back to the bowl. "I love you so much that I don't feel as though I can ever get enough of that feeling. And I want more. My need for you is insatiable. That's why I licked all the blood from your right side first. I thought by tasting you, tasting what I had done, that it would help. It didn't. I only wanted you more. But the only way to do that was to physically take you inside of me. That's just ridiculous. I don't want to eat you. Then I wouldn't have you. Unless, of course, it was just a tiny part of you that could grow back and heal." His eyes came back to me. "So I did it. I took the tiniest piece of your skin and I ate it. It wasn't enough. I came to realize I'm never going to be sated. This power you have over me is forever torturing. Now I'm trying to decide if I suffer through it, or I kill you and be done with it once and for all. What will be better for me?"

My body jerked to the side as I gagged. Pain was crippling and I didn't want to know how bad it was. To the bone … close … it had to be. But I wasn't as weak as before. Each second that passed, his drug wore away and I was becoming the smallest amount stronger.

"You're sick," I managed, between heaves. "You need help."

"Perhaps. But tell me what can be done? Tell me and I will listen because I don't want to lose you. *Not really.* This is killing me," he growled pulling me back to face him. "Don't you see?"

Still, I couldn't stop the constant gagging that kept coming at envisioning him eating my skin.

"Tell me!"

I jumped. Not at the anger or power of his voice, but at the how it combined with the look in his eyes. Rarely did I get frightened, but this Marko scared me. "Heal me and we will talk this out. We will find a way. I l-love you, and you're scaring me."

Marko's face hardened and he glimpsed back down to my chest. After a few seconds his expression softened and he was pulling me into his arms. "I'm sorry, ma minette. I am. If you could feel this love, this force that exists in my heart because of you, you'd see how bad this is. You say you're scared, but so am I. And I don't fear anything. For the first time, I think I'm truly in trouble."

His voice cracked and I lifted my shaking fingers to touch his cheek. "We're going to make you better, I promise. I'm sorry for upsetting you. This was my fault. I did this."

"Do you love me so much that you can so easily convince yourself of that lie?"

"We fight. It's what we do. My love is still the same."

Emptiness settled within as Marko's arm rose and he savagely tore into his forearm with his fangs. The crazed look was still there, buried behind the sadness and confusion that he was battling. I knew I had to tread lightly if I was going to prevent something like this from happening again.

Blood poured onto my chest, soaking into the slices that were covering me. Pain was present, but so was the tingling that came along with healing. I braved a look up, taking in the dark circles beginning to appear under Marko's eyes. God, I had to make sure my Marko was okay. If Aetas was showing these signs, how bad off was Marko?

"It's me," I whispered. "You need stronger blood than my own. Is there anyone you can feed from within headquarters?"

His eyes darted to mine. "I will not taint myself with anyone else's blood. They'll dilute yours."

I paused, trying not to look as rocked as I felt. "Maybe just this once to see if it makes you better? I want us back to normal. I want you to love me again without being angry at me."

"I don't want anyone else's blood, ma minette."

My lips pressed together to stifle the scream that wanted to come. If I let my temper show I'd only upset him more. That could be fatal for me if he was already teasing the thought of killing me to ease his suffering.

"Alright." My voice was calmer than I felt. I reached for his wrist, bring the cut to my mouth to lick over. The power of his blood was stronger than the night before. He and Marko together may have been an explosive combination, but the power wouldn't mean anything if Aetas didn't get better.

"I need you to help yourself. For me. For us. I know you don't want to taint my blood. I *understand*," I stressed. "I wouldn't dream of tainting yours within me, either, but I'm afraid of losing you. I love you. Please consider trying to feed from someone else, if only just once to see."

Marko pulled me into his arms, holding to the back of my head as he wrapped himself around me. Our bodies slid together from the massive amount of blood covering me, but I tried not to think about it. Or the fact that he'd eaten a part of me. *Jesus.* I was going to be sick, again.

The vibrations in my chest grew as I shut my eyes. My wounds weren't closed yet, but they were in the process. I could continue to do this. I'd just make myself forget. I'd block it out. I had to. I didn't want to remember this day. Ever.

"Hunter?"

I looked up, making sure this fake Marko hadn't detected my internal communication with my bonded. He didn't appear to. His eyes were still closed as he held me.

"Fuck, I've been so worried. How are you? I feel sick. My equilibrium has been off and I've been so tired. What the hell is going on there? Does Aetas know about Marko yet?"

I swallowed passed the nausea. *"No. Not yet. Aetas isn't well. How is Marko?"*

"Sleeping. I'm driving."

"Where are you going?"

Hunter paused. *"North. We held up in an abandoned house until sunset. It's bad out here, Tessa. The humans, they're doing searches of every place they can, trying to weed us out. It's a fucking war zone up here. Army, National Guard, fucking every military force you can imagine is patrolling the streets. Our kind is in big trouble. I'm not sure we're going to find many of us left."*

My heart thumped hard and Marko stirred above, brushing back my hair. "Shhh," he breathed out.

"I will come to you soon. Hunter, don't tell Marko, but Aetas is losing his mind. He ... hurt me. Bad. While I was unconscious ... he ..." I couldn't go any further, I wasn't sure if I could even say it in my thoughts.

"He what?" A growl roared through and I took a deep breath. How could I have forgotten Hunter's overprotective nature? I was talking to him as a friend, but he was so much more to me again. *"Tell me, Tessa. What the fuck did he do to you?"*

"He ... ate a piece of my skin."

"He fucking what?!"

"I don't want to talk about it," I rushed out.

"I hate this. You're coming back to us the moment we get settled somewhere. Fuck you staying there. No. Hell no. If you don't come within the first few minutes that we stop, I'm coming to you. And it's not going to be pretty, Tessa."

I opened my lids, staring in a daze. Did I have a choice? Hunter would come. I knew he would. And staying was risky. But if I left, Aetas would surely come looking, himself, and he'd bring the enforcers with him. Did we stand a chance running from not only our kind, but the humans, too? I just didn't know the best course of action to take.

"Let me see if I can make Aetas better. I'm trying to get him to feed from someone besides me. He doesn't want to, but I might have luck. If that's the case, he might become more stable."

"And if he doesn't? If he kills you or hurts you enough to incapacitate me? Marko is too weak to help anyone right now. He is the answer to this, Tessa. He's the only one that stands a chance to save us. Don't put everyone at risk trying to fix this yourself. Trying to help Aetas is like trying to tame a rabid dog. You just can't do it."

I cringed. *"You're probably right. Just keep trying to get as far away as you can. I'll come to you when I'm able. Feed Marko as much as you can. If you find a vampire more powerful, make him feed my mate, too."* I closed my eyes, letting myself experience the butterflies that came along with my feelings toward Hunter. I'd done so well at pushing them away, but I didn't have to anymore. *"I miss you."*

My heart exploded in rhythm and it wasn't from me, it was from him. *"And I miss you. I ... love you. I've always loved you, even when I hurt you."*

"I know. I love you, too. Take care of Marko. I have to go. I'll see you soon."

I cut off my thoughts, not allowing Hunter to come back through. The longing to be with him and Marko was almost too much. I shifted and Aetas' eyes—Marko's eyes—flew open. The intensity had me momentarily frozen. Did he know I was talking to Hunter? Could he hear? I wasn't wearing my crown, but I was hoping his blood within me was enough to keep him out of my head.

"Let's take a bath. I want to hold you some more, but I need you clean. The blood is too much. I can't think with the smell."

"Of course." I tried to lift, but didn't get a chance to make it far before he jerked me into his body and eased us to the end of the bed. When he stood and made his way into the bathroom, I tried to calm the nervousness. It wasn't the bath that I feared, but him. I wanted to escape his presence. The energy he was throwing off was only getting worse. *Darker.* I'd felt this before. This evil, and it had been in my own Marko.

"Can you stand?"

My feet hit the ground, but he held on, letting me test my strength. I gave a quick nod as I gripped to the countertop. He cautiously let go of me and made a dash to the large marble tub. He had the water on and was back at my side within seconds.

Up and down, his stare traveled over my face. From my eyes to my lips, he went back and forth for what seemed like ever.

"What are you thinking?" Fuck, I was afraid to ask, but I had to know.

Slowly, I was led to the tub. He bent down, testing the temperature before he glanced back at me and turned the water off.

"The strongest hero besides myself is Lucille, I will take her blood. For you," he said between clenched teeth. "Not because I want to."

"Thank you." The whisper was forced. I was too afraid to say anything else.

Marko walked up the four steps that led to the massive tub and I held his hand, following. When my toes dipped into the water it was ice cold. I gasped, jerking my foot back, but he was ready for my reaction. Arms locked around my waist and he was suddenly spinning me. Water engulfed me as he stood at the edge, holding me down. At the frigid temperature, I couldn't breathe. It stole my oxygen, rushing into my open mouth and nose from the shock.

"What did you tell him?" He yelled. "What did you tell Hunter? I know you were talking to him. I felt your change. You were afraid, but then you were happy. You love him more than me, don't you?"

Coughing wracked my body as I clawed at his hold. Half of my head was out of the water while the other half was submerged. His words were distant, but all too clear.

"M—ark—o!"

"Admit it! You love him more than me. I would kill for you. I would kill you for myself!"

My screams were muffled through the gurgling. The heat that burned inside of me from my powers sizzled, but if I used them on Aetas, they would hurt *my* Marko. Panic left me fighting with everything I had. *I didn't need air to survive.* I didn't. But the tortuous feeling of drowning was enough to fuck with my head to make me think I did.

Air collided with the remaining water in my mouth and I gagged as I tried to take a deep breath. I was pulled up so fast that it forced the water down my throat. One minute Marko was there, the next gone. My body shook violently as I scrambled out of the tub.

Where had he gone? *Hunter ... was he looking for my bonded?* I had to get out of here. There was no saving Aetas. I thought there might be hope, but I was wrong. All I could do at this point was save myself.

Chapter 29
Hunter

Tap. Tap. Tap.

Over and over, my finger connected with the trunk of sedan I'd stolen. My mind was racing as I filled up the car with gas. I couldn't breathe. What the fuck was happening at headquarters? Something bad, that was for sure. I wanted to go to Tessa. No, I *needed* to go to her.

Marko was awake and trying to strengthen his legs by walking the length of the car on the passenger side. He watched me as he did so, his eyes studying my every move.

"What's happening? You're not telling me something. Have you heard from Tessa?"

My jaw clenched and I nodded, still trying to catch my breath. "She's coming to us the first chance she gets. Soon. Very soon."

I was beginning to stumble over my words. I hated not being truthful with Marko, but it was for the best. Worrying would only make things worse for him.

Brown eyes narrowed as he stopped and rested his arms on the top of the vehicle. "Very soon. What happened? Is she okay? Does Aetas know, yet?"

My head shook. "No. He doesn't know."

"Is she okay? You avoided the question."

Again my jaw tightened. "She's okay."

"As in at the moment or in general?"

"Look, she's fine. She'll be here soon."

My body was trembling uncontrollably and I gasped as my breath disappeared.

"Hunter?"

Like a fish out of water, my lips opened and closed. Air wouldn't come. The panic left me stumbling a few steps behind me. I looked around wildly, not sure what to do. I had to go to her. I had to, but what about Marko? What about our kind? The questions were easily dismissed as I knew she was my only concern at the moment.

"Hunter!"

Marko's voice tore my eyes away from the daze my anxieties caused. Before I could answer a weird thickness edged to the back of my throat. I didn't think, I ran to the side of the building, trying to conceal what I knew was coming.

Tessa.

Dark smoke poured from my mouth as my palm pushed into the brick of the building. Footsteps pounded and I staggered a few steps to take my mind off of the gagging sensation.

"Holy shit. Are you sick? Hunter."

Marko came closer and tears filled my eyes from the sensations. Feet began to appear and relief took the prominent role as Tessa began to become solid.

"Oh …God. That's amazing." Marko walked closer and within seconds, Tessa was before us. She wore a pair of jeans and a t-shirt. She'd never looked more human since I'd become a vampire. She was hugging her chest and tears were already streaming down her face. Marko didn't hesitate to pull her into his arms. Her stiffening might not have been noticed by him, but I saw the haunting look in her eyes. Hesitantly her hand reached for me and I threw my weight forward, wrapping myself around both of them. I didn't care what Marko thought. Tessa needed me and fuck if I was going to withhold myself from her for a second.

"Where are we?"

I kissed her forehead, wrapping around them tighter for only a split second before I glanced up to Marko. His confliction and awkwardness was obvious, but there was something else—an acceptance.

"An hour or so south of Dallas."

"Not nearly far enough," she said, wiggling out of us. "We have to go. We can't waste any time."

"What happened?"

Even as Tessa stepped away, I held to Marko, helping him walk as I followed Tessa's impatience steps. I pointed to the car at the gas pump and she nodded, avoiding Marko's question.

"Ma minette. What happened?"

Her shoulders drew back and she let out a deep breath, glancing over her shoulder. When she got to the back driver's side door, she gave him her attention, frowning as she did so.

"Aetas isn't well. He's losing his mind. His obsession with me is out of control. I could have not saved him or either of you if I would have stayed. He would have killed me."

"He hurt you. Let me see." Neither was a question, but a demand as he broke away from me and went toward her.

"I do not think it would be best," she whispered under her lips.

A tear raced down her cheek as she turned away from him. Marko mirrored her actions, moving to the side, putting himself in front of her. When he pulled her into him, Tessa's hands shot to his chest, gripping into his shirt.

"Look at me, love. Let me see what he did to you. I *have* to see."

Tessa's energy pulled me in and I felt her mind open. Our bond fed me images. Ones I knew Marko was seeing as I was. It started with him wanting her to feed from him, and then went into the drugging—the accusation of rape. From there … the attack. My mind reeled and reality and what I was seeing blurred through the rage that engulfed me. When it got to him trying to hold her under the water, I was shaking so much that my legs felt like they were going to give out.

"There has to be a way for him to die." Marko jerked her into his body holding on tightly. "Fucking … Jesus. To see myself do that, knowing it's not me … I have no words. My heart hurts for you, ma minette. I'm sorry. I tried to tell you not to go back."

"I thought I could distract him enough for you both to get to safety, but I did what I could. When he left, I had to go, too. I think he's looking for Hunter. I think he went to kill him."

Her eyes came to me and I shrugged. "Let him look. He's not going to find any of us." I took the nozzle from the tank and glanced at Marko before holding my hand out to Tessa. He let go and she threw herself into me while I hugged around her.

"We will figure this out. You know me, I won't stop until we're all safe."

"I know. I'm glad you're on our side. After all the predictions," her stare came up. "I was so sure we'd be fighting you at the end."

"Everyone doubted my love for you. Maybe even I did, too."

"I didn't," Marko said, pulling open the back door. "Never doubted it for a second."

A smile came to my face and I eased my hold. Tessa stepped back, moving in closer to Marko. When she went to join him, I got in, leaving the small store. I wasn't sure how much longer we'd make it. The cash I'd stolen from one of the houses we'd broken into on our way out of the city wasn't much. Soon, we'd need more. There had to be another way.

"What do either of you know about the Dallas circle? Is it worth heading there? Can we risk it? We need resources and allies."

My eyes shot up to the review mirror and I took in Marko holding Tessa. He looked huge in the confined space.

"It's risky. You saw what met us when we left our city. I have no doubts it'll be like that everywhere. Besides, our kind would have fled."

"Where to?"

Marko's eyebrows drew in. "It's hard to say. Abandoned houses, small towns outside of the city … as far away from danger as they can get, I assume. This has never happened to us in my lifetime. I don't know."

Silence lasted for a few minutes before Tessa's head lifted from his chest. "What if we found a place and you projected your power. The survivors would come. They'll want someone to lead them."

Marko's head tilted as he thought. "Yeah, but if they feel me, who else will? If there's any enforcers in the area, they'll come as well."

"True," she whispered, "but perhaps they'll be on our side. I mean, if they see you here, and they can confirm that you're also at headquarters, maybe they'll follow us. Maybe they'll see what Aetas is doing and get people to join our side."

"Can we risk it?" I looked back at their reflection. "That's what it comes down to. It's only going to take one mistake for Aetas to find us." My brain pushed through the fog of my past. Although I had remembered so much, I almost felt like I was forgetting something. Or someone. "What about the humans? Is it possible to get them to fight with us to end this war?"

"Whoa." Marko's head shook, forcefully. "No way. Even if by some miracle we win, we want them to think we're dead. We have to go back into hiding. It's going to take time to recover from this massacre. And this could be far from over. We have no idea how many of us are left, but Tessa is right in the fact that we have to find them. We have to figure out a location where we can hide and not be found—by humans or Aetas. Somewhere good."

I scanned the dark sky, looking out into the far stretches of the horizon. "We have a few hours of night left. Do we stop outside of the city or do we keep going and push to see how far we can get? We can grab a hotel, but truthfully, we can't afford it."

Tessa looked between us and I saw her features turn serious as she began to think.

"Dallas will have survivors. Their city was bigger than ours. We should stop there before we continue on."

"We can't actually go into the city," I said, glancing at her. "They have the roads blocked. They're checking everyone who goes in and out. At least that's how it was in Austin. We had to steal a car outside of the check point. I told you, it's bad. Worse than you could imagine."

Her hand rose and her fingers pressed into her forehead as she closed her eyes. "I should have known that. Alright. So we steer clear of the city. We find a place for the night—a house, and we see if anyone comes. Maybe we spread the truth and keep going. We tell as many as we can, and we get them to wait for our call."

"Always a leader." Marko's lips tugged at the side and his head lowered to nuzzle against hers. "I knew there was a reason I fell in love with you. It was in your blood from the beginning. We're lucky to have you."

"A leader would have stayed. She would have sacrificed herself for her people. I left, Marko. I may have just doomed us all."

"Do not for one second blame yourself." Her eyes met mine in the mirror. "This sacrifice you speak of was a suicide mission. Your death would have been inevitable. You did the smart thing. You got out of there. The time makes no difference. One day, one year, if Aetas wants us dead, he'll come looking."

"He's right," Marko agreed. "He *ate* your skin while you were unconscious. He is not well, ma minette. Not even close."

Tessa's face dropped color and she took in a slow deep breath. I had to take one too for the nausea that hit me.

"How are you? Are you healed well enough?"

Tessa pulled the t-shirt away from her chest, glancing down. At Marko's gasp, my head lifted higher to try to see.

"Well?

Neither answered me as Marko let out a threatening sound. "I saw it in your memories, but you wouldn't look directly at what he had done. Fuck!"

"It is healing," she whispered.

"I will make this up to you. I swear to you that I will. I should have never tied with him in the first place. I don't know what I was thinking."

"I want to see," I snapped. "She's my mate, too."

Tessa's frowned as her eyes met mine and her head turned to the side as she pulled the t-shirt down to her cleavage. The bright, red gouges were still embedded deeply into her chest. Although the muscle was healing, the deep lacerations still looked horrific, even in the dim surroundings.

My eyes darted back to the road, only to return as she let the t-shirt go back into place. Bile burned my throat and I knew there was no stopping what was coming. I hit the brakes hard, pulling to the shoulder. I barely managed to get the door open before I barreled out. I felt sick with myself. I'd felt the pain, but I never imagined. I should have gone—should have fucking tried to do something.

"Hunter." Tessa jumped from the car, walking over at a fast speed where I paced approximately ten feet away. "Don't be upset. You—"

"Should have stopped it," I yelled. "I should have fucking—God!" I spun around only to head back to her. "Let me see, again. I want to see every place he marked on you."

"This is not the time." Her voice was low but firm. "We have to find somewhere to stay."

I pulled her into arms, burying my face in her hair. Her stiff posture eased into my hold and she loosened completely, molding herself into my body as her arms wrapped tightly around my neck.

"I'm sorry. I'm starting to think that I'm not a very good mate to you. You deserve someone like Marko who can protect you. I'm just not there yet."

Tessa's head leaned back while she looked at me. "You're so much stronger than most newborns. Look at you. You're rational, you're beginning to tap into your gifts. Hunter, you have to give yourself time. Within the next year or two, you're going to be unstoppable to most.

My head shook. "That doesn't help you now."

"Hold me," she breathed out. "I've missed you."

A frown began to appear only to vanish at her words. I held to her tighter, going back to breathe her in. A car approaching in the distance had me tightening my grip for only seconds before I pulled back.

"We have to go. You're right. We have to get settled for the night. We'll stop in the next town. Then, I will hold you."

Tessa's eyes searched mine and I couldn't help but delay our separation. My fingers dug into her back and it was almost impossible to move passed the desire to kiss her. I couldn't though. Not yet. I wouldn't ruin this with Marko by jumping the gun. Our new relationship was going to work and nothing was going to stop it.

Chapter 30
Marko

I broke from Hunter's neck, moaning at his increasing power. It'd only been a few hours since our last feeding, but the truth couldn't be denied. He was growing in power and was a lot stronger than any newborn I'd ever come into contact with. Even Tessa when she was close to his age, and that was scary.

"You good?" He glanced back, searching my face.

"Yeah. I'm better already. Thanks."

Tessa was sitting on the sofa, her mouth twisted as she stared at the human we had tied to the chair. The only reason he was alive was for food. We needed a different source amongst ourselves and although his blood was weak, it would do us good. He was young. Healthy. A community college kid who lived alone. Tessa couldn't have picked a better place. And her getting him to let her enter … it was a phenomenal show to watch. She'd been all manipulation and seduction—her true self as a vampire. And the human hadn't expected a thing. He'd let her right in, and in turn, she'd locked her gaze on his and made him invite us passed the threshold. It was too easy and gave us confidence when we were low on the emotion. Aetas knew we were gone. I could feel his rage within and I didn't doubt that somehow Tessa and Hunter could too.

I walked around Hunter, trying to ignore the slight ache in my legs. Already they were supporting me better. A few more feedings and I'd be thriving with my new blood. It wasn't affecting me like Aetas. Why it had taken such a bad turn for him I could only assume. I prayed time didn't have it turning on me, too. What would that do to Tessa? To myself?

"You need to feed, Hunter."

Tessa's voice left him shifting. He was already staring at her. Already … *wanting her*. I didn't miss the longing that stayed absorbed deep inside of his depths. The more I fed from him, the more it became my own. I understood it. I was aching for her too.

"Later. The human isn't going anywhere."

"No, but he's mine. You need stronger blood. You haven' fed in days. I'm surprised you haven't attacked anyone yet."

His head dropped. "Probably because there's only one person I want."

Tessa's gaze came to me and the clenching of my jaw was automatic. The action was all reflex and I breathed through the jealousy that still stirred at the thought of anyone feeding from my mate. Tessa had always been mine. Always been who I wanted. And now she was his, too.

"You need to feed. Let Tessa take care of you."

Hunter gave a quick shake of his head. "It's not a good idea. She can feed from me. I'll feed from the human."

My eyes went from him to her. She was waiting patiently for what I had to say. Still, she looked to me for overall guidance. It had a smile tugging on my lips.

Jealousy … I had to let it go. Tessa was mine even if I shared her with her best friend.

"You're afraid of the lust you will feel when feeding from her?"

"Yes. And she's not completely healed yet. She needs to keep her strength."

He was so in tune with her. So loyal and yet careful of her needs. "I bet her wounds are already healed. She's stronger now. Maybe you should let her feed you if she wants to."

Hunter's stare darted to me and stayed as his brow creased. "And the lust?"

There was that heaviness—that pit in my stomach at the thought of the two of them being sexual. "Why don't we see what happens. If it becomes too much, I will tell you to stop. *And you stop.*"

"Come Hunter." Tessa patted the sofa, moving to sit at the edge as she waited. "Marko, I want you to come, too."

"Me?"

"That's right," she said, nodding. "I'm afraid." She stopped and I knew. It left my pulse hammering in my chest.

"You want him, too."

I was already walking, being sucked in at the confusion masking her features. It was just as hard for her as it was for me. She was bonded to him. They shared things she and I would never share again. And she'd deny him if I wanted her to. I knew that in my heart. But I couldn't do that. Not to either of them. *Not anymore.*

Hunter sat down and I followed, taking my place next to him. Tessa paused before she stood and lowered to straddle him. While she read my face, she moved in closer to his lap.

"Let me have your hand, ma minette." I lifted mine and she slid her fingers over my palm. My show of support had her lowering. Hunter's energy was all over the place as she settled her breasts against his chest and exposed her neck. "Go ahead," I said, lowly.

My pulse was beginning to race as I braced for his bite. It came cautiously—slow and gentle. I knew the moment his fangs breached her skin. Her grip tightened on my hand and a gasp broke through the room. To deny that it was filled with pleasure would have been a lie. She loved their joining and I knew the way that connection felt. Especially with her.

The pain was all too real as it ate at my heart. My sweet ma minette. We'd never share the sensation brought on by a bond that deep, ever again. And it was all my fault. Sure, we'd feel love when we fed from each other, but that special tie to another was gone for good.

As I watched Hunter's arms wrap around her with love, grief sunk my heart. Anger wasn't present. Not even at myself. My conscious new this was our new reality. That's why my rage wasn't present. No … rage couldn't live where credence thrived. My mind knew this was right, even if my heart was trying to accept.

My finger traced down the length of Tessa's and she mirrored the action as she stayed faced away from me. Her head was resting on Hunter's wide shoulder and she was turned into his neck. Deep breaths left him and I could see his digits twitching to tighten on her back. He'd start, only to let them ease.

How far would he go if I wasn't present? Would he even try? Even as a vampire, he held respect for Tessa. It was so unlike a newborn … unlike our kind.

Movement across the room had my stare leaving Hunter and Tessa to settle on the human. He was watching in horrific fascination. The way his eyes were glued to us didn't sit well with me. The human was aroused. I could see his hard cock bulging through the gym shorts he wore. It left my instincts flaring. I may have been alright with Hunter, concerning Tessa, but no one else.

"Shit. God." Hunter broke from Tessa's neck, breathing heavily while he licked over the wounds to close them.

"But you barely took enough." Her voice was slightly pouty, and her lids were heavy with lust as she pulled back to look at him. Hunter went to respond when his gaze stopped dead on the human. The college kid was still locked on Tessa. Still, raking his eyes over her back, and down to her ass.

A slight growl broke through the air and Hunter's fangs stayed lowered while his lip pulled back, threateningly. Slowly, he moved Tessa to the side, standing, and I couldn't help but follow. We were killers, plain and simple. This human should have feared us. Should have had his head down, or crying through the terror he was faced with. Not fantasizing about what we were doing.

"Are you looking at what doesn't belong to you? Marko … is he looking at what's ours? I know he's not *fucking* checking out our mate."

"Oh yeah," I said, stepping forward. "Someone has a death wish."

"Not from either of you," Tessa said, butting in. "He's my meal, remember? The kill will be mine."

The tips of my fangs cut into my lip as I watched the human's eyes widened. There it was. *Fright*.

"Mmph. Mmmmmph." His head started shaking as he yelled into the cloth secured into his mouth. The evil smile that broke onto my face couldn't be stopped.

"Look at my concubine one more time and I'll burn your eyes out of their socket until there is nothing left. You don't believe I can, go ahead and take one more look."

Tears streamed down the boy's face and his head lowered through the sobs. My anger didn't last as I turned my attention back to Hunter. He was still staring, still ready to attack.

"You didn't feed enough."

My words brought his black eyes to mine. Within seconds they lightened, but not entirely.

"I can't take anymore of her blood. Let's leave it at that."

"Because you want her?"

"Of course I do, but she's not ready. None of us are. After what she's been through—" He stopped, glaring once more at the human before focusing on me. "I'm done letting anyone push themselves on her. I'm tired of her making decisions based off of what she feels has to be done, versus what she wants to do. Tessa wants me, I know this. But even if you weren't in the picture, she wouldn't be ready. Her mind needs time to heal. I felt her anxieties. She's a mess."

"I beg your pardon?" Light green disappeared behind her narrowed lids as she came to a stop a few feet away from the human. Her energy flared defensively and I sighed, knowing her wrath all too well. She didn't like to be told she was weak, and that's exactly how she took Hunter's care for her.

My hand shot up and I shook my head. "He loves you and he wants what is best. You're about to argue. Don't. Now is not the time."

"I am not a mess. Take it back," she said to him, hurt. "I'm fine."

"Tessa." Hunter let out a deep breath. "You're tired. I feel how mentally exhausted you are. And there's nothing wrong with that. I want to help you get better."

"I said I'm fine." She growled, grabbing the human's hair and jerking back. "And I am far from tired. There are things to do—vampires to save. We have to plan for a way to take down Aetas. I will rest when he is incapable of hurting any more of our kind."

Hunter's lips pressed together. At his silence, Tessa dove forward, embedding herself into the human's neck. The loud cry buffered in the gag and his tied legs struggled at the rope binding him down. Minutes went by while Tessa fed. As she did, her strength emanated throughout the room. Human blood may have been weak compared to ours, but the length of time that had passed since her last taste empowered her strength.

She broke free, panting as blood raced down her chin. The breaking sound of the bones in his neck cracked through the room and she dropped his head, walking away from his lifeless body.

"Hunter will feed again, and then we will talk of a plan. Tonight we bring as many vampires as we can to our side. Aetas wants a war. It's time we give him one he will never forget."

Chapter 31
Aetas

Empty. Gone. All three of the vampires connected to me the most had betrayed me. *They knew,* and now they were going to pay.

How had I convinced myself that Tessa's feelings for me were real? How I had thought they hadn't seen Marko when they lifted the marble lid that kept him entombed?

I was going to kill them. All three of them. Well, not Marko. I couldn't do that. But Tessa and Hunter, they were dead. What I had in store for those two wouldn't compare to the carnage I'd already brought down on our kind. Tessa was going to suffer for what she was doing to me. Fuck, I couldn't breathe without her by my side. If I was going to go through this agony, wasn't it better to go through it knowing I'd made her hurt worse than me before it was over with? *Betrayed me, for them?* Didn't she see how powerful I was? Didn't she know she didn't stand a chance without me?

My voice roared through the bedroom as I drew my hand back and slammed it through the wall. I felt no pain. I felt nothing but loss and rage. Every enforcer under me was searching the world for those traitors. And my men would find them. They'd capture them and bring them back to me. What they'd do when they saw Marko was beyond me. I hadn't thought that far ahead. But I couldn't think of anything at the moment. Nothing but her.

"Your Highness?"

I spun, snarling at Colin as he stopped in the doorway.

"Are you not out looking? Did I neglect to make my orders clear?"

"No, King Delacroix, I just thought you'd like an update."

"I don't want an update, I want them here! Unless you're telling me they're downstairs waiting, you're wasting my time."

A hard look came to the lead enforcer's face and he nodded, closing the door behind him. I immediately spun back around, beginning to pace the long length of the room. Perhaps I should try to summon them again. At least Marko. He was my fucking bonded. Yet, nothing I did could bring him back to me. How was that possible? Why couldn't I even call out to the one I created? My blood was ruining everything. If I wasn't so powerful, *so pure.*

"Fuck!"

My voice tore through the room for what had to be the millionth time since I found Tessa gone. I had thought she'd run to the memorial, but she wasn't there. That only led me to go in to take out my anger on Marko ... but he was missing, too. *And then I knew.* I knew with Hunter gone, along with the king and queen, that Hunter had rescued my bonded. He'd taken Marko, and Tessa had followed. And here I was, the fool in it all.

Heat blazed along my insides, damn near burning a hole in my core as I tried latching onto the link with Marko. I could feel it. The connection was there, but I couldn't reach it.

My attention went to Hunter and it was even worse. I couldn't feel him anymore than I could a ghost. It was just like after I'd created him. Unless he was before me and opened, he didn't exist to me.

"Tessa! You fucking bitch."

I tore into my hair, nearly crippled with her loss. Had I fallen in love with her so much? My heart said yes. My mind couldn't help but drift to Marko. He loved her more than what was fathomable. Naturally so would I, too. Especially in this form. But I'd switched back to myself already. The misery was still there. It was real.

"Tessa!"

Blood raced like lava through my veins as I searched out her blood within me. She was all I had consumed since my bond. All I fucking lived off of. She *was* my life, and I wanted it back. I was dying without her. Yes, I could feel it. My adrenaline made me stronger, but she was the one keeping my heart beating. Her blood was what made my existence worth living. I didn't want to be here because of anyone else's life force. I wanted her, despite the fact that I wanted to torture her. I wanted both her life and her death. God, I was losing my mind.

"There has to be a way. There has to be."

Darkness engulfed me as I shut my eyes and tried to concentrate. Throughout the centuries, I'd done nothing but expand my mind. I had done things no one ever knew existed. There should be no reason why I couldn't bring her to me. Marko and Hunter may be closed off from my blood, but Tessa wasn't created from it. There were no ties to me, and I had her crown. Sure, she may have been bonded to Hunter, but my blood within him wasn't powerful enough through her yet. *She had fed from me a lot though ...*

I tried to stop the need to lash out at the thought as it barreled its way through. Bringing her back had to be possible. It had to. I just needed to figure out how to make it happen.

Impatience had me lunging forward before my lids were even lifted. I raced toward the door, to the only place I could think of. My real room. I had books in there. I had everything that I'd ever experienced as phenomenon of our kind written down. There had to be an answer somewhere within the pages. And if not ... I'd track her down with every resource I had and she would pay. Whether it was with her life or not, I just wasn't sure. Maybe her death wouldn't be any different than Marko's. Maybe it truly would kill me. I felt as if her disappearance already was, and I knew she was alive. Not being able to bring her back might just do me in for good.

"Move."

A servant rushed to sidestep out of my way as I stalked down the long hall. I saw nothing but a blur as scenarios took root and turned into visions before me. *The dress, those eyes.* My fantasy come to life was going to haunt me forever. She'd pretended to want me, then. Had she known it was me when she'd materialized herself to portray something she wasn't? When she'd made love to me all those times? Did Tessa know it was her leader giving her such passion?

I couldn't help but think she at least suspected it. And if she had … maybe she really did love me. *Yes, she'd see her mistake. She'd come back to me.*

"Your Highness."

My jaw tensed as I looked toward the door I passed. Eleanor, one of the newest and lower members dropped her head as my murderous glare stopped on her.

"What is it?"

"I would like to enquire on our next meeting. I feel as though it is imperative we select new members as soon as possible. You have been away in your room and I fear the outside news has not made its way to you. We are in trouble. I ask that you please consider this in your time of … woe."

"My time of woe?" I inhaled deeply, pushing my unstableness aside long enough to take in her words. "What is the news I have missed? Is it so dire that you feel as though I cannot make decisions on the wellbeing of our kind?"

"I—" Her mouth opened, only to shut. "I mean no disrespect, my lord. I know you are more than capable of dealing with a crisis. That is why I ask of you, please meet with us. Choose new members that way we can help the ones who are lost to us. The humans have run everyone from their homes. We are in hiding and losing this war they have brought upon us. We need your guidance."

"We are vampires," I ground out. "Our instincts guide us. We were made to withstand these measly humans and rule this world. If we are not tested, how will we know who we are?"

Eleanor grew quiet as her expressions turned to shock.

"We will meet at sunrise tomorrow. Inform our strongest."

"Thank you, Master."

Relief was evident in her tone as I turned my back on her and continued to my room. Perhaps choosing new members would come to benefit me. After all, they had gifts. If I couldn't find the answers I was looking for to bring Tessa back, maybe one of them held it.

Chapter 32
Tessa

Twelve. Twelve vampires.

A yawn came from my mouth as I took in the ten males and two females that sat around the small living room. For two days Marko projected his power off and on, and only the few before us had shown. Stress and panic were wearing me down and it was almost impossible to focus through the growing anxieties.

"I almost didn't come. I didn't want to. The stories going around, they're not good." Cedric pushed back his long dreads, keeping his dark eyes low as he stole glances at Marko. "They say you're killing our kind. That you're setting us up to be wiped out by the humans. I'm not even sure why I'm here. I guess I got tired of trying to find a place to hide and curiosity got the best of me." He paused. "Is it true?"

"No." Marko shook his head, shoving his hands into his suit's jacket pockets while he leaned against the far wall. "It is like I told the ones before you. Who everyone is seeing is not me. It is Aetas portraying me, and you're right by what you say. He is trying to destroy our kind. He and I are bonded. Did you know that?"

Cedric gave a quick shake of his head.

"We are. His blood is very powerful. Not only with him, but within me. I believe it is the reason he can't bring me back to him. If he could, I most certainly wouldn't be here. He knows I'm missing from where he entombed me, and I have no doubts that the enforcers are searching for me even as we speak. That's why it is imperative I reach out to as many survivors as I can. You all must know the truth. Aetas is not dead. He is very much alive and he's using me as the face of this war. I assure you, the culprit behind this massacre is not me. I want us to live. When I leave here, you must let everyone know that."

"Leave?" Confusion flickered on Cedric's face. "But where will you go? Who will lead us if you disappear?"

Marko sighed, glancing over to me. I felt his pain as a natural leader. He wanted to stay. To protect what we'd found of our kind.

"I must reach out to as many as I can before they catch me. Staying in one place only increases the odds. But we're going to find a safe place for you all before we leave. During the time I'm gone, I want you to use your own powers and project them as I did. Collect and try to rebuild until I can deal with Aetas. If I am able to overthrow him, I promise you all my protection. If that means moving what is left of us to Axis to provide that safety, so be it."

Daisy, one of the first to arrive came forward, clutching her hands nervously. "What if you fail? Aetas is the strongest of our kind. If he's truly the one behind this, there's no beating him. Look at what he's already done. What hope is there for us if he kills you? Can't you stay with us for a while? We will find a place. We can hide you until our numbers grow. Then ..."

She didn't continue and I knew why. To speak against our leader was sure death. It was ingrained in us not to do, even in these times of distress. Yet, we all knew what she meant.

"I wish I could remain here, but I can't. Trust me when I say that I don't plan to lose. Aetas may be our leader, but he is not invincible. Anyone can be overthrown. It just takes finding a person who wants it bad enough to win. I am Aetas' match. Because of him, I am the strongest. I plan to use that to my advantage."

"I feel him in you," Cedric whispered. "I met Aetas once when he visited our city here in Dallas. It was decades ago, but there's no mistaking his power. You have it. You could win if you go about this the right way."

A smile tugged at Marko's mouth. "You have any ideas that could help me out? I'm not opposed to suggestions."

I moved closer to Marko, watching the way the vampires' faces drew in as they thought. They were looking to him to be their savior, and so was I. He was our only hope. Hunter and I wouldn't be able to do it on our own, and Marko was so much stronger now than he was before Aetas bonded him. His powers were incomparable to anyone outside of our leader. And if I wanted to be truthful, they were quite possibly matched. Marko felt stronger in the sense of his aura, but I couldn't be for sure.

"You can't kill him. Not if the two of you are bonded." Cedrick licked his lips, keeping his eyes downcast as he thought. "You mentioned he entombed you. Is it possible to get him in there … to stay for good?"

Marko let out a sound that I couldn't quite read. "I'm sure we could manage it. His powers would be useless there. Mine were. But even if I did entomb him, the risks involved go beyond what I'm comfortable with. Someone could set him free. He could overpower me at some point and get out all over again. During the time there, he had to personally feed me to keep me alive. I'd have to do the same with him. It'll only be a matter of time before he or someone else figures out a way to turn the tables. Then we'll be right back here, or worse."

An older vampire, a male who looked to be in his late thirties slowly eased from the chair.

"Nelson, correct?"

Marko's voice had the vampire nodding. Surprise lit his face almost as if he couldn't believe Marko remembered. Even I was a bit surprised. I hadn't recalled his name.

"I was a doctor before I was turned. I've stayed one for our city for the last twenty years. I have a suggestion. One I'm not sure is much better than the entombment, but it's worth a shot."

"Go ahead." Marko pushed from the wall.

"The tomb was obviously well shielded by Aetas' powers. He prevented you from using your own. Once you become leader, it will be up to you to take his place in that. Let's say you are strong enough to prevent him from succeeding in escape. What if while contained, instead of feeding him the original way, we were to make it intravenous? You told us before that he had a tube in your neck. He obviously thought this though. That was his plan for you. His failure was feeding you weak blood. Probably human, or someone of lower rank. If we were to bag your own and keep him isolated and contained—guarded even in a hospital-type setting, the plan could succeed. Of course you'd have to have trusted guards. And the person switching out the bags would have to be you or someone you confided in so he couldn't try to manipulate his escape. But it could work if he were completely in lockdown and monitored."

"You would bag my blood?"

"I could, yes. We could set up times for you to donate. Once or twice a week. We could afford to feed him enough to keep him healthy without going overboard to give him too much power. We could study the effects and monitor his output of energy. Ultimately, we could control him by monitoring how much of your blood we provide."

"Fascinating," Hunter breathed out. "But won't his powers grow as Marko's increase, too?"

Well yes," Nelson admitted. But the king can always be the stronger one by thriving in his life, while … Aetas is only fed enough to survive in a healthy state. It may be a little hard to understand, but I believe it is possible." He paused. "Aetas will live regardless if the king is to rule. It could work or not, but this way, even if Aetas' powers are impossible to control, at least the intravenous input keeps Master Delacroix at a safe distance, and Aetas restrained at all times.

"And in a hospital type setting?" Marko was beginning to pace. I could see that his mind was racing as he went over the possibilities.

"Yes. Somewhere close to where you'll take up residence. A place where only you and a select few know of."

Marko's hand came up as he looked around the room. "We'll talk more about this privately." He scanned the vampires and I wished I knew what he was thinking. By looking into their eyes, he could see their intentions. Were they good? Did they believe and want to help us? It appeared so.

"Protect the doctor and you protect yourselves. We will all have a role to play if we're going to be safe. I need you all—"

I blinked passed the change in the air. I felt it the moment Marko's head whipped around to the front door.

"We are not alone. You all must go and stick together. I will call to you." Marko's hand flicked and that was all it took to send the vampires surging to their feet. Some had their fangs exposed while the others' claws were out, including my own.

"Come." I rushed forward, leading them to the back door. My pulse was rising as I jerked to a stop not feet away. *Enforcers.* One in the back, one in the front. Two. I knew their numbers even if I couldn't physically see them yet.

"There's two," I announced, glancing at Hunter who was feet away, closer to Marko. "Do we kill them?"

"Not yet. Just … wait. They're …" Marko's lids closed as his head tilted. "They already feel me. They're confused … and communicating. I can't hear what they're saying. It's just a jumble of broken words, by I can pick up on some of it."

My lips separated as I locked my stare with Hunter's. It wasn't possible. Marko shouldn't be able to read their minds without making eye contact. He wasn't bonded to them, yet he was breaking through the barriers of the impossible.

"You hear their thoughts? From here?"

"I hear more than their thoughts, ma minette. I see their lives. I feel their desires. I am everything and everywhere if I choose. Right now, I am nothing. I am not here. You are not here. *None of us exist.*"

The last was barely audible as his tone dropped. Tingling vibrated against my skin and true fear developed inside of me as I watched the man I love open his black eyes. Ones that used to only change where the color was. Now they were like mine and Hunters. Even the white part was gone.

Who was Marko becoming? How strong would he get? Would it be too much—enough to make him lose his mind like Aetas? The thought terrified me.

One of the males shifted next to me as an almost nonexistent shadow crept along the back wall. On instinct my hand came out to still him. I wasn't sure what was going on, but I trusted that Marko's words meant something. If we didn't *exist*, perhaps the enforcers didn't know of our presence.

Another dark shape became visible from the corner of my eye and I slowed my breathing as I quietly stepped to the side. Marko was still staring ahead as if in a daze. His black eyes were as dark as a void. He was gone, but where I wasn't sure.

Hunter's steps were silent as he made it to my side. The vampires around us were trembling. If we were caught—if Marko was caught—we were as good as dead.

Darker the shadows became, becoming more visible as they moved in closer to each other. One shot up the stairs while the other stayed rooted not feet away. Marko still stood like a statue, appearing oblivious to what was happening around us. Banging erupted upstairs and Daisy jumped, grabbing to my arm. She seemed to catch herself, immediately dropping the hold.

"They're gone!" The shout had the other enforcer turning into his normal, vampire self. He let out a sound of aggravation as an enforcer with a paled out version of olive skin stomped down the steps. His black clothes matched the darkness of his eyes as he scanned the room.

"I told you we should have been more cautious. The queen probably felt us coming from a mile away. She'll be long gone now."

"That wasn't just the queen and we both know it." The blond enforcer turned and studied the room. His mouth was tight and uneasiness was embedded in his features. "We both felt it. If I didn't know better, I'd swear the king was here. The power ... it went well beyond what the queen holds. Hell, my skin is still crawling. Look." He pulled up the long sleeve black shirt exposing his forearms. "Fucking goosebumps."

The other enforcer knock his arm out of the way as he came toward us. "Something wasn't right, I'll give you that. But the king ... we both know he's buried away in that fucking room, scouring through all those books. He's been in there for over a day now. He's damn near lost his mind."

"His mind was gone from the beginning," the blond said lowly under his breath. "I don't like this. I don't like any of it."

"Then perhaps you'll help me."

Marko's head turned in their direction and his eyes were still black. Both men jumped, automatically lowering in a defensive position. Their eyes were wide as they dropped even further to their knees to bow.

"Your Highness. Please, forgive us. We weren't aware you had left your chambers."

The dark haired one, peeked up, but he couldn't hide his fear. He was nervous.

"Stand."

Marko blinked rapidly, but never lost the authority he projected as his eyes faded back to normal. I knew he was somehow still keeping us hidden, and the talent amazed me.

"Your Highness—"

At Marko's hand lifting, the blond snapped his mouth shut.

"Let me ask you a question. It a simple question, but the answer will not be an easy one."

At his pause both men nodded.

"Who am I?"

The dark haired one looked over at his partner, only to return. "You're King Marko Delacroix. You're our leader."

Marko smiled but it was far from happy. "Wrong. I am King Marko Delacroix, but I am not your leader. Not yet."

"I don't understand."

"Let me ask you a question, Fernand. You just came from Axis, correct?"

The dark haired vampire stole a glance at the blond, once again, and nodded. "We did. This is our territory we were assigned to search."

"And you say I was in my chambers, reading books. Yes?"

"Yes, Your Highness."

"If I confide something in you, can you keep your word to be honorable to my request?"

"I can. On my life," he said proudly.

"And you?"

Marko glanced at the blond who eagerly nodded his head.

"I will. To the death."

Marko flicked his wrist and the men's eyes widened as their heads snapped in our direction. Confusion had their mouths opening, only to close.

"Fernand. I ask that you go back to Axis and knock on the door you believe me to be in. You will probably get yelled at to leave, but I don't want you to until the door opens and you come face to face with who you're speaking with. He'll ask what you want and I don't care what you say, but you're not to speak one word of what you just saw here in this house. After all is settled, I want you to come back to me. So you can believe I'm not playing a trick on you, I want Adam, here, to stay at my side. You trust him?"

Fernand's head turned to the other enforcer. "Yes. I trust him."

"Good. Now go and tell me who is behind that door."

Marko's hands clasped and Fernand's gaze came right to mine before he vanished completely.

"What's this about? Who's behind the door?" Adam swallowed hard. "And I thought the queen was missing. But you have her? She's here, and so is The Black Prince."

"Patience, Adam. You trust Fernand?

"Yes, Master."

"Then soon you will know."

The blond turned his attention to me. His mouth opened to speak, but he shut it, obeying the king. A minute rolled by, and then two. When Fernand appeared, his paled features were damn near ghostly.

"Who the hell is that if not you?"

One of Marko's eyebrows rose. "Who do you think it is?"

"No, tell me. I …"

"Who was it?" Adam's impatience was thick in his tone. "Fernand, who?"

"I was there when they put him in the memorial. I saw him with my own eyes. *He was dead.*"

"Our leader was never dead. It was me you all put in the memorial, and it was all his doing."

"Aetas?" Adam's head cocked to the side. "Are you saying the king we believe to be you is indeed our prior leader?"

I forced myself forward, not able to stop the anger dwelling within. "He fooled us all. Even me. What he has done cannot be ignored. Aetas has to pay for his crimes. He is killing us off."

"But why?" Fernand rushed out. "I see what he is doing, but why deplete our numbers? Why destroy all that we have worked for? We've come so far."

Marko shrugged. "Because he can? Because he grows bored and wants to start over? I search through the blood he and I share and all I feel is his need for destruction. For death and meaning of something I don't understand. And I don't think he understands it either. All I know is he has to be stopped or else more of our kind will perish. Already our numbers die by the hour. *I feel them.* I feel us fading into nothingness, and the stronger I grow, the harder it is for me to remain here. Aetas needs to be stopped. *I will stop him.* But I need your help.

Chapter 33
Hunter

Pitch black was all around as Marko led us through Dallas' underground city. Where I thought it impossible for us to get in, he'd been here before. His powers grew frighteningly stronger by the hour and he was far from the weak state he'd been even a day ago.

After the vampires and enforcers left, he'd turned to me and Tessa, his eyes darkening all over again. *"We must be sure before we leave this place."*

With that one sentence, we were suddenly here, surrounded by cement walls. Marko's motivation left him racing forward with no explanation. We knew nothing of what went through his mind. And there had to be a mass of information he was picking up on with his growing intuition. He was distant. Driven as he moved at a speed Tessa and I could barely match.

The eerie emptiness left my pulse skittering as we went deeper into the tunnels. If anyone was here, they were hiding their powers surprisingly well. We took a left and I felt Tessa's adrenaline slam into me.

"There's humans ahead." Her hand jerked out, barely able to touch Marko's arm as he stayed a step ahead. Her breathless voice had him slowing and coming to a stop. "Will we kill them or stay hidden?"

Marko turned to look back at both of us. With how dark the area was, it was almost impossible to see him clearly.

"I will keep us hidden like before. We stay quiet and we go fast." He paused, and I knew he sensed our unease. "Humans aren't the only ones here. A former member is waiting out his time until they leave, but they have no plans of going anywhere. We need Nico alive. Hunter." Marko stepped in closer. "This vampire will trust you more than me. We don't have a good history, but he knows of you, and the plans meant for your future. You *must* use authority with him. You have to tell him to go to the others and wait for us."

"Me? What if he doesn't listen? You said he's a member. I am no one."

"*Yet.* You hold great power, Hunter, your mind just refuses to acknowledge the truth. You must remove the barriers set on by the tragedies of your past. You are not human anymore." He glanced at Tessa, only to come back to me. "You've won that battle. You have her and she loves you. The fight is over. Now embrace the new war you're in and be the vampire our kind needs. The vampire *she and I* need. We can't do this on our own. We're running out of time. With each word I speak, Aetas gets closer to finding a way to take her away from us. His motives are my own, even if I can't hear his thoughts. He wants her. If he succeeds … what then? How will you fight when you won't embrace all of what you are? He will kill you when you attempt to save her, and then she will die. And then so will I, because without her, I have nothing left to live for. Our kind will fall and it will be all on you. *Rise.* Be the leader you're meant to, right now. You don't have the time or the choice."

My mouth shut and I tightened my fists. I felt like a soldier getting my ass handed to me from a superior. It's what had driven me to the top. I always led and I didn't question my judgment. Yet, that's all I had done in this new life. My instincts were there, as was the power in my blood, so what was I waiting for?

"Will he manage to take her?"

Marko's face turned impossibly harder as he stared at me. "I feel as though he won't stop until he finds a way. Like I said, every second that passes, he grows even more desperate. My blood is driving him crazy. *She*, is driving him crazy."

"Because of your love for her …"

"Tessa is everything to me," he ground out, stepping so close his face was but inches from mine. "Aetas is finding out firsthand the depths love can go, and while we're talking about it, you should know, too. There is more to the emotion than the good side. People die for love. They *kill* for it. Just because you have her, too, never forget about the man whose love goes as far as obsessive madness. She's what flows through my bloodstream. She's my life source—my entire fucking existence. I allow this because I love *her*. You ever cross me to keep Tessa to yourself, the powers above better help you because no one else will be able to."

"Don't fucking threaten me. Who the hell do you think I am?"

"Enough," Tessa hissed. "There will be no backstabbing between the three of us. We are one. That is never-ending from this moment on. You both have love for me, but I asked that you love each other. That is what I want. We don't stand a chance unless you do."

Marko and I held stares for only a moment before his expression softened and a grin pulled back the side of his mouth. "You see that, Hunter? Tessa is the calm to the chaos. She's also the storm that ignites it."

He turned, pulling her in his arms. His lips brushed against hers and whispers in French filled the space. The interpretation in Tessa's mind left their conversation as clear as day to me.

"I love you. Don't be upset with me, ma minette. It had to be said."

"It's said. Never again does it have to be repeated. We love each other. He knows that."

"I know, but I still have to make my feelings clear. We may not be bonded anymore, but that changes nothing. You will always be mine."

"Always," she said, lower. "The fact that I can even have this conversation with you in a language foreign to me proves that. The bond we shared may be no more, but the effects will last forever. All that you are is imprinted in me. Hunter will love you, because I do. And you will love him, because you love me. This will be a beautiful joining, and stronger because of our trials."

Her hand rose and she traced down his cheek with her fingertips. The kiss that followed from him was deep and I didn't miss the way he clutched to her.

"I will have you tonight. If." He paused. "Can you … be with me yet? Here," he said, moving his finger to her temple. "You're unsure."

Tessa's confliction ate at me, just as it did her. I felt her sadness and confusion.

"You want me after what I did?"

"After what I did?" he corrected. "This is my fault. Everything that has happened after my decision to tie with Aetas is my doing. I don't blame you, nor do

I look at you any differently for your actions. I know your heart. It's here, inside of me. You love me and I love you. That's the end of it. Let it go. *I already have.*"

Prickling stabbed at my skin and my head whipped to the side. "We have to go," I cut in. "Something's not right."

"Everything is fine." Marko spoke to me, but still faced Tessa. "What you feel is Niko. He's detected us. He's coming."

Coming? All I could do was nod as I pushed Tessa's emotions far away. I was expected to take charge of this member. The vampire could probably end my life in seconds if he wanted, and yet I had to order him from the place he called home. I could do it. I knew the words and authority would come, but could I back them up if it came down to it?

I wasn't so sure.

"Hunter, step closer."

I obeyed, still trying to focus. When Marko grabbed my hand, I couldn't help but look down at the connection. The warmth emanating from his touch crept up my arm, branching out into my chest as it took me over. My pulse was increasing and sweat began to coat my skin as his power filtered through. "I need you to see, nothing will change unless you believe. Feel your source—you're path, as I do. Feel your greatness as only I can."

His grip tightened and the electricity that followed jolted my body rigid. Air gushed from my mouth, devoid of tone. It was meant to be a yell, but I was incapable and it was all because of Marko.

Flashes blinded me. Vivid colors swirled and I could see myself panting as I glared ahead … right into Marko's eyes. It was of our first meeting after my change. I was going wild, tearing at the invisible shield. My power surged, building and growing as I went crazy to get to him. Even then, as Marko, I could feel it.

Time drew out, and still I increased. Outside of the memorial, my aura hovered through the air like a heavy fog. It mingled with Marko's and I could feel how the vampire tested it against his own.

"Don't fucking threaten me. Who the hell do you think I am?"

My early anger sent a tidal wave sweeping over Marko's skin. He was so sensitive now. He picked up everything and I almost couldn't believe that it had come from me.

The room warped and I suddenly saw the memory of a man I knew had to be Nico. His light brown hair was short and his piercing blue eyes were so close to my own light color. Marko was staring him down and I could feel their anger toward each other, but there was only one thing I cared about above all. Marko was testing him, just as he'd done with me, and even now with as young as I was, I knew I surpassed him. It didn't seem possible for the lack of skills I seemed to possess.

"Aetas' blood mixes well with those who are below him, but his biggest mistake was tainting the source. There is no future to rule," Marko said, dropping my hand and bringing me back. "We are already there. Now face the truth. Take charge and tell him to go. Make him by any means you feel is necessary. This is all you."

The heaviness of the member grew closer, but I didn't wait for him to appear on his own. My core was on fire, coming to life inside of me as I searched out the male who was made to serve *me*. Marko was right. I couldn't wait for this to come on its own. It was there and I'd force it to me, just as I planned to do to the member.

Instinct.

There was no room for humanity in the height of war. It was lead or follow—fight or die. Fuck not having a voice in this disaster we were facing. This city was technically mine and it was overtaken. I had the say on what happened to it.

My power burst from my body, seeking out my target. The moment our powers clashed, a shockwave took my breath away. I could feel his location. Feel how he was momentarily stunned as I drew him in to me. I had control. Only me as his tall frame stumbled forward. Vibrations of thoughts left my hold shaky, but I refused to be weak. More, I lured him in against his will, holding to our connection tightly.

"You don't belong here." My voice was deep as I closed the distance between us. "This is my city and I'm ordering you to leave. Do you hear me?"

A strangled sound left him and I dropped the web I had invisibly woven. When he didn't answer, my hand locked around his throat. Anger, it was all I knew. Reality of our world was beginning to sink in as my true self tore through the confines of my newborn status. The change was still so fresh that the buffer kept me only focused on Tessa—my mate. She'd be taken or end up dead if I didn't do as Marko said and break through the restraints of my condition.

War. War. War.

Blood boiled within as I turned and slammed him into the curved cement wall.

"I think I gave you an order and you still haven't acknowledged it."

"You're … The new Black Prince."

"Answer me," I growled. "Are you going to leave my city or am I going to have to remove you myself?"

Niko's eyes flashed to Marko's. "This is your fault. You did this to us."

Power exploded from my core, right into Niko. His limbs jerked while a muffled cry left him. "I believe I am the one talking to you. Not him. You speak of something you do not know. Your leader and my creator, Aetas, is not dead. He's killing us off. He's impersonating the king you attack."

"Aetas is n-not dead?"

His teeth were chattering from my powers and I didn't ignore the way that fed the vampire within. It made me stronger. More aware of who I was, and I loved it.

"No. He wants us to think he is, but he is very much still alive and soon the world will know. I need you to listen to me, though, Niko. You have to leave here."

He struggled in my grasp and I flexed my jaw as I let him fall to the ground. Trembling was still shaking his body as he struggled to stand.

"Why do I have to leave? W-why can't the humans? I will fight with you. W-we can kill them all now, and with your power radiating from here, they'll stay away. The survivors will come back and we will be safe again."

"I cannot stay. I must help the king overthrow Aetas. We will never be out of harm's way until he is taken care of."

"You can't overthrow Aetas. It's impossible. He's Aetas!"

My throat vibrated with warning as I slammed my hand over Niko's mouth. "Aetas will fall. It is not impossible. Do you not feel the power of the king? He and Aetas are bonded. They share the same blood. Marko will rule, Niko, and I *will* serve him. And you," I added more pressure, leaning closer in to take in the scent of his blood. It had my fangs lowering, hungrily. "And you will serve me. Won't you."

It wasn't a question, but an order.

His teeth clenched under my hold and he nodded, slowly.

"That's what I thought. Now get out of here and head south. The vampires will be putting off energy. You're the strongest of them all. I expect you to take care of them—protect them until I come for you. Is that understood?"

Again he nodded.

"Good," I said, dropping my hand and stepping back. "And Niko …" The vampire stumbled away, watching me cautiously.

"Yes, Prince?"

"If you hurt any of them, or they are mistreated while you're representing me, you will pay. Is that clear?"

"Yes, Prince."

He took fast steps until the darkness swallowed him whole. I faced Marko and Tessa and couldn't stop my grin from coming at theirs. I did it. I was finding myself, and I couldn't help but like the person who was beginning to show. For the first time, I felt confidence. Meaning, in who I was inside. I'd always been a soldier and leader, and wasn't this sort of the same thing? I was ruling, and I was in a war. The only difference was this time I had Tessa and Marko on my side.

Chapter 34
Marko

I knew the moment we appeared in the tunnels of New York's underground that we were walking into a blood bath. Panic and mayhem were surging through the air and screams echoed along the cement walls. I'd only been here once, but the ruler in me pulled Hunter and Tessa straight toward the heart of the massive city where their members were. My speed was so fast that I could feel them struggling to keep up. Yet, I couldn't slow. These were my people, and they needed help.

"Clear. Go, go, go!"

The loud yelling had my hands breaking loose from my mates. Beams from the flashlights broke through the darkness in all directions as the humans poured from a room ahead. Power burned, sizzling in the background as the killer in me took over. Bloodlust hit hard and my fangs and claws shot down in my need for revenge.

"Marko, wait."

Tessa voice should have stopped me, but it had the opposite effect. I had to protect her. I had to make sure that a single human didn't make it passed me. Hunter was there. I knew he would keep her safe, but as her mate—her husband and soulmate—it wasn't in me to let that fall to chance.

"Marko, please!"

Lights jerked in my direction, blinding me, but I was already diving for the closest human, tearing through his face and throat as I swung my arm to fillet through the next. Shots rang out, pinging with pressure as they connected with my impenetrable skin. Aware of a possible threat, the bullets didn't stand a chance in harming me. The protection was child's play, and an act I mastered long before I even found Tessa.

Blood flooded my mouth as I tore into the side of one's neck. Only when the sweet flavor hit me, did I tap into my gifts. Time slowed and the chaos ceased as I sucked the human's life-force into me greedily. I had wanted carnage and murder and for the briefest moment, I had had it. But it didn't have to be this way. I had to think. I …

I broke away, slicing through the necks of the remaining few so fast that my hand and body were but a blur. Just as the last of my claws ripped through the skin, I brought the present back and let them fall to the ground. Tessa was running again, only to slide to a stop feet away. She blinked, confused as she stared at the bodies around me.

"I didn't feel you stop time. I didn't even know."

Nor would she ever went I used that gift. But she knew what I did. For her it would appear one minute I was fighting, the next, it would be like someone took out a frame and the humans were suddenly on the ground.

"Hunter, guard her, and stay a few feet behind me. The city is overrun. I'm going to call them forward. Don't let human or vampire anywhere near my queen."

"You don't have to worry about that."

He was already moving closer to her as I stepped over the bodies and continued toward the great room. My powers flared, surging out for as far as I could push them. The calm I projected was nothing more than bait to hungry wolves. Yet they wouldn't act on their impulses. They wouldn't be able to think at all. Not with my persuasion. It was Aetas' gift and one I hadn't tested, but I knew what it was capable of.

The screaming faded as I neared the glow emanating from ahead. Shuffling of feet in the distance grew louder, the closer we got. Fuck, I hoped this worked. I felt it would, but my gifts were just as new to me as Hunter's were to him. I knew if I put my mind to it, anything was possible, but I hated the thought of failing at such a critical time.

"I told you he would come. I told you!"

A vampire yelled out crazily as I broke into the light. Both vampire and human were gathering, all looking confused and fearful as I neared. The amount of living filled the space until they were practically wedged against each other. Both wanted to act from their instincts. They wanted to murder one another, but I wasn't going to let them. I had plans of my own.

"Your Highness. Thank you, Your Highness. I told them you'd come and save us. No one believed me. No one would listen."

My eyes went back to the older, crazed male vampire. That he could speak at all was enough to give me pause. He shouldn't have been able to, but he was clearly not of sane mind, therefore unaffected by my persuasion.

"I am not who you seek. You put your faith in an imposter. Your leader, your messiah, Aetas still inhabits his headquarters. *As me*," I snarled. He will let you all die. I, the true King Marko Delacroix, will not. So yes, old man, I am here to save you. But know the truth of who it is that protects you on this day. It is not that fraud, Aetas."

Eyes followed me as I neared the blood soaked members that remained at the very heart of the room. Their backs were facing each other, guarding who they could, yet protecting themselves.

"You. Mistress Price." My finger pointed to a dark skinned woman in what was once a dark blue dress. She was looking over her shoulder at me, watching my every move. She was older than most, but not any more powerful than I was before Tessa's change. "You're the strongest here. Your ruler?"

She cleared her throat, turning to face me as I allowed it. "Dead, my king. We are all that is left."

"I see. And you know who I am?"

"I do. I saw you once, but it was a very long time ago. I'm regretful to say that I missed meeting you when you graced our city decades back. You weren't a member then, but we all knew you would be in time."

I saw the truth in her black eyes as I neared.

"I'm going to clean up your city, but I need you to do something for me before I allow you to return to it as leader."

"Leader?" She blinked rapidly. "I never—"

"No, you never thought it because even as a vampire you are humble and smart. You know someone more powerful than yourself should lead, but I'm telling you that it will be you, and I will be make sure your strength surpasses anyone who will think to try to take it away from you. I need allies. Rulers I can trust after I overpower Aetas. I can trust you. I see that."

"Of course." Her words came in a gush of breath. I could feel her mind racing and I didn't have to tap into it to know she was going over what this would mean. "What will you have us do? You mentioned us returning, so that must mean we are to leave?"

I nodded. "Yes. Vampires are collected in a safe haven. Right now they are held up outside of Dallas, but come tomorrow night, they will move. They will be projecting their energies to call in more of our kind. You and your people must do the same. I will take you all. Except him," I said, pointing at the old man. "He doesn't go. He's a risk."

"Hey, now."

"No. You can stay here until this passes." My head shook and I turned back to her. "I will clear the humans out and between you, your members, and Niko, you should be fine there until I call. And I will call. I cannot promise that you or any of your people will live past that day. I may not even live, but if any of us stand a chance, we have to try. All I'm asking is for your support during, and your backing afterwards. I am not asking you or your people to fight. I just want you all to witness the fall of a king, and the rise of another. A new beginning for us all."

"You are bonded with him, yes? I feel him in you. And I have heard rumors."

"I am. I will not kill him, but I will contain him to where he will never be found or free He will be as good as dead to our kind. I promise you that."

The woman turned to look at her fellow members. The four besides herself that remained were strong, but not like I had hoped. Dammit, I had so much work to do to rebuild our kind. My blood—Aetas' blood—would solve that over time.

"Aetas has gone too far. He wishes for our deaths, but I will not give it to him. We will go and we will stand with you."

"Thank you." I glanced around the room to the humans holding their bows, daggers, and guns at their sides. Simultaneously, their hands all rose to rest their weapons at the hollow point behind their chin. Panic flared in their eyes while they held steady. "My gift to you and your city."

BANG!

The unison of explosions, tears of skin, and cries, rang through the room and a wave of bodies fell to the ground. The energy of the vampires spiked in an array of different emotions and some even jumped away from the dead humans that lay at their feet. Before I let them adjust, we were in an all too familiar room. One almost identical to where we'd just been. Austin's underground. *My city.*

"Your Highness." Mistress Price spun and took in the surroundings. "Your powers are great. More than I have ever seen. To bring us all here. At once …" She swallowed hard, meeting my eyes. "I am honored you chose me. We will not let you down."

"I count on it. Let your people go to their rooms and rest. Our time is running out."

Although I spoke, I tested the air for humans. They weren't here. Not underground anyway.

I let my power stretch out, guarding the city. Before I could turn, an all too familiar power mingled with my own. I turned in fear, rushing to Tessa and Hunter. He had his arm around her, practically holding her up. Pain laced her face as I tore her from his side.

"Let me see." My hand settled on her stomach and I cursed as I felt heat flooding out through the material of her sweater.

"I'm not sure how much longer I can hold him off. I'm trying, but …"

Sweat beaded her skin and I pushed my own powers into her core. She seized, her knees buckling as she clawed into my suit's jacket. "He's trying to locate you. To bring you back. He's getting closer."

"He will take me." Her voice struggled as she barely got the words out. "You must not stop getting everyone together."

My head shook and I met Hunter's pained eyes. He was clutching to his stomach as well.

"Marko, we lose if you stop now. Move your hand."

"No."

A loud cry burst from her lips and all I could do was try to guard her as best as I could. But it wasn't working. Not enough to stop the pain.

"Hunter, come." I made it to the nearest table, laying Tessa down while keeping my palm securely in place. He barely made it to my side before I locked on his wrist with my free hand. "Help me. Use every ounce of your abilities to locate Aetas' power and try pushing it away. Aetas'," I stressed. "Not mine or Tessa's. You have to know the difference. Feel."

He lowered, just to the side of my hand. I let go of his wrist, watching his lids close as he focused.

"I feel three. I know Tessa's, but … the other two are so closely matched."

My jaw tightened. "Weigh them against your own powers. The one closest to yours will be Aetas'. You hold his blood, not mine. Pay attention to the way it pulls you. Do you feel it?"

Sobs left Tessa as her head shook through the fire and tugging that was no doubt twisting inside of her.

"I think I know which one is his. There's so close though."

"You have to know for sure," I snapped. "If you push mine away, she's gone. He will have her."

"Fuck! Don't yell at me. I'm trying."

Deep breaths were leaving me as I forced myself to calm. "You're right, I'm sorry. Just … focus. Weigh them against your own again."

Seconds stretched out for what seemed like eternity. I could feel Hunter's aura changing with time. Out of nowhere, a shockwave of heat scorched up my arm. Black eyes stared down at Hunter's connection and his face was flushed through his surge. Tessa screamed in agony only for it to die out midway. Her head rolled to the side and with her unconsciousness … Aetas' powers grew. But not enough to take her. Our leader's attack on our mate left a hunger in Hunter. I could feel it growing as he did what he meant for—fight.

Chapter 35
Aetas

"No. No!"

I pushed from my knees, swaying as I stood. My shoulder connected with the wall and my glare landed on Domnius, one of the older vampires who was new to my member's circle.

"You said it would work. You said I could bring her back. I've tried seven times so far! Every time, she doesn't come."

Fast steps took him closer to the door. I could smell his fear as it perfumed the room thickly.

"King Delacroix, it should have. The powers on the other side must have prevented it. I don't understand. You're the most powerful vampire alive. Right?"

"Of course I am you fool! You deceived me. You lied to me."

"No. I swear I did not." Faster he stumbled back. My pace was swift as I matched his steps. I lunged as he spun for the door, pinning him with my body against the barrier.

"I don't like manipulators. Did you use me to become a member? Did you feed me false information for status?"

"No, please! You felt her. You were so close, I heard you say it."

"You heard nothing," I yelled, spinning him to face me. "If I didn't need you, I'd kill you right now. As it is, you may still have information I need. Do you? What are you hiding up there in that mind of yours?"

My eyes tried to search his but he wouldn't meet my gaze. With my other arm, I gripped his chin, squeezing for his attention.

"Look at me. Show me your secrets. Perhaps if you show me yours, I will let you in on one of mine."

"Your Highness, I beg of you."

"Begging is for the weak. *Look at me!*"

My grip became crushing. Domnius thrashed as his face turned a deep shade of red. Just when I knew he couldn't take anymore, his eyes shot up. My trap was immediate. I plunged into his mind, shredding through his memories like a tissue paper. Murder, rape, all the pettiness I expected was there. It wasn't until I got to his developing gifts that I let time play out. What happened with Tessa was what he had said. I was doing it right, so then why couldn't I bring her to me? Yes, Marko and Hunter had a role in preventing me, but I should have been stronger than the three of them combined. I should have had no problems bringing her back.

"Show me," I growled under my breath. "Show me how to get to her."

The repeat of the memories had me searching other routes to take. When I was still left without answers, I let his body drop to the floor. Coughing filled the room as I turned and began to pace again.

"We will try again. This time it will not fail!"

"She …" Again, he coughed violently. "She is not your mate anymore. The challenges almost make the task impossible. It works only on bonded and creations. You have neither."

I stopped, turning my head to look over my shoulder. "Can you guarantee that it works?"

"Well … yes," he said, standing. "I don't see why it wouldn't. That's what it's for. It is the easiest thing and usually the first we learn when we bond."

"What if a person was so strong that their blood protected their creation or mate against them? That it guarded them just as well as it did its source?"

His eyebrows drew in. "Well, there's bound to be a way. But."

A smile tugged at my mouth. "I'm ready to let you in on my secret now."

My skin rippled and I could feel my body morph to my true self. Immediately hatred gushed through my veins. With it, a roar tore from my lips. Domnius' hand shot to his chest to cover his heart while his head shook.

"Aetas. You were dead. We saw you."

"You saw what I wanted you to see. Fools. All of you."

"Yes," he whispered. "We are that."

"What is that supposed to mean?" I stepped forward as he cast his stare toward the ground.

"Nothing." He stole a glance up, edging back at such a slow pace that I knew he didn't think I was aware of his need to flee. "You bonded the king, and you created the Prince. Which is it that you wish to bring back?"

A chuckle left me. "So impatient to escape me. I don't blame you." I tapped into Marko's blood, letting it once again take me over. My pulse was getting out of control being away from his form for too long. I was … slipping from thought, going back into his frame of mind. The need to have Tessa kept coming through. She was all I wanted and the fact that I couldn't get her was driving me even madder. If I could just see her—touch her—choke the fucking life from her. Fuck!

"We will go for Hunter, but I don't want him. It will be a distraction. Marko has to be helping block me. When he turns his attention to Hunter, I get Tessa. Now, come forward so I can channel them through you."

The resistance was in every step Domnius took toward me.

"What will you do with her, Your Highness? Do you have plans to hurt the queen? There is t-talk."

Talk of what?

He hesitated as he got in position before me. "Of screams," he said quietly. "From when she was here. People believe she ran away because you hurt her."

"The queen is my business. No one else's. You don't worry about my plans."

My palm slammed into his stomach as I cast my strength into him. The anger and experience left my powers exploding from me and going right for Tessa. The moment I caught her energy, I ripped back with everything I had. The resistance was immediate, leaving me enraged.

I searched for Hunter's blood within me and growled at how weak it was. I hadn't fed from him since his change. It was a mistake I couldn't change, but it made no difference. I let the essence filter through, throwing my powers toward nothingness—searching. It was like trying to find needle in a pitch black room. My energy pushed out, spreading as I grasped at the tiniest sensation. What felt like half an hour went by before I brushed against the tinge of something all too familiar.

"Got you."

My mass drew in so fast that I felt the wavering in my core. With a punch of what I knew must have felt like a bag a bricks, I hit Hunter with everything I had. He was so unguarded that I felt the lock on him almost immediately. Instead of pulling back like I knew I could have, I squeezed, letting my heat burn into him so he would think I was trying.

Whimpering echoed in the distance from Domnius, but I cared not of his wellbeing. I was focused on only one thing and I got it.

"Marko … that's it. Push me back. Fight me."

Blood trickled into my mouth as I bit into my lip at the sheer strength that clashed with mine. Just when I was sure his was peaked, I switched gears, jumping right back to Tessa. My internal hooks sunk in and with a force I wasn't aware I process, desperation had me bringing her forward.

Black smoke poured from Domnius's mouth and I couldn't stop my claws from embedding into his stomach at my excitement. "Come to me, baby. That's it." Harder I gripped, until I felt the warmth of his blood pooling over my hand. The fog rolled out onto the floor and I pushed him back as her unconscious body began to take shape.

"Get out." I waved blindly. "If one word of anything that happened in this room gets out, I'll know immediately, and I will torture and kill you."

I didn't even watch him leave. The door slammed closed, but I was already lowering to kneel in awe at her curled up body. She was wearing a black nightgown and she was paler than I liked. No doubt it was caused from the constant battle I'd waged trying to get her back.

"Ma minette." Damp curls were forming at her temple and I stroked them back, not able to stop myself from lowering to pull her in my arms. Seeing her face again was like having my heart back. I couldn't catch my breath, yet I was more in love with her than ever. "I've missed you. God, I've missed you so much. You have no idea what I've gone through without you with me."

I pulled her higher in my arms as she began to stir. Her lids fluttered and she smiled, curling more into me. "Marko?"

"That's right. I've got you, and I'm never letting you go again."

Again her eyes opened. She blinked hard, trying to lift her head, but I held on tighter, keeping her against me.

"Aetas?"

"Marko," I corrected through clenched teeth. "And you must feed. You're not well. I want you better. I want us back to where we were. I'm dying to taste you. I'm so hungry for you."

Each breath left my cravings unbearable. I hadn't fed since she'd left. I couldn't bear to taint her blood within me. I needed it. I fucking … was dying. God, help me.

"Take my blood."

My hand was shaking as I brought it to my other wrist. Adrenaline and the wear on my body was starting to take effect.

Blood seeped over my claw and I tore down my skin another inch before lowering it to her lips. Tessa didn't fight me as she stole a glance at my eyes and hesitantly separated her lips. Her blinking was fast. She was thinking, but what about, I wasn't sure. I didn't care as her suction pulled the very life from me. The release was magical. Everything I needed and more. All the pent up anger, all the fears and anxiety over her disappearance, gone in our moment.

"Take as much as you need. Take it all," I moaned. "Fuck, I don't care. I'm yours. My heart. You break it, you mend it. I am nothing but broken pieces of a man lost to your love. Why must it be this way?"

Harder she suck. My mouth opened and I took a big breath from the puncture of her fangs.

"Yes. Like that."

As fast as she'd bitten, she withdrew, and tugged my hand further down, biting into the soft bend of my arm.

"*God.*" I dragged the word out, pushing my fingers to her hair as I held her mouth to me. My cock was so hard. So unbelievably ready for her. I couldn't think of anything passed the point of needing to be inside of her. *To have her inside of me as I drank her in.*

French poured from my lips, leaving me as easily as the blood that filled her.

"I'm going to show you how much you've been missing from me. We're never going to be separated again. Come closer. Hold to me. I know you had to have ached for me like I did for you. Show me."

Tessa's jaw locked and she tore my skin as her arm lifted and her hand clamped to my shoulder, pulling me down until I was curled around her. The scent of her skin had me closing my eyes and resting the side of my face on the top of her head. I could feel the slight lightheadedness but it added to the bliss I was floating in. For minutes she fed, rubbing her face over my arm numerous times before biting into me again at a different location.

Before I knew it, I was lying on the floor with her still using my body as her personal buffet. Crimson stained her cheeks and chin, and her beauty as she finally faced me left me speechless for the first time in minutes.

"Let me see you."

I blinked passed the spell, trying to decipher what she meant.

"Aetas. Please."

"Aetas. No," I said shaking my head. "He's dead, now."

Tessa lifted, moving in closer to my face. "He lives. I feel him in me. I want *him*. I want you," she whispered. "Show me, Aetas. Show me your true self."

I stared into her eyes, mesmerized at the world that seemed to live inside of her depths. Yes, there was something calling me in. Calling me home. I loved it there, within her.

The warmth of her hand heated my cool cheek and I moved into the touch, never breaking the contact of her lure. I didn't want to. I couldn't bear another minute outside of the peace she brought me. Had I been mad at her only minutes ago? Days ago, before she left? I couldn't remember. I cared about nothing but right now."

"Come to me." Her soft palm fitted against me, firmly, and I let Marko fade from me. Negativity crept in, but had no control over the love of my heart. "Stay like this. This is who I want to see from now on."

My lids grew heavy and each blink was harder than the next. I was … tired. Content now. No. I needed something. The longing. It was still there.

Tessa broke from my eyes, nuzzling her face into mine. The slight irritation buzzing in the background had me battling with my mind on what I was supposed to be doing. I couldn't quite remember.

"You're so weak." Her breath tickled my ear, moving along my cheek as she grew closer to my mouth. "I think you should sleep. Perhaps you'd like me to help you relax?"

"Sleep …" The word registered and my head jerked back. Awareness plowed into me like a cannon blast. "The last thing I want to do is sleep. I want you and I intend to have you right now."

Tessa stiffened, searching my face as I pushed to stand, pulling her with me.

"Take this off. Let me see what's mine." I grabbed the straps of her nightgown to pull down when my eyes jerked to a stop at the reflection of my face in the mirror. The perfect, handsome, younger features were unfamiliar to me. The thinner nose, the smaller lips. I looked like a child in my eyes now. Early twenties yes, but a boy, not a man like the way Marko made me feel. That stranger wasn't me. He wasn't the real me.

"What is it?" Tessa turned, meeting my eyes in the mirror. Still, my head was shaking. "Aetas, what's wrong?"

"That's not my name. That's not me."

"What? Yes it is. That's you."

"No." My voice was forceful now. The rage was returning and I was more confused than ever.

Tessa turned back to me, placing her hands on each side of my face. "I like this, you. This is the Aetas I know. The one who has taught me so much. He's my leader … my lover. Not the other version. I want his one. Please stay like this."

"Why? Because you don't want me to taint the memory of your precious Marko?"

"No. Because this is who you are."

My lids squeezed shut through the throbbing that was beginning to take place in my head. "It is not. I don't know him anymore." My words were mumbled as I blindly reached for Tessa, bringing her closer. The love wasn't as strong when I was this way. It was there, but not like when I was Marko.

I stepped back, opening my eyes as I pulled us to the bed. The resistance that met me wasn't a match as I threw my weight down and brought us falling back onto the mattress. The moment we landed, I rolled on top of her, lowering my face into her neck. The sweet perfume that was her enveloped me and I couldn't help but suck against her skin.

"Aetas?"

My head shot up and I snarled, slamming my palm over her mouth. Marko's blood swirled within and I embraced it, letting it transform me back to him—back to me.

"Aetas is dead, ma minette. I never want to hear his name leave your pretty little lips again. *Ever*. Now enough of this before my mood is spoiled and I make you pay for leaving me."

The pressure from her anger radiated through the room and she jerked her head to the side. "Do you truly love me so much that you will deny your own identity?"

"You *are* my identity. I can think of nothing but you. Each breath I take is meaningless unless the smell of you has masked it. Your blood is all I want keeping me alive. You, you, you. You are my foundation of being and there's nothing I can do to change that. I've thought of everything. To kill you would be killing myself. Even then I wouldn't have you like I need. I am doomed to live in this torment eternally. At least if I am to suffer, I will do so with you at my side. *In my bed*." I lowered back to her neck, letting my fangs come down to scrape along the surface.

"If you love me, why do hurt our kind? Why do you not do what you can to make me happy?"

"I'm going to make you happy, love. I'm going to make you so fucking happy right now."

Chapter 36
Tessa

I couldn't move through the sickness I felt. I wanted nothing more than to kill the vampire sleeping with his body wrapped around my own. Blood had dried over my chest and limbs long ago, but I cared not for how much I had lost, or the fact that he'd gotten his pleasure and fix from nearly draining me so he could sleep. My smell would calm him, he'd said. As if I cared whether or not he was at peace.

If his death wouldn't take the life of my mate, I would have poisoned him and tore his heart out of his chest to crush in my palm. Let him love me, then. God, his death would be so simple. I could do it. I knew I could. It was hell not being able to. It was even worse pretending.

To give my body to a monster over and over was destroying me. *Hate.* The emotion didn't even scratch the surface for how I felt about Aetas. The moment I began to pull back, he sensed it. The anger that came from him at that was one that scared me. I couldn't afford to screw this up. Marko and Hunter couldn't afford it. Aetas' attention would zero in on them for sure. He needed *me*, to have all of his focus aimed at the one person who could keep him distracted.

The grip tightened around me and Aetas drew me in impossibly closer. I tried not to tense or shove him away from me. The worst part was knowing I could leave. I could disappear right now and be free of this. But what would that do? He'd bring me back and the next time, his *love* might not so easily forgive. I was in a lose-lose situation no matter how I looked at it. The only thing I could do was buy Marko and Hunter time. At some point Aetas was going to realize he needed to get them back and with what I saw last night between unconsciousness, Hunter was just as susceptible to the summoning as I was.

"You're awake. I feel your thoughts. They run so deep. They coax me from such a good sleep."

I stared up at the ceiling, trying my best to rein in the negativity. "I apologize. I didn't mean to wake you. I was thinking over what needed to be done today. Have you chosen a new circle, yet?"

"I have." Stubble from his cheek scraped against the side of my forehead as he buried his face into me even more.

"Surely you have duties. May I attend as your queen? I know I'm not member-worthy yet, but—"

"You're more powerful than most selected. I killed off the strongest."

I blinked passed the information, trying not to let my pulse increase. He trusted me more than I expected. Or … he thought himself above needing protectors.

My mouth opened to speak, but his hand quickly covered it.

"Too early. I care not for any of that. Politics are the last thing on my mind right now."

I resisted the urge to attack him for cutting me off with his hand. Hostility was my first reaction toward him every time he touched me.

I turned my head under the weight of his hand and he let me, lowering it to begin to massage into my breast.

"I should …" My mouth closed and my thoughts died off. I was going to say bathe, but the flashbacks of the last time I was around water with him nearly took my breath away. Fear engulfed me so intense that Aetas' head rose. I stole a glance, hating that Marko's face was what met me. I tried to avoid looking at it as much as possible, but I couldn't escape the truth. Aetas wasn't going to turn back into his old self. Ever.

"What is it? You're afraid."

I paused, trying to recall who I caught a glimpse of. Something wasn't right with his looks. I knew that even as I stared at his shoulder. "I don't want to fear you." I let my eyes dart up once again to his cheek. "Marko, I must be honest with you. You scare me sometimes. Just the thought of getting clean leaves me shaking. If I embrace this … you won't hurt me again, will you?"

"Oh, ma minette. Come here."

His arms drew me in until my face was level with the front of his throat.

"Just love me. That's all I want."

My fangs thickened with the need to tear out his throat, and they lowered the smallest amount as I moved in. When my lips pressed into him, his fingers laced through my hair, keeping me there. My vampire wanted to react violently. To attack at the lack of control I had, but somehow I managed to move back and place more kisses across his skin.

"God, yes. Keep going. I knew you loved me. You just had to see for yourself. That's all it was. That's the only reason you were gone so long."

I paused, blinking through the lies he was feeding himself to cope.

"You're back now, though, and my love will keep you here. You'll never want to leave me again."

"No," I whispered, placing one last kiss. "This is my home now. With you."

"Look at me. Look me in the eyes and tell me that."

I hesitated as my intuition told me not to. But if I were to deny him, he'd get angry. I couldn't allow that yet. Slowly, I angled my head back and nearly gasped at what I saw. The brown color of his eyes were lighter, almost golden as he stared down so full of desperation. And his features … they were different.

"This is my home," I choked out. "I choose you. I want us to be happy together."

"Tell me you love me as you look at me. Right here," he said, pointing back to his eyes.

"I … love you."

Never before had I felt so uncomfortable saying those three words, but Aetas wasn't himself, or Marko. The realization of what he was becoming left me unbalanced. Shocked to the core. This vampire before me, he was new. Almost a mix of them both. It was as though Aetas' mind had warped the two together. He truly in his mind was a version of Marko, now. I saw a slightly thinner nose, smaller, yet still full lips. And those eyes. My stare kept getting sucked into their depths. They were so entrancing. So mesmerizing to look into.

"I love you," I repeated through a fog. "I love you."

Time slowed as I felt my mind stall. *Love. Love.* God, it was so nice to be looking into his eyes. So ... calming. *Love.* He did love me. I could see it.

"Yes, you do. You love me so much that you didn't even know the extent until you returned. That Marko you were with, he wasn't who you truly love, and you saw that while you were away, didn't you? That's why you so easily let me bring you back."

"*Yes,*" I breathed out.

"And Hunter, you hate him more than ever. He killed you, *but I gave you life*. Remember? You even loved me, then, when I taught you how to use your powers. You love me so much that you never want to see them again. You hate them, just as I do. They tried to break us apart, but what we hold is so much stronger than they are."

"You're right."

Lips crushed into mine and my lids lowered heavily through the tingling in my mind.

"I love you. I do."

"Again," he growled, pinning me to my back. "Here. Keep looking into my eyes. Keep telling me so I can feel it."

"I love you."

Power radiated from above me as the golden color almost seemed to come to life in his intense stare. It was suffocating, and yet addicting. And I couldn't turn away. I suddenly didn't want to.

"You've been surging. You're surging," I repeated from nowhere.

Marko froze at my words, his eyes going wide as something seemed to dawn on him.

"Yes ... I don't know how I missed it. Don't think about that now, though. Keep looking at me. Keep loving me."

"I am."

A big smile burst onto his face. "I got you. Fuck, I finally got you." He moaned, lowering his body to mine. "Now I can go through with my plan. Now we can start our reign."

Where I expected him to kiss me again, he didn't. All he did was grin and gaze into my very soul as minutes went by. And I didn't care. The silence and connection left me in a blissful peace. I was floating and happy for the first time in as long as I could remember. There was no worries. No burdens or fears when I was taken over by the void within him.

"Such a beautifully broken mind you have, my queen. I see into you clearer than I've ever seen into anyone. Your thoughts, your dreams, your secrets, they're mine now. You've been misled by our enemy, but our new connection changes things. You love me, and I forgive you for your hatred and deception. But none of that matters. You have shown me what I need to know. Together, we will fix this."

His words didn't make sense. All I knew was his love for me, and my need to return it.

"You wish to shower and meet with my members. I will give you what you want. But not for the reasons you had hoped for. I've erased those from your memory. I've erased it all. Now you will go to lead them. You will show your support for your king, and you will kill anyone who tries to turn you against me. Your loyalty is to the one you love. And you do love me, don't you?"

"Yes."

The grin faded as he rose and pulled me to my knees to face him. The hold on each side of my head was light and gentle as he continued. "You will lead the plan of attack on Austin's underground city. We will kill all those who try to rise against me. They are traitors and we can't tolerate their rebellion. As laws go, we as leaders can't kill royalty without reason. This imposter, Marko, this unknown stranger who is impersonating me will not be harmed until he admits to his true identity. He and his accomplice, The Black Prince, will be brought in and put in lockdown for their crimes. We can keep them there until we decide a better course of action. Perhaps we will let the doctor, Nelson, live down there with them for his crimes. And you will stay far away from the mate and former best friend who wants nothing more than to kill you. *Yes*. This will work."

"It will work," I agreed in a monotone voice.

Marko leaned in, kissing me before pulling back and standing from the bed. My mind blanked out and only one thing registered as I stared around the room in a daze. *Planning*. I had to meet with the members. I had to rule them.

"First, a shower," he said, as if reading my mind. "Then we will work."

I looked down at the dark, dried blood from our lovemaking. "Yes, of course. I don't know what I was thinking."

"You weren't. The fake Marko did something to your mind, but I fixed it. It'll take a little time, but you'll be better than ever before too long."

"Thank you." I stared up at him in awe. My heart fluttered as I took his extended hand and followed him into the bathroom.

"No need to thank me. Thank you, ma minette. You have no idea what you've done."

He was right, I didn't. I didn't know anything at the moment except the way I kept wanting to look deep into his eyes. It was as though I was searching for something within. Trying to figure out a deep rooted mystery. But there were no answers, only the pull to keep trying to find the solution.

"I feel better than I have in weeks. It all makes sense now. I haven't grown stronger in so long. But that's what it was. That's why I was losing my mind all of this time. I was surging, like you said. I don't believe it is over, but now that I know, I can at least try to control it. I don't want to hurt you."

He leaned forward, turning on the shower before facing me again. Uncontrollably, my stare shot up to his.

"Look at you." He smiled, brushing the hair back from my face. "My queen. This is really happening, and it couldn't have come at more perfect time. Fate works in mysterious ways. You leaving when you did brought out all the traitors, and now they'll be collecting in one place. We can destroy them all at the same time. It's so perfect. You did well. I'm so proud of you."

"You are?"

Confusion had me trying to search for thoughts that weren't there.

"Yes. You did this for us. That's what we will tell everyone when they see you've returned. You were protecting your king and leader. You were scouting and you knew I'd object to you putting yourself in harm's way, so you left without me knowing. But you came back and you told me of the traitors' plan. Now you're back to help me rule."

Marko pulled the shower door open, leading me inside. "You're going to be the heroine in this. Centuries from now when our kind looks back at this moment in history, they will see the bravery of the one and only queen that will ever be again. They will see a world that was at war with itself, and how we persevered through chaos. How we rose from nothing and against all odds, we became great again. We're starting over and this time will be different. Aetas' reign will not matter compared to King Marko Delacroix's. This is a clean slate. One that will be better than the last."

"The last?"

"It matters not." Marko positioned me in front of the spray. "Lift your arms."

I obeyed, raking my mind for what was even happening. He talked of a clean slate, but that's exactly how I felt. I knew things, but they didn't feel right.

"Spread your legs."

Again, I followed his direction. In swift circular motions he lathered me, caressing and fondling as he worked his way down.

"Look at me." My eyes rose, stopping on his lips. "You're thinking too much. Let me help."

His fingers drifted down to the top of my slit and I reached for his shoulders as he added pressure over my clit and began to tease me.

"Is that better? Is this what you want?"

Before I could answer, his lips met mine and the cold marble connected with my back. I broke away gasping as he lifted me and held under my ass with one of his forearms. When the tip of his cock traced my opening, tears slid down my face. I wiggled through the panic that was beginning to form within me.

"Marko? What's happening?"

The break in my voice has his head rising.

"No, no, no," he whispered. "Look into my eyes, ma minette. Do you see my love? Look deep."

The snap in my mind was like a rubber band as my gaze connected with his. Vertigo left me feeling as though I was falling. Memories began to blind me in vivid color. I watched as a stranger to the scenes that soaked into my brain. I was scouting. Yes, watching this fake Marko and Hunter turn people against my king. I hated them. I wanted to kill them, but I knew I couldn't. Not without hurting the real Marko or myself. But that was a secret, now. I wasn't meant to speak of it anymore. And my Marko, he wanted me better. He loved me more than anything, and I loved him. He loved me. *Loved me. Loved me.*

A cry broke from my mouth as Marko's cock plunged into me. My mind was still scattered and the room wasn't coming in clear, but the pleasure was great. So much so that I wrapped my arms around him, driving myself down to meet his swift thrusts.

"You love me," I stated.

"Fuck yes I do, baby."

Marko's mouth met mine and reality wasn't clear. My body was taking over, but nothing else was adjusting right. For some reason, I prayed clarity would never come back. I wasn't sure I could face the truth buried deep below. And it was there, just out of reach. It scared me. It was going to destroy me. What had I done?

Chapter 37
Hunter

Tessa. Answer me, dammit! Tessa?

"Well?"

Marko's impatience left me gritting my teeth.

"She doesn't answer. I'm not even sure she can hear me."

"Tessa has to be able to hear you. You're bonded. Fuck! What has he done to her?"

Marko paced the living room of the house we were staying in outside of L.A. For almost a week we had travelled around collecting survivors, taking them back to Austin. But it seemed the strongest of our kind was gone. Dead, during their own attempts to protect the vampires they were meant to rule. From Seattle to San Francisco, the numbers barely reached a handful at a time. We were seriously in trouble, and from what we had heard from the ones who had escaped in time to save their lives, it was worse on the East Coast. Martial law was in full effect. Military tanks and vehicles patrolled the streets twenty-four hours a day. Everyone who was visible was screened, and homes were constantly being raided. So far we had been lucky, but we didn't stay in one spot long.

"Try again. We have to make sure she's okay."

"She's physically okay," I growled. "I feel her, Marko. She's more than okay. She's on some kind of fucking mission. I can feel her focus—her determination. She's … like a fucking robot or something. She goes, goes, goes, but then her mind crashes. She gets almost hysterical, and then it's like she reboots or something. She goes from the lowest of low, to okay again. Happy, even."

Marko moved in closer. "You feel all of that?"

"It's getting stronger as I do. She still won't talk to me though."

"Is that all you feel?"

The hesitancy was obvious as I broke my stare from him and turned to grab the black hoodie to pull over my head.

"Hunter. I asked you a question."

"And I don't want to answer it."

"Hunter."

The warning left the hair on my arms standing on end. I turned at my vampire's defensiveness, baring my fangs through the rage that exploded.

"She sleeps with him and it makes both of us sick afterwards. She is confused and then she changes. What more do you want me to tell you?" I yelled. "I don't understand what is happening any more than you do. Or she does, I think."

The sheetrock caved like powder under Marko's fist. Energy heated the air, swirling through his own fury and I reached out to the wall as the ground began to shake.

"He's done something to her. He's fucking done something. God, I will kill him. I will kill him, if I have to kill myself!"

"Calm. Down."

The roar that left him only caused the surroundings to quake even worse.

"Marko, enough!"

Black eyes met mine and Marko had me pinned to the ground with his weight before I could so much as stop him.

"Show me what she sees. Show me through your connection. I want to look through her eyes. I want to know her thoughts." His grip was trembling as he held to my face like a vice. "Show me! I want to know what's wrong with our mate."

My mouth opened but it was too late. Marko's powers pushed into me and I felt us freefalling through nothingness. It all happened so fast that I wasn't able to catch my breath before I was looking at a group of people sitting at a table. At the end sat Marko, grinning smugly as Colin stood behind him, at the door. But … it wasn't Marko. I went back to his face. He looked oddly different. Even as I stared at him, I couldn't quite figure out what was off. His eyes were a lot lighter, but that wasn't it.

The enforcers will go in first. They can get through the perimeter the members' inside have set. Once they have taken their position, we will appear in the heart of the city's great room. At that point, we will make the traitors pay for their treason against our king. I believe their deaths will lure in the imposter and the prince. Things may get heated, but they are not to be harmed under any circumstance. The king and I are more than capable of taking care of things from there.

I could feel us moving with Tessa's steps and I knew we were exactly where Marko wanted us. We were seeing what Tessa was. We were … listening to her plan our capture.

"If there are no questions, I call this meeting to an end."

At the silence, she nodded.

"We attack in one hour. Be ready."

Air burned my lungs as I sucked in oxygen. Marko's weight was crushing me and on reflex I pushed his body from mine.

"We have to go," he panted. "We have to get everyone out of there."

"What the hell is she thinking?" Coughing left me curling to my side. My body felt as weak as water as I tried to move. "She ratted us out. She …isn't out our side?"

"Don't you dare say that. Tessa would never turn her back on us. She said I was an imposter. He's gotten into her mind. Reprogrammed her like Margo used to do. He took her gift once, and I felt the blankness in Tessa's thoughts. She is confused, acting on what he is telling her to do."

My hoodie was grabbed from behind and Marko pulled me to my feet. I could tell he was straining almost just as much as I.

"We have to save the city. We have to get back."

"How? Look at us? I can barely fucking stand. And you, you're swaying."

Sweat was pouring down his face as he shook his head. "Excuses, my friend. That's what you're giving me. You're the soldier. Did you ever quit because your body was incapable of going on?"

I frowned. "No. There was no quitting, only a mission."

"This is our mission. We can't afford to lose. All that is known will be lost if we don't get there before they do."

A loud bang had both of our heads spinning for the door. Military uniforms registered and men poured into the living room. The shots were immediate—no orders to stand down or to surrender. They were shooting to kill. From the burning of my arm, I knew what they were using weren't regular bullets.

"The city!"

Marko's hand locked on mine, but I was already fading. Pain shot through my shoulder and I felt myself get knocked to side. Warm raced toward my fingertips and the distraction made me whole again.

"Dammit, Hunter. *Defense.*" The air ripple as Marko's hand shot up to shield us. "I thought we went over this in Seattle."

"Get us out of here!"

"I can't yet. Not both of us. I'm still too weak."

Shots kept going off in the background and my eyes widened as one made it through his protective wall.

"I'm drained. I need time to recoup. I never considered how much it would take out of me to break into Tessa's mind. And I haven't fed in three days. We've been going nonstop."

My lids closed as I tried to focus on healing myself. It didn't work. He wasn't the only one who was drained. I needed to drink, too. I was bleeding out way too much.

"We have a fucking menu ten feet away. Let's get better and get the hell out of here." I groaned, stepping forward on shaky legs.

"You sure you're up for it?"

My eyes cut over to his. "I took a bullet through the brain and survived. Drop the shield long enough for me to reach over."

One of Marko's eyebrows rose. "You're brave to mention that."

"You're weak, I decided to take my chances. Besides, it happened. I can't erase the past. Tessa lived, as did I. No one hurts more over that than I do. Now drop the wall when I get close enough."

"And you expect them to just stand there and let you take them? Look, they're already backing away."

"Drop the damn wall," I yelled.

"Fine. When you get shot up because you don't know how to protect yourself like I taught you, don't come crying to me."

"I won't get shot, old man. Drop. The. Wall."

Marko growled, but dropped his hand. The shots were immediate. I felt my skin thicken as I forced myself to rush forward as fast as I could. Men scattered, but they were like fish in a barrel. I grabbed two, throwing one toward Marko as I drug the other back. The air rippled again and I didn't wait as I let my fangs plunge into the soldier's neck.

Flashes of his life began to blind me and like Marko had taught me, I pushed them away, focusing on the human's pulse. Warmth gushed into my mouth, so sweet that I moaned at the flavor. Marko hadn't fed in three days, but it had been longer for me. Four? Five? I couldn't remember anymore.

An explosion sent ringing into my ears and I knew I was flying through the air. The connection against the wall left air bursting from my lungs. And heat. Yes, was I on fire?"

The high pitch sound wavered and loud yells began to break through. I blinked, seeing men rush upon us. My head jerked to the side and I scrambled to Marko's body, grabbing his wrist as I faded us out. The panic left my adrenaline going, giving me enough strength to will us away, but I'd only ever made myself disappear, and only a handful of times in the last few days.

Gravity was nonexistent and my free arm flailed as the floor to the city was suddenly underneath us. The drop was a good thirty feet down and I knew we were going to hit hard.

"Shit!" My voice echoed around me as I braced myself for the impact. Just as I was sure it was coming, we were suddenly hovering an arm's length away. Footsteps were rushing in our direction and I grunted as we landed the two feet to the floor.

"What happened?" Mistress Price reached for Marko, lowering to her knees as she flipped him over.

"RPG, I think. Fuck I don't know. We were already weak. He needs blood. Yours. You must feed him. He needs all the strength he can get. Aetas will be here in an hour. They know about us. They mean to kill you all and take me and Marko to lockdown."

"No." Mistress Price's eyes were wide as she looked around at the vampires crowding in. "We must get him better. We have to leave immediately. Where will we go?"

"Not L.A.. Damn place is overrun with military."

"Dallas?" Niko cut his wrist, placing it before me. I stood, throwing him an appreciative look as I brought it to my lips. The power was so much more than what the human provided. I drank him in deep, feeling my wounds heal almost instantly. My strength surged back through and I watched Marko wake up and clutch to the Mistress's wrist as he stared in my direction.

For minutes we fed and watched each other. We didn't need words to communicate our thoughts. He knew I had saved his life, and the proof of my loyalty was one he had needed to see. And, I was getting stronger. We were a team. Just as much mates as we were with Tessa.

"We must go," Marko said, breaking away from her wrist.

"Dallas?" I wiped the blood from my chin as I followed his suit.

"They will expect that. We go to no cities. We need somewhere closer, but secluded."

I scoured my thoughts, grinning as the answer became clear.

"The City of the Dead. What place is closer to Axis than that? We'll be within the walls. No one will ever think to check there. And we'll be in."

Marko hesitated for only a moment before he returned my grin. "You're a fucking genius, my friend. To the City of the Dead."

Chapter 38
Marko

I swore I would never come back here. That I would avoid the City of the Dead for as long as I could manage. Being faced with the memorial that had kept me imprison for nearly two months was almost unbearable. It was like facing a nightmare I couldn't escape. But Hunter was right. This was the safest place for our kind. No military would ever be able to breach Axis, and here, we were within reach to both Aetas and Tessa. It didn't mean we could drop our guard. Even through the city was miles wide and we resided at the far reaches, we stayed on alert at all times. Three days now, to be exact.

"You okay?"

Hunter's voice had me taking a deep breath as I nodded.

"Yeah. I just had to see it again. You know, face yours fears, so they say."

"You were bad off when we found you. *Real* bad."

My eyes closed as I tried to stop my jaw from clamping down at the memories.

"It was hell. Absolute fucking hell."

Hunter's steps grew closer and I glanced over as he became even with me. "You'll never have to worry about it again. We will not lose. We can't."

All I could do was nod. During our three days, we'd made it to Denver and Miami, and didn't bring many survivors back. My biggest hope was that they were in hiding and they'd come to us when I overthrew Aetas, but nothing was for sure. This might be it for our kind. One hundred-thirty-seven. That was it.

"Tessa just had another episode. Her mind is too strong for Aetas to control for long. The attacks are starting to grow closer together. I worry how much longer this can continue before she breaks completely. Every time he does this, I can't help but feel he does more harm than good."

My stomach turned and the sickness was all too real.

"What if we took her, like him?" The question was more of one to myself, but Hunter responded.

"He may find us. You heard Tessa, she wants us to continue with the plan."

"You feel her—I felt her," I snapped. "She's not well. He's hurting her." I paused. "But she'd be pissed if she knew I put our kind in jeopardy. I am torn. I have to go to her."

"You?" Hunter gave me a look of disbelief. "Are you insane? She thinks you're a traitor. She'll either try to kill you or have you arrested. Then Aetas wins. Use your head. You're smarter than that."

"I am. That's why I won't go as myself."

A confused looked crossed Hunter's face only to melt away as I felt my skin crawl and tingle.

"Jesus. It's like what Aetas did with you. Who are you? I don't recognize your face."

I shrugged, smiling. I take note of everything. I'm one of the enforcers I saw during Margo and Gina's trial."

"And if you run into him up there?"

"Pray I don't."

"I want to come. Change me, too."

I turned, walking toward headquarters.

"Marko. Take me with you. It's too risky for you to be alone. You need me."

Hunter caught up to my side and I frowned. "Two of us puts us more in jeopardy. I have to go alone."

"Bullshit." He grabbed my arm, pulling me to a stop. "We're in this together. We're mates, dammit. Or, we're mated. Whatever. I have your back and you have mine. We don't split up. We haven't throughout our time together and we won't now. I can protect you if need be. I'm stronger every day. Take me."

I groaned and locked on this throat, forcing my powers into him. The color of his skin darkened and Hunter jerked as his features changed shape.

"Can't ...breathe."

I let go, letting him catch his breath.

"Was the throat thing necessary?" Coughing came from his mouth and I rolled my eyes, pulling him in closer to me.

"No, but it was better than the alternative. You really piss me off sometimes."

"Because I'm right," He said, rubbing where I had held.

"No more talking or I make you incapable. And no doing anything stupid. We want to blend in, Hunter. I don't care what you see up there, you restrain yourself, understood?"

My pace increased as we headed through the memorial of the fallen enforcers.

"You're the one who needs this talk, not me. I'm the one who uses my head. You're the loose cannon."

My eyes cut over and Hunter kept the slight smile on his face as he stared ahead.

Never in a million years would I have thought myself able to tolerate the man I once longed to kill. The man I could have killed had I not prolonged it for reasons unclear to me now. Hunter was fast becoming more than a friend. A part of me loved him, and no matter how big or small that part was, it was love. The kind that didn't fade over time, but prospered. Seeing him grow as a vampire, seeing his trials and protectiveness over me, and the longing he held for Tessa that matched my own—I'd sacrifice myself for him, just as I would for Tessa. Just as I feared I might have to do.

"Hunter." I slowed, running my fingers through hair that wasn't there anymore because of the change. "I have to talk to you about something. It's about what will happen if things don't go our way. I don't want you to say anything, but I need you—"

"Nope. We're not having this talk. Do you know how many soldiers came to me over the years and tried to do this same thing? Do you know how many I listened to? Not one. No, this isn't happening."

"Hunter," I growled. "You have to listen. We're talking about the existence of our kind. Of the last of us if something happens to me."

My shirt was fisted and Hunter jerked me inches from his face as his fangs bared. "Nothing is happening to you. *Nothing*. I won't let it. Get that through your fucking head right now. You will win and you will rule. That is the outcome."

I jerked free, shoving at him hard as I headed toward the elevator. I didn't bother to turn around to look at him as I continued. "Get Tessa and have her take our kind far away. You all are to stay put until you are able to rule. Tessa has the strength, but not enough to beat Aetas if it comes down to it. You will. You—"

Hunter slammed into my back like a freight train, and I never heard him coming. We hit the ground hard, sliding over the dirt path from our force. Our hands went for each other at the same time and Hunter swung, hitting me right in the jaw.

"Take it back."

We rolled and I threw my energy into him enough to knock him off.

"You heard me. I won't take it back."

"Take it back!" He clawed his way back to his feet and lunged back at me. He was all emotional aggression and I knew he was doing it because he was afraid of something truly happening to me. The realization was enough to deplete my anger. My hands shot up and I quickly sidestepped his attack.

"Fine. Fine."

"Say you take it back."

I twisted my mouth at the pants leaving his mouth. "I take it back."

His anger faded and I couldn't help the smile that tugged on my lips. "Can we take back your hit, too? Fuck that hurt." I rubbed my jaw and he laughed, reaching out and pushing against my shoulder as if we hadn't just been fighting like adolescents.

Was this what it was to have a close friend? I wasn't sure, but I had something with Hunter and I liked it. Even if he did get under my skin at times.

"I can't believe you attacked me. Look at us. We're filthy." I dusted at the clothes but opted to use my powers instead to clean us up.

"It's your fault. I told you not to go there."

"It had to be said, whether you wanted to hear it or not."

An eyebrow lifted in warning, but I kept quiet, forging on as we neared the elevator. When the doors opened and shut behind us, I swallowed hard, knowing this was probably a mistake on my part. I was risking a lot by breaching Axis' walls, but I had to see Tessa for myself. I had to make sure she was okay. That I had restrained this long was torture.

"Don't say anything," I rushed out. "Let me do the speaking if anyone addresses us. And … just don't do something stupid. We go in, we check on Tessa, and we get out as fast as we can. Clear?"

"Crystal." Hunter paused. "Actually, maybe I should do the talking."

"*Hunter*."

"Okay, okay. Just joking. Bad timing I guess. Sorry, I get like this when I'm nervous. That talk you gave. I hate that shit. It's like bad karma. You tempt fate when you invite in death. I can't shake the feeling I got when you continued after I told you to stop." He frowned, shoving his hands in his pockets. "Marko, you can't lose. You just can't. Tessa needs you. She'd be lost without you."

"What about you? Wouldn't you be happy to have her to yourself?"

He gave me a hard look before he moved his attention to the floor. "No. It wouldn't be the same. I used to think she and I were perfect for each other, but she loves you, too. And I, well, I like you. A lot. Don't take that the wrong way, I just." He shifted, glancing up at me. "You're dear to me. Let's leave it at that. You're a good guy."

"So are you."

The door opened and I gave him one last look before leading us out of the elevator. Silence met us and I felt even sicker than before as I led us down the long hall. So clear I could feel Aetas and Tessa's energy. It only made me rein mine in even more. Fuck, they were close. So damn close.

I slowed, letting Hunter come up, even with me. "They're on the main level. There's a lounging area for enforcers to the far right. I think if we head in that direction, we may pass them. Stay at my side. Not behind me. We are equal here. Brothers."

"Always." He kept his stare ahead, hard and devoid of emotions. Mine were almost impossible to control at his word. *Brothers.* Yes. In a weird way, perhaps we were.

The hall opened up into the main room and the news filled the space as it always did. I ignored the chaos and destruction sounding in the background and tapped more into the powers around me. When I glanced toward the thrones in the back, I almost stumbled. Aetas was seated in his, and Tessa sat erect at his side. Members were split and stood to the side of both. All were glaring in our direction. All but one. *Tessa.* Her eyes were swollen and red as if she had been crying and was still trying to manage to keep it in.

"I was wondering how long it would take for you to grace us with your presence. How are your lodgings? Did you long for death so much that you would inhabit a city of dead vampires?"

Enforcers poured from the surrounding doors, moving in to surround us. Hunter grabbed my bicep, but I shook my head at him. There was no more running. Our people were here and there was no getting to them fast enough.

I let our true forms take us over as I faced my enemy. Tessa's hands reached for the arms of her thrown and I watched her knuckles turn white while tears rolled down her cheeks.

"That is not your true form," she said, wiping them away. "You are not Marko. You are an imposter. Show yourself to us and confess your crimes."

I laughed under my breath, giving her a smile. "Ma minette, somewhere deep in your mind, you know who you face. It is why you cry. The man you sat by is not me. He is Aetas. Aetas," I repeated louder for all to hear. "You've all been deceived. This man is none other than our leader. He did not die the day you placed him to rest, that was me. Me! Think back to Margo and Gina. Think back to the predictions made before their deaths. They knew this was going to happen. It is why he killed them. Isn't that right, *Aetas*?"

"Aetas?" he repeated.

The members turned his way, but kept still as shock began to settle into their features.

"Do your lies go so deep?" he continued. "Aetas is dead. Everyone saw him before he was laid to rest."

"Saw me! See." I changed into Aetas form and gasps filled the room. "It is easy to become anyone when you have the power to. Isn't that right, my dear ruler? How am I able to do this if I were not pure of blood like you? It is because we're bonded. I grow because you grow. It is time to end this charade. You have hurt our kind long enough. I am the one who gathered the survivors to save. It wasn't you. You care not for us. You have *killed* us. You have committed treason and by your own law, and I say you should be arrested."

Laughter filled the space as he stood. Regardless that he felt this was a joke, the enforcers around me were humming with energy. My words were enough to confuse them, I just hoped what I was doing worked.

"No one here has committed treason except you. You held an uprising to overthrow your king. You have your rebels—"

Aetas' words died off as a group of vampires came walking from the hallway that led from the City of the Dead. Mistress Price walked side by side with Niko and with each second, more followed.

"What is this? Are you all so ready to face your deaths?"

"No." Niko walked around an enforcer and came to stop next to Hunter. "We're here to watch one, though. Or an arrest. Either works for me. As long as it's you."

"How dare you speak to me like that!"

I threw up my shield just in time to deflect Aetas' power. The blow was like a punch in the gut and I gritted passed the pain.

"How can I do that if we aren't equals?" I stepped closer to him, glancing at Tessa as she scooted to the edge of her chair. "It's over Aetas. Your reign is finished. You must submit and go with the guards to lockdown. I'm asking nicely. You would be smart to take me up on my offer. It beats the alternative."

"And what's that?"

He stepped down, walking toward me. Footsteps pounded from behind and I could feel the enforcers closing in.

"Admit you are not me, or you will find out."

Tessa stood, rushing toward us. My hand shot out for her to stay back, but she didn't stop. She only widened her steps away from us.

"What is this? Is it true, Marko?"

Aetas glared at me and slowed as he turned to face her. "You love me, yes?"

"...Yes."

"Tell him I am Marko and you love me."

"You are not me! Tessa is *my* concubine, not yours, and what you have done is also against your laws. Now admit who you are Aetas and submit to your fall. You have failed us—killed us. You are guilty of treason."

"**NO!** I am not him! I am not Aetas."

A frustrated sound came from my mouth and I looked down at my hand, watching a knife appear. In one strike, I let the blade slice through my forearm. Blood simultaneously poured from our skin, trickling to the floor. The steady downpour that left both of us mingled with the whispers that were exploding in the room. "I am you. You are me. We are one. Do you remember that, ma minette? You once said that to me. Now I say it to him."

I cut through my arm again, deeper this time. Aetas growled, holding to the wound as he lunged for me. Hunter jerking me back was the only thing that saved me from getting caught in his grasp.

"Admit who you are," Hunter said, putting half of his body in front of mine.

"I should have killed you instead of made you in my creation. You betray your maker!"

Tessa raced in our direction, only to be cut off as Aetas disappeared, only to appear between us.

"Don't listen to them. Look back into my eyes. You love me. Remember? None of this matters. None one matters but us."

"Don't do it, Tessa!" I pushed passed Niko, moving more in their direction. "Don't look at him, love, look at me."

"No! You do not speak to her." A blast of energy sent us all flying back and even as I hit the ground, I didn't take my eyes off of Tessa. He had her, pulling her toward the side of the room. The enforcers didn't stand a chance as they tried to stop him. Power kept coming toward us in blows, weighing us down.

I scrambled to my feet, fight through the heaviness. I fell over one of the vampires as I ran in their direction. Each step was harder than the last, until it ceased for a few seconds. He was talking to her, beginning to wrestle her fighting form.

"Aetas! Wait! Don't make me do it. Aetas!"

The closer he got to the main doors, the more panic registered. He could disappear at any time and then Tessa would be lost to me for good. He could come back and do this again if he got free now. I couldn't lose her or let my people down. *I had no choice.*

"Tessa!"

I laced my fingers, gripping to the handle of the knife. My heart ached more at seeing her struggle to break free than any blade was capable of producing.

"Marko? Marko!" Hunter's energy blasted against my skin, but it was too late. I forced my hands toward me with every ounce of strength I possessed—right over my heart. The pain was but a blessing for the goodbye my soul was saying.

"Marko!"

Tessa blood-curdling cry for me echoed in the distance and in a blur of color I watched Aetas drop as I did. Heat gushed down my chest even as the mix of mine and Aetas' blood filled my mouth. None of it mattered as I watched Tessa step over his dying body to rush back to me.

"Jesus. Somebody get me something!"

Hunter was suddenly over me and the horror on his face sent tears trailing down the sides of my face.

"If you live, so help me. Fuck," he cried out.

Agony flared in my chest as he removed the knife and pushed down over the wound.

"No." I tried to turn out of his hold. "I … must die. It's the only way." Sobbing sounded as Tessa threw herself down next to me. I let out my own heartbreak at her pain, not able to stop the crying that poured free of me. "I'm sorry. I … love you."

"Not this way," she sobbed. "Take my blood. I can save you. I've seen it."

"You can't."

The room was already fading and each word was getting harder to speak than the last.

"Marko?"

"Shh. Kiss me. One … last time."

The sobbing grew louder as she lowered, but I couldn't tell if it was coming from her, me, or Hunter. Everything was so dark. I didn't like the dark, but I had Tessa. Her energy was my light and I held to it with every last breath that struggled free from my lips.

"I'm sorry. I'm so sorry. Please forgive me. I love you," she cried.

The pressure only lasted for a second against my numb lips, but it was everything to me. She and Hunter had been together when I first saw her, and I was leaving them together. Something in that gave me peace as I felt myself drift away. I had never been the hero of my story, but somehow the love of a woman and a dear friend had made me become one in the end.

Epilogue
Tessa

"Do you think it will always be this way?"

More tears rolled down my cheeks and stopping them was impossible. My heart ached and there was no removing the heaviness that was weighing me down. My eyes rose back to the memorial and I wiped away the new stream that trailed down my face.

"I feel as though we've had this conversation before."

He wrapped his arm around me, pulling me close. The kiss on the top of my head had a sob leaving me and I buried my face into his shirt.

"That's because in a way, we have. I showed you my memories of us again last night."

"That's right. High school. I'm sorry. I can't think straight these days."

Hunter turned us, walking toward headquarters at a slow pace. "That's because your plate is full of responsibility. Ruling a race isn't easy work, you know. Not to mention everything else you do. You need to feed, and then you need rest."

I nodded, hearing his words, but barely processing them. Since Marko's death, I had the weight of the world on my shoulders. We were in hiding again here at Axis, and we'd stay that way for at least another century until we braved going back to our underground world. Days were spent training our gifts. Growing them so we could establish our foundation again. We were off to a good start, but it was hard work.

The humans were still on guard—still patrolling and killing us off. They had luck with large groups that didn't make it to us in time, but even now, almost two months later, vampires were showing up at our door. They didn't know that when they arrived. Axis was always hidden, even from our own kind, but the pull would always be there for us to find.

I made sure of that.

I made sure of a lot. Maybe too much.

My eyes squinted as more thoughts rushed in. Ones I was thankful to even be having. Aetas has screwed up my mind good. Even now, after all this time, I still didn't recall my past. At least, not any of it that didn't come from Hunter. I was a mix of truth and lies fed to me by my former leader. Deciphering truth from fiction was almost impossible. All I did know for sure was my love for Marko. The emotion was real, even if I couldn't recall the majority of our life together.

"Mistress Price was meant to put a call out to the cities this morning. I forgot to remind her. Do you know—?"

"She took care of it," Hunter assured. "I talked to her just after she finished.

"And the enforcers? How's the recruiting going?"

Hunter brought us to a stop, turning me to face him. "You talked to Colin yesterday. Nothing much has happened since then. Calm. Everything is going smoothly. You worry for nothing."

My arms wrapped around him and he angled my face up, brushing his lips against mine. "I love you, and you're doing an amazing job. Please try not to push yourself so hard."

I sniffled, meeting his eyes as more pain nearly crippled me. "I'm so afraid."

"There's no reason, I promise. Aetas is dead. We burned his body. His ashes are guarded by enforcers just to put you at ease. We just checked, they're there at the memorial now. There is nothing to fear."

"It's not that," I choked out.

Hunter made a sad expression, turning us to head back toward the elevator.

"Then I will put your mind at ease."

Silence last between us until we got off the elevator and made it to the main stairs. When we started down the long hallway, my feet rooted to the floor and I couldn't continue.

"Why do avoid him so much? He misses you, Tessa. You saved his life. You didn't leave his side for weeks. Now you rarely go to his room."

Another sob left me and I felt myself falling to pieces. "This is my fault. I killed him."

"You saved him," Hunter stressed. "He lives, baby."

"Barely. Jesus, help me. He teeters on life and death I just know I'm going to lose him for good. I go in the middle of the night. I sit with him and I confess my love. I cry, and he doesn't wake for me. I've tried everything and it makes no difference."

"It makes *all* the difference. Do you not see him get better when you're around? He has more color. He breathes easier. You have to go to him. You have to be there for Marko. He needs you, Tessa. And he does wake now. Not for long, but he wakes. He's getting better. Come see."

Hunter's hand lightly settled around my bicep and I let him lead me down to the end of the hall, regardless that I was afraid. Could I do this? See what I had done to the man I loved? Why had I even stayed with Aetas? Shouldn't I have known something bad was going to happen? *My fault.* I had failed Marko.

The door opened and Hunter had to physically pull me inside. My pulse was pounding and I felt like I was going to be sick. When my eyes settled on Marko's pale face, my heart constricted just as it always did when looking at his beautiful features.

"Lay down on the bed with him. I'll get on the other side. He needs to feel his mates. We are everything to him, and he is everything to us. We love him and he has to know that."

My mouth opened, but I was already walking, already being pulled in by the love within. What I told Hunter was true. I may have avoid and buried myself in work during the day, but I always came at night. Always begged him to return to me. Each time he didn't, my soul mourned even more.

Deep breaths lightened as I approached and I stole a glance at Hunter as he moved in sync with me on the other side of the bed. When I climbed onto the mattress, he joined me.

"Now lay down and hold him. Tell him how well you are running things in his absence. Tell him how much you miss him and how you're madly in love with him."

I smiled, lowering myself. My head was propped on my hand and I reached over with hesitation to trace my fingers over his stomach. I could feel his core energy so close and the location and connection seemed right.

His shirt moved with my touch and I soon lost myself in the motions as I began to speak about my every day routine. Hunter's hand at some point had settled on Marko's shoulder and being so close to the men I loved did put me at peace. Separate, we were incomplete. Together, we were whole.

"I've missed you more than you'll ever know. Sometimes when I'm giving orders, or holding a meeting, I find myself stopping and wondering what you would do if you were awake and in my position. You were meant to lead. Even as I do, I feel it is not my place."

I paused, lifting to rub my face over the stubble on his cheek. "God, your scent calls to me. Do you feel my emptiness without you? This is tearing me apart, Marko. You have to come back to me. This is killing me."

"I … think it's killing me more."

My head shot up at the scratchy, weak voice that made my heart plummet to the floor.

"Don't stop." His lids fluttered open and I nearly began crying all over again as his eyes connected with mine. The stinging left my vision blurred and I quickly blinked it away as I moved back. My hand cupped his cheek and the sob couldn't be stopped as I hugged myself to him.

"I won't stop," I managed. "I won't stop until you're better. God, I love you. I'm sorry."

Marko's head turned toward me, yet he tried to pull back. I lifted, not able to control the clutching sensation around my heart.

"What are you sorry for?"

His eyes blinked heavily and fear that he might leave me again so soon had me rubbing my hand over his rough cheek to try to keep him awake. I couldn't lose him. Not yet.

"For this. For not running away from Aetas fast enough. Or …"

"Oh, ma minette. None of this is your fault. This was the only way. I knew that before I even saw the two of you sitting there." He took a ragged breath, closing his eyes for a few seconds before opening them again. "A sacrifice had to be made in order to save you and our people. I would have done it a million times over. I love you all that much." He turned to Hunter, a grin pulling at his mouth. "I do believe I have reason to worry when I get better. Do you usually threaten dying men?"

Hunter laughed under his breath. "If it's appropriate. In this case it was. You killed us that night, too, you know. We thought we lost you for good. You died twice more after Tessa brought you back the first time. She wouldn't stop, though. None of us would."

"None?"

Marko looked between us and I wiped the wetness from my cheek. "It wasn't just me who gave you my blood. I lost so much during the first attempt that Hunter, Mistress Price, and Niko mixed theirs during the following two … We were desperate. We were trying everything we could think of while Nelson worked on you."

Marko's hands were shaking as he lifted them. Hunter and I slid our palms over his and held to him as he closed his eyes.

"I am indebted to you all."

"No. What you did can never be repaid. And never repeated," I stressed. "Hunter and I … we can't lose you."

"She's right. We're absolutely miserable. Especially me," Hunter said, throwing me a wink. "I've been moping around, bugging the shit out of poor Colin just so I can have someone yell at me when I screw up. It's bad. You have to get better. I don't think he can take much more."

Marko laughed, groaning through the pain. His lids opened and the smile remained. The beauty it possessed took my breath away. Hunter was right. His strength was growing. *Marko was going to live.* And we were going to be okay. Everything was going to be just as it should.

"I'm really tired. Will both of you stay?"

He was already yawning, trying to pull me down to lay with him. I smiled, looking over to Hunter as he pulled back the covers on Marko's other side. I rose, doing the same.

"We're not going anywhere, and there's nothing that could make us. I should have never of left your side to begin with, but I can promise I'll never leave it again. I love you."

The side of Marko's mouth pulled back and he opened his eyes, searching my face as I made the dress vanish into my nightgown. The moment I curled into his side, I felt his energy surge the smallest amount. He was happy, and *he was healing.*

"I love you, too … He paused. "I loved you to death, ma minette. I really did. Now I will love both of you for life."

The End

About the Author

Alaska Angelini is a Best Selling Author of dark, twisted happily-ever-afters. She currently resides in Wisconsin, but moves at the drop of a dime. Check back in a few months and she's guaranteed to live somewhere new.

Obsessive, stalking, mega-alpha hero's/anti-heros are her thing. She loves to twist horror and romance. Throw in some rope, cuffs, and a whip or two, and watch the magic begin.

If you're looking to connect with her to learn more, feel free to email her at alaska_angelini@yahoo.com, or find her on Facebook under Alaska Angelini or her new horror/thriller name, A. A. Dark.

Made in the USA
Las Vegas, NV
24 December 2024

15294260R00378